The
Hurricane
Years

CAMERON HAWLEY

The Hurricane Years

LITTLE, BROWN AND COMPANY · BOSTON · TORONTO

Published simultaneously in Canada
by Little, Brown & Company (Canada) Limited

PRINTED IN THE UNITED STATES OF AMERICA

More than ever
for Elaine

The
Hurricane
Years

I

For the rest of his life—a span that was, at this moment, far more indeterminate than he could possibly have realized—all that was about to happen would be instantly recallable.

The time was a minute or two after 7:10 P.M., established by the glance that he had given the toll-booth clock as he came off the Pennsylvania Turnpike, fixed in his mind by having calculated that, with an hour and twenty minutes to drive the forty-two miles to New Ulster, he could easily enough keep his promise to Mr. Crouch that he would stop by his house with the proofs of the stockholders report before eight-thirty.

He was noticeably tired, but no more so than he had often been after two days in New York, and he had no consciousness of being under unusual stress. True, he was behind schedule on the sales convention, only five weeks to go and most of the script yet to be written, but that did not seriously concern him—he always did his best work under the whip of time—and from here on out there would be no more lost evenings, no more bon voyage parties for Kay. All that had ended with the bash in her stateroom this morning, a champagne-and-caviar crush from which the sailing whistle had finally rescued him, freeing him to get back to the advertising agency for a showdown session on the assignment of a new art director to the Crouch Carpet account.

The sun had been out when he left New York, but the sky had gone gray before he crossed the Delaware Bridge, a storm threat in the air, and now as he came down the tight cloverleaf turn, rain spattered the windshield. The wipers made an oily smear and he pressed the washer button. Water spurted, the blades picked it up and the glass cleared. There was an amber light at the highway and he made a whipping turn before it changed to red. The big envelope of printer's proofs slid off the seat beside him, an oblique reminder of all that would have to be done if the stockholders report was to be mailed on Tuesday. The printer was holding the forms on the press waiting for a final okay . . . if Mr. Crouch cleared it tonight . . .

There was no warning, no foretelling symptom, no premonition of disaster. The pain struck not as a blow but as a revealed presence, instantly full-blown, unwavering, unrelenting. Despite its stunning intensity, there was no veiling of consciousness, no diminution of any faculty. His senses were, in fact, noticeably sharpened. Ahead there was a flashing sign, alternately a red SAM's and a yellow DINER, and his visual perception was so acute that he would later remember that there were two missing bulbs, one in the cross-stroke of the A, the other splitting the second s.

He turned off the highway at the first possible moment, as soon as he reached the near edge of the diner's paved lot, quickly stopping the car, leaning back as he reached out with his foot to set the parking brake, hoping for relief as he squared his shoulders and arched his back. But there was no change in the intensity of the pain. He took a deep breath. The pain was still there, fixed and unchanging. He tried to belch, attempting to relieve the pressure that seemed about to burst his lungs. He was unsuccessful. But now there was the greasy aftertaste of the cheeseburgers he had gulped down a few miles back at the turnpike lunch counter. Nausea suggested both an explanation and a promise, and he got out of the car, gagging himself, trying to vomit. He could not.

Something urged him to walk—this he would later have occasion to recall—and drawn by the lighted windows of the diner, it now became his objective to buy some Alka-Seltzer tablets. This was logical enough since, as his medical history would reveal, he frequently suffered minor gastrointestinal disorders and was a habitual user of such proprietary products.

There were three steps up to the entrance of the diner. The door was a sliding one, and when he reached out to pull it open, his hand slippery on the bar, he first realized that he was perspiring heavily.

Three people came out, two men and a girl, forcing him back

down the steps. Groggy, he staggered. One of the men looked at him, nudging the other. They laughed.

He climbed the steps again and entered the diner. The cashier's stand was at his right. There was no one behind it. He waited. The diner seemed very hot. He felt soaked through. Taking off his hat, he saw that the sweatband was already darkened by perspiration. He tried to catch the attention of the waitress. She was talking to three men at the counter, saw him, but made no move to come.

He would later maintain that he did not, at this time, suspect the seriousness of his state, but that would be in conflict with the admission that he made an attempt to telephone someone. He would not, however, be able to remember whom he intended to call. Nevertheless, there was the positive memory of having walked the half-length of the diner to the telephone booth, of discovering that he did not have a dime, of returning to the cashier's stand, of seeing the waitress still talking to the men at the counter. At this point he fell. There was, almost certainly, a momentary loss of consciousness, but his memory was of an unbroken awareness, a feeling not of collapse but of a slow-motion downward drifting, his bones softened by the heat, his body without structure, limp and formless, a damp rag draped over an unyielding rock. The rock was the pain in his chest.

Although he was now aware of some fogging of the senses of sight and hearing, he nevertheless heard the muttered exclamations of individual voices, and he could see, to knee height, the legs of the men sitting at the counter. One of the pairs of feet came off the ledge and moved toward him. He expected the feet to stop, a voice to ask a question, and he prepared himself to answer. But there was only the rattle of coins on the glass counter top. The feet circled, edging around him. The door opened and closed.

A second pair of feet moved toward him. But they, too, circled him, stepping around his head as if avoiding a puddle of filth. With great effort—he had not realized how difficult it would be to speak —he said, or thought he did, that he had to make a telephone call. The feet went out the door.

With enormous effort he turned, trying to get off the rock. He succeeded. But now the rock was on top of him, crushing him down, making his second attempt to speak all the more difficult. But he must have managed it because now there was an answer, a snorting laugh, a man's voice saying, "Yeah, call your buddies in A.A., huh?"

And he heard the waitress say, "Geez, we sure had more'n our share of 'em lately."

The last pair of feet left the counter and he was looking up into a fat man's face, impossibly distant, peering down at him over the bulge of a jutting belly. The belly jiggled and was gone.

He saw white then, brown-splotched and red-spattered, the dirty uniform of the waitress, purple-nailed hands pressing the skirts to her legs, false modesty that struck him as ludicrous—he would remember the temptation to smile as proof that he felt no panic—and again he tried to speak.

For an instant, he thought she would help him, a hope lost when he heard her say, "Geez, mister, you gotta get out of here. We can't have nothing like this."

"Call—" he began and then, confused, he tried to remember who he had been planning to telephone.

"I can't make no call, mister," the waitress said, the waggle of her chin the only movement in the foreshortened ugliness of her face. "It's a pay phone. You got to have a dime."

He tried to sit up, heaving against the weight of the rock, thinking that his wallet was somewhere under it, then clearly recalling that he had been trying to get change, that there was a dollar bill in his hand. He found it, crumpled and sopping. But the girl was gone.

The door was open. He could feel the draft icing the rivulets of perspiration on his neck. The waitress was calling to someone outside, her voice rising to a throat-cracking scream.

Footsteps were coming in. "Okay, miss, take it easy."

He looked up at a questioning face, ominous, shadowed by a state trooper's wide-brimmed hat. Now he was conscious of fear, not of what had happened to him but that he might not be believed. With all the strength he could muster he said, "I'm not drunk," trying to hurl the words upward. But they were weightless puffballs, falling back in his throat, choking him.

The hat became larger and larger, coming closer and closer, the face materializing out of shadow, the nose enormous, sniffing.

The nose retreated. "Okay, mister, take it easy," the trooper said, routinely repetitive, strangely comforting. "You ever had any heart trouble?"

He shook his head, trying to say that he knew what it was, only indigestion, reasoning that it could not be his heart. Your heart was on the left side. That was not where the pain was. The pain was in the center of his chest.

But the hat was gone before he could speak. The will to argument faded, pressed out of his mind by the crush of weight.

The hat was back. "Okay, mister, we're going to give you a little whiff of oxygen. Might help. Won't do you any harm."

The mask came down, covering his mouth, stopping him from saying anything more.

At this point there must have been a pronounced dulling of perception but not—or so he would later insist—a complete loss of consciousness. He would remember that the trooper asked for permission to take his wallet from his pocket, even recalling a concern that his driver's license might not be there. He also remembered being told that an ambulance had been called, but there was no certain awareness of the passage of time until it arrived, nor was there any precise recollection of his being moved, only the memory that somewhere, sometime, he had felt the cold spatter of rain on his face.

The return of coherent consciousness came after the ambulance was underway. It was, however, a borderline state in which he found it difficult to discriminate against the irrational. There was, for example, the illusion that he had already traveled a great distance —the total route was slightly less than three miles—and that he was being taken to some faraway place. The white-coated man who sat beside him spoke English as if it were a foreign language learned from a British tutor. There was something about his oddly accented pronunciation that was hauntingly familiar but he could not then dredge up the memory with which it was associated.

From time to time the white-coated man reminded him that he must not speak, make no movement, expend no effort. The continued cautioning was unnecessary. He was drained of will, totally acquiescent, accepting what now seemed foreordained and inevitable. He did not associate this feeling with the needle that had been jabbed into his arm.

What seemed most strange—on this point he would remain adamantly convinced—he was experiencing no sensation of fear or panic. What he did feel, as nearly as he would later be able to describe it, was a sensation of being detached and uninvolved, as if his mind had been freed from his body, almost as if he were an observer rather than a participant. It was a feeling so strong, so clearly recognized, that he wondered, as an oddly dispassionate inquiry, if it was a phenomenon of death.

He did not recoil from this thought. Instead, it gave him a sensing of important revelation, the discovery that death did not come as a terrifying struggle against the will to live, a mighty battle to hang on to the last breath of life. But neither was it at all like falling asleep.

"The pain is less severe?" the strange voice asked. "Please, you must not speak—only nod."

He nodded, wondering how he could speak even if he wanted to, the oxygen mask covering his mouth.

"I wish now to check the information I was given by the police officer," the voice said. "It is for the admission record."

Turning his eyes, he saw a pair of dark-skinned hands, an aluminum clipboard, a poised ballpoint pen.

"You are Mr. Wilder—Mr. Judd Wilder?"

He felt an impulse to correct the pronunciation, but concern was fleeting and he disregarded it, nodding again, seeing now that his driver's license was under the clip, that and the identification card that had been removed from the windowed pocket of his wallet.

"Your home address—it is 1226 Vixen Lane, New Ulster, Pennsylvania?"

He started to reach for the mask. The brown hand restrained him. "You will please not speak, Mr. Wilder. I will read to you. It is necessary to let me know only if something is not correct. You are—" He was reading from the card now, speaking as if in some language even stranger than English, the words individualized, disassociated, "—Director—Advertising—and—Promotion—Crouch—Carpet—Company."

The hand held the pen like an engraving instrument, precisely copying word for word, even letter for letter as he inscribed *Crouch*. Obviously, the name was unfamiliar, heightening the illusion of being in some distantly foreign place, so far away that Crouch Carpet was unknown.

"Person to be notified—ah, yes, I see—your wife."

He lifted the mask. "You can't call her. She just sailed——"

Brown fingers shot out, clamping down, forcing the mask back, leaving a hospital odor in his nostrils. "Please, sir, in your own best interest—there is nothing about which you are needing to be concerned. Everything will be taken care of in the proper way."

He was hearing Kay's voice as he had heard it in the crowded passageway outside her stateroom . . . "Now take care of yourself, Judd" . . . remembering the tone more vividly than the words, the thin brittleness of a worn cliché, lost then in the enveloping roar of the ship's foghorn blast, lost now in a simple fading away, long distance over an impossibly distant span. For a panicked instant, he thought he was losing consciousness, a fear quickly dissipated when he heard, "Yes, everything is in order—except—it is only your age we do not have."

Lifting the mask, he said, "Forty-four," expecting protest, but hearing a grateful "Ah, yes, very good."

The pen inscribed 44 in the one blank space on the form. The aluminum cover of the clipboard plopped down with the sound of a satisfied sigh.

Silence made him suddenly aware, as he had not been before, that a siren had been wailing over his head.

"Ah, here we are," the voice said, expressing both relief and the triumph of accomplishment.

He was about to ask "Where?" but remembered the legend printed across the top of the form, as readable now as if it were still before his eyes:

COUNTY MEMORIAL HOSPITAL

« 2 »

Dr. Aaron Kharr typed the last words of the sentence, punched the period key with resigned finality, and picked up the telephone, his quiet "Dr. Kharr" a mildly critical rebuke for the tone in which the corridor squawk-box had blasted his hope that this might be an undisturbed evening. He needed it. If his book was to be finished by the end of September, he had to complete a chapter every nineteen days. It was a promise that he had made only to himself, but that made it no less binding.

"Dr. Raggi wants you in Emergency," the operator said, echoing the harshly reverberant demand that was only now dying away in the corridor.

"Very well," he said, curbing annoyance, knowing that she was falsifying the tone of young Raggi's request. Whatever else might be said of the two young foreign interns that County Memorial had been forced to take on in order to provide some semblance of a resident staff, Raggi from India and Chang Lee from Malaya, neither could be fairly criticized for a lack of courtesy or professional deference.

Standing, lifting his white coat from the back of the chair, he read again the last sentence that he had typed:

Confronted with the businessman patient in his middle forties, the discerning physician recognizes that this is often a period of peak stress, a time when the forces of long-building tension swirl up into an emotional hurricane that is the common causation of a wide range of psychosomatic and psychogenic disorders.

He hesitated, questioning his use of the "hurricane" metaphor, wondering if it might smack too much of the *Reader's Digest* for professional taste. He would have to think about that. But later.

His coat on, he automatically inventoried pocket bulges. Finding his stethoscope missing, he picked it up from the desk, flipped the OUT card on the door, and started down the hall, grimacing as he anticipated being confronted in Emergency with the mangled victim of another automobile accident.

County Memorial Hospital, only three miles from a Pennsylvania Turnpike interchange, was the focal point for maimed bodies dragged in from a seventeen-mile span. This was one of the drawbacks that he had overlooked on that day eleven months ago when he had come down from New York to be interviewed for a position that had then seemed a heaven-sent opportunity to find a happier and more rewarding life than he had known during his two years with the Allison Clinic, or in his prior situation as Chief of the Cardiovascular Section of the Berringer Research Institute. Two weeks before, not entirely by chance—he had been scanning the classified columns in medical journals for the past month—he had seen an advertisement describing a position so perfectly fitted to his needs that he could hardly believe what he read. But there it was: "small but completely modern and fully equipped community hospital, located in a beautiful rural section of Pennsylvania" was looking for "a fully accredited internist to serve as a constantly available consultant to a staff of general practitioners." His duties, the advertisement had promised, would be "exclusively diagnostic, with no requirement to serve as a resident physician." What had most intrigued him was that concluding "unusual opportunity for a qualified internist desiring a light enough work load to permit research, writing, or similar activity."

The nine days that he had waited for a response to his letter had been all but unendurable, and when a reply had finally come from County Memorial Hospital, signed by Jonas Webster, Chief of Staff, suggesting that he come over for an interview at his earliest convenience, he had boarded a bus that very afternoon. A bus, he had found, was the quickest way to get there, but with all the stops it had still been a five-hour trip, a cruelly extended anticipation of probable disappointment. Every few miles he had reread the letter from Dr. Webster, and each time his eyes had settled upon the left-hand margin of the letterhead where the names of the staff doctors were listed. All were, if not unmistakably Anglo-Saxon, at least threateningly Christian. He had been a fool, he thought, not to have made it clear in his original letter that he was a Jew.

When he discovered, as he did early in his interview with Jonas Webster, that the Chief of Staff had known from the beginning that he was a Jew—Berringer Institute had been the giveaway—hope had risen to a crescendo of desire. Everything he saw and heard sustained it. The rolling Pennsylvania countryside, a green valley seen in the bloom of early May, offered such peace as he had never before dared think attainable. The hospital was an architectural gem, fresh enough in design to be assuringly contemporary, yet completely at home in a countryside of lovely old stone farmhouses. Inside, it was no less appealing. The laboratory, although small, was beautifully equipped, really a little showplace, and the adjoining X-ray department looked as if it had been lifted directly from one of the color pages in a General Electric catalogue.

He had failed to note on that first visit that the laboratory was staffed only by a technician, a dull-witted girl who could not be trusted to do anything beyond the few routine tests that she had learned to perform by rote, and that the X-ray department was the semi-private domain of Dr. Mallaby, whose only qualification as a roentgenologist was a brother-in-law who had been instrumental in securing one of the federal grants that had financed the hospital's construction. Nonetheless, even though he had known all this, Aaron Kharr would not have been deterred. He was fully qualified, if necessary, to read his own X-rays, and whether necessary or not, always preferred to do his own laboratory work.

County Memorial was the result, he now knew, of a rebellion against a little clique of city-based specialists who, through their tight control of Marathon General Hospital, were enacting a galling tribute from all of the general practitioners in the northern half of the county. These country doctors, denied staff privileges at Marathon General, were being forced to relinquish their primary hold on any patient requiring major surgery or extended hospitalization. Earlier, when there had still been some element of competition among the Marathon specialists, fee-splitting had kept the situation reasonably tolerable, but when the surgeons got together and decided that their union was strong enough to stop this deplorably unethical practice—and, by no means incidentally, keep all of that perfectly good money in their own pockets—the country doctors were goaded beyond endurance. Jonas Webster had led the rebellion.

Banding together with five other country doctors, and staging a vigorous assault not only upon the public coffers of Harrisburg and Washington but also upon the private purses of community residents, Webster had brought the hospital into being. Later, he had attracted George Garrison, a retired Army doctor looking for a rural retreat, a capable if somewhat eccentric surgeon who, as Aaron Kharr now knew, had been responsible for creating the opening that he had been called in to fill. It was Garrison's low regard for the diagnostic skill of the other doctors on the staff that had inspired the unorthodox idea of hiring a staff internist, so radical a departure from normal small-hospital organization that he had been able to sell it to the others only by using the argument that avoiding the necessity of sending difficult cases to Marathon specialists would mean that their own pocketbooks would be fattened rather than thinned. As Garrison had set it up, the Chief Internist—he had invented the title—would be on salary and would accept no fees himself, and their practices would be protected from pilferage by a clause in his contract that prohibited him from ever hanging out his own shingle anywhere in Marathon County.

On that initial visit to County Memorial, Aaron Kharr had been interviewed by only Webster and Garrison, both of whom had struck him favorably, and they in turn had quickly decided that he was the man they wanted. They had obviously been impressed by his biographical outline in *Who's Who in American Medicine*—no doctor on the staff of Marathon General was even listed—and the number of his papers was greater than the combined total published by all members of the Marathon County Medical Association.

Rather quickly, the high glow of Aaron Kharr's initial expectation had become somewhat tarnished. County Memorial had not proved to be, as he had imagined, a desirably scaled-down version of the hospitals he had known in New York. In truth, it was little more than a medical motel serving a group of resolutely independent doctors who recognized no authority other than their own self-interest. In a free spirit of live-and-let-live, there was no review of case records, no inquiry into questionable practices, and most assuredly no attempt at professional discipline. When, on rare occasions, there was a staff meeting, it was exclusively devoted to financial matters. Aaron Kharr's idealization of the small-town G.P. as a warmhearted and largely selfless healer, the antithesis of the impersonally self-serving doctors he had known in New York, had been seriously challenged if not largely destroyed. The pecking order at Community General was no less determined by annual income, and it was solely on that basis that, in a few weeks now, Harmon Teeter would displace Jonas Webster as Chief of Staff.

Harmon Teeter was very much on Aaron Kharr's mind as he left his office and started down the corridor toward Emergency, acutely conscious that if Teeter had been on duty this evening, as the hospital's duty schedule required, Kharr himself would have been spared this interruption. This was no new problem. He had been initially assured that he would not be called upon to serve as a resident physician, told that one member of the staff would always be at the hospital, each serving his turn as resident physician for the day. He had questioned this arrangement in his original interview with Webster—actually, he had been more than a little shocked to discover that County Memorial had no resident staff at all—but Webster had assured him that it worked very well and explained that there was a built-in motivation. The doctor on duty picked up for himself all the emergency cases that turned up—unless, of course, the patient of another County Memorial doctor was involved—and the turnpike was constantly producing what Webster described with a shrug as "some very desirable cases." Webster had been right—it was indeed a powerful motivation—but all too soon some of the staff doctors, Teeter the first and most frequent offender, had discovered that by getting Aaron Kharr to cover for them, they could skip several hours of duty, occasionally the whole day, and still pick up any juicy plums that dropped while they were away.

At first, anxious to get along with new colleagues, Aaron Kharr had been unwisely accommodating. Since he was always in the hospital anyway, it was difficult to refuse to "keep an eye on Emergency." But this extra duty, coupled with the things that he had to do simply to make up for a lack of ordinary competence—Carruth, for example, was still incapable of getting a simple I.V. going—had quickly become so great that, in his first two months, he had added only fourteen pages to the manuscript of his book. Enlisting the sympathetic support of George Garrison, who was no less up in arms because of the hospital's failure to supply a competent anaesthetist, there had been a showdown with Webster. As a result, Garrison had been told to find and hire the man he wanted, and Aaron Kharr had been authorized to bring in a young intern who could at least take over some of the scut work. The authorization came easier than its fulfillment.

Garrison had eventually dug up a young Malayan, Chang Lee, and guided by that example, Aaron Kharr had gone to New York and prevailed upon a young Indian, Chavan Raggi, to follow his internship at Bellevue with six months at County Memorial before returning to India. Raggi was proving a great help, but a burden as well. Since he was, in effect, serving a residency, Aaron Kharr had shouldered not only a teacher's role but also a substantial measure of responsibility for his medical judgments. The worst aspect of the new situation was that, with Raggi available, the doctors on the staff were more inclined than ever to cheat on their days of duty. Teeter, he was quite sure, had not been in the hospital since early morning.

Nevertheless, despite his annoyance with Teeter, and as distasteful as he found the prospect of handling another gruesome accident case, Aaron Kharr strode purposefully down the corridor. For all of County Memorial's shortcomings, his eleven months here had greatly enhanced his confidence in himself as a competent all-around physician, and late in life though it was—he was forty-four —he felt that he had finally found himself. There was something of this satisfying discovery in his quick stride, self-confidence at a level where there was no need for a slow-paced cultivation of professional poise.

Raggi was waiting for him at the door of Emergency, character-istically tense and somber, and Aaron Kharr greeted him with an exaggeratedly casual "Good evening, Dr. Raggi," hoping that it might suggest the professional composure that the young Indian so badly needed. "What's up?"

"I hope, sir, that this time I have not again inconvenienced you unnecessarily," Raggi said, a reference to a case last night where he had mistakenly suggested a diagnosis of coronary occlusion.

"Don't worry about that," he said, relieved by this suggestion that it was a heart case, the area in which he felt himself most completely qualified. "Cardiac disorders are sometimes difficult to differentiate. They fool the best of us at times."

"This time I am thinking I have not been fooled," Raggi said, tautly earnest, handing him the admission card.

He glanced at it, scanning the meticulously inscribed: *male . . . white . . . 44 . . . Director of Advertising and Promotion . . . Crouch Carpet Company . . .*

Inescapably, his mind was drawn back to his typewriter, and then by obvious association, to the subject of the chapter on which he was working. Quickly, guiltily, he caught himself up, curtly asking, "Where is he?" and assuring himself that he was long past the stage where he needed any more case studies to establish mid-forties stress as a causative factor in under-fifty coronaries.

"Here, sir," Raggi said, leading the way, opening doors.

Aaron Kharr stopped in the doorway, caught in mid-stride as he saw the patient flat out on the examining table, an oxygen mask on his face, electrocardiograph leads connected, a nurse standing by with the EKG tape looped in her hand. He curbed a flash of temper, quickly excusing Raggi, blaming himself for not having impressed upon him before the seriously traumatic effect of hitting an unpre-pared patient with this brutally blunt evidence that he had suffered a heart attack. As he knew only too well from his years at the Berringer Institute, the country was full of men who had physically survived heart attacks only to remain mentally crippled by blundering doctors who, in their organic preoccupation, were carelessly unaware of the mental damage they so often inflicted. He would have to talk to Raggi about this—but later.

Inquiring eyes watched him over the top of the mask, and he responded with what he hoped was a confidence-inducing smile. "I'm Dr. Kharr," he introduced himself, taking out his stethoscope. "Let's see what's going on in this belly of yours."

He opened the shirt wider, starting low on the abdomen, sustaining the pretense that the heart was not his prime concern, following the same course that had dictated the use of *belly* instead of *heart*, the same reasoning that had restrained him from beginning his examination with a heart-associated taking of the patient's pulse. With a half-dozen quick moves of the stethoscope bell, he worked up toward the chest area. But what he heard was of far less importance than what he had already seen. Faster than any possible process of conscious thought, his brain had reacted to simultaneously registered visual impressions, so quickly producing a diagnosis that it seemed more intuitive than reasoned. But he continued listening for a moment, warning himself that his God-given keenness of perception was a gift not to be flaunted before a young resident to whom diagnosis must still be a process of deliberate step-by-step deduction.

But he was also preoccupied with the making of a decision. Made, he quickly implemented it, stepping around behind the patient, stealing a quick glance at the admission card to pick up his name, saying, "Mr. Wilder, I think we'll relieve you of this nuisance," lifting the oxygen mask from his face.

Raggi gave him a stricken look, thinking himself again convicted of an erroneous diagnosis. But that was less important for the moment than the reaction of the patient who, the instant his lips were freed, burst out with "I knew it wasn't my heart!"

The vehemence of the outburst startled Aaron Kharr. He had assumed that the important need would be the usual one of lifting the patient out of the peculiarly depressed state commonly associated with coronary occlusion—that was why he had removed the oxygen mask, why he had made no move to look at the electrocardiograph tracing—but he guessed now that the problem here was of a different order. This man was refusing to believe that his heart was involved. It could be a sign of strength, evidencing a will to fight back that would be all in his favor. On the other hand, it might evidence a psychic barrier against fear that, once breached, would loose an overwhelming terror. But there was still another possibility, no less dangerous. No coronary patient was harder to rehabilitate than the man who, ostrich-like, stubbornly refused to believe that he had really had a heart attack, hiding the truth from himself. He was the man who too often left the hospital only to go plunging ahead down the same suicidal path that had brought him there in the first place.

Undecided, Aaron Kharr searched the patient's face, hunting for some clear indication of character and personality, acutely aware that he knew nothing about him except what could be drawn from his being a corporation executive, and even more revealingly, perhaps, engaged in advertising and promotion, an area of business activity that was not only notably stress-producing, but also one that attracted men of a type more than ordinarily susceptible to psychogenic influence.

"Just this damn belly of mine," the patient said, again explosively insistent.

"You've had this same trouble before?" he asked, a testing question, intently watching the man's face, searching for any hint of what lay behind those belligerently narrowed eyes.

"My own fault," the patient said, angrily self-critical. "Grabbed a couple of cheeseburgers. Should have known better. Always does it—this damn belly——" He winced sharply.

"Still feeling some pain, are you?" he asked, noting from the card that Raggi had already given him morphine. "When did this start, Mr. Wilder? How long ago?"

"Ten after seven," was the instant reply, the quick and precise response of a man who lived by the clock, a significant indicator of the precoronary syndrome. "Be all right in a minute or two." He tried to prove it by starting to sit up.

Aaron Kharr reached out, restraining him with a hand on his shoulder, testing the strength of his resistance, finding it significantly weak.

"This belly trouble you've had, Mr. Wilder—how serious has it been? Ever had an ulcer?"

"No, nothing like that. It's just——"

"How did this pain hit you?" he asked, guided by Raggi's note that the patient had been picked up at Sam's Diner. "You said you'd eaten these cheeseburgers at the diner——"

"No, that was back on the turnpike. I'd just come off——"

"You were in your car—driving?"

"Yes, I——"

"This may seem a foolish question, Mr. Wilder, but it may help me get at what's wrong here. You were driving along—this pain suddenly hit. Now what was your first reaction? What did you do—stop immediately?"

"No, I—had to drive on a little ways—find a place where I could —get off the road."

"Then what? Did you sit there in your car for a while, feeling as if you were paralyzed, as if you couldn't move?"

"I knew what it was, just this damn belly. I got out—tried to walk it off. Then I saw the diner—thought I'd get some Alka-Seltzer——"

"I understand," he interrupted, saving the patient from the effort of further speech, positive now that his diagnosis was correct. That first walk-it-off reaction was the classic symptom of coronary occlusion, differentiating it from an anginal attack. "Have you ever had any reason, Mr. Wilder, to think that there might be anything wrong with your heart? Have you been worried about—?"

"It's not my heart! That state trooper—that's all that started this crazy heart business."

Dr. Kharr responded with a calculated smile. "Oh, I don't think Dr. Raggi would accept a trooper's diagnosis," glancing at the young resident, belatedly aware that Raggi had absolutely no sense of humor. Quickly excusing himself to the patient with "Let's see if we can find something to make you a little more comfortable," he made a finger gesture toward the door.

Raggi opened it, following him out, dead-seriously pleading, "Please, sir, I was not accepting the—"

"I concur in your diagnosis, Dr. Raggi."

The young resident's face lapsed into a smile of ineffable gratitude. "Thank you, sir."

"But not in your procedure."

Stricken, Raggi asked, "How is that, sir?"

"I fail to see any evidence of a need for an oxygen mask," he said mildly. "And you do have to think of the traumatic effect on the patient."

"I know, sir, but Dr. Sippleton always told us that it was the safest procedure to——"

"Safest for whom—the doctor or the patient?" He cut him off, needled to the flare-point by Raggi's quoting of Sippleton. It was understandable, perhaps—Sippleton, as a celebrity lecturer, had the knack of impressing all medical students—but Aaron Kharr could not hear his name without a galling memory of how the old cardiologist, moderating an Atlantic City panel on the etiology of coronary occlusion, had cut the ground out from under the paper Kharr had written on his work at the Berringer Institute, Sippleton throwing all the weight of his considerable reputation behind the pronouncement that there was no definitive evidence whatsoever that stress was a causative factor in coronary occlusion. But now as a triumph of self-control, Dr. Kharr asked quietly, "Did you give him heparin?"

"No, sir," Raggi said, perceptive enough not to say that the use of heparin was not a Sippleton-approved procedure.

"I'd suggest a hundred milligrams at once."

"Yes, sir," Raggi snapped back, wheeling to the drug cabinet.

"Have you called Dr. Teeter?"

"He is out of town, sir."

Suppressing comment, he looked at the admission card. "New Ulster—how far away is that?"

"Miss Pearson says about forty miles, sir."

"I don't suppose you've called his wife yet?"

"I am afraid, sir, there will be some difficulty on that score. She is on a ship that has only today sailed for Europe."

"We'll have to notify someone," he said, turning to reenter the examining room, noticing that the patient's eyes flicked away at the opening of the door, reaffirming a stubborn refusal of acceptance.

The nurse was still standing with the electrocardiograph tape in her hand. Purposefully, he reached out for it. As he had expected, it offered no evidence of a coronary occlusion—it was too early for that—but he continued to stare at the tape, calculatedly putting on the pressure, waiting until the patient's eyes came back to him, silent until he heard him say, "You still think it's my heart, don't you?"

"I think this," he said firmly. "It would be an extremely dangerous gamble to assume that it's not. What I would suggest, Mr. Wilder, is that you let us put you to bed—" He allowed his voice to lapse, watching the patient's reaction, seeing his eyes narrow, his jaws clamp, the left hand secretively clenching the table edge.

Aaron Kharr braced himself for the inevitable next question. It never came. Instead he heard a firmly courageous "What about my car?"

He called out to Raggi, "What about Mr. Wilder's car?"

"It will be brought here, sir. I have been so informed by the police officer."

"Don't worry about your car, Mr. Wilder. We'll see that it's taken care of."

"Not worrying—about the car," the patient said, speaking now in short bursts as if fearful of a deep breath. "There are some proofs—front seat—stockholders report. Somebody'll have to—come up for them. Will you call—Mr. Crouch?"

Recalling the corporate name on the admission card he said, "He's the president of your company, I take it?"

"Yes—Matthew R. Crouch—New Ulster. Call his home. The number——"

"Don't worry about the number, Mr. Wilder. The operator can get it easily enough."

"Just tell him—have someone—pick up the proofs."

"I'll see that he's called," he promised abstractedly, his attention preempted by this significant revelation of job obsession. There was no more certain evidence of a stress-induced coronary than the patient who, at this critical juncture, thought not of himself but only of his work.

"Tell him—call the printer. They're holding the press—waiting for an okay."

"All right," he agreed. "Now what's this about your wife? I understand——"

"You can't call her. She's on a ship—just sailed—for Europe."

"Is there anyone else we can call?" he began, but stopped as he saw a flash of fear suddenly freeze the patient's face, explained by the question: "It's not that bad—is it?"

"Let's hope not," the doctor said, purposely withholding positive assurance. "Get a good night's sleep—tomorrow morning we'll be able to tell a lot more than we can now."

For a moment the patient seemed amenable enough, apparently accepting the situation, a supposition canceled as he burst out with "But I've got to get out of here before noon! Got a big convention coming up—only five weeks——" His voice was choked off by a spasm of pain.

Aaron Kharr stared down at the momentarily contorted face, positive beyond any doubt that he was on solid ground. This was no unique case. There were, in the research studies he had accumulated at the Berringer Institute, a hundred or more reports on men who had been driven to a coronary by this same singleminded obsession with a business enterprise. He had seen them in an earlier stage at the Allison Clinic, men who were plainly headed toward this same end, deaf to any warning, madly insistent upon sacrificing themselves for a purpose that, strangely, none of them was ever able to define. They were like religious zealots searching for some mystic revelation, so obsessed that the quest itself had been perverted into a goal. And this was the result, the wreckage left in the path of the hurricane, the heart torn by the wild winds of the madly driven mind.

How could any cardiologist with even half-open eyes fail to see what was so plainly obvious, so undeniably true? Sippleton must have seen a thousand cases like this . . .

Reminiscent anger flushed his face as he heard again the echo of those never-to-be-forgotten words with which Sippleton had dismissed his Atlantic City paper . . . "If I correctly interpret Dr. Kharr's imaginative little hypothesis, he would have us all turn over our practices to the psychiatrists" . . . and then that wave of laughter, sweeping toward him from the audience, crest-breaking as he came down from the platform, crushing him into his seat. It was the worst defeat he had ever suffered, beaten down again by the tight-ranked cardiologists who, securely entrenched behind their self-saving specialist's creed that the organic heart was their only concern, would go on proudly chalking up a statistical "recovery" for every patient who became ambulatory, unmindful of the thousands they had turned into heart-fearing neurotics who would never again be the men they had been before, or at the opposite pole, men so blindly unaware of what had really happened to them that they were completely unprepared to protect themselves from a second attack.

For an instant, as a reflex reaction to contained anger, Aaron Kharr thought of taking this case himself, swept along by the captivating prospect of proving again that a patient could, with the right kind of handling, be rescued from the traumatic effect of a stress-induced coronary, cured not only in body but in mind as well. Why not? There was a provision in his contract that allowed him to take a limited number of cases "of particular scientific interest" . . . he could easily enough maintain that . . .

Fantasy collapsed with an intruding anticipation of what would happen when this Mr. Crouch was called, all but hearing the presidential voice proclaiming that "the best heart man in the country" would be called in, the voice of the corporation belligerently asserting its humanitarian concern. And tomorrow morning Dr. Big Name would drive up from Philadelphia in his big black Cadillac with a shiny gold caduceus on the bumper, a specialist with a reputation big enough to hide corporate guilt, a fee high enough to assuage presidential conscience. Whoever he was, he would set a rigid regimen that the attending physician would not dare to violate. And the attending physician would be . . .

In his mind's eye he saw Harmon Teeter's moon-shaped face, that fat gargoyle smile with which he tried to mask the leer of avarice. These turnpike coronaries were the juiciest of plums, particularly when they involved a corporation executive, affluent himself and backed by company insurance, who would not quibble about a five-hundred-dollar fee for medical attendance during a three-week hospitalization. And under County Memorial's lottery system, this was Teeter's jackpot payoff. Even though he was not in the hospital, this was his assigned day, giving him a proprietary right to the case. No physician on the staff was more poorly qualified, temperamentally, to handle a cardiac rehabilitation, but by the same token there was no doctor who would more surely resent the loss of a five-hundred-dollar fee.

Raggi was standing by, ready to inject the heparin. Almost without thought, surely not as a conscious effort to salvage what little he could, Aaron Kharr held up a momentarily restraining hand, snapping an order to the nurse. "Get me four tubes of blood."

Impatiently, he snatched the syringe from her hand and drew the blood himself, unmindful of Raggi's look of puzzled inquiry. "Now the heparin, Dr. Raggi."

The patient asked, "You'll call Mr. Crouch?"

"Yes, right away," he said, adding, "I'll do it myself," as a penance for momentary rebellion against the professionally demanded blind support of colleagues like Teeter. "We'll get you to bed now, Mr. Wilder, and I'll see you again in a few minutes."

There was a telephone in the outer room but he passed it up, striding down the corridor, needing an extra minute or two to prepare himself for agreement that whoever this Mr. Crouch named as the corporation-approved cardiologist was indeed a highly accredited specialist.

« 3 »

Over the years Matthew R. Crouch had done a reasonably successful job of teaching himself to control his emotions. Under most circumstances, he could now maintain a dignified self-restraint appropriate to his late-in-life role as a man of wealth and substance, the principal stockholder and chief executive officer of the Crouch Carpet Company. But this was his home, not his office, and he clumped down the telephone receiver, wheeling like a taunted terrier, glaring at his wife.

"What is it, dear?" Emily asked quietly, a calming reminder that after thirty-nine years of marriage, there was no point whatsoever in trying to conceal anything from her.

He took a deep breath, finally able to say, "Judd Wilder's had a heart attack." Once it was out, a barrier breached, there was no holding back. "What in God's name are we doing to these men? Sam Harrod—Mac—now Judd. If we lose him, too——"

"Now listen, Matt," she commanded, standing, her hands reaching out to clamp his arms. "It's not your fault. Get that out of your head right now."

"Something's wrong. You don't lose three men in a year—young men——"

"Mac was almost sixty."

"But Judd's only—he can't be more than—" He made a quick

calculation, remembering that Judd Wilder had been thirty-two when he had hired him in 1952. "My God, Emily, he's only forty-four!"

Her hard-gripping hands shook his shoulders, a rough gesture, a sharp contrast with the voice that calmly declared, "He's not dead, Matt."

"Sam Harrod didn't die either—but look what it's done to him."

"Matt!" There was the sting of a slap in her voice.

"All right," he conceded. "But it's true. Before his heart attack, Sam was the best damn wool buyer in the industry. Now he goes around like he's walking on eggs, scared to death——"

"Some men lick it," she cut in, the sting still in her voice.

For a moment he did not get it. Then it hit him quick and hard, and he counterpunched with a fast "It wasn't my heart!"

"And it isn't Sam Harrod's heart either—not now."

He sidestepped with "Judd's been pushing too hard. I knew it. I tried to get him to slow down but—damn it, I should have *made* him!"

"Stop it, Matt. It's not your fault, you know it isn't."

He took a deep breath, expelling it expressively, a concession to authority.

"Where is he?" she asked, a reminder that she had heard only one side of the telephone conversation.

"Way up above Marathon. Some little country hospital—County Memorial. I remember seeing the place—just before you get to the turnpike."

"Is that where it happened, on the turnpike?"

"On his way back from New York—the same way it hit Mac," he muttered, shaking his head groggily, trying to dislodge the nightmare that had plagued him for so long, sharing the terror that Mac must have felt, mortally stricken, trying to flag down someone who would help him, dead when a patrol car finally stopped. "I hate that damn town!"

Emily was staring at him, her blank face a prelude to a suddenly exclaimed "Oh, Matt, if he was coming back from New York—how awful for her!"

"Her?"

"Kay. She sailed today."

"She would!"

"Now Matt——"

"Would you go gallivanting off to Europe all by yourself——"

"She won't be by herself. Rolfe's there. And she has this old aunt of hers——"

"All right, all right, but I still say——"

"Matt, be reasonable. Kay couldn't have known something like this was going to happen."

"She *should* have known. *I* should have known. I *did* know. I kept telling him he ought to slow down, take it easier. Damn it, I should have *made* him!"

"Matt, stop blaming yourself. You couldn't have——"

"There he is with a heart attack, and do you know what he's worrying about—getting the proofs of the stockholders report okayed so we can mail it on Tuesday. Damn it, it *is* my fault. I was pushing him to get it in the mail before——"

"Matt!"

"All right, all right, but it wasn't that important. Nothing is."

Emily said placatingly, "It can't be too bad. If he was conscious enough to have someone—who called you?"

"Oh, some doctor—said his name was Kharr. Chief internist up there, whatever that means, a little hospital like that."

"What will you do—have a heart specialist go up?"

"I suppose so," he said grimly. "But I'll tell you one thing—it won't be that Philadelphia character we had for Sam Harrod."

"Matt, you can't blame any doctor for——"

"The hell I can't. I do. Before he got to Sam——"

"You just don't like doctors, that's all."

"Why should I? You know what they tried to do to me. If I'd listened to them——"

"How did Dr. Kharr sound?"

"As good as any of them, I guess."

"You could call someone about him, couldn't you? At least you could find out how well he's qualified. I know when Margaret had that kidney trouble down in Florida, Harry checked up on the doctor who——"

"Who could I call?"

"Who's Judd's doctor here, do you know?"

"Oh, that pretty-boy Hewes," he said angrily, jut-jawed, blaming himself for having let Roger Stark talk him into retaining Dr. Lyman Hewes to supervise the setting up of the company's fancy new Executive Health Appraisement Program, an opening that Hewes had quickly capitalized upon for the benefit of his private practice. "What I ought to do is get up there myself."

"Matt Crouch, you're not leaving this house. It's at least forty miles up there, and the way it's raining——"

"Damn it, I've got to do something!"

"Why don't you call Howard Robbins? He used to be president of the medical association, didn't he? At least, he could tell you something about this hospital, whether they have the facilities to——"

He wheeled to the telephone, snatching up the directory, action always his best antidote for tension.

"His home number is TRinity 2–8604."

He gave her a quickly questioning glance as he dialed, wondering how she happened to know his doctor's number. She must have memorized it. But why? Was she still worried about him? Why should she be? There was nothing wrong with him, not now. He'd gotten over that hump a long time ago. That's what every man had to do—get over the hump, learn how to take the pressure. That's what he'd tried to tell Judd. He *had* told him, time and time again. Judd just hadn't listened. But he would now . . . a man did a lot of thinking in a hospital bed . . .

He felt himself suddenly staggered, struck by a sneak blow . . . the *convention?* This was the first of April . . . only five weeks . . . Judd would be out for at least two months . . .

Behind him he heard Emily murmur, "I just can't get over how awful this will be for Kay."

« 4 »

As Judd Wilder was being wheeled down the long corridor there was a recurrence of the same illusion that he had experienced in the ambulance, the feeling that he was being transported to some very distant place. But now, as had not been the case before, there was an alarming measure of movement. Lying on his back, staring upward, he saw the ceiling lights as blazing mileposts along an unearthly blue boulevard, repetitive proof that he was being carried farther and farther down a one-way road that was tangibly existent only within the circle of his vision, disappearing behind him, leaving no way to return, no route of escape.

Confused by incongruity, he tried to fight off a demanding sensation of lethargy by arousing himself to a desperate effort to hold on to what was so rapidly slipping away, frightened now by the realization that everything he had accomplished in New York was about to be lost. No one would know the promises that he had exacted, the assignments that the agency had agreed to undertake . . . there must be a Dictaphone around here somewhere . . . get it all down before it was too late . . .

"Now, now, Mr. Wilder, just take it easy," someone restrained him, a voice seemingly but not certainly feminine. An echoing resonance made it seem both male and female, a neuter mingling of Kay and Mr. Crouch, of Gloria and the state trooper, of the brown-skinned doctor in the ambulance and the cold-fingered nurse who had opened his shirt, the massed voices of all of the people who were always telling him to take it easy . . . take it easy . . . take it easy . . . *take it easy* . . .

No, he didn't dare! Not yet. He had to get everything tied down . . . get Allen Talbott up here . . . tell him what had to be done . . . no time to waste . . . *only five weeks to the convention* . . .

He was suddenly overwhelmed by suffocating heat, the hospital as hot as the diner had been . . . he had to think before it was too late . . . remember everything that he had done in New York. Begin at the beginning . . . yesterday morning . . .

"We're almost there, Mr. Wilder."

Desperately, he made a last attempt to think, closing his eyes, clenching his fists, feeling his brain a heat-dried sponge that, no matter how hard he squeezed, yielded nothing. New York was too long ago, too far away.

He did hear a voice, a sharply concerned—"Mary, get Dr. Kharr" —and then there was the sound of running footsteps fading away down the corridor, farther and farther, finally lost in the distance beyond distance.

« 5 »

For the third time in the last hour, Aaron Kharr gently pushed open the door of Room 24, scowling another acknowledgment of his guilt as he saw the ghostly outline of the oxygen tent over the bed. Mrs. Cope, the head nurse on the floor, was still on watch, sitting under the small-bulbed floor lamp, the only light in the darkened room. Absenting herself from the desk was a violation of rule and practice that should not be condoned, but after what had happened he was in no mood to criticize anyone but himself.

Plainly, he had lost his head, panicking when that young nurse had burst into his office proclaiming that the patient was going into shock. It had not been shock, nor had there ever been any such danger, but hurrying down the corridor, accused by the memory of how he had taken off that oxygen mask in Emergency, he had ordered a tent before he had fully appraised the situation. Once committed, there had been no turning back, particularly after Mrs. Cope had appeared and taken charge.

All he could hope now was that Mrs. Cope had never read his *Annals* paper "The Trauma of the Tent," an accusation that the indiscriminate use of the oxygen tent, so frightening to the patient, was a significant cause of the neurotic aftermath so frequently encountered with coronary cases. He had even written, "Too often, the ordering of the tent is the act of an attending physician thinking first of himself and only secondarily of the patient, primarily concerned with protecting himself against criticism."

The moment his fingertips had touched the patient's warm skin, he knew that it was not true shock, only a neurogenic simulation, but by then Mrs. Cope had already gone into action. He might still have stopped her had he not been momentarily diverted by consciousness of another error. This, too, was something of which he had too often accused his colleagues: failing to give weight enough to the psychological impact of a coronary occlusion. It was not that he had overlooked it—it had been in the forefront of his mind from the moment he looked at Wilder's admission card—but somehow he had deluded himself into thinking that the patient was refusing to accept the reality of his heart attack. After his years at the Allison Clinic, he of all people should not have been fooled by the false front of self-control so often observed in men who had lived their lives in big corporations.

Seeing him now, Cope rose and came to the door, her flat-footed stride telling him that the patient had finally succumbed to sedation. "He's sleeping like a spanked baby," she reported with a satisfied smile, sounding like the Pennsylvania-Dutch *hausfrau* that he had taken her to be when he had first come to County Memorial. He knew better now. She had, indeed, been a Marathon County farm girl, raised near Five Corners, but unlike her earthbound family she had escaped the soil, her nurse's cap a passport to far places. She had worked, it seemed, in hospitals all over the country, even serving an enlistment as an Army nurse. In the course of her wanderings she had acquired a rough-and-ready competence that, he had soon found, visibly awed most of the G.P.'s on County Memorial's staff. Although she accorded them—at least within a patient's hearing—the outward obeisance that the profession demanded, it was only too evident that they reacted to her raised right eyebrow as if it were a threat of loss of license.

"Has Mrs. Potts located a night nurse yet?" he asked, a reference to his having told her before that the president of the patient's company had authorized private nurses around the clock.

"Oh, I took care of it," she said casually, adding a tossed-away "But I told Pottsy," as a minor concession to protocol. "Mary Welch just happened to come by. She'll be all right."

"Welch—I don't believe I know her," he said cautiously, unable to equate the unusual personal interest that Cope had shown in this case with the casual picking-up of a nurse whom she credited with being no more than "all right."

Cope planted her hands on her ample hips, a gesture that in her lexicon was roughly equivalent to a tongue in the cheek. "She's had three years of psychiatric at Eastern Veterans."

Was this her oblique way of criticizing him for overemphasis on the psychosomatic aspects of medical practice? It seemed a likely possibility. Cope had given him more than a little reason to suspect that she had her own ideas of the proper division between *psyche* and *soma*—the mind the rightful province of the more perceptive and understanding nurse, the physician wisely confined to the treatment of bodily ills. "This isn't a psychiatric case, Mrs. Cope."

"No," she said, making it almost a question. "Anyway, she ought to be able to handle him when he wakes up and finds himself in an oxygen tent." Her hands were still on her hips. "That's what's worrying you, isn't it?"

He gave her a crisp nod, hoping that he was not revealing the way she made him feel, a boy again, confronted by his too-perceptive mother.

"He's the kind of a man it could hit," she observed pointedly.

"Yes."

"I've seen plenty of it."

"I'm sure you have," he said, sensing that all this was a prelude to something else. He stepped back into the corridor.

Cope followed him, half closing the door. "I guess you know about his wife being on this ship going to Europe?"

"Yes, she sailed this noon."

"She won't get there for six days—nothing she can do, anyway—so he doesn't want any message sent to her." She shrugged. "Anyway, that's what he says."

He nodded, responsive to her suggestion of a deeper truth, recalling his work at the Berringer Institute, the clear evidence that there was a significant coordination between marital difficulties and under-fifty heart attacks. A substantial percentage of the men he had studied had, in the beginning, singled out their wives as a major cause of precoronary stress. Later questioning had often proved it to be misdirected blame, a convenient way to hide honest acceptance of the real cause, but there were cases where it was a justified accusation, and none were harder to bring around.

"No matter what he says, she ought to be told," Cope said, surprising him not only with the vigor of her statement but also with a concern that was strangely out of character. As was the case with so many men-biased older nurses, she had always before acted as if she regarded wives as the curse of the nursing profession.

"I notified the president of his company," he said. "That should be adequate for tonight. I'm sure we can safely leave any further notification to whoever will be taking care of him tomorrow."

She regarded him with bold intensity. "Aren't you taking this case yourself?"

"Of course not," he said, more brusquely than he intended, then lamely excusing it with: "No doubt his company will be sending up a cardiologist in the morning. They usually do—one of their top executives."

"He'll be here, he'll be gone," she said tartly. "Then what?"

"Once he's laid down the regimen to be followed, it will be simple enough for one of our staff doctors to follow through."

"Dr. Teeter," she said, only the name, not a word more, but her tone, had it been quotable, would have been good and sufficient reason for taking away her certification as a registered nurse.

Escaping a frightening temptation to agree, he pushed past her and went into the room, crossing to the bed, looking down at the sleeping patient, seeing his face as a blur, less because of the screening plastic than because of the intruding memory of another face, Harvey Allison's on that last day at the Clinic, his quietly angry voice cutting like cold steel . . . *"For the good of your own soul, Dr. Kharr, I hope that you will very soon find yourself in a situation where you will be proved no less fallible than the doctors you are always so ready to criticize."*

With a trembling hand he reached down and lifted the plastic skirt of the oxygen tent, looping it over the support, clearing his field of vision. Intently, he studied the patient's face, a vigil maintained for a long time. He saw not the slightest hint of distress. Judging by the relatively short duration of pain, the myocardial infarct was small. No matter who the attending physician was, the heart would heal itself. In three weeks, Teeter would dismiss him from the hospital, close out the case, chalk up another uneventful recovery, and send him on his way with a conscience-free five-hundred-dollar bill for professional services. And who could say that Teeter was wrong? There was a limit to a doctor's responsibility. There had to be.

Behind him, Cope asked, "Worried about him?"

"No."

"Mrs. Welch will be back in a few minutes. Do you want to talk to her before she goes on duty?"

He started to say no, that it would not be necessary, but heard himself say yes.

At least for tonight, this was his case.

« 6 »

Six hours out from New York, the *Bretagne* was overtaken and swiftly passed by the *Queen Elizabeth*. No more than nodding her bow to the majestic English queen, the small French ship continued on at her own pace, following the eastbound steamship lane into the night as surefootedly as an old duchess crossing the familiar grounds of her ancestral château. In the matriarchal peerage of the open seas, the *Bretagne* had a place that was all her own, well maintained by the stoutness of her iron heart, supported by that small but influential coterie of ocean travelers who, with cult-like devotion, regarded a *Bretagne* crossing as one of the few civilized experiences still available is a madly scurrying world.

Kay Wilder was not one of those devotees—she had originally planned to fly—but Miss Jessica most definitely was, and that was largely why Kay was now on board. This was not, however, the first time she had been a *Bretagne* passenger. Twenty-six years ago this summer, Miss Jessica had hurried her aboard at Le Havre, a twenty-year-old girl treated like a helpless child, sent back to the States to escape a France threatened by war. Now, a quarter-century later, two months past her forty-sixth birthday, she was finally returning to Paris, again on the *Bretagne*, again with the feeling of forced escape. But what that force might be was indefinable. What she was running away from was something too amorphous to be named, too unnamable to be acknowledged.

Except for the persistent memory of having been horribly seasick that first night out of Le Havre, Kay Wilder had almost no recollection of her 1939 crossing, and what little she had seen of the ship since she had come aboard had aroused no sense of familiarity. For one thing, the vessel's interior had been almost completely rebuilt after the war. For another, instead of being cramped into a four-berth cabin with three other women and three tiny children as she had been in 1939, she was now alone in one of the eight choice cabins on the boat deck, accounted by all *Bretagne* devotees to be the best of accommodations on the best of all ships. Up to now, however, she had had no chance to appreciate whatever special charm her cabin might have. Coming aboard in New York, she had no more than glimpsed it when it had been suddenly overrun by the incrushing hordes of that awful sailing party.

Judd had insisted that he'd had nothing to do with it, that he'd known nothing about it—it was possible, of course, as blind as he was to everything that did not directly concern Crouch Carpet—but he must have said something around the advertising agency or they would not all have come piling down to the ship, everyone on the Crouch Carpet account plus a miscellaneous assortment of space peddlers and time salesmen, all eagerly embracing an excuse to start drinking at ten-thirty instead of waiting until lunchtime for their first martinis. Her cabin door, it seemed, had been open to anyone with an expense account big enough to cover an admitting bottle of liquor, or one of those incredibly tasteless baskets done up in flame-colored cellophane that, seen in Madison Avenue shop windows, had always made her wonder who would ever be stupid enough to buy one. There were five of them now at the bottom of the Atlantic—or at least that was what she had told the cabin steward to do with them, throw them overboard, anything to get rid of them, not only the baskets but everything else that had been carted in and dumped upon her.

But nothing, it seemed, could rid her cabin of this terrible after-party smell, this rank compound of a dozen foul odors, the gagging stink of fire snuffed out in canapes, of soggy cigarette butts smoldering in dung-like heaps, of the stale dregs of whiskey spilled and wine splashed, of cheese ground into the carpet and caviar smeared on the upholstery, of the man-smell of sweat and the non-man stink of fruity perfumes. After the steward had done his best, she had gone on brushing and scrubbing, both portholes open to the cleansing sea air, trying not only to clear her nostrils but also to shut from her mind all that even the faintest whiff suggested.

She thought she had succeeded but now, as she opened the hanging locker to take out the black Italian knit that she planned to wear down to dinner, the moving door fanned out a hidden pocket of redolent odor. Hurriedly struggling with the heavy wing nut on the porthole latch, breaking a fingernail, she got the forward port open, shivering then in the blast of cold air as she hurriedly finished dressing. Until a half-hour ago, she had not planned to go down to dinner, so vividly recalling herself as a bad sailor that she had thought it best to get her sea legs firmly under her before chancing a public meal. But then, assured by the calm sea and her continuing sense of physical well-being, she had decided to at least give it a try. Now the decision was clinched. She had to get out of this cabin.

Starting down the passageway, feeling it swaying unfirmly under her feet, she again wished that she had taken a plane. But quickly set against that regret was the prospect that, in the end, had made her bow to Miss Jessica's insistence. This way—if she could only control her mind—she would have six days of total escape, completely cut off from Judd and Crouch Carpet and New Ulster, not yet called upon to face Miss Jessica and Paris and Rolfe. Yes, most of all Rolfe. Safely alone now, she could admit that it was because of her son that she had felt it so urgently necessary to make this trip. She no longer needed to fear that she might betray to Judd, by some inadvertent word or intonation, that the idea had come not from the reminder in Rolfe's letter that April 9 would be Miss Jessica's seventy-fourth birthday, but from that terrifyingly veiled threat in Rolfe's last paragraph. Judd had read the letter, too, of course, but as usual he had impatiently skimmed the last paragraph —either that or he had been so fortunately obtuse that he had missed its implication. In either event, she had aroused no suspicion when she had said, as offhandedly as she could manage, that she wished she could be in Paris for Miss Jessica's seventy-fourth birthday. "Well, why not?" Judd had responded, alarming her only for that moment when it had seemed that he might be thinking of going with her, a crisis safely passed as soon as he realized that, on April 9, he would be right in the middle of staging his precious convention.

She had written both Rolfe and Miss Jessica that same night, spending most of the evening on her letter to Rolfe, weighing every word, knowing that it would be suspiciously unnatural if she were not to say how anxious she was to see him, yet knowing too that everything would be lost if Rolfe got the idea that she might try in any way to influence what he was planning to do after Paris. Her care and skill had been rewarded. His reply had sounded, if not overly enthusiastic about the date of her arrival—he might not be able to meet her because of something at the Sorbonne—at least fully approving a surprise birthday party for Miss Jessica, even offering to start at once on the arrangements.

Her note to Miss Jessica, much too hurriedly written, had brought the kind of response that she should have known it would get. Her thoughtlessly scrawled sentence about being uncertain of getting an airline reservation had set her aunt off in true Miss Jessica fashion. Impatient as always of all bureaucratic underlings, she had called her dear old friend, the chairman of the steamship company, and her letter enclosed not only a prepaid ticket but a firm and non-cancelable assignment to one of the boat-deck cabins signed by the chairman himself. Miss Jessica's letter did not mention the *Bretagne* by name—that was to be assumed, just as her oblique comment, "We Cannons have always been ship people," expressed her opinion of those below-the-salt New Yorkers who were always popping in and out of Paris on their flying machines.

Uncertain of the dining saloon's location, Kay went down one deck, and directed by the sound of laughter, walked aft. But it was only the bar, Café des Boulevards, as phonily Parisian as the new cocktail lounge at the New Ulster Country Club. Instantly retreating, she went back to the staircase, but inescapably reminded that this was Thursday, visualizing all the Vixen Valley crowd at the country club, grateful that she was at least missing the torture of another Thursday-at-the-Club, stuck with all of those sheep-brained females inanely chattering on about the only three subjects that interested them—children, beauty parlors, and cleaning women—while the men holed up at the bar, totally engrossed with their single-minded subject, Crouch Carpet.

On the deck below she saw the purser's office. Two couples stood before it, and catching quick snatches of their conversation, she gathered that the passenger list was out. Stalling until they moved on, she picked one up, and starting with the first name, worked her way through to the last, testing every one for any overtone of familiarity. From *Abbey, Mrs. J. B., Detroit, Mich.* to *Zwinker, Mr. and Mrs. John, Charlottesville, Va.* there was not a single name that suggested any threat to six memory-free days of isolated anonymity. There was no one from anywhere near New Ulster, a few Main Line names but none who would recognize her—at least not as Kay Wilder.

Turning, she found herself confronted, but only for an instant, by a woman whose face seemed startlingly familiar. There was the flicker of an exchanged smile, but actually no more than a mutual acknowledgment of presence, and as Kay stepped aside to clear the way she realized that it was the woman in the Givenchy coat. Kay had noticed her coming aboard, hurrying up the gangplank at the last minute, breasting the downrushing tide of visitors blasted off by the all-ashore whistle. She had been on deck only to wave goodbye to Judd on the dock, but he was already in a huddle with two of the agency men, checking some proofs that had been spread out on a dockside packing case, and she had started back to her cabin when her eye had been caught by this woman, actually not as much the woman herself as by the coat she was wearing. Unmistakably, it was the Givenchy that she had looked at yesterday on her brief foray into Bergdorf's, the coat that she herself might have bought had it not been such a madly unjustifiable extravagance. But this woman had bought it, and obviously as a last-minute impulse purchase. Whoever she might be, she had money and was accustomed to spending it lavishly, hardly a recommendation, yet as Kay went down the last flight of stairs, the thought crossed her mind that, if she were looking for a shipboard acquaintance—which, of course, she was not—this woman in the Givenchy coat was the only prospect she had seen for even a half-interesting conversation. There were plenty of other unattached women, at least a dozen names on the passenger list, but she had seen enough of them on deck at sailing time to mark them off as a bunch of uniformly blue-rinsed and be-diamonded widows whose sole purpose in life had become that of finding another listener to another agonized recounting of poor dear Henry's heart attack—or if it wasn't Henry, it would be Joe, or Frank, or Bill, but always a heart attack.

Well reminded of the dangers of involvement, Kay came down the last flight of stairs, finally at the open doors of the dining saloon, resolved to insist that she be given a table alone, prepared to counter any argument with the sure knowledge, gained from her count of the passenger list, that with First Class no more than half filled, there were plenty of open tables.

"Ah, Madame Wilder," the chief steward greeted her, hands up in a Gallic expression of joyous fulfillment. She had no idea how he recognized her, or why he seemed so greatly relieved by her presence, until she picked out of his effervescent bubble of words something about the captain's table.

For a first moment she was silenced by incredulity, her voice no more than recovered when it was choked off again by the realization that all hope of Nirvanic anonymity had been shattered by Miss Jessica's call to the chairman of the steamship company. Protest was useless. She was already being guided down the full length of the saloon, every pair of eyes in the room watching her.

An empty chair loomed ahead, and she wanted nothing so much as to slip into it unnoticed, but no, she must remain standing to meet everyone at the table, an exercise in willpower made all the more difficult by the chief steward's insistence upon formal introductions. Names blew through her mind like leaves tossed into the wind, nothing registering except the suddenly terrifying illusion that she was back in New Ulster, that this was another Thursday-at-the-Club, the same faces around the same table.

At last she could sit down, nodding dumbly to the chief steward's sycophantic murmur as he pushed in her chair, gratefully accepting the screening shelter of the huge menu that someone slipped in front of her face, hiding the trembling of lips frustrated by their inability to voice the despair of a soul imprisoned in a maze that, no matter how hard she struggled to escape, always brought her back to the same place.

Glancing away, she saw the woman in the Givenchy coat being seated alone at a table against the wall.

II

UNKNOWN TO JUDD WILDER, lost in the drug-hazed oblivion of this first night in the hospital, a fervent prayer had been said for his recovery. The supplicant, conscious of her lack of grace, had begun her prayer with a confession of unworthiness, begging forgiveness for calling herself "Mrs. Welch," certain that the all-seeing, all-knowing God was aware, as she hoped no one here at County Memorial was, that her name was still Mary Hostetter. The substance of her prayer was that this case would last the full time that coronary patients were normally kept in the hospital. With three weeks of private duty, she would earn enough to pay her room rent and still leave a substantial sum against the weeks when she would not be able to work. Beyond all reasonable doubt, she was now pregnant.

This last month had been a series of small disasters. Despite what everyone said about the demand for nurses, her total earnings in four weeks had been less than two hundred dollars. She had gone off registry at Marathon General because of the fear that the Supervisor of Nurses would guess why she had been sick that morning, and transferring up here to County Memorial had put her at the bottom of the private-duty register. She had waited five days for a call, worked two nights, the patient had died, and then she was back at the bottom of the list again. That was the way it had gone all month, more time off than on, her longest duty a burn case that, horrible though it was, had disappointingly ended after four days when the patient had been transferred to Philadelphia.

Last night had been pure luck. There were still names ahead of hers on the registry, little chance of being called for at least another forty-eight hours. Too jittery to stay alone in her room, frightened of taking any more of the tranquilizers that she had snitched while on the burn case, she had walked to the hospital through the wind and rain, offering free help to Mrs. Cope. It had been a crazy thing to do—Mrs. Cope had probably guessed, the funny way that she had looked at her—but, anyway, it had worked out, that was all that mattered. Everything would work out if this case would only last.

Dr. Kharr had given her an alarming few minutes, acting as if he didn't quite believe that she had been at Eastern Veterans, asking so many questions. Anyway, he had finally let her stay. But there was no guarantee that she would be kept on. She was still on probation with Dr. Kharr, desperately anxious to prove herself. But the night had given her no chance.

"Blood pressure every half hour," Dr. Kharr had ordered. "Call me at once if it drops below one-ten or if his pulse gets above a hundred." But there had been no drop of blood pressure, no rise of pulse. Neither had there been any coughing, wheezing, or shortness of breath. There had been no chance to record, as Dr. Kharr had ordered, any intelligible words that the patient had said. The NOTES space on the chart was as blank as if she, too, had slept through the night.

The day was coming now, a thin watery light. Two minutes to six. She picked up the blood-pressure apparatus and lifted the clear plastic shirt of the oxygen tent. The patient's eyes opened and for the first time he seemed aware of her presence. She thought he was about to speak and she leaned in, listening intently, offering an encouraging "How are you feeling?" His voice was low, the words mumbled but nevertheless audible.

Elated, she wrote:

> 5:50—*Talking in sleep, patient said, "Don't have to be San Francisco until tomorrow"*

« 2 »

Turning off the alarm before it sounded, Dr. Aaron Kharr wearily pushed back the bedclothes and swung his feet to the floor. He felt tense and worn, unrefreshed by sleep. His mind was full of the

Wilder case, not as something recalled upon awakening, but as something that had been with him all through the night, endlessly explored. Introspectively, he recognized his preoccupation as a neurotic symptom, and purposely forced himself to admit that he was being a fool, wasting his concern on a case that would very shortly be taken over by someone else.

He got up, tiptoeing into the bathroom, gently opening the lavatory faucet to prevent a noisy gush of water, a precaution against awakening Mrs. Stine, whose bedroom was on the first floor, directly under his. Every consideration that he could show her, small though it might be, was more than justified. Fresh towels every morning, line-dried and smelling of the clean air and the bright sun, was a luxury that he had never known in New York.

When he had first come to County Memorial, discovering that there was no such thing as a rentable apartment within reasonable distance of the hospital, he had been faced with the problem of finding a place to sleep, his only essential requirement for a suitable home. Mrs. Potts, mother-henning him as she had during those first days, had come up with a list of nearby householders with spare rooms to rent. From the name alone he had almost automatically selected Mrs. Isaac Stine as the best bet, greatly surprised when she had said, "I'd sure like to have you, Doctor, but you're a Jewish gentleman, aren't you?"

"Yes, I'm a Jew," he had said, belligerent avowal collapsing when she had gone on: "I know you people got special ways of eating, and like I say, I'd be glad to have you, only I wouldn't know how to cook right for you."

He had assured her that his diet was not limited, that in any event he would be eating most of his meals at the hospital, and seeing the spotless room, fluffy white curtains at the window and a bright patchwork quilt on the big soft double bed—he had slept for the past two years on a ridged and lumpy daybed—he had suggested a trial tenancy for a month. Long before that month was over, he was taking as many of his meals as he could manage with Mrs. Stine. On Sundays, only the most serious of emergencies would keep him away from her dining room, filled as it always was from the seemingly inexhaustible reaches of the Stine family, his presence accepted with neither deference nor discrimination, always ready to squeeze in a place for him at the table.

After his second week, Mrs. Stine had stopped asking about his laundry, simply taking over, startling him into an awareness of what was happening when, one evening, he came home to find on his dresser a paid sales slip for six pairs of new socks and a dozen handkerchiefs. After that, no medical obligation at the hospital was of greater moment than his constant surveillance of Mrs. Stine, desperately anxious that, despite her seventy-two years, no affliction should ever be allowed to reduce her capacity to take care of him.

Dressed, still on tiptoe, he came down the stairs, mildly surprised to find Mrs. Stine already up, watching him through the kitchen doorway, sharp-elbowed arms akimbo. "Now what are you doing up at this hour of the morning?" she demanded. "You never got in until ten after one."

"Did I make a lot of noise?" he asked, obliquely apologetic.

"Anyway, you can have your coffee," she said, the forgiving matriarch giving him no chance to refuse.

He followed her into the kitchen, bright with the just-risen sun on red-striped curtains, the air redolent with the cinnamon-nutmeg odor of something already baking, amusing her with his purposely wrong guess that she must be up early because company was coming.

"Missionary sale today," she corrected him. "And I'm not having anybody come to a Trinity sale and buy something that was baked yesterday. How about my making you an egg?"

"No, just coffee," he said, knowing that she would produce at least a plate of doughnuts, perhaps even a piece of her coffee cake.

It was coffee cake, buttery yellow and raisin-dotted, and she stood waiting for the reward of his first-bite exclamation of delight. He gave it willingly enough, then casually asked, "Do you happen to know a young nurse named Welch—Mrs. Welch?"

"No Welches around here," Mrs. Stine said, significantly tight-mouthed.

"In her middle twenties, I'd say," he went on. "Medium height, round-faced, rather attractive——"

"Umhum," Mrs. Stine agreed. "What about her?"

"We needed a private nurse in a hurry last night and Mrs. Cope just happened to catch her. But if you don't know her——"

There was a twinkle in Mrs. Stine's eyes. "What I should have said—there aren't any *Mister* Welches around here. At least none that I know about. Neither does Annie Wirtz. That's where she's staying. One room, that's all, just her alone."

"Oh," he acknowledged, guessing that this must be what he had sensed, that uneasy feeling about her, converted now to self-criticism for having foolishly missed a diagnosis that probably should have been obvious.

"Nothing against her," Mrs. Stine said, generously tolerant. "Happens to nurses just like all the rest of them. You'd think they'd be smarter about it—nurses—but they ain't, not a bit. Human nature's human nature, I guess, and most of us got too much of it." She paused, waiting for encouragement and, not getting it, shifted to "Bad case last night?"

"No, not especially," he said, breaking off a piece of coffee cake, moved to add "Another coronary" by his awareness that there was nothing Mrs. Stine appreciated more than being made a party to his hospital life.

"That seems to be about all you're getting these days—coronaries."

"There are a lot of them all right, more all the time."

"Sure seems that way. When I was a girl, somebody having a heart attack—now that was something unusual. Now everybody's having them. Maybe it's just that I been noticing them more since you been here."

"No, it's true, the incidence is way up. It's at least twice as high as it was twenty years ago."

"You don't mean it. Now what in the world would cause—?"

"Oh, that may be a bit on the high side," he granted. "Some of the cases that used to be diagnosed as acute indigestion would now be recognized as occlusions, but still there's been an enormous increase."

"Why would that be?" she asked, answering herself with a quick "It's the kind of life people are leading, that's what it is—all this drinking, all this sex stuff."

"There's nothing new about sex," he smiled, knowing that it would be appreciated.

"Well, you'd think there was, the way they're all chasing around," Mrs. Stine sniffed, visibly suppressing the temptation to go on with what, rather surprisingly, was one of her favorite subjects. "Seems like the whole world's just gone crazy. And if it ain't sex, it's something else. They're always chasing something. Mostly, I guess, it's the almighty dollar. That's what our minister was preaching about Sunday—what shall it profit a man if he gain the whole world but lose his own soul."

He nodded, sipping his coffee.

"Or have a heart attack, huh?" she asked.

He nodded, again thinking how strange it was that everyone, even doctors, commonly attributed the increase in coronary disease to the heightened tensions of modern life, yet the profession went on stubbornly refusing to acknowledge emotional causation and treat it accordingly.

Mrs. Stine broke the moment of silence. "This case you had last night? Someone from around here?"

"No, a man from New Ulster. Executive with a big company down there—Crouch Carpet."

"I bet that's your answer right there," Mrs. Stine retorted. "These big companies—you remember Wilmer, don't you? The one that was here that Sunday, the one with the New Jersey wife—Selma? He's with this big oil company, kind of in charge of all their service stations down around Camden. She was telling me there ain't a blessed day in that poor man's life when he don't have to take these pills to keep his nerves from going to pieces. Seems just terrible, a company driving a man like that."

"Maybe he's in the wrong job."

"That's what I says to Selma—why don't he get into something sensible? But she says, no, he just loves it, wouldn't do nothing else. I guess it's kind of like dope, what these companies do to 'em. Once it gets into their blood, they just got to have it."

"That's a good simile," he said, draining his coffee cup.

"Sure you won't have a little more? There's plenty."

"No, I've got to get along. Want to catch this night nurse before she goes off duty."

"Who you got on seven-to-three?" she asked, a reflection of her never-flagging interest in County Memorial's nurses.

"Oh, I believe they've called Miss Harsch," he said, offhandedly.

"Umhum," she said, unimpressed. "But you've got Mabel Cope three-to-eleven?"

"No, she was on the desk last night, just took over until we got someone in."

"Mabel's a good nurse," she said, half question, half challenge.

"Yes," he agreed, but conscious of the moment of hesitation before his reply, he balanced it with a firm "Yes, she's very competent."

"No reason why she wouldn't be," Mrs. Stine said positively. "They're good people, the Weavers. That's who she was before she married this fellow Cope. I guess you know about that?"

"No," he said, submitting to conscience, reminding himself that one of his faults had always been an inadequate interest in the personal lives of the people he worked with.

"Well, he was kind of an artist, I guess you'd say—painted them big pictures they have on billboards. He was good, they said, awful good. Made big money. They said if he stayed in New York, he could have been rich—they was after him all the time—but, no, he no sooner gets one place than he wants to be someplace else. Some men are like that—itchy feet."

"Yes," he agreed, understanding now why Mrs. Cope had worked in so many hospitals.

"Then he has this heart attack."

"Heart attack?" he repeated, wondering if this might explain the special interest that Cope had shown last night in the Wilder case.

"I don't know how bad it was—some people said one thing and some said another," Mrs. Stine went on. "Anyway, it did something to him. He just kind of lost his nerve, I guess you might say. Anyway, they came back here and went to living in an old tenant house on one of the Weaver farms. Well sir, from the day he got here he didn't do a lick of nothing—to earn a living, I mean—not one blessed thing. I don't know, maybe he couldn't—maybe it really was his heart—but if you ask me, no man in his right mind would do what he done."

"What happened?"

"Well, they *said* he was cleaning a gun." She paused. "Anyway, that's the way it came out in the paper."

He stared, shattered by this revelation of how brutally he had misjudged Mrs. Cope last night. Groping for something to say, he let his subconscious mind ask, "How old was he when it happened—the heart attack?"

"Well, now let's see, I ought to be able to figure that out. He was a year younger than Mabel—I remember that from what they had in the paper—and they'd been here—yes, it was just after Ruth's Joanie had her first baby—" Her voice drifted off into a continuing mumble, undisturbed by his protest that the answer was not important, finally coming up with, "as near as I can figure, I'd say he must have been forty-four, maybe forty-five."

He nodded, abruptly standing, aware that he was beginning to victimize himself with this neurotic fixation about middle-forties coronaries. He thanked her and hurried out, deciding to take his car instead of walking the quarter-mile to the hospital, impatiently annoyed when the motor failed to catch with the first twist of the key. It was almost seven o'clock. If he didn't hurry . . .

A sensation of sudden tightness gripped his chest, quickly relieved by a deep breath. But, warned, he sat back, purposely slowing the pace of his mind, regaining composure with the calmly constructed argument that there was no reason to hurry. It was not his case—at least it wouldn't be in an hour or two. Crouch had said nothing over the telephone last night about sending up a cardiologist, but it was almost a certainty that one would appear this morning. Whoever he was, he would have nothing to criticize. The treatment of choice had been followed in every regard—yes, even to the use of the oxygen tent.

The motor caught, purring softly, and he drove slowly ahead, concerned now with only a minor decision, wondering whether he should call Dr. Teeter immediately or wait until after the big-city cardiologist appeared.

« 3 »

For what seemed a very long time, Judd Wilder had been attempting to break through the misty barrier that separated him from full consciousness. Times without number he had tried and failed, never quite able to penetrate the last thin veil that still denied him the full use of his senses.

He lay back now, not as an acknowledgment of defeat but as a calculated maneuver, waiting for his strength to build up. Finally, determined to succeed, he lifted his arms and struck out with all the force that he could muster. His doubled fists hit a slick surface, oily smooth, weightless and yielding, defying penetration. Flashes of reflected light danced about him, a net of laced lightning that hemmed him in, arousing a claustrophobic fear. Blindly, he struck out again, a clawing motion now, trying to tear his way through.

There was a distant cry of alarm. White-clad figures, ominously distorted by the light-crackled haze, were rushing in to block his escape. The only one he recognized was Kay, a recognition that incited instant apprehension, reality challenged by the fear of hallucination, seeing her not as she was now but as she had been so long ago . . . that night in Philadelphia . . .

Suddenly, miraculously, the misty barrier was gone, swept out of the way by the pass of a sorcerer's hand. He caught a quick breath, exhaling a sigh of gratitude, quickly searching out the face of his benefactor. It came into focus now, so sharply detailed that he knew he was no longer dream-deluded, yet he could not immediately solve the riddle of surely familiar identity.

"Don't be concerned about this oxygen tent, Mr. Wilder," the white-coated man said, his voice as puzzlingly familiar as his face. "We've been making you a little more comfortable, that's all. But if it bothers you, we'll get rid of it." He smiled. "In case you don't remember, I'm Doctor Kharr."

It all came back, a torrent of memory that threatened to overwhelm him. But, strangely, it did not, leaving him with the embarrassed feeling of foolish fear. "I guess I'm a little fuzzy."

"Of course you are," the doctor said. "This fuzzy feeling, Mr. Wilder—listen to me now—it's very important that you understand this—the way you're feeling has nothing to do with your heart, absolutely nothing, nothing at all. We've been giving you sedatives to keep you asleep. That's the reason you're feeling so woozy, the only reason. It's entirely the result of these drugs we've been giving you. Do you understand that?"

He nodded, wanting to say something more, to express his gratitude, to thank Dr. Kharr for worrying about him, but words were difficult to form, his lips so far away from his brain, the effort of speech so demanding.

"This is Miss Harsch, who'll be with you today," he heard the doctor say, and rousing himself to full attention, he saw the nurse who stood beside the doctor, her broad-hipped figure, iron-girdled, rising to the plastic-dimmed haze of her face. "And Mrs. Welch, of course, who was with you last night."

The second nurse was behind the doctor's chair, her face in the clear, and seeing it was a relief from illusion. He recognized now that it was her face, not Kay's, that had drifted in and out of the night fog. Reminded, he said, "You didn't send any messages—the ship—my wife?"

"No, not yet. But if you want us to——"

"No!" burst out, an exclamation self-formed, independent of thought. "I'll be out of here before—" Before what? "Before—" He remembered. "Before noon. I've got a convention meeting——"

"No, you haven't." Dr. Kharr was smiling down at him. "Don't you remember my telling you last night—what Mr. Crouch said when I called him?"

Mr. Crouch . . . the stockholders report . . . yes, that's what he'd been trying to remember. "The proofs—is he sending up some-one—?"

"It's all been taken care of, Mr. Wilder. Mr. Crouch said to tell you not to worry about anything. Someone will get the proofs."

"Good."

"And you don't have to get to San Francisco," the doctor concluded, his smile sardonically knowing.

San Francisco? Then it was true . . . he hadn't been dreaming . . . that meeting at the Los Angeles Biltmore . . .

He closed his eyes. Memory came instantly, sharp and clear, everything explained now, even this feeling of reminiscent alarm . . . standing there at the lectern, his mind suddenly gone blank, unable to recall a single word of his speech, the same speech that he had made day after day all across the country, words and phrases so firmly fixed that, day before yesterday in Dallas, he had not even turned the pages of the script. And then Los Angeles, the biggest contract carpet market in the country, all of the contractors sitting there waiting, his mind rebelling, refusing to go through with it again.

But he had gone through with it. Somehow, the dam had broken and the words had started coming. And he had gotten away with it. No one had known, all the contractors coming up afterward to tell him that it was the best manufacturer's meeting they'd ever attended. Hugh Iverson had said that it was the biggest shot in the arm that the Los Angeles office had had since he had come out as District Manager.

But then it had hit him again at the cocktail party, his brain refusing to fit names to faces, tangling his tongue. He had been a little frightened at first, wondering what was wrong, but now he knew . . . just tired, that's all . . . sixteen cities in twenty-three days . . . too many meetings, too many cocktail parties, too many names to remember. But he was all right now. All he had needed was a little rest.

That telephone call—yes, that had been his lucky break. Actually, it had been only the hotel's convention office calling to tell him that his exhibit panels had all been packed for shipment, but his desperate need to escape had made him turn it into a demand that he leave at once for San Francisco. Hugh Iverson had willingly enough believed him, his expressed disappointment no more than the act that every district manager had to put on to cover his relief at getting the home-office brass out of his hair, particularly when some of his best customers were starting to get a little sloppy, threatening a real Saturday night brawl, not at all in keeping with the Crouch Carpet image that district managers were supposed to maintain at all company affairs.

With an escape route open, Judd Wilder had taken it with a blind rush, stuffing his bag, checking out, hurrying the taxi driver who was taking him to the airport. There had been a colossal tie-up on the freeway, and the driver had gone off to detour around it, losing him in a flatland of matchbox houses, nothing seen beyond the smog-choked beam of the headlights. The street had been torn up, the taxi bounding wildly until it had hit that last chuckhole, dropping into it with a metallic crunch, crazily canted, a front wheel spindle broken. The driver, when his anger had been exhausted by cursing, had said, "Guess you'll have to call another cab. There ought to be a phone in that little motel over there."

He had seen the neon sign—LOS JUNTOS M TE—the O dark, the L flickering . . . yes, he knew where he was . . .

But why, instead of asking for a telephone, had he asked for a room? But he had. The old woman in the gray sweater had put down her knitting, getting to her feet to stare at the full key rack, pretending a difficult decision, finally handing him No. 6. He had given her a twenty-dollar bill and she had stepped back through the bead-rattling curtain, returning with the change, still without a word until she said, "On your left, three doors down."

He had found No. 6 easily enough, stopped on the threshold by a strange odor, unrecognizable until he saw the upholstered chair, the embroidered daisies that scalloped the edges of the pillowcases. He had known then why it was familiar—the smell of Iowa.

But it was gone now. Or was he used to it? All he could smell was the doctor's-office stink of that disinfectant gadget in the bathroom . . .

But he had been right about Iowa. He had proved it this morning when she had come to check up on him, knocking on his door, calling, "You all right in there?" For a minute, he hadn't known where he was, groping blindly for his robe, going to the door, startled by the blaze of sunlight into realizing how long he had slept . . . yes, that was when he'd been sure about Iowa, that Grant Wood look, the way her thin gray hair was drawn back to a tight little bun, the cameo pin clutching the high neckline of her gray dress.

What was it that she had said? Something about wanting to make sure that nothing had happened to him. "No, nothing's happened," he had said. But he was wrong. Something had happened to him. He had slept for almost twenty hours. He'd never done anything like this before.

What time was it now? He must have gone to sleep again after she had brought the creamed chipped beef . . .

Chipped beef?

Yes, she had made him something to eat. But, no, that was afterwards, after she'd made sure that he wasn't a lush holed up with a bottle, after she had found out that he was an Iowa boy, raised just twenty-two miles from where her husband's farm had been . . . the crazy old guy, giving up everything he'd had to come out here to California, leaving her stuck with this crummy little motel, nothing but a hotbed joint, a hideaway for drunks . . .

Drunk? Yes, that's what they'd thought in the diner . . .

Diner? He hadn't gone to a diner. No, she had brought him that tray, creamed chipped beef and baking powder biscuits . . . good . . . the first food all week that hadn't knotted this crazy belly. Yes, he'd gone to sleep again after that. But it was all right, still daylight, and he didn't have to be in San Francisco until tomorrow morning.

He burrowed his head into the pillow, feeling the safety of total isolation, absolutely cut off. No one knew where he was, not Kay, not

Mr. Crouch, not a soul in the world. No, not even the old lady. She didn't know his real name . . . *Floyd Fulton* . . . why had he done that, signing Floyd's name on the registration card? But she probably wouldn't recognize it, so long ago . . . not many farmers had taken *Collier's* . . .

Thought ran out, leaving an emptiness, a vacuum suddenly filled with apprehension, meaningless until he was struck with a frightening incongruity—he hadn't signed that registration card when he had checked in! No, the old lady had brought it when she had come back for the tray, leaving it on the dresser top, asking him if he would fill it out before he left. And that's what he had done . . . yes, now he could remember it all . . . flying to San Francisco, the clerk at the Fairmount giving him all those messages . . .

He wasn't at the Los Juntos . . . that had been weeks ago . . . *where was he?*

"Now, now, Mr. Wilder, we must relax, mustn't we?" a woman's voice said.

He saw a face, blinking at it until the image cleared, the white cap perched on lacquer-set gray curls, the painted marionette mask of a frozen smile. Her lips were moving again but the voice came from far away, the puppeteer behind the curtain saying, "Now, now, we mustn't be alarmed, Mr. Wilder. All we're doing is taking our blood pressure."

And as if his lips, too, were being pulled by strings, he heard his voice say, "It's true, huh—I have had a heart attack?"

"Now, now, we'll just have to ask Dr. Kharr about that, won't we?" the puppet face said, the smile cast in wax, hand-colored.

Dr. Kharr?

Yes, now he knew . . . COUNTY MEMORIAL HOSPITAL.

« *4* »

Returning to his office after his morning rounds, Aaron Kharr called Dr. Teeter's home, determined to turn over the Wilder case at once, aware that the longer he delayed the more difficult it was going to be. Mrs. Teeter had answered the telephone. Her husband, she said, had been suddenly called to Washington, and there was very little chance that he would return until late tomorrow. Anxiously apologetic, she had sounded worn and harried, no doubt a reflection of the dilemma her husband had faced, torn as he must have been between the counterpull of two purse-filling days of office calls and the ego-puffing experience of being summoned to Washington for a meeting of a committee that had been formed, apparently by drawing names out of a hat, to advise the Department of Health, Education, and Welfare on administration of the new Rural Health Act.

Obviously, the Wilder case could not be carried along for two days without an attending physician. A possible solution was to turn it over to Dr. Carruth, who was on duty today as resident, but that raised some questions about County Memorial protocol in which Aaron Kharr had no desire to become involved. Looking for a way out, he decided to toss the problem into the lap of the Chief of Staff. Jonas Webster usually stopped at the hospital sometime between eight and nine. He had not yet arrived, the operator said, but she promised to call him when he did.

With his conscience cleared, checking the time—it was 8:22—he turned to his typewriter, hoping to get in an hour of work on his book before the 9:30 appointment to examine a patient that Dr. Neilson was bringing in. Taking out his script book he hurriedly flipped pages until he came to the last paragraph he had written, expecting that rereading it would restore the flow of thought that had been broken when he had been called to Emergency last night. Instead, it served only as a reminder of the Wilder case.

He was still staring at the blank sheet of paper in his typewriter when the telephone rang. Recognizing Dr. Webster's bass grumble, he started to raise the question posed by Teeter's absence, cut off when Webster asked, "You admitted a coronary last night, Doctor—man by the name of Wilder?"

"Yes, that's what I wanted to see you about."

"President of his company is outside. I've been talking to him but you're the one he really wants to see. Will you come out?"

"Of course," he said, surprised. He had anticipated the arrival of a cardiologist but hardly that of the president of Wilder's company. A man who would drive forty miles to visit a stricken employee seemed misfitted to the voice he had heard last night over the telephone, but two years of examining corporation presidents at the Allison Clinic had taught him that startling incongruities were by no means unusual. Nevertheless, he was stopped in his tracks when he first saw the man who was waiting for him, glimpsed from behind the screen that separated the lobby area from the main corridor. Had there been anyone else in sight, he would never have picked this gnomish little man, hunched over the magazine he was reading, as the president of a big corporation.

Abruptly aware of his presence, however, the man bounded to his feet, a quite different person, supercharged with a terrier-like show of energy, almost instantly assigning himself to a fixed classification in Aaron Kharr's character-conscious mind. Beyond question he was a self-made man, lacking those physical attributes that, in the modern corporation, are so commonly judged the hallmarks of leadership. Undersized and far from commanding in appearance, he could never have been, as a younger man, a candidate for advancement that any personnel manager would have picked for his executive potential. Plainly, he had battled his own way to the top, no doubt driven by that intensity of ambition frequently observed in men of small stature, even more certainly motivated by the self-taught truth that confidence, belligerently enough displayed, is usually accepted at face value.

But Matthew R. Crouch was no fool. The questions that he asked were knowingly pointed, evidencing an understanding that caused Aaron Kharr to say, "You seem to know something about heart attacks, Mr. Crouch."

"Ought to," he snapped back. "God knows I've had enough of them. Lost two men in the last year. Judd's the third." His face contorted like a fist clenched in anger. "And, damn it, I'm not going to lose him, too, not if there's anything in God's world that can be done to save him."

"I don't really think there's too much cause for concern," he said placatingly. "All the signs indicate a relatively small infarct, and one that isn't going to be too difficult to heal. But, of course, there's always the possibility of an unfavorable development."

"That's a gamble you have to take," Crouch said. "Nothing much you can do about it anyway. Right? But, damn it, there is something you can do about what comes afterward. That's what I'm worrying about."

"I'm afraid I don't quite understand," he said warily, resisting belief that Crouch could really mean what he seemed to be saying.

"You don't?" Crouch asked with a twisted smile. The magazine he had been reading was still in his hand, tight-rolled, held like a scepter of command. He unclenched his fist and the magazine sprang open, exposing its cover. Aaron Kharr saw that it was a copy of the *Annals of General Practice*, the issue that carried his "Emotional Rehabilitation of Cardiac Patients," the paper that he had read at the Atlantic City meeting.

Fanning pages, Crouch demanded, "You wrote this, didn't you?"

"How did you get hold of that?" he asked tautly, responsive not only to the rankling memory of that Sippleton-inspired fiasco but also to finding, in lay hands, something that he had written only for professional consumption.

The president's little smile took a cocky twist. "When I'm depending on a man, I want to know who I'm dealing with. After you telephoned me last night—maybe I should have known who you were, but I didn't, so I called my own doctor. Asked him if he knew anything about you. All I figured was that he'd be able to look you up in some kind of a directory. Didn't have any idea you'd be somebody he knew."

"Really?" he said, a blank response. "Who is your doctor?"

"Howard Robbins," Crouch said, giving him only a moment for recollection, quickly adding, "Said you probably wouldn't remember him. Said he just met you once—Atlantic City—the time you read this paper. First thing he thought about when I told him what was worrying me about Judd. Said this was something I ought to read. So I drove around and picked it up. That's what I've been doing while I was waiting for you—reading it."

"I see," Aaron Kharr managed, attempting to mask an ebullient awareness that his paper had not been the failure that he had always thought it, a feeling quickly transmuted into a joyous sense of righteous victory over Horace Sippleton.

"What you say here is absolutely right," Crouch drove ahead. "Got a case of my own right now. Sam Harrod. Used to be our purchasing agent. Best damn wool buyer in the business. Brought him up myself. A year ago every mill in the industry was trying to hire him away from me. Then he has this heart attack. That was six months ago. Heart's perfectly all right again. Anyway, good enough so that he ought to be back on the job again. But every time he comes near the office—it's just no go, that's all." He met his eyes, fiercely proclaiming, "I don't want that to happen to Judd Wilder!"

"No, of course you don't," he murmured, wishing that more of his colleagues shared this layman's understanding that it was the mind rather than the heart that deserved major attention in cardiac therapy.

"You're the first heart specialist I've run into that seems to know what the hell it's all about."

"I'm not a cardiologist, Mr. Crouch."

"All right, all right," Crouch said impatiently. "Internist—whatever you call yourself. But you've done a lot of heart work. Must have. Couldn't have written this if you hadn't."

"Well, I did spend several years in cardiovascular research at the Berringer Institute."

"I thought so," Crouch said with a snort of satisfaction. "Most of these damn heart specialists—all they worry about is a man's heart. If that heals up, that's the end of it as far as they're concerned. But, damn it, it isn't the end of it."

"No, indeed," he agreed, yet quickly conscious of the professional demand that he defend his colleagues against all charges, even those that he himself had made. "I'm sure, Mr. Crouch, that any doctor who has ever done any amount of heart work is aware that there are emotional consequences."

"Being aware of it is one thing," Crouch shot back. "Doing something about it is something else."

"Quite true."

"I'll just say this—if Judd had to have a heart attack, he was sure as hell lucky to land in your hands."

Aaron Kharr's inexperience in the reception of compliments left him without a ready-made reply, confusion compounded by this suggestion that Crouch seemed to be expecting him to handle the case. The prospect, glimpsed as through a suddenly opened door, was brightly appealing—a mid-forties coronary, not serious enough to make organic recovery a paramount consideration, the way open to concentrate major effort on emotional rehabilitation. Most of the case reports he had collected were negative instead of positive, illustrating mistakes in procedure rather than the constructive course that should be followed. If he could handle this case himself, in-

timately involved from beginning to end . . . and why not? He was
sure of his ground . . .

Last night came back, a specter accusing him of that panicked
moment when he had ordered an oxygen tent. But it had not been
his case then . . . all he had been doing was holding the fort for
some cardiologist . . .

"—afraid you weren't free to take a private case," he heard Crouch
conclude, missing whatever it was that he had said before, totally
attentive now as the president explained, "That's why I went to this
fellow—what's his name, your Chief of Staff?"

"Dr. Webster."

"That's right. Doc Robbins said I'd better see him first. Anyway,
it's all cleared with him. He said there was no reason why you
couldn't take the case if you wanted to."

Aaron Kharr looked away, pretending preoccupation with the
grossly pregnant woman who had just come up to the information
desk. He did not need the Chief of Staff's permission—there was a
provision in his contract as Chief Internist that permitted him to
take a limited number of private cases—but it was a privilege that
he had never before exercised, and there could be no doubt of the
goodwill that he had gained by never preempting a fee-paying
patient.

His concern must have been evident because Crouch's face
twisted into a gargoyle scowl, an expression vocalized in a demanding "What's wrong, Doctor?"

Somehow, the question fathered the answer, and once born it
became quickly dominant, feeding on the memory of his last months
at the Allison Clinic, the losing battle that he had fought with Harvey Allison over the ethics of medical privacy. It had been his
contention that anything an examination revealed should be disclosed only to the patient. Allison, with all the authority of prosperous proprietorship, had decreed that the clinic's prime obligation
was to whoever paid the bill, arguing that if corporations were to
go on spending the kind of money that the clinic got for examining
an executive group, there was no alternative to disclosing everything
to the company president, often giving information to him before
the patient was told, sometimes telling him things that the man
himself never learned. Ethics aside, Aaron Kharr had argued,
Allison's policy was forcing all of the doctors on the staff to pervert

their whole point of view, making them see a patient not as a human being but as a corporate asset to be as coldly X-rayed as a steel casting, marked for downgrading or discard if any hidden flaw was revealed.

"What are you thinking—that I'm interfering in something that's none of my business?"

"No, of course not," Kharr said quickly, evasion excused by adding, "With his wife out of the country, and no one else to—I'm sure he'll appreciate your concern."

"All right, Doctor, whatever is bothering you, let's get it out on the table. Damn it, I want you taking care of that boy. If anyone can bring him around, you're the one to do it."

"That's very flattering," he said slowly, stalling for the moment that it took to compose "But I'm not at all certain that I can do what you want done."

"What do you mean—what *I* want done? All I want is to get him through this without letting it lick him."

"By which you mean," he carefully restated, "that you want him to come out of it the same man he was yesterday. That's impossible, Mr. Crouch. No man ever walks up to the brink of death and comes away quite the same man that he was before."

"I know that," Crouch said, stubbornly refusing retreat.

"And that is especially true in these heart cases," he went on, more easily now, feeling himself on solid ground as he paraphrased something that he had once written. "There are any number of worse things that can happen to a man—the medical books are full of them—but for some reason the psychological impact of a heart attack is particularly severe. Perhaps it's because our minds are so heart-oriented, because we are so aware that we've been struck in the very *heart*—we even use the word—of life itself."

"I know that, too," Crouch said, unyielding.

"And there's a further danger in the treatment we have to employ," he went on, feeling himself oddly disoriented as he fell back on the same argument that his critics had so often used against him. "In order to give the heart a chance to heal, we have to enforce a regimen of almost total immobilization—there's no alternative, it's the only cure we know—so we can't escape the bad psychological effect that it's bound to have. We can immobilize his body—that's largely the point of hospitalization—but we can't stop that mind from working. Oh, we can keep him under sedation for a while, but at most that's only a few days. Then that mind starts working. He begins reviewing his life, weighing what he's done against what he's gotten out of it, asking himself whether it's been worth the price he's paying. If he's the dynamic driving type who's been completely wrapped up in his work—and most under-fifty coronaries are, of course—that may well be a question he's never faced up to before. More often than not, he winds up with a new set of values."

"That doesn't have to be bad. If a man gets his thinking straightened out, it can be a damn good thing."

"Of course. But it may mean that he doesn't want to go back to his old job. He may want——"

There was a screech of protest from the settee springs as Crouch sat bolt upright, belligerently asserting, "Sure, I want Judd back on the job. Of course I do. Why shouldn't I? He's a damn valuable man. But if it isn't the best thing for him—to hell with it! He doesn't owe me anything. He doesn't owe the company anything. It's the other way around. If it hadn't been for Judd Wilder—" His voice cut off as if choked by the inexpressible. His face went blank, and in that instant when it was free of expression, Aaron Kharr had a distinct sensation of opaqueness suddenly gone transparent, of experiencing that intuitive vision that was always the end point of a diagnostic search, the feeling that he had been given a glimpse into some hidden recess of a human mind, an insight that always made him feel a close-to-mystical sense of privilege.

Crouch said in a harsh whisper, "What a man goes through—lying there in bed—thinking—damn it, I'm not talking about something I don't know anything about. I had eight months of it."

"Heart attack?"

Crouch shook his head, jaws set, lips barely parted as he muttered. "Just cracked up, that's all." He caught a quick breath, expelled with an explosive "But I licked it! And no thanks to those damn doctors. In spite of them! You know what they kept telling me? The same thing you say here—relax—take it easy—telling me I was done, that I couldn't take it any more. Almost had me believing it. If it hadn't been for—" He was cut off by a sudden awareness that the receptionist was eavesdropping.

"Let's go into my office," Kharr quickly suggested.

"Good!" Crouch exclaimed, so mercurial a change of tone and

temper that it seemed less an expression of relief than a claim of victory, an impression all the stronger as he turned back to pick up the big envelope with PROOFS red-printed across it, the package that had been, last night, the patient's first concern. Plainly, despite Matthew R. Crouch's protest that he was thinking only of Judd Wilder's welfare, Crouch Carpet Company would never be far out of mind.

« 5 »

Of all the people who were to be shocked this morning by the news of Judd Wilder's heart attack, no one was more profoundly affected than Allen Talbott. It was Gloria Frey, the secretary he shared with Judd Wilder, who told him—blurting it out with no preliminary warning other than a quickly asked "Have you heard about Mr. Wilder?"—hardly giving him time to shake his head before she said, "He had a heart attack last night."

Stunned, he had to reach out for the doorjamb to steady himself.

"I know," Gloria said. "You just can't believe it, can you?"

What he truly could not believe was that he, yesterday afternoon in Philadelphia, had by so narrow a margin saved himself from making a terrible mistake. At the last minute, blindly guided by something that now seemed awesomely extrasensory, he had said, "I'm almost certain that I'll accept your offer, Mr. Winninger, but I would like a chance to talk it over with my wife." Had he not kept open that one loophole, there would be no alternative this morning to resigning his position as Assistant Director of Advertising & Promotion for the Crouch Carpet Company.

"How bad is it?" he asked, seriously shaken, yet clear-witted enough to see that Gloria would safely misinterpret his lack of poise.

"I don't know," she said. "All I really know is that Mr. Crouch drove up there this morning."

"Up where? Where is he?"

"Some little hospital up near the turnpike. County Memorial. He was on his way back from New York. That's the awful part of it— he'd just put Mrs. Wilder on her ship, you know, and now there she is, six days until—there isn't any way they can get her off, is there? I mean—you know, a helicopter or something?"

He shook his head, brushing aside concern for Kay Wilder, preoccupied with his own wife problem, wishing now that he had not gone so far overboard last night to sell Carol on Philadelphia—and Winninger & Company. All this past year she had been hounding him to get back to New York, telling him that he was never going to get anywhere here, calling him "Judd Wilder's coffee-boy," never missing an opportunity to rub salt in his wounded pride every time she forced him to admit that some advertising piece he brought home for his scrapbook was not really his own, that Judd had edited the copy, altered the layout, more often than not switched the whole selling slant.

What had kept him hanging on at Crouch Carpet as long as he had—the first of next month would be his third anniversary—was the persistent rumor that Judd was to be made Vice President for Merchandising, thus opening the way for his own elevation to Director of Advertising & Promotion. But there had been a limit to how long he could hold out against Carol's constant needling. A month ago he had registered with Willcox & Pratt, giving Carol her victory but, afterwards, not telling her about any of the New York interviews he turned down. He wanted no more Madison Avenue, no more commuting to Connecticut, no more agency job-jumping. What he really wanted—this he knew—was Judd Wilder's job. Yesterday, becoming Advertising Manager for Winninger & Company had seemed as close as he was likely to get. Now, suddenly, he saw it as not even a reasonable facsimile. Even with the extra two thousand a year he would be earning, it would be a bad second best to the prospect that had now so abruptly opened before him.

He turned to the door of his office, stopped by Gloria's "I guess we'll have to cancel the convention meeting—" not adding "—won't we?" until he was looking squarely at her.

His instant reaction was one of verified distaste—he had always thought Gloria a cold-blooded little bitch—but that was quickly overridden by the overwhelming impact of the prospect that her words incited—*he would have to take over the convention!*

Awake in the night, he had tried to prepare himself for what he had expected to be the most unpleasant aspect of his resignation: facing Judd's accusation that he was walking out on him at the worst possible time, only five weeks to the convention and all of the major work yet to be done. Last night, it had seemed a fair retort that it was not his fault that Judd had, as always, let everything drag until the last minute. Now, today, his fault or not, that was the measure of his problem. There wasn't even a plan, at least on paper. That was to have been the purpose of today's meeting, to tie down what Judd had in mind.

Without answering Gloria's question, he turned again to his office, closing his ears to whatever it was that she was saying about the proofs of the stockholders report, sleepwalking to his desk. He lit a cigarette, an act made conscious only by his awareness of the wildly wavering flame of his lighter. He stared at the calendar, seeing the numbers as boldly blank warnings of all that had to be done—speeches to write, skits to stage, actors to be cast, rehearsals to be directed, color slides to be made—there was no end to it.

Allen Talbott was not lacking in what, by his own standards, passed for self-confidence. He did not doubt his competence to put on a successful convention, providing only that he was given time enough to isolate and define objectives, to draw up an orderly plan of procedure, and to implement it with precisely defined delegations of authority. But he could not—he dared not—attempt to match the one-man show that Judd Wilder put on every year, the virtuoso performance of a man self-driven by neglected deadlines, script tumbling from his typewriter to be snatched up by actors already on stage, everything in a mad disarray that seemingly defied untangling until, at the last moment, it all fell into place, another great convention. "The best ever!" everyone always said, the applause deafening when Judd stepped on stage to thank all who "contributed so much," everyone knowing that it was *his* convention.

Allen Talbott stubbed out the half-smoked cigarette. He would be a fool to try to follow Judd's act. No matter how good a convention he put on, it would come off as a bad second best to one of Judd's showy theatricals. And he would always be under that cloud. Even if Judd didn't come back . . .

The telephone rang, the caller identified by a coolly composed "Good morning, Allen—Roger Stark," the tone a portrait of the man.

Allen Talbott had never more than glanced inside the office of the Vice President for Administration—Advertising & Promotion was one

of the few departments that still reported directly to Mr. Crouch
—but with Roger Stark's general supervision over all financial matters, he had now and then called with some question about the
advertising budget, and the sound of his voice had always incited
the same mental picture: a man in an Eames chair at a Danish desk-
table, as coolly detached as the precisely geometric Mondriaan-like
paintings on his walls, his emotions so admirably controlled that
there was never the slightest betrayal of feeling. It was, perhaps,
this sophisticated inscrutability that most appealed to Allen Talbott,
but whatever the foundation for his intuitive respect, he had never
been able to share Judd Wilder's dislike for the man, nor his distrust of Roger Stark's rapidly expanding weight in the company's
management.

"If you aren't too seriously occupied at the moment," Stark said,
his voice as lightly rising as a lazily drifting upward spiral of cigarette smoke, "perhaps you'd like to drop by my office for a chat."

"Yes, sir, Mr. Stark, I sure would," Allen Talbott said, sounding
entirely too eager, too concerned, too worried, not at all the cool,
detached, dispassionate man that he wanted to be—and really was
—when he was not unfairly caught off guard.

« 6 »

Although Aaron Kharr was finding out a great deal about Matthew
R. Crouch and the Crouch Carpet Company, he was learning little
about Judd Wilder. It was largely his own fault. Prompted by the
president's revelation that he had once suffered a mental episode, he
had nudged him into talking about it, expecting reticence, surely not
anticipating that the old man would pour out his whole life story.
Nevertheless, it was an intriguing case, all the more so because it
supported something that he had turned up during his first year at
the Allison Clinic.

With so many medical histories of corporation executives available
in the clinic files, he had undertaken an analysis of them, thinking
that he might find some significant relationship between health patterns and executive success. He had discovered little along that
path, but while following it he had stumbled into something that

he had never before suspected—the surprisingly high percentage of corporation presidents who, on their way to the top, had suffered some near-catastrophe of body or mind. In some cases, it had been a heart attack, in others a serious gastrointestinal disorder, in still more something vaguely designated as a "nervous breakdown." Charted separately, they had revealed nothing significant, but when he had put them all together, and included divorces and other personal-life upheavals that were no less attributable to emotional stress and strain, it had been evident that there was an explosively rising incidence during the middle forties when, as he had written last night, ". . . the forces of long-building tension swirl up into an emotional hurricane."

That in itself had been an important revelation but what had particularly intrigued him had been the why and how of survival. A few men had somehow managed to surmount disaster, going on to corporation presidencies while their less fortunate fellows, under a seemingly comparable impact, had been knocked out of the race. Why? What had been the secret of their recovery and rehabilitation? This was a subject that he was planning to explore in his book, and Crouch seemed to offer the prospect of some valuable insights. No case in his files evidenced a more phoenix-like rise from the fiery ashes of self-destruction, but what made it even more appealing was the unusual precision with which the cause of Crouch's crackup could be pinpointed.

Young Matt Crouch had started life as a yarn boy in a Philadelphia carpet mill, and with the thoroughly credible energy of driving ambition, had climbed the ladder until a superintendent's job was within his grasp. Precipitately, the mill had been closed by a strike, never to reopen. He had found another ladder, again climbing toward the top rung, only to be knocked off by circumstances beyond his control. In the climactic situation, he had taken over a family-owned carpet mill during the Depression, brought it through the war years by converting carpet looms to the weaving of Army duck, piling up a hoard of profits earmarked to use in the building of a revitalized carpet company of which he had been promised the presidency. Instead of going ahead, however, the proprietary family had decided to cash in its chips, divide the profit hoard and liquidate the mill, a traumatic frustration that had knocked the emotional props out from under Crouch. Given a man so singlemindedly driven by an obsessive need to be the top dog, it was easily understandable why he had landed in a sanitarium.

From Crouch's references to the treatment he had been given, there could be no doubt that his mind had been severely afflicted, yet only eight months later, professedly without capital or financial backing, blackmarked in financial circles by his crackup, he had somehow got control of a small, near-bankrupt carpet mill in New Ulster, Pennsylvania. On that shaky foundation he had gone on to build, in less than twenty years, a large and successful company. Opening the big envelope that had been in Wilder's car, he was now displaying the proofs of the company's forthcoming stockholders report, proudly proclaiming that Crouch Carpet's profit last year represented a higher return on both sales dollars and invested capital than that of any other company in the carpet industry.

Lost in a mathematical maze, Aaron Kharr backtracked to the area of his preeminent interest. "Tell me this, Mr. Crouch—going back to your days in the sanitarium—how did you manage to shake out of it? What got you on your feet again? Was there any particular doctor who——"

"Hell, no! If I'd listened to any of those damn doctors I'd have given up right then and there. You know what they kept telling me? The same things you say here in your article. You're sure as hell right about the stupid things these damn doctors do."

"That's not what I——"

"You asked me what got me back on my feet again, didn't you? All right, I'm saying that you don't get a man up off the canvas by telling him that he's licked for good. There was this one character, some kind of a doctor—psychiatrist, I guess. Oh, he was a smart cookie, all right. Had me all figured out. So he came in this one day to tell me what I'm going to have to do. What it added up to was that I had to forget the carpet business. Never think of it again. You know, the old burned child and the fire business. He had a fancy name for it but that was the general idea. Well, that was a hell of a dose for me to swallow. Asking me to give up the carpet business was like asking me to give up my whole life. That's what it had been, ever since I was a fourteen-year-old kid. But how did I know—maybe he's right. As groggy as I was, all that dope they kept giving me, I didn't know what the hell to believe. But just about then, Emily comes walking in. You know what she brought me? All the floor-covering papers that had come out since I'd been in there. I grabbed at them like—I don't know how to describe it— like I'd been dying of hunger and here's somebody bringing me a feast."

"Your wife must be a very understanding person," Aaron Kharr said, wondering how any doctor could have been so blindly obtuse.

"Anyway, she knew what had been eating my guts out," Crouch said, the reserved compliment of an egocentric man. "And that's a hell of a lot more than any of those damn doctors did."

"How old were you then, Mr. Crouch?"

The old man started, peculiarly struck. "Funny you should bring that up. That's almost the first thing that hit me—Judd being the same age I was." He paused, his eyes questioning. "Just a coincidence, I guess."

"Perhaps less so than you might think." He studied the old man's face. "The mid-forties are often a time of great stress. The emotional pressure builds up, something has to give."

"What are you saying—that what happened to me and Judd's heart attack—they're something alike?"

He hesitated, guarding himself with "There's no consensus in the medical profession on the cause of a coronary occlusion."

"I'm not asking what the medical profession thinks," Crouch snapped back. "I'm asking what you think."

Again he hesitated, held back by all the prohibitions against exposing professional dissension to the lay public, urged on by the reasoned argument that since Crouch had already read his *Annals* paper it was better to talk it out than to risk misinterpretation. "Yes, in my view, there's usually an emotional involvement, particularly in these under-fifty cases."

"Is that what you mean here by—" he flipped pages, searching the *Annals* paper, "whatever it is you call it—this precoronary syndrome business?"

"Substantially, yes. I didn't go into it in very much detail there— you'll notice some references to my earlier publications—but in the work that I did at the Berringer Institute, we definitely established an almost invariable association between an under-fifty coronary and a certain quite specific behavior pattern—what we eventually came to call the precoronary syndrome."

"You mean there's a certain type of man that just naturally gets hit with a heart attack?"

"I wouldn't say *naturally*, Mr. Crouch. A mid-forties attack is distinctly *unnatural*. But, yes, there's a coronary-prone personality, no question about it. It's been recognized for hundreds of years, way back to the times of the Greeks and the Romans. There are references to it in some of the oldest medical literature that's come down to us. But it's never meant very much in practice because it wasn't truly differentiating. You'd have ten men, all with coronary-prone personalities, but only one would actually wind up with a mid-forties heart attack. What we were trying to do at Berringer was to narrow the focus, to see if we couldn't isolate a behavior pattern that was more positively predictive."

"And you did?"

"Yes—at least to my own satisfaction. Again I'll have to say that this isn't something that's been widely accepted by the medical profession."

"To hell with that," Crouch brushed it off. "I'm not arguing with you—I've always thought it was something like that—but I still don't understand what happens."

"What happens?" he repeated, looking away, feigning a moment of thought-gathering, trying to decide how far it would be wise to go. "This is only speculation, of course, but the results do seem to support a tenable hypothesis." He shifted his position. "If we begin with a man who is aggressive, highly motivated, ambitious, strongly oriented to superior accomplishment, something of a perfectionist——"

"That's Judd, all right."

He disregarded the interruption, but not the warning that everything he said would be specifically applied. Cautious now, he went on, "Given that personality pattern, and the rather high level of emotional tension that it induces, the normal life expectancy of a man of that sort—this may not be actuarily sound, but we'd not be at all surprised if he had a heart attack sometime in his early or middle sixties. That would be about par for the course. But suppose that isn't what happens. Instead, he gets hit in his middle forties. Why?"

"That's what I want to know."

"All right, let's go back to what we were talking about a few minutes ago, the high incidence of emotionally induced episodes during those years. I'm sure you've seen a great many examples—I don't mean just your own case, I don't mean just physical illness— all the men who've suddenly gone off the deep end, changed jobs, gotten themselves involved with other women, divorced their wives—"

"I know what you mean. Got a case right now. Our District Manager in Chicago. Damnedest thing you've ever seen. Hell of a good man, too. Or at least he was until this thing hit him. Sweet wife, three kids, hell of a nice house out in Lake Forest. And you know what the damn fool is doing? Throwing it all overboard and going down to South America, one of these crazy government things, teaching in some little college down there." He stopped abruptly, nodding sudden comprehension. "It could have been a heart attack —is that what you're saying?"

"More or less. The pressure builds up, something has to give. With some men it's a heart attack, with others it's a mental disorder——"

"But, damn it, I wasn't throwing anything away. I didn't have anything *to* throw away. Forty-four years old and what did I have to show for it? I'd worked my tail off—" He broke off, embarrassed. "I didn't mean to get off on that again."

"No, it makes a good point." Aaron Kharr leaned forward, intrigued by this chance to get a testing reaction to one of the key premises of his book. "You always knew what you were working for, didn't you? From the time you started out as a yarn boy, you'd had your heart set on being president of a carpet company, right? If anyone had ever asked you what you wanted out of life, you'd have told them, wouldn't you? Even when you were in the sanitarium?"

"If they'd ever asked me. But they never did. That was the trouble —those damn doctors were so full of their own ideas——"

"Let me make my point, Mr. Crouch. This is one of the most significant things in the whole precoronary syndrome. I've put that question—what do you want out of life?—to I don't know how many under-fifty coronaries, and do you know that I've never gotten even a half-specific answer, never, not once in all these years."

Crouch stared, his expression one of concentrated speculation.

"The man who gets hit with an early coronary, Mr. Crouch, isn't the man who knows what he wants out of life and has been frustrated in getting it. That man may wind up with an ulcer, or a diaphragmatic hernia, or what have you, but rarely with a heart attack. Your typical coronary is what you might call a runner without a goal. He's the man who has been running like mad all his life, running not only because it was the thing his innate character urged him to do, but also because it was what our society told him that he *had* to do, if he wanted to get anywhere. In his twenties, it was easy. He ran as naturally as an exuberant young animal. In his thirties, it was harder, the going got a little heavier, but there was always something to keep him running—a better job, a bigger salary, more status in the organization. And then he hits the forties. He's getting tired now but he has to keep on running. His natural energy is exhausted, but still he runs. He doesn't know why. If he ever had a goal, he's lost sight of it. He runs like a man in a nightmare, driven by a neurotic compulsion that he can no longer control, an obsession that his body can no longer sustain." He caught his breath, then quietly added, "That's what we call the precoronary syndrome—and when a man gets caught up in it, a coronary occlusion is by no means an illogical consequence."

"You think that's what happened to Judd?"

"That was only a broad generalization," he said. "Whether it applies or not, I don't know."

The old man sighed audibly. "Anyway, I guess that's water over the dam now—what caused it. That's no longer the question."

"Oh, but it is," Aaron Kharr quickly caught him up. "That's the all-important question—at least for Mr. Wilder. He has to see what it is that he's done to himself, how self-destructive his behavior has been. Unless he sees it, he'll never break out of it. And if he doesn't——"

"He'll wind up like Sam Harrod."

"That's only one of the possible reactions to a heart attack, Mr. Crouch. It's the one we see most often—it's easiest to observe—but there are others that are almost as common, and at least one that's far more dangerous. The worst possible aftermath, Mr. Crouch, is the one that looks best on the surface. It's the man who seemingly makes the perfect recovery, who comes out of it the same man he was before. I'm sure you've known cases like that—the man who tells you afterwards that it wasn't a real heart attack, just a little warning bump. What's happening, of course, is that he's simply refusing to accept reality."

"He has to change?"

"Exactly. If he doesn't, another attack is almost inevitable—and the prognosis on a second coronary in a man under fifty is not good. That's the essential problem in rehabilitation, Mr. Crouch—the patient must be frightened enough to be jarred out of that precoronary syndrome, yet not so frightened that he loses his ability to function as an effective human being. It's a narrow line. And the only way you can walk it without making a dangerous misstep is to know the man you're dealing with, and know him far more intimately than——"

"What do you want to know?" Crouch broke in, an abruptly explosive interjection. "Everything, I guess. All right, let's see how much I can tell you." He braced his shoulders as if rising to a challenge. "Judd was born out West somewhere. Iowa, I think. Yes, I'm sure that's right. Some little town out there. Father ran a newspaper. Still does, as far as I know. His mother is dead, I do know that. She was a daughter of a senator from out there—Simon Judd. Maybe you remember him? He was on that committee that raised so much hell with carpet wool tariffs."

He shook his head, impressed again with the narrow gauge of Crouch's one-track mind.

"Anyway, that's where Judd got his name, from his grandfather. Well, let's see what else I can remember." A thought struck. "Maybe this will tell you something about the kind of a boy he was. Out there in Iowa—yes, it was Iowa, I'm sure of it now—he put on some kind of a pageant. I guess that's what you'd call it. Anyway, it was one of those affairs where they act out the history of a place. Must have been quite a show, I guess. *Life* had a big article about it—I think it was *Life,* maybe one of the other magazines. Anyway, it was all about Judd, how he'd written the whole thing and put it on. Really something for a kid that was still in high school, putting on a show that was good enough to get written up in *Life* magazine."

"Yes, indeed," Aaron Kharr granted, a cautiously understated reaction. Despite resistance, he was beginning to be intrigued. He had long suspected that a strong vein of creativity suggested susceptibility to the precoronary syndrome, and there was no better indicator of inherent creativity than a youthful revelation, particularly when it had been carried to fruition.

"That's how he happened to come back East to college," Crouch went on. "All that publicity, Colfax College offered him a scholarship. I guess you've heard of Colfax. It's over here at Millburgh. They go in a lot for theatrical stuff. That's one of their big departments."

"Then the theater was Mr. Wilder's original interest?" Aaron Kharr asked, recalling the number of frustrated playwrights he had turned up in his Berringer study of advertising men. "Before he went into business, I mean."

"Business isn't so different," Crouch objected. "This convention he puts on for us every year—I've seen a lot of Broadway shows that weren't half as good."

"And there's one coming up very shortly, I understand."

Crouch started, regarding him narrowly. "He's not worrying about that, is he?"

"Yes, quite definitely, I'd say. When I first saw him last night, he was insisting that he had to get out of here by noon today—some big meeting on the convention. And when they were taking him up to his room, he tried to get one of the nurses to get him a dictating machine so that he could——"

"Good God! But that's Judd for you. Now look—you tell him to forget that damn convention. We'll just postpone it, that's all. What the hell, there's no reason why it has to be in the spring. Fall is just as good. Maybe better. You tell him that. Tell him that we're postponing the convention until he gets back on his feet. That ought to relieve his mind."

"I'm sure it will," he said, a warm response to the president's humanitarian attitude.

"Anything else worrying him?"

"Not that I know about," he said, reminded then of Mrs. Welch's note on the chart. "Oh, he did say something in the night, I believe —a trip to San Francisco."

"San Francisco?" Crouch puzzled. "But he was just out there a few weeks ago. No, I don't know what that's all about. Anyway, that's out too. Anything that needs to be done, we'll take care of. Tell him that."

"I will," he agreed, favorably contrasting Matthew R. Crouch with the coldly unemotional corporation presidents he had so often encountered. Without conscious decision, he reached for a notepad.

"All right, let's go on from college. He's forty-four now—must have graduated about the time the war broke out."

Crouch cocked his head, nodding, "I remember him mentioning that one time, how they let him graduate early so that he could enlist."

"Know anything about his service record?"

"He was in the motion picture end of it, I know that. Directing those training films they used."

A spark caught, lighting the hope that there might be a personal association here, a point of contact that would help to establish rapport. "Do you know, by any chance, if he was at Astoria? That was the Army's big motion picture center during the war. They took over the old Paramount studio out on Long Island."

"I know he was somewhere near New York for a while."

He made a note, explaining, "I grew up out there in Astoria, only a few blocks from the studio. That's how I happen to know a little something about it."

"I don't know how long he was there—if that's where he was," Crouch continued. "He was overseas quite a while, I do know that."

"Europe?"

"Maybe so. But it was India I remember him talking about most."

"India?" Kharr repeated, fanning another fire-catching spark. "This is a coincidence. The young doctor who was on the ambulance with Mr. Wilder last night is from India."

Crouch nodded absently. "We used to get a lot of carpet wool from out there—Kashmir, Afghanistan, Tibet. That's how I happen to remember Judd talking about it."

He nodded, conscious again of the limited focus of the presidential mind. "And he came with you when?"

"August, 'fifty-two," Crouch instantly supplied.

"Assuming that he got out of service in 'forty-five or early 'forty-six," he calculated, "that leaves roughly seven years before he came to work for you. What had he been doing?"

An elfish smile appeared on Crouch's face. "Good thing it was back in the days before we had this fancy personnel setup. The way things are now—the kind of a job record Judd had, they'd have said thumbs down before he even got an application filled out. He'd never stuck with anything more than a year or two—movies, radio, television, stage shows, I don't know what all he'd been in."

"But you hired him as an advertising man?"

"That's what I thought he was," Crouch chuckled. "I didn't find out until afterwards that he'd only been with this advertising agency for a year. Anyway, not much more than that. Maybe I ought to tell you how I came to hire him?"

He nodded assent, hoping that he was not agreeing to a further extension of Matthew R. Crouch's life story.

"This was the spring of 'fifty-two," the president launched off. "I was in a hell of a spot. About as close to the bottom of the barrel as a man can get. Hard to believe, the way things are rolling now, but there were some weeks there when I didn't know how the hell I was going to meet the payroll. Everything I had in the world was riding on being able to sell a quality piece of tufted carpet. Some of the mills had gone to rayon and they were flooding the market with some of the damnest junk——"

"Yes, you told me about that," he interjected, hoping to leapfrog a repetitious recounting.

Undeterred, the president went on. "These damn department-store buyers—guess you couldn't blame them, all the complaints they were getting from this crap that had been shoved off on them—anyway, the minute you said 'tufted' they'd throw you out of the store. We weren't even getting a chance to tell our story."

"It was advertising that finally put it over," he suggested, trying to hurry the old man along.

"I'm getting to Judd," Crouch promised. "I'd always been a wool man—still am—but one of the chemical companies had been after us to try a new synthetic. We'd made a couple of test runs and they wanted some pictures for something they were getting out. That's how Judd happened to come down to New Ulster. Well, I'd seen some advertising men in my time. Most of them, you start telling them how a machine works, you might as well be talking Greek. They just aren't interested. But not Judd. The minute he saw that tufting machine, he was like a kid with a new toy. Had to see everything for himself. Down on his belly under the needle bars to see how the loopers worked. Climbing up on the reel. Back on the latex line. Over in the dye house. That always impresses me—a boy who's got push enough to really dig in and find out what the hell it's all about."

"Yes, indeed," Kharr said, his real agreement with himself, seeing

Judd Wilder's compulsive drive as a key confirmation of his intuitive first judgment.

"And another thing," Crouch added. "Anybody else, coming down from New York, would have brought a photographer along. But not Judd. No, sir, he took his own pictures. And anything else that needed to be done. Damnedest fellow I'd ever seen—I mean for being able to do anything that came along."

Versatility, too, was a prime indicator, and Kharr pressed on with "So you hired him?"

The old man's face softened reminiscently. "Judd was staying overnight, going over to Millburgh the next morning, so I invited him home to dinner. Naturally, we got talking about the business—all the hell I was going through, the tough spot we were in, so Judd starts firing questions at me. What was our merchandising program? Why hadn't we done this? Why hadn't we done that? I don't mind admitting that he had me squirming. I'd always been a mill man—production was my end of it—I'd left the selling side to my sales manager. And he was a good man, a damn good man, best personal salesman I've ever known, but he'd never come up with anything like the ideas that Judd was shooting at me."

"But if he'd had no experience in merchandising—?"

"That's what I'm trying to tell you. Judd's got the kind of a mind that—well, he's just quick, that's all. Of course, when you get right down to it, merchandising is nothing but common sense. Still you've got to have a feel for the way people are going to react. I guess that's what Judd's got, that as much as anything else—plus a brain that's always running in high gear."

"So you hired him?" he repeated.

"I wanted him right from the start, sure I did. But I didn't think there was a chance of getting him, not for the kind of money I could pay. But he kept telling me that what I needed was a merchandising man, somebody who'd get in and really promote tufted carpet as a quality product. So I told him to let me know if he ever ran into anybody who could do a job like that. Didn't have the slightest idea he'd be interested himself, but damned if he wasn't. The first thing I knew I'd made a deal with him."

"And I take it he's done a good job for you?" he suggested, the answer obvious, the question asked only to hurry Crouch along toward the area that he wanted to explore.

"That's what I was thinking about all the way up here," the president said with a heavy sigh. "Our whole merchandising plan, our franchise setup—that's what really got us off the ground, the way Judd figured out to tie up those big contract accounts. The convention, the regional meetings, the contractor seminars—it's been one thing after another. And it hasn't been just on the merchandising side. He's been into everything. The training course we're using for our salesmen—that's Judd's. Our employee relations program—he worked that out. This union business—I told you before how I was figuring on maybe moving South back in 'forty-nine?"

"Yes."

"Almost did in 'fifty-six. Hadn't had any labor trouble up to then. Boys were too scared of their jobs, I guess. But then we started really growing. Had to bring in a lot of new people. So the international sends in this gang of organizers. I was all for getting out, to hell with it. But Judd kept saying, no, let's see what we can do. So he organized a little campaign. All nice and quiet, nothing that wasn't absolutely legal, but before we got through with it, there wasn't anybody around town who didn't know what was going to happen if the union won. So they had their election. Damnedest thing you ever saw. We beat the bastards so bad they haven't shown their faces around New Ulster since. That's meant a hell of a lot."

"I'm sure it has."

"The great thing about Judd, you turn him loose on anything, I don't care what it is, he'll come up with an idea. I don't say it'll always be a bell-ringer—sure, he's had his flops, all of us have—but his percentage has been good. And that's what counts. That's why it's so tough to think of losing him."

Aaron Kharr nodded, tempted to offer the sympathetic encouragement that Judd Wilder was by no means a lost man, yet cautiously aware that by saying even that much he would be dangerously close to a commitment. He could hardly be wrong in his judgment that here was a clear-cut case of stress-induced heart attack—he had rarely seen a life history that, at least in broad outline, so perfectly anticipated the precoronary syndrome—but there was still a great deal that he had to know before he could be reasonably sure that rehabilitation was a good gamble. The few notes he had made were only a start. Now, his pencil poised, he asked, "Tell me this, Mr. Crouch—what kind of a man has he been to work with? A little difficult?"

"No, I wouldn't say so. Oh, he takes a little handling sometimes, sure he does. Gets raring ahead, you've got to rein up on him. But I'll take that every time over a man you've got to whip."

"In other words, he's a self-starter, a man with a lot of energy, a great deal of drive?"

"I just wish we had more men like him. The trouble with—"

He blocked him with a quick "You say you've had a good relationship with him—how about the other men in your organization?"

"Oh, I guess Judd ruffles a few feathers now and then. He comes up with an idea that shows up somebody—naturally, you're going to have some jealousy. Somebody like Vance Nichols, our chief stylist —burns the hell out of him that the best-selling quality we've got in the line right now was one of Judd's ideas. But that's what you get into with a big organization, everybody worrying about protecting his own little bailiwick."

"I know," Aaron Kharr acknowledged, thinking of the internecine warfare that had gone on at the Berringer Institute, the jealousies that had plagued him at the Allison Clinic.

"I'll tell you how I feel," Crouch said expansively. "Organization is all right—you got to have it—but damn it, it's *ideas* that keep a business going. You can hire plenty of men who can do what you tell them, that's no problem. But when you start looking for a man who can think up something that's really new, something that hasn't been done before—there just aren't many of them around."

"And that's what Mr. Wilder has been—your idea man?"

The president stared at him for a silent moment, acting as if it were a new thought. "Anyway, it's meant a lot to me, having him in the company."

"What about the people who work directly under him—how does he get along with them?"

"Oh, he's had a little trouble, I guess. Who hasn't? These young fellows today—all they care about is getting by. But they don't get away with any slipshod stuff with Judd. Everything's got to be right up to snuff."

"In other words, he's a perfectionist," he said, clinching a vital point, a characteristic as certainly significant as anything in the whole coronary-prone personality pattern.

"Damned if I'll criticize him for that," Crouch said testily. "Some of our fellows do. They say he's too fussy about little things that don't really matter, but what I always say——"

"Tell me this, Mr. Crouch—this perfectionism—has it been a more pronounced characteristic recently? Say over the last year or two?"

"No, I wouldn't say so," Crouch said, but his voice had an uncertain undertone.

"What's his health been like, anything significant there?"

Crouch snorted. "He just had his physical examination—this fancy setup we've got now—Executive Health Appraisement, whatever that means. Not a hell of a lot, something like this happening right after this damn doctor says everything was fine."

"Those things happen," Aaron Kharr said, passing it off with a minimal satisfaction of professional demand. "What about his work, the load he's been carrying, the amount of pressure he's had on him. Have you had him under——"

"No!" Crouch exploded, an angry outburst unaccountable until he added, "Damn it, I've never had the whip on Judd. I've never had to. Just the opposite. God knows how many times I've told him that he ought to slow down, take it a little easier." He stopped, self-consciously aware of a lack of self-control. "I don't want you to get the wrong idea, that's all. A lot of people do. They think that's all a president does—whipping the hell out of his men."

"No, I doubt if you have any cause to blame yourself, Mr. Crouch," Aaron Kharr said quietly. "The man who winds up with a coronary seldom has anyone to blame but himself. The whip on his back hasn't been in anyone else's hand—it's been in his own."

Crouch nodded, but clearly without full acceptance, still searching for absolution as he said, "There are a lot of things besides a man's job that can keep the pressure on him."

"Of course."

"With some men it's wife trouble."

Alerted, Aaron Kharr asked, "Are you suggesting that might be a factor here?"

"I guess you know his wife's off to Europe. Sailed yesterday. You sent her any word yet?"

"No, Mr. Wilder was quite insistent that it not be done. He said he didn't want to worry her, that there was nothing that she could do anyway—which is true enough, of course, but still it does raise a question as to what ought to be done."

"Don't know what to say," Crouch said with a grimace. "Never have been able to figure that woman out."

"How long have they been married?"

"Oh, it goes back—they've got a boy who must be twenty-one, twenty-two."

"Then they were married while he was still in college, or not too long afterwards. Perhaps a war marriage?"

"Maybe so," Crouch said as if accepting a not quite valid excuse, the same tone prevailing as he added, "Kay's an odd one, all right. The way she was brought up, I guess. Raised by this old aunt of hers. One of those old dames that spends most of her time in Europe. That's where Kay went to school as a girl. Didn't come back here until the war started. Then she went to Bryn Mawr."

"Sounds like money in the family."

"Used to be. Don't think there's too much any more. But they were quite a family, the Cannons. Shipping money. The old Cannon line. Then they got into politics. Well, not politics exactly—more the State Department, I guess. One of them was an ambassador to—oh, I don't know—France, I guess it was. He was a bachelor and this old aunt of Kay's—Miss Jessica, that's what everybody calls her—she was sort of a hostess for him. He's dead now, but she still spends most of her time living over there."

"Is that the reason for Mrs. Wilder's trip abroad—to see her aunt?"

"Maybe so. But I'd say it was more this boy of theirs. Rolfe. He's over there now, going to some university in Paris." He paused, his voice dropping to a rough grumble as he said, "If Kay was half as interested in helping Judd as she is in boosting that boy—" He shrugged it off.

Tentatively, Kharr ventured, "Then it hasn't been too successful a marriage?"

"Oh, I wouldn't say that. Not at all. Wouldn't have any reason to. It's just that—well, the right wife can do a hell of a lot for a man."

"Yes, indeed," Kharr said quickly, blank agreement, feeling the discomfiture of inadequate experience that, as a bachelor, he so often felt.

"The trouble with Kay—oh, I don't know, maybe this isn't fair to her. Everybody's got a right to live their own life, I guess. But somehow she just doesn't fit in. All the rest of our wives—the company means just as much to them as it does to their husbands. But with Kay—I won't say she's exactly *anti*-company, but still—she's just an odd one, that's all."

"I think I understand," Kharr said, not at all certain that he did. But at least he had a lead worth exploring. "What about the boy, what's he like?"

"Oh, I don't know—these kids today, I can't figure any of them out. He's smart, I guess. Must be. Went through college in three years. Now he's over there in Paris getting another degree, studying —oh, I've heard but damned if I can remember—seventeenth-century something."

"Doesn't sound like he's following in his father's footsteps."

"No chance of that, not with a mother like Kay."

The telephone rang. The call was from old Dr. Leebow, who, substituting loquacity for common sense, insisted on detailing all the symptoms of one of his cases. Kharr tried his best to cut him off, but long before he achieved that happy end, Crouch had grown restive, on his feet before Leebow finally gave up.

"I'm taking too much of your time," Crouch said. "And I been thinking—we've got this fancy personnel department now, might as well get some good out of it. The minute I get back I'll have Judd's file sent up to you. That'll give you everything we've got on him. And I'll get his medical record for you, too. I told you, we've got this setup to give all our men physical examinations every year. Don't think much of the doctor we've got doing it, this fellow Hewes—he sure as hell missed on Judd—but, anyway, I'll get his records for you."

The vision of a subservient doctor meekly surrendering a patient's file to a company president brought back Aaron Kharr's worst memories of the Allison Clinic. And he was all the more apprehensive as he felt himself being pressured by Crouch's scowl, a look of squint-eyed inquiry that culminated in a taut "You're not going to tell me, are you, that you won't take care of Judd?"

Suddenly he saw the way out. "I think it would be a serious mistake, Mr. Crouch, to force upon Mr. Wilder a doctor not of his own choice."

Crouch looked staggered, but only for a moment, quickly recover-

ing with a sharp, "How can he? He's in no condition to decide anything."

"He will be in a day or two. For the time being—naturally, I'll
carry on. Beyond that, it should be Mr. Wilder's own decision—no
one else's."

Matthew R. Crouch was plainly a man unaccustomed to reversal,
reluctant to yield any power of decision. For a moment his expression
was stonily resistant. Abruptly, it broke. He thrust out his hand. "All
right, Doc, I'll buy that."

There was no alternative to taking his hand, yet Aaron Kharr felt
himself somehow trapped, caught in a bargain that was no less
worrisome because he himself had offered it.

« 7 »

Since his first awakening, which had been achieved only after a long
and difficult struggle, Judd Wilder had been drifting in and out of
consciousness, a strangely cyclical phenomenon. Every time he felt
himself threatened by fear, he floated off into another world, resting
there in a state of torpor until, with the clearing of his mind, he was
again challenged by another alarming intrusion. He had gone
through this cycle an uncounted number of times, drifting from one
world to another, unoriented as to time and place, reminiscence
largely indistinguishable from fantasy, the here and now marked
only by the frozen waxworks smile of the nurse. Every time he
opened his eyes, there she was. No matter how he turned his head
or shifted his gaze, she would be looking directly at him. It was some
kind of trick—one of those novelty-sign faces that followed you as
you walked past a show window—but, impatient of its eeriness, he
wished that someone would pull the plug and turn it off.

Looking straight up at the ceiling was the only way he could
avoid seeing her. He tried it now, attempting to break the cycle,
knowing that if he closed his eyes it would happen again . . . walking down that long flight of gray concrete steps, down and down
and down to some deep basement . . . the echoing snap of the
switch, the green flicker and then the burst of harsh fluorescent light

. . . wheeling out the shrouded corpse . . . the crayon-marked red tag . . . JUDD WILDER . . . *No!*

But the old man's gnarled hand was reaching out, a talon-fingered claw slowly peeling back the white sheet . . . "You know him?"

"No, I don't know why he used my name." How many times did they have to ask that? "Yes, I know who he is . . . Floyd Fulton . . . F-l-o-y-d F-u-l-t-o-n . . ."

He had to get out . . . too hot . . . he was going to vomit . . . *get out of here* . . .

The nurse's face was staring down at him again, hideously distorted by the watery shimmer of the plastic tent. Nausea was still a threat, a persistence that brought back the Jersey City morgue, now as a conscious memory. Dry-mouthed, he slipped his hand out under the plastic tent, reaching for the water glass on the bedside stand.

The nurse grabbed for his hand, a prohibition made all the more sadistic by her unbroken smile, by the sugar-coated cruelty of the smirking voice that said, "We can't have water, Mr. Wilder, not with a heart attack."

Heart attack . . . yes, that's what the doctor in the coroner's office had said . . . "No, it wasn't suicide, we're certain of that now . . . we've definitely established the cause of death as a coronary occlusion with myocardial infarction . . . what is popularly known as a heart attack . . . if he had only gone to a hospital instead of holing up in that motel" . . . the Los Juntos . . .

He was getting things mixed up again. He wasn't at the Los Juntos . . . he *had* gotten to a hospital . . .

Or was this a dream, too? No . . . Sam's Diner . . . the ambulance, that doctor . . . what was his name?

"Dr. Kharr," he said aloud, a triumph of recollection, a welcome assurance of reality.

But the Jersey City morgue had been no dream either, that life-empty face so brutally exposed in the harsh glare of those greenish lights, so different from the face that he had seen that morning in the *Herald* office . . .

He had been twelve that summer, big for his age, long-armed enough to run the folding machine. That was what he had been doing, folding that week's edition of the *Herald*, trying to keep from smudging the fresh ink, everything wet and sticky in the August heat, hurrying so he could get away and out to the scene of all the excitement. All day long men had been coming into town, not stopping on Main Street but driving straight through to the fairgrounds. By now, there must be a hundred men out there, armed with everything from shotguns to hickory axe-handles. At dawn tomorrow morning, they would throw a blockade across every road by which milk or grain or hogs could be hauled to Des Moines or Sioux City.

The newspapers back East—his father had quoted some of them in the *Herald* this week—were still saying that Farmers Holiday Association was nothing to worry about, that at worst a "farmer's strike" would be no more than a political demonstration staged by the same radical crowd that had just nominated Franklin D. Roosevelt for President. It was hardly credible, one editorial writer had said, that any serious trouble could start in Iowa, the richest agricultural state in the union, the birthplace of Herbert Hoover. But his father had written, "As we go to press, our neighbors are gathering in Haygood in a scene only too reminiscent of the way our forebears gathered a century and a half ago at Lexington. Let us hope that freedom from oppression can be regained here without the firing of another shot that, we fear, would again be heard around the world."

Obviously, that was not the hope of the reporters who, drawn by the possibility of newsworthy violence, had been coming into Haygood all day, stopping at the *Herald* office to get their bearings. Most of the big Midwest dailies had sent men, newspapers as far away as the *Chicago Tribune* and the *Denver Post*, men who had been awesomely impressive until Floyd Fulton's dramatic arrival reduced all of them to nonentities. Judd recognized him the instant he stepped inside the door, looking exactly like the frontispiece picture in his wonderful book *With My Own Eyes*, wearing the same khaki coat, the one with all the pockets, the silk scarf at his neck, the authentic garb of a real foreign correspondent. At least once a month, there was a Floyd Fulton article in *Collier's*. There had been one in the last issue, all about the Bonus Army marching on Washington. Now he was right here in Haygood!

The other reporters had brushed Judd off with a nod or a wink, treating him like a kid—not Floyd Fulton. He gave him a real handshake and a solid, "Glad to meet you, Judd," saying it as if he really meant it. The others had treated him as if he were nothing but a twelve-year old kid.

The papers were quickly folded, but the mailing labels still had to be put on, a rankling task that kept him in the back of the shop while his father told Floyd Fulton about the Farmers Holiday Association. But he could still catch words and phrases, enough to follow the story, and when his father went to get some back copies to show Floyd Fulton how a full page of the *Herald* had been filled every week with legal notices of mortgage foreclosures, Judd thought of showing him the March 9 issue with the three suicide stories on the front page, all farmers who had lost their homesteads to big Eastern insurance companies.

"You've got what it takes, Judd," Floyd Fulton had complimented him, going on then to tell him how he, too, had started on a little county-seat weekly like the *Herald,* not in Iowa but back in Pennsylvania, and to prove that he, too, had been a printer's devil he picked up a stick and went to a type case, setting a line in 18-point Cheltenham Bold. The line he had set had been BY JUDD WILDER.

Friday, with the paper in the mail, was always a light day in the *Herald* office and Judd knew that he did not have to appear at the shop. He was awake long before dawn, slipping out of the house into the black night, at the fairgrounds before the sun came up. The scene was an exciting resurrection of *The Red Badge of Courage*— the bivouac on the night before the big battle, fires scattered over the plain, black figures silhouetted, the flickering light catching the grim thrust of unshaven jaws. Muttered curses rose over the continuous rosin-can screech of the night locust, accented now and then with the sharp metallic click of a rifle bolt being thrown, the loose rattle of the pump being tested on a Winchester Model 12. Somewhere in the distance there was singing, a parody of the "Battle Hymn of the Republic." Running from group to group, he tried unsuccessfully to find Floyd Fulton.

As the sun came up, the scene lost some of its magic, the night-uniformed troops materializing into straw-hatted farmers in overalls, the assembly looking more like an enormous threshing crew than an army, the bold curses of the night watered down into sky-looking observations that it was "gonna be another hot one." Even more disappointingly, the farm trucks that were now pulling away from the front of the grandstand were loaded not with arms and cases of ammunition but with old threshing-machine belts studded with spikes, long chains to stretch across the roads, bales of hay to be thrown in the path of trucks. He made several attempts to catch a ride, pushed off by pig-smelling farmers who treated him like a kid. He countered by thinking them a bunch of play-acting old fools— until, suddenly, Floyd Fulton appeared. He was standing up in the front seat of a touring car with the top down, a brand-new Ford that had been driven out from Des Moines by the reporter for the *Register*. Floyd was wearing the bush jacket with a scarf at his neck, not the blue-and-white bandanna that a Haygood thresherman might wear to keep out barley chaff but a square of paisley silk.

The *Register* reporter, even though he was driving his own car, looked as though he was only Floyd Fulton's chauffeur, and the other two newspaper reporters in the back seat were acting as if what was happening was not as important as what Floyd Fulton was saying about it. Judd, cautious after his many rebuffs, did not run to the stopped car until, bursting with elation, he saw Floyd Fulton beckoning him. He asked what was happening and Judd told him all that he had learned on his tour of the encampment.

"Good stuff," Floyd Fulton said, throwing open the door for him, whipping out a hand to help him in, introducing him to the man from the *Des Moines Register,* the man from the *Omaha World-Herald,* the man from the *Sioux-Falls Argus-Leader* . . . "Judd Wilder from the *Haygood Herald.*"

They drove east to the Des Moines road, crossed the railroad tracks and turned north. Where the Sioux City road came in, a milk truck had been stopped and the big ten-gallon cans were being dumped. Two miles farther on a load of hogs was stopped, the truck driver cowering before the crowd, wanting to know what a man could do with his hogs if he was not allowed to take them to Sioux City. They told him in jeering curses. But there were other farmers standing back, silent, troubled, nodding when the driver asked if they didn't know what would happen to a load of hogs if you kept them all day in a truck with no protection from the August sun. Oscar Sonnenberger, whose farm was nearby, finally offered the use of an empty pen. The spark of revolution seemed to be flickering out. Judd, anxiously identifying faces and spelling names, was acutely conscious that Floyd Fulton was disappointed.

Nothing was happening at the next crossroad, men standing around in little clumps, whisker-scratching, wandering off into the cornfields beside the road, coming back buttoning their flies. At Judd's suggestion, Floyd Fulton ordered a south turn, retracing their path. It was getting hot now. The gravel where the milk had been dumped was beginning to smell like the backyard of the creamery. Most of the men were sitting in the narrow band of shade under the cottonwood trees along the road, chewing tobacco, swatting flies.

Waiting, they heard a distant gunshot. The man from the *Register* sent the Ford roaring down the road to the next blockade point, Floyd Fulton standing up in the front seat again. One of Marvin Aungst's sons, the one with the harelip, had shot a crow and everybody was laughing at the funny way he was talking, trying to collect a ten-cent bet from Elmer Weidler. "Hell, if I had ten cents to my name I wouldn't be here," Elmer said, getting a big laugh, but the *Argus-Leader* man was the only one who got out his wad of notepaper.

Floyd Fulton took off his scarf, stuffing it in his pocket. Trying to divert him, Judd called his attention to the Indian mounds that could be seen from the road, surprised when he showed great interest. In a whisper guardedly concealed from the three reporters, swearing Judd to secrecy, he confided that he was planning to write a novel about the American Indians. They wandered off, Judd telling him about all the stuff that his grandfather, Senator Simon Judd, had dug out of the mounds, hope fulfilled when Floyd Fulton promised that someday he would come back to Haygood. When they returned to the car, the *Register* man was talking about starting back to Des Moines, and the *World-Herald* man was studying a schedule trying to find out when he could get a train to Omaha.

Heavyhearted, Judd directed them back to Haygood, taking the long way around, not turning west at the schoolhouse corner but driving on to the Sandy Creek bridge, courting the last thin hope that something might be happening there. The gamble paid off. From a half-mile away they saw the dust, cars still coming, men running. Closer, they saw a log chain across the bridge.

Floyd Fulton jumped out without opening the door, his feet no more than on the ground when he was confronted by two men with shotguns. One was Jake Kipp, moonshine-smelling the way he always was, telling Floyd Fulton to get the hell out of Mound County, that they could handle their own affairs. Most of all they didn't need any help from any damn foreigners. "If you Khaki Shirts are so all-fired crazy about Russia, why the hell don't you go back there!"

Judd did not know, until he heard the *Register* man telling the *Argus-Leader* man, that the Khaki Shirts were a gang of city rowdies, imitating Mussolini's Black Shirts but actually led by Communist organizers out from the East. Jake was mistaking Floyd Fulton's bush jacket for a Khaki Shirt officer's uniform, and nothing that Judd could say would change his mind. "Sure, I know you're Harry Wilder's boy," Jake said. "And you can just tell that old man of yours—some of the crap he's been running in his paper lately—he can go back to Wall Street, just like them Reds can go back to Russia! We got no place for any damn foreigners, one brand or the other!"

Floyd Fulton started to talk to Jake then, but he gave Judd a side glance—that was the wonderful thing about Floyd Fulton, the way he could make you understand something without saying a word— and he got the idea, slipping off into the cornfield like he had to take a leak, wading the creek, then running down the corn rows again until he got to where he could hear and see what was happening. There were three old Model T's full of Khaki Shirts, most of the shirts so new that you could still see the store wrinkles. They were trying to horn in and take over, but the Mound County farmers would have none of it. There was a sharp scuffle, quickly ended when Lars Oliafsen knocked down one of the foreigners and bloodied up his new shirt. The intruders, impotently cursing, turned around and headed for Des Moines.

Judd ran back to the bridge where Jake was still holding up Floyd Fulton and the reporters. He told them what had happened, and because Jake was as interested as they were in finding out what was going on, he let him talk while Floyd Fulton wrote it all down.

Jake finally let them through. Encouraged, they turned away from Haygood and spent the rest of the forenoon touring the roadblocks. But they encountered no more incidents. At noon, calling Des Moines long distance from the *Herald* office, the *Register* man learned that a big battle was developing up north around Sioux City. They took off immediately, all four of them, not even waiting for dinner. But as the car pulled out, Floyd Fulton called back, "You'll be hearing from me, Judd."

For days that promise was his consoling hope, all but lost when a telegram arrived. Luckily it came over the wire just before he arrived at the depot to meet the 5:35 to look for local items, so Otto Backe gave the message to him instead of sending it to the *Herald* office where his father might have seen it. The telegram was from New York, signed FLOYD and the message read: YOUR STUFF IN NEXT ISSUE STOP THOUGHT BEST NOT USE YOUR NAME STOP WRITE ME LOCAL REACTION CARE COLLIERS.

Judd did not tell his father about the telegram, thinking it would be better to surprise him with the magazine. In that aim he failed, but as things turned out it was all for the best. Rachow's Drug Store got only four copies of *Collier's*—magazine reading in 1932 was a luxury that few could afford, even at five cents a copy—and by the time Judd got there, running down from school at recess, all had been sold. At noon, he haunted the post office, eyeing the subscription copies that could be seen through the little beveled-glass windows in the lockboxes, waiting for someone to claim one of them, finally successful when old Mrs. Tolken came in. He fast-talked her into letting him carry her groceries home. And that was where he read it, on the Tolken's front porch. No peak of elation, before or since, equaled the thrill of reading that long paragraph about the Khaki Shirts being turned back in Mound County. It was exactly as he had told it to Floyd Fulton, word for word. No, his name wasn't there, but that didn't matter—they were his words—and in *Collier's!*

He ran all the way home from Tolken's, cutting through backyards, climbing fences. The noon dinner had already been eaten but his father was still at the table, a copy of *Collier's* in front of him. It was one of the few times that Judd ever saw him openly furious. Mound County had been held up to ridicule and disgrace before the eyes of the nation, he said, and he would like nothing better than to get his hands on the fool who had filled Floyd Fulton full of all those lies, making everyone in Haygood sound like a bunch of stupid hayshaking hicks. Judd Wilder's greatest joy was reduced to a black secret, bursting within him but unrevealable.

Everyone in Haygood felt the same way about the Floyd Fulton article. Judd, reading and rereading it behind the locked door of his bedroom, could not find one line that was untrue or inaccurately reported, but that did not stop the Main Street big-talkers from saying that if Floyd Fulton ever showed up in Haygood again he would be tarred and feathered and ridden out of town on a rail. For months, until they were finally diverted by Franklin D. Roosevelt being elected President, there was still talk about finding the blabbermouth. Judd had no idea why they did not suspect him—Jake Kipp could have given him away, and dozens of people must have seen him in Floyd Fulton's car that day, but apparently everyone thought him too much of a kid to know as much as Floyd Fulton had learned. Their failure to credit his competence was enough to spawn a driving ambition. He would, he swore, leave Haygood as soon as he could. He would never come back, but when those stupid yokels read his articles in *Collier's* they would know what he thought of them.

As the telegram requested, Judd wrote a report on the local reaction, absolutely factual as a good correspondent had to be, leaving out nothing, not even the tar and feather threat. He sent it off in a plain envelope with no return address, knowing that old Cass Priestly in the post office had no regard for the privacy of the U.S. mail. Either the trick worked or old Cass was too dumb to realize that he was someone a lot more important than just Harry Wilder's kid. Anyway, the letter got through and there was an answer from Floyd Fulton, short but wonderful, telling him what a "big kick" he got out of the report. It was, he wrote, "good stuff," and he was sending a package in which he hoped Judd would find something of interest. The box arrived on December 17, close enough to Christmas so that old Cass didn't pay any special attention to it. Judd sneaked it up to his bedroom, finding the cardboard carton a fabulous treasure chest—five books and a dozen copies of magazines that he had never before seen. Beyond all comparison, this was his best and most significant Christmas. Floyd Fulton had sent him the *New Republic* and the *Nation;* his mother and father gave him a year's subscription to *Boy's Life*.

He kept writing to Floyd Fulton, composing every letter as if it were an article for *Collier's*, reporting everything that was going on in Haygood, always hoping that there would be at least a paragraph that Floyd Fulton might use. That never happened, but he always answered. A half-dozen times he sent books or magazines, once the galley proofs of a new book about the Russian Revolution that was not even published yet.

Then it all stopped. After three of Judd's letters had gone unanswered, apprehension all the greater because there had not been a

Floyd Fulton article in *Collier's* for a long time, he finally wrote a letter addressed to "Editor, Collier's Magazine" asking for information. The reply confirmed his worst fears—"Mr. Fulton is no longer on our staff and we do not have a forwarding address for him."

Almost two years passed. Then, one night after supper his father interrupted his reading the *Des Moines Register* to exclaim, "Well, what do you know—Mr. Floyd Fulton finally comes out in his true colors, I see." He read the item aloud, an account of how Floyd Fulton, one of the Americans who were fighting with the Communists in the Spanish Civil War, had been wounded, and after escaping over the Pyrenees, was now recuperating in the American Hospital in Paris. Secretly, Judd wrote that night, hoping against hope that a letter addressed only to "American Hospital, Paris, France," would somehow get through.

Weeks later, coming home from school one afternoon, his mother met him at the door with a letter postmarked Paris, France. She handed it to him, asking, "You wrote to Floyd Fulton, didn't you?" When he admitted it, she said, "I don't think we'll tell your father," turning away then, allowing him to read his letter in privacy. Long afterwards, that memory of her would persist, that longer than any other.

Floyd Fulton's letter from Paris said that he was finally ready to start work on his Indian novel. He was planning to base it on the Black Hawk story, and as soon as he got back to the States, would be coming to Iowa to do some research in the state historical library. Would Judd come to Iowa City to see him? He wrote back that he would, wondering how he could manage it without letting his father know, a problem that faded off into nothingness as the weeks went by with no further word. Then, startlingly, Floyd Fulton telephoned one night to say that he was actually in Iowa City. Judd was nonplussed, hardly knowing what to say. He was helping Mr. Dwight direct the senior class play, starting to work with him on the script for the pageant, and the Floyd Fulton episode was beginning to seem something out of his distant grade-school past. By now he could see that old Floyd was a pretty corny character, all of that big foreign correspondent act. And he knew, too, that *Collier's* was nothing but a "slick," almost as bad as the *Post*, full of what Mr. Dwight called "encapsulated boob-culture," nothing that really meant anything to someone who was genuinely interested in the Art of the Theater.

His decision was made by coincidence. Had there not been, that weekend, a meeting in Iowa City for participants in the Iowa State High School Drama Contest, he might not have gone. After he had, he wished that he had not. He would have much preferred to remember Floyd Fulton in his bush jacket and paisley scarf, not the startlingly aged man, at least forty-five, with whom he had spent a long afternoon in a gray soot-smelling hotel room. There had been a pretense of talking about the novel, a pitiably brave prediction that it was sure to be bought by the movies as soon as it was written, but Judd had quickly decided that it would never be anything more substantial than the dream of a defeated man. Floyd Fulton's fame, meteoric in its rise, had fallen back to earth like a spent skyrocket, leaving a trail of debts, unpaid alimony, empty bottles, a hundred madly broken promises that had now, apparently, closed all the editorial doors through which he once so jauntily strode. Much of this, Floyd Fulton ruefully admitted; the rest was close enough to the surface to be easily seen. Over and over again, he bemoaned the mess he had made of his life, excusing self-pity by turning it all into a warning, begging Judd not to be the fool that he had been. Judd needed no such admonition—the example was enough.

That was the last time he had seen Floyd Fulton alive. The next time there had been only that lifeless face in the Jersey City morgue, viewed after a nightmare episode. Judd had been a freshman at Colfax then, awakened one night by a frantic pounding at his bedroom door, opening it to find the dean of men, backed by a half-dozen boys, staring at him as if he were a ghost. The police in Jersey City, it seemed, had telegraphed Haygood, Iowa, that Judd Wilder had been found dead in a local motel. His father, of course, had telephoned the dean. Judd himself had called his father back, vouching for his aliveness, less impressed by the depth of his father's relief than by his quick about-face, his certainty that Judd had been somehow involved in a gruesome prank.

Whoever the dead man was, he must have known Judd Wilder, and the dean, fearing that Colfax College might be unfavorably involved, had sent him to Jersey City to help the police with their identification. Somehow Judd had known, even before the sheet was turned back, who it would be. Guilt-stricken, recalling how much

Floyd Fulton had once meant to him, thinking that he must some-how have failed him that day in Iowa City, he had done what he could to help the authorities. They had finally located Floyd's sister, a life-embittered woman who seemed to have been struck the last blow by having her brother commit suicide. Judd, too, had assumed that it was suicide, as relieved as Floyd's sister was when the doctor in the coroner's office had said, "No, it was not suicide, we're certain of that now. The cause of death was a coronary occlusion with myo-cardial infarction, what is popularly known as a heart attack . . . if he had gotten to a hospital instead of holing up in that motel . . ."

But he had gotten to a hospital . . . the red tag . . . JUDD WILDER . . . *he had to get out of here!*

Fighting his way, he struggled up through the enveloping fog, searching for the face of the nurse . . . *where was she?*

Lost, he thought for an instant that he had drifted off again. But, no, the fog was gone, a face coming into focus now, a different face, tantalizingly familiar but unrecognized until identification burst upon him . . . *Dr. Kharr* . . .

He must have said it aloud because there was a responding smile, a softly asked, "How are you feeling now?"

"All right," he said, blinking, trying to clear his mind of the sticky web of panic. Glancing right, he saw that the oxygen-tent apparatus had been pushed into the corner, the nurse furling the plastic against the upright arm.

"You don't need that any more," Dr. Kharr explained. "Actually, you didn't need it at all, just a precaution that it seemed best to take until we could be sure. I hope it didn't frighten you?"

"Why should it?" he demanded, striking out against what seemed an accusation of cowardice.

"It sometimes does," Dr. Kharr said, still looking at him suspi-ciously.

"What time is it?" he asked, made to seem a fool when Dr. Kharr glanced at the wall clock, saying, "As you can see, almost noon."

"I guess I've been asleep," he said, shifting from a recognizably weak excuse to a quickly accusing "You slugged me with a lot of dope, didn't you?"

"Yes, we've been giving you sedatives—but I told you that's what we were going to do. Remember?" The doctor paused, demanding a nod. "A little extra sleep isn't hurting you any, Mr. Wilder. And why not? You haven't anything else to do."

"The hell I haven't."

Dr. Kharr was smiling, shaking his head. "If you're still worrying about that convention of yours, you can forget it. It's been postponed."

"Postponed?" he reacted, his mind cocked by recoil, an automatic weapon instantly loaded with explosive objection. But when he pulled the trigger, nothing happened. It was a terrifying sensation, one that he had never experienced before, this feeling of utter helplessness, of being unable to fight back.

"That's what Mr. Crouch told me to tell you," Dr. Kharr was saying. "He said that fall would be as good as spring, perhaps even better. Anyway, that's what he's decided to do, postpone it until you're back on your feet again."

"Back on my feet," he whispered to himself, hearing it as a command, trying to rise . . . *he had to get out of here* . . . He was drifting off again . . . the red tag . . . JUDD WILDER . . .

Dr. Kharr's voice snatched him back, lost words that were only now filtering through, telling him that he might be feeling uncomfortable this afternoon, that he would probably have a little fever, "—but no more than with a common cold. In any event, it will be completely normal, exactly what we're expecting. By tomorrow at this time you'll be feeling very much yourself again—so it's nothing to worry about."

"I'm not worrying," he said, a frightening truth.

"If there's anything else I can tell you, anything you want to know—anything we can do to make you more comfortable—?"

"I'm all right," he said forcefully, prompted by hoarseness to add, "It's just this no-water business. Why can't I have a drink?"

"A drink? Of course. Why not?" Dr. Kharr was on his feet, turning to the door with a sharply commanding "Nurse!"

Her face popped into the opening, a mask on a puppet-show stage. "Yes, Doctor?"

"Have you been restricting water?"

"But, Doctor, it's a heart case. We never allow heart cases to——"

"I gave no such order. Get him a drink, please."

Her doll-face melted, wax exposed to heat, her lips drooping into an expression incongruous with the startled stare of her marble-round eyes. Her offstage voice, late in picking up the cue, finally said, "Yes, Doctor," and she flounced off toward the bathroom as if suspended by too-taut strings.

"Sorry about that water business," Dr. Kharr whispered apologetically. "Once these nurses get started on some routine—but it's my fault, really. I should have told her. But don't worry about it. We'll get things straightened out here. If there's anything else——"

"I'll be all right," he said. "But thanks for—" He suddenly realized that he should be thanking him for more than a drink of water, "for everything—last night—all that you did."

"Oh, I did little enough, Mr. Wilder. Actually, there wasn't too much that needed to be done."

"Thanks anyway," he said, aware that he had reached out only when he felt Dr. Kharr's hand, the responding grip of the doctor's fingers strangely tentative, the same feeling that was in his voice as he said, "I happened to be in the hospital when you were brought in last night, that's all. But that doesn't mean that you have to accept me as your doctor. It may well be that someone else——"

Too quickly to be stopped, a protest burst from Judd's lips, the words unconsidered, an instantaneous response to what seemed a terrifying threat of abandonment.

For an endlessly prolonged moment the doctor's face remained an unreadable enigma. Then almost too quickly to be seen, there was the flicker of a smile, off and on, gone, no hint of it in the measured voice that said, "All right, Mr. Wilder, I'll be very glad to take care of you."

« 8 »

As Emily had reminded him when he left the house this morning to drive up to County Memorial, the regular monthly meeting of the New Ulster City Planning Commission was today, called for 12:15 at the country club. Matt Crouch was not particularly interested in city planning but he had accepted chairmanship of the commission because, as Emily had said, it was high time he started thinking of something other than the Crouch Carpet Company. If he retired at sixty-five—he was only a few months away from it now—he would need some outside interests.

Hearing the noon whistle as he approached the Administration Building, he decided that there was not time enough to go up to his office. Stopping at the curb, he picked up the proofs of the stockholders report and called out to the watchman, about to order the envelope sent up to Mr. Stark's office when he saw Roger Stark come out through the revolving door.

He called, catching Stark's attention, irked as he always was by the glacial quality of the vice president's response, the slow turning of his head, the chilled expression with which he resisted the indignity of an informal summons. Watching Stark come up to the car, hound-thin and high-headed, his Phi Beta Kappa key glinting on his vest, Matt Crouch downed his instinctive dislike by again reminding himself of what Elbert Coe had said when he recommended employing Stark as Vice President for Management. "He's a cool character, perhaps not the sort of man you'll cotton to as a human being, but you'll like him for what he can do for your company—and that's the important thing, isn't it?"

There had been no alternative to agreement. Elbert Coe was his last hope to get the financial help that Crouch Carpet had so desperately needed to surmount an embarrassingly unanticipated emergency. Finance, as Matt Crouch ruefully admitted, had never been his long suit. His prime interest had always been in production, his business philosophy based on the premise that if he made the best possible piece of carpet, and backed it with the best possible service, profit would take care of itself. And it had—up to a point. But that point had fallen far short of what had been needed to finance the company's booming expansion. Suddenly the treasury had gone dry, all the more shocking because he had thought everything was going so wonderfully, the mill on three shifts and the backlog of orders growing larger every day. Stunned though he had been, he was not too deeply alarmed at first, imagining that it would be easy enough to bring in some new capital. A week in New York and Philadelphia had been cruelly disabusing. One investment house after another had turned him down, their rejections inexplicable until he had talked to Elbert Coe.

"Since you've asked me to be frank, I shall be," Coe had said. "To be quite brutal about it, my dear sir, it's no wonder you frightened them off. Take this past half-hour—what have you done? Shown me your samples, told me what a good product you're making, what a fine mill you have—that's all, nothing more. And I suppose you did the same with the others. If so, it's quite obvious why they turned you down. There's nothing more suspect these days, you see, than a product-minded company president. In the modern management view, product is only the means to an end, that's all. The all-important end, my dear sir, is profit—and as you've made only too obvious, you are not essentially a profit-minded president."

He had defended himself vigorously, arguing that of course he was interested in profit, that he had built Crouch Carpet out of earnings. But he could not resist saying, too, that his company's growth had been at the expense of competitors who were so "profit-minded" that they had forgotten the necessity of turning out an honest piece of goods and selling it at a fair price.

Elbert Coe had remained unimpressed, further condemning him with "Ah, yes, the old-fashioned view that profit is a reward for the performance of a service to the community. Socially commendable, of course, but sadly out-of-date in our contemporary corporate society."

He had all but given up then, saved from final despair only when Coe, speculatively regarding him over the top of his half-moon spectacles, had observed, "But now, of course, if you were to add a keen, young, profit-minded executive to your management staff—and if you were willing to accept his guidance in financial matters—yes, under those circumstances, it's just possible that Tilden, Coe & Company might be interested in underwriting a stock issue for you."

Not too surprisingly, Elbert Coe had just happened to have such a keen, young, profit-minded executive in mind. That was how Roger Stark had come to Crouch Carpet. And there could be no doubt that he had done what he had been brought in to do. When this stockholders report was released, the financial community would learn that Crouch Carpet had earned $3.16 a share last year, another record high, another assurance that all stockholders would remain fully content and safely silent. That, to Matt Crouch, was vitally important. His greatest concern with Elbert Coe's plan of financing had been that a big issue of common stock would so dilute his own holdings that he would no longer have majority control of the company. "Don't worry about that," Coe had assured him.

"You'll never hear a peep out of a stockholder as long as your earnings statement looks good enough. Keep that profit figure up where it ought to be and Crouch Carpet will still be your own show."

That, above all else, was what Roger Stark had done for him, and Matt Crouch was by no means ungrateful. He had learned the hard way, years ago, that he had to accept the limitations of his own ability, and just as Judd Wilder's flair for merchandising and promotion had filled a need that he himself could not supply, so Roger Stark's talent for financial control had countered another regretted weakness. That, in the beginning, was all that he had expected of him.

The title that Stark had been given at Elbert Coe's suggestion—Vice President for Administration—had been, it was true, unfortunately broad in scope, but at the time it had seemed the best way to avoid a direct conflict with Fred Hanford, who, as Treasurer, would have been badly hurt if a Vice President for Finance had been brought in over his head. In any event, Matt Crouch had never had any intention of making Roger Stark his number two man. Yet in less than three years, by a process so subtly evolutionary that it had gone largely unnoticed, that was what Stark had undeniably become.

Stark's first move had been to computerize the office operations, and although Matt Crouch had been shocked by the high rental cost of an IBM 1401, the expense was quickly justified, not only by direct savings but also by the way it had cleared his desk of paperwork and freed him to get out in the mill again. Tight budgetary control over both mill costs and overhead expense had been quickly achieved. Then, with the computer available, it had seemed reasonable enough to approve Stark's suggestion that it be used to control finished-goods inventory, and when that proved so successful, its use had been extended to raw materials and scheduling. After that, only the human element had remained fallible. That weakness Stark had moved to counter by developing C.O.C.—Coordinated Operating Control—a system that had so simplified day-to-day procedure that all any department head had to do in order to find the answer to any operating question was to consult the appropriately keyed paragraph in the C.O.C. manual.

Matt Crouch had hesitated before approving C.O.C., arguing that any man worth his salt would rebel against a system so mechanistically dehumanized, but his last lingering doubts had been dissipated by the applause that had followed announcement of the adoption of the system at one of Stark's new Co-worker Information meetings. Secretly, he had been shaken, made to seem an old man no longer able to trust his instinctive judgment, shocked that otherwise intelligent men could be so easily fooled into thinking that they were being given a new delegation of authority when, in truth, their responsibility had been reduced to finding the right page and paragraph in the C.O.C. manual.

With too-revealing hindsight, Matt Crouch could easily enough trace the nefarious process by which Roger Stark had nibbled away control of the company. He was still president, still the ultimate authority, still in control of company policy, but these days there were fewer and fewer problems that reached policy level. What the computer did not decide, the C.O.C. manual did, and Stark, as both master programmer of the computer and author of the manual, was building an ever higher wall around the president's office, keeping everyone out, diverting all of the traffic into his own lair. It was getting so bad now, Matt Crouch frequently told his wife, that he was having a hard time finding out what was going on. A lot of things were happening that he didn't know about. No one ever told him anything.

Emily offered no sympathy. It was, she said, high time that he gave up active management of the company, insisting that he ought to think himself lucky, grateful that he had as good a man as Roger Stark to take over. And in some ways, of course, it was true—this earnings report was proof enough that Stark would keep the company financially sound—but now as the Vice President for Management bent down to the car window, an obviously begrudged obeisance, his coolly anticipatory expression again chilled Matt Crouch's visualization of what the Crouch Carpet Company would become with Roger Stark as its president.

"Here are the report proofs," the president said curtly. "I suppose you'll want to check them."

"Naturally," Stark said, a faint smile of withdrawn satisfaction playing about his gray-blue eyes, silent then, not a word about Judd.

"I've been up to the hospital," Matt Crouch prompted, his tone censorious.

"Yes," Stark said, sounding as if he were granting permission to speak.

"It's not too bad, thank God. Bad enough, but still he's going to pull through all right."

"It was a heart attack?"

"Yes, but we're lucky there, this doctor we've got. Fellow named Kharr—Dr. Aaron Kharr. That's why I went up, to check him out. If anyone can bring him around, he's the man to do it."

"Splendid," Stark said, his tone flat, incongruous with the word. "I've been doing a bit of checking-out myself."

"So?"

"I called in Talbott to see where we stand on the convention."

"You did, huh?" he said, bristling at this evidence that Stark had invaded one of his few remaining private preserves. Advertising & Promotion still reported directly to the president's office, Judd Wilder one of the few men in the company who had not gone over to Stark's camp.

"Am I not right—you were under the impression that the convention preparations were well in hand?"

"There was still a lot to be done, I know that," he retorted, curbing anger. Stark had frequently implied that Advertising and Promotion needed tighter executive control, but this was the first time he had openly accused him of not knowing what was going on.

"From what Talbott tells me, *everything* is yet to be done," Stark said sardonically, a cutting correction. "Oh, I suppose Judd had some sort of plan in mind, no doubt he did, but unfortunately nothing was reduced to paper."

"Paper be damned," he exploded. "There's nothing *to* be done."

"Nothing?"

"That's what I said—*nothing!* The convention's canceled."

"Canceled?"

"Postponed," he conceded, irked by the need for even this minor retreat.

Stark eyed him coolly. "I'm sure that's not a final decision."

"The hell it isn't!" he shot back, his body stiffening, his foot inadvertently touching the accelerator. The car lurched ahead, Stark's head snapping back out of the window. Quickly, Crouch tramped down on the brake, the car lurching to a stop. But Stark's face did not reappear in the window. Looking in the rear-vision mirror, he searched it out. For the first time in three years, he saw Stark's face stripped clean of its habitual expression of confident superiority. Crisply nodding his satisfaction, Crouch called back, "I'll be at the country club," and drove ahead.

His hand was trembling on the wheel, accusing evidence that he had lost his temper. That was what he had to watch. Justified or not, it wasn't good for him. If Emily found out, she'd raise the devil. But, damn it, there was a limit to how much any man could take!

He was halfway to the country club before he realized that, not having gone up to his office, he had failed to pick up the folder of notes from which, as chairman, he would guide the meeting. He slowed down for a moment, then abruptly decided that he could get along without them. If he brought up rezoning again they'd squabble their way through the whole hour. If anything was ever going to be done about city planning, somebody would have to knock a few heads together. He couldn't do that, not as long as he was President of the Crouch Carpet Company. Maybe after he retired—but, damn it, there was no reason why he *had* to retire. No one could make him. And even if he did, he'd still be Chairman of the Board.

As he entered the clubhouse, heading for the private dining room where the meeting would be held, old Doc Robbins flagged him down with a palsied hand. Obviously, he had been waiting for him, anxiously inquiring, "How'd you make out up at County Memorial?"

"Oh, everything's fine," he said. "You were sure as hell right about this fellow Kharr."

"That's what I wanted to talk to you about," the old doctor said with a nervous quaver. "I got worrying about it after I talked to you, thinking that maybe I'd—I told you about knowing this man who used to work with him?"

"You called him?"

Robbins nodded, clearing his throat, triggering a dry hacking cough, a lapse that Matt Crouch filled with a positive "Well, he knows a hell of a lot about heart attacks, nobody has to tell me that."

Wiping his rheumy eyes, Robbins nodded agreement, "Yes, that's the report I got—very able, very talented——"

"So what's wrong with him?" he demanded. "If you're going to tell me that he's a Jew—all right, so what?"

Robbins seemed taken aback, but only for a moment. "No, no, it's not that, not at all. We have some very able Jewish doctors." He reached out for his arm. "All I wanted you to know—some of his ideas, some of the things he may be telling you—" He glanced about as if fearful of being overheard. "Just don't take it all as gospel, Matt. From what Dr. Firth told me—well, it seems Kharr's something of an individualist, a bit of a rebel."

"Good God, that's terrible," Matt Crouch exclaimed, a mockery of shock. "You don't mean, do you, that he might tell me something that hasn't been approved by all you—" Overdone, irony could not be sustained, and he burst into laughter. "Forget it, Doc. Come on, let's go in."

"Well, I thought—after what I'd told you last night—I don't want you to——"

"All right, maybe some of his ideas aren't what all the rest of you have been saying—he told me they weren't——"

"He did?"

"But, damn it, does that make him wrong? I've talked to a hell of a lot of doctors about heart attacks, what causes them—you know I have."

Robbins retreated with a weaseling "Matt, I've never taken the position that——"

"Kharr makes a hell of a lot more sense than anybody I've ever talked to. At least, he's worrying about what comes afterward—and that, by God, is the important thing."

"I'm sorry, Matt. I didn't mean to disturb you."

"Hell, you haven't disturbed me, Doc. Not a bit. Grateful to you. Appreciate it. Come on, I'll buy you a drink."

« 9 »

Kay Wilder had spent most of the late forenoon blanket-wrapped in a deck chair, sampling the three books that she had brought out with her. One of the advantages of going by ship, she had told herself, would be this chance to really do some reading again—there had been a time in her life when she had read, read, read—but nothing had caught her up this morning, everything either a too-insistent reminder of what she had left behind in New Ulster, or a too-evocative suggestion of what lay ahead of her in Paris.

She had eaten breakfast late, successfully avoiding the others at the captain's table, thinking that she might skip lunch altogether. But as the morning had worn on, conscious that she still had five full days ahead of her, she convinced herself that she was being a little ridiculous. Surely they couldn't be as bad as they had seemed last night. And there was a chance, the waiter had said at breakfast, that if the weather remained as good as it was, Captain Davideau might put in an appearance this noon.

But the captain was not at the table when she came down. And there had been no overnight improvement in her tablemates. Crowley was a bit more subdued, perhaps, put in his place now—he was, after all, only a Vice President for Foreign Operations, while the other two men were both Presidents—but that slight gain had been more than offset by the duel for status that had developed between Johnson and Skarbo. Skarbo's company, it seemed, had the larger gross volume, but Johnson's the better net profit record, a first-round standoff that had set them sparring for some further advantage. Their common strategy, it developed, was to probe each other's corporate operations with seemingly innocent questions and then, no matter what the answer was, to profess amused surprise that anyone was still using such an obviously obsolete procedure. They warmed up with a skirmish over computers, Skarbo scoring with his company's recent installation of some fabulous new system, but Johnson had countered with a diversionary attack upon Skarbo's pocketbook, demonstrating with his ballpoint pen on the tablecloth how much tax money Skarbo was losing by not having a Swiss headquarters for his European sales company, seemingly a victory until Crowley's smirking comment, resolutely unexplained, that they both ought to look into what could be done with what he called the "Antwerp maneuver."

Once, Mrs. Skarbo, a sad little creature who clutched her platinum mink stole as if afraid that she was about to be accused of shoplifting, reminded her husband that they were taking this ship instead of flying so that he could get away from business for six days, only to be hushed with the curt retort that he had never felt better in his life. With that, Mrs. Skarbo, her wifely duty fulfilled, had gone back to listening to Mrs. Johnson, who, in a stage-whispered conversation with Mrs. Crowley, was extolling this wonderful, wonderful cook that she had—of course she was really a caterer, at least that's what she called herself now, and you had to date her up weeks and weeks in advance because nobody in their crowd would think of entertaining without her because, you see, she cooked everything over at her own place and brought it over hot, so you didn't have to worry about a thing, not even what you were going to have to eat, because she always knew where everybody had been the night before and what they'd had there, but whatever it turned out to be was always wonderful, just wonderful—

That was when Captain Davideau appeared, interrupting Mrs. Johnson's description of the best of all those wonderful, wonderful dishes—inevitably beef Stroganoff—and the introductions, an honor performed by Mr. Johnson with unexpected formality, raised Kay's hope that the conversation might now be elevated to at least a listenable level. They were no more than seated, however, when Skarbo, after only the briefest of deferential pauses, blasted out, "Captain, I think we'd all be interested in what you think of this character de Gaulle."

Seated as she was at Captain Davideau's right, Kay could not see his full-face reaction, but a profile view of a hooded eye in the dark shadow of his arching seahawk nose was more than enough to explain why he suddenly found his command of English inadequate to the occasion. Thereupon, as if retiring behind a glass curtain through which he could see and be seen, but which was impenetrable to sound, he ordered his lunch as a command to the waiter, and sat back as if his presence alone was all the sacrifice he intended to make to what was obviously a demanded but unpleasant duty. He seemed a very old man then, too irretrievably embittered by a lifetime of having suffered fools to have any interest in conversation, and after a briefly appraising glance, Kay decided against the effort. But she had no more than lifted her fork, when she heard a whisper obliquely directed at her ear. Because her French was rusty, it took her a moment to realize that what he had said, freely translated, was a plea that she exonerate him from blame for seating her with these very stuffy people—"*ces gens embêtants*"—and then, glancing at a porthole as if he were commenting on the weather, he added that being seated at the captain's table these days was largely a matter of how much ocean freight your company shipped—or might ship—on the line's vessels. It was a rare occasion, he said, when he was permitted the indulgence of pleasant company, flattery that was made to seem more sincere by his totally expressionless face.

By then, the table talk having gone back to the Antwerp maneuver pursued against a counterpoint of recipes for hot canapés, Captain Davideau switched to a guarded but perfectly fluent English, and with a twinkling smile in his voice, of which there was not the slightest evidence on his face, he chided her for not remembering him. She guessed that he must have been on the *Bretagne* in 1939. But no, it was much longer ago, he said, when he had been no more than a third mate on the old *Marseille*.

It came to her then, not as a true memory but as a vague recollection fleshed out with what Miss Jessica had afterward told her, all that she really knew about that ghost-ridden winter of wailing winds and unearthly creakings when Miss Jessica had rescued her from Hill House and taken her back to Paris on the *Marseille*. She should, perhaps, have recalled more than she did because she had been nine years old that spring, old enough to have had an impressionable mind—indeed there were older memories of unquestionable authority—but the great need then had been not to remember but to forget, and her response to that need had left her forever uncertain of what had been real and what illusory. And there was so little left any more to which reality could be tied. Hill House was gone, of course, every acre of the old Cannon estate gobbled up by the locust plague of humanity that had come swarming out of Philadelphia and, insectlike, devoured all the beauty in its path, egg-laying endless rows of drearily repetitious little houses. But for three generations of Cannons, Hill House had been the family's pastoral retreat during the months of July and August, and most of Kay's authentic memories of early childhood were of those summers when she had been sent to Hill House to stay with her grandfather, who, although a lightheartedly admitted failure in the family shipping business, was a master architect of tree houses, possessed a surgeon's skill in the setting of broken bird wings, and spun the loveliest yarns about the lives and loves of all of the wild creatures that lived in the Hill House woods and meadows. But he had died that winter before Kay had been brought back to Hill House for the last time. She had returned, not for a vacation but rather because, as she was later to learn, her father had gambled and lost the last installment of his inheritance in some blue-sky stock scheme, forced then to send his wife and child back to Hill House in order to keep a roof over their heads.

Not having been told what had happened, her recollection of those next few weeks remained mistily vague, becoming sharply clear only after that early morning when she had been awakened in the dawnlight to find her mother bending over her bed, already dressed in a traveling suit, frantically clutching her for a moment and then running out of the room. That had been the beginning of uncounted days of horror, climaxed by her father's funeral. He had, they told her, accidentally discharged a gun that he had been cleaning, a falsehood in which she found no comfort because it was so patently an insult to her nine-year-old intelligence. After that, she had lived on at Hill House for an indeterminate time, perhaps only a few weeks, with her aunt and uncle, her Aunt Bess perpetually sniveling over her as a "poor, dear child," her Uncle Charles always looking at her with the same frown of puzzled distaste with which he regarded the purple sports that turned up now and then to mar the pristine whiteness of the potted petunias whose raising he had made his principal interest and only occupation.

Neither her aunt nor her uncle had told Kay that her mother had left to divorce her father, nor that there had been far more involved in her father's total defeat than the loss of money. The sordid truth she had finally learned when Miss Jessica had appeared on the scene, as bluntly explained as if Kay were an adult, shock heightened by the strangeness of this starchy woman whom she had never before seen, saved from bursting into tears only by the feeling, immediately sensed, that Miss Jessica was someone before whom she would never dare to admit either weakness or fear.

"You'll go back to France with me," Miss Jessica had ordained, intriguing her with a matter-of-fact account of what her life in Paris would be like, curtly rejecting an attempted expression of appreciation. "You may as well understand this, child—I'm not taking you away from here because of any silly sentimentality. I'm not that sort of person. I'm doing it because you're the only Cannon left who might be worth saving. Our family blood seems to run to weak men, but we've had some strong women and it's possible that you may be one of them. At least you're not a whimperer, so I've decided to give you a chance."

On the *Marseille*, crossing the stormy Atlantic, seasick that first night out, encouraged by the blanking darkness, she had moaned, "Oh, Aunt Jessica!" Instantly, she had been cut off with a sharp correction. "Never call me that. You'll address me as *Miss* Jessica. That's what I wish to be called, and that's what I am called, by everyone, everywhere."

And it was true. Not only was she Miss Jessica to the nice young man who, that next morning, had started to teach Kay to speak French, but also to the stewards, to the ship's officers, even to the wonderfully bearded old man who had the next cabin and never met her aunt without kissing her hand. And she was no less universally Miss Jessica after they got to Paris—to the servants, to the gendarme on the corner, to all of the strange people who came to that house hidden away around the corner from Rue de Henri Martin, slipping out of taxicabs and limousines in the inner courtyard, some of them speaking little or no English, yet all so well briefed in diplomatic protocol that they invariably addressed her as *Miss*, never as *Mademoiselle* or *Señorita* or *Fraülein* or whatever else the equivalent might be in their native tongues. At first, Kay had not known why they came, her youthful imagination supplying all sorts of fanciful reasons, particularly after her awareness that Miss Jessica's guests were almost invariably men. Finally revealed, the truth had been more intriguing than fantasy. When, as Miss Jessica explained, two diplomats wished to meet without either one being forced to take the initiative, she would invite them to luncheon or dinner, thus allowing both to maintain the fiction that the meeting was accidental. Whatever the international circumstance or situation, Miss Jessica had always been ready to help, playing a marginal but often important role in the diplomatic maneuvering that went on during those years between the two world wars.

Miss Jessica's peculiar status in the world of diplomacy, unique though it was, had nevertheless been understandably achieved. In her late twenties, still unmarried, she had gone abroad one summer and in the course of a European tour had called upon her older brother, Jeffry Cannon, who was a career diplomat, then attached to the American Embassy in Rome. A bachelor, and the only Foreign Service officer in Italy with enough personal wealth to afford proper social representation of the United States, he was badly in need of a hostess. Miss Jessica had taken on the job, at first as a family duty, then as the beginning of the life-filling career for which she had been searching.

Kay had never met Jeffry Cannon—he had died several years before Miss Jessica had brought her to Paris—but from what she had pieced together, it was plain enough that his relatively illustrious career, finally culminating in an ambassadorship, had been largely built upon his Cannon inheritance, first of wealth, then of Miss Jessica. Fortunately, he had recognized the linkage, and his will had left her enough money so that she could go on living as she wished. And what she had wished, obviously, was to continue the life she had been living, broadening it by extending her base of operations, dividing those first years when Kay had lived with her between her Paris home, a little vacation villa on the Costa Brava, and the Georgetown house that had been left her by Jeffry Cannon.

When the war had forced a return to the United States, instead of going to Georgetown, Miss Jessica had chosen to reopen the old Cannon home on Walnut Street in Philadelphia. She had not returned to the Washington area, she had said, because she had lost her taste for old friends who had so incompetently made such a mess of the world, but there was also the more-than-suspected reason that she was establishing her niece in a city where, as a Cannon, she would be able to reclaim her social birthright.

Although Kay had protested that she had no such interest, she had found Philadelphia excitingly dull, a perfect setting in which to make the most of accomplishments that, although commonplace in Paris, gave her a differentiating distinction from all the other girls at Bryn Mawr. That next summer she set herself apart even more by picking off the prize of all vacation jobs: personal assistant to Nellie Potter Tyler at her Orangerie summer theater. In order to qualify, she had been forced to put herself through a cram course in drama, but the transition from her major in art history was not too difficult, and she had found it enormously exciting, all the more so after she discovered Judd Wilder and began to see what a wonderful future he had. She had often, in girlish dreams, tested the sound of married names—she had, until Miss Jessica intervened, most seriously weighed *Mrs. Paul Vallors*—but no fantasy had ever so excited her as the prospect of being *Mrs. Judd Wilder*, the wife of the famous theatrical director. This time there had been no objection from Miss Jessica, only a caution, brushed aside at the time but recalled later as a pertinent warning—"Just be certain, Kay, that you're in love with the man he really is and not the man that you're so sure you can make him."

It was true that she had misjudged what Judd would do with his life, committing herself to an existence that was quite different than she had imagined, a never-healing wound that was reopened now as Captain Davideau said, "It is so long ago that Miss Jessica told me—perhaps I am wrong—but as I recall—your husband, is he not in the theater?"

Long practiced, she contained the automatic flinch, setting the little smile with which she always preceded a lighthearted denial, a pause instantly filled by Mrs. Skarbo, who, obviously eavesdropping, burst in with an awed "Oh, is he really! Did you hear that, Frank—Mrs. Wilder's husband is in the theater."

Kay started to protest but was squelched by Skarbo's rumbling "You don't say," immediately followed by Mrs. Johnson's "Well, I just *knew* it must be something like that—I said so last night, didn't I, George?"

And then they were all looking at her with the righteousness of confirmed suspicion, understanding now why they had uneasily sensed her presence as that of an alien bird who had somehow invaded their flock, and with the falsetto laughter of a hostess forced to save a bad situation, Mrs. Johnson was saying, "Well, I'm sure he didn't have anything to do with that awful, awful thing we saw our last night in New York—oh, George, what was it called?"

"I know what I'd call it," George Johnson said, bellicosely righteous. "Filthiest thing I've ever seen. How anything as rotten as that could be produced on a public stage——"

"And what was it you had to pay for the tickets, George?"

Captain Davideau said in English, addressing the table, "Unfortunately I am needed on the bridge," making it sound not unfortunate at all, even chancing a faint smile as he said to Kay in French, "I promised Miss Jessica that I would take care of you."

She rose with him, murmuring an honest "*Merci,*" but her gratitude was to him, not to Miss Jessica, and she left the table with an unbanishable feeling that this whole trip was a mistake—with Miss Jessica's penchant for managing everyone else's life, it was almost a certainty that she had had something to do with whatever it was that was disturbing Rolfe.

Walking out, glancing away to avoid responding to the steward's obsequious bow, she saw that she was being intently watched by the woman she had seen wearing the Givenchy coat.

« *10* »

Driven by the racing clock—it was already 2:30—Aaron Kharr headed back to his office. He had wasted an hour examining two patients, both referred by Dr. Carruth, who had obviously sent them in for no reason other than to rid himself of a couple of hopeless hypochondriacs.

There was no note on his desk from Mrs. Campbell. Tight-lipped, he snatched up the telephone and called the supervisor of nurses, drumming a fingertip tattoo on the desktop as he waited for her to answer.

"This is Dr. Kharr," he snapped at the first sound of her voice. "Haven't you been able to find me a three-to-eleven nurse yet?"

"Oh, but didn't she talk to you? She said she would. I thought she had. Oh, dear, then you don't know, do you? Mrs. Cope is taking it."

"Mrs. Cope? But she—isn't she on the desk?"

"Oh, I know, and I do wish we could keep her there, but she's given us five weeks already, and with private duty paying fourteen dollars more a week—I really think we ought to do something about that, Dr. Kharr, I really do. I know the hospital has its budget problems, of course it does, but I don't see how we can go on paying a charge nurse so much less than——"

"Yes, something ought to be done about it," he cut her off, hanging up before she could launch off again, trying to think his way through all the implications of this turn of events. At noon, after a futile talk with Miss Harsch in the corridor outside Wilder's room, unable to make the slightest lasting impress upon the too-yielding softness of that marshmallow brain, he had gone to Mrs. Cromwell, attempting to make her understand how much he needed a nurse on the all-important three-to-eleven shift who was at least intelligent enough to understand what it was that he was trying to do, and flexible enough to break out of the time-fixed routine that was habitually followed on all heart cases.

He could hardly question Cope's intelligence—she was the smartest nurse on County Memorial's registry—but by the same token, knowing it, she was the most independent, the least amenable to direction. And now, recalling what Mrs. Stine had told him this morning about Cope's personal life, his apprehension was further heightened by a strong suspicion, almost a certainty, that because of her experience with her husband she would regard herself as an unchallengeable expert on cardiac rehabilitation.

Hearing a sound behind him, he snapped a glance over his shoulder. Cope stood in the doorway. How long she had been there he had no idea, but her stolidly settled pose suggested that she had overheard the conversation with Mrs. Cromwell.

"I thought you might want to see me," she said.

"Yes, I was just talking about you," he said. "I understand that you're going on the Wilder case."

"If you want me."

Given no alternative, he responded with a quick "Of course," asking her to come in, offering her a chair, aware too late that unguarded courtesy had carried him beyond the line that must always separate doctor and nurse, according her a status that would make it all the more difficult to exert his control of the situation. Disconcerted, he fumbled, "This is—quite a surprise. Had no idea that Mrs. Cromwell would call you."

"She didn't call me, I called her," Cope said crisply. "I'd had five weeks of desk duty, that's enough for a while."

"Yes, we really ought to do something about our pay scale," he let slip, made instantly aware by Cope's reaction that it had been a mistake, trying then to excuse himself by explaining, "That's what I thought Mrs. Cromwell said—the extra money—but if I misunderstood, I'm sorry, Mrs. Cope."

She said stiffly, "I thought I might be of some help."

"And I'm sure you can be," he put in hurriedly, attempting a saving change of subject with a fumbled comment about its being an interesting case.

Relenting, Cope asked, "You are going to keep it yourself, aren't you? You aren't going to turn it over to Dr. Teeter?"

"No, I'm taking it myself."

"That's all right then. I just wanted to make sure." Her expression softened, signaling a change of mood. "I always thought I'd like to be on a case of yours. I read one of your papers once—Dr. Raggi had it—about what happens to heart patients. One of the cases you described reminded me of one that I was on once, one that I've always wondered about."

He nodded dumbly, silenced by a recognition of the paper she had read, that the case to which she referred was that of her own husband, and he could not help but admire the self-control that kept her face so passively immobile, and the dedication that had turned personal tragedy into a subject of professional inquiry.

"Any special instructions?" she asked. "I know you don't want him scared into thinking that a coronary has to change his whole life."

"Yes, reassurance is important," he agreed, "but we don't want to overdo it. I used to think that the too-frightened patient was our big problem, but the longer I've gone, the more cases I've studied, the more convinced I am that the patient who comes out too frightened is no more of a problem than the man who isn't frightened enough."

"Not frightened enough? I've never seen one yet who wasn't scared to death."

"Yes, in the beginning—the initial impact—but surely you're familiar with the man who refuses to believe that he's ever had a heart attack. Do you remember that coronary of Dr. Webster's, the chicken hatchery man—Schwartz—wasn't that his name?"

"I guess you know he died last week."

"Yes, that's my point, Mrs. Cope. No man under fifty-five should ever have a *second* coronary. If he does, there was something wrong with the way he was handled on the first one."

"It wasn't my case," Cope said. "But it was a bad one, I do remember that."

"But do you know what Mr. Schwartz told me when I examined him last month? He said that he'd never had a heart attack, not a real one, anyway. I sat right here with his cardiogram tracing, showing him the evidence, but he still insisted that it had been nothing but a little 'bump,' as he called it."

"You don't think Dr. Webster told him—?"

"All I'm saying, Mrs. Cope, is that if Mr. Schwartz had come out of this hospital realizing that he had to completely change his behavior pattern, he'd be alive today."

Mrs. Cope's face went taut. "How do you want Mr. Wilder handled?"

"Frankly, Mrs. Cope, at this point, I don't know enough about him to be sure what course we'll follow. I've had a talk with the president of his company, and I got a fair amount of background, but at best it's no more than a high-spot outline. He's sending me his personnel folder. I may get more out of that, I hope so. The rest we'll have to dig out by talking to him. I'm keeping him under moderately heavy sedation today and through the night, but if the signs look as good in the morning as they do now, I'll let him come out from under and start talking to him tomorrow afternoon or evening."

"About what?"

"Everything," he said firmly. "His work, his family, every aspect of his life. I don't want this hospital experience to be an escape from reality. Too often, that's what we make it—keeping a patient so comfortably assured, so pleasantly isolated, that he never faces up to the truth. I want to prod him into thinking through his whole life. Why did he do this, why did he do that? How did he work himself into the behavior pattern that gave him this coronary?"

"What do you want me to do?"

"Where you could be most helpful at the moment—as I said, I think I'll be able to get the necessary background on his business life, but the more personal side—his wife is unavailable, we can't talk to her——"

"You think that's where the trouble might be?"

"I don't know. It's possible. In any event, it's something to be explored."

For a moment, it seemed that Cope was on the point of argument, but then her lips tightened. She looked at her watch and stood up. "I'll do the best I can, Doctor."

"I'm sure you will," he said. But as he saw the positiveness of her turn to the door, the flat-footed stride that carried her out without a backward glance, he felt himself warned that what she thought would be "best" would be a matter of her own judgment.

He turned back to his desk, conscious now of the stack of mail. He was still winnowing the drug company advertising, looking for something that might merit attention, when he was again conscious of someone in the doorway. Turning, he saw that it was Jonas Webster, thumbs hooked in his vest, regarding him over the top of spectacles that, characteristically, had slipped halfway down his nose.

"Come in, Doctor," he greeted him warmly, an honest enough expression of genuine liking for the man—of all the doctors at County Memorial, Webster came closest to fulfilling his pre-arrival anticipation of what a "country doctor" would be like—yet he was impelled, too, by a secret twinge of guilt for having criticized his handling of the Schwartz case.

"You fooled me," Webster said.

"How so? About what?"

"You're taking this coronary case?"

"Yes."

"I didn't think you would."

"Why not?"

"Didn't think you'd stick your neck out that far."

"Stick my neck out? In what way?"

"Promising that you'd send him back to his job just as full of beans as——"

"I made no such promise as that."

"But that's what he wanted, this man that—what was his name —the president of his company."

"I made no promises of any sort," Kharr said levelly, everything under control until he saw the odd smile on Webster's face as he asked, "Have you told Teeter yet?"

"He's out of town."

Webster's smile took on an even more peculiar quality. "If you had to take a case, Aaron, it might have been a bit more diplomatic to have snitched it from one of the other boys——"

He flared on *snitched,* saved from a flashback only when Webster continued, "—someone with a little less sensitivity in the general area of his pocketbook."

Webster winked, making it seem a joke, and Aaron Kharr managed a little laugh, but then the Chief of Staff was gone, and whatever humor there may have been was lost in the realization that he had issued a warning. A long moment passed before he became suddenly aware that, for the first time, Webster had called him

Aaron. Under other circumstances, he would have been pleased, but now it served only to sharpen the warning—and by a reflex reaction, to harden his determination to hang on to the Wilder case no matter what pressure might be put upon him.

« *11* »

Judd Wilder felt reasonably certain that he was now awake, yet he had so recently crossed the indeterminate boundary of sleep that he could not be sure which side of the line the voice had come from. Someone had asked, "Remember me?" and he had nodded, bluffing, thinking that he would be able to solve quickly the riddle of familiarity . . . yes, he had been dreaming . . . Mrs. Gorman . . .

But the face that was slowly impressing itself upon his consciousness, coming up like a photographic print in a tray of weak developer, was not Mrs. Gorman's.

"I was with you when you came in last night," the voice said. "I'm Mrs. Cope."

"Yes, I remember" he said aloud, trying to convince himself that he did, and as if it were a reward for effort, her face began to take on some aspect of familiarity. But that, too, was confusing because the longer he stared at her, the more she looked like Mrs. Gorman, standing there now with her hands on her hips, the illusion so vivid that he found himself waiting for her to demand, "Young man, are you going to get up out of that bed, or aren't you?"

Instead, but in the same tone, she demanded, "What in the world—" looking not at him but at the bed, plunging an exploratory hand under the covers, discovering something that brought a quick snort of righteous disdain, a sound totally reminiscent of the way Mrs. Gorman had reacted when she discovered him putting on a torn shirt that his mother had failed to mend, snatching it off his back with the same show of suppressed indignation with which Mrs. Cope now remade his bed. With her arm slipped under his back, lifting at the same instant, she gave the undersheet a sharp tug, snapping it to drumhead tightness. Her hand cupped his head, up before he could react, and the pillow went back feeling entirely different than it had before. Her arm swept out, leveling the bedcovers, no less a miracle than the instant calming of a stormy sea, leaving him with all sense of physical being lost in the pleasant sensation of floating free of support.

He started to thank her, put off by the way she flicked her sleeve cuffs, the concluding gesture of a woman who, beset by someone else's incompetence and neglect, had again put the world to rights. He was no longer concerned that he had confused her with Mrs. Gorman, illusion excused by a remarkable similarity, less of appearance than of manner, most pronounced in a quiet radiance of controlling power, of a dominant ability to impose an ordered calm upon a frenetic world, to take over as Mrs. Gorman had always done when his mother had been away.

As a boy, Judd Wilder's early-blooming interest in politics had been largely generated by the discovery that there was an unvarying association between elections and Mrs. Gorman. Every time Simon Judd was running for office, his mother disappeared and Mrs. Gorman came to keep house for them. It did not, that early, seem strange that his mother should go flying off whenever his grandfather needed her—Simon Judd was, he knew, a far more important man than his father—and if, on his own part, there had been any feeling of regretted abandonment, it was more than offset by the wonderful changes that took place every time Mrs. Gorman appeared. And the most evident of all changes was in his father.

Harry Wilder was a man who cherished order and tranquillity, and although he taciturnly accepted what had to be, there was always the feeling that he regarded Mrs. Gorman's appearance as a reward for forbearance, a sabbatical when his dinner would always be ready when he came home from the newspaper office, when he could eat it without being forced into talking about politics, uninterrupted by having to get up to answer the telephone calls that were almost always for Judd's mother. And after supper he would be free to smoke his pipe in the living room, to go to bed whenever he wanted to, secure in the knowledge that, no matter how early he got up, a real oatmeal-and-sausage breakfast would be ready and waiting for him. "I don't know how she manages," he had once said, speaking only of a torn coat sleeve that had been made whole overnight, but Judd had heard it as an expression of his father's quiet bewilderment that Mrs. Gorman, with no evidence of harried frustration, made a pleasant life seem so simply and easily achievable. When the inevitable day came, he always said, "Your mother'll be home tonight," with a curiously flat voice, never with discernible regret, yet neither was there any clear evidence of pleasure.

Judd's reaction had never been so neutral. Although he always welcomed Mrs. Gorman's appearance, he usually came to feel before the end of her stay, an anticipatory excitement at the prospect of his mother's return, an instinctive craving for the driving energy that, like a magnetic field, radiated from her presence. But since the need for that stimulation was largely unconscious, it seemed instantly satisfied the moment she walked into the house. No less quickly, but far more observably, his father reassumed his other character, tight-lipped and uncomplaining, patiently waiting for his supper until Judd's mother got home from some meeting, invariably pleasant when he took her telephone calls, usually going back down to the newspaper office afterward, something that he rarely did when Mrs. Gorman was there.

As soon as his father was out of the house, often without bothering to do the dishes, his mother would get back to her lists and file cards, a game she played night after night as if it were a kind of solitaire upon the outcome of which her very existence depended. She had lived, it seemed, in one world and his father in another, the orbits of their lives impinging only at mealtime. They did, of course, share a bed, but what happened there was largely unimaginable to Judd, not because of any lack of understanding of what usually went on between husbands and wives when they were in bed together but rather such intimacy suggested an interdependence of his parents that was too out of character to be easily credible.

As the years went by, his mother's absences became more frequent, Mrs. Gorman's stays longer, but he never came to think of her in any sense as a substitute mother. He was, for one thing, too old for that, too conscious of the maturity he was finding in freedom from maternal attachment. For another, his relationship with Mrs. Gorman was incompatible with the mother-image that had been impressed upon him. Judged by example, a mother was someone whose prime concern was intellectual—the grades he got in school, the books he read, the unspecified dangers that she attributed to "trashy thinking," the undefined but horrendous prospect of "wasting his mind." Mrs. Gorman's preoccupation was almost totally physical. She watched over him as if he were a bull calf being grown out for exhibition at the Iowa State Fair—her father had been a locally famous breeder of Aberdeen Angus cattle—her duty that of seeing that he was well and regularly fed, perfectly cared for, and kept free from unsightly blemish. Once, on a Boy Scout hike, he had gone into the bushes, unaware until the fiery itching had started that he had squatted in poison ivy. That evening, seeing him scratching, unsatisfied with his evasive explanation, she had bull-dozed him as easily as if he were a roped calf, quickly overpowering him, stripping his pants and underwear. Unlike his mother, who from his earliest youth had never entered his bedroom without knocking to make certain that he was not indecently exposed, Mrs. Gorman had made no more of anointing the affected area than if she were rubbing liniment on a charley-horse. Uncontrollably, there had been a physical reaction, to which Mrs. Gorman had paid no evident attention, yet somehow it had given rise to a persisting sense of intimacy, unexplainable yet subtly affecting their relation-ship, and in the weeks that followed he had felt himself free to ask her questions that he could not have put to his mother. Mrs. Gorman was never shocked, never evaded an answer. There were things she didn't know, but nothing known was ever a prohibited subject of conversation. Even as late as his last year in high school, sophisti-cated as he then thought himself, Mrs. Gorman had been the one to whom he had turned when the Leslie Dwight bombshell had exploded, the whole town in an uproar that had, for a few days, threatened to destroy the Centennial pageant as expiating sacri-fice to atone for Leslie Dwight having blackmarked Haygood with his unspeakable perversion. Judd, torn as much by his own unsus-pecting innocence as by his fear that the pageant might not go on, had found Mrs. Gorman's the only voice calm enough to make sense. "Sometimes it happens that way," she said. "You get a bull calf that's all mixed up, not knowing why God put him on earth, so all you can do is get him out of the herd as fast as you can." And there had been, he thought, the hint of a smile when she had added, "But it's nothing you'll ever have to worry about." It was not her point, he knew well enough, that he could take over the pageant and run it himself, but somehow that was what it had meant to him. Later, when he had been casting the scene about the first white child born in Mound County, he had asked her to play the part of the mother. She had, as he had expected, refused, saying that if she did something as foolish as that she'd never get her catsup and piccalilli made, but he could not forget the way she had reached out for his hand, a gesture that was, for Mrs. Gorman, the equivalent of an impulsive kiss.

There were few such high points in his memories of Mrs. Gorman. What most often came to his mind—as it had a moment ago—was the way she awakened him in the morning. First she could call from the bottom of the staircase, quietly, almost as if she didn't expect him to answer. And he never did. Then she would come up the stairs, quickly, surprisingly light on her feet for a woman of her age and heavy-boned build. The door would be thrown open—it would never have occurred to her to knock—and she would be standing there, hands on hips, her face set in a never quite successful expression of anger, demanding, "Young man, are you going to get up out of that bed, or aren't you?"

Mrs. Cope's hands, too, were on her hips, but there was no encouragement of continued illusion in the way she said, "You're feeling better than you did last night, aren't you?"

"I guess so," he said, searching himself for some physical response to self-inquiry, aware now that the sheets were no longer cool, that he was beginning to be suffused again with a steamy warmth. He reached up to turn back the bedclothes from his throat.

Her hands were there before his, anticipating even the need to wipe his forehead, leaving a lingering sensation of coolness that persisted until she said, "You've got a little fever, that's all. But it's nothing to worry about. It will be over by tomorrow."

Tomorrow . . . "Your mother is coming home tomorrow" . . .

But his father's face was all wrong.

And why was he wearing a white coat?

❖ III ❖

JUDD WILDER's second night at County Memorial Hospital ended with a sudden breakthrough into consciousness, an awakening so abrupt that he began a hurried search for cause. But there was no hand on his shoulder, no hovering face, no one waiting to stab a drinking tube into his mouth or another stinging needle into his arm. He raised himself on his elbows, looking about him. There was no one else in the room . . . he was alone . . .

Aloneness was somehow meaningful, but he could not grasp immediately what that meaning might be, comprehension fogged by incipient panic. For an instant, he thought himself the victim of a nightmare's aftermath, but memory did not support him and he quickly grasped at the explanation that it was no more than something he had often experienced, the momentarily frightening disorientation of waking up in a hotel room that he had checked into late at night, so tired that he had flopped on the bed with no attention to his surroundings, not knowing where he was in the morning . . . but he did know where he was . . . COUNTY MEMORIAL HOSPITAL . . .

But why had they left him alone?

It hadn't been his heart . . . they'd been wrong . . . they knew it now . . . that's why they'd left him alone. He had to get up . . . get dressed . . . check out . . . *the convention* . . .

He waited for his spurred mind to respond with the expected rush of thought, the inpouring of all that had to be remembered, the outpouring of a hundred demands for action. Nothing happened. His brain was dead, dead as a stopped watch. It took a moment for full awareness to strike, a moment that ended with a seizure of sudden terror . . . they'd lied to him, telling him that it was his heart . . . it wasn't his heart, it was his mind . . . that colonel in India . . . *he'd had a stroke!*

A shiver that started in his jaw muscles spread as a racking tremor through his whole body. He clenched his fists, gripping the bed-clothing, trying to stop the trembling of his hands, choking back a cry for help.

His eyes, darting about the room, caught a flash of movement in the mirrored face of the half-opened bathroom door, the reflected upsweep of a white skirt, exposing a thigh bare to the eye-focusing incurve of tight panties, quick fingers darting down to a garter fastening, hesitant there for an instant before the dress was whipped down again, swirling out of sight. All that he could see now was green tile and the top rim of the bathtub, yet vision persisted, a powerful stimulant to which he found himself terrifyingly incapable of normal response.

His arms went limp, no longer capable of supporting his shoulders, dropping him back into a steamy warmth, dominantly aware of a groin-centered emptiness, an in-sucking vacuum so physically real that he stiffened his back against its multi-fingered pull. Then, as suddenly as if a sharp edge had cut a straining purse string, every-thing went slack. There was no longer a feeling of fear, only the slow acceptance of a peculiarly total fatigue, instantly reminiscent. It was as if he had slipped into a dark theater to see a motion picture that he had viewed uncounted times before, anticipating every word that was to be spoken, every move that was to be made, the flash of a single frame enough to tell him where he was in the film . . . that last morning . . . watching her in the mirror . . .

He had never known who she was—she had neither asked his name nor volunteered her own—and that anonymity, enhancing the feeling of fantasy that had pervaded the whole weekend, had after-ward helped him to surmount a shattering experience, a period of madness beyond comprehension, the loosing of forces within him-self of which he had never before been aware.

For eleven days he had been out in the Everglades, filming the location sequence of *Jungle Survival*, the Air Force picture that Huck had given him as his first assignment as a unit director. They had finished shooting late Friday afternoon, but it would be Monday at the earliest before the rushes could be reviewed at Astoria, and with Huck's approval, the crew had been taken into Miami for a three-day leave. Within minutes of their arrival they had scattered like exploding shrapnel, leaving Judd alone with that Medical Corps major who, with no apparent qualification beyond a peacetime medical practice among Washington's elite, had been serving as a technical adviser on the picture. Useless though the major had been in the Everglades, he proved quickly valuable in Miami, turning up a two-room suite at the Alcazar when no hotel rooms were supposed to be available. Immediately on the telephone, the major's second call had produced an invitation to a party aboard some millionaire's yacht. Although reluctant to place himself any deeper in the major's debt, and further put off by his snidely lecherous remarks about the evening's possibilities, Judd had been unable to resist what had seemed a glamorous prospect, excusing himself on the ground that a millionaire's yacht party was an experience that might stand him in good stead when, after the war, he would be directing Hollywood pictures.

In the mail forwarded from Astoria, there had been a note from Kay Cannon, telling him that she had taken a job in New York, giving him a telephone number to call. Before leaving the hotel that night he had answered her letter, promising that he would call her as soon as he got back, filling out the page by telling her that he was about to attend a party on a millionaire's yacht, wondering after he had sealed and mailed the letter if he had not sounded too naïvely impressed with something with which Kay, as a Cannon, would not be impressed at all.

He and the major walked from the hotel to the waterfront, picking their way through the blackout darkness, passing a half-dozen docked yachts, all alive with the muffled sounds of music and laughter, coming at last to the biggest of all, a houseboat that seemed a floating palace in the purple night. He had approached it as something seen through a viewfinder, the long trucking shot of the waterfront intercut with close-ups of clipper bows and rope patterns, silver-edged clouds racing across the sky, the emergence of the moon a cue to cut to a medium shot of the canvas-sided gangplank, the whole sequence violin-scored, unabashedly romantic until, following the major's charging lead, he suddenly found himself sucked into a packed mass of gold-braided uniforms and multicolored chiffon, the air blue-hazed with smoke, stiflingly hot, raucously vibrant with a cacophonic roar of straining voices, punctuated every now and then with screeching laughter and the crash of breaking glass. Instantly deserted by the major, who had plunged in like a bull turned loose in a pen of heifers, Judd squirmed his way along the wall, hunting for breathing room, saved from total revulsion by his camera-eye construction of a montage of grotesque close-ups, the only way that the scene could possibly be pictured. He felt himself detached by exclusion, outranked by every officer present, most of them old enough to be his father, but as he pushed through to the bar, the only girls he saw who were anywhere near his own age were more frightening than attractive. Most of them looked like the society-girl dress extras that Huck had used for his V.D. film.

He had one highball, and then out of desperation, another, but there would never be any real validity in the hopefully self-saving excuse that alcohol was in any way accountable for what had been about to happen. Finally, satiated, all but suffocated by the ever-increasing crowd, he squirmed through to a door, finding himself out on the deck, thinking he was alone until, as his eyes grew accustomed to the darkness, he saw a feminine figure standing against the rail, long-cloaked, a filmy scarf haloing gold-glinting hair. Unexplainably, she seemed to be expecting him because she said with a throaty little laugh, "I'd almost given you up." He took a step toward her, ready to reveal that he was not who she thought him to be. But looking squarely up at him she said, "I was afraid you didn't see me come out." And then before he could say that he had never seen her before, she held up a cigarette for him to light. In the glow of the flame her eyes were dancing with silently mischievous laughter, taunting him after her first puff with a rippling "Can you handle a right-hand drive?"

If he had not so brashly responded, "I can handle anything"—and he could never explain, afterwards, why he had—it might never have happened. But that was the beginning, as much as anything could ever be accounted the beginning, and what followed was beyond all explanation. Why she had wanted him to drive her English-made Daimler was accountable only as a means of keeping him so preoccupied with the strangeness of a right-hand-drive automobile that he was unaware of where her turn-right and turn-left directions were taking him. "Turn in here," she finally said, and when he brought the car to a stop they were in a high-walled courtyard. Then she was in his arms, and when he was next capable of observing anything beyond arm's length, all he could see were patches of blue sky glimpsed through a bedroom window, framed in cresting palm fronds, an artificial horizon of purple-flowered bougainvillea cascading over the railing of a high balcony.

He had seen no more than that of Miami until Monday morning when she sent him back to his hotel in her Daimler, chauffeur-driven now, burdened with the last demand that she had made upon him. "Forget me," she had said at the door of the bedroom, and he nodded quick acquiescence, too honest to pretend that he did not know that it was what he had to do—either forget her and everything that had happened or be forever degraded by the orgiastic madness with which he had allowed himself to be overwhelmed. He had thought that such behavior existed only in barracks bull sessions, wild stories to which he had never more than half listened, finding them impossible to believe. His own prior experience, limited though it had been, had offered no hint that his midnight fantasies had been so close to an existent reality.

There was a telegram from Huck waiting at the hotel desk, enthusiastically approving the rushes, canceling any need for a return to the Everglades for retakes. The crew were all in the coffee shop, waiting for what he knew they would accept as the best of news—eleven days of Everglades muck and mud and dive-bombing mosquitoes had been more than enough—yet he had delayed facing them, going first to his room, scrubbing himself from head to foot, wearing dark glasses when he came down, desperately attempting to maintain the cool sophistication that, because he was so conscious of being younger than any man in the crew—he was only twenty-two—he had thought the essence of his ability to command and direct. He need not have bothered. The crew had their own hangover problems. Red-eyed, yawning, they had sat staring blankly into their coffee cups. He gave them the pack-up instructions, finally getting enough response to be sure that nothing important would be left behind, and caught a cab to the airport. On the plane, Miami behind him, he slowly recovered from his sickening awareness of a revolting second self. Guilt could not be dissipated, yet there was also the deeply secret satisfaction of having survived such a dregs-stirring excursion through the lower reaches of human behavior. It was a little like, a hundred times magnified, the aftermath of having smoked, that dance night at Colfax, his first and last reefer.

Nausea, although a potent argument against repetition, could not destroy a newly acquired feeling of knowing maturity, an assurance that he had satisfied a curiosity that would never again plague him.

Nevertheless, back in New York, he had waited until the end of the week before he called Kay Cannon. Meeting her in the lobby of the hotel, there had been a bad moment of fear that his degradation might still be somehow visible. But she had said, "You're looking wonderful, Judd," seemingly an absolution of guilt. She had tickets for a new play, the second night of something that every New York reviewer had panned, bad enough so that, afterwards in Schrafft's, it had been easy to believe her when she told him that he could have done a hundred times better. They had talked for a long time, her every word making Miami seem farther and farther away. The only moment of threat had been in the taxicab on their way back to her apartment. Kay had impulsively kissed him, something that she had never done before, and, surprised out of caution, he had unconsciously responded in a way that almost betrayed him. Instantly, however, she had fended him off. And when they got to her apartment house, she had quickly countered his experimental suggestion that he go up with her by inviting him to come that next night to meet some Broadway people that, she said, he ought to know. On his way back to the hotel, it occurred to him for the first time that, remote though the possibility of acceptance seemed, he might some day ask Kay Cannon to marry him.

One month and four days later they were married, time compressed by his precipitate orders to leave in nine days for the India-Burma Theater to film the story of the airlift operation over the Hump. The ceremony was in Philadelphia, in Miss Jessica's Walnut Street living-room, everything arranged by Kay during those madhouse days when he had been assembling the personnel and equipment for the India unit. Miami had come back as an incipient concern, particularly after Huck had told him that the Everglades film had been a secret test of his ability to handle a unit of his own, heightened when common sense had dictated taking along three of the crew members who had been waiting for him that Monday morning at the Alcazar Hotel. But all that had been put out of his mind by the time he got to Philadelphia, resurrected for only one frightening moment on their wedding night at Buck Hill Falls. Someone had given Kay a bottle of perfume as a gift, and holding the glass stopper for him to smell, he had experienced an instant of almost disabling recall. Fortunately unperceptive, she had said only, "I can see you don't like it," and tossed the bottle in the wastebasket, a gesture sufficiently dramatic to cleanse his mind, a promise that, once and for all, this was the end of it.

And for those three days it had been. His fear of appearing too knowing, too practiced, had quickly disappeared in an accepted normality so satisfying that there was no temptation to abandon it. And if normality was his prime hope, Kay fulfilled it. By the second day, they were living a married life. Almost all of their third and last day at Buck Hill Falls was spent working on the India film, breaking down the tentative script that he had brought along but had been unable to concentrate upon on the train down from New York. Inevitably, there had been talk about the Everglades film, even some mention of Miami, and his lack of reaction had seemingly consigned it to a safely lost past.

Later, however, there had been irrepressible flashes of memory—there were too many palm trees in India, too much blue sky, too many cascades of purple bougainvillea—but by the time he got out of the service in December 1945, aged by the forced maturity of war, anything as long ago as Miami had happened not to him but to a naïve kid who had been too young to know what it was all about. Thereafter, Miami had been something too deeply buried to ever be consciously recalled, and the vividness with which it had been resurrected this morning by that glimpsed view in the bathroom door mirror was strangely alarming, all the more so as his mind translated that groin-empty feeling into an awareness that, in a terribly emasculating accident, he had been made into an impotent old man.

And the nurse who came out of the bathroom made him seem all the older, so young that she appeared as a child playing a make-believe game. "How long have you been awake?" she demanded, wide-eyed with an adolescent's earnest concern.

"Oh, a long time," he said, feeling as if he were teasing a child.

"Oh, but you haven't," she exclaimed, darting an anxious glance at the clock. "It's only been four minutes since—" She broke off with a little laugh, a childlike acknowledgment that she knew that she was being kidded. "You're feeling better, aren't you?"

"I'm fine."

"I knew you'd be," she said, youthfully confident. "I could tell it by the way you were sleeping. You didn't wake up once, not even when I took your blood pressure." She laughed, teasing him now with a petulant "You didn't even know I was here, did you?"

She was using one of those feminine tricks little girls all learned so early, bidding for attention by accusing you of not noticing them. And you always said, "Don't be silly."

"You were asleep before Mrs. Cope left," she argued brightly. "You don't remember her leaving, do you?"

She misinterpreted his hesitation, supplying, "She's your three-to-eleven nurse," adding a meticulously pronounced "Mrs. Cope," as if she were recalling for him something that she thought he had forgotten.

"I know her name," he said, tricked by a need for proof into a quickly added "And you're Miss—" suddenly defeated by inability to resurrect her name.

"I'm *Mrs.* Welch," she supplied, the emphasis sharply correcting, the sparkle strangely gone from her voice.

"I know," he said. "I remember."

But what he knew was that all of the kids who were getting married lately seemed unbelievably young, and what he remembered was that he was an old man now.

He closed his eyes.

« 2 »

Over the past year, Matt Crouch had come to feel that Saturday was the best day of the week. Monday through Friday he too often felt himself a figurehead captain, isolated on the bridge of a ship grown so large that he could no longer exercise personal control. He was still in ultimate command—no one could doubt that—but since Roger Stark's system of Coordinated Operating Control had been installed, fewer and fewer problems were being brought to the president's office. Often now he was genuinely lonely, hour after hour going by without anyone asking to see him. In the old days, there had been a constant parade in and out of his office, every department and section head coming in at least once during the day, usually oftener. That was how he had once kept his fingertips on the pulse of the business. Now, every day he was getting more and more out of touch.

As captain of the ship he could, of course, call in anyone he wanted to see, and keep him there as long as he desired, but it was a privilege that, Monday to Friday, he rarely exercised. With the big ship plunging ahead at an ever faster pace, there was the feeling that he dared not take any ship's officer away from his post, further restrained by the realization that there were a lot of things going on with which he was no longer familiar—the computer remained an awesome mystery—and there was always the threat that, just as he was getting someone to really open up, Roger Stark would walk in.

On Saturday mornings, however, an entirely different situation prevailed. With the ship at dock, the general offices officially closed, he could indulge himself as much as he wished. At one time or another during the forenoon, almost all of the key men would come in for a quiet hour or two at their desks, and by leaving the door of his office open, he could stop them as they went past, calling them in for a little session, protected from intrusion by the fact that Roger Stark, still a dedicated Philadelphian, almost always left New Ulster on Friday evening for a Main Line weekend.

But this morning, as he headed his gray Cadillac into the presidential parking space, he saw that Stark's black Riviera was already in the No. 2 spot. His first thought was that Stark had been kept in town by the proofs of the stockholders report—he had insisted yesterday upon restoring every word of copy that Judd had cut in order to make the text fit the layout—but that hardly explained why there was a car in every front-row parking space except Judd Wilder's. To have everyone turn up at the same time on Saturday morning was unusual enough to arouse suspicion. Obviously, Stark was up to something.

Doing his best to curb unwarranted suspicion, Crouch reminded himself that he was still president of the company, still in control, still capable of putting down any disloyal opposition. As he entered the executive suite lounge, he saw shadowy figures through the translucent glass door of Stark's office. There were three of them, identification supplied by the cars in the parking lot—Kelsey, Campbell and Locke—making it clear that Stark had called a secret rump meeting of the executive committee. His first impulse was to throw open the door on them, exposing their perfidy, but in the moment that it took to suppress a flare of head-bursting anger, he had a second thought, deciding that if there was to be a battle he wanted it on his own ground.

Stomping into his office, he demanded of Miss Fox, "What's going on in there?" in no way mollified by her watery "I don't know," proof again that he had been entirely too softhearted in hanging on to an old maid secretary after she had lapsed into placid senility.

But now she said, "Mr. Stark came in awhile ago for some of the old convention files."

He stared at her, stunned by a lightning-flash revelation, recalling now that Stark had not only admitted talking to young Talbott yesterday morning, but also that, after lunch when he had asked Miss Fox to have Stark come in, she had told him that he had Talbott in his office.

"He said they'd probably want to see you a little later."

"Tell him I'm ready," he said, jut-jawed, not meaning it as she took it, but making no move to stop her as she got up and went out the door, heading for Stark's office.

Seated in his chair, fists clenched over the arm ends, he felt his desk a fortification against frontal attack, but experience warned him against underrating an opponent who had so nefariously packed the executive committee with his own men. All of them—Kelsey, Campbell and Locke—owed their vice presidencies to Stark.

Admittedly, there had been a need to expand the simple executive organization to which Matt Crouch had clung ever since the company's first days—he had been thinking about that long before Elbert Coe had brought it up—but it had never seemed a matter of great urgency until he had been so suddenly confronted with a cash-empty treasury. For that situation, he had blamed himself rather than Fred Hanford, his Treasurer, but as Roger Stark had pointed out, the president of a company was impossibly handicapped if he did not have adequate financial information upon which to base his decisions. What was needed, Stark had said, was a modern accounting system. That was what Miles Campbell had been brought in to set up. Giving him the title of Comptroller had been necessary, Stark had said, to get the caliber of man that was needed. And because it was Stark who had found Miles and brought him in, it had seemed logical enough that the Comptroller report directly to the Vice President for Administration.

Matt Crouch had not realized how much of the Treasurer's responsibility was being absorbed by the Comptroller—Fred Hanford was not a man given to complaint—but when Fred had unexpectedly retired, saying only that his doctor had advised him to move to a warmer and drier climate, there had been no argument against Stark's quiet contention that Miles Campbell was the only man in the company who was prepared to step into the breach. He had questioned, but only momentarily, Stark's further suggestion that Campbell be given the title of Vice President for Finance, granting that it had more of an appropriately big-company sound, but uncomfortably aware that Stark, by putting in his own man to do everything that he himself had been brought in to do, was not only retaining all of his original authority but also was lifting himself to a new and higher level in the company. That was when Stark had started applying computer control to the mill operation.

George Wilson had not been as quietly acquiescent as Fred Hanford. Before, although always as stubbornly show-me as any good mill man had to be, George had nevertheless been amenable to the president's personal direction, granting not only the authority of his office but also his superior experience and demonstrated ability as a production man. With the very first application of computer control, however, George had seen red, and all he could see through that bloody haze had been Roger Stark.

Matt Crouch had done his best to quiet George, but the more he talked the more madly unreasonable he had become. In a violently unpleasant session one Saturday morning, George had really gone off the deep end, calling him a stupid fool for letting Stark pull the wool over his eyes. Wild-eyed, his voice overstrained, he had shouted that "letting that computer-brained bastard inside the mill is going to wreck everything we've been working for," arguing that "it's going to be cut-a-penny here, cut-a-penny there, and we'll wind up making nothing but the same kind of crap everyone else is turning out." He had tried to make George understand that Stark had no control over quality, that no one would ever be allowed to change Crouch Carpet's production standards, telling him that all Stark was trying to do was to help them make the profit that they deserved, and had to have, but George's mad jealousy had already driven him beyond the reach of reason.

Roger Stark knew how George Wilson felt about him—it could hardly have been otherwise, the way George was sounding off to anyone who would listen to him—but Stark had remained as cool as always, excusing George's eccentric behavior as, perhaps, an evidence of genius, seemingly pouring oil on the raging sea by suggesting that some of the control function of the Comptroller's Cost Section be transferred to a new Assistant General Superintendent. Norman Kelsey had been brought in for that job, picked by George himself out of a dozen or more applicants. For several weeks an armed truce, if not a real peace, had prevailed. Then, through an unfortunate slip, George had discovered that Norman's original application had come in as the result of a contact that Stark had made through an undercover connection with a bank that had financed the bedspread mill in which Norman Kelsey had previously been employed.

Unquestionably, there had been some truth to George Wilson's allegation that Norman Kelsey was "Stark's man"—it was even conceivable, as George claimed, that the deck of applicants had been stacked so that Kelsey was sure to be the man that George chose for the job—but at the time there had been no presidential alternative to supporting Stark's quietly reasonable contention that Norman was doing the job he had been brought in to do. Nor could he disagree that George Wilson was a sick man. Something had to be done about him, a dilemma horribly resolved when George had been suddenly struck down by a cerebral hemorrhage that left him totally paralyzed. Mercifully, he had not lived out the week. Norman Kelsey had been made Vice President for Production.

As severely as Matt Crouch had been shaken by George Wilson's death, coming as it had so soon after Fred Hanford's retirement, neither loss had hit him as hard as that of Jim McIntyre. In some measure, perhaps, shock was cumulative, all three of the men with whom he had started the company gone within fourteen months. But there was more than that involved. In a not entirely reasonable way, he had felt closer to Mac than to either of the others. Fred Hanford had been, at least until the job had got too big for him, his financial guardian. George Wilson had been his good right hand in the mill, often reaching out to wisely curb him when he might otherwise have driven ahead into trouble. Mac had served him in a very different way—never a guardian, never a curb, always his unquestioning disciple, his most enthusiastic apostle, the zealous missionary who had gone forth to spread his creed. Without Jim McIntyre, Crouch Carpet could not have survived its infancy. Time after time in those lean first years, he had gone out when there was not an order on the books, and sent back a stream of life-giving business. There was no man in the whole carpet trade who had been better known and better liked. Even before his death, he had become a legendary character, spawning undying yarns about the big orders he had written without even a sample to show, about his refusal to burden himself with a briefcase, never carrying anything but a price list which, so the stories always went, he was never quite able to decipher.

Like most great personal salesmen, Jim McIntyre had had his weaknesses. Fortunately, he had been able to transmit some of his selling skill to the men under him—Crouch Carpet still had more topnotch salesmen in its field force than any company its size in the industry—but he had lacked the breadth of a truly top-level sales manager. He had never had more than a limited appreciation of modern merchandising, little feel for the artful use of advertising and promotion—all that Judd Wilder had supplied—but his most evident shortcoming had been his almost total lack of administrative ability. He admitted it, acknowledging that his department's paperwork was always in a mess, answering all criticism by saying that what he needed was someone who could take over the inside job and free him to spend all of his time out on the firing line. Roger Stark had answered that plea.

Warren Locke had been, until the whole accounts receivable operation was computerized, Crouch Carpet's Credit Manager, his work so efficiently done that there had seldom been any reason to call him to the president's office. He had thus preserved a corporate anonymity that, from any lack of evidence to the contrary, he was perfectly willing to maintain until the end of his working life. When Stark had suggested that Locke be made Assistant Sales Manager to relieve Mac of all office operations, Matt Crouch had judged it no more than a move to find a spot for a displaced man, made logical by the truth of Stark's argument that Locke, through his credit work, was already familiar with every account on the books.

Unquestionably, it had worked out. Within six months, Mac was answering questions by saying with a rumbling chuckle, "Darned if I know—you'll have to ask Warren." It was Warren Locke who had administered prices, realigned territories, established sales quotas, settled commission squabbles, and generally supervised the day-to-day operation of the sales force and the district offices. Surprisingly, when he made his first appearance on a convention program that next June, he got almost as much applause as Mac.

Matt Crouch had taken a newfound pride in Warren Locke's success—after all, having hired him he thought of him as one of his boys—and when Stark had suggested, after Mac's sudden death, that Warren be made General Sales Manager, he had delayed his approval only long enough to assure himself that there was no real alternative. It was, however, a decision that he quickly had cause to question. When they had called in Warren Locke to tell him the news, it was to Stark that Warren had expressed his real gratitude, even going so far as to say, "If it hadn't been for you, Roger, this would never have happened." It was then that Matt Crouch had awakened to the realization that Stark had pulled off another slick maneuver, getting his own man in Sales just as he had already done in Finance and Production.

It had been too late then to do anything about it other than to block Stark, a few months later, from giving Locke the title of Vice President for Marketing. If anyone was to have that title, he had decreed, it should be Judd Wilder. With that, Stark had immediately backwatered, admitted that Marketing might be a bit too broad, implying a control over Advertising & Promotion that, with Judd's independent temperament, Warren Locke might find difficult to apply. Under the circumstances, he had agreed, Vice President for Sales would be adequate. But the president had temporarily balked at going even that far unless Judd Wilder, too, was given a vice presidency for what was surely a no less valuable contribution to the company. Yes, that was worth thinking about, Stark had granted, but was he really prepared for the organizational consequences of giving a vice presidency to the head of a nonoperating department? If you made the Director of Advertising & Promotion a vice president, how could you deny the same status to the Director of Styling, the Director of Research, the Director of Personnel, even the Director of Purchasing? Once you broke into the Director level, where could you stop? "But let's talk about it sometime," Stark had put him off.

Somehow that sometime had never come—Stark had never brought it up again—but it had haunted Matt Crouch last night, linked in his mind with the guilt he had always felt for having stalled off, until it was too late, telling Mac about his bonus allotment of company stock. Fortunately, there would be a second chance with Judd. This time he'd go through with it, Stark or no Stark. He would award Judd his vice presidency as soon as he was well enough to listen and understand. And it would be even better this way, a real morale boost just when Judd would need it most—right after he came out of the hospital.

Reminded, he stabbed a buzzer button, wanting Miss Fox's assurance that the driver had left as planned to deliver Judd's personnel file to Dr. Kharr this morning, but she opened the door to ask, "Are you ready for them?"—a question made rhetorical by the way that, without waiting for his reply, she stepped back to clear the doorway for the vice-presidential parade. They came in single file, as always in the strict order of reverse seniority of appointment—first Locke, then Kelsey, then Campbell—stopping as they reached chairs, deferentially turning back to the door for Stark who, hesitant for a surveying instant at the threshold, made himself seem a crown prince being escorted to the throne by three henchmen of whose sheeplike loyalty he had already assured himself.

Matt Crouch felt a particular aloneness as he looked at their strangely rubber-stamped faces, thinking of the old days when there had never been the slightest chance of confusing a sales manager with a bookkeeper, when you could tell a real production man as far as you could see him. Now they all looked alike, faces put through a duplicator, copies of the Roger Stark impression. There wasn't a real carpet man in the bunch, not one. With Judd Wilder gone, there was no one left any more who went back far enough to know what *Crouch Carpet* really meant.

Stiffly on guard, he turned to watch Stark, who, seating himself at his right hand, was going through a standard ritual so coolly precise that it could hardly be unstudied, sitting down as if his only concern was the preservation of the crease in his trousers, flicking a bit of nonexistent lint from his coat sleeve, smoothing his center-parted hair with his fingertips, adjusting the metal-rimmed spectacles that made his eyes seem like photoelectric sensors guiding some electronic instrument.

Knowing Stark's game of always waiting for someone else to make the first move, Matt Crouch decided to use the same tactic, but his challenging silence was too quickly broken by Warren Locke's politely inquiring, "Mr. Crouch, any new word this morning on Judd?"

"I talked to his doctor just before I left the house," he said, going on to relay Dr. Kharr's morning report that Judd had had a very good night, the prognosis even more favorable than it had been last evening, intending to tell them something about Dr. Kharr, but discouraged by a positive impression that they were not really interested in what he was saying, only in Roger Stark's reaction to it.

Again there was silence. This time it was Campbell who stepped into the breach. "But I suppose, sir, that it will be some time before he's fully recovered?"

"Oh, a couple of months and he'll be back on the job as good as new," he replied optimistically, again tempted to tell them something about Dr. Kharr, put off by a quick-striking hunch that this talk about Judd was no more than an opening gambit, positive when he saw the conspiratorial glances that were exchanged, centering on Locke who had apparently been given the cat's-paw's role.

Clearing his throat, obviously uncomfortable, Locke said, "But even at best—two months—that does give us something of a problem about the convention." He swallowed hard, looking to Stark for support.

Stark remained silent, employing his standard strategy of always letting someone else carry the ball. Matt Crouch blasted him out of it with a demanding "Didn't you tell them we're going to postpone the convention?"

Purse-lipped, readjusting his spectacles, Stark said, "We've been exploring the alternate possibilities."

"What do you mean—alternate possibilities?"

Locke started to answer but Matt Crouch hushed him with a raised hand, not taking his eyes off Stark, pinning him down with a sharp "If you've got another Judd Wilder up your sleeve—all right, let's hear about him."

Annoyingly unruffled, Stark said quietly, "I quite understand the way you feel about Judd, Mr. Crouch. And we all share your high regard for his—even *genius*, perhaps is not too strong a word—but is it really your firm judgment, sir, that it's impossible to stage a convention without him?"

"How can we?"

"Other companies do."

"Not the way we do it. We hear it every year—there's nothing like a Crouch Carpet convention. Everybody says that. What would happen if we brought our whole crowd in here and put on some kind of a half-baked affair that—damn it, we can't afford to make that kind of an impression."

"Quite so," Stark agreed, aggravatingly composed. "But on the other side of the scale—must we not also weigh the impression that would be created if we were to cancel it?"

"I didn't say cancel—I said postpone."

Stark was undeterred. "The impression we'd give, I'm afraid, would be substantially the same—and I, for one, would regret projecting a corporation image of Crouch Carpet as a company so organizationally weak that the loss of one man makes it impossible for us to function normally."

Matt Crouch felt himself staggered, caught off guard by a blow that he had not anticipated. "All right, what would *you* do?"

Stark fanned his hands, a gesture of modesty strikingly inconsistent with his crisply confident voice. "I would proceed from the premise, Mr. Crouch, that our organization is strong enough, and resourceful enough, to meet any challenge that's put to it."

The president felt even more shaken now, disoriented by the incongruity of having someone else evidence superior confidence in the Crouch Carpet Company. Groggily, he struck out, hearing himself demand, "Just tell me where we've got another Judd Wilder, that's all I want to know. Who've we got that can fill his shoes?"

"No one," Stark granted. "But is that what we really want? Surely the situation in which we now find ourselves points up the danger of dependence upon any one man, no matter how brilliantly capable that man may have been."

"All right, so what are we going to do—appoint a committee?" he feinted, poised for a counterpunch, ready to cut down Stark by reminding him that his fancy Product Development Committee, after more than a year, still had not come up with its first usable idea.

"I think this is something that has to be organizationally integrated, Mr. Crouch. As a general principle——"

"Let's forget the damn principles and get the hell down to brass tacks," he cut him off, in no mood for another Stark lecture on corporate organization. "You say we've got to have a convention. All right, I come right back to what I asked you before—who's going to put it on? Who've we got? This assistant of Judd's—whatever his name is——"

"Talbott," Locke supplied. "Allen Talbott."

Matt Crouch wheeled on him with a quick "Can he do what Judd's done?"

"Well, he wouldn't go about it in the same way, of course," Locke said uneasily. "What I mean is—well, Allen has a different approach——"

"How so?" the president tried to nail him down, thwarted by Stark, who came in with a quickly coaching "Warren, you're not saying, are you, that you find Allen difficult to work with?"

"Oh, goodness, no. All of our boys like Allen. The thing they really appreciate—well, he's always willing to sit down and talk things over, listen to their ideas. That means a lot. They all like to feel that they're making a contribution."

"Understandable enough," Stark encouraged him.

"We were talking about this only a couple of days ago," Locke went on, "wondering if there was some way this year that we could get Judd to—please don't misunderstand me, Mr. Crouch. I'm not saying anything against Judd. He's put on some wonderful conventions for us, and they've done us an awful lot of good. Nobody could appreciate that any more than I do——"

"But he doesn't soft-soap you enough—is that what you're saying?"

Locke flushed but stood his ground, courage gained from a glance at Stark. "No, sir, it's just that—well, take Ed Fowler, the speech that he made at last year's convention. You may not remember it——"

"I don't?" Matt Crouch caught him up. "All right, I'll just tell you —it was the story on the contract follow-up plan—right?"

"Yes, sir," Locke granted, impressed but stubborn. "The only point I wanted to make—when you take an Assistant General Sales Manager, and all you let him do is read a speech that someone else has written——"

"Just tell me one thing, Locke—did it do what it was supposed to do? Did it sell the plan? Or didn't it?"

Stark stepped in to take him off the hook. "I think Warren's point here, Mr. Crouch, is not that it wasn't an effective presentation. It's simply a matter of morale and spirit, of what you——"

The president cut him off with an axing gesture, stopping the sweep of his hand with a stab at Kelsey. "What about you, Norman? You boys in Production all stewed up because Judd's been writing your speeches for you?"

"No, I wouldn't say that exactly," Kelsey said. "We've always been glad to get all the help we can. But still—I'm like Warren, not wanting to say anything against Judd, particularly at a time like this—but still I think there's something in what he says. Speaking of last year's convention—we all thought that the high-draft creel was something we ought to play up in our production presentation. It was an exclusive then, nobody else had it yet, and we felt that it would give us a pretty darned good story. Some of our boys spent a lot of time on it, working up all the dope, but when Judd finally got around to talking to us—I don't know, maybe he was right, maybe it was too technical to get over—but still it was pretty rough on the boys, all the work they'd put in and then having Judd—well, he hasn't always been the easiest man in the world to work with."

"Neither have I!" Matt Crouch exploded. "And, damn it, if I had been there'd never have been a Crouch Carpet Company."

Their silence was an accusation that he had lost his temper, his embarrassment all the greater because of the way that Stark, avoiding a direct response, quietly asked Campbell, "Miles, what's your impression of Allen Talbott? You've been working with him on the budget, haven't you?"

"Yes, he's been our point of contact for the past two years," Campbell said. "And I must say it's been a very nice relationship, much pleasanter than—well, that's neither here nor there—yes, Allen's been fine, just fine. He's very cooperative, very amenable, a very nice chap. Gets along with everyone."

Gruffly, Matt Crouch demanded, "What in hell are we doing here—judging a popularity contest?"

"Not at all," Stark granted. "But it does seem that there's something that might be gained from having everyone pulling together. After all, we do have a lot of good minds that can be brought to bear on this convention project. Why shouldn't we take full advantage of them? Isn't that what you fellows are really trying to say?"

Matt Crouch looked from face to face, seeing their mimicking obeisance to Stark as a measure of what small men they really were, so quick to forget all that Judd had done for them, so full of all of the petty resentments that they had stored up against him. Jealousy! Yes, that was a lot of it. That's why they resented Judd—because he showed them up, because he had something that they didn't have. *Ideas!* And, damn it, that's what built a company, what kept a company growing. And you didn't get ideas out of soft minds, out of these three-in-a-row monkeys who thought that it was the nice guys who always got the most peanuts. Why couldn't they see that? Business wasn't a popularity contest. You had to get in there and fight. And when you did you couldn't help stepping on a few toes. That's all Judd had done . . .

"—and I do think there's more involved here than a judgment of Talbott's individual competence," Stark was going on. "Our real objective, it would seem to me, should be the establishment of an organizational structure that will bring to bear on the convention all the personnel resources that we have at our command. Warren mentioned the desire of his men to contribute—Norman made the same point—I'm sure it's equally true in other areas. And I see no reason whatsoever why we shouldn't avail ourselves of all the strength we can muster. Surely we need it. Don't you agree, Mr. Crouch?"

Matt Crouch felt suddenly overcome by a consuming weariness, the last of his strength abruptly drained. He was tired, frighteningly tired. He closed his eyes, the night coming back, Stark's voice a drone in the darkness, vaguely ominous but no more than a wordless threat until his ears suddenly caught a phrase that snapped his eyes open. Blinking, he demanded, "What's that you just said?"

"It's only a suggestion," Stark replied offhandedly. "But with the convention so undeniably a sales function, it does seem reasonable that the Vice President for Sales should exercise general control over the nature and character of the program. In the past—yes, with Mr. McIntyre the sort of man he was, and with Judd's peculiar talent—unquestionably, some violation of organizational structure was justified. But that special situation no longer prevails."

Finding new strength in alarm, the president demanded, "Let's have it straight, Stark. What are you trying to do—put Advertising & Promotion under Sales?"

"It's a quite normal relationship, Mr. Crouch, one that you'll find in the vast majority of well-managed companies. And in our case, it's a move that's justified not only by sound organization but also by the exigencies of the situation. We have only five weeks and there's an enormous job to be done. As for Allen Talbott, I've felt for a long time that he might well be given more—"

For a long time?

Suddenly, it all came clear . . . yes, he could see it now, the way that Stark had infiltrated Talbott into Advertising & Promotion, planting him there to wait for this chance to stab Judd in the back . . . the same way that Kelsey had struck down George Wilson . . . Mac dead on the turnpike and Locke all ready and waiting . . . *If it hadn't been for you, Roger, this would never have happened"* . . .

He tried to break out of it, but the circle of expressionless faces hemmed him in, coming closer and closer, the wolf pack closing in on its old leader, thinking that he was so near to death that he could no longer fight back . . . *damn it, he'd show them who was* . . .

Pain stabbed behind his eyes, a jagged lightning flash from temple to temple. He reacted instantly, terrorstruck despite all the years that had passed since he had experienced this awful headache, anger rising until it had become a pressure too great to confine, ending in an explosion that, in his mechanically oriented view, he had always visualized as a bomb-burst in the delicate watchworks of his mind, blasting everything apart, pinions unseated, gear trains unmeshed, a mainspring wildly unwinding, a ratcheting sound that had gone on and on, quieted only when Emily had finally made him see that everyone was not against him, that his persecution complex was unjustified. Recognition had been the key to cure, a slow process then, but now it came so quickly that the watching eyes across the desk had hardly blinked.

He took a deep mind-cooling breath, slowly gaining assurance that he was thinking clearly. Maybe he had been a little too panicked last night, worrying so much about Judd that he had overlooked the strength and capacity that had been built into the organization. Stark was right . . . this was a big company now . . . maybe Judd had run a little too much of a one-man show . . .

"After all, what alternative do we have?" Stark was asking. "Judd is out—that we must accept. And with only five weeks to go——"

"All right," he broke in. "Go ahead. See what you can work out."

They were all on their feet, up to claim their victory before it could be snatched away.

"Just a minute," he stopped Stark at the door, waiting then until the others were outside. "This is only temporary, just until Judd gets back—you understand that, don't you?"

"Of course," Stark said blandly. "If Judd comes back the same man he was before—if this new approach appears less effective—no organizational decision is ever irreversible." Without waiting for a response he switched to "About the stockholders report—I thought you might like to know—Allen Talbott talked to the printer this morning. There'll be no difficulty about the changes. They can still make the Tuesday night mailing."

Matt Crouch remained silent, hoping to discourage Stark, wanting nothing so much now as to be left alone.

But Stark stayed on. "With a news release for the Wednesday morning papers, I'd guess that the stock will hit 40 by the end of the week. It might not be a bad time to consider a secondary offering of some of your stock. As a matter of fact, Elbert Coe mentioned it only yesterday."

This time, silence worked. Stark went out, the sound of the closing door echoing his confident prediction, eighteen months ago, that the stock would hit 40 before the middle of this year.

Subconsciously directed, Matt Crouch's hand reached out for a pencil and a scratch pad. No less without recognized volition he inscribed a carefully drawn 40, retracing the lines until they were deeply impressed . . . maybe Emily was right . . . maybe he ought to retire. Why not? If he cashed in his stock now . . .

Quickly, as if it were a surreptitious act, he multiplied 167,300 by 40, then hurriedly tore off the sheet and crumbled it in his hand. But the answer remained in his mind.

« 3 »

As the forenoon had gone on, Judd Wilder had drifted into a state of strange euphoria. He felt now as if, after a long upward climb from some hot and steamy tropic lowland, he had finally reached a high plateau where the air was clear and cool—but oddly unin-vigorating.

He felt no urge to get out of bed. That in itself was most unusual because, all of his life, except on those rare occasions when he had been ill, he had never been able to lie abed once he was awake—and now, quite definitely, he was no longer sick. Several times, ex-perimentally, he had taken a series of breaths, cautiously shallow at first, then deeper and deeper until his lungs filled to their utmost capacity, yet he had not felt the slightest twinge of chest pain. The threat of nausea was gone. He knew that he had no fever. The heartbeat that pounded in his ear when he lay on his side was steady and strong.

He had gone through a heart attack—and survived it. He should be feeling, he thought, some sense of victory, of accomplishment, at least of great good fortune. But his only recognized sensation was one of an all-pervading emptiness. His mind was a well that had gone dry, drained through some subterranean crevice that, momen-tarily open, had closed again. With patience, the well would refill—and as the strangest phenomenon of all, he found himself willing to wait.

Again, he felt impelled to do something about canceling orders that he had placed in New York for things that would not be needed now that the convention had been postponed, but there was a pe-culiar absence of any propelling urgency. This, in itself, was un-natural enough to contribute to a recognized feeling of strangeness, but that same lack of urgency kept him from searching for an ex-planation. Neither did he attempt to weigh or measure, either as regret or relief, his reaction to the postponement of the convention. If he thought about it at all, it was only as a coincidence. Once, quite clearly, he did recall the elated relief that he had felt when, that last year in college, after Pearl Harbor, it had been announced that the seniors who were enlisting in the armed forces would be given their degrees without final examination, but he did not feel himself moved to pursue why he had resurrected that old and long-forgotten memory.

Several times he had thought of Kay—it was unavoidable, the way that stupid nurse kept talking about her, asking over and over if he didn't think that some message should be sent to her—and again there was that same sense of fortunate timing, the feeling that everything had worked out in the best possible way. Vague though all of his thoughts were, he could clearly visualize what would be happening if Kay were here, all but able to see her standing there at the end of the bed, looking down at him with the self-righteous justification of a fulfilled prediction, reminding him of how many times she had asked, "What are you trying to do—kill yourself?" And then, as always, she would add, "And for what?" Here, pinned down in a bed, he wouldn't be able to walk out on her, the only way he had ever found to express the hopelessness of trying to make her understand.

Unlucky though he had been—his mind did not dwell here, conditioned as it was to quickly override adversity—he felt that this could not have happened at a better time, a better place, or under better circumstances. Here and now, he could lie back with that same sense of safe escape that he had experienced at the Los Juntos Motel. That memory kept coming back again and again, so insistently intrusive that it challenged his ability to distinguish fantasy from reality. He knew with full certainty that his heart attack had struck as he was coming off the Pennsylvania Turnpike, just after he had made the turn at the light, yet the memory of having been stopped by hitting a chuckhole was so persistent that he found it difficult to banish. There was no confusion about the diner, all that had happened there was too vividly impressed to be questioned, yet the face under the state trooper's hat kept reappearing as the face of the doctor at the Jersey City morgue.

The surmounting of confusion was not so much a differentiation between illusion and truth as it was a separation of one truth from another. What had happened at the Los Juntos Motel was no less real than what had happened at Sam's Diner, and that earlier episode was undeniably pertinent to the way he now felt. There had been this same sensation of suspended time, this same feeling of secretive escape, this same need to shut out the world and lie back in undisturbed aloneness. The only threat to tranquillity was Miss Harsch—and now she was bearing down upon him again, another glistening gold capsule tipping the lance head formed by her thumb and forefinger.

"Time for our medicine," she said.

"What is it?" he demanded, closing his lips against the threatened quick thrust of her hand.

"Doctor's orders," the voice said, mechanical, tape-recorded, as lifeless as a laugh-track.

"I'm not taking anything unless I know what it is."

The tape ran on. "We wouldn't want to have to tell Dr. Kharr that we're being difficult, would we?"

"Tell him anything you want to."

The tape ran out. The lips no longer moved. But, staring up at her, he suddenly saw her eyes, not as a part of her fixed expression but as if he were seeing them through eyeholes in a mask, revealing an interior bewilderment that was grotesquely incongruous with her unchanging smile.

Quickly, he reached up for the capsule and popped it into his mouth, a surrender induced by the feeling that he had been unfairly teasing a child-minded moron, pointlessly demanding an admission of something that he already knew. Dr. Kharr had told him this morning that he would no longer be given narcotics, only these mild tranquilizers that would have no more effect upon him than a weak martini. It was true. He had felt nothing from the others, he would feel nothing from this one.

He drank from the drinking tube without protest, accepting the pointlessness of reminding Miss Harsch that Dr. Kharr had told her, when he had come in and found her spooning breakfast food into his mouth, that he was not to be treated as a helpless invalid. He drank deeply, long after the capsule had been swallowed, and her smile might have indicated gratitude had it not been the same expression with which she had responded to everything else that had happened, as unchanging after Dr. Kharr's sharp criticism as it had been when, while bathing him, the rough-surfaced washcloth envelopment of his genitals had been so startlingly interrupted by the unmistakably lingering contact of flesh with flesh, only for a moment but long enough to make him see her fixed smile as a shockingly lascivious leer.

Forget her, he counseled himself, remembering something that Huck Joyce had once said about an imbecilic old actress—"Don't blame her, pity her"—closing his eyes then, purposefully trying to blank his mind.

He must have succeeded because there was an otherwise unaccountable lapse between seeing her walk away with the water glass and a sudden awareness that she was coming in from the corridor, bearing down upon him again, now with an armload of riotously jumbled flowers.

"See what a beautiful surprise we have!" she exclaimed, thrusting the flowers toward him, smothering his nostrils in a suffusion of sickening sweetness.

He gagged, trying to fight off a return of last night's nausea.

"Lovely, aren't they?" she burbled, demanding agreement as the price of release, fortunately not waiting for his complete capitulation, turning then to put the flowers on the dresser, confronting him with the vast expanse of her tightly corseted buttocks. Distantly, he heard her say, "Now we're going to play our little game." She turned back, holding up a small white card with a teasing gesture. "Now what dear friend do you suppose sent us these lovely, lovely flowers?"

He clenched his eyes, trying to escape into sleep, pursued by her outreaching voice, raised now to a falsetto pitch. "Best wishes for your speedy recovery—Eloise and Roger Stark."

Stark?

Arrested, his runaway mind came to an abrupt stop, his breath held as if he had heard a warning shout. Involuntarily, he glanced toward the open door, all but seeing Roger Stark looking down at him with an expression of cool triumph, a fleeting aberration that slowly gave way before a pre-reasoned assurance that Stark was not the threat that he once seemed.

Roger Stark's sudden appearance at Crouch Carpet as Vice President for Management had climaxed a month of wild stories that the company was in financial difficulty. At first, Judd had given the rumors no credence, unable to believe that anything could be seriously wrong when the factory was running three full shifts, thinking that no more was involved than another of Mr. Crouch's periodic attempts to frighten everyone into cutting expenses. Even when construction of the new warehouse had been halted with the steelwork half up, he had not been overly alarmed, truly concerned only after Mr. Crouch had called him in one morning and peremptorily ordered him to cancel the entire magazine campaign. After that, it had been all too easy to believe that the bankers were taking over the company, a grim prospect seemingly fulfilled by Roger Stark's appearance.

During Stark's second week on the job, he had asked Judd to

have lunch with him, a transparently contrived attempt at camaraderie, a pretense made false not only by the knowledge that Stark was making the rounds, a department head a day, but also by the strong impression that his bid for friendship was an exercise prescribed by some management textbook, his lack of sincerity betrayed by a smile that flashed on and off with no relevance to what was being said, as oddly mistimed as if it were a trick that he had not yet perfected.

Judd had gone to that luncheon meeting resolved to keep his mouth shut, to listen and learn, to appraise what was going to happen to the company. Afterwards, angrily aware of a lack of self-discipline, he realized that he had done the opposite. It was Stark who had listened and learned, constantly prodding him with questions so sharp-pointed that it had been impossible to refuse response. By contrast with the easy give-and-take of any session with Matt Crouch, that luncheon with Roger Stark had been a chilling experience, frightening enough that he had gone back to his office and immediately dug out of his personal file a letter that had arrived a few days before from a Manhattan executive placement agency inquiring whether or not he would be interested in a position as advertising and promotion manager for a company that, although unnamed, was almost certainly General Carpet Corporation.

He had received a dozen or more such feelers from other companies—Crouch Carpet's merchandising success had attracted widespread attention in the booming carpet and home furnishing industries—but this was the first time that he had ever followed up one of them. Instead of answering by letter, he made a telephone call, and when his guess about General Carpet proved correct, it seemed prescient of an ordained fate, the move to a new job so clearly predicted that writing a résumé seemed a needless annoyance, the preliminary interview at the agency's office a pointless waste of time.

His first direct contact with General Carpet had been a luncheon meeting with the Chairman of the Board, Harrison Horter, at the Pinnacle Club in New York. There had been, some weeks before, an article in the Sunday *Times* magazine section about the corporation executive as an art patron, citing Harrison Horter as one of a band of enlightened industrialists who were doing for the arts in the twentieth century what the Medicis had done in the Renaissance, and Judd had approached the Pinnacle Club with a pleasant anticipation of working for a man so different from Matt Crouch. Instead of meeting a latter-day Lorenzo, cultured and urbane, he had been confronted across the table by a great monolith of a man, as unresponsive as granite, as cold as marble. Flanking him were two all but perfect replicas of Roger Stark. They did the talking. Luncheon with a lone Roger Stark had been bad enough, but at the Pinnacle Club it had all been a double-barreled attack, each in turn prodding him with barbed questions, all of which demanded answers with dollar signs in front of them. He had felt justified in his inability to answer them—if he had wasted his years at Crouch Carpet figuring cost ratios instead of working on merchandising ideas, he could not have done a good enough job to make them want to hire him away—but the simplest escape had been to say that he could not, in good conscience, reveal any information about the operations of Crouch Carpet. By then he had all but decided that he would not take the job even if it were offered to him, and from the chill that had settled over the luncheon table he guessed that it would not be, almost certain of it when they had broken up with no invitation from Harrison Horter to come back with him to General Carpet's offices. Actually, as he would later recall, Horter had not said more than a dozen words to him all during that long lunch hour.

It had been an experience more disappointing than he had acknowledged, threatening the destruction of his long-held conviction that staying on at Crouch Carpet all of these years had been a matter of his own choice. Nevertheless, defeat had been strangely transformed into a kind of victory. He had told no one—not even Kay—about the General Carpet opening, and he had never known who had seen him at the Pinnacle Club, but word had somehow got back to Mr. Crouch. That very next morning he had been called to the president's office and accused of consorting with competitors, the most serious crime in Mr. Crouch's book. Reacting to emotions too complex to be quickly sorted out, Judd had bypassed the honest claim that he had revealed nothing about Crouch Carpet's operations, resorting instead to a defense that, somehow, by some uncharted course, had brought him around to talking about Roger Stark. Although he could not afterwards recall having actually said so, Mr. Crouch had got the idea, apparently as a shocking first revelation, that everyone in the company thought that he was abdicating in Stark's favor. Judd had rarely seen him so upset, his anger diverted from the Pinnacle Club luncheon to Roger Stark, culminating in a desk-pounding pronouncement that, damn it, he was still running the company, that Roger Stark didn't have one damn thing to do with advertising or promotion, and he'd damn soon take care of Stark if he tried sticking his nose into any place where it didn't belong. More to the point, that very afternoon, he had called a meeting on the advertising budget. Not only had the magazine campaign been restored, but right down the line, on every item that Stark questioned, there had been a presidential ruling in Judd's favor.

When, a few days later, he received a surprising letter from Harrison Horter, suggesting that he drop in to see him the next time he was in New York—"with a view to finalizing our interesting conversation last week at the Pinnacle Club"—he had replied that he was no longer interested. With Stark effectively excluded from any interference with Advertising & Promotion, and with Mr. Crouch always ready to support him in any argument, he had been given even more freedom of action than he had had in the past.

Nevertheless, Stark's continued presence had remained an intuitively sensed threat, the danger indeterminate, hidden as it always was behind his unvarying expression of chill insouciance, his secret plotting revealed only when someone else turned up with a proposal that bore the unmistakable mark of his behind-the-scenes manipulation. Warren Locke had, of course, been a Stark stooge from the very beginning. With his bookkeeper's mind, and shaky in his new job, Warren had quickly embraced all of Stark's ideas for computerized sales-cost analysis and merchandising control, trusting the computer read-out more than he did his own judgment. At this year's budget meeting, Warren had actually proposed that Crouch Carpet shift its major promotional attention from the top-quality lines, with which its reputation had been made, in order to capitalize upon the booming mass market for promotionally priced carpet. That threat to the founding concept upon which the company had been built had, of course, been easy enough to handle. A nudge had been all that was needed to trigger an explosion from Mr. Crouch, demolishing poor Warren, who had crumbled like a straw man in a big wind, unsupported by Roger Stark, who had sat through the whole thing without once coming to Warren's aid, letting his stalking horse take the punishment while he maintained his own pose of detachedly innocent observation. And yet, after it was all over, the budget approved—with only those items stricken out that Judd had put in to satisfy Mr. Crouch's need to cut something—Warren had gone out with Roger Stark, figuratively if not literally arm in arm, apparently unaware that he had been betrayed, obviously blaming Mr. Crouch rather than Stark for his ignominious defeat.

How anyone, even someone as naïvely unknowing as Warren Locke, could be taken in by Roger Stark was difficult for Judd Wilder to understand, yet it was undeniably true that Stark's following in the company was constantly growing, particularly among some of the younger men who apparently accepted him as the prototype of the modern business executive, judging his lack of sensibility as a creditable suppression of unseemly emotion. And yet they were the first to fall for his corny little tricks—those anniversary messages, the birthday cards to their wives, those little notes when somebody's kid made the newspaper with a touchdown or a class office—all triggered by a system that his secretary operated, Stark's way of insuring that he would always do the right thing at the right time. It was no surprise that Stark had sent him flowers—it was automatic—and no less inevitable that they would be so badly chosen, such an overblown mess of incompatible colors, so gaggingly overperfumed, accompanied by such a cliché message.

"—play our little game again!"

He raised his hands, trying to block his ears, but Miss Harsch's voice came through in an irresistibly penetrating sing-song: "'Sure hope that very soon you'll be in perfect health once more, and feeling even better than you ever felt before'—now isn't that a pretty sentiment—Warren and Anne Locke."

Everything was a blaze of red, a bloody explosion, his lungs choked with the stink of cheap rosewater hair tonic . . .

". . . Norman and Barbara . . ."

". . . Allen Talbott . . ."

". . . Susie and Ed . . ."

. . . they were all outside, trying to get in . . . they'd found out where he was . . . someone had betrayed him . . . this damned nurse! Yes, that was what she had done . . . called them. But how could she? She didn't know who he was . . . she thought he was

Floyd Fulton . . . yes, that was the way he had registered. But someone had told them . . . they knew he was in here . . . calling his name . . . *Mr. Wilder!* . . . *Mr. Wilder!* . . .

"Mr. Wilder!"

Consciousness came as an abrupt surfacing from dark depths, a sudden breakthrough into blinding light . . . the ambulance was here . . . he must have passed out for a minute . . . lying here on the floor . . .

"If you do not remember me, sir—I am Dr. Raggi."

"I know," he said. "On the ambulance," memory confirmed by the aluminum clipboard that he saw in those dark-skinned hands. But there was another connection that he could not make, unable to explain why that strangely accented voice sounded so tantalizingly familiar.

"Dr. Kharr will be coming to see you later—he is very busy today —so I am stopping by to see if there's anything we can be doing to make you more comfortable."

"I'm all right," he said, turning away to escape the too-knowing look of those searching black eyes, wondering how long they had been watching him, feeling as if he had been caught in a moment of embarrassingly childish behavior. Catching a quick breath, he involuntarily gagged.

Instantly anxious, Dr. Raggi asked, "You are still feeling nauseated, sir?"

"Just those damn flowers" burst out before he could stop it, afraid then that he had betrayed himself, expecting a too-knowing chuckle of understanding.

But what he heard was a crisply commanding "Nurse—you will please remove all of the flowers."

He closed his eyes, shutting out the quick glimpse that he had had of Miss Harsch's face, her smile crookedly affixed, the mask knocked askew.

"I understand, Mr. Wilder, that you have been in my country?"

"Your country?" he asked, puzzled, but for only an instant, somehow knowing before he heard it that the answer would be "India." And now everything came clear, realizing now why that accent had seemed so familiar in the ambulance, awareness so abruptly achieved that it seemed as if his mind had been suddenly restored to complete rationality, the threat of fogging illusion as quickly banished as if a limitless sky had been wiped clear of the last cloud.

"That's a long time ago," he said, automatically excusing incomplete recollection, yet quickly aware that it was unnecessary. Memories of India came back in a series of flashed images, brilliantly sharp and clear, all the more surprising because it had been so long since he had resurrected them.

« 4 »

Dr. Aaron Kharr, hunched in his office chair, scowled up at Dr. Raggi, his face wracked by a conscious effort to contain an explosive mixture of doubt and disappointment behind an expression of professional aplomb. He wished now that he had not asked Raggi to see Wilder—what had happened, it seemed, was something too important to be judged upon secondhand evidence—but as busy as he had been, his schedule as jammed as it always was on Saturday, there had been no other practical way to keep a running check on how Wilder was responding to the switch from phenobarbital to amitriptyline.

"Sit down, Dr. Raggi," he said, abruptly cordial, trying to make amends for what he now realized had been a too-sharp expression of disbelief. "Do you suppose it possible that that fool nurse didn't follow my drug order?"

Raggi sat down slowly, considering his answer. "I will say this, sir—I would think it unlikely—but not impossible."

"She's stupid enough," he agreed. "But still—yes, it's hard to imagine her not doing what she was told."

"Is it not true, sir—these mood-elevating tranquilizers—is it not difficult to anticipate precisely the effect they will have?"

"Apparently," he said grittily, feeling himself obliquely accused of having taken a bad gamble, of having tried to move too rapidly in order to get Wilder into a state of mind where he could have a solid talk with him before the day was over. "Tell me this, Dr. Raggi—you say that you watched him for several minutes before you woke him?"

"Yes, sir."

"And it seemed that he was having a bad dream?"

"Yes, sir, his face was very animated."

"Was there any indication at all of what he might be dreaming? Did it seem that he was fighting against something? What was the expression on his face? Angry? Belligerent?"

"I would say—" Raggi paused, seemingly a search for words. "If I were forced to guess, sir, I would say that he was trying to hide from someone—something—whatever it was that was frightening him."

Aaron Kharr stifled a groan, fighting acceptance of this evidence that Wilder had already been caught up by that traumatic heart-attack fear which, once fixed, would be all but impossible to dislodge. "And you say that he was nauseated."

"Could it not be, sir—I am recalling something in one of your papers—is it not possible that a patient who awakens to find himself surrounded by flowers—"

"I know," he cut him off, sidestepping what had already occurred to him: the death-fear that had been plainly induced in several cases that he had studied by the funereal aspect of a flower-banked hospital room. "But it doesn't make sense, not after the way he talked when I examined him this morning. He wasn't frightened then. If anything, he wasn't concerned enough. That's what I was planning to do this afternoon—try to jar him into taking this as seriously as he should."

"Perhaps, sir, if you were to wait a few days——"

"There's no time to wait. These first days are crucial. This isn't psychoanalysis, Dr. Raggi—you can't fumble around week after week, session after session. You've got to move quickly. And you've got to know where you're going. That means that you've got to know your man. If you don't——"

"Yes, yes, I know what you have written, sir," Raggi said, making it sound like an expression of sympathy, almost as if he were saying that he understood how embarrassed he must be to have written, as he had in several of his papers, that any general practitioner who was willing to make the effort could easily acquire enough understanding of a heart patient's character to guide a successful psychological rehabilitation.

With an angry sigh of impatient self-criticism, Aaron Kharr twisted around to his desk, certain that the fault lay not in his method but in its execution. He picked up the four long sheets of yellow paper on which, working last night until almost midnight, stealing time that should have been spent on his book, he had constructed a biographical outline of Judd Wilder's life. Against marginal numbers from 1920 to 1965, providing a space for every year of the patient's life, he had set down everything that he had learned, not only from his talk with Matthew R. Crouch but also what he gleaned from the material that the president had sent him. The package, arriving late in the afternoon, had fulfilled the president's pledge but not the anticipation that had been aroused by its promising bulk. The big envelope, tape-strapped to hold in its bulging contents, had proved to be overstuffed with Crouch Carpet annual reports and advertising booklets, a great deal of information about the company but little that bore directly upon Judd Wilder's character. His personnel file, anticipated as a treasure lode, had proved a disappointing magpie's nest of relatively meaningless forms, most of them apparently having something to do with group insurance or the company's retirement plan. They had, however, given him a few bits of useful information. More had come from some newspaper clippings that had been scattered through the file. Over the past two years, it seemed, Wilder had been quite active in outside organizations, suggesting that he had recently turned to other sources for the gratification that he was no longer finding in his job, by no means an uncommon mid-forties phenomenon. The most valuable clipping was from the *Colfax College Alumni News,* reporting that Judd Wilder had been the recipient of the Hopkins Award for "outstanding contribution to the practice of advertising as an honored profession," and containing a biographical sketch that had given the doctor several good notes.

He had learned almost nothing from Wilder's medical record. As Crouch had promised, it was all there, the full file, but despite all the tests that had been made, the record offered no evidence that Dr. Lyman Hewes had seen Judd Wilder as anything other than an assemblage of disassociated organs, all of which had been functioning normally. Two weeks ago there had been no clinical evidence of cardiovascular disease, negative evidence that confirmed Wilder's coronary as psychogenic, rooted in a behavior pattern that had to be corrected.

Last night it had seemed that he had a biographical outline well enough delineated to serve at least as a working guide. But now, his key insight contradicted by Raggi's report, it appeared that all he had really put together was the barest of barebones skeletons, fleshed out with entirely too much imagination, too many conclusions drawn from equating Wilder with other seemingly similar cases. Worse, it appeared that he had been guilty of what Dr. Steinfeldt had styled "diagnosis by fantasy," the charge that his old mentor had always leveled at the psychoanalysts who, taking some scrap of information and interpreting it on the basis of some "pseudoscientific classification," would puff it up into an assessment of personality that "reveals far more about the unquestionably neurotic analyst than it does about the questionably adjusted patient."

Scanning the outline, a marginal note reminded him of the opening gambit that he had suggested to Raggi. "I don't suppose you got anywhere trying to talk to him about India."

"I'm afraid not, sir. He was not very responsive."

"But you did try?" he asked, clutching at a straw. "What happened? What did you say, what did he say?"

"I said, 'I understand, Mr. Wilder, that you have been in India.' He seemed surprised that I should know this."

"As if it were something he didn't want known?"

"Perhaps, sir," Raggi said. "But I would say that it was more—this is only my impression—it was my feeling that he was not wishing to think about it."

Aaron Kharr searched the second page of his outline. He did not have the date that Wilder had left for India, but it must have been shortly after he had been married in March 1943. Except for the entry that a son had been born in December '43, there were no more notes until his discharge from service in December '45. Last night that blank gap had not concerned him because, since Wilder had continued in motion picture work afterwards, it had seemed that his war service had not diverted the forward thrust of his career. But now there was the sharply prompting memory of one of the case studies at Berringer. In that instance, a wartime marriage, immediately followed by a long separation and a child born while the man had been overseas, had plainly been the beginning of a stress-producing marriage. In that case, too, the man had been reluctant to talk about his military service. Thinking aloud, he mused, "It may be that there's some unpleasant association with India—or perhaps with something that happened while he was away."

"I do not think it was India," Raggi said firmly, embarrassed then by his positiveness. "Perhaps I am wrong, but I am thinking, sir, that it was not India alone that he did not wish to recall. I felt, sir, that he does not wish to think about anything. All he wants—" His voice trailed off.

"All he wants is what?"

"I am afraid, sir, that what he is wanting is to be left alone—not thinking, not talking, just left alone."

Aaron Kharr nodded dully. If Raggi was right, it was almost hopeless. He had studied many cases of coronary victims who had reacted in this way, exhibiting neither anxiety nor bold disdain, simply pulling back from life as a mortally wounded animal retires from the arena, crawling away into some dark and uninvadable retreat. The only such case that he had ever seen successfully handled had been Dr. Steinfeldt's, but he had learned long ago that he did not have Steinfeldt's gift. Whatever it was that he lacked—and no shortcoming had been so agonizingly examined—he knew that he dared not count upon being able to establish with Judd Wilder that personal rapport which had drawn men to Dr. Steinfeldt as the healing warmth of the sun draws a wounded animal from its hiding place.

"If there's nothing else, sir—" Raggi suggested, starting to rise.

"No, that's all—but thank you," he said, struck by the weakness of his voice, almost the sound of surrender. Reacting instantly, he reached out for his work pad, ripping off the top sheet and crumpling it in his clenched fist, hurling it at the wastebasket. As a completion of the same sweeping motion, he reached out for a fresh pencil.

« 5 »

Kay Wilder's quest for solitude was proving almost too successful. Her only conversational exchange of the day had been at breakfast, when, eating alone, she had brushed up her French by talking to the waiter. At noon she had come down to find all of her tablemates, even the wives, engaged in a spirited three-way argument over the relative merits of the Camelback Inn, the Homstead, and the Broadmoor Hotel as convention sites, a debate interrupted only long enough to acknowledge her arrival with a circle of briefly flickering on-and-off smiles. The captain had not appeared.

This afternoon had dragged endlessly. The good weather of the first two days was lost behind gray-black clouds so low that sea and sky were inseparable, the decks fog-shrouded and dripping. She had twice gone out to walk, both times driven back to her cabin by drizzling rain. But her cabin was impossibly hot—control valves that no longer worked were, it seemed, an accepted attribute of the *Bretagne's* charming antiquity—and when the steward, at her insistence, had opened a port, his reluctance had been immediately justified by an I-told-you-so inpouring of oily black smoke swept down from the ship's funnels.

She had spent a few minutes in the chill and deserted writing room, and then gone to the library, aimlessly browsing, fingering the cracked leather bindings of a few mold-smelling volumes. The only book in which she might have been interested was in a glass-doored case for which, the steward explained, the key had been lost for many years. The lounge, warmly yellow-lighted, had seemed at first a gray-day haven, but all of the nooks and corners had been preempted by one or another of the little groups into which, by this third day out, all of the passengers had coalesced. Self-excluded though she was, her too obvious aloneness was becoming a burden, inciting boldly questioning glances from the more repulsive males, and even more repelling smiles of smug sympathy from the blue-rinsed widows who, birds of a kind, had settled into their gaily chattering little flocks.

She finally found an out-of-the-way chair, but the old copy of *L'Illustration* that she had picked up from the reading table was too potent an anticipation of Paris, the overheard conversation from the bridge table around the corner a too-virulent reminder of New Ulster. She was about to return to her cabin, wondering whether the chance that she might be able to nap was worth the price of a gauntlet run through the lounge, when she looked up to see the woman with the Givenchy coat standing in the doorway, hesitant for a surveying moment. Kay felt again, a bit more than subconsciously, that same community of character that had been suggested when she had first seen this woman coming up the gangplank. A dozen times since, passing her on deck or coming in or out of one of the public rooms—for some reason, they always seemed to be meeting—Kay had been tempted to speak, encouraged by the slight but perceptibly growing warmth of each successive smile of recognition, yet held back from making the first move by the feeling that they were somehow engaged in a duel of poise. Beyond the obvious fact that she had money, all that Kay knew about her was what she had learned from the passenger list, that she was "Kemble, Mrs. Ritchie, New York."

Watching out of the corner of her eye, Kay saw that Mrs. Kemble was walking in her direction, coming directly toward her. Somehow she sensed that she would stop. She did. A low-pitched voice, tense but controlled, asked, "Are you by any chance the sort of person who might think four o'clock a not-too-inappropriate time for a drink?"

"Well—yes," Kay said, hesitant as she tried to come up with a reply in kind, belatedly settling for "I'm precisely that sort of person." She put the magazine aside and rose, confronted by a quickly offered hand and an introductory, "I'm Chris Kemble."

"Kay Wilder."

Chris Kemble's handshake, although a woman-of-the-world gesture to which she was plainly accustomed, was oddly overpressed, suggesting a nervous tension that was verified in her face. A spider-web of sharply incised lines radiated from the corners of her eyes. But it was the eyes themselves that were most telling. Overly bright, they seemed jewels polished to a surface hardness that might, at any instant, shatter into either fire or liquidity. There was something about her, perhaps no more than her invitation, that aroused the apprehension that she might be an alcoholic, a possibility furthered by her suggestion that they go to her cabin rather than the bar.

Sure enough, there was a bowl of ice ready and waiting, a tray of bottles and glasses on top of her buffet, and the instant they were inside, Chris Kemble said, "Scotch?"

"Please—but a light one," Kay said, measuring her hostess as she turned away to make the drinks, trying to guess who she was, what her background might be. Her beautifully cut copper-colored suit and her recognizably Ferragamo shoes bespoke a showcase newness, the same impression that Kay had gathered from all of her other clothes, not only the Givenchy coat but everything else that she had seen her wear. She could, of course, be someone wealthy enough to toss away expensive clothes as if they were disposable tissues, but that hardly explained why everything in sight, even the things on her dressing table, looked as pristinely fresh as if she were a bride on a gift-furnished honeymoon.

And there was an extension of the same tantalizing riddle when, handing Kay her drink, she raised her own with an enigmatically accented "To a better tomorrow," almost certainly a reference to something beyond the weather.

"Tomorrow," Kay responded, drinking sparely.

"You're from Pennsylvania?"

"Yes. And you're New York?"

"Not really. Actually, Connecticut. More recently Reno."

"Oh really," Kay said blankly, wondering why she had not guessed, uncertain as she always was when confronted by someone newly divorced, never knowing whether to offer congratulations or sympathy.

"A week ago today," Chris Kemble said, a defensive edge in her voice. "I'm sure to tell you sooner or later—there's really no secret about it—so let's bury the past right now and have done with it. Until seven days ago, just about now—" She glanced at her watch, continuing with a flamboyantly theatrical air, "I was—if you can believe what you read in *Time*—the queen bee of the Westport hive, the consort of the reigning king of Madison Avenue, the wife of the fabulously successful James Stuart Kemble." Her voice collapsed at a peak of brassy irony, obviously because Kay had been unable to hide an expression of recognition. "Oh, God, don't tell me that you know him?"

"Not really," she said hurriedly, embarrassed by transparency. "I've heard Judd mention his name, that's all."

"Judd's your husband?"

"Yes."

"He's in advertising?" Chris Kemble asked, immediately answering herself. "I knew it. From the very beginning—I'd have spoken to you before if I hadn't had this feeling that it was sure to be one of those isn't-it-a-small-world things. He's with a company?"

"Yes."

"Don't tell me that it's one of Jim's clients?"

"No, they're with the Coleman agency."

"At least you're not Madison Avenue and Connecticut."

"No," Kay said, evading revelation with a quick change of subject. "How long were you married?"

"Twenty-two years."

Kay blinked.

"That shocks you."

"Just a coincidence, that's all."

"You, too?" Chris guessed. A smile twisted her lips. "Now I'll tell you something really silly. Do you know what I thought—about you, I mean? I was certain that you were divorced, too. I don't know why, unless it was the way you—no, what it really was, I'm sure, was the hope that you might be someone who would tell me that I've not been the fool that everyone thinks me." She gulped at her drink. "Do you mind terribly—my talking about it for a minute or two?"

"Not at all," Kay said, startled, yet oddly gratified by this unusual experience of finding herself chosen as a confidante. Other women occasionally came to her to be told something they did not know, more often to ask her to do something that they were incapable of doing themselves, but almost never to share their innermost lives.

"Cigarette?"

"No, thank you," Kay said, watching as Chris Kemble snapped a light to her own, jangling the coppery bracelet on her wrist, catching a first deep puff.

"I was all right until today," Chris said. "And then I ran out of courage. It does take that, you know. I wanted so terribly to be free —but free for what? There's an answer, I'm sure there is. There has to be. But you can't help thinking about it."

"No, of course you can't," Kay agreed, sipping her drink, studying Chris Kemble's face over the rim of her glass, wondering what it would be like to be suddenly free, sheltering a guilty awareness that it was not an entirely new thought.

"Oh, I should have made the break years ago," Chris Kemble said. "But you keep hoping. Trying. And God knows, I did try. I even went to a psychiatrist. All I got was a lot of lip-licking talk about a happy sex life." She injected a bitter little laugh. "All that sex was to Jim these last few years was a substitute for counting sheep. I'd had enough of being taken for a sleeping pill."

Kay forced a smile, a quick cover for embarrassment, repelled as she always was by this kind of talk, yet restrained from a totally unfavorable judgment of Chris Kemble by the feeling that this brassy boldness was a surface manifestation, a hard façade behind which a much softer woman was almost certainly hiding.

"Oh, I don't know, maybe I could have been a better wife—I was never the jolly little concubine. I'm just not the type. But, no, that wasn't it. If it had been, he'd have taken up with another woman. Oh, I don't mean that he didn't have his little romps, of course he did. But they were pills, too—tranquilizers. There was never anyone who meant anything to him. I almost wish there had been. It would have been so much easier that way. That's what made it so awful, really. If there'd only been a reason, something to pin it on, anything. But there wasn't. At least anything that made any sense to anyone but me. And least of all to Jim. Do you know what he said when I told him I wanted a divorce? He said—oh God, I can still hear him—"Now, now, dear, just simmer down, this is something that happens to all women about your age—we know all about it, we just did this market survey for Medford Drug—this wonderful new product that they're bringing out—*Menocalm*—"

"Oh, no!"

"I mean it. He really did. That's when I knew that it was hopeless, absolutely and completely and totally hopeless. Up until then, I'd always been able to invent some excuse for not going through with it. For a long time it was Barbara."

"Your daughter?" Kay asked, brushing aside an irrelevant thought of Rolfe.

Chris Kemble closed her eyes, nodding. "She had to go to Bennington, of course—daughter of the fabulously creative James Stuart Kemble—she simply *had* to be artistic. So it was off to Bennington in her brand new Mercedes 300SL—Jim was trying to get the Mercedes account for Kemble International—" She bit her lip. "But she never got there."

Kay choked back a gasp, visualizing a tragic accident.

"When we finally found her—it was weeks and weeks—she was in San Francisco, living in this horrible place with this awful boy—" She blinked as if trying to clear the glaze of dried tears. "After that, I couldn't go on pretending that there was anything I could do for her—'All I want, Mother, is to live my own life in my own way.' So that was that."

"What are your plans now?"

"Paris first. After that—" She shrugged it off.

"You've been abroad before, I'm sure."

"Oh yes. Twice this last year. Kemble International—that's Jim's new world to conquer. And you do it according to schedule, of course. Nine o'clock breakfast with branch staff—be sure to get all their names right. Ten-ten—visit office—remember to speak to all the little people. Ten-forty—visit factory of prospective client—don't forget you met Mr. Whoozis at your cocktail party last night. Eleven-thirty—"

"It sounds a little ghastly," Kay interjected, smiling.

"More than a little. Horrible. The last time we were in Paris—three days, three big luncheons, three dinner parties. All for prospective clients, of course. Oh, but it was all very worthwhile—three new accounts—two million dollars' worth of new billings—three more years and Kemble International will be the biggest agency on the Continent."

"You traveled a lot with your husband?"

"Only this last year. I thought—well, if the agency is the only thing that means anything to him—all right, I can't lick it, I'll join it. So I started going along."

"But it didn't work?"

"Oh, it worked wonderfully," Chris said sardonically. "Before the plane was off the ground, he was treating me like an old employee —the twenty-year veteran—you know, the old battle-axe secretary that you have to sleep with every now and then, just to keep her morale up."

Kay squeezed a nervous laugh from a guarded smile, still uncertain of what sort of woman might be hiding behind Chris Kemble's overstressed façade.

"Oh, it was much too late, I knew that," Chris went on. "But I couldn't make myself accept it. I kept saying this isn't the man I married, this isn't the real Jim Kemble. This is all a front, all an act that he's putting on. And for a while it was, I'm sure it was. We used to laugh about the three-name business—James Stuart Kemble. But then one night I heard him answer the telephone that way. I should have known then that he'd never go back to being Jim Kemble again."

"And who *was* Jim Kemble?" Kay asked with forced lightness.

Chris looked at her and through her. "I know what you're prob-ably thinking—that there never was such a person, that Jim Kemble was just someone that I'd dreamed into being. And it does seem that way sometimes. But it isn't true. He did exist. And I can prove it. I still have some of his short stories—half of his novel."

"He was going to be a writer?"

"He *was* a writer. He'd sold two stories to *Cosmopolitan,* one to the *Post.* He had a contract for his novel—" She broke off, catching a quick breath, proclaiming the recapture of self-control with a dis-missing smile. "Oh, I know I'm not the first woman who fell in love with one man and woke up married to someone else. But it's so terribly unfair. You don't marry just a man, you marry a way of life. Or at least I did. I don't mean that I didn't love him. I loved him more than—well, I just did, that's all. But as much as I loved him, as much as I wanted to spend the rest of my life with him—if he'd told me that night that he asked me to marry him that it was going to mean Westport and a Rolls-Royce, a dinner party every night of the week, never a weekend without—love him or not, I'd have started running right then. Do you know the kind of life we'd planned?"

"I can guess," Kay said, hoping after she heard herself say it that it was not revelatory.

Chris closed her eyes. "The day the war was over, the minute he got out of the Navy—my family had this place in Maine, an old house up the coast from Rockport—that's where we were going to live. Money wouldn't have been any problem. Even if the novel hadn't been a success, there would have been enough. We didn't need a lot. We'd talked about that, over and over again."

"But you never got to Maine," Kay suggested, sure of her ground, the parallel with her own life too clear to be missed, yet what struck her was not a feeling of strange coincidence but rather an impres-sion of universality, a sensing of justification.

"No, we never got to Maine," Chris repeated, her voice suddenly detached, freed of emotion, clearing a view that supported Kay's impression that Chris Kemble deserved sympathy and understand-ing.

"Jim got into Navy public relations," Chris went on in that same faraway voice. "At the time it seemed such a wonderful break—I could go to Washington to be with him, and at least he'd be writing something, even if it wasn't what he wanted to write. But it didn't work out that way. Instead of Washington, it was London—we had five weeks together, that's all. And he didn't write a thing all during the war—except, of course, guest lists and menus. Oh, it was my fault in a way, I suppose—one of those silly things that seem so clever at the time, but that you go on regretting for the rest of your life. But Jim was trying so hard to get a commission, and he wanted it to be the Navy—well, Father had been doing a lot of business with the Navy, and he'd known Admiral Dandridge for years, so I talked him into having Dandy out for the weekend. He was simply mad about pheasant shooting and we knew some people that had this private preserve. Of course, I got Jim invited too, and before the weekend was over—I'm sure you can guess what happened from what I've already said. If Jim sets his mind to it, he can charm anyone. That's how he got his commission, and that's how he wound up as Dandy's aide. It was supposed to be public relations, but all he did, really, was arrange the admiral's parties. Oh, it was legitimate enough, perhaps even important—it was Dandy's job, you see, to maintain liaison with all of the people the Navy was working with over there. How he ever picked Jim for the job I have no idea—he was still a meat-and-potatoes boy from Michigan, didn't like French cooking because everything had *gravy* on it——"

A too-quick "I know what you mean" inadvertently slipped out.

"But when Jim puts his mind to something, there's nothing he can't do, really—that's always been one of his troubles—so, naturally he made a terrific success of it. And of course he got to know everybody, simply everybody. And one of them was Skip Kingsley—the tobacco Kingsleys, you know?"

"I've heard of them," Kay said, cautiously refraining from saying that she had lived in the same house with Ann Kingsley at Bryn Mawr.

"Skip had always been the ne'er-do-well son," Chris went on. "Or at least that's what everyone thought—the yachting crowd, Bermuda races, all that—but his father died just before the war was over, and the day Skip got out he was made president of the company. Well, Jim got out too, of course—oh, God, I'll never forget that day, meeting him in Boston—the Navy Yard, that's where his ship docked. I had everything ready to go to Maine. I'd been up there off and on all summer, getting the house in shape. I'd taken the back bedroom, the one that overlooked the cove—all his books, all his reference material, his typewriter—that was to be my coming-home surprise." She closed her eyes. "But his surprise came first. We had to go to New York. He had a date with Skip. The cigarette company was taking on a new advertising agency and Skip wanted Jim to sit in on the presentation. It was only going to be a week—" She spread her hands, loosing a sigh. "But the week turned into a month, and a month into a year, and then it was too late."

"He went with the agency that got the account?"

"Of course. That was part of the deal. Skip insisted on it. Jim made almost twenty thousand that first year. That doesn't sound like much now, but back in those days—I don't think he'd ever made more than a hundred a week on the paper, I'm sure he hadn't. Anyway, once he started seeing that kind of money—well, he was just hooked, that's all. It was like dope—money, money, money—more, more, more. I kept saying why, why, why? and he kept saying —Oh, why go on. I'm sure you understand."

Kay nodded, but with considerably less certainty than she had felt before. The illusion of parallelism that had carried her along, so vivid that she had been visualizing James Stuart Kemble almost as Judd's blood brother, had been shattered by this revelation. Money-making had never been Judd's concern, at least not for himself—but was money-madness any worse than company-madness? And in the end wasn't it almost the same thing?

"So that's how the brave young eagle gave up the wild blue yonder," Chris said with a toss of her head, continuing in a fairy-tale voice, "and became the silly goose who never gives up hunting for another golden egg."

Kay's smile was no more than appreciative. "I don't suppose he ever looked at his novel again?"

"Once," Chris said, abruptly crisp. "Three years ago. It was right after the agency had gone public. Jim had sold off a lot of his stock, so we had all this money, far more than we could ever use up, no matter how long we lived—oh, it was a silly thing to do, I know that, but we were alone at home that night, the first time in weeks, and I dug out the old novel. I didn't mean it seriously, really I didn't. I knew he'd never go back to it, but I still thought then there was a chance he might get interested again in *something* besides money. Do you know what he said?" She closed her eyes, an expression of total despair. "He said, 'Chris, why the devil are you always trying to embarrass me by reminding me what a naïve kid I was?' He even tried to take it away from me and throw it in the fire. And then he said, 'Aren't you ever going to get over the ridiculous idea that writing a book means anything? The woods are full of guys who have written books. They come into our employment office every day. You can hire as many of them as you want for two hundred a week.'"

"So that was that," Kay observed.

"Yes, that was that," Chris sighed. "That's his only standard of judgment—money. I remember once—more than once, really, he does it all the time—but I'd met this quite attractive woman, someone I thought might be interesting to have over sometime, so I asked Jim what kind of a man her husband was. And do you know what he said? He said, 'Oh, about thirty thousand, I'd say—at the outside, fifty.'"

"Oh, not really," Kay exclaimed, laughing in spite of herself.

"I laughed too," Chris admitted. "And the awful thing was that he couldn't see what was wrong." She rose abruptly. "Here, let me have your drink."

Despite instant resistance, even an automatically voiced protest, Kay Wilder surrendered her glass.

« 6 »

Lying flat on his back, Judd Wilder stared up at the grid of flame-colored light that the setting sun was casting on the ceiling, a fire glow black-barred by the Venetian blind. As he watched, the light slowly faded, a stage effect controlled by a dimmer, down to a cherry red and then snapped off. As if cued, the click of a switch broke the blackout stillness, a pool of light instantly setting a new scene, drawing his eyes to the window corner where Mrs. Cope was opening her knitting bag.

He had, until now, been no more than half conscious of her presence, knowing that she was in the room, yet with no loss of that pleasant sense of protected isolation that had come when, with the change of shift at three o'clock, Mrs. Cope had taken over from Miss

Harsch. His relief at her arrival had been so pronounced that he had wished there was some way to express his gratification, but it had been a difficult thing to put into words, all the more so because there was an inexplicable conflict between his desire to be let alone and the deep-seated pleasure that he had found in the way that Mrs. Cope had instantly sensed that he was starting to get jumpy, bathing him with no silly false modesty, then strong-handedly kneading the muscle knots out of his back and buttocks. When his dinner tray had come, his reaction to the first spoonful of the thickly gelatinous and completely flavorless mess that had been sent up from the kitchen had caused Mrs. Cope to taste it herself. Then, with a snort of disgust, she had disappeared, coming back twenty minutes later with a rich beef-tasting soup that she had gone down and made herself, somehow knowing that it was the only thing he could possibly have eaten with any appetite.

Watching her now as she took out her knitting, he was reminded again of Mrs. Gorman, remembering those winter nights when he would go out into the kitchen, excusing his intrusion by claiming that it was too cold to do his homework in the dining room. Sometimes they would talk, but never unless he started it. More often than not they would sit in silence, he working on his math or writing a theme, Mrs. Gorman mending and darning, never a word unless it was to remind him that there was a spice cake in the cupboard or lemon pie in the punched-tin box that his Grandfather Judd had brought home from Mexico.

Now, abruptly aware of footsteps in the corridor, he heard the Indian-accented voice of the young doctor who had been with him on the ambulance. Mrs. Cope heard it too, alert for a listening moment. But the footsteps faded away, leaving only the memory of Dr. Raggi's promise that Dr. Kharr would stop by before he went home to dinner.

"I guess Dr. Kharr isn't going to make it," he said.

"Anything worrying you?" Mrs. Cope asked, eyebrows up. "I can call him."

"No. I was just wondering about him, that's all," he said, thinking of what she had told him earlier about Dr. Kharr, all the research work that he had done, all the papers he had published in medical journals. "Why would a doctor with all that going for him wind up in a little hospital like this?"

"We're just lucky to have him," Mrs. Cope said, pointedly preoccupied with needles and yarn. "He'll probably stop in after a while. He comes back almost every evening. I don't know how he stands it, the hours he puts in. I guess he'd rather be here than sitting in his room."

"Doesn't he have a family?"

"No, he's a bachelor. Lives over at Mrs. Stine's."

"Oh," he said, and then aimlessly: "There aren't many Jews around here, are there?"

The knitting needles stopped. "Is that bothering you?"

"No," he said, startled by the sharpness of her question. "Why should it?"

"It shouldn't. But with some people it does."

He started to reply, but did not, put off first by the oddly intense quality of her voice, then by the often experienced difficulty of proving his freedom from prejudice, never able to say that he had worked all his life with Jews—there were as many in the carpet business as there had been in motion pictures and the theater—without making it sound as if he was using that old "some of my best friends" cliché. The thought crossed his mind that Mrs. Cope, too, might be a Jew, but if so it meant no more than something to be avoided in the same way that he had always refrained from saying anything about Catholics when Mrs. Gorman was around.

As a calculated change of subject he asked, "What are you making?" recalling the khaki sweater that Mrs. Gorman had knitted as a present for his twelfth birthday, the day that he joined the Boy Scouts.

"Oh, just a cardigan for one of my sister's girls," Mrs. Cope said, flipping out the half-made sweater, arranging it on her lap. "You have a son, don't you, Mr. Wilder?"

"Yes. He's in Paris now."

"I guess that's why your wife's going over."

"No, not really," he said, denying his own conviction, voicing the explanation that Kay had given him. "She has this old aunt living in Paris. Her seventy-fourth birthday is coming up so Kay thought she ought to be there."

"Your wife French?"

"No, but she lived there as a girl, with this aunt of hers."

"I guess that's where you met her, over there?"

"No, she came home to Philadelphia when the war broke out. This is the first time she's been back."

The knitting needles were clicking again. "How old is your boy, Mr. Wilder?"

"Twenty-one."

"Then he was born during the war."

"Yes, when I was overseas," he said, his mind slipping into the groove that had been cut this afternoon by Dr. Raggi talking about India, the shadowed room suddenly transformed into the corrugated iron shed that had been the Signal Corps headquarters, night-black when he first came in out of the blazing sunlight. For a moment, he had been unable to read the gray-penciled message that the radio operator had picked up from Calcutta, all but unbelieving when he finally had. It was three weeks before the date Kay had given him, a too-early confrontation with a reality for which he had only begun to prepare himself. Kay had waited two months before she had written him that she was pregnant, another month gone before the letter had caught up with him, leaving him torn then by the ambiguity of her 'Don't worry, dear, I'll take care of everything.' He had imagined her in the hands of some back-alley abortionist, a nightmare unrelieved by two vague letters, then sustained for more long weeks by the failure of any mail to get through. Eventually, he had learned the relieving truth that she would have her baby, but by then it had all come to seem so far away, so remote and disassociated, that it was difficult to think of himself as a married man, let alone the father of a newborn son.

"He was two years old before I saw him," he said, barely hearing Mrs. Cope's reply that it was something that happened to a lot of wartime fathers, already lost in a memory kept alive by frequent resurrection. He often recalled that first time he had seen his son, the look of fear in those baby eyes, the cry of alarm when he reached out to him, the child's frightened escape to his mother's arms. "He'll soon get to know you," Kay had said. And he had, of course, but never in quite the way it might have been. He had often heard other fathers talk about the problem of understanding their sons, knowing only too well what they meant, yet rarely feeling common ground, convinced that his own difficulty traced to those unrecoverable years when Kay had preempted a parental relationship that, by the time he got home, was too firmly fixed to be invaded by a stranger.

"I guess a lot of boys are doing that these days," Mrs. Cope said. "Taking a year abroad before they graduate."

"This is postgraduate," he said. "He got his B.A. last spring. He's working on his master's now."

"Must be a smart boy."

"Yes, he has a good mind," he said, agreement limited by habitual reservation, doubting that Rolfe, bright though he was, had been the child prodigy that Kay had come to imagine him. It was not unusual, he knew, for a mother to think her son a genius, but there had been something disturbingly strange about the way Kay had so suddenly picked up that fixation. It had started, of course, with Dr. Loftberry, the headmaster at Sedgefield Day, the private school where they had sent Rolfe after they moved to Connecticut. The tuition was ridiculously high, an extravagance that demanded continual justification, and he had been certain that Loftberry's pitch about Rolfe being an unusually gifted child was no more than a hard sell to hang on to a paying customer. Kay, however, had fallen for it completely, a reaction all the stranger because she had, up to then, shown no signs of being a too-doting mother. There had, in fact, been times when he had thought her guilty of neglect, so wrapped up in all of her activities that Rolfe was treated almost as a burdensome responsibility, accepted, but never without the evident consciousness that, without him, she would have had more time to spend on things that interested her more. All that had changed with startling abruptness. From then on, Rolfe had become her major project, superseding the campaign to restore the Sedgefield Opera House, the interest to which she had turned when the move to Connecticut had broken her connection with the New York group that was trying to raise the supporting endowment for a repertory theater in the Village.

By the time he had taken the Crouch Carpet job, Kay was firmly fixed in her new orbit. On her first inspection trip to New Ulster she had no more than walked through the house that he had rented, shrugging off its shortcomings, but she had spent a whole day at the public school, agonizing over the lack of any special provision for gifted children, then assuming for herself the responsibility of making up for its shortcomings, becoming Rolfe's tutor, zealously throwing herself into an unremitting drive to enhance his education.

Later, he had often regretted that he had not protested more forcibly, and he might have done so, he told himself, had he not been so tied up those first few years with Crouch Carpet. When he had finally reached the point of open apprehension about Rolfe becoming an owl-eyed grind with an unhealthy lack of interest in anything but books, the situation had seemed beyond retrieval. Often, finding mother and son with their heads together over a table-ful of books, he had felt himself as much the excluded stranger as he had on that day when he got home after his discharge from the Signal Corps.

He had hopefully anticipated that the apron strings might loosen when his son went away to college, a belief encouraged when Rolfe unexpectedly chose Colfax over his mother's strong advocacy of Princeton. Although Rolfe had never actually said that he had picked Colfax because it was his father's college, there had been that heartening implication. The Saturday morning when they had driven up together to look over the campus—Rolfe had suggested it on a day when his mother was in Philadelphia—had been one of those rare occasions when Judd Wilder had felt himself reasonably close to his son. But that small gain had been quickly offset by the vigor with which Kay, overriding one defeat, had thrown herself into a new campaign to maintain her son's dependence. Until Rolfe entered Colfax, Judd had taken no part in alumni affairs, but with Kay's prodding they had gone up for Homecoming Day, attending all of the alumni meetings, and before the weekend was over she had snagged an appointment for herself as a member of the Aux-iliary Committee in charge of redecorating Hanscomb Hall. There-after, she had an unchallengeable excuse to drive up to Colfax at least once a week.

Rolfe, seeing his mother as often as he did, rarely wrote letters. Between vacations, all that Judd heard from him was through Kay, and what little she told him was limited by the preamble that Colfax today was a long way from the little freshwater college that he had attended, suggesting a lack of understanding on his part that be-came embarrassingly valid when, upon occasion, he found himself exposed to some of the work that Rolfe was taking. Admittedly, Kay understood more than he did, her secret undisclosed until, rummag-ing around for an old briefcase that he wanted to take along on a

West Coast promotion trip, he stumbled on her cache of books, duplicate copies of every text that Rolfe was using.

Judd Wilder's one major victory had been scored in the spring of Rolfe's junior year. That winter, the Professor of Marketing in Colfax's School of Business had asked him to come up to lecture on the use of theatrical techniques in modern merchandising. Although he had been badly jammed at the office—he was up to his neck in the spring promotion campaign—he had accepted, largely because it would give him a day with Rolfe. Actually, he had seen very little of him, but the lecture had been enthusiastically received by both students and faculty, and a few weeks later he had received notice that he had been selected as that year's recipient of the Hopkins Award.

Kay's appreciation had been limited by the reminder that the Awards Program had been inaugurated by the Development Office as an obvious bid for bigger contributions from alumni who were honored—he, too, had thought of that—but Rolfe was clearly impressed. Although Rolfe had never before shown the slightest interest in business—he was majoring in something called History of Science—he had sat through the whole day-long Management Seminar that had preceded the award banquet, and afterwards at the cocktail party he had stayed at his side, stubbornly resisting all of his mother's attempts to draw him away. That evening had encouraged Judd Wilder to consider asking Rolfe if he would like a summer job with Crouch Carpet, even concocting the argument that his understanding of History of Science would surely benefit from some firsthand observation of modern industrial technology. But before he could broach the subject, however, Kay came up with an opening for Rolfe on an archaeological expedition that was setting out to dig for traces of pre-Columbian Norse settlement on the Maine Coast. Everything had been arranged before she revealed that one of her distant relatives, Julia Lancey, whom Judd had never before heard her mention, had invited them to spend July and August at the Lancey cottage at Northeast Harbor. Judd could, she said, fly up for weekends and his vacation. Weekends had, of course, been out of the question, and his vacation had been cut short by the price war that had threatened when the cost of synthetic carpet yarn was unexpectedly slashed by all the producers.

Unexpectedly, Kay had come home from Northeast Harbor a week before Labor Day, alone, not with Rolfe as she had planned. Something had gone wrong, evidenced not only by the number of times that he caught an expression of unguarded bitterness on her face, but also, and even more strangely, by the way that she had thrown herself into his arms, demanding affection as if it were something that could be taken by assault. She had come to his bed that night, her forwardness strange enough to be strongly arousing, gratifying him with a fiercely physical desire that he had imagined long since dulled beyond revival. It was afterwards, lying there in the darkness, that he had learned that Rolfe had spent only two weekends at Northeast Harbor, both times with a crowd of friends that he had brought along, and that he had deserted Kay on the trip home in order to go around by Syracuse with a girl he had met on the dig —"some grubby little thing in a tight sweater and stretch pants."

"Anyway, I guess your wife will be glad to see him," Mrs. Cope said, simultaneously counting stitches.

"Oh, sure," he said, yawning, an overdone attempt to put the best possible face on a worrisome situation, the same pose that he had maintained when Kay had suggested that she ought to go to Paris for Miss Jessica's birthday. Transparently, it had been a blind. There must have been, he thought, a letter from Rolfe that she had not told him about, another declaration of independence, a climax of the breaking away that had begun in Maine. Nothing had come of the stretch-pants girl from Syracuse—Rolfe had afterwards been so vague about her that Judd had wondered if she had not been more excusing than enticing—but that incident had clearly been the beginning of a rebellion against maternal domination. Judd had welcomed it, hoping that Rolfe would turn more to him. Instead, he had turned away from both of them. They had seen less and less of him during his senior year at Colfax—he had spent his spring vacation on a trip to Florida—and when he won the fellowship that had taken him to Paris, all of his expenses paid by the research grant that Dr. Brook had obtained, their relationship had become even more remote. Money, it had then come to seem, had been Rolfe's only real parental tie, the break emphasized when he had summarily rejected his father's offer of a continuing allowance.

Dr. McClelland Brook had become Rolfe's idol, endlessly quoted, his exalted person the source of all guidance. Judd Wilder's strongly unfavorable reaction to the bearded Brook could hardly be acknowledged as jealousy—at least it was something of an entirely different order than Kay's disturbance—yet, if only as a sharing of the bitterness of rejection, it had helped him to understand Kay's attitude. He had been unable, however, to translate that understanding into a closer relationship. From the beginning, even in the first days of their marriage, Kay had prohibited trespass upon her innermost thoughts, and her continued self-containment had so buttressed the wall between them that he had abandoned any real hope of ever being able to break it down. He had wanted to talk her out of the Paris trip, compassionately aware that she would surely be badly hurt if she tried to keep her hold on Rolfe, but he knew her well enough to realize that objection, instead of dissuading her, would almost certainly have the opposite effect. Nevertheless, he had hoped until the very last that she would change her mind and cancel her sailing.

"What's your son studying?" Mrs. Cope asked. "What's he going to be?"

"Darned if I know," he replied, shrugging to lighten the weight of his concern, hearing her question as a paraphrase of the one he had asked Rolfe, getting no reply beyond a quoting of Dr. Brook's pronouncement that the pursuit of knowledge was an end sufficient unto itself. "He's majoring in something they call History of Science. It's not actually history. It's more—well, philosophy, really—the philosophic background that brought on the scientific age. One of his professors at Colfax got a grant to study the seventeenth-century period in France, so now Rolfe's working on that for his master's."

"I suppose he'll teach, then," Mrs. Cope said. "That's what happens to most of them—the smart ones, I mean, the ones that don't seem to fit into anything else. And it's not too bad a life, I guess. This hospital where I worked when I was out on the Coast was right close to UCLA, so every now and then we'd get some of their people. There was this one old professor. I'll never forget him. There wasn't one blessed thing that man said that anybody could understand—I mean somebody like me with no more education than I've got—so the trouble was, I could never figure out when he was out of his head and when he wasn't. Either way, nothing made any sense."

Judd smiled appreciatively, encouraging her to go on.

"But you know it was a funny thing about that old man. Here he was, seventy-some years old, almost eighty, and he'd never done one blessed thing in his whole life but study this one writer—oh, what was his name now? I ought to remember, goodness knows I heard it often enough, on the case almost six weeks. Anyway, he was back there about Shakespeare's time. The only thing he ever wrote was this one little book—anyway, that's all anybody's ever found out about—but here he was, this old professor, spending his whole life studying him. That's all in the world he'd ever done, not one other blessed thing. But you know it's funny, a lot of old people come down to the spot he was in, and they're full of regrets for the way they've lived their lives. But not him. He was just about as satisfied a human being as you'll ever find anywhere."

"I can believe it," he agreed, thinking of old Dr. Coggle at Colfax, still teaching History of Drama, still worshipping Racine as the greatest playwright of all time, blind to everything that had happened in the theater over the past two hundred and fifty years.

"Maybe that's the way to be happy," Mrs. Cope observed. "You find yourself some little niche somewhere that's all your own, nobody else trying to crowd in on you, so you just hole up and stay there."

"But what do you ever accomplish?"

"How much do most of us accomplish?" she asked tartly. "It's like this knitting. Knit, knit, knit—and what's it mean? All I get out of it is 'Oh, thank you, Aunt Mabel' and then it goes right down in the bottom of a drawer and there it stays."

"Oh, I don't believe that," he said with a placating smile.

"It's true," Mrs. Cope said tersely. "But I still go on knitting. Why?"

"Busywork," he suggested.

"Umhumm," she agreed, pausing to pick up a dropped stitch. "But isn't that what most of us fill our lives with—just a lot of busy-work? It's rush, rush, rush—we got to do this, we got to do that, we got to go here, we got to go there—*why?*"

A too-emphatic gesture flipped her knitting, displacing the ball of yarn in her lap. It bounded to the floor and rolled under the bed, a distraction that kept both of them from hearing the door open. Mrs. Cope was still down on one knee when, suddenly glancing up, her face froze in an expression of shock, quickly colored by a flush of embarrassment as she hurriedly got to her feet with an out-of-breath "Good evening, Doctor."

Judd did not immediately recognize that the man standing in the doorway was Dr. Kharr. Without his white coat, he seemed a quite different person, not only in appearance but in voice and manner as well, yet it was not until after his light exchange with Mrs. Cope, that it began to seem a calculated informality, his claim that he had only stopped in to say hello on his way back to his office after dinner too plainly an attempt to make this appear a social occasion rather than a medical call. His smile, a shade too firmly fixed, was unmistakably the expression of a man for whom easy camaraderie had always been an elusive goal, unattainable because he could never restrain himself from pressing a bit too hard, always adding that extra little push that Judd now felt as he heard him say, "I understand, Mr. Wilder, that you were around my old stamping ground during the war."

"Where's that?"

"Astoria. Or am I jumping to a conclusion? I heard you were in the motion picture end of the Signal Corps so—I thought you might have been at Astoria."

"Yes, I was there for a while," he said, a cautious admission, certain now that this was a buildup to something unrevealed.

"That's where I grew up, right near the studio," Dr. Kharr went on. "Do you remember the subway station, the downtown entrance? That's where my father had his office, in the building just behind it. There was a drugstore on the first floor—?"

"It's been a long time," he excused himself.

"No, of course you wouldn't remember something like that," Dr. Kharr granted. "But that was a wonderful neighborhood when I was a boy. It was a Paramount studio then, you know, before the Army took it over. All the kids would hang around, waiting for some big star to come or go. And a lot of the big ones did make pictures out there, Adolphe Menjou and—oh, I don't remember all their names. My brother could tell you, he was a great fan—had all their autographs. But I'll never forget Adolphe Menjou. Do you remember him?"

"Of course."

"I saw him once—a rather amusing incident. Father wasn't the regular studio doctor, but his office was so close by that they'd sometimes call him for an emergency. On this particular afternoon I was in his office—I always went there the moment I got out of school—and this call came from the studio. There'd been an accident, something terrible had happened to Mr. Menjou, so my father went flying off, and with me right at his heels, of course. This was too good a chance to miss, to get right inside the studio. And sure enough, I managed to slip in—thanks to my father, who was understanding enough to let me carry one of his bags. So there was the great Mr. Menjou lying on a cot, gasping for breath, choking. You see, they'd been using some sort of smoke effect——"

"And the poor guy had got a lungful of the stuff," Judd supplied, instantly visualizing the scene, recalling that madhouse day when they had been shooting *They Also Serve*, the battlefield scene that Huck had tried to do indoors, everything fouled up by a prop man who had dumped in too much hydrochloric acid, filling the studio with a choking smudge that had driven everyone out into the street.

"Actually, it wasn't at all what it seemed," Dr. Kharr went on. "What had really happened—this was always one of Father's prize stories—there'd been something that Mr. Menjou didn't want to do, some lines that he didn't want to speak——"

"And the minute they changed the script his lungs cleared right up," Judd put in, again a response to memory, almost at the point of offering a matching anecdote about Edmund Gwenn when he was stopped by a resurrection of caution. But his mind was filled now with crowding recollections of the old Astoria studio, and when Dr. Kharr asked, "How long were you there?" he quickly answered, "Not quite a year—April to March," feeling no restraint as he added, "But it was a great experience."

"It must have been," Dr. Kharr said. "You were just out of college?"

"Yes, they'd let us graduate early, all of us who went into service," he said, remembering those weeks after Pearl Harbor, impatiently waiting for his commission to come through. He had been working for WMBG almost on a full-time basis that last year at Colfax, and the owner of the station, Miles Brinker, had promised to get him a Navy commission. Brinker had claimed as one of his innumerable "good friends" a former network vice president who, so he said, was in charge of producing all radio propaganda shows for the Navy. Judd was exactly the kind of radio director that they were looking for, Brinker had said, and it was only a matter of pulling the right strings to get him at least a lieutenant commander's stripe and a half. Although there had been reason enough to suspect Brinker's honesty, tainted as everything he did was by an obsessive showoff complex, Judd had nevertheless believed that the Navy might really want him, an illusion supported by his having recently won a citation for the Atlantic Charter show that he had written and directed for WMBG, cited as "The Best Locally Produced Contribution to National Preparedness by a Class C Radio Station."

The bubble had burst when, fanning through *Variety*, he had discovered a little item about the man whom Brinker claimed he had been calling in Washington every few days for the last month. According to *Variety* his good friend had been transferred to London six weeks before. Confronted, Brinker had crumbled, making only a weak attempt to bluff it through, all but admitting that he had been lying in order to keep him on at the station—working, of course, for half the salary that anyone else would have been paid.

"You must have had a little luck, getting into the motion picture end," Dr. Kharr suggested, hurriedly adding, "Yes, I know you'd had some theatrical background, but still—a lot of men had a hard time landing in the right spot. My brother worked his heart out trying to get into Army public relations, and wound up writing meat orders in the Quartermaster's Department."

"Yes, I got a break or two," he said, a reserved admission, unable to credit luck for what had been his own doing. Again in *Variety*— he had read nothing so faithfully those last two years at Colfax—he had learned that the Signal Corps was recruiting Hollywood personnel to set up an organization for the production of training films. One of the directors mentioned was Norman Joyce, winner of two Academy Awards, three all-star wives, and the hero of endless fanmagazine tales about his international roistering, a truly fabulous character. Judd had met him only a few weeks before at one of Miss Jessica's Sunday salons. Brief though their conversation had been— there had not even been a chance to mention Floyd Fulton—that one chance encounter gave him excuse enough to write Joyce a letter, making it sound as personal as he dared, yet afraid to go so far as to address him as "Huck," the name that he knew was used by all of his friends.

He got no direct answer, but a week or so later he had received an application blank from the Signal Corps. In desperation—his draft number was sure to come up in the next week or two—he bought a bus ticket to Washington, trying to get through to the colonel who had signed the note that had accompanied the application blank. He never located him, but in the course of his search he encountered Ronnie Chadreau from Philadelphia, one of the extra-man bachelors who, as a loyal courtier of Nellie Potter Tyler, had been a constant hanger-on at the Orangerie, where Judd had spent the previous summer as an assistant director under Nicholas Kodansky. As a newly commissioned major, Ronnie was apparently in charge of recruiting theatrically experienced personnel. At first, Judd had felt himself seriously set back, his fate in the hands of a man whom he had avoided, shunned, and, on more than one occasion that past summer, openly insulted. To his astonishment, Ronnie greeted him with twittering delight, proclaiming to everyone within earshot that here was the young genius who had actually directed the Orangerie productions for which Nicholas Kodansky, the old faker, had been given public credit. For the first time since his Labor Day escape from Nellie Potter Tyler's domain, Judd had felt his summer had not been completely wasted.

Nellie Potter Tyler, as the most openhanded of Colfax College's rich patrons, had not only provided the funds that had built the Workshop Theater—officially it was the George P. Tyler Memorial Workshop Theater—but also, as an unrelenting theater buff, she supported the Orangerie. The name derived from its quarters, the great glassed wing that had been built by George P. Tyler as an addition to his Main Line mansion in order to celebrate one of his more spectacular financial coups. After his death, Mrs. Tyler had converted it to a summer theater. It was never called that—always the Orangerie, never the Orangerie Theater—a reflection of her eccentric delight in pretending that her little "divertissements" were not the elaborate productions that they so obviously were. At least publicly, she maintained the illusion that they were something spontaneously created by her coterie of extraordinarily talented friends who, quite by chance, happened to find themselves together on a stage set designed by a top New York scenic artist, reciting lines miraculously learned without study or rehearsal, supported by a pit orchestra drawn from the Philadelphia Symphony—which, by no means incidentally, was always a substantial beneficiary of Nellie Potter Tyler's largesse.

Judd had never actually seen an Orangerie production—after both his freshman and sophomore years he had gone home to Iowa for the summer—but what he had heard about the Orangerie had made it seem a rich woman's plaything, and when, after his direction of *Tamerlane* at the Workshop, he had been offered a summer job as an assistant director, he had hesitated before accepting, deciding to take it only after learning that it meant a chance to work under Nicholas Kodansky, originator of the Kodansky Approach and the current idol of all of the dramatic critics who supported the New Theater movement.

Before the end of his first week at the Orangerie, he had discovered that Kodansky's talent was almost totally verbal, his effervescent talk foaming up a sparkling head of frothy theory, masking his shocking inability to put any of it into practice. Kodansky's rehearsals were shambles, his directions to actors madly incoherent, his conception of a scene completely unrelated to the reality of performance. If he was in any way aware of his incompetence he never acknowledged it. At the point of crisis—this had happened on Judd's second day—Kodansky would wave his hand in a magnificently regal gesture, utter a lightly imperious "Carry on, my good fellow," and vanish from the stage. Judd, although secretly frightened—he had never before directed professional actors—had taken Kodansky literally. Thus, he quickly became the real director of the Orangerie. But the credit was never his, always Kodansky's. All through the summer, even the actors and actresses who stayed on week after week to support the visiting stars, continued to treat him not as their director but as Kodansky's interpreter, crediting him only with some special ability to translate the gibberish of genius into intelligible stage directions. When they asked questions it was never "What do you want?" but always "What does he want?" Until that day in Washington when he had run into Ronnie Chadreau, he had never known that anyone else was aware of what a phony Nicholas Kodansky really was—anyone else, that is, except Kay Cannon.

The first time he had noticed Kay, at least as an individual set apart from the hangers-on who were always lurking in the shadows, had been on the first walk-through day for the Orangerie's second production. Kodansky had disappeared after a particularly wild and incoherent interpretation of the play's significance, and Judd had only started to get the rehearsal going again when, glancing toward the wings, he had seen this girl watching him, her expression one of suppressed amusement, her eyes so coolly knowing that he found it difficult to keep up the bluff that all he was doing was translating Kodanskyese into intelligible English. Obviously, she knew what was going on, and fearing that she might cause trouble—Kodansky, for all his madness, was a cannily ruthless protector of his reputation—he had resolved that tomorrow he would exclude all visitors from rehearsal.

Kay Cannon had proved unexcludable. She was serving that summer as a secretary to Nellie Potter Tyler. Her principal duty, it seemed, was that of judging the social acceptability of applicants for tickets to Orangerie productions, but he soon learned that she was, as well, the best of all emissaries when Nellie Potter Tyler's pocketbook had to be tapped to cover a production-cost overrun. And since Kodansky's budgets were as wildly unrealistic as everything else he did, Judd found himself continually forced to turn to Miss Cannon. Although he tried to maintain the pretense that he was acting only to protect Kodansky from mundane affairs that might interfere with the exercise of genius, she was not fooled. Pleased though he was by her recognition that he was the Orangerie's real director, he nevertheless remained strongly resistant to any threat of a more personal relationship, his guard never higher than when she asked him, as she so persistently did, about what he planned to do after he got out of Colfax. He had by then seen enough of Nellie Potter Tyler to know that he wanted no future entanglements with rich society women, young or old, who had a perverted taste for artistic patronage. Even if Kay had not been Bryn Mawrish, so obviously Old Philadelphia, he would have been put off by seeing her hanging around with the likes of Ronnie Chadreau, always talking about things he did not understand, their English hardly more intelligible than the French in which they so frequently conversed.

When on the last day of the season he had found a note from Nellie Potter Tyler in his mailbox, he had spent a bad half-hour fighting off the temptation to return the hundred-dollar bonus check that was enclosed, knowing well enough that Kay had inspired it. He finally decided to keep it, convincing himself that he had surely earned it, that he really needed it to get through his last year at Colfax, and certain that he would never again see Kay Cannon. As soon as the curtain was down on the last performance, he caught the bus to Millburgh, purposefully running out on the big party at the mansion house, returning to Colfax College and his waiting job at WMBG. Two days later, he received a note from Kay, expressing her regret that she had missed a chance to say goodbye to him, wishing him the best of luck in "what I am certain will be a brilliant career in the theater." He saw no need for a reply.

Not many days later, however, there was another note, not from Kay but only too obviously prompted by her, handwritten in an all but undecipherable scrawl.

> Dear Mr. Wilder:
> As I'm sure you must know, Maxwell Anderson's new play, "The Land Is Bright," is opening its Philadelphia try-out next week. Mr. Anderson and some of the people in the cast are stopping by for tea on Sunday about five. Would you come, too?
>
> JESSICA CANNON

He thought of a dozen reasons why he could not, should not, and would not, waste a whole Sunday afternoon and evening on a society tea party, let alone spend $2.47 on bus fare to Philadelphia. Jessica Cannon, Kay's aunt, the Orangerie gossip had it, was a screwy old dame who was trying to carry on in Philadelphia with the same kind of salon for which she had been famous in Paris before she had been driven out by the German occupation. But there was one strong argument in favor of his going—in less than nine months he would be out of Colfax, in desperate need of any Broadway contact that he could make. So he went to Philadelphia, not knowing what to expect, fearing that he would find himself embarrassingly misplaced, a boy from Iowa whose only knowledge of high society had been supplied by Noel Coward's plays.

He need not have worried. Everyone, even the Old Philadelphians, treated him as if he belonged, responding warmly to Kay's introductions as she escorted him around the crowded room. He had a short but excitingly intimate talk with Maxwell Anderson about the tryout difficulties they were having with his play, and all the members of the cast, after they found out that he had been Kodansky's first assistant at the Orangerie, gave him a reassuring sense of eventual acceptance in the profession. He committed, so far as he knew, only one social error—"Miss Cannon" instead of the demanded "Miss Jessica"—and he was quickly reprieved by being asked to bring his hostess her next bourbon, a privilege that brought with it a satisfied smile from Kay and a guardedly whispered "I knew she'd fall for you."

When a second invitation had come from Miss Jessica, he accepted it without question. And then there had been a third and a fourth. It was on that fourth Sunday, the week before Pearl Harbor, that he had met Norman Joyce, unfortunately without recognizing at first who he really was. The dominantly fascinating guest had been Lucretia Lane, the only authentic Hollywood star that he had ever seen at close range. She was in Philadelphia for the tryout of her first legitimate play, and although Judd was on guard against accepting the theater's automatic downgrading of anyone who had not served a Broadway apprenticeship, he could not deny its validity in this case. Lucretia Lane was a stock character, the beautiful but brainless product of exploitation, an ill-poised and inherently vulgar creature who had been cleverly sold to the public as the embodiment of sophisticated womanhood. Norman Joyce, as Judd had first thought, was there only as Lucretia Lane's current husband, a hulking figure doubled into a hideaway corner chair, a craggy face under a shock of iron-gray hair, scowling morosely into a frequently replenished whiskey glass. It was only at the last minute, hearing someone call him Huck that Judd had recognized him as the famous Hollywood director who had been with Floyd Fulton in Spain. By then it had been too late to have anything like a real talk with him. All that he had managed, and that only after Kay had reintroduced him, had been a brief exchange about Kodansky—Huck knew the score, there had been no doubt about that—and then a badly fumbled attempt to compliment him on his newest picture. That was all, really, that supported his statement to Ronnie Chadreau that he knew Huck Joyce. Ronnie was far less impressed by this claim than by Judd's casually tossed-in remark that he had seen Joyce only a few weeks before at Jessica Cannon's. "But my dear fellow," Ronnie had exclaimed, "if you're a good enough friend of Miss Jessica's to be invited for one of her Sundays, for heaven's sake, man, why haven't you had her call the colonel for you? He's one of her oldest friends."

With Ronnie's urging, he had taken the next train for Philadelphia, arriving unannounced on the doorstep of Miss Jessica's Walnut Street house. Kay answered his ring, so elated by his coming to see her that it had taken him a long time to get around to the real purpose of his visit. Miss Jessica, she explained, was in New York working on her French refugee project, but that didn't matter—she'd take care of everything herself—and now how about a drink and some dinner? She knew a wonderful little restaurant, insisting that he be her guest. In the end she had allowed him to pay the check, but by then the evening had become something that he had not intended. Somehow, he had started talking about Iowa, telling her about how he had put on the Centennial pageant, and he had been astounded to find out how understanding she was, how intelligent and knowing, surely more interesting than any girl he had met at Colfax. Still, when he gave her a quick kiss upon parting, no more meaningful than one of the kisses that his Orangerie experience had taught him was the proper reward for an actress's good performance, he had felt himself a hypocrite, never for a moment forgetting why he had come. But Kay, too, had remembered. The last thing she had said had been, "Don't worry about a thing, Judd—leave everything to me. Where can I call you?"

She had called him two days later. Before the end of the following week he had his commission in the Signal Corps.

He spent his last evening as a civilian with Kay in Philadelphia, an evening that began strangely, all of his attempts to express gratitude countered by Kay's regret that she had been able to do no better, at that late date, than a second lieutenancy. Then, no less strangely, she had changed into a person that he had never suspected her of being. There had been more than a single goodnight kiss that evening, an intimacy well beyond anything that even his fulsome gratitude suggested. Had it not been for the atmosphere of Miss Jessica's Walnut Street townhouse constantly reminding him of who Kay Cannon was, he might not have stopped where he had. As it was, he awoke the next morning with the feeling that he had surely demeaned himself by his lack of sophistication, making Kay Cannon think of him as a boy from Iowa who still hadn't learned to keep his primitive sex urge from being too evident.

Dr. Kharr asked now, "Had you had any previous motion picture experience?"

"No, but I'd worked in radio, and with my stage experience—it's all pretty much the same ball of wax."

"You were doing what—directing?"

"Not at first," he said, recalling his battle to get out of the recording studio. On his application blank, listing everything that he had ever done, every talent to which he could make even a remote claim, he had included "Radio announcing." And that, of course, was the one thing that the classification office at Fort Monmouth had picked up. He and four other men had been given auditions. He was the only one to be sent to Astoria.

The only Astoria he had ever heard of was a city in the state of Oregon, and that was where he thought he was going until, when his transportation came through, he discovered that he was being sent to New York City, that this Astoria was a section of Long Island where the Signal Corps Photographic Center had recently been established in a studio taken over from Paramount Pictures. It was his first time alone in New York, the trip out to Astoria his first subway ride, but the excitement of new adventure was largely neutralized by apprehension. Certain that he was in danger of being exposed as an imposter, and in the mood of a criminal concocting an alibi, he invented a cover-up story that he hoped would at least justify what he had written on his application blank. It proved a waste of effort.

No alibi was ever needed. For a week no one paid any attention to him. Then one morning he was ordered to the studio where records were being made for filmstrips. The recording was done directly on a master wax, no errors could be corrected, and the narrator had to read for fourteen minutes and thirty seconds without a break. Waiting for his trial, Judd saw a big-name network announcer, after nine attempts, finally get within fifteen seconds of the end, only to crack under the strain, stumble over a word, and wind up a chattering wreck. In a do-or-die effort, Judd, after one dry-throated false start, got through to the end. Elated by accomplishment, he did not realize for several days that he had trapped himself, seemingly sentenced to the recording studio until the end of the war. Before the end of the first month, he was hunting for escape, tempted to pretend a crackup under the strain—all he would have to do was to start fluffing—but somehow he could not bring himself to do it.

After his third week he was shifted to the Sutton, a Manhattan hotel that had been taken over as quarters for the permanent staff. His roommate was Abe Weiss, a Hollywood cameraman. Susceptible as Judd was, he quickly caught the fever to get into movie production. Abe's friends were all Hollywood men, and by joining their nightly bar-hopping rounds, he put himself through a concentrated course in movie argot. During the day, whenever he could get away from the recording room, he slipped down to the sound stage, a violation of regulations but easily enough managed by staying in the shadowed background. Before long, he felt himself so comfortably at home that he no longer held his breath when the bells sounded for a take. Hopefully, he bucked for a change of work. Nothing came of it. His captain said that he was too valuable in the recording studio.

He had by then largely forgotten about Norman Joyce. Then, one night in a Second Avenue bar, one of Abe's pals exploded the news that Joyce had arrived at Astoria and would start tomorrow morning to pick men for his special production unit. A rip-roaring argument had been touched off, one camp maintaining that they would rather work for Old Huck than any other director in Hollywood, the others insisting that he was a blackhearted, slavedriving Irish bastard and that they would rather go over the hill than be drafted into his unit.

Not entirely by accident, Judd was down on the sound stage when Norman Joyce walked in. All work immediately stopped. Hollywood celebrities were too common around the Astoria studio to attract attention from any but the rawest recruits, but Huck Joyce's arrival made even the hardened old-timers act like stagestruck kids. In the world of the grips and gaffers, the propmen and the cutters, the cameramen and their assistants, Huck Joyce merited attention—and they gave it to him in fullest measure, the bolder edging up to remind him of pictures where they had been in his crew, accepting his nod of recognition as if it were an Oscar. Judd got no nod. Worrying about the claims he had made to Abe and the gang about knowing Huck Joyce, he had avoided the danger of being publicly rejected by making no attempt to speak to him on the set, but he maneuvered his position so that when Huck went upstairs, he passed within a few feet of him. Despite a face-to-face moment, there was no evidence whatsoever of recognition, not even a hint that Huck remembered meeting him that Sunday at Miss Jessica's.

He attempted to get his name on the list of men who were being interviewed for the Joyce unit, only to find himself excluded—there was no call for anyone to do voice-over narration—but he haunted the corridor outside Huck's temporary office, eventually rewarded by seeing him go into the men's room. Staking everything on one bold gamble, he slipped up beside him at the urinal. Bypassing the chance to remind him that they had met in Philadelphia—he was afraid that it might be an undiplomatic reminder that Lucretia Lane had recently divorced him—he said boldly, "I believe, sir, that you know an old friend of mine." When there was no response, he added, "Floyd Fulton."

Huck reacted like a pinpricked lion, a flick of his eyes and then a slow turning of his grizzled head.

Tense, Judd took an inventive gamble. "He used to mention you in his letters from Spain."

"How'd you happen to know Floyd Fulton?" Huck demanded, a testing thrust.

"I worked with him once on a story he was doing," Judd said, hoping that he would not be pressed for details. "We got to be pretty good friends, so he kept writing to me."

"What's happened to him?" Huck asked, barked as if it were a demand for a password.

"He's dead, sir."

"Dead?"

"I thought you might not know—that's why I spoke to you." He told him then about the call from Jersey City, about identifying the body in the morgue, about the funeral.

"What a hell of an ending," Huck muttered, a shuddering paean of angered grief. "But that's what happens—one day you're on top, king of the beasts, then one slip and the jackals are tearing your guts out." His eyes were glowering coals in black sockets. "Why the hell couldn't they have shot him in the streets—let him die like a man. But they never do. No, that's too easy. They have to make it tough —crawl off in a corner and die alone, you poor Godforsaken bastard." His sigh was the groan of a tortured soul. "They blacklisted him—I suppose you know that?"

Judd nodded, not knowing exactly what he meant, but bluffing it out.

Joyce zipped up his trousers. "What do you do around here, Lieutenant?"

Judd plunged. "Not what I want to be doing, sir. They've got me stuck in recording."

"What do you want to do?"

"What everyone wants, sir."

"You bucking for a job?"

"Yes sir."

"Doing what?"

"Anything you'll let me do, sir."

"What *can* you do?"

"Anything, sir."

"Cocky, huh?"

For a moment he thought he had lost, that long moment before he saw a glint in the dark caverns where Joyce's eyes were hidden. "Don't think you're fooling me, kid. You're running a long bluff and I know it. But come on, I'll talk to you."

Before the week was over the roster of the new Joyce unit was posted. Judd's name was on it, listed without duty or assignment, but that didn't matter. Even if he was never given a chance to do anything but lug a camera case or wrestle lights, he had made the grade—and on his own.

That night, going into the hotel, stopping at the newsstand for a paper, his eye had been caught by LUCRETIA LANE'S LAST LOVE on the cover of *Photoplay*. He bought the magazine and sneaked it upstairs, hurriedly reading the article before Abe came in, concentrating on the paragraphs about Lucretia Lane's stormy two-year marriage to the great director Norman Joyce, whose "Academy Award picture, *The Hills Beyond*, is still remembered as one of the most sensitively poetic love stories ever brought to the silver screen."

There was little of the *Photoplay* Norman Joyce in the man who presided over the first assembly of his unit. Two-fisted and glowering, Huck stood above the crowd on a shoulder-high platform, his voice rough and gravelly. "If there's one thing I hate, it's a goddam goof-off," he rumbled. "I've tried to keep them out of this outfit, but if I've let one slip through, now's the time for him to get down on his belly and start crawling out of my sight."

He went on like that, tough as an old drill sergeant, an inexplicable contrast with the sensitively poetic director of *The Hills Beyond*.

Coming to the point, he began to describe the series of pictures he was about to make. A serious problem on the war fronts, he explained, was the failure of fighting equipment because some factory worker had goofed off. The films would be two-reelers which would be shown in munitions plants, retelling the old fable of the war that was lost for the want of a horseshoe nail, updated now to the plane that crashed because some goof-off on the production line had missed putting in a vital cotter pin.

After that it was plain to Judd that Huck was, as every director had to be, something of an actor, his manner in any situation less a reflection of character than of the mood he wanted to get into his picture. Whether this was, in Huck's case, something calculated or subconsciously induced, Judd could not be certain. In any event, it was startlingly effective. Glancing around him, seeing that even the hard-shell old-timers were slack-jawed and staring, he decided that Huck himself was either the greatest actor that Norman Joyce had ever directed, or that the secret of great direction was a degree of personal involvement beyond anything that he had ever imagined. He could not then be certain where the truth lay, nor was it a mystery that was ever to be completely resolved. Close though his relationship with Norman Joyce became—within a month he was accepted by the entire unit as Huck's personal man Friday—there was always a gap between them, a protective moat that Judd suspected no one was ever allowed to cross. Huck was king, alone on his throne, always assuming the ultimate responsibility, and by that assumption driving himself to so high a level of accomplishment that his unquestioned superiority preserved the mysterious aura that was the essence of his command.

To the other men in the unit, Huck was an unrelenting autocrat, frequently cursed but always obeyed, less because of a recognition of his authority than because he was respected. To Judd, Huck Joyce was living proof that accomplishment was all that mattered, that if a man had enough ability it was unnecessary to demean himself by brown-nosing everyone whose friendship he might ever need. But to get away with it, you had to be good, capable of doing anything, able to humble any recalcitrant crew member by pushing him aside with a firm "Let me show you how to do it." How Huck had mastered so many diverse skills was hard to understand, but Judd wasted no time in puzzled incredulity. He pestered Abe into teaching him how to run a camera, hungrily soaked up the craft knowledge of the scenic artists, the propmen, and the electricians. He learned most of all in the cutting room, where he spent every moment that he dared be away from Huck's call.

Consciously, he was trying to avoid Huck's biting scorn of incompetence, initially unaware that he was becoming more goal than goad. Unrealized until it became a full-blown ambition, the image of himself as a motion picture director had already begun to take form in his mind.

Nevertheless, despite his capacity for respect and admiration, he did not give way to blind hero-worship. By the time his ambition had crystallized, he too plainly saw Huck as a crazy Irishman who profligately squandered his energies in the meaningless bedding of the endless parade of dames who heel-clicked their way in and out through the marble-floored foyer of 301.

That number, 301, was the code designation of Huck's hideout, not the street number but the suite number of the Park Avenue apartment that he had rented soon after he had come on from Hollywood. The address, supposedly known only to the inner circle, was a badly kept secret, known as it was by a growing army of party girls, and as Judd was later to discover, by a never-ending parade of bill-collectors and process-servers. Judd was prepared to accept some degree of eccentricity as an artist's right, a Hollywood hallmark, but he could not understand why Norman Joyce, so brilliantly capable in the management of all the complexities involved in the making of a motion picture, could be so wildly irrational, so carelessly unconcerned, so downright stupid in the living of his personal life.

Judd's introduction to 301 came one Saturday afternoon when Nick Tresh, the scenic designer, sent him into Manhattan with a sheaf of sketches for Huck's approval. Although by then, Judd had been in New York long enough so that the first glitter had tarnished, the very words "Park Avenue" were still endowed with glamour, a feeling sustained by the uniformed doorman who guarded the entrance of the apartment house, enhanced by the silver-haired old servitor who took him up in a velvet-padded elevator, directing him to the door of 301 with a courtly bow and the palm-up gesture of an English butler granting an audience with the lord of the manor.

Huck shattered the Park Avenue illusion when he finally appeared at the door, wearing nothing but a pair of shorts, red-eyed and yawning. But the apartment itself was no disappointment. The entrance foyer, floored with a bold checkerboard of black and white marble, opened into what Judd was sure must be a drawing room, its Oriental rugs, crystal chandelier, and French furniture incongruous with any less elegant designation. There was a dining room beyond, no less elaborately furnished. When Huck, still yawning, told him to come back with him while he dressed, Judd saw that there were three bedrooms, all shimmering and satiny, ruffles upon ruffles, the bedside tables loaded with fancy bric-a-brac, lamps whose bases were all porcelain figurines of hoop-skirted ladies or dancing couples performing frozen minuets.

Impressed though he was, Judd could not imagine a setting more ill-fitted to Huck, and he wondered why he had rented it, all the more so after he discovered that he was living in only one room, a bedroom that had become, in the short time of his occupancy, a magpie's nest of half-emptied suitcases, tangled clothing, film scripts, books and magazines, empty whiskey bottles and crusted glasses, overflowing ashtrays and crumpled cigarette packs, a junk heap overlaid with a scatter of mail, most of which had never been opened.

"Place is getting kind of mussed up," Huck grumbled, as if aware of it for the first time. "Have to get somebody to come in. Suppose you could dig up a maid to keep the place clean?"

"I'll get someone," he said, knowing an order when he heard it, suspecting that this was the real reason Huck had had him sent in with the sketches. He had no idea how to go about hiring a maid, even where to make a start. He talked first to the elevator man, then the doorman, and by following a maze of vague directions, draining his own purse to pay taxi fares, he eventually found Clara. The wage she demanded was shocking, but it would appear less so, he imagined, to a Hollywood director rich enough to rent an enormous Park Avenue apartment. Sure enough, Huck dismissed the cost with a shrug, engaged Clara on the spot, rewarding Judd with a "Good work, kid—nice casting. But you better drop by now and then to keep an eye on things." With that, he tossed him a key.

From that beginning, never by designation, never by anything that even remotely approached a direct order, Judd took over the management of 301. Clara came to him with her problems and he solved them. He kept the liquor cabinet filled and a supply of snacks in the icebox, and made an arrangement with the restaurant in the building next door to provide food service, eventually to station a waiter in 301's pantry every evening when Huck was in town.

When the studio crew started calling him the "bat boy" he became mildly worried that he might be maneuvering himself into a domestic dead end, concern dissipating as Huck gave him more and more responsibility on the set and in the cutting room, never to the point of final authority but often tantalizingly close to it. But there was always that last step. After Huck started letting him work with actors, drilling dialogue before they were brought before the camera, he became possessed by a fierce desire to bring at least one scene to a state of perfection where it would be shot exactly as he had rehearsed it. He never succeeded. Invariably, Huck frustrated him by finding some change to make.

Judd found slight comfort in knowing that he was not the only victim. Sam Springer, whom Huck had brought along from Hollywood, and who had won two Oscars for film editing, took it for granted that no sequence would stand exactly as he cut it, that Huck would always find some change to make, a scene to clip short, a close-up to be shifted, a forgotten take dug out of the can to supply that one last note that filled the crescendo chord. Judd could see, when it was Sam rather than himself who was being frustrated, that it was Huck's hand that added the final fillip, the highlight that gave life to the portrait's eye, the indescribable something that was the "Norman Joyce touch." Sam could shrug it off—"He's just got it, that's all"—but Judd could not. He castigated himself unmercifully every time Huck did something that had not occurred to him, even angrier when what Huck did was something that he had thought of doing himself, passed over because of a lack of confidence in his own judgment.

More and more surely as the months went by, the *Goof-off* series finished and *They Also Fight* brought to the production stage, Judd came to understand that Huck's talent was largely intuitive, that he was guided much less by reason than by an innate sense of the theatrical. When Judd asked him, as he was occasionally bold enough to do, *why* he had done something, Huck would either shrug it off, or if he happened to be in a good mood, explain that it "felt better that way." Once, when Judd came back to 301 on a rainy Sunday afternoon with a copy of Valenkoff's *The Artist in Celluloid*—he was buying every book he could find that he thought might help him—Huck had angrily snatched it from his hand and hurled it toward the wastebasket. "Forget that art-of-the-cinema crap," he growled. "Making a picture is like laying a dame. When you start intellectualizing about it, what the hell have you got— nothing! All you're after, kid, is a *feeling*. If you get it—okay, you're in business. If you don't get it, to hell with it. Never try to talk your- self into it. Forget you've got a brain. That's the trouble with these art boys—they try to *think* their way through. To hell with that. Remember this, kid—making a picture is like having a dame—all that matters is what it does to you down inside."

Huck's similes, vivid though they were, would have struck Judd Wilder with more impact if he had been as experienced as he felt himself forced to pretend. Actually, no open pretense was ever re- quired. In the atmosphere of 301, it would have been as laughably incredible to say that he had never been to bed with a girl as it would have been to say that he had not yet learned to breathe. That had been before Huck had made him a unit director, before the Everglades assignment, before Miami, before the girl with the right- hand-drive Daimler.

"No, I wasn't really directing, not at Astoria," he said now. "As long as I was there, I was an assistant to Huck Joyce. I don't suppose the name means anything to you—Norman Joyce?"

"No, I'm afraid not. I was never enough of a movie fan to remem- ber the names of directors."

"Not many people do," he said. "But back in those days Norman Joyce was pretty close to the top of the heap, maybe a little over the hump, but still right up there."

"Even being his assistant must have been quite a feather in your cap," Dr. Kharr observed. "After all, you were just out of college. You couldn't have been more than—what were you—twenty-two or -three?"

"I was only twenty-two when I got my own unit," he said, re- calling all the fuss there had been with the colonel when Huck had picked him for the Florida assignment. "I wasn't twenty-three until —I'll never forget my twenty-third birthday. We were hung up in Cairo. The DC-3 we were on had blown a cylinder head trying to take off, so there we were, ditched in a field down off the end of the runway. We had a couple of tons of camera gear that we had to get off-loaded and stowed until we got another way out. We had to have some help, so I went back and rounded up a gang of porters and a couple of carts and finally got them out to the plane. That's when the lid blew off. Most of my crew, you see, were Jewish boys, five out of the seven—and the porters, of course, were all Arabs. I probably should have known that it was an explosive mixture—" He broke off with a chuckle, able to laugh now at what had then been no laughing matter. "I never did find out what touched it off —maybe just spontaneous combustion—but, anyway, it was one hell of a birthday party."

Dr. Kharr responded with no more than the brief flicker of a humorless smile, pressing on with "You were on your way to India?"

He nodded, suddenly struck by something strangely cool in the doctor's manner, seemingly a confirmation of his earlier impression that something lay behind the pretense that this was only a friendly visit.

And now, unmistakably probing, Dr. Kharr asked, "That must have been quite an interesting experience—the time you spent in India? You were there for—am I right—something over two years?"

Goaded by suspicion, he sharply countered, "You seem to know a lot about me."

Dr. Kharr blinked, plainly taken aback. "Well, I did talk to Mr. Crouch. You do remember my telling you that, don't you?"

Bypassing admission, he demanded, "What the hell's this all about?"

"What's what all about, Mr. Wilder?"

"All this India business. First, it's this other—what's his name— Raggi. And now you're off on it, too. What goes?"

Dr. Kharr's face visibly reddened, his voice taut as he said, "I'm sorry, Mr. Wilder, but I had no way of knowing that your experience in India was something that you don't want to talk about."

"What do you mean—I don't want to talk about it?" he flashed back. "I just want to know what goes, that's all. What's this all about? Why all this India business?"

Dr. Kharr regarded him narrowly, making him feel like something under a microscope, pinned down and unable to wriggle free. "Yes, Mr. Wilder, I'm interested in what happened to you in India—but no more than I am in every other aspect of your life. If I'm to help you, I need to know as much about you as I possibly can."

"I thought this was a heart attack?" he challenged, closing his ears to an inner voice that was crying out against him, telling him that he was being a fool.

"Do you have any idea *why?*"

"Why what?"

"Why you've had a heart attack?"

"How should I know? You're the doctor—you tell me."

"Has it occurred to you, Mr. Wilder, that there may be a connection between your heart attack and the kind of a man you are—or at least the kind of a man you've driven yourself into becoming?"

"You've got me pegged for the emotional type, is that it?" he said, reacting to the store of resentment that he had accumulated over the years, all of the doctors who had taken his money and given him nothing in return, telling him that there was nothing wrong with him that was not his own fault.

The twist of Dr. Kharr's lips suggested a cynical smile. "It's possible, I suppose, that I may have gotten the wrong impression but, quite frankly, Mr. Wilder, you don't strike me as being exactly the stolid type—impassive—phlegmatic—unemotional——"

"All right, maybe I do get a little steamed up at times," he said, finally yielding to that insistent inner voice, but some uncontrollable perversity made him add a challenging, "So what?"

"So this—" Dr. Kharr said quickly, leaning forward, a movement of attack. "Beyond any question, Mr. Wilder, there's an association between coronary occlusion and behavior pattern. You may not accept that at first, but if you're openminded enough to be convinced—" He paused, waiting.

There was more than one inner voice now, a whole chorus of discordant cries, all clamoring to be heard, and the one that broke through was a demanding "What the hell is this—a couch session?" Then, reacting to the doctor's flinch, the same voice rushed in with "What are you—some kind of a headshrinker?"

Too late, Judd tried to add a tempering smile. Dr. Kharr was already on his feet. He had another chance—the doctor was still standing at his bedside—but, staring up into that black scowl, he was too stunned to act quickly enough, the opportunity lost as Dr. Kharr turned away and started for the door. He might have stopped him—there was an instant of hesitation in the doorway as he turned back with a quiet "I'll see you in the morning," but Judd's impulse to cry out in apology was overwhelmed by the incomprehensibility of what had happened. Dazed, he stared at the closed door, attempting to blame Dr. Kharr for walking out on him, trying to put down the damning realization that it was his own fault.

Made suddenly aware of Mrs. Cope's presence by a sound of movement, he twisted his head on the pillow, surprised to discover that she was already standing beside him, her close presence a promise of sympathetic understanding.

"Have you always been like this?"

The voice was unmistakably Mrs. Cope's but the tone was unbelievable until he looked up into her face, seeing then an expression of tight-lipped disapproval that was shockingly unexpected.

"What do you mean?" he asked, dry-mouthed. "Like what?"

"Why are you so afraid to let anyone help you?"

❖ IV ❖

JUDD WILDER AWOKE with a start, unaware of what had awakened him, yet knowing that whatever it was had been a prelude to a quick closing of the bathroom door. Listening, he heard the sound of vomiting. Then the toilet was flushed. Another wait and he could hear water running in the lavatory.

The door opened and Mary Welch came out, her face ashen.

"What's the matter?" he asked.

She started, seemingly terrorstruck by the discovery that he was awake.

"You're sick," he said. "You'd better——"

"No, no, no, no," poured from her lips, a torrent of frightened denial, abruptly halted with a pitiable attempt at a self-saving smile. "I'm all right, really I am. It's only—nothing, nothing at all."

"It has to be something. You don't——"

"You know, don't you?" she demanded, almost an accusation. Before he could reply, she burst out, "All right, I'm pregnant. I thought I was all over this part of it—" She bit her lip, seemingly fighting another attack of nausea.

"Why don't you get out of here?" he suggested sympathetically. "It's almost seven. Miss Harsch will be here in a few——" Her eyes stopped him. They were wide, unblinking, staring at him as if he were now the object of a new fear. "I'll be all right," he assured her. "It's only a few minutes——"

"Don't tell Dr. Kharr! Please don't! Promise me that you won't!"

"What's so awful about being pregnant? Do they have some kind of rule here that nurses can't—" Suddenly it came clear, the memory of yesterday morning, the way that she so insistently called herself *Mrs.* Welch. A wordless sound of understanding escaped his lips.

"You knew yesterday, didn't you?" she said, distraught. "I thought you did."

He said nothing, canvassing his experience, thinking of all the pregnancy cases he had dealt with over the years, all the typists and file clerks and mail girls he had been forced to talk to, driven to his office by the never-understandable vindictiveness of female supervisors who, claiming that gossip was interfering with efficiency, sent him their unfortunate girls as if they were consigning them to the outer depths. He had never had any taste for criticism or moralizing, and trial and error had taught him that dissembling evasion was no help, either. The best thing to do was to give them a chance to talk—that, strangely, more often than not was taken as a great kindness. One girl, in what could have been an embarrassing misdirection of gratitude, had afterwards written him that she had named her baby Judd.

"Who's the man?" he asked, the bold question that he had found to be the best opening gambit, rarely answered but almost always accepted as an invitation.

"He doesn't know," Mary responded, sounding as if she thought it a direct reply. "If he did, he'd insist on marrying me—and that would spoil everything."

"Why do you say that?"

"It's true," she said. "He would."

"But why would that spoil everything?"

"He's just starting his surgical residency," she said, surprisingly controlled now. "That means three years—at least—maybe more. He'd never go through with it if he had a wife and child to support. He'd take some little job, a clinic or something—and he shouldn't! Surgery is what he's always wanted. It's his whole life. I can't take that away from him."

It was impossible to doubt her sincerity. "Sounds like you really love the guy."

"Too much to do something like this to him."

"So you haven't told him?"

"He doesn't even know where I am."

"That's a little rough, isn't it?"

"I'll be all right."

"I didn't mean rough on you—I mean rough on him."

"He'll never know," she said, turning away, making a pretense of putting the dresser top in order.

He watched her appreciatively, wondering how many girls there were who would make such a sacrifice for a man, inevitably recalling that letter from Kay, the one in which she had told him that she was pregnant. "Are you going to have the baby?"

"Of course."

"But you aren't going to tell him."

"It's my problem."

"But it's his baby, too."

"Not if he doesn't know," she said, picking up a water glass, starting for the bathroom. But the door did not close and she came back immediately with the fresh water, putting it on the side table with an embarrassed, "I'm sorry, Mr. Wilder."

"Sorry about what?"

"Subjecting you to—I shouldn't have told you."

He smiled. "You didn't."

"Yes, that's going to be the trouble," she said. "Before long, I won't have to tell anyone."

"Are you sure you're right?"

She nodded vigorously. "You don't know Ralph—how much surgery means to him."

"I know this," he said. "If you're enough in love with him to want to do what you're doing—for his sake—whether he was in love with you before or not——"

"Oh, but he was. He is. It's not that—" She wheeled, alerted by the sound of the door opening.

Miss Harsch was peeping in through the narrow slit of the partly opened door, her face set in the fixed mask of her perpetual smile, her entrance as inappropriate as if a miscued burlesque queen had burst upon the stage at a moment of high drama.

He clenched his fists, the physical suppression of a groan . . . he couldn't stand another day cooped up with that moronic face . . . if there were only some way to get rid of her . . .

Urged on by a feeling that rose in intensity until it approached desperation, his mind finally responded, suggesting what seemed, momentarily, the perfect solution . . . talk to Dr. Kharr . . .

But the instant that the doctor's image flashed upon the screen of his mind, his thought stream was diverted from Miss Harsch, chan-

neled again into the raw-nerved rut that had been so deeply worn
in the night, feeling again the agony of regret that had haunted his
dreams. He had been awake several times, only briefly, but long
enough to let him see, as if those moments of lucidity were peep-
holes into a nightmare world, how ridiculously he had acted with
Dr. Kharr. He could not excuse it, much less explain it—that "head-
shrinker" crack kept coming back and back as an echoing accusation
of mad stupidity—but neither could he accept the validity of Mrs.
Cope's question, no less endlessly repeated in the echo chamber of
his mind . . . *"Why are you so afraid to let anyone help you?"*

It was not true, he had tried to tell her that; but distracted, still
reeling from the shock of Dr. Kharr's abrupt departure, he had compounded his error by making Mrs. Cope think that he was rejecting
her help, too. She had passed it off, saying nothing more, but there
had been a perceptible coolness, an absence of the warmth that he
had felt the evening before, a loss of something for which he had
waited all day. Despite the depth of his disappointment, experience
had prepared him to accept being misunderstood. All through his
life, it seemed, he had been accused of being too cockily self-suffi-
cient, of always running his own show, of always insisting upon
going his own way. Somehow he had never been able to make
people understand that he was not rejecting their help, that he was
only preserving his right to *know*, to think things through for himself, to arouse the urgent energy that came only from being able to
see with his own eyes. Mrs. Cope was not the first person who had
turned against him because of what had been misjudged as the
disdainful rejection of a generous offer, unwilling thereafter to lift
a hand to help him no matter how dire his need might be. It was
by no means true that he was unconcerned by the friends he had
lost—Kay had never hurt him more deeply than when she had once,
in a rare moment of vocalized anger, accused him of not caring
how many people he alienated—but his regret, genuine though it
had often been, had always before been countered by the feeling
that the injustice of an unfair judgment could only be righted by
driving ahead as hard as he could, never losing faith in himself,
eventually vindicating himself by leaving his detractors far behind.

But now he was the one who had been left behind. Flat on his
back, helplessly invalided, prohibited from defending himself, he
was seeing again that nightmare vision of Dr. Kharr turning away

from him, hearing again that terrifyingly final sound of the door being closed.

From somewhere in another world, distance upon distance, he heard the lonely wail of a siren. As he listened, it came closer, materializing into the reality of an approaching ambulance, turning off the highway and coming up the drive, the siren sound rising in pitch as it approached, then suddenly cut off, dying with a rattling gasp directly under the window of his room.

Turning his head on the pillow, he saw Miss Harsch looking down through the parted slats of the Venetian blind. Her fixed smile, so meaningless before, seemed now the expression of a gleeful ghoul.

« 2 »

Awake, lying in bed, Aaron Kharr had heard the siren when it was still a long way off, approaching from the direction of the turnpike interchange. He had tried, soon after he came to County Memorial, to limit the use of the siren to those few occasions when it was really needed, but old Oscar who drove the ambulance was no more amenable to suggestion than most of the hospital employees—and it did have the advantage of an early-warning system.

Raising himself to a sitting position, he heard the ambulance pass the house, listening until a change of tone marked its turn into the hospital drive. Wearily, he swung his feet to the floor, accepting the inevitability of a telephone call. It was Sunday, Webster's day of duty, but there was no chance of his being at the hospital this early. Raggi, alone, confronted with an emergency situation, would call him even before he tried to get in touch with Webster.

He stood up, feeling groggy and thick-headed, thumping his temples with his doubled fists, reacting to the sensation of a brain that seemed to have been choked into insensibility by the pressure that had built up during the night. He had slept badly, awake countless times, unable to escape a damning awareness of how horribly he had messed up his attempt to talk to Wilder.

He shed his pajamas and pulled on his shorts and trousers, prepared now to hurry down the stairs at the first sound of the tele-

phone, hoping that he would be able to cut it off before it awakened
Mrs. Stine. But no ring came.

Opening the hall door so that he would be able to hear it in the
bathroom, he went in and shaved, listening over the buzz of his
electric razor. Still no call. He came back and sat on the edge of
the bed, tempted to lie down again. The stimulation of a response
to emergency was beginning to wear off, exposing a strange exhaustion. He was accustomed to ordinary early-morning fatigue,
usually able to override it by opening his mind to an anticipation
of the day that lay ahead, but now that stratagem did not work. His
purposeful visualization of the hospital, instead of providing its intended attraction, strongly repelled him. Even the prodding thought
that a quiet Sunday forenoon would give him a much-needed
chance to work on his book fizzled out like a spark tossed into damp
tinder. His book seemed almost a lost cause now, its very premise
challenged by what had happened last night with Wilder.

Or did the fault lie, not with his premise, but with himself? Now
wide awake, he was forced to the latter conclusion, clearly seeing
the fool that he had made of himself, turning up without his white
coat, pretending that it was a social visit instead of a medical call,
stupidly imagining that he could establish an easy rapport with
Wilder, a relationship out of which everything he needed to know
would bubble up as freely as water from a spring.

A part of the trouble lay with Wilder—the man was difficult, no
doubt of that—yet not a thing that he had said or done should have
been unanticipated. His aggressive penchant for argument, his
suspicious questioning of every statement, even his rather vicious
needling, were all to be expected. Actually, they proved, if proof
were needed, that here was an almost classic case, a perfect example
of a man with a coronary-susceptible personality who, in his middle
forties, had driven himself into an occlusion-precipitating behavior
pattern. If there had been any cause for surprise, it lay in the clear
evidence that, despite the supposedly traumatic effect of a heart
attack, there had been, even after two full days, no modification of
behavior, no lessening of obsessive compulsion, no disposition to understand why he had been struck down. But that, too, should have
been anticipated—it *had* been!

No, he couldn't blame Wilder. The fault could only be charged
against himself, its magnitude measured by the realization that he

had done nothing, absolutely nothing, to turn Wilder aside from the suicidal path down which he was still driving himself. He had tried—and failed. Again, as had happened too often in the past, he had counted upon an ability that he did not possess.

The creation of warmly personal relationships had always been to Aaron Kharr, ever since his youth, a gallingly mysterious process. He had never been able to understand why what seemed, for most people, something as natural and unconsidered as breathing, should be so difficult for him. In high school, he had made only one close friend, a relationship based upon a mutuality of background and interest. Sammy Harris, too, had been a doctor's son, also committed to a medical career, and their sharing of plans and apprehensions had drawn them together. He had looked ahead to medical school as a place where there would be a lot of Sammy Harrises, a wealth of potential new friends. And there had, indeed, been plenty of prospects, dozens of fellow students whose friendship he would have welcomed. But the only ones he attracted were the bottom-enders, the parasites who were looking for a notebook to copy, or for some-one to tutor them through an examination. The others passed him by. He attributed it largely to envy. He was always at, or very near, the top of his class—he could do nothing about that—but there were times when a high place on the honor roll seemed less desirable than a bar stool at one of the beer-drinking bull sessions to which he was never invited.

When, surprisingly in his third year, he had been elected to Alpha Omega Alpha, the medical-school equivalent of Phi Beta Kappa, he had thought that he was finally being admitted to the inner circle. He was not. After that, it seemed, he was even more pointedly excluded. Aware of how important personal relationships were to a doctor, he had grudgingly stolen enough time from his medical books to read some popular volumes that he hoped might help him —even, surreptitiously, Dale Carnegie's *How to Win Friends and Influence People*—but all that he got out of any of them was the feeling that they had been written by men who put too low a value on self-respect and intellectual honesty.

As an intern, exposed for the first time to the inner workings of a big hospital—and by extension, the whole medical profession—he had become increasingly aware that success in medicine depended less upon competence than connections. A number of specialists who, as he observed them, were little better than clever quacks, nevertheless waxed fat from referrals generated within the circle of self-serving friends to which they had attached themselves. Unattached, you were an outcast. There were a dozen or more such doctors on the hospital staff, destined to spend the rest of their lives grubbing about in the charity wards, manning the outpatient clinics, or doing the real work of the friend-makers who had formed the right professional alliances. To escape that fate, an intern had to start early. Those who made the right friends quickly got the good duty, the juicy plums, assignments that brought them into the orbit of the right doctors and the right surgeons.

Aaron Kharr had seen all this—it could hardly be missed—but somehow he could not bring himself to do what had to be done. He simply could not grovel convincingly before empty pomposity. When he attempted insincere flattery, he always wound up with a fiery blush and a giveaway stutter. More seriously, he had never been able to stand mutely by when silence could be taken as agreement with something that cried out for challenge. Most often it was a diagnosis, and with his fast-blooming skill in that area, he had scored a succession of triumphs, several over big-name staff doctors. Instead of gaining status, however, he found himself regarded with ever more obvious disfavor by the men upon whose favor he would be dependent.

Necessarily, he had learned to live without the camaraderie of his colleagues, to steel himself against the way they fell silent when he approached their coffee-break table in the cafeteria, even to convince himself that their attitude toward him was, in one way at least, an evidence of respect. What he could not down, however, was a growing realization that his inability to generate friendship within the profession was paralleled by a matching deficiency in his relationship with patients. Somehow, despite the sincerity of his total dedication, few patients responded to him, seemingly unable to appreciate his earnest desire to help them, or to understand how desperately he wanted to transmit the human warmth that was in his heart. No incident in all his internship had more deeply puzzled him than the anguished disappointment on the faces of all the patients in one of the wards when, one time, he had to tell them he was taking over for Dr. Hackett, all of them apparently oblivious to the truth that of all the interns, Hackett was the most blatantly incompetent. He found no comfort in the observation that private-room patients, able to pay the highest fees for the best of care, were no more discriminating.

Consciously or not—surely more so than he had, at the time, been able to admit—his eventual decision to go into research had been influenced by his fear that he did not have, and might never be able to acquire, the kind of personality upon which a successful practice seemed to depend. His dream image of himself as a famous consulting internist had been eroded away by a realistic awareness that specialists were dependent upon referrals from friendly colleagues. But the thought of going into general practice raised the no less frightening specter of dependence upon the whims of undiscriminating patients, a prospect viewed all the more apprehensively after he had spent several loose-ended weeks in his father's office. Although he had no more than vaguely entertained the idea of going in with him, and eventually taking over his practice, that possibility had been ruled out when he found himself unable to attract even a peripheral share of the affection that all of his father's patients lavished upon the old man. His father must have recognized it, too. Gently, with unmistakable regret but nevertheless pointedly, he had agreed that it might be wise for him to go into research.

There was more required, however, than decision. His medical-school record got him interviews, but nothing came of them. Over and over again, in a dozen paraphrases, he was asked if he thought he was temperamentally suited to the team play that research required, an oblique way of telling him that he had been spotted for an outcast. Eventually he was offered a job—not a fellowship, not an appointment, only a job—in the research laboratories of Palmer-Rand. He took it with a sense of temporary defeat, almost as if he were accepting charity to tide him over a bad time, thinking that whatever he was called upon to do would use only a fraction of his ability.

Hired by a bow-tied personnel man in the drug company's Manhattan headquarters, he was sent to the Newark laboratory and told to report to Dr. Roy Lorents, the group leader of the team to which he had been assigned. Expecting at least a clean-slate start, he had been stunned by immediate attack. Dr. Lorents was a biochemist, with a second doctorate in clinical psychology, who had made his life's work the development of drugs to be used in the treatment of mental illness. But his avocation, apparently, was un-relenting derogation of medical-school education. He said that he had not asked to have an M.D. on his team, that he did not want one, and he had proceeded to justify his attitude by forcing Aaron Kharr to admit that, in his four years in medical school, he had been given no training in the psychiatric area. Aaron Kharr was by no means unaware of this shortcoming in his education—he had even tried, unsuccessfully, to take a clinical psychology course as an elec-tive—but he had attempted to defend his alma mater by offering the same excuse he had been given: that with all that had to be learned in general medicine there was no time for such sidetrack excur-sions. "Which means," Lorents had come roaring back, "that you have no training whatsoever to handle at least seventy-five per cent of the complaints that you have been licensed to treat."

Unrelentingly, Lorents had pounded him with a barrage of ques-tions about psychosomatic relationships and psychogenic diseases, leaving him staggered, groggily agreeing that he was no more than twenty-five per cent educated for the practice of medicine, even less so for research, so beaten down that he felt himself fortunately reprieved when Lorents had finally said that he would give him a probationary chance at animal work.

Had his pride not been so seriously challenged, Aaron Kharr would have walked out. Instead, he spent his work days observing and dissecting cats, his weekends and nights boning psychology and psychiatry, driving himself with a fury unmatched in his worst skull-cracking sessions in medical school. A whole new world opened up before him, his prior ignorance so obvious that he could almost for-give Lorents for blackmarking him as an M.D., discouraged only be-cause the dark stain seemed unerasable. Even after he got to the point where he could hold his own in weekly review sessions, he had remained an intruding outsider, the only man on the team who had never been invited to Lorents's Short Hills home for a Saturday night cook-out. Anti-Semitism was a possibility—he was not only the only M.D. in the group, but the only Jew as well—but he convinced himself that suspecting prejudice was a too-easy way to excuse his own shortcomings.

That next fall, by then convinced that Lorents was right in his cynical claim that internal medicine would never give adequate weight to emotional stress as long as treating its effects remained so profitable, he decided to switch to psychiatry. Surprisingly, Lorents helped him get a psychiatric residency. He stuck it out for ten months, his research-conditioned sense of logic and reason continually insulted by the irrationality of psychoanalysis—and that, it seemed, was about all there was to psychiatric practice, that and the fascination with abnormal psychology, particularly when it had a heavy erotic content. If the internists were neglecting the mind, he decided, the psychiatrists were no less seriously neglecting the body. He could see the area in which he wanted to work, a middle ground where there was a balanced weighing of all factors, physical and emotional. It was a field with a name—psychosomatic medicine—but it was not a recognized specialization. There were a few lonely men working in the area, attempting to bridge the gap between medicine and psychiatry that no one acknowledged but everyone knew to be there. They were largely unknown and unsung, hidden in their bunkers, kept there by the crossfire of the profession's undeclared war. One such man was Dr. Hugo Steinfeldt. His book *Psychosomatics in General Practice* had greatly impressed Aaron Kharr and after digging out everything else that Steinfeldt had written—paper after paper in little offbeat journals, none of which he had ever read before—he had gone to a sparsely attended symposium where Steinfeldt had read a paper suggesting a positive linkage between emotional stress and coronary occlusion. There had been only the briefest spatter of applause. Afterwards, Aaron Kharr had been the only one who had gone up to talk to him.

That very night he had asked Steinfeldt to take him in for what would be, unofficially but in full effect, a residency in psychosomatic medicine. Never before had he tried so hard to sell himself. Eventually he succeeded. Steinfeldt accepted him as both pupil and co-worker, and if what grew up between them was not *friendship* in all of the common connotations of that word, it was nevertheless enormously satisfying, the warmest human relationship that Aaron Kharr had ever experienced.

Dr. Steinfeldt divided his time between a private practice, which was considerably larger than Aaron Kharr had expected, and what he called "research," largely an analytic extension of his practice. With no more evidence than his own cases, but analyzing them with acute perception, often illuminated by brilliant intuitions, he had made great progress toward the identification of stress-disease relationships. He had been particularly successful with ulcer cases. That was the area where his practice had grown, one patient telling another. He got few referrals. His approach—at least what was known of it—smacked too much of psychiatry to win the support of medical men, and too much of medicine to appeal to the psychiatrists.

Aaron Kharr's first task was to codify and reduce to writing, hopefully as a scientifically acceptable treatise, Steinfeldt's system of stress diagnosis. He could hardly have been given a more educative assignment. Steinfeldt, burning for recognition after so many years of professional neglect—modesty was not one of his many virtues—opened up to his new assistant as he could never have done if teaching had been his only purpose. Beyond that, the old man liked nothing better than to test his theories in argument, and Aaron Kharr was more than willing to be the flint for Steinfeldt's steel. The sparks flew, but they were warming rather than destructive, and before the first month was over, Steinfeldt invited him to live in the back room of his apartment. Thus, instead of stopping their verbal jousting at midnight, they could carry on until the small hours.

The more Aaron Kharr learned from Dr. Steinfeldt, the more respect he gained for his father, who, he now recognized, had in thirty years of general practice, come remarkably close to Steinfeldt's key insights. He had said as much one evening and Steinfeldt had immediately agreed. "Of course! Thousands of old general practitioners know most of this—but only after they've been in practice for ten, or twenty, or thirty years. We talk about medicine being a science, but we practice it as if it were an esoteric cult to which illumination comes only after you've wandered around in the desert until your hair turns gray. Nonsense! In this day and age, how can we justify a profession in which a man has to get ninety per cent of his education in on-the-job training? And if a man can start from scratch and work it all out for himself, then why can't it be taught? It can! All we have to do is get it down on paper. That's your job, my boy."

It was an assignment more easily accepted than fulfilled. The essence of Steinfeldt's approach was an incisive understanding of the patient's personality and life situation. To secure it, Steinfeldt brushed aside most of the conventional history-taking that Aaron

Kharr had been taught in medical school. "Why waste time finding out that a patient's grandfather died of acute flatulence at the
age of ninety," Steinfeldt would demand with a rumbling chuckle,
"when you might be discovering why he's screwing his secretary?"

Steinfeldt was no less the iconoclast about clinical tests. If a test
promised something significant, he used it—the private laboratory
that opened off his office was a little gem—but he inveighed endlessly against doctors who studied lab reports instead of their patients. "We spend too much time with our ears plugged up with a
stethoscope," he said, "when we ought to be listening to what the
patient says, not to sounds that we can't interpret anyway." Continued blood-pressure testing was another of his targets. "No matter
how many times you look at that column of mercury, it's never going
to tell you why."

Why? That was Steinfeldt's endless cry. Clinical diagnosis had always been, for Aaron Kharr, and for all the doctors with whom he
had worked, the point and purpose of examination and history-
taking. With Dr. Steinfeldt, it was only a beginning, at best no more
than a definition of the problem. An X-ray revealing duodenal ulcer
did not answer a question, it asked one—and the question was always the same—*why?* If he could answer that, a cure was in sight,
less importantly for the ulcer itself than for what had caused it.

Superficially, Dr. Steinfeldt's intense study of the patient's personality and background bore some resemblance to psychiatric
investigation, but the departures were more significant than the re-
semblances. He was almost violently anti-Freudian, not against
Freud himself but against his disciples who, he said, were so badly
misinterpreting "poor old Freud" that he would almost certainly go
down in history as "the author of modern man's most dangerous delusions." With Dr. Steinfeldt, no patient could ever get away with
blaming irresponsible behavior on some traumatic childhood experience. "Learning how a man was trained to the pot won't tell you a
thing that you can do anything about," he had once said, "but you're
getting somewhere when you find out that he's eating his belly out
because he isn't allowed to defecate in the executive can." The past
was never as important as the here and now, the distant experience
buried in the subconscious never as significant as the current situation that the patient was failing to face realistically.

Dr. Steinfeldt did share the psychoanalytic premise that the patient had to be made to see that the cause of his illness lay within himself, but he preached no doctrine of abject submission. To him, every man was the master of his own fate, and fate was not a millstone of past mistakes and misdeeds but something that was fashioned anew with every rising of the sun, not a deadweight burden to be meekly dragged along but a treasure to be joyously shouldered and carried forward to an ever-renewed life. He did not always succeed. Occasionally, he sent his failures on to a psychiatrist. One of them had once called back about a referred patient, saying that he seemed a well-adjusted man. "Yes, and I'm afraid I'm responsible," Dr. Steinfeldt had said. "But I'm hoping you'll be able to jar him out of it—he's much too valuable a man to lose."

Aaron Kharr had no easy time distilling out the essence of Steinfeldt's free-wheeling methods. Suspecting that the old man's notes were at best inadequate, at worst shaded by a serious tendency toward inductive thinking, he rigged up a dictating machine to record all of Steinfeldt's patient interviews. Listening to the recordings, he learned a great deal. And from what he learned he attempted to construct a standardized procedure, setting up a series of questions to be included in the interview, then a grading scale that weighed not only the content of the answers but also the tone and manner in which they were given. Dr. Steinfeldt's approval was reserved—for all his desire to earn scientific kudos, he was enough of an egoist to cherish a bit of priestly mysticism—but he agreed that it should be tried. Whenever a new patient turned up who was not too firmly pre-sold on Dr. Steinfeldt, he would be assigned to Dr. Kharr and these new tests made upon him.

Apprehensively recalling his earlier difficulty in getting patients to respond to him, yet certain that his better understanding of psychology would now carry him through, Aaron Kharr made a first trial. It was a horrifying experience—feeling himself instantly disliked, totally rejected, something within him freezing, blocking him from going on. After revising his procedure, he tried with another patient. And again, and again, and again. He finally became convinced that it was not his method but himself, a realization all the more disabling when, at his insistence, Dr. Steinfeldt had finally tested the procedure himself and pronounced it a tremendous advance, immediately insisting that he do a paper on it.

That paper—"Stress Differentiation as a Diagnostic Tool"—was

Aaron Kharr's first publication. Even though it appeared in a little journal that was rarely read by practicing clinicians, it was recognition almost rewarding enough to make him think that research, after all, was what he really wanted to do. That rationalization was supported by an unexpected development. The one letter that came as a result of the paper was from Dr. Cyrus Bernathy, Chief of Cardiology at East Manhattan Hospital. Bernathy, it seemed, had been carrying on a research project for some years, investigating the pathology of coronary occlusion, and the Steinfeldt-Kharr paper had suggested a possible explanation of some of the anomalies he had turned up. Lacking the time to pursue the project himself, he offered to open his files. Steinfeldt was suspicious. Such professional generosity was unprecedented, all the more so coming from a top-level cardiologist, a leader of the clan that he had always regarded as implacably resistant to truth. Nevertheless, Steinfeldt had agreed to a luncheon meeting. After an hour's talk, Aaron Kharr, thinking that he was reflecting Steinfeldt's attitude, tried to duck by saying that he had not had enough training in pathology to undertake the study that Bernathy had in mind. Instantly, the cardiologist had offered to take him under his wing as a research fellow. To Aaron Kharr's surprise, Steinfeldt suggested that he take the appointment, inevitably a reminder of his father's agreement that he was better suited to research than practice. Obviously, he had not been paying his way in Steinfeldt's office.

But that was by no means the end of his relationship with Dr. Steinfeldt. He kept in touch with him all during the two years that he spent at East Manhattan, prizing a receptivity to new thinking that Bernathy could not supply. Nevertheless, he had learned a lot of cardiology, not only from Dr. Bernathy but from those long sessions at the autopsy table. Still it was a trying two years. Sometimes it seemed that Bernathy was genuinely interested in searching out the truth, perhaps even conscience-stricken that he played some part in suppressing it, but at other times he appeared terrified by the consequences of admission. "Think what would happen if we ever acknowledge that occupational stress is a primary cause of coronary occlusion," he had blackly speculated one night. "A million workmen's compensation cases would spring up overnight." It was no coincidence that most of Dr. Bernathy's personal friends were corporation presidents.

For all of Bernathy's ambivalence, he was personally kind and considerate. The same could not be said for the rest of East Manhattan's staff. Aaron Kharr had never before felt himself so completely shut out, an exclusion too blatantly explained by the number of times he had overheard himself called "Bernathy's young Jew." Almost for the first time in his life, he was unable to talk himself into believing that being a Jew was an imagined handicap.

When, at the end of his two years, he was offered a chance to head up a research project that Steinfeldt had induced the Berringer Institute to undertake, he accepted it, not only as an opportunity to do work for which he was eminently fitted, but also as an acceptance of his lot in life. Berringer was unequivocally a Jewish institution, endowed by a German-Jewish refugee, almost completely staffed by men with his own ethnic background.

Outwardly, Aaron Kharr got along well enough with his colleagues, protected as he was by the stipulation that, except for budgetary control and an annual review, he was to be let alone to direct his own activities. Most of his papers found publication somewhere—his known association with Bernathy had given him, if not admission to the big show, at least standing room on the fringe—but as the years slipped away it became difficult to satisfy his need for accomplishment with no more than publication. For all that he had written there was no evidence that his work was making any impress whatsoever on the medical profession. What was the point of the search for truth if, after you finally dug it out, it was to be buried in the dusty pages of some little journal that would never be opened except by some later research worker who would then discover the pointlessness of his own pursuit?

He talked himself into leaving Berringer and going to the Allison Clinic with the argument that it offered a way to bridge the gap between research and practice. The more he thought about it, the more it seemed a chance to justify himself, to prove that what he had learned could contribute to the clinic's avowed purpose of helping business executives solve their health problems. And he might have succeeded had it not been for Harvey Allison's attitude that preserving organizational harmony within the clinic staff was more important than anything else. All disputes, diagnostic as well as procedural, were resolved by a majority vote, and the majority always favored the politic course, never countenancing anything that might displease the bill-paying corporation and thus jeopardize the clinic's profit-producing goodwill. Almost from the beginning, he had found himself unable to accept the premise that maintaining good relationships with his colleagues was more important than honest service to the patients they examined.

His first serious clash with Harvey Allison had come when, on his own responsibility, Aaron Kharr had told a forty-six-year-old New Jersey corporation executive that he was in imminent danger of a coronary, a direct contradiction of the group judgment that there was no clinical evidence of heart disease. Less than a month later, the man had dropped dead. And when the company canceled its contract with the clinic, Allison irrationally charged the loss to Dr. Kharr's lapse of sound professional judgment. Nevertheless, he had continued to talk frankly to an occasional patient, the deterrent of Allison's disapproval less potent than the lift of spirit that came when he found himself getting through. One man had sent him a gift of a handsome AM-FM radio manufactured by his company. The set was of little use because he had no time to listen to it, but the enclosed card, *"For my good friend and benefactor,"* was both a treasured reward and the promise of a better future.

Until last night he had thought that promise still fulfillable, his old inadequacy something left far behind. But now he was right back where he had been twelve years before, as hopelessly and stupidly inept with Wilder as he had been with that first patient he had tried to handle in Dr. Steinfeldt's office. Why did patients instinctively dislike him? Why wouldn't they give him a chance? What was wrong with him?

His tie knotted, he stood staring at the mirror-image of his face, fruitlessly continuing an unrewarded search, finally abandoning it with a weary sigh. He walked to the window, looking out toward the distant hospital trying to decide what to do. Obviously, the ambulance case had not been an emergency. Whatever it was, Raggi had been able to handle it. There was no need to go to the hospital this early—but what else was there to do?

Suddenly, as he heard the pan-rattling evidence of Mrs. Stine's presence in the kitchen, his indecision was resolved by a positive sensation of hunger. Quickly, he went down the stairs, pleasantly anticipating Mrs. Stine's every-morning demand that, for once, he take time enough to sit down and have a decent breakfast. But not today.

She was up to her wrists in sticky noodle dough, advance prepara-tion for a big Sunday dinner that could be hurried to the table as soon as she got home from church. Harried as she was, all he got was an invitation to pour himself some coffee—there was a plate of sugar doughnuts already on the table—and when it became evident that his attempts at conversation were only adding to her nervous distrac-tion, he gave up and started for the hospital, walking instead of driving, justifying his still-puzzling lack of zeal by telling himself that he had not been getting enough exercise lately.

He stopped at the front desk, asking the girl at the switchboard about the ambulance call.

"It was a D.O.A.," she said, brassily professional. "Another turn-pike coronary."

"Local?"

"Camden, New Jersey."

"Relatives been notified?"

"His wife was with him. She's in the booth now, talking to a Harris-burg number."

He walked around the corner to the telephone booth. Raggi was standing outside the closed door, only now aware of his presence. After a checking glance inside the booth, Raggi came toward him, silently offering the clipboard that he was carrying. It was all there, the same old story—*Sampson, Peter, T. . . . male . . . 49 . . . died prior to arrival of ambulance . . . signs suggest massive coronary occlusion with immediate heart failure . . .*

"I would have called you, sir, if there was anything that could have been done," Raggi explained. "As it was, sir, I felt competent to handle the situation."

"Of course," he said, trying to make it a compliment, noting with satisfaction that Raggi was finally beginning to show some self-confidence. A head gesture toward the telephone booth asked a si-lent question.

"I would say, sir, that she is taking it remarkably well," Raggi said. "I am thinking it was not too much of a surprise—a shock, yes, yes, but you see, sir, he'd had a coronary before—"

The booth door opened and Mrs. Sampson stepped out. Her ex-pression, though drawn, seemed relatively composed, suggesting not an absence of grief but a wife who had long since learned to live with emotional stress. It was a face that Dr. Kharr had often seen before, a face that reminded him of many of the wives that he had interviewed at Berringer when he had been working up his post-coronary background studies, exhibiting a practiced control that was almost as significantly differentiating as a husband's behavior pattern.

Raggi introduced them, and Aaron Kharr, after expressing his sympathy said, "If there is anything more that we can do, Mrs. Sampson, anything at all, I do hope that you'll call on us."

"You're very kind," she said. "But I think everything is taken care of now. Dr. Raggi has been most helpful. And luckily I was able to reach my brother in Harrisburg. That's where we'd spent the night —what little there was of it."

"You were on your way home?" he suggested, difficult small talk.

She shook her head. "No, Sam thought he had to be in Wilmington today. Altoona yesterday—Harrisburg last night—that's the way it's been these last few weeks. And it was all so unnecessary. There was no reason for it. But you couldn't stop him. I tried last night. I knew what was going to happen. It was the same way he had acted the other time, this terrible drive, drive, drive—" Her voice broke with a shudder.

Forced into saying something, he needlessly asked, "There had been a previous attack?" instantly regretting his ineptness.

But, strangely, the question seemed to help her regain composure. "Yes, last year," she said firmly. "It should have been a warning—it was—but I could never make him see it that way." She closed her eyes as if trying to shut out some awful vision. "It's a horrible thing to have to remember, Doctor—seeing something like that happen to someone you love—knowing what it means, but not being able to stop it."

"You mustn't blame yourself," he murmured abstractedly, impressed by how clearly she saw the relationship between behavior pattern and heart disease, baffled again by the medical profession's reluctance to accept a causation so obvious that even a layman could recognize it.

"I tried to get him to change doctors," she said. "Sam and Paul were such close friends—I thought that someone new, someone who didn't know him so well, might be able to crack down hard enough to make him see what he was doing to himself—"

Her voice went on but all he could hear was the boomingly repetitious echo of words already spoken ". . . *someone new . . . someone who didn't know him so well . . . able to crack down . . .*"

« 3 »

Judd Wilder had made up his mind what it would mean if Dr. Kharr did not appear by ten o'clock—and now it was five minutes past the hour. Obviously, he had washed his hands of him, not even bothering to turn him over to another doctor. What other explanation could there be? If he was tied up on another case, he would have sent up that young Indian—but he had not appeared either. No one had. Not a soul had entered his room since Miss Harsch arrived three hours ago, not even the blood-sample girl from the laboratory.

Miss Harsch, apparently with that same intuitive perception with which dumb animals sense a change in the atmosphere, seemed to know that Dr. Kharr had taken himself off the case. She was no longer paying any attention to the doctor's orders, back again to treating him like a helpless invalid, stubbornly insistent upon spooning the breakfast gruel into his mouth, not even allowing him to raise his head high enough to drink from a glass, countering his every objection with a smirking "But Mr. Wilder, don't you understand—we've had a *heart attack!*"

He had looked forward to Dr. Kharr's arrival as a way of getting Miss Harsch under control again, but as that hope faded, he had become increasingly conscious of his disability. Once, surreptitiously feeling his wrist under the bed sheet, he had been startled into a state of near-panic when he was momentarily unable to find his pulse. He was being foolish—and knew it—but no amount of self-reassurance could banish his apprehension of abandonment, the near horror of finding himself left alone in Miss Harsch's hands, not another soul in the world caring whether he lived or died.

His earlier self-criticism, blaming himself for having so foolishly alienated Dr. Kharr last evening, was becoming harder and harder to sustain. The longer he thought about it, the more difficult it was to believe that he had said anything at which the doctor could have been justifiably angered. Yes, there was that "headshrinker" crack, but he would only have been seriously offended by that if he were a psychiatrist—and he was not. Mrs. Cope had confirmed that. It had to be something else. But what? Again he combed his memory, reconstructing their conversation, reweighing every word that had been spoken, finding nothing until he suddenly heard himself saying . . . *"most of my crew were Jewish boys."*

Could that be it . . . Abe Weiss again . . . ?

He had roomed with Abe at the Hotel Sutton during three months of his stay at Astoria, learning from him almost everything that he came to know about a motion picture camera. Abe's free-handed instruction, so generously given and so gratefully received, had blossomed into what he had thought to be genuine friendship, solid enough to stand any amount of give-and-take needling. But one night in a Second Avenue bar he had made a kidding remark that had unaccountably offended Abe, causing him to push away his glass and walk out. At the time, he had thought only that Abe had belted a couple too many, certain that his resentment would not survive the night. That next morning, however, Abe had applied for a change of quarters. Days had gone by before Judd had learned, by a circuitous route, that Abe had misinterpreted something that he had said as being anti-Semitic. He had gone to him and tried to establish his innocence of prejudice. Baffled by the impossibility of proof, he got nowhere.

Concerned not only by the loss of Abe's friendship but also by the fear that his blackmarking might spread to the other Jews in the crew, he had talked to Huck, asking for advice. Somberly squint-eyed, Huck had asked him how he honestly felt about Jews. And he had been truly honest in his reply: "I won't say that I'm not conscious of someone being a Jew when I first meet him—sometimes I am. But it's no different than recognizing that somebody else is Italian, or Irish, or what have you. Beyond that, I just forget it, that's all."

"Yup, that's what you're supposed to do," Huck had said. "It's what the copybook says. But sooner or later you always cross yourself up, just the way you've done with Abe. Here's the only rule to follow, Judd boy—when a Jew has forgotten it himself, then you forget it, too. Otherwise—never!"

And he had, last night, forgotten that Dr. Kharr was a Jew. Yes, that must have been it . . . Cairo . . . the Jews and the Arabs . . . but what was there about the story that could have offended him?

That was the trouble, you never knew. He hadn't known with Abe Weiss. Or that time in St. Louis with Sol Rivkin . . . Myron Wolf . . . Harold Freeberg . . . no, not with Harold . . . there'd been a reason then, the company turning down his son as a sales trainee . . .

A click of the latch sent his eyes to the door. It opened on Dr. Kharr. Recognition brought an instantly upwelling sense of reprieve, a feeling that he had been forgiven. But a second glance disabused him of that hope. The curt nod with which Dr. Kharr responded to Miss Harsch's surprised "Why, good morning, Doctor!" was as starchily stiff as the white coat that he was now wearing, and his manner as he stepped into the room made last night's informality seem an untrustworthy memory.

Miss Harsch, her hands in a helpless flutter, fumbled the chart off its hook on the end of the bed. Dr. Kharr took it, transferring to his left hand the thick ring-binder notebook that he had been carrying in his right. He looked at the chart but only as a routine gesture, his eyes unfocused. Still without a word, he handed it back to Miss Harsch, turning to pick up a chair, bringing it to the side of the bed, positioning it precisely, reaching down to place the big ring-binder notebook on the floor beside it. And now, finally, he asked, "How are you feeling this morning?" But his tone made it plain that he was no more interested in the answer than in what he had seen on the chart.

"Better," Judd said, and then much more vigorously, "A lot better," embracing the hope that whatever it was that he had said last night would be excused as the result of an illness from which he had now fully recovered.

Abruptly, apparently a diversion from plan, Dr. Kharr took out his stethoscope and bent over him. Judd, given a moment to think, decided to apologize for last night, at the point of speaking when the doctor suddenly straightened up, crumpling the black stethoscope tubing in his hands. "What are you so steamed up about, Mr. Wilder?"

"I'm not," he said, automatic denial, struck then by the disabling impression that Dr. Kharr, through his stethoscope, had been listening to his secret mind.

Silent, the doctor stuffed the instrument back in his pocket. Without taking his eyes from Judd's face, he sat down, stiff-backed, a hand on each knee. "You've no cause to worry about your heart, Mr. Wilder. As I told you last evening——"

"I'm sorry about last night," burst from his lips, words hair-triggered to this first chance for release. "I didn't mean to give you the impression that I didn't want your help——"

Having gone this far he stopped, expecting at least understanding, perhaps even a gracious acceptance of apology, unprepared for the kaleidoscopic sequence of expressions that crossed the doctor's face —surprise transmuted into questioning disbelief, disbelief into tentative gratitude, gratitude into the look of a sensitive man embarrassed by some emotion that he found peculiarly difficult to contain. For an instant it seemed that Dr. Kharr, too, might be about to apologize, but then as if an inner light had been snapped off, his face went dark again. "This is your third day, Mr. Wilder. We know now what the score is. It's time to face up to what this means."

"All right," he said, implacably agreeable, resolved to say nothing that could possibly give rise to argument.

Dr. Kharr leaned forward, a simple enough movement but it somehow conveyed the impression of a planned assault. "When you hear the term 'heart attack,' Mr. Wilder, what sort of an image comes into your mind? How clear a mental picture do you have of what's really happened?"

"Not very, I guess," he said, hoping that it was the reply that Dr. Kharr wanted.

"Are you interested?"

"Of course. Why not? Why wouldn't I be?"

"Some people aren't. They prefer to let their bodies remain impenetrable mysteries—which is unfortunate, of course, because it makes it so difficult to talk things out."

"I'm interested," he said flatly, forcing a smile over the resistance of concern, wondering what was meant by "talk things out."

Dr. Kharr lifted his hands, placing them palm to palm, fingertips down, forming an image so graphic that it was not at all difficult to accept. "This is your heart, Mr. Wilder."

He nodded, feeling a strange prickle of apprehension.

"Compared to some of the other organs—the kidneys, for example —the heart is a relatively simple mechanism. Essentially, it's nothing but a compartmented muscular bag. That's where we get the term *myocardial—myo* for muscle, *cardial* for heart—the heart muscle. If I'm being too elementary—?"

He shook his head, trying to break the grip of an unaccountable alarm as he saw Dr. Kharr begin to flex his palms in heartbeat rhythm, giving the double-handed image a reality so vivid that he had almost the feeling of watching his own dissected heart.

"Think of my wrists as the large vessels through which the blood is drawn in and forced out. Here's where some people become confused—those vessels are *not* the coronaries. So when we talk about a *coronary occlusion* we're not talking about anything that directly affects the flow of blood to the rest of the body. The coronaries are a separate system. All they do is bring in the blood that nourishes the heart muscle. Clear?"

"Sure," he said, aware of the dryness of his mouth.

"All right, the coronaries come in up here, big at the top like the taproot of a tree, and then they spread down through the heart muscle like an underground root system, the blood vessels getting smaller and smaller until, when we get way down here"—he wiggled the tip end of a finger—"the twig ends are quite small. Now if something stops the blood flow high up in the coronary system, way up here in one of these big main roots—yes, that's serious—but down here in these little twig ends, an occlusion cuts off the blood supply from only a small area of the myocardium, not enough to seriously detract from the heart's normal functioning."

"And that's all that's happened to me?" he asked, a question so forced that it sounded like a challenge of veracity, regretted as he saw the look that momentarily shadowed the doctor's face.

But with no more reaction than a tone of tried patience, Dr. Kharr replied, "Yes, all the tests show that your infarct is a small one —I'll come back to that later—but first let's follow through the whole sequence. We use the word *infarct* to describe this area of muscle tissue that's been cut off from its blood supply. We call it a *myocardial infarct*—a blood-deprived area within the muscular structure of the heart. Clear?"

He nodded.

"All right, here's what happens within that infarcted area. Essentially, it's the same thing that happens when you wound the muscular tissue in any other part of your body. Suppose you cut your finger and leave a little flap of flesh that's isolated from its blood supply. Those deprived cells die, of course, and they slough off as the wound heals. Scar tissue builds up to replace them, the arteries sprout new root ends to take over, and everything is patched up as good as new again. But there is, of course, this difference between a myocardial infarct and a cut finger. The heart has to keep on beating, and it's always more difficult for the healing process to take place in muscular tissue that's constantly in motion. For example, if I cut this finger near a joint, the wound won't heal very fast unless I immobilize the finger with a splint. That's our problem in myocardial infarction—we can't put the heart in splints."

It seemed one of those tired little jokes that doctors forced on captive patients and he responded with a smile in kind.

"So we have to be content with the next best thing. And that's to keep the heart beating along under a minimal load, and with no demands upon it that will increase either the rate or amplitude of its pumping activity. That's the principal reason for bed rest—we can't immobilize the heart, so we try to help out as much as we can by immobilizing the body. But that doesn't solve the whole problem. As I'm sure you realize, the heart responds to mental stimulation just as it does to physical exertion——"

"And with a steam-up character like me, that's quite a problem," he cut in, aware as he heard himself say it that he had missed the light note that he had tried to strike, hitting instead a cynical discord that brought an instant reaction to the doctor's face, a storm-cloud expression that threatened a lightning flash of anger.

Instead, surprisingly, Dr. Kharr replied with icy calm, "If you weren't that kind of character, Mr. Wilder, you wouldn't be here—at least not with a heart attack."

Argument leaped to his lips, but he caught it in time, silent then, recognizing that this was where he had got in trouble yesterday.

"You don't accept that, do you?"

"I'll take your word for it," he said, anything to avoid an argument.

"I don't want you to take my word for it. I want you to see it yourself."

"See what?"

"*Why* you had this heart attack."

He attempted a smile, settling for a shrug, groping for some unobjectionable way to ask what difference it made.

"What are you thinking?" Dr. Kharr demanded. "That it's water over the dam—too late to do anything about it now—so what's the point?"

Thrown off guard by the doctor's perception, he let a smile of guilty admission break through.

"The point is this, Mr. Wilder," Dr. Kharr said, his voice vibrant with intensity. "If you are able to see why you've had this first attack—and are concerned enough to do something about it—there's a good possibility that you may be able to avoid a second one." He paused. "You've been lucky this time—you've gambled with your life and won—but don't count on getting away with it again. The prognosis for a second coronary occlusion in a man under fifty is bad, Mr. Wilder, very bad indeed. If you persist in the same suicidal behavior pattern that you've followed up to now——"

"—suicidal—" rebounded from his lips, a missile deflected, but not soon enough to stop its impact, jarring loose the echoing memory of Kay's voice . . . *What are you trying to do—kill yourself?*"

"Yes—suicidal," Dr. Kharr struck again. "What else can you call behavior that can result only in self-destruction?"

Blinking, Judd stared at the doctor's face, searching for some explanation for this sadistic attack, diverted as he saw his eyes flick toward the window. Following his glance, he saw Miss Harsch shrinking back into the window corner, her hitherto unbanishable smile displaced by an expression of shock, staring at Dr. Kharr as if she could hardly believe what she had heard. Judd clenched his hands under the bedclothing, feeling himself released now from his vow not to fight back, poised to counter the next blow.

But there was no next blow, only Dr. Kharr's quiet "If you want to take a little break, Miss Harsch, go ahead," spoken in a voice so controlled that, by contrast, what he had said before could only have been a calculated attack.

For a moment Miss Harsch seemed not to comprehend. Then, snatching up her purse, she hurried out, stopping at the door for a backward glance, not at Dr. Kharr but at him, seemingly asking his forgiveness for desertion in the face of danger.

Watching her leave, Judd was peripherally aware that Dr. Kharr's eyes were still fixed upon him, exerting a magnetic pull that he consciously resisted, successful until he heard; "I hope that you're not thinking, Mr. Wilder, that you've been the victim of an unfortunate accident. You've not. This is no accident. This is something that you've done to yourself."

Silent, he measured the doctor's face, trying to gauge the depth of his vindictiveness. He was no longer thinking about what had happened last night; his concern now was that he do nothing more to incite further retaliation.

"What do you think occluded that artery?" Dr. Kharr asked. "What blocked it? What stopped the blood from flowing through?"

"Some kind of a clot, I guess."

"Yes, that's the popular conception. Even in the medical profession, there are still a great many doctors who use coronary *thrombosis* as if it were a synonym for coronary *occlusion*. It's not. In your case, Mr. Wilder—this is not an absolute certainty, but I'll wager my reputation on it—there was no thrombus, there was no clot."

"Then what was it?" he asked emptily, suddenly recalling a house-organ article that he had approved for publication only last month. "This cholesterol business—arteries gunked up like old water pipes?"

"Yes, you may have a bit of atherosclerosis—we all do," Dr. Kharr said humorlessly. "But surely not serious enough to cause an occlusion." He edged forward on his chair. "How much do you know about fat metabolism—the reduction of the triglycerides in the presence of heparin?"

It was such a far-out question that a smile broke through, uncalculated; yet it had an instantly evident effect on Dr. Kharr, his expression, that of a humorless man who had found himself being laughed at. But then his lips twisted, an effort at a smile, and he said, "I don't suppose you've ever heard of Dr. Hugo Steinfeldt?"

"No."

"Not many people have. But he was a great man. It's only now that he's beginning to get some recognition. There was a paper in one of the journals just this past month, quoting him on the psychosomatic nature of diabetes, something that he'd written fifteen years ago. That was his field—psychosomatic medicine. Not *psychiatric* —not mental illness, not diseases of the mind—*psychosomatic*. The psyche *and* the soma—that's where the name came from—diseases of the body that are caused by something going wrong in the interplay between the mind and the body."

"I understand," he said, guessing that Dr. Kharr's insistent differentiation from psychiatry meant that he had not forgotten that head-shrinker crack.

"Gastrointestinal ulcers, for example," Dr. Kharr went on. "As a young man, he'd been in the thick of that battle, trying to get the profession to acknowledge their psychogenic origin. Today, of course, most doctors do, but still—" He cut himself off. "Anyway, by the time I came to work with him, his big interest was heart disease. There'd been an enormous increase since the war in the incidence of coronary occlusion—not as much as there's been since, the rate is still going up, particularly in men under fifty—but even then Dr. Steinfeldt was very much concerned. Diet was the popular answer—it still is in most quarters—but there'd been no change in the American diet significant enough to account for any such upturn in coronary occlusions. Or at least that was Dr. Steinfeldt's view. I remember when the polyunsaturated fad started—this was later, I was at Berringer then—we were sitting together at this meeting, listening to a paper on the polyunsaturates. When it was over there was a question period, so Dr. Steinfeldt stood up and asked, 'Doctor, when you want to accelerate the development of atherosclerosis in laboratory animals, what do you use as the principal constituent of their diet?' Right away, of course, there was laughter, at least from the research men who were there, because we all knew that the answer was corn oil."

"Then all this polyunsaturated business is bunk?"

Dr. Kharr spread his hands. "The vegetable oil industry picked it up, of course, and from then on—I'm sure I don't have to tell you, Mr. Wilder, when the profit motive is strong enough, it's not too difficult for big business to overlook an inconvenient truth."

Judd quenched a flashback, suppressing the retort that big business was no more profit-driven than the medical profession, adding another dimension to his estimate of Dr. Kharr, equating him now with some of the other Jews he had known—Professor Klein at Colfax, Leo Wolf in Connecticut, Sam Kirschbaum at the agency—all of the Jews whose anti-business bias had been so transparently a protection against the excessive materialism with which they were so often charged. But he could not restrain himself from a needling "Don't you think the medical profession has to take at least part of the blame?"

"Of course!" Dr. Kharr shot back, startling because it was the first time that Judd had ever heard any doctor make such an admission. Always before, the lightest needle-prick had brought a touch-us-not reaction, the professional turtle pulling into its shell at the first hint of criticism. He would never forget, not always as a positive recollection but ever-present in his subconscious mind, what old Dr. Noble had done after his mother's death, Dr. Noble who had been their family physician for longer than Judd's lifetime, standing there lying—yes, *lying*, there was no other word for it—to protect a physician a thousand miles away, a doctor whom he had never seen, let alone known, whose only claim upon him had been a professional vow that no damaging truth about a fellow practitioner must ever be admitted.

"I'm not defending the medical profession—far from it," Dr. Kharr said. "And I'm not asking you to believe what I'm going to tell you on the basis of professional acceptance. I'll give you the evidence and you can make up your own mind."

"Fair enough," Judd said, chancing a smile, seeing Dr. Kharr in yet another light. Unquestionably he was an oddball—a rebel in the medical ranks would have to be—but at least he was no Dr. Noble. "You were talking about Dr. Steinfeldt," he reminded him.

"Yes," Dr. Kharr said with a quick nod. "There was nothing particularly new in his concept that emotional stress was somehow involved in coronary occlusion. But how? What was happening? What was the physiological linkage between cause and effect? We had all sorts of theories, of course—one of them, as it turned out, was right on the mark—but we couldn't tie it down, not then at least, not until after I'd gone over to the Berringer Institute."

The corridor door opened a crack, Miss Harsch peeping in, but Dr. Kharr went on without interruption. "The real break came in May 1958. *Circulation*, one of our medical journals, appeared with a report on some work that had been done by two San Francisco investigators. They had studied tax accountants, a group of men all under the same occupational tension, all heading for an annual stress peak at the same time—April fifteenth, the date when the income tax returns had to be filed. They bled these men biweekly, testing for blood clotting time and serum cholesterol. It was a beautiful demonstration. The closer they got to April fifteenth, the lower the blood clotting time and the higher the cholesterol level. And it couldn't be anything but stress, everything else was controlled. I'll never forget reading that paper. There it was, as plain as could be."

"But I thought you said that this cholesterol business was a lot of—"

"We didn't know what the role of cholesterol was—we still don't," Dr. Kharr said. "We did know that there was an association between high serum cholesterol and coronary occlusion—that had been demonstrated by several investigators—and in our own work, wherever we were able to get a blood test immediately after occlusion we almost invariably got a high reading. But did that necessarily mean that cholesterol was the culprit? Or was high cholesterol merely an indicator of something else? We'd already begun to suspect that it was because we had established that the relationship between cholesterol and diet was far less significant than the quite remarkable coordination with stress."

"So there's nothing to this low-cholesterol diet business either," Judd suggested.

"No, I'm not prepared to go that far, but I'm inclined to think that a low-fat diet is more—" He broke off with "But let me go on and you'll see for yourself." He raised a clenched fist. "Think of this as a molecule of glycerine. There are millions of them in your bloodstream. They're there to serve as carriers of fat. As fat is released by the digestive process, it's picked up by this glycerine carrier. Three molecules of fat attach themselves to each molecule of glycerine—one, two, three." Three fingers snapped up in time with his count. "That's why we call it a triglyceride. Clear?"

He nodded.

"All right, now we have this triglyceride in the bloodstream, flowing along until it comes to a fat storage cell. If everything is functioning as it should, those three fat molecules break away from the glycerine carrier and are absorbed into the cell. But that happens only if there's heparin present. Heparin is a substance created by the body, specifically to separate those fat molecules from their carrier. If there isn't enough heparin present, the triglyceride can't get rid of its fat—right? So it goes on riding along in the bloodstream. And more and more triglycerides are being formed all the time, of course. All right, as the triglyceride concentration builds up, the blood gets thicker and thicker. It's not unlike what happens to lubricating oil in an engine. As the oil sludges up, it becomes too thick and heavy to get through and do its job. Essentially, the same thing happens in the heart. When the capillaries get sludged up, and the blood can no longer flow in to nourish the heart muscle—all right, you've got an occluded coronary."

"That's quite a theory," he said, his quick smile an involuntary antidote for apprehension aroused by the vivid image of a sludge-plugged heart.

"It's more than a theory, Mr. Wilder," Dr. Kharr said tautly. "Do you recall—when you were still in Emergency—that I had a blood sample taken?"

"I guess I wasn't paying too much attention."

"That night I ran a triglyceride determination. It was over 300 milligrams per cent. That's extremely high—normal is somewhere around 125—surely high enough to strongly suggest what had happened. I was even more convinced after I saw the precipitate drop that we got when we gave you heparin to make up for what your body hadn't been producing. By midnight, you were back to normal. But it had taken a lot of heparin to restore the balance. Obviously, there'd been a serious depletion of the heparin in your bloodstream." He paused. "Clear?"

"Yes, but—I still don't see why——"

"Why you weren't producing enough heparin?" Dr. Kharr supplied. "Yes, that's the whole point. All right, let's see if I can explain it. I'm not going to get into all the biochemistry that's involved—it's all very complicated, and there's some of it that we still don't understand—but we do know what happens, at least in terms of the end result. You know what adrenaline is, of course?"

"More or less."

"Actually, it's not adrenaline—more precisely, it's norepinephrine that we're concerned with—but all this will probably be more understandable if I use the popular term. In any event, it is produced as a response to psychic challenge. The amount of it that a man produces depends on his personality and the situation in which he finds himself. If he's naturally competitive and aggressive, and in a situation where he feels himself continually challenged, his adrenal glands have to work overtime to keep up with the demand. Clear? All right, think of it this way—it's not this simple but this is one way of looking at it—think of your body as being capable of producing either adrenaline or heparin, but not both at the same time. Normally, there's only an intermittent demand for adrenaline. A challenge arises, the gland responds with a charge of adrenaline, the challenge is met, and you go back to making heparin again. Now here's what I want you to see, Mr. Wilder—if a man has driven himself into a behavior pattern where he feels himself constantly under stress, where he never gives up pumping adrenaline into his arteries, where there's no time to replenish his depleted stock of heparin—" He spread his hands. "You see it now, don't you?"

He was hit hard, much harder than his governing instinct of self-protection would permit him to reveal. All of his adult life he had been told that he had to learn to relax, to slow his drive, to take things easier, but never before had it made any sense. Understanding had always been blocked by his inability to visualize any tangible connection between mind and body. He knew there was an interrelationship—his bouts of belly trouble were clearly linked to periods of nervous tension—but he had always been disinclined to explore the mysterious workings of his mind, accepting its machinations as a religious man accepts the nature of his faith, intuitively fearing that the magic might be lost if it were too closely examined. Now, almost as if he had acquired a new character, he saw the haziest of intangibles revealed as a reasoned reality. And yet, for some reason that he made no effort to understand, he was unable to reply with an unqualified "Yes" when he heard Dr. Kharr ask if he understood. All he could manage was a cautious "You think that's why this happened to me—is that it?"

"You don't see it?"

"Oh, I'm not saying that you're wrong——"

"But you don't think it applies to you?"

"I don't see how it could."

"Why not?"

"If that's what it was—stress—whatever you want to call it—it wouldn't have happened now."

"No?"

"It would have happened sometime when the whip was really on." Encouraged by his own argument, he added more strongly, "I haven't been under any pressure lately. Actually, I've been—I won't say exactly coasting, but still—well, March is always my easiest month. That's when I catch my breath before I have to start going all-out on the convention."

"Catch your breath after what, Mr. Wilder?"

"The spring promotion tour. If you want to talk about pressure—sixteen meetings in twenty-three days, all of our district office cities—Boston, New York, Atlanta, Kansas City, Chicago—all the way out to the Coast. By the time I got out to San Francisco——" He saw a look of sharp inquiry and explained, "That's where we wound up—San Francisco."

"In other words, if something like this had happened then you wouldn't have been too surprised—is that what you're saying?"

"No, all I meant was—" Whatever it was that he had been about to say was swept away by a flooding memory of the Los Juntos Motel, his mind no more than cleared when he was struck again by the blanking image of Floyd Fulton's death mask in the Jersey City morgue. He knew that he had to throw it off, to say something that would break the grip of Dr. Kharr's eyes, but all that came out was, "It just doesn't make any sense—not now."

Dr. Kharr removed his spectacles. The effect was startling. His eyes were now dominant, making him seem a different man, his face no longer a coldly probing lensed instrument. And there was a change, too, in the voice that quietly asked, "You were on your way back from New York?"

"But it hadn't been a tough trip. I'd just gone over to put Kay on the boat, that's all."

"You'd driven over that morning?"

"No, the day before. Kay's ship was sailing at noon, so we thought it would be too tight a squeeze to try to make it that morning. Anyway, I had some things to do—a lot of stuff to line up for the convention. And Kay had some last-minute shopping."

"What did you do that evening? Out on the town?"

"No. We were going to the theater, but I got tied up over at the advertising agency so—well, it was pretty late when I finally got back to the hotel, so we just grabbed a bite downstairs and turned in." A muscle spasm clenched his jaws, a reaction to the memory of Kay's dry-lipped kiss across the gulf between their twin beds, the instant loss of hope that he might challenge her indifference with a show of passion, but knowing then that there was no way out . . . sex that was only a last-night formality, Kay's final payment on the ransom price of escape . . . unable to sleep . . . sitting at the window looking out into the night . . . the big VEGA sign over on Broadway . . . remembering Ilsa Lang, the first time that he had thought of her since . . .

"And the next morning you took your wife down to the ship?"

"Well, no. Actually, she went over by herself. I had to pick up the proofs of the stockholders report. They weren't going to be ready until ten, so Kay went ahead. But I knew some of the agency crowd were coming down to the boat to give her a little send-off, so I got there as soon as I could."

"Ah, then there was a sailing party?" Dr. Kharr asked, acting as if he had picked up a significant clue. "How much did you drink, Mr. Wilder?"

"Not enough to—couple of glasses of champagne, that's all. I've been laying off liquor."

"Why?"

"Oh, I don't know, it just hasn't seemed to agree with me lately."

"What do you mean lately? The last few weeks?"

"No, longer than that. It's been—oh, I don't know that I can pin it down—the last year or so." Conscious of the sharpness of the doctor's surveillance, he twisted away with "Champagne never did sit right—or maybe it's just all the junk you eat at one of those affairs. That's what I thought this was—indigestion."

"Yes, that's what you kept telling me," Dr. Kharr said with a mercurial smile, too quickly gone to have any real meaning. "To get back to your wife's sailing—was that in any way a stressful situation?"

"What do you mean by that?" he asked, abruptly supplying his own meaning. "Look, if you've got the idea that there's any sort of trouble between—forget it, there isn't."

"Forgive me," Dr. Kharr quickly apologized. "But it did seem—your wife going abroad by herself—and then your not wanting any word sent to her——"

"Why wreck her trip? This is something she's been looking forward to for years. If you sent her a cable—wireless, whatever it would be—she'd be on the first plane back. And what could she do for me? Nothing. Right?"

Dr. Kharr's only response was another question. "How long is she planning to stay?"

"Oh, I don't know—a month or so—depends on how things work out." A thought of Rolfe was quickly put down. "You can forget the wife-trouble angle."

"Then what kind of trouble *have* you had, Mr. Wilder?"

The sharp thrust of the question loosed a vigorously defensive "What do you mean—trouble?"

"Anything that would put you under sustained emotional stress."

"Look, I'm sorry to upset your little theory, but it just doesn't pay off. I haven't been under any stress—emotional or otherwise." It seemed a too-weak defense and he tried to buttress it by adding, "I mean it. It's true. I haven't."

"What time did you leave New York—do you happen to remember?"

"Leave New York?" It took a moment to refocus his mind but the instant it cleared, the memory was there, reassuringly precise. "Sure I remember—I went through the Lincoln Tunnel at five after four."

"And you had your attack just after seven?"

"Seven-ten. I'd just come off the turnpike—I'd looked at the clock on the tollbooth."

"Three hours and five minutes from New York," Dr. Kharr observed. "That's fast time."

"I usually make it in two-fifty, two-fifty-five. But I stopped for something to eat."

"But not a full dinner?"

"No, I just grabbed a couple of cheeseburgers."

"Why were you in such a hurry, Mr. Wilder?"

"Well, I had this proof to get to Mr. Crouch by eight-thirty."

"Tell me this, Mr. Wilder—" Dr. Kharr put on his glasses again. "Had Mr. Crouch asked that you have that proof at his house by eight-thirty? Or was that simply a goal that you had set for yourself?"

"I don't know what you're trying to prove but—what's this all about?"

Dr. Kharr reached down beside the bed, coming up with the thick ring-binder notebook that he had put there when he first sat down. He placed it on his knees, squaring it precisely, opening it to a place that had been marked with a slip of paper. With no word of explanation he began to read. "'This precoronary behavior syndrome, first identified by Dr. Hugo Steinfeldt, is somewhat more difficult to describe and define than the causative situation in other psychogenic manifestations. With gastrointestinal ulcer, for example, the precipitating anxiety is usually easy to unearth since the patient is well aware of it and typically willing to discuss it. By contrast, the coronary patient characteristically insists that he had not been under any unusual stress. He will often maintain that quite the opposite is true.'"

Unavoidably, Judd shot a suspicious glance at Dr. Kharr, thinking that the doctor was tricking him—but, unquestionably, he was reading, not improvising, and the page had been marked before he had come into the room.

Dr. Kharr did not look up. "'Although there is always the temptation to suspect that the patient, consciously or not, is suppressing the truth, this is rarely the case. Typically, he is honestly unaware of the stressed state into which he has driven himself. Nevertheless, he will frequently reveal a secondary consciousness that something untoward has happened to him. He may, for example, remark that some particular food that he used to enjoy no longer agrees with him. Not infrequently, he will have made a recent attempt to give up smoking. Often enough to be notable, he will have stopped drinking, again with the explanation that alcohol doesn't seem to agree with him any more.'"

This time, Dr. Kharr did look up, but it was only the briefest of glances, no more than a check to make certain that what he had read had hit the mark. Even so, Judd's eyes broke away first.

"'Needless to say,'" Dr. Kharr read on, "'no one behavioral trait can be taken as surely differentiating. It is only when the examining physician observes the whole syndrome that a positive diagnosis can be safely made. In practice, this is not as difficult as it may seem. There is a pattern that, once observed, is rarely missed thereafter. Initial identification can be aided, perhaps, by adopting a view originally suggested by Dr. Leon Schain, one of the writer's associates at the Berringer Institute. Dr. Schain observed that the precoronary behavior pattern was manifestly similar to that of a drug addict. Although this analogy can be carried too far, it does have a certain legitimacy. There is indeed a drug involved—adrenaline—and the course of a growing addiction is not too difficult to postulate in a typical case.'"

Dr. Kharr turned a page, reading on, his voice flatly expressionless, yet relentlessly driven. "'The type of man in whom the development of a precoronary behavior pattern may most logically be suspected, almost invariably exhibits those character traits which, as previously noted, have long been accepted as signs of a coronary-prone personality. He is inherently aggressive, competitive, energetic and ambitious. To put it another way, he is naturally geared to operate at a high adrenaline level. In his earlier years, the necessary psychic challenge was ever-present. However, as he comes into middle age, typically in his mid-forties, adequate stimulation becomes difficult to find. The old challenges have lost their potency. There are few situations that he has not faced before, few problems for which his experience will not quickly supply an answer. The hope for further advancement has often dimmed. His personal life has commonly become routine, equally lacking in future promise. For most men, this is a period of crisis. A few respond by radically reordering their lives, changing jobs or even entering some entirely new field, but it is only the exceptional man to whom that opportunity is available. Most men, surely the majority, settle back and adjust to a lower level of adrenaline stimulation. But not the man we are examining. He has, in the idiom of the drug addict, become so hooked on adrenaline that he can't kick the habit. Unable to find sufficiently stimulating major challenges, he begins to rely on a multiplicity of minor ones. When they do not exist, he invents them. Quite unknowingly, he starts playing little adrenal-stimulating games. One of the most commonly observed is a running battle with the clock and the calendar. By constantly fighting the pressure of time, he can generate a continuing air of crisis, and thus keep giving himself repeated shots of adrenaline all day long. In our psychological appraisement tests at Berringer, one of the most surely differentiating overt signs proved to be the frequency with which a subject looked at his watch. When we asked him to remove it, as we did in one series of tests, he would continue to look at his bare wrist with substantially the same frequency.'"

His voice lapsed for an instant, suggesting that something was being skipped, continuing: "'More than ninety per cent of those we eventually graded PCS–1—that is, those we judged to be in a critical stage of the precoronary syndrome—readily admitted that they never took an automobile trip without calculating minutes against miles, estimating an arrival time and then pushing themselves to meet this self-imposed and usually meaningless deadline.'"

Dr. Kharr's voice had come to an abrupt stop, suspended as if he were anticipating an explosive response, and Judd found a perverse pleasure in denying him that satisfaction. Exercising rigid self-control, he kept himself from looking at the doctor, fixing his expression in an unrevealing mask, caught up only when he suddenly realized that he was staring directly at the wall clock. Instantly, he averted his eyes, looking now toward the window, wondering if Dr. Kharr had noticed it, relieved by the slow-dawning realization that, by then, he had already started to read again, his eyes on the notebook . . . or whatever it was . . . probably something that he had written . . . trying it out . . . Ken Malling coming up to Connecticut that weekend with his new play, not realizing until he heard himself reading it aloud how full of holes it was. Yes, that's what this must be . . . all of Kharr's little crackpot theories . . . hoping that someday he could get it published . . . the big dream!

Again, he opened his ears, listening, but now more conscious of tone than content, increasingly convinced that his guess was right. A tentative quality had come into Dr. Kharr's voice, an air of growing self-doubt, every sentence advanced as if he were afraid of its being challenged . . . and it would be easy enough to do . . . like all this psychological testing crap. All right, maybe he had set eight-thirty himself . . . so what? Didn't Mr. Crouch have a right to know what time he'd be there? If he hadn't told him . . .

"—and the PCS, of course, will deny any such interpretation, not only because he is inherently self-defensive but also because of the obsessive tendency toward argument that is so commonly a differentiating sign of the precoronary behavior syndrome. Again the drug addiction analogy is pertinent. In his never-ending search for adrenal stimulation, the PCS must constantly find new challenges. One way to do so, he finds, is by regarding everyone he meets as a potential sparring partner, always hoping that he can goad someone into offering him the challenge of argument. His friends will often characterize him as a "needler," always trying to incite a flashback. Such behavior is rarely appreciated, and is at least partly accountable for the deteriorating social relationships that, as the syndrome develops, become more and more evident. Investigation will usually disclose that his business relationships also have been adversely affected, particularly with those who work under his direction. Since by nature he is something of a perfectionist, this trait is commonly heightened to obsessive proportions as the syndrome develops. When a piece of work is submitted to an advanced PCS by a subordinate, he overlooks merit and sees nothing but fault. The smallest error is magnified to crisis proportions. Often he brushes the subordinate aside, declaring that he will do the job himself, thus generating a double shot of adrenaline, stimulation supplied not only by artificially aroused anger with a supposedly incompetent assistant, but also by the challenging necessity of outperforming—"

Inescapably, Judd flinched, trying to blink away an apparition . . . John Weller's scowling face looking down at him, pinning him to his desk chair . . . "*All right, you bastard, let's see what you can find wrong with that!*" . . . throwing the envelope at him, missing the desk, slamming the door on his way out . . . picking up the envelope, knowing before he opened it what would be inside . . . "*It is with the greatest satisfaction that I herewith present my immediate resignation . . .*"

"I'm sorry, I hadn't intended to go this far today," Dr. Kharr's voice broke in. "You're getting tired, aren't you?"

He thought, "What are you going to do—walk out on me again?" —unaware until he looked at the doctor that he must have said it aloud. Dr. Kharr's whole body had gone slack, his shoulders slumped as if some inner support had collapsed under a crushing blow. But his face, drained and gray, was much less an acknowledgment of defeat than an accusation of some terrible unfairness.

Convulsively, feeling as if something were being torn from his mind, Judd flung out, "You're probably right," an admission so difficult that he could not restrain the physical reaction of throwing out his arm.

Dr. Kharr caught his hand, ostensibly no more than simple restraint, his fingers a slack netting. But then, strangely, they gripped down, the pressure slowly increasing as if hope was flowing back into his veins. And when Judd twisted his head to look at his face, he saw that the grayness was fading. And as if the return of life had restored his power of speech, he said, "All I'm trying to do is help you, Mr. Wilder. I've probably gone about it in the worst possible way——"

"No," he denied. "You're right. I guess I was a—whatever you call them——"

"What you were doesn't concern me—it's what you're going to be from here on out, that's all that matters. I don't want this to happen again, neither do you."

He lay back, feeling a strange emptiness that was, in itself, a kind of fulfillment. "But what's the payoff? What do I do? What's the answer? I'm what I am. I can't be someone else. I can't be something I'm not. I've got to be myself. If I can't, there's no point in——"

"But you haven't been yourself, Mr. Wilder, not for the last year, or the last two years, or however long it's been since you got off the track. This didn't happen to the man you were two years ago, it happened to the man you were last Thursday evening." He paused. "Let me read you one last thing—I know that I'm going much too far for one day——"

"Go ahead. I'm all right."

Dr. Kharr turned pages until he found what he was looking for, marking the paragraph with a finger as he looked up to explain. "This is something that Dr. Steinfeldt once said. I'd asked him what he saw when he examined a PCS. This is what he said, as nearly as I could get it down—'I see a man who is a runner without a goal. He has been running all his life. He runs because it is his nature to run, because running is the expression of his being. Once, there was an open road ahead, up the hills and down the valleys, and no valley was ever so deep that it dimmed the promise of what lay over the next hill. But then he lost his way. Somewhere he took the wrong turning. Now he's off the main road. He's in the deep woods. The dark shadows are closing in. He can't see ahead. But still he runs. Unless he finds his way back to the main road, he will run until he is swallowed up in the black shadows of the deep woods.'"

There was the sound of a heavy book being closed, strengthening the priest image that Dr. Kharr's oddly enriched voice had brought to Judd Wilder's mind, preserved in the silence that followed. Somewhere in the distance a church bell was ringing.

"Let me ask you one last question," Dr. Kharr said. "If I were to give you a sheet of paper and a pencil, would you be able to put down—right now, this very minute—a clear statement of what you want to accomplish in the last half of your life?"

Silence was enough of an answer.

"When you can do that, you'll be back on the main road," Dr. Kharr said quietly. "Think about it."

And then he was gone, not as he had left yesterday, but now as if he had slipped through the curtaining mist of a dream . . . the black shadows of the dark woods . . . Kay . . . "*What are you trying to prove? . . . What do you want?*" . . .

« 4 »

At the accelerated pace of shipboard life, Kay Wilder's friendship with Chris Kemble had reached, in a single day, a state of intimacy that could not have been achieved in months of more normal association. Last night Kay had listened to an outpouring of self-revelation that made Chris totally believable when she said that she was telling her things that she had not told even her psychiatrist, her lack of reserve credibly explained when she had added, "I couldn't possibly tell you all this if I didn't know that we'll never see each other again." By then, Chris had been on her third husky highball, yet it had been Kay's conscious judgment that alcohol was releasing rather than distorting the truth. She had listened with the fascination of first experience—never before had any other woman talked to her like this—captivated by the evidence that some of her own deeply buried thoughts were not as uniquely personal as she had imagined.

The initial attraction of similar situation had, however, been substantially weakened—Judd and Jim Kemble could hardly be more different men—but that original motivation toward friendship had been replaced by something that, although accepted as sympathy for a fellow creature torn by emotion, was more truly a recognition of appealing fallibility. Chris Kemble was apparently unaware of the incongruity of her position, attempting to justify divorce because of a money-mad husband, yet in the next breath gloating over the alimony settlement that her lawyer had managed to extract, measuring her ultimate victory by the same yardstick that she so violently decried. And now she was looking ahead to a life where she could "be herself," a happy state that visibly involved occupancy of a First Class suite, a casually purchased Givenchy original and a closet full of clothes no less fabulously overpriced, everything paid for with money that had seemingly lost its obsessive taint the instant it passed into her hands.

The most telling change, however, had been in Chris's attitude toward "all this sex business." What she had said earlier about never having been the "jolly little concubine type" should have been a dead giveaway, but Kay, thrown off by that brassy declaration, had missed its implication. And she had accepted at face value, too, Chris's declaration that there had been no other woman involved. The second highball had dissolved that façade, and Chris Kemble had emerged from behind it as a distraught woman desperately anxious to have someone tell her that her husband's compulsive philandering had not been the result of her own inadequacy. Kay had gone as far as she could by way of comforting response, using words that she had read but never before spoken aloud, yet finding herself incapable of responding in kind to Chris's frankness. She had revealed very little about herself. It had been a conscious containment, not difficult to preserve. Chris had been too self-centered to be seriously interested in anyone else's life, and Kay, with an example before her of how easy it was for an emotionally disturbed woman to reveal more than she intended, had held her tongue.

Today was a different story, Chris a different woman. They had met after breakfast, Chris coming out of the little Boutique des Indes, surprising her by saying that she had decided against buying a lovely Cambodian brooch because she couldn't afford it, a prelude to an embarrassed reference to the way that she had "let go" last night. A strong sense of guilt was evidenced not only by the sincerity of her apology but also by the way that, as they walked the deck together, she turned away all questions about herself, countering every one with a question about Kay. By the time they had completed their six laps and sat down together in a sheltered corner of the deck, Kay was talking almost freely, feeling now that Chris, after last night's emotional purge, was a more likable person than she had imagined. They would never be friends ashore, all this would end at Le Havre, but at least Chris was more interesting than anyone else on the ship, and talking to her was a buffer against the intrusion of Mrs. Skarbo and Mrs. Johnson, who periodically toured the ship as if they were circulating at a Chamber of Commerce cocktail party, exhibiting their president's-wife status by exchanging chitchat with everyone in sight.

Yesterday, avoiding anything that might destroy her protective anonymity, Kay had said nothing about Judd ever having worked for a New York advertising agency, nor that they had once lived in Connecticut, but now something slipped out about Sedgefield.

Chris picked it up immediately. "Sedgefield? You mean you lived there?"

"Oh, that was a long time ago," Kay said, starting a change of subject.

But Chris insisted, "When were you there? We used to know a lot of people in Sedgefield."

"Everyone we knew is gone now," Kay said. "I remember at Christmastime—the card list—there wasn't a Sedgefield name on it any more."

"But you did say that it was just before you moved to Pennsylvania. And you said you'd been there twelve years."

Giving up, Kay said, "Yes, we lived in Sedgefield until 'Fifty-two."

"Then you must have known Jack and Mary Ellis. They had that lovely old house—you know, on the right, just after you cross the bridge?"

"Yes, I remember the house," Kay acknowledged, suppressing a far more vivid recollection of Jack Ellis himself, expecting everyone on the Opera House board to fall into a swoon every time he opened his mouth, invariably some pompous pronouncement prefaced by a reminder that he was a network vice president. "I really don't know Jack. We were on the Opera House board together, that's all."

"The Opera House!" Chris exclaimed. "Oh, isn't it a gem? We were over there—oh, I've forgotten exactly when, sometime last winter. Jim had gotten them these folksingers, whatever they call themselves. Anyway, they're on TV and it's one of Jim's programs. They were horrible, I thought, simply horrible, but the Opera House itself—so many of these restoration things wind up so quainty-cutesy but that isn't at all. You must be awfully pleased with the way it turned out."

"I haven't seen it since it was finished. We were only getting started when I left, not much beyond the planning stage, really."

"Then you must have worked with Ben Kassoff?"

Kay attempted a poised "Yes," but the word stuck in her throat, affirmation swollen to choking proportions by the unreasoned fear that she was trapped, even more alarmed when Chris went on, "I got to know Ben awfully well when he did over our house. Wasn't he the most fascinating man? Of course he was mad, absolutely mad—"

Kay set a fixed smile, hoping that it was sufficiently opaque to hide her memories of those last months in Sedgefield, all the more vivid because they had been so long submerged, protected from exposure by the impossibility of imagining herself ever having been involved in anything as completely insane as that unaccountable affair with Ben Kassoff.

For an instant, she was caught up again by the ancient argument that it had all been Judd's fault for throwing them together the way he had, but that escape was as quickly blocked as it had been that last night, as invalid as her frantic feeling that Judd had been unfair, suddenly appearing when he should have been safely hidden away in a television control room. But that made no sense either. Nothing did. Nothing ever had.

It had never meant anything, nothing at all. That's what made it so horrible. If there had been anything genuine between her and Ben, it would have happened long before it did. Ben had been a part of their life ever since the move to Connecticut.

There had, of course, been the unbalancing elation of finally getting out of Greenwich Village. She had, by then, all but abandoned hope that Judd would ever break out of his starry-eyed attachment to Huck Joyce, directing those stupid little industrial motion pictures, not clearheaded enough to see that MGM or Twentieth Century were not going to be impressed by one of those little commercial pictures that he was grinding out. But one of them won some kind of a prize for the best industrial film of the year, meaningless until it had brought an out-of-the-blue offer to go into television direction. Judd had vacillated for a week, and afraid that any attempt to influence him would do more harm than good, she had done no more than repeat what the network had already told him: that with all his motion picture background and his earlier experience in radio he was exactly the man they were looking for, certain to have a bright future. True, at the beginning his earnings would be low—the network could not afford to pay very much to a director until a sponsor could be found—but that would come. Even though the number of sets in use was still too low to make television an economically attractive advertising medium, a few of the big companies were beginning to be interested, if only for the prestige that it would give them.

Judd had professed to see the change as a big gamble—he was still hoping, she knew, that Huck would get himself straightened out—but in the end, to her delight, he had decided to make the break. She was certain that it was the right move for Judd, still not what he ought to be doing, but a step in the direction.

Judd's first television production had been enthusiastically reviewed, *Variety* calling him a "welcome new director" whose professional skill had "lit up the tube with a glow that should warm the hearts of those buffs who have been pitching TV as an artistic medium." After his fifth production—Ilsa Lang in *Dust Bowl*—the show had been bought by Vega Cosmetics. His salary immediately skyrocketed from a hundred and twenty-five to four hundred dollars a week, and he had finally agreed that it was time to get out of the Village. Rolfe was almost six, ready for school, and they couldn't go on bringing him up in an environment where he never saw anything but asphalt streets and brick walls.

She had spent the next four days in a hard-driven canvass of Connecticut, paying far more attention to neighbors than houses, rejecting all areas that had been too heavily infiltrated by the advertising crowd. Her search had finally centered on Sedgefield, pinpointed to the area called Papertown, a name derived from the paper mill that once operated there. The mill itself had long since disappeared but around the millpond there were still the little cobblestone houses that the paternalistic millowner had built for his employees. First discovered by painters—serious artists, not commercial hacks—Papertown was then in the process of being taken over by people from the legitimate theater, precisely the influence that Judd most needed.

Snatching at the chance, she signed a purchase agreement on the best house that was still available, making the down payment out of her own money, hoping that it would not bring on a repetition of the horrible scene that Judd had made when he had discovered that she had been secretly subsidizing part of the rent of their Greenwich Village apartment with the interest money from the bonds she had inherited from Uncle Charles. There had been no scene this time. Completely immersed in his job—with sponsorship, the production budget had been more than doubled—Judd had been blissfully uninterested in anything outside the studio walls, agreeing by default to let her take over the job of getting the place remodeled. That was how she had met Ben Kassoff.

Ben was, according to his most-used story, a refugee architect from Russia who had escaped to the United States after he had been taken prisoner by the Germans at Leningrad. But he was quite capable of revising his biography to suit the occasion, and there was a cynical suspicion in some quarters that his escape had been only from Brooklyn. Whatever the truth, he was the only building contractor around Sedgefield who had any interest in remodeling Papertown houses. All the others had abandoned the territory, frankly saying that they would rather work for people who had more common sense. Ben had taken over Papertown like an occupying conqueror, driving his pickup truck as if it were a chariot, roaring around from job to job, goading on his largely imbecilic workmen who, hired at half union scale, nevertheless accomplished miracles under his direction. When they failed him, he stepped in himself. And then, it seemed, there was no limit to his abilities. When he had decreed that half of their dining room had to be replastered, Kay had agonized over losing the lovely old mural that had been painted by some primitive artist. Ben had blithely said it would be simple enough to restore the lost portion, and that was exactly what he had done, turning up one Sunday morning with a fistful of caked brushes and a cardboard box of old twisted color tubes, painting away like a madman for the whole day to the accompaniment of a wild yarn about how he once fooled the best of Parisian art dealers with his fake Cézannes, a tale that began to take on some essence of credibility when, by nightfall, he had so perfectly matched new work to old that the juncture was undiscernible. Then, until long after midnight, he and Judd had sat in the kitchen drinking wine, excluding her by the coarseness of their language. Eavesdropping, she had been shocked to hear Judd use words that he could only have picked up in the service. Ben's tongue, of course, had been as unrestrained as his behavior—and that, according to the gossip she was picking up, confirmed by the stories she heard him tell Judd, was as uninhibited as that of a wild stallion. Even from the bedroom she could hear their ribald laughter, and when Judd finally came to bed, she pretended to be asleep, justified by seeing him, for the first time in their married life, unmistakably drunk.

But it was not entirely because of Ben's bad influence on Judd that she had begun to look forward to getting rid of him. Beyond question, he was doing a wonderful job on the house, but having him around all the time was beginning to make her nervous. Hopefully, she thought the job would be finished by the holidays, but it had dragged on and on, the house seemingly haunted by gremlins that made roofs leak and doors come unhinged. Ben usually answered her calls for help himself, but he always turned up on evenings when Judd was there, the two of them invariably winding up in the kitchen. When she had once suggested that spending so much time with Ben was a waste, Judd had flashed back that Ben Kassoff had more on the ball than all the rest of the Papertown crowd combined.

As the weeks went by, Ben started coming around every Saturday night, not at her request but at Judd's, and although there was always an overtone of lusty ribaldry drifting in from the kitchen, where they insisted on having their sessions, most of the talk she overheard was about Judd's television show. Ben had started working with Judd on set design. Although his story that he had once been a scenic designer for Ziegfeld was patently ridiculous—even Judd laughed at that—it could not be denied that Ben's contribution, whatever it was, made an enormous improvement in the pretty-pretty sets that had previously been turned out by the faggoty little designer that the network had assigned to Judd's show. Ben did not have a television set of his own, so Judd had invited him to come around on Wednesday night to see the program on the air. "You don't mind, do you?" he had asked her, obviously deaf to what the gossips would be saying. Nothing had happened, of course, but thinking of what everyone was no doubt imagining, every Wednesday evening had been a nervous trial. It was a great relief when Ben finally bought a television set of his own.

That summer, during the thirteen weeks when Judd's show was off the air, she had seen almost nothing of Ben Kassoff, but Judd had gone out several times on Ben's boat with a crowd of men, fishing off Montauk, usually staying out overnight, returning red-eyed and uncommunicative. Foolishly, she had let an acid comment slip with the result that, when the fall season started, Judd had stopped those sessions at their home, going instead to Ben's house, or having him come in to New York.

She had of course called Ben when there was something that had to be done at the house, but he usually sent one of his men. The explanation that he was getting too busy to handle repairs himself was believable enough—he had a half-dozen crews going by then, a new office in town and a decorating shop out on the highway—but he was never too busy to see Judd. Obviously, he was avoiding her, and the search for a reason had been only too easily satisfied. The number of rich-bitch Cadillacs that she saw parked in front of Ben's office was proof enough of what was going on.

It was Judd who had thrown them together again. The Sedgefield Chamber of Commerce had declared itself open to some community project that would serve as a tourist attraction. With no difficulty at all, Kay had nudged the Papermill crowd into supporting the idea of restoring the old Sedgefield Opera House, and staging there each summer a festival of early American theatrical revivals. With the Chamber's approval of her proposal, she had been made a member of the planning committee, immediately frustrated by a chairman whose greatest concern was for *Robert's Rules of Order,* with which, week after week, he thwarted any progress toward getting a tangible plan down on paper. Judd had never been involved—his television program took too much of his time—but, desperate, she had talked to him one morning at breakfast. "Have you thought of talking to Ben?" he asked, safely unaware that she had been thinking of little else for the past week. But even with Judd's approval, she waited three days before calling Ben, strangely fear-filled, explaining her trepidation by telling herself that she was afraid that he would refuse to help. And yet, when she had called him, and he had quickly and enthusiastically voiced his interest, promising that he would come around to see her that very evening, her fear-like titillation had been in no way appeased. Her hand, she remembered, had trembled violently when she opened the door for him.

Although Ben's chariot pickup had given way to a canary-yellow Buick convertible, he was still the flamboyant conqueror, interested now in extending his domain. The big money crowd was moving into the Sedgefield area, buying up the old estates along the Sound, and Ben had said with a conniving chuckle that what he needed to break in with them was a big showpiece remodeling job. The Opera House was exactly what he had been looking for. He would, he said, take over the whole architectural job, first surveying the old theater to uncover any weaknesses in its structure, then completely planning not only the basic work that had to be done to bring it back to structural soundness, but also all of the decoration, interior and exterior, that would make the Sedgefield Opera House a showplace for the whole East. She had thanked him profusely, particularly for his offer to do all the planning at his own expense. But when he told her that it would take the whole summer to draw the plans, leaving her with a blithe, "I'll get together with you again sometime after Labor Day," she had experienced an emotion no more definable—and no less frightening—than her original fear of his coming.

Before September, however, the Sedgefield Opera House was pushed out of her mind by a new and overwhelming excitement. In the first year of Judd's television show, he had salted his line-up of former Broadway hits with an occasional new play. One had been *Dust Bowl*, an adaptation of an unproduced play by Kenyon Malling, starring the Hollywood actress Ilsa Lang. When Kay had seen it on the air she had thought that Judd's script judgment must have been distorted by nostalgia. It was a play with a small-town background, the action set in the Depression period, the whole thing terribly dated, obviously the effort of a passed-over playwright desperately trying to recapture the success he had once had on Broadway. The *Variety* review, however, had been surprisingly good, even going so far as to call Ilsa Lang's performance *magnificent*. At the time, there had been some talk of a Broadway production, but nothing had come of it. Unprepared, Kay had been hit as by a bomb-burst on the night when Kenyon Malling had stopped by the house, telling her that a producer named Bernard Solleman was going ahead with an adaptation of his play, renamed *Head of the House*, and that Judd was being offered the chance to direct. When, a few minutes later, Judd had arrived, she could hardly believe that he was actually hesitant about doing it. When he asked, "Do you think I should?" she had responded as if answering a cry from her soul, thinking only of what it would mean to have him make the great leap to Broadway, too excited to share Judd's worries about Bernard Solleman, too elated to doubt Ken Malling's assurance that the new script was a far better play than the old one had been, too blindly happy to see what lay behind Judd's peculiar reluctance to accept Ilsa Lang as the play's star.

She had urged Judd to quit the network at once so that he could put his full time on the play, but he had already agreed to direct a summer replacement, and the way their debts had piled up argued strongly for keeping a regular paycheck coming as long as possible. As a result, Judd had carried a double load all through the summer.

That overburden, however, had the good result of opening the way for her to help him, at least with some of the clerical work connected with getting ready for production. For the first time since that pre-marriage summer at the Orangerie, she was deeply involved with her husband's working life, happier than she had ever been before. She sat in on all of the early script sessions with Ken Malling, and Judd had even asked her to come into New York for the first reading with a full cast, but as rehearsals got underway, her sense of intimate participation was more and more dulled by Judd's increasing resistance to suggestion. She could understand his dictatorial handling of everyone in the company—a director had to be god on the set, she knew that—but it was difficult to excuse his treating her as if she was no more than a script girl, her suggestions given no more weight than those of pimple-pocked nephew of Bernard Solleman that Judd had been forced to take on as a stage manager.

More disturbing than anything else, however, had been the hard-to-down sensing that there was something more between Judd and Ilsa Lang than a legitimate director-star relationship. She had tried to talk herself out of it, attempting the sophisticated view that it was only one of those transient pseudo-intimacies that every Broadway director's wife had to learn to accept, and she had managed several coffee-break conversations with Ilsa Lang without once letting a catty overtone slip through. It had been Judd, not Ilsa, who had always broken it up, peremptorily demanding Ilsa's presence on the stage.

She might have been more concretely worried had she not known from her own experience that Freud had been wrong about man's strongest motivation. The harder Judd drove, the less interested he was in sex—and never had she seen him so totally and blindly driven. Many nights he stayed in town, but she could hardly blame him for that, acknowledging that there were no hours to waste on commuting in that last big push to get the play on the boards. She had even managed to forgive his cutting her out of a trip to Boston for the tryout week, overlooking the lameness of his excuse that she had to stay home to get Rolfe started at Sedgefield Day School, hurt but willing to endure any pain that would help make *Head of the House* a hit.

The Boston reviews had not been encouraging. One of the critics had recognized the play as a rewrite of a television show and had hung his whole review on that peg. Ilsa Lang, he wrote, had been wasted in a moth-eaten play that should never have been taken from the trunk. The other two critics, although praising Ilsa Lang's performance, found little favorable to say about the play as a whole. Talking to Judd over the telephone, on the one night he called her from Boston, she learned that he was trying to get Bernard Solleman to hold off opening in New York for another two weeks, but that the producer was insisting that he could not afford the extra expense. They were coming directly into New York.

She went into Manhattan early in the forenoon before the opening night, catching Judd in his hotel room for only a moment, shocked by how haggard and gray-faced he looked, her natural sympathy chilled by his manner toward her, acting almost as if she had no right to turn up unbidden to his room. The rest of the day was no less miserable, New York on one of those early autumn days of cold wind-driven rain, her long walk past the theater minimally rewarded by seeing Judd's name in the smallest type on the posters.

It was quite by accident—this would always be in her favor, a refuge for conscience—that she ran into Ben Kassoff in the lobby of Judd's hotel, an encounter as plainly surprising to him as it was to her. He had come in for the opening of Judd's play, picking the hotel because it was one where he had occasionally met Judd when they had worked together on television settings. Explained, it all seemed reasonable enough. He had been going to call her, anyway, he said—the revised plans for the Opera House were ready—and with that excuse they had first had a drink together and then gone to Sardi's for dinner, both of them repetitiously voicing the hope that Judd would appear. He had not, of course, but they had spent the dinner hour talking about him. It was only after they left, on the way to the theater, that Ben revealed that he was one of the play's backers, having bought a thousand-dollar share. And then, prophetically as it had turned out, he said, "But even if it's a big hit, I don't expect to get my money back, not with Bernard Solleman in the picture."

The opening night performance was a hazed memory, the too-familiar lines no longer hearable, the Boston changes heard as jarring surprises. Seated as she was among relatives and friends of the cast, the observable reaction was an untrustworthy index of audience reception, but the applause at the end of the second act was more substantial than at the end of the first, and when the play ended there were enough curtain calls for Ilsa Lang to support the hope that even if the play did not prove a smash hit, it might nevertheless have a substantial run.

Afterwards, backstage, Judd had seemed strangely lifeless and deflated, withdrawn and impenetrable, and that mood had persisted at Bernard Solleman's apartment, where they had all gone to wait for the reviews. When they finally came, they were better than Kay had dared to hope. The television-play origin had been mentioned by only one critic and he had used it positively, citing the superiority of the stage production. Ilsa Lang's personal notices ranged from a warm "more than adequate" to an ecstatic "stunningly and unexpectedly authoritative." One of the reviews was pegged upon Kenyon Malling's return to Broadway after an eleven-year absence, the play cited as a notable comeback, the third-act seduction scene—which, of course, was all Judd's—singled out for special praise. Judd got no more notice in any review than a single line. Sensing his disappointment, she tried to tell him that everything favorable in all of the reviews was really a tribute to his work, but he had brusquely cut her off, turning to snatch Malling away from a circle of flattering admirers, insisting that they immediately go back to the hotel and start trimming the first act of the deadwood that had caused the *Times* reviewer to criticize the play's slow start. Ilsa Lang had left with them. Ben Kassoff had driven Kay home to Connecticut.

Head of the House settled down to its run. Judd, although he went into New York every day, ostensibly to keep polishing the play, never came home with any news other than a report on the box office. Despite the good reviews, the feature articles about Ilsa Lang in both the Sunday *Times* and the *Herald Tribune*, there was no encouraging buildup in advance sales. Although decrying Judd's increasing commercialism, Kay could not deny the validity of his concern about money. He had taken a cut in salary in order to do the play, and his personal expenses, living in New York hotels as much as he had to, left little to apply to their Connecticut bills. His share of the profits, which he had taken in lieu of a higher weekly salary, and from which he had hoped to draw a continuing reward, began to look more and more like a mirage, disappearing into thin air when Bernard Solleman abruptly closed the play.

She had not been immediately concerned, certain that Judd, now that he was established as a Broadway director, would be offered other plays to stage. Now and then someone did give him a script to look over—Ken Malling came out to Connecticut to read him his new play—but as the season wore on, nothing tangible turned up. She used her own money to pay Rolfe's tuition at Sedgefield Day, forced to admit it when Judd found the receipt, afraid then that he would go back to television. What happened was worse. Without talking to her, without as much as a hint of what he had in mind, he took a job with an advertising agency, degrading himself to the direction of television commercials. That, she knew, was the end of the legitimate theater, her heartsickness heightened by the way Judd threw himself into his new job, as obsessively concerned with a little one-minute Vega Nail Polish spot as he had been with *Head of the House*. Fortunately, there had been the Sedgefield Opera House to fill her life—and less fortunately, Ben Kassoff.

After all these years, the memory twisted and tortured by countless contrived explanations, nothing remained but the bitter ashes of a temporary nymphomaniac madness, all the more unaccountable because she had never before been enough stirred by physical passion to lose her controlling sense of reason. But she had. And it had not been Ben's fault. Madly, she had called him at his office, leaving messages for him when he would not answer the phone, inventing excuses to get him to the house on Wednesday night when Judd had to be in the studio to get the commercials on the air, once even stooping so low as to get Rolfe out of the house by having him stay at the Ellisons' for the night.

Nothing had been a surer proof of insanity than the way she had gone on and on, telling herself every Thursday morning that it had to stop. But that good resolution was always lost before another week came around. She had known full well that the end could only be horrible, yet she had psychotically driven herself toward it. Despite the near-maniacal subtlety of her contriving, she had slipped up, failing to notice in the evening paper that President Truman had preempted the 9:00 P.M. time for a broadcast on the Korean situation. A full two hours before she expected him, she heard Judd's car pull into the driveway.

Somehow, she and Ben had managed to get into the living room before Judd came in the back door, but their attempt to pretend a conference on the Opera House had been too shallow a burlesque to fool anyone. Judd had carried it off far better than she had, leaving them alone, going into the bathroom, showing no emotion when he came back to find Ben gone. But there had been a terrifying cruelty in his silence, denying her any chance to loose the awful pressure of guilt within her. By forcing her to live with it, not only that night but through all the days that had followed, he had punished her as nothing else could have done. When she found, not too long afterward, positive evidence of Judd's continuing relationship with Ilsa Lang, she was prohibited from even hinting her displeasure. She thought of divorce, but never as anything but a terrifying end to everything. All she could do was wait. When, eventually, Judd told her that he was taking a job with Crouch Carpet and that they were moving to Pennsylvania, she had seen it as a justification for her patience, a chance for a new life for both of them.

"You really should drive up some time and see how the Opera House turned out," Chris was saying. "You remember—I don't know whether this was a part of your original plan or not—all those little stores? Well, they've torn those down so you can really see the theater. And on the right side—you know, toward the inn—they've built a lovely terrace."

"Yes, that was a part of the original plan," Kay said, a testing admission, wondering if she was strong enough to face a full recollection of that night when Ben had talked to her about the idea of ripping out all of those old ramshackle stores, surprised to discover that a memory so long avoided could be faced. Reassured, she boldly asked, "And Ben is still in Sedgefield?"

"Ben? Oh, don't you know? He's dead."

"Dead?"

"Oh, it was horrible, really it was. They were having a big dinner for him, giving him some kind of an award—the Civic Association, you know—man of the year, something like that. Reggie Bellows was making the presentation. You probably didn't know him. He came in from the West Coast, president of this electronic company out in Ben's industrial park. Well, anyway, Reggie was making his speech, the big buildup—Ben didn't know a thing about it, you see —so when Reggie announced that they were making this award to

Ben—man of the year or whatever it was—everyone stood up. Naturally, they were expecting Ben to get up and go to the platform. Well, they kept on applauding and applauding—oh, it must have been horrible—Ben just never got up out of his chair. It was a heart attack, of course. All the excitement, I suppose. Anyway it was too late, there wasn't a thing that could be done. But you can imagine how Reggie Bellows must have felt."

"Yes," Kay said, but there was no room in her mind for any feelings other than her own, overwhelmed as she was by an ebullient sensation of release, total and final.

« 5 »

Aaron Kharr had worn away the afternoon as if it were a hard stone that could only be ground down with unremitting effort. He had gone back to Mrs. Stine's for Sunday dinner, anticipating the relieving sabbatical that he had come to expect at her family-crowded table. Today, however, he could not forget the hospital, his mind inescapably occupied with an urgent concern about how Judd Wilder was reacting to the talk that he had had with him.

After dinner he went up to his room, physically logy from having eaten too much—he always overate when he was keyed up—encouraged to think that he might manage an hour's nap. Ten minutes later he was on his way to the hospital. Another ten minutes and he was at his desk, fighting off a compulsion that drove him toward Wilder's room, telling himself that he dared not see him again this afternoon. He had made his move. He had talked too long, pushed him too hard, really made a mess of it—but what had been done had been done. There was nothing to do now but wait. If he had been wrong, the damage was already done. If he had been right, the worst thing he could possibly do would be to barge in on Wilder when he was only starting to think his way through.

Two-thirty. The whole afternoon ahead of him. A good chance to get in some work on his book. But when he got out the manuscript, it was a too-vivid reminder of what he was trying to put out of his mind. He had to do something with his hands. That recognition sent him to the laboratory—Sunday was always a good time, no one around to bother him—but some fool had turned off the water-bath control and it would take at least a half hour to get the temperature down and stabilized. He didn't have that much time to waste. Better to use it checking out those references—if that stupid janitor had not again ignored the DO NOT DISTURB sign that he had left on the journals he had dug out last night.

Flinging open the door of the little storeroom that, since his coming to County Memorial he had converted into a library, he discovered Raggi slumped over the table and dead asleep, his head pillowed on a magazine that, as he abruptly awakened with a back-stiffening reflex, was revealed as a dog-eared copy of *Playboy*, open to a nude girl seductively lounging across a double spread.

"Boning up on your anatomy, Dr. Raggi?" he asked, his smile too late to dull the edge of sarcasm.

Dark as Raggi's skin was, a flush showed through, but the fire in his black eyes suggested anger rather than embarrassment. "Am I expected, sir, to be on duty every day and every night? Was it not our agreement that I was to be given one free day in each week?"

"Of course, of course," he said, an impatient acknowledgment, transferring his annoyance with "Dr. Webster hasn't shown up, is that it? All right, go along. I'll be here for the rest of the day."

Raggi stood up, the set of his lips suggesting that his protest had not been completed, that there was more to come.

Moving quickly to forestall it, Aaron Kharr asked, "Anything happen? Anything hanging fire? Anything I ought to know about?"

Raggi swallowed, evidencing the choke of sudden embarrassment. "I'm sorry, sir, I was writing you a note when I—it is about your heart patient, sir."

"Yes?" he asked thinly, fear constricting his throat.

"The nurse was calling, sir. She was saying he was refusing to take his twelve o'clock medication."

He slumped with relief. "Oh, that's all right. It was only a tranquilizer."

"Yes, sir, he is knowing that. That is why he is refusing it. He is saying that he is not wishing to take anything that will be stopping him from thinking."

"He said—what?" he asked, hope flaring.

"He is saying, sir, that he is wishing to think."

A burst of joyous triumph overwhelmed Aaron Kharr's consciousness, an elation beyond measure, a sensation that demanded some outlet over and above anything that could be said. Jamming his hands into his pockets—an exercise in emotional restraint so practiced that it had become habitual—his fingers touched his car keys. Before there was time to think, he pulled them out and thrust them at Raggi. "Here, take my car! Go for a drive. Do you good. It's a beautiful day."

Across the corridor, his telephone was ringing. Turning away from Raggi's still unbroken stare of incredulity, he went to answer the phone, anticipating that it would be the call from Mr. Crouch that he had been expecting since early morning. His intuition betrayed him. Dr. Leebow was on the other end of the line, launching at once into a quavering recital of signs and symptoms. Too elated to be intolerant of senility, Aaron Kharr let him babble on, holding the receiver to his ear with a hunched shoulder, meantime spinning a fresh sheet of paper into his typewriter. Finally permitted to hang up, he began to type his notes on the Wilder case. Quickly filling a page, he glanced back over what he had written, seeing that he was going into far more detail than was necessary, actually a verbatim transcript. But why not? It could be a valuable record . . . might even use it in his book . . . maybe a whole chapter . . . a transcript of the rehabilitation process, every word that had been spoken . . .

He started a second sheet, the words coming as fast as he could type. He had no difficulty recalling exactly what he had said, the words double-engraved upon his memory, first by rehearsal, then by recital, but now as he finished recording a long speech of his own, he found it difficult to recall exactly how Wilder had responded. Actually, he had said very little. At the time, his responses had seemed at least adequate, all that could be expected, but now those single typewritten lines, rarely more than half the width of the page, raised the clear possibility of misjudgment. He had thought of Wilder as being insufficiently impressed by the seriousness of the situation, too little changed, too much the man he had been before— his whole plan of attack had been based on that assumption—but if that were truly the case, why hadn't he talked more freely? Nothing was more characteristic of a PCS-1 than volubility, a compulsive need to argue, an unremitting drive to dominate every conversation. Could it be that, underneath, he was more frightened than he had allowed himself to appear? Yes, he had got him think-ing—but what was he thinking about?

The flow of remembered words that had sent his fingers racing over the keyboard had stopped. He looked at his watch. The af-ternoon was slipping away at an alarming rate. Any minute now he might be called. Sunday, with all the holiday traffic, was sure to produce an accident case or two. Driven, he began to type again, one ear cocked for the sound of the ambulance.

His telephone rang. Again his intuition betrayed him. It was the front desk, asking if Mr. Wilder was permitted to have visitors. There was a Mrs. Ingalls to see him.

"I'll be out in a minute or two," he said, giving himself the time that he needed to decide what to do. With a patient so far from home he had thought himself free of the visitor problem—he wanted no intrusion, particularly today—but it would be difficult to deny a visiting privilege to someone who had driven forty miles. He stopped at the entrance of the lobby, half hidden by the screen of artificial philodendron. A woman stood waiting at the desk. She was fortyish, overweight, wearing a cocoa-colored knit suit that can-celed the wariness that he always felt when confronting a smartly dressed woman. Her face, more clearly seen now as she shifted her position, reminded him of a nurse he had known as an intern, a wonderful old gal who could walk into a twenty-bed ward and make everyone, even the geriatrics, feel as if Mother was home and every-thing was right with the world again.

"I'm Dr. Kharr," he said. "You were inquiring about Mr. Wilder, I believe."

"Daphy Ingalls," she responded, tossing in "Mrs. Ray Ingalls" as if it were a nuisance formality. "We're old friends of Judd's, Ray and I. How is he, Doctor?"

"He's coming along fine," he said, his resolve weakening, begin-ning to think that it would be an unjustified disservice to Wilder to deny him this buoyantly pleasant visitor. "These first days, of course, we're trying to keep him as quiet as possible——"

"Oh, I know. I wasn't really expecting to see him. But I was going right by, taking my daughter back to Cornell—I just had to stop. And with Kay away, the house and all—I thought there might be something I could do for him at home."

"You're neighbors, I take it?"

"We were for years and years—until they built their new house. We came to the company about the same time—Judd and Ray, I mean. Ray's a dye chemist—we'd been with du Pont—and then we came up here—New Ulster, I mean—and we rented this house on Diversion Street. We hadn't been there more than—oh, I don't know how long it was, not more than a month or two, when Judd and Kay came. They moved in right next door, and they were there all those years so—well, naturally we got to know them awfully well."

"Yes, of course," he said, seeing the possibility that had opened before him. "I wonder, Mrs. Ingalls—I know you've a long drive ahead of you, but if you could give me a minute or two—I do have a problem, you see, trying to get a little background on Mr. Wilder. With no member of his family available, it's rather difficult."

"Well, sure, anything I can tell you," she said, amiably enough, yet now with a hint of reservation, enough to let him know that she was no loose-tongued gossip. But she did accept his invitation to sit down, tugging her skirt over her plump knees, brushing back the lock of once-red hair that feathered out over her forehead, volunteering, "Judd's the company advertising manager, sales promotion and all that."

"Yes, I know that much."

"And wonderfully talented. Ray always said that he could never understand why Judd stayed with the company, all the other things he could do—you know, Broadway, Hollywood."

"But he did stay on," he supplied. "And it's been—am I right—twelve years?"

"It doesn't seem that long, but I guess it is. Yes, Julie was nine when we moved—and she just had her twenty-first birthday. My daughter, the one I'm taking back to Cornell."

"Fine school," he said, recognizing her attempt to divert him, wondering if it was wise to go on, gambling with "Why do you suppose he did stay on?" He got only a blank look. "His wife's influence?"

"Kay?" she shot back, her tone sharp. But it was quickly softened with "I don't really know. I've never been as close to Kay as—I don't mean that she isn't a wonderful person, I don't mean that at all. It's just that—well, I do know when Judd decided to build—they'd been renting all these years, you see—I know Kay wasn't too enthusiastic."

"When was that, Mrs. Ingalls—building this house?"

"Oh, a couple of years ago. Actually, I was a little surprised myself, the way that Judd had always said that he didn't want to tie himself down, owning any property."

"Did it strike you—?" He stopped, cautiously rephrasing his question. "Was it your impression, Mrs. Ingalls, that the decision to build a house represented any significant change in his attitude or outlook?"

"I don't think I get what you mean, Doctor."

"Did you by any chance say—or think—'This is a different man than I used to know'?"

She laughed. "Not with Judd—you never know what he's going to do next." Her smile faded, lost in the soberest expression that he had yet seen. "The only thing that might have made me think anything—well, it *was* a surprise to have him build over in Vixen Valley —I mean, right in with all of the other company executives. That's something he'd always avoided—running with the company crowd."

"Was there anything else that struck you as unusual?" he asked, quickly explaining, "This may seem unimportant to you, Mrs. Ingalls, but I can assure you that anything you can tell me will be very helpful."

"No, I don't think so," she said. "Of course, we haven't seen so much of Judd and Kay since they moved. Actually, it's only a few blocks, but—" She stopped, thoughtstruck. "It's such a little thing, probably doesn't mean anything—I'm sure it doesn't—but I do remember Ray laughing about Judd buying a Riviera."

"A Riviera?"

"Oh, it was one of those silly things that we always laughed about —you know, Judd always insisting on driving a different car than anyone else had? For years, it was Chryslers. But then when he moved over to Vixen Valley—well, everyone else had Rivieras, so Judd bought one, too. Ray thought maybe they were getting a special deal or something—but still it wasn't much like Judd."

Struck by this confirmation that Wilder's behavior had indeed slipped over into the precoronary syndrome area, he mused, "Yes, that's interesting, very interesting, indeed." She was starting to rise, forcing him to acknowledge, "Yes, I know you have to be on your way."

"Will you tell Judd——"

Suddenly, he saw a chance to extend this talk. "Will you be coming back this way?"

"Why yes—tomorrow."

"Won't you please stop? By then I'm sure—yes, tomorrow he'll be in good enough shape to have a visitor."

"It'll be early. Before noon. I have to be back in time——"

"Whenever it is, Mrs. Ingalls—do stop. Just ask for me. I know Mr. Wilder will be glad to see you—and so will I."

❖ V ❖

WITH HIS EYES STILL CLOSED, Judd Wilder fixed his unseeing gaze at the spot on the wall where he knew the clock to be. Cautiously, he stole a one-eyed glance. Twenty after seven. Mary would be gone by now. If he looked left, he would see Miss Harsch's waxworks smile. He closed his eyes, feigning sleep. But now he heard feminine voices in the corridor, and glancing toward the door, saw that it was not completely closed. He could not hear what was being said, but one of the voices was unmistakably Mary's. He could not identify the other but it was certainly not Miss Harsch's.

The door opened, Mary backing into the room. "No, really, I don't mind at all, honestly I don't."

He could not see the face in the corridor, but the voice—something about not calling another nurse until she saw Dr. Kharr—could only have come from a scrawny throat and thin blue lips.

"I really mean it—I'll be happy to stay on," Mary said, emphatically stressing the *happy*, and when she closed the door and turned, her face looked as if she meant it.

"What's happened to Miss Harsch?" he asked, startling her but not enough to dislodge her smile.

"She's not coming in," Mary said, unsuccessfully attempting a show of sympathetic concern with "She isn't feeling well."

He almost said, "Nothing trivial, I hope," but she stopped him with an earnest "Don't worry—I'm not going to leave you alone."

"I'm not worrying," he said. "But you don't have to stay on."

"I want to!" she said, gaily emphatic, turning with a schoolgirl skip to return her purse to the dresser top, reaching up to repin her cap. "At least I'll have a chance to do something for you now."

"What do you mean—now?" he puzzled, amused.

"I've done so little and—" There was an odd catch in her voice. "I owe you so much."

"You don't owe me anything. It's not your fault that——"

"Oh, but I do!" she exclaimed, turning then. Looking up into her face, he saw her bite her lip, a child trying to contain some bursting secret. But her eyes were strangely misted, as if tears were a more likely possibility than words. Quickly, she made a show of activity, straightening the bedclothing, her face averted as she said, "I called Ralph yesterday—and you were right. We're going to be married as soon as we can work it out." And then, choked, she said, "That's what I owe you," looking directly at him for an instant, then spinning away in a flurry of swirling white, a child offering a gift of affection and then running away from the embarrassment of gratitude.

Dazzled, he was still trying to think what he could say when he heard a crisply professional "Do you feel as if you could void now?" —unable to believe that it was Mary's voice until he saw the perfectly composed face that was now looking down over the edge of the chartboard. "Dr. Kharr wants a urine sample before you've had your breakfast."

« 2 »

Aaron Kharr learned about Miss Harsch's defection almost as soon as he entered the hospital. There was a message at the front desk, asking him to call Mrs. Cromwell at once, that need eliminated as the Supervisor of Nursing caught him on the way to his office. Miss Harsch, it seemed, had called in to say that she was ill, asking to be taken off the Wilder case.

"Hannah Weimer is next up on registry," Mrs. Cromwell said, "but I didn't want to call her until I was sure that she'd satisfy you."

He did not in the least mind losing Miss Harsch—whoever he got could hardly be worse—but he was stung by Mrs. Cromwell's implication that the fault was his, an accusation that he might have brushed off had not his mind been sensitized by the knowledge of how often, in years past, he had been unfairly accused of being difficult to get along with.

"So Miss Harsch is ill?" he asked, pointedly disbelieving it.

"We'd have to get someone in a day or two, anyway," Mrs. Cromwell said evasively. "She's got an O.B. coming up, one that she'd promised."

"I see," he said, suddenly recalling Harsch's face when he had sent her out of Wilder's room yesterday.

"They do make promises, some of the older nurses. Patients they've had before. And she is good on maternity cases. Very popular. Dr. Teeter always asks for her."

He flinched at the sound of Teeter's name, but quickly said, "I'm sure he does," cynicism successfully enough restrained so that there was no visible reaction from Mrs. Cromwell. "Who've you got with him now?"

"I asked his night nurse—the little Welch girl—to stay on until we found out what you wanted to do." She waited. "Of course, the floor nurses could take care of him perfectly well—but I didn't know if that would satisfy you."

"Am I so demanding, Mrs. Cromwell?"

She mumbled something, seemingly put in her place, but then she said, "The only thing is, with the other doctors I know what they want, but with you—well, you're just different, that's all."

Different rebounded from the hard-calloused scar tissue of countless wounds. "I'll let you know," he said, wheeling away, hurrying down the corridor, so preoccupied that he did not notice the man coming toward him until, no more than a stride away, he found the way blocked by Harmon Teeter, his pear-shaped figure surmounted by a face so full-mooned that, as always, it seemed incapable of any expression other than a Toby-jug grin. Teeter badly needed to lose at least fifty pounds, something that Aaron Kharr suspected he had not done because he was afraid that it might detract from the jolly-good-fellow image upon which he had built the most lucrative practice of any County Memorial doctor.

"Got a message for you from an old friend of yours, Doctor," Teeter burbled. "Met him down at our Washington meeting."

"Who was that?" he asked guardedly, certain that all this was no more than Teeter's small-talk way of getting around to the Wilder case.

"Dr. Kelstein," Teeter replied. "Said he used to work with you when you were in research."

"Oh, yes—Sam Kelstein," he acknowledged, trapped in a demeaning recollection, unable to put down the memory of that day when, weak-kneed and silent, he had sat through a Berringer staff meeting when Sam had tried to launch a rebellious uprising against the Institute's secret but obvious policy of restricting all research fellowships to Jews. Sam had been right—Berringer was being needlessly preserved as a scientific ghetto, all of the work that was being done subtly but surely downgraded, an extra hurdle placed in the way of publication in the big journals, a handicap imposed upon every young research worker who was trying to break through the safety-glass wall that invisibly but surely divided the medical profession—and Sam had counted upon him for support, upon him more than anyone else. But he had sat silent, as stunned as everyone else had been by hearing the truth spoken aloud, joining all the others in assuaging his conscience by accusing Sam of intemperate frankness. That had been the end of the rebellion—and, as far as Berringer was concerned, the end of Sam Kelstein. He had disappeared into the world outside the walls, so completely lost that Aaron Kharr could not now put down a feeling of mild alarm that Sam had kept track of him, somehow finding out that he was here at County Memorial, still haunting him with the memory of a defection that could never be excused. But all of that lay hidden behind his tautly controlled "What's he doing now? I haven't heard from him in a long time."

"Oh, didn't you know?" Teeter said, his full-moon smile again unclouded, expressing the pleasure that he always found in being the all-knowing informer. "He's in Washington. Just been made head of this big section—passing out research grants under the Rural Medicine Act. Said he's always had a lot of respect for you—be glad to see you again." He cocked his head, winking his smile into an arch smirk. "One of those grants wouldn't be bad to have, not bad at all."

He stared blankly at Teeter's face, trying to visualize what he had in his mind—surely he could not be imagining that any government agency, as madly irrational as some of them were, would consider giving a research grant to County Memorial Hospital—yet Teeter's expression was unmistakably related to that tongue-licking smirk with which he always greeted the arrival in Emergency of a well-insured turnpike case.

"It just might turn out to be something pretty good," Teeter said, his thick lips working. "Anyway, keep yourself clear for Friday. We'll be driving up to Harrisburg. Kelstein is coming up for a regional meeting. I've set up a luncheon date with him." He winked. "Just a nice little get-together, the three of us."

"I'm sorry," he said, trying to make his regret sound at least passably sincere. "I won't be able to make it—not Friday."

Teeter's underlip ran out, his "Why not?" a bass rumble.

"I have to be in Baltimore that day," he said. "I've agreed to be on a heart disease panel—it's a big meeting, a conference on executive health problems—I really don't feel I can get out of it, not at this late date."

"Well!" Teeter exclaimed, a collapsing exhalation that twisted his smile into a leer, ominously chilling. "I'd counted on you, Doctor, but if that's the way you feel about it—all right, we'll just have to get along without you."

Helpless, he watched Teeter's roly-poly progress down the corridor, wondering if he knew yet about the Wilder case . . . probably not . . . this wasn't going to make things any easier . . .

« 3 »

When he heard the door open, Judd Wilder thought it was Mary returning, surprised when he heard Dr. Kharr's curt "Good morning," feeling himself caught unprepared. Quickly, he attempted to resurrect all of the questions that, last night, had gone unasked. Dr. Kharr had stopped by after dinner, but only for a minute or two, no more than a quick look-in, giving him no chance to talk, spending more time out in the corridor with Mrs. Cope than he had with him. Again it seemed that his prime interest was nurses, asking now about Mary.

"She went out for something," Judd said. "She'll be back in a minute or two."

"I presume you know—we've lost Miss Harsch?"

"I'll manage to survive without her," he said, suggestively cynical, recalling a dagger look that Dr. Kharr had given her yesterday, almost certain that his own relief at getting rid of her was shared.

But there was no break in Dr. Kharr's oddly disengaged expression. "Since we do have to make a change"—he pulled up a chair and sat down—"perhaps this is as good a time as any to review the situation. There's really no need for round-the-clock nursing, Mr. Wilder. You're not that ill. Of course, it's entirely up to you. There is the matter of expense—that's a minor consideration, I'm sure, but still—" He shot a guarding glance at the door. "What I had in mind, really, was that you could get along easily enough without a night nurse."

He felt a choke of alarm, visualizing Mary's face when she was told that she was fired . . . that pregnant kid from the mailing room, the blonde one with the watery blue eyes . . . breaking up in his office . . .

"She's young, of course," Dr. Kharr was saying, "but her training has been good, and there is the advantage of her having been with you from the beginning——"

"You mean Mary?" He blinked his relief. "Put her on instead of Miss Harsch?"

"If you'd prefer someone else—or if you feel that you'd still like to have a nurse here at night——"

"No, no, she's fine with me," he said hurriedly, noting the quality of Dr. Kharr's satisfied smile, wondering if he knew that Mary was pregnant.

"Well, she will appreciate it, I do know that," Dr. Kharr said, crisply businesslike. "I'll talk to her—see how she feels about it." He made a move to leave, stopped as if by an interrupting reminder, intoning, "You had a good night, no pain, no discomfort, nothing worrying you?"—too ritualistic a recital to be seriously questioning.

Anxious to hold him, but unable on the spur of the moment to come up with anything else, Judd said, "I've been doing a lot of thinking," gratified when he saw the doctor's head snap around, instantly alert, sitting down again, giving him his full and undivided attention. But now there was the problem of answering his "About what?"

Feeling like a schoolboy who had raised his hand too quickly, he fumbled, "Everything—what we were talking about yesterday—that I'm going to have to change——"

"You find that difficult to accept?"

"If I argue, I suppose it will only prove your point"—he interjected a quick smile—"just giving myself another shot of adrenaline."

"I wasn't trying to prove a point, Mr. Wilder. My only objective was to make you see that——"

"That I can't go back to Crouch Carpet," he heard himself supply, a thought that sprang from the shadows, not at all what he had planned to say, almost as startling to him as it obviously was to Dr. Kharr.

"No, no, Mr. Wilder, please. I said nothing like that. There's no reason why you can't go back to your job, no reason at all." He paused, and then as a quick thrust, added, "Providing that that's what you want to do."

"Of course. What else?"

"That's a question for you to answer."

"All right, the answer is yes. Why wouldn't it be?"

Dr. Kharr shrugged. "I can't make that decision for you. How could I? I know next to nothing about your company, your work——"

"Sure, it's a pressure job, it has to be, but there's nothing new about that. It's the same job it's always been."

"But are you the same man?"

"What do you mean by that?"

"Let me ask you this—" Dr. Kharr began, hesitant for a question-framing moment. "Have you been conscious of any change in yourself over the last couple of years—in your reaction to your work, the satisfaction you get out of it, the sense of accomplishment that it gives you?"

His automatic reaction was one of sharp denial, almost instantly neutralized by the realization that argument would be taken as proof of what he wanted to disprove, and he responded with a mild "No, I don't think so."

"How about your personal life, your way of living—has there been any change there?"

He sensed a peculiar note in Dr. Kharr's voice, enough of a warning to arouse caution. He shook his head, silent.

"You've gone on living in exactly the same way that you always have, the same circle of friends, the same house—?"

"Oh, we built a new house a couple of years ago, but that was only —well, it was too good a deal to turn down, that's all. Mr. Crouch picked up all this extra land when we built the new mill, so he turned it into a housing development. Vixen Valley. It's a beautiful layout, right across the creek from the country club. A lot of us have built out there."

Dr. Kharr cupped his chin in his hand. "Did building this house —deciding to build it, I mean—represent a decision on your part to spend the rest of your life with the Crouch Carpet Company?"

"I never thought of it that way, but—well, why not? I've been with the company twelve years, I'm perfectly happy——"

"Perfectly?"

"Well, maybe not *perfectly*. Who is? But as far as the company is concerned—I can't imagine working for a better one."

"You've never thought of leaving?"

"Oh, I've had offers."

"I'm sure you have. Any that you ever seriously considered?"

"No, not really. There was one a couple of years ago that—" He stopped, aware of what Dr. Kharr might think if he told him about General Carpet. "It turned out to be with one of our competitors. I could never do a thing like that, walk out on Crouch Carpet, not after——"

"Suppose it had been something completely different, something more appealing than the carpet business—?"

"What's wrong with the carpet business?" he flashed back, instantly recognizing that it was an irrational response. Contrite, he backtracked, answering Kharr's original question. "Oh, I won't say that I haven't changed. Sure I have. Twelve years—you're bound to change. And it's a lot different situation—the company, the whole carpet industry—everything's changed. As for getting as much kick out of things as I used to—I don't know, maybe I don't. Those first few years, trying to build something, battling to keep our heads above water—one wrong move and the whole company could have gone down the drain. It was a great experience."

"I'm sure it was," Dr. Kharr agreed, taking off his glasses. "How'd you happen to go to work for Crouch Carpet? You'd been with an advertising agency in New York, am I right?"

"Yes, Frederick Coleman. It's Coleman, Bradford and Brown now, one of the big agencies."

"Yes, I know. We studied some of their men in one of our test groups when I was with Berringer Foundation. And I met Mr. Coleman himself once. An odd sort of man, I thought. Rather a difficult man to work for, I should imagine?"

"I never had any trouble with him," he came back, picking up the ready-made proof with which, afterwards, he had assuaged his conscience for the way he had quit with so little notice. "When things got to the point where we needed an agency at Crouch Carpet, that's where I took the account."

"How long were you there?"

"At the agency? Not too long. Less than a year. They were trying to set up a department to produce their own television shows. Or at least that was the idea. That's what I'd been brought in to do. But it didn't work out. Television was in the shake-out stage then, everybody battling to get control of the shows that were going on. The networks had all the cards, so they raked in the pot. All that was left for the agencies were the commercials."

"And that wasn't enough to satisfy you?"

"Oh, that wasn't the only reason I left. It was more—well, I'd just had it, that's all—New York, the Madison Avenue rat race, commuting to Connecticut, the whole bit."

"Then you'd been looking for another job?"

"No, not really. Oh, I won't say that I hadn't been keeping my eye open—sure I had. That's the way you live in New York. It's the Madison Avenue way of life. But I didn't have a job in mind that first time I went down to New Ulster."

"What happened? Why were you there?"

Judd Wilder hesitated, almost certain that Mr. Crouch had told Kharr the story, but a moment's thought suggested that Dr. Kharr might well have got a wrong impression from the Crouch version.

"It was just one of those things, a lucky break," he began, pushing down the bedclothing, clearing his arms. "My TV shows were off the air—summer hiatus—so I was filling in with a motion picture that one of our clients wanted made. It was one of those institutional things—you know, the great future for synthetic fibers. One of their big hopes was the carpet industry, so I'd spent a week in some of the old carpet mills around Philadelphia, trying to get something in the can that would back up their story. It had been pretty much of a washout. Synthetics just wouldn't work in the old weaving looms. If there was any chance, it had to be in the new tufting process. But that was still a long-shot bet. Some rayon had been tufted—it had been an awful flop, bad enough so that a lot of people thought there was no future at all for tufted carpet—but these people had come up with a new fiber that they thought might work, and one of their salesmen had given a test lot of yarn to somebody named Crouch who'd taken over an old bankrupt carpet mill at New Ulster. He was supposed to have developed a new tufting machine, one that would really turn out a quality piece of goods."

He shifted his position, lying on his side now, deciding not to reveal his later discovery that he had been sent to New Ulster as an unwitting spy, the company far less interested in getting a sequence for the film than they were in getting some pictures of the Crouch tufting machine. "They'd told me Mr. Crouch was a crusty character —they'd written him, trying to get a report on how their yarn had worked, but he wouldn't even answer their letters—so I figured there wasn't too much chance that he would let me inside the mill, let alone take any pictures. And when I got there, the way the place looked—even if I did get in, I couldn't imagine finding anything that was worth the bother of unpacking a camera. But there I was —I'd driven all the way from Philadelphia, so I thought I might as well have a go at it."

"You had no idea that's where you'd be spending the next twelve years," Dr. Kharr said with a smile, more relaxed than Judd had ever seen him.

He laughed. "The reception I got—it didn't look like I'd be there even twelve minutes. In those days Mr. Crouch was pretty short-fused, it didn't take much to get an explosion, and he really blew off about that lot of yarn they'd sent him. He'd thought he was doing them a favor to test it—if anything they ought to be paying him— but instead of that they'd sent him a bill for it. It was only a mistake, some stupid clerk, but that didn't stop him—he'd be damned if he was going to pay any damned company for testing their damned no-good yarn——"

"I can hear him," Dr. Kharr chuckled.

"Oh, he's tamed down a lot in these last few years. But I figured I had nothing to lose, one way or the other, so I handed it right back to him, damn for damn——"

"Which, of course, was exactly the right way to handle him."

"Anyway, something clicked, I don't know what, and the first thing I knew he was insisting that I come back to his laboratory to see how bad this damn no-good yarn really was. What he called his laboratory was really a laugh—just a cleared space in the middle of this old junk-filled machine shop—but this testing setup that he'd worked out was really something. You could stand there and watch a year's wear in fifteen minutes. And when I saw the way his tufted carpet was standing right up with a good grade of Wilton—and then when he told me that he could turn it out for half the cost— well, naturally I was interested. Anyway, I must have said the right things, because then he offered to show me his mill. That's what really bowled me over. I don't suppose you've ever seen a tufting machine operate?"

"No," Dr. Kharr said, his tone and manner definitely encouraging.

"You know what a tufted bedspread is, don't you?" he began, slipping easily into an explanation that he had recited times without number. "With a bedspread you start with a sheet of fabric and punch in little tufts of yarn to form a decorative pattern. All right, it's the same principle. Instead of starting with muslin or percale, you use a very heavy fabric, usually burlap, and instead of punching in only enough tufts to form a design, you punch it in solid with carpet yarn. That's your wearing surface."

"That's what a tufting machine does?"

"Right. Actually it's a mammoth sewing machine. Instead of one needle you have hundreds of them. They're set like teeth in a comb, a straight line across the width of the fabric. If you're making twelve-foot carpet, for example, five picks to the inch, that's seven hundred and twenty needles. So every time the head comes down, you put in seven hundred and twenty tufts. And it goes just like this." He lifted his hands, fingers extended in a downpointing straight line, and beat a rapid tattoo on the bedclothing over his midsection. "You can't believe the way that carpet comes rolling out."

"It's faster than the old weaving methods?"

"More than ten times," he said, impressed by the quickness of Dr. Kharr's understanding. "A Wilton loom will weave—say, three yards an hour. On velvet you might get up to four, maybe four and a half. But we've got a tufter now that is running over sixty yards an hour."

"And this is what you're doing at Crouch Carpet?"

"It's what the whole industry is doing. Tufting has completely revolutionized the carpet business. When I came with Crouch Carpet—except for cotton rugs, of course—everything was woven. Today, woven carpet is practically gone. Oh, there's still a little being made—eight or nine per cent of the industry—all the rest is tufted."

"And you saw this coming?" Dr. Kharr asked. "That's why you went with Crouch Carpet?"

"Oh, I won't say that I didn't see the possibilities—you couldn't listen to Mr. Crouch for a whole day without getting a little steamed up—but, no, I can't honestly say that I visualized what was going to happen."

"Then why *did* you take the job?" Dr. Kharr asked, his voice low yet tautly insistent.

He started to repeat what he had said before about wanting to get out of New York, stopped by Dr. Kharr's probing eyes, finding himself in a clouded haze of unresolved thought. Groping, he said, "As much as anything else, I guess, it was Mr. Crouch."

"In what way? As an individual? A man you liked personally, someone with whom you felt it would be pleasant to work?"

"No, he wasn't going to be easy to work with, I could see that. It was more—" He paused, trying to distill out the essence of that vaporous cloud. "I didn't know too much about business then, and most of what I did know—the sponsors I'd had on my television shows, the clients I'd met at the agency—frankly, I didn't think too much of businessmen. As far as I was concerned, most of them were a bunch of con men, all out for the quick buck, and not worrying too much about how they got it. Until I saw Mr. Crouch—he was the first man I'd ever met who made business seem like something that—well, something that you could go into without feeling that you were getting your hands dirty."

"He must have done quite a selling job on you."

He shook his head. "He didn't sell me—I sold myself. Oh, he sold me on giving it a try, sure he did, but I still had my fingers crossed. When I first went down there, I didn't know whether I'd stick with it or not. But the deeper I got into it, the more I saw—anyway, I've never been sorry that I made the jump."

"Never?"

"Why do you find that so hard to believe?"

"What I believe is of no importance. All that matters——"

"I know this—there's nothing else that I could have done that would have given me as much satisfaction as I've gotten at Crouch Carpet."

"In what way?"

"In every way."

"Oh, I'm sure you've done very well financially——"

"It's not that," he said, turning, starting to raise himself on his elbow, impelled by an impulse to argument that almost immediately collapsed, deflated by a recognition of pointlessness. Times without number, trying to make some of his old New York friends believe that he had no yen to get back on Broadway, he had failed to make them understand how rewarding life in a good company could really be. It wasn't the money, it wasn't anything you see or count or measure, it was something you *felt*—and you could never make an outsider feel it, someone who hadn't been on the inside, someone who hadn't experienced it himself. No outsider could ever understand. Even those business-school professors up at Colfax . . .

Reminded, pushed by Dr. Kharr's expectantly waiting expression, he made a hurried attempt to recall the script that he had written for that talk he made at Colfax last year, trying to give those business-school kids a feel of what corporate life was really like, hoping to counteract some of the cockeyed ideas they were getting from, of all people, the very teachers who were supposed to be preparing them for business careers. He had not made too much of an impression, he knew that—you couldn't undo in an hour what had been done over months and months—but at least he had made a few solid points, and snatching at the first one that came into his mind, he started to speak when the door opened.

Mary stood in the doorway. "I'm sorry to interrupt, Doctor, but there's someone waiting for you."

Dr. Kharr scowled, stubbornly resistant for a moment, then submissively rising. "I'm afraid we'll have to continue this later, Mr. Wilder. I do have some appointments."

"I hadn't meant to hold you up," Judd said, genuinely apologetic, yet unable to fend off a feeling of abandonment.

"I'll be back as soon as I can," Dr. Kharr said, going out, closing the door.

Judd lay back, his thoughts spinning under the impetus that they had been given, interrupted when he heard the door open. He glanced right, expecting to see Mary, but it was Dr. Kharr again. "I'd meant to tell you, Mr. Wilder, but it slipped my mind. You had a visitor yesterday. I put her off then, and I will again if you'd prefer not to see her—she's out front now—a Mrs. Ingalls."

"Daphy? What in the world is she doing up here?"

"I believe she said yesterday that she was driving her daughter up to Cornell. I think she's on her way home now. If you'd prefer not to see her——"

"No, no, tell her to come in," he said, accepting the rightness of Daphy's appearance on the scene, his smile an anticipation of the way she always made him feel. "She was our next-door neighbor for years."

"Yes, so she said. I'll send her back."

The door closed and did not open again—Dr. Kharr, he guessed, was holding up Mary's return, talking to her about taking the day shift—and waiting for Daphy's appearance, he remembered that first time he had seen her . . . the moving truck no more than out of the drive, and there was Daphy at the back door with a steaming-hot casserole for their first dinner in New Ulster . . .

Kay had been flabbergasted, never having experienced anything of the sort. To him, it had been a heartwarming experience, a return to the small-town neighborliness that he had known in Iowa—Daphy was from Minnesota, just across the line—but to Kay it had been oddly disconcerting, perhaps because it was a gesture that she would find so difficult to return in kind. She had been embarrassingly stiff in her thanks, but if Daphy had noticed it, there had been no evidence of it. She had gone on doing things for them, as she did for everyone else, asking no more gratitude than a mother does of her children, taking everyone's friendship for granted, dispensing generosity and goodwill as naturally as she breathed.

Eventually, Kay had accepted Daphy as a friend—she could hardly have done otherwise—yet there had always been a noticeable reserve, most evident when Rolfe was concerned. Frequently back in those first years, Daphy would gather Rolfe up with her own brood—"When you've got seven of your own, an extra's no trouble"—taking them all off on some wildly improbable expedition, returning a dirty but exhilarated Rolfe, sometimes scratched and brush-burned but always excited by some great adventure, never more disappointed than when Kay would say, "No, you can't stay over there for dinner again."

Judd always understood with Rolfe's disappointment. Sometimes when Kay was away, he would go over for dinner himself, responding to an over-the-fence hail, the dinner as last-minute as the invitation. Daphy was a slapdash cook, never able to give anyone a recipe for anything she made, yet everything that turned up on your plate was wonderful—or if it wasn't, you laughed it off. It was that kind of house. Kay had once said that it was a good thing that Ray was as easygoing as he was, that he would never be able to stand it if he weren't. And it was true that Ray was easygoing, too much so for his own good—with a little more push he could have been Director of Research . . . *"but at least I'll never wind up with a heart attack."*

Those remembered words struck now with delayed impact . . . Pine Creek . . . the tent pitched under that big rock ledge . . . the watery chuckle of the dark-hidden creek, the little slapping sounds that Ray said were night-feeding brown trout rising in the lip of the run at the end of the pool . . . *"This is what living is all about, Judd . . . this is what you have to do to keep your soul alive . . ."*

Kay had looked at him as if he were out of his mind when he first told her that he was going to take two days off and go trout fishing with Ray, even more incredulous when he had said they were going to take a tent and camp out . . . "But, Judd, you've never done anything like that in your life." That was untrue, at least in a total sense—he had camped out with his Boy Scout troop back in Haygood, and he had fished for pickerel and catfish and sunnies in Indian Lake, and for flounder off Long Island with Ben Kassoff— yet he had been embarrassingly aware that he had never handled a fly rod, never cast to a trout, let alone hooked and landed one. He had gone to the library, taking out every trout-fishing book he could find, an armload of bound copies of *Field & Stream* and *Outdoor Life,* up most of the night trying to learn enough to keep from making a total fool of himself.

He had started off that next morning with too little sleep, edgy and tense as he always was when he found himself in a spot where he could not avoid coming off second best. But by the time they got up to Williamsport, it didn't seem to matter too much, and after they had turned north at Renova, really up in the mountains, it didn't matter at all. They had loafed along, stopping every now and then to see something that had caught Ray's eye, walking down to turn over rocks in a little stream they had crossed, letting a half-hour slip away while they waited for another glimpse of a bear with two cubs.

He had come home from that weekend prepared to buy his own tackle, thinking that he might even start tying his own flies—they could have taken some beautiful trout in that pool below Cross Forks if they had only had a better match for those little yellowish-white mayflies—but by the time the next season had come around, it was impossible to get away. That was the year he had staged his first convention.

Mary came in now, bubbling over with effervescent gratitude, thanking him for giving her the day shift, brushing off his denial that he had had anything to do with it. "Oh, but you did! Dr. Kharr said it was your idea. And I'm terribly grateful. I just can't tell you how much it means."

Almost regretfully, he told her that he had a visitor coming, the warning no more than given when there was a knock on the door. Daphy peered in, her face blooming when he called out a hearty greeting.

She came in, looking at him as if he were one of her kids who had fallen and bumped his head, needing only a motherly assurance that it really wasn't so bad. Whatever she said, that's what it meant, and he heard himself agree, "Sure, I'm fine—it's nothing serious." He caught the glance that Mary gave him, a darting look of critical concern, but there was still the need to convince Daphy. "They're trying to tell me it was a heart attack—you know how these doctors are, always trying to scare you into being a good patient."

"Well, you'd better be," Daphy said, more than half-seriously severe. "But I must say you're looking better than I expected."

"Why not? Why shouldn't I? This isn't anything. I mean it. It isn't."

Daphy gave him a tolerant smile, the knowing look of a mother who has listened to all the white lies of seven smart kids, but also with that special understanding that always made him think of Ray as being a lucky man.

"Well, I'm not going to stay long—I can't," Daphy said. "Sue's going to be in some kind of a do at school this afternoon and I've got to be there. I'm on my way back from Cornell. Took Julie up. She wanted me to drive her. I didn't know why, but I found out—boy trouble—and she wanted a chance to talk."

"Isn't that supposed to be something that kids don't do these days —talk it over with mama?"

"I'm lucky, I guess," Daphy said, stopping to blink suddenly misted eyes. "All of our kids have been wonderful that way—talking things over, I mean. Oh, they've had their spells—Chuck's going through one right now—but they always come around." She sighed. "But it's so hard to know what to tell them these days. Everything's so different. Sometimes I feel so terribly out of step. What in the world do you say to a girl when she says, 'Mother, I'm so terribly in love with him that if we don't get married before long I'm just not going to be able to keep from—'"

She had let her voice drop, seemingly because she had said enough to make her meaning clear, but there was also the possibility that she had seen, or sensed, some reaction from Mary. Mary was at the window, occupied with the chart, giving no indication of eaves-dropping, but he nevertheless warned Daphy off with a flick of his eyes.

She got it, instantly switching away with "But I didn't come to talk about me. Or Julie either. What can I do for you, Judd?"

"Nothing. I'm fine."

"Well, let me tell you what I have done. I don't know, maybe you'll think I was butting into something that wasn't any of my business——"

"Never."

"Anyway, I knew you still had Annie coming in—I have her Wednesdays, you know—so I called her to see if there was anything around your house that needed taking care of. All she could think of was the milk delivery piling up, so I stopped that. I didn't know what to do about the mail, whether to have it forwarded up here or not. I didn't know whether you'd want to be bothered——"

"Why not? Sure, have it sent up. At least anything that's impor-tant."

"Would you want to have it sent over to the office? Maybe Helen could sort it over and——"

"I don't have Helen any more," he cut her off, a bold front against a feeling of guilt that, unreasonable though it was, he had not been able to erase from his mind . . . one of those crazy things that hap-pen when you're too keyed up, that last night before the convention, the dress rehearsal so fouled up, Helen trying to get him to simmer down . . . all right, he'd been a fool, letting it get out of hand. But there was no excuse for Helen, particularly after what she'd said about forgetting it . . . yes, that was the whole trouble, she hadn't forgotten it . . . never a word but it couldn't be missed, the way he'd catch her looking at him when she came into his office, the way she'd edge up to him, the supposedly inadvertent brush of her breasts against his shoulder when she stood beside him to see something on his desk . . .

"Goodness, I didn't know you'd lost Helen," Daphy said. "What happened, anyway?"

"Oh, she went out to California," he said, thrusting away an insistent image of that wild note she left for him, managing a casual "She's got some relatives out there, an uncle or something."

"I bet you miss her, don't you?" Daphy asked. "You had her a long time."

"Eight years," he said curtly, trying to cut it off with, "Don't worry about sorting the mail, just send it up."

"What about the magazines—newspapers—?"

"Forget the magazines, at least for now. But the New Ulster paper —I don't know, maybe you could call and have them send it up here for the next couple of weeks."

"Well, if it's all right—?" Daphy said, glancing in Mary's direction. She must have got a nod of approval because she said, "I'll take care of it as soon as I get back. Anything else?"

He hesitated. "There is something that I ought to call the office about. I guess I could do it myself——"

"No, let me do it," Daphy insisted. "Tell me who to call—what to say."

"Well, if you don't mind, call Allen Talbott——"

"Allen Talbott," Daphy repeated, fishing a pencil and a scrap of paper out of her purse.

"Tell him to get in touch with Eaves in New York and cancel the costume order that I gave them. And do the same thing with Century Lighting—" He paused, waiting as she wrote. "And the slides from Sales Graphic. It may be too late there, they were going to go right ahead, but at least he can try."

"Sales Graphic," she repeated. "I guess Allen will know——"

"He'll know all of them. It's all stuff that I had ordered for the convention. We won't need it now that it's been postponed."

Daphy's pencil stopped. "Postponed?"

"The old man has stalled it off until September." Her incredulous look amused him. "So I'm going to get a little breather this spring. Tell Ray I might even be doing some trout fishing again."

"All right," she said, but her voice had the sound of a mother humoring a sick child. "Eaves, Century Lighting, Sales Graphic—just these three?"

"That's all," he said, experiencing a strange sensation of finality, a wiping-out that was all too easy.

Daphy put her notes in her purse, seeing something that prompted her to say, "Oh, I almost forgot—what's Kay's address in Paris? I called Lydia and she said she thought she'd be staying at the Hotel Louis something—however you say it in French—so that's where I wrote her. But Marj thought she'd be staying with——"

"Wrote her?"

"Well, of course I wrote her, the minute I——"

"About me? About this?"

Daphy's face froze in an astonished expression. "Judd Wilder, don't tell me that you haven't sent word to Kay? You don't mean that she doesn't even know—?"

"Why wreck her trip?"

"Oh, Judd, how could you?" she agonized. "Here you are with a heart attack——"

He waved her off. "It's not—not a real one, anyway."

Startlingly, he heard Mary's voice, unaware that she had come up to the side of the bed until he heard a low but firm "It *was* a heart attack, Mr. Wilder."

"I'm sorry, Judd, if I did something that you didn't—"

"No, it's all right. Forget it. All I meant was—well, I'm going to write her. Thanks for coming, Daphy. It's meant a lot, you more than anyone else. I mean that."

She blushed her pleasure, hiding it with a firm "I'll call Allen Talbott. And if there's anything else—well, you know." Unexpectedly, she bent down to give him a quick kiss on the cheek. "God bless you," she whispered, strangely choked, and for no discernible reason he thought of Iowa, the same feeling that she had given him that night when she came over with the hot casserole.

"I'm sorry," Mary said after the door had closed.

"About what?"

"Butting in like that," she explained. "But you mustn't start saying that you haven't *really* had a heart attack. If you do, the first thing you know you'll have yourself believing it."

He laughed at her. "Don't worry, I'm not kidding myself," he said, his mind drifting off, trying to picture Kay when she got Daphy's letter . . . this was Monday . . . she'd get it as soon as she got to Paris . . . Wednesday . . .

« *4* »

Chris Kemble's original declaration that she had no plans beyond Paris was proving untrue. She had, it seemed, a tour of Spain all planned, the arrangements already made. Kay Wilder, although trying to make herself believe that this belated revelation was coming out now because of their developing friendship, was nevertheless finding it difficult to see why Chris, after having so freely revealed all the intimacies of her married life the first time they talked, should have waited three days to tell her about this trip to Spain.

"I'll fly to Seville and get a car there," Chris was saying. "It's much the best plan, I'm told, starting south and working your way north. That way you have the weather with you, north with the spring. From Seville, over to the coast—down, really—the Costa del Sol, you know? Málaga and all that. We've some friends there, but I'm not at all certain that I'll bother to see them. They're Jim's friends, really. He was in the agency until he had a heart attack. Or at least that's what he said it was. Jim thinks it was just a good excuse to get out from under. Anyway, they're living somewhere near Málaga. He's supposed to be writing a novel but—well, you know how it is—forty-seven, forty-eight—you don't go back at that age and start over again, not and make a success of it, at least something like writing a novel."

"No, probably not," Kay agreed, suspecting that Chris was cueing herself into talking about Jim again.

But she went merrily along her tour. "From Málaga we'll go up the coast as far as—oh, I've forgotten the name of that town—" She reached down into the string bag beside her deck chair, bringing out a guidebook stuffed with a thick packet of papers, extracting what Kay saw was an American Express itinerary. "Of course— Granada," Chris exclaimed, impatient with herself. "I don't know how I could have forgotten that—the Alhambra, you know? I want to see that almost more than anything else. Daddy was an awful Washington Irving buff. He used to read me *Tales of the Alhambra* as if they were fairy stories—which they really are, I suppose. I just hope I'm not disappointed."

"I'm sure you won't be," Kay said abstractedly, diverted by a recollection of one of Rolfe's letters, his hope that he would be able to get down into Spain before he came back to the States.

"Then we'd go up through the Don Quixote country," Chris went on, studying the itinerary, reading a snatched phrase here and there —Toledo, Madrid, out to Segovia and then back to Madrid. "It's open after that. We could give up the car, turn it back in Madrid. Or we can keep it and go down to Valencia and then up the coast to Barcelona. Or there's another possibility—leave the car in Valencia and go out to Majorca." Her tone inscribed a question mark.

"Oh, I couldn't possibly advise you," Kay said. "It all sounds so wonderful."

"Then you're interested?"

"Interested?" she asked blankly, abruptly aware of what Chris must be suggesting. "You don't mean—?"

"Of course," Chris laughed. "Didn't you understand? That's why I've been telling you all of this. Why not? Oh, I know you have to stay in Paris until after your aunt's birthday—you'll still have plenty of time. I'll be taking this trip down through the château country, anyway. I won't be back in Paris until—" She checked her schedule. "We won't be leaving for Seville until the morning of the seventeenth."

"I really don't know what to say," Kay said, hiding her instant rejection of a trip with Chris Kemble, her mind suddenly alive with a counter possibility . . . she could do something like this with Rolfe . . . get a car, just the two of them . . . and it wouldn't be her idea . . . Rolfe had said in that letter that a trip to Spain was what he wanted more than anything else . . . "I don't suppose it would be too terribly expensive."

"Of course it wouldn't," Chris came back, a startling response to a question that Kay was only half aware that she had asked aloud.

"I've engaged the car, anyway—Kay, I'm not asking you because I want someone to share expenses, no, no. All I want—Kay, we'd have a wonderful time, the two of us, you know we would. There aren't many people I'd want to spend a month with, but——"

"Thank you, Chris. I'd love doing it, and I do appreciate your asking me. The only thing is——"

"Here, take this." Chris forced the stuffed guidebook into her hand. "Think about it."

"I will," she agreed, sheltering a deception, already glancing at the American Express folder to see if there was any indication of what it would cost . . . they could do it more cheaply than a travel agency tour, of course . . . Rolfe had made that trip to Rome on practically nothing . . . no, they wouldn't go that way. Rolfe deserved at least one good trip . . . she had her own money . . . Judd would fuss, of course, but . . .

"There's no hurry about letting me know," Chris said. "Any time before we get off the boat."

« 5 »

Judd Wilder had half expected that Mrs. Cope would arrive early, and she did, but only by a few minutes, not having heard about Miss Harsch until she reached the hospital. She came rushing in as if she were responding to an alarm bell, jumping on Mary for not having called her, shooing her out, telling her to go home at once, but then following her into the corridor and talking a long time. When she came back, she was preoccupied, her lips moving in a silent dialogue punctuated with little snorts and sniffs, easily enough interpreted as her observations on any nurse who would so irresponsibly desert a patient. And as if it were comment by example, she launched off on a round of flurrying activity, giving him a bath, changing the bed linen, rubbing his back so vigorously that he felt himself less an invalid being soothed than an athlete being readied for battle.

Kneading his shoulder muscles, she suddenly asked, "What do you think of Dr. Kharr?"

Surprised, he twisted his head, looking up at her. "What do you mean—what do I think of him?"

"Do you like him or don't you?" she asked, a no-nonsense demand.

"Sure I like him. Why wouldn't I? Oh, I don't know that I buy all of his ideas, but still—well, he makes a lot more sense than any other doctor I've ever had. Why?"

"That's just what I thought you'd say," Mrs. Cope said, bearing down again.

Wincing under the pressure of her fingers, he finally managed an intelligible, "Why? What's up?"

"Nothing," she said with a dismissing smack on his buttocks, open-handed and final.

« 6 »

All through the day, curbing impatience, Aaron Kharr had restrained himself from going back to continue his session with Judd Wilder. He was not stalling because of any lack of confidence—quite the opposite. He had picked up from Mrs. Ingalls, after she had left Wilder's room, the lead for which he had been searching. Actually, she had told him little that he had not already known, or had strongly suspected, but that one remark about the Crouch Carpet conventions had, like a catalytic agent, congealed all of the fluid possibilities that had been coursing through his mind, fixing both a point of attack and a continuing plan of action. He saw now how Wilder could almost certainly be made to understand what he had done to himself, and once that was accomplished, the battle to bring him around would be all but won. He would need at least a half-hour, perhaps longer, and it was to get that much time free of interruption that he had decided to wait until seven o'clock.

He went home early for dinner, sitting down to the table as Mrs. Stine's mantel clock was cuckooing six, earning a compliment—"Now you're showing some sense, Doctor, being here to eat when it's ready"—back at the hospital at a quarter to seven. After making sure that Raggi was on duty, ready to guard him against any interrupting calls, he holed up in his office for a quick review of

Wilder's biographical outline, refixing every date and detail in his mind, knowing that there was nothing more inhibiting to a patient than a physician who, while pretending personal involvement, was constantly checking his notes. Furthermore, it was vitally important that he never again be caught off base, as unprepared as he had been this morning.

At precisely seven o'clock he left his office, striding confidently down the corridor, telling himself that his feeling of tension was normal, purely anticipatory, in no way apprehensive. Rounding the corner, he saw Mrs. Cope leaving the floor desk, carrying the little paper cup that held Wilder's evening medication.

"You can take a break if you'd like, Mrs. Cope," he said. "I started a little session with him this morning—had to break it off, but I'm free now so—"

Mrs. Cope's "Umhumm," intoned without lip movement, suggested no more than pique at being excluded, but then she said, "You had a session with him yesterday, too, didn't you?" looking directly at him, her eyes unblinking.

"Has he been talking about it?" he asked, anxiously alert.

Her eyes did not drop. "He's not the one who's been doing the talking."

"But who else—?"

Cope's eyes gave him the answer, even before she said, "She didn't stay sick very long—came in at three—for one of Dr. Teeter's cases."

"Yes, I knew that she'd promised—" he began, his voice drifting off, the pretense of normality impossible to sustain against a rising tide of apprehension, vividly recalling that look on Harsch's face . . . the same thing he had seen in that Atlantic City audience when he had described the "suicide" approach . . . "*Surely, Dr. Kharr, you're aware of the dangerously traumatic potentiality of hitting a third-day coronary with any such radical procedure . . .*"

"I heard Dr. Teeter telling Dr. Webster about what she'd told him," Cope said. "It was pretty wild."

He choked back an exploring question, prohibited by propriety from saying or doing anything that might condone her blatant breach of the professional code.

Cope must have sensed what he was thinking because she said, "I didn't know whether to tell you or not—maybe I shouldn't have."

All he dared say was, "The patient is coming along all right—that's the important thing."

"I guess so," she said, looking down now.

Following her eyes, he saw her fingers nervously working to re-shape the little paper cup inadvertently crushed by the grip of her hand. He thought of what Mrs. Stine had told him about Mrs. Cope's husband, an impulse to sympathy still unresolved when unexpectedly she looked up.

"Maybe it's not my place to say anything—I guess it isn't—but if it was me, I wouldn't push him too hard."

Startled, he asked, "Do you think I have?"

"I'm sure you know a lot more about it than I do, Doctor."

"None of us know enough," he said with the earnestness of apprehension. "I need all the advice I can get. And you're much closer to him than I am."

"I could be wrong, but I'm guessing he's a lot more scared than he's letting on."

"Yes, I suppose that's possible," he admitted, pausing to frame a question, an effort made futile as she turned away with "If you want me you can call."

He watched her walk back to the desk, hesitated for an indecisive moment, and then started down the corridor toward Wilder's room. Despite his respect for Cope's intuitive judgment, he could not give any great weight to her feeling that Wilder was truly frightened—surely there had been no hint of it this morning—yet there was only the narrowest of margins between traumatic fear and reasoned concern, and there was at least an outside possibility that, in his anxiety to bring Wilder around, he had pushed him over the line. If that happened . . . Teeter waiting to cut him down . . . everyone talking . . . East Manhattan . . .

Memory was a quaking image, shuddered by the anger of recalled inequity, remembering his defenselessness against Dr. Bernathy's silent charge that it had all been his fault. And it had, at least in the sense that he was the one who had finally made a dent in the hoary dogma of standard practice. Bernathy had decreed that every coronary occlusion patient, regardless of the severity of the attack, must be kept flat on his back for three weeks. Endlessly quoting Dr. Steinfeldt, Aaron Kharr had tried to convince him that this procedure was one of the prime causes of the heart-fearing neurosis that incapacitated so many patients, making no progress whatsoever until he had happened upon a paper in which Dr. Samuel Levine of Boston advocated getting coronary patients out of bed as soon as possible, the less severely afflicted as early as the third day. That support from so eminent a cardiologist had turned the trick, and the new approach had been cautiously inaugurated. Twenty or more selected cases had demonstrated uniformly satisfactory results when, in one of those freak coincidences with which the practice of medicine is plagued, a patient who had been allowed to sit up in a chair on the fourth day had gone into heart failure. Although the autopsy had unequivocally established an entirely different cause of death, the new procedure in no way implicated, Bernathy had been driven into panicked retreat, frightened out of his wits by his vulnerability to the criticism of his peers. Thereafter, regardless of circumstances, no patient on his service was allowed out of bed until the twenty-first day. That was the safe way—no cardiologist could ever be blackmarked for the death of a patient who was still in bed.

Aaron Kharr had no fear that anything like that would happen to Judd Wilder, but he was nevertheless aware of risk of another sort. Ever since the publication of his first paper on the psychological rehabilitation of the coronary patient he had known that, having touched a raw nerve of professional conscience, he would be mercilessly pilloried if he himself failed to bring off what he claimed any conscientious doctor could easily do. The trouble was—he saw this now for the first time—Teeter had a two-edged sword with which to cut him down, and with his resentment at having had a high-fee case snatched away, he would not hesitate to use whichever edge served his own purpose. Every doctor on the County Memorial staff knew that he had taken the case after Mr. Crouch's intervention, and no denial would ever convince anyone that he had not promised to send Wilder back to his job. If that was the outcome, Teeter would make the most of it. On the other hand, if Wilder decided against returning to Crouch Carpet, Teeter would be in a position to discredit his whole approach. Unavoidably, he felt a rising sense of alarming entrapment, but his response was not an impulse to caution. Instead, there was a vigorous surge of renewed purpose, an adrenaline-driven exhilaration that lengthened his stride and quickened his pace.

A few steps away from Wilder's room, however, he abruptly slowed to a tiptoed advance. Seeing that Mrs. Cope had left the door partly open, he approached cautiously, hoping for a moment of preparatory observation. The room was deeply shadowed, only two lights on: the small-bulbed floor lamp at the window where Mrs. Cope had been sitting, and the reading light over the bed that, fortunately, fully illuminated the patient's face. Wilder's expression was reassuringly neutral, revealing neither the fear that Mrs. Cope had suggested, nor the impatience of a man restrained against his will. Unquestionably, it was the face of a man rapidly regaining his health. In two weeks he could be dismissed as a fully recovered patient. Another attack within a year was extremely unlikely. After that, no doctor could conceivably be blamed for what happened. Why go on?

Abruptly, with no consciousness of decision, he stepped into the doorway, reminding himself that his key objective was to work Wilder around to talking about his Crouch Carpet conventions, a little surprised by the tremor that he heard in his voice when he launched a calculatedly casual "Good evening."

Wilder's instantly responding "Come in!" was a warm enough response, but his smile was noticeably quick-fading, and there was an overtone of reproach behind, "I thought maybe you weren't going to make it."

"Sorry it took me so long to get back," he said apologetically, pulling up a chair, trying to make it seem an offhand act, masking the precision with which he spotted the chair, close enough to the bed so that he would have the clearest possible view of Wilder's face, yet far enough away so that his own would be shadowed. He sat down. "Getting a little bored with hospital life?"

"No, not particularly."

"We'll try to ease things a little for you tomorrow. Let you sit up in bed." He got no response. "In a day or two, get you out in a chair."

"All right."

"Would you like a television set?"

"Oh, I don't know, it doesn't matter."

"I'm afraid our library facilities are rather limited, but we can get you almost any of the magazines. Anything you particularly want?"

"I haven't felt much like reading," Wilder said. "Too much to think about." He glanced toward him, a little smile twisting his lips. "That's what you wanted me to do—isn't it?"

"Yes, of course," Kharr said, trying to put the best possible face on alarm, wondering now if Mrs. Cope was right, blaming himself for having waited so long to come back. Forced to recapture lost ground as quickly as possible, he said, "Sorry our talk was interrupted this morning. I was very much interested in what you were telling me."

"Oh, I had to see Daphy."

"Of course," he replied, suddenly seeing the opening that he wanted. "I met her on the way out, talked to her a minute or two. She seemed a very nice person." Wilder gave him a suspicious glance but said nothing. "She was telling me something about these conventions you put on. They sound like very elaborate affairs. Must be an enormous amount of work."

"They are," Wilder agreed, but immediately cut away with "There's something I want to ask you, something that's been bugging me."

"Yes?"

"You said this morning—or maybe it was last night, I don't know —that there's no reason why I can't go on doing my job. Right?"

"Right," he agreed, bracing himself.

"How do you square that with this stress business? If this has happened to me because of what I've been doing—if you're right about that, then how can I go on doing it?"

It was the same old question, the one with which his critics had always opened their attack. Prepared, he came back confidently, "I've studied a great many cases, Mr. Wilder, and I've yet to find one where I could fix the blame on a man's job. No matter how demanding his work may be, that's not what creates stress—or at least not the kind of stress that we're talking about. It's not the job itself, it's the way the man reacts to it. More than anything, I think, it's a matter of motivation. The man who is soundly motivated, with a tangible objective and a real sense of purpose, rarely winds up with an early coronary. The man who gets in trouble is the man who is driving ahead without——"

"The runner without a goal business?"

"Exactly."

"And that's the way you've got me pegged?" Wilder demanded, his tone close to belligerence.

"Well, you *have* had a heart attack," he countered, a reflex response that, for a moment seemed too blunt, defeating his purpose of getting Wilder to talk. He saw that his lips were tight-set now, his expression unreadable, but like the surface of a deep river it suggested that a powerful stream was flowing underneath, turbulent depths that Aaron Kharr was more than anxious to explore. Taking a long gamble, he said, "Let's talk for a minute or two about these conventions you put on."

Wilder's expression did not change. "What about them?"

"They're very important to you, aren't they?"

"Sure, that's the way we built up our whole distribution system."

"I don't mean important to the company—I mean important to you."

"If it's important to the company, it's important to me."

"But perhaps in a different way."

"You don't think they're worth the work I put into them, is that it?"

"It might be a question worth exploring for a minute or two."

"All right, go ahead—explore," Wilder said, a cool smile briefly flickering, his tone unmistakably challenging.

Summoning patience, reminding himself that if Wilder were not this kind of a man he would not be here, his voice slipped into the precut groove of his prepared approach. "Suppose we go back to your boyhood days—your first ambition, your first dream of what you were going to do with your life."

"My first ambition?" Wilder repeated. "I never had one. I didn't know what I wanted to do."

"Surely you weren't very old when you decided on a theatrical career?"

"I never made any decision like that," Wilder said stubbornly. "The closest I ever came—well, as a young kid I got the idea that I wanted to be a foreign correspondent."

"Yes, I can see that—your father being a newspaper editor——"

"No, not because of my father," Wilder said, momentarily hesitant as if he were going on, then wiping it out with "That didn't last very long."

"How old were you when you put on this pageant, the one that was written up in *Life?*"

"I don't know, seventeen or eighteen. Eighteen, I guess. It was the summer after I got out of high school."

"You're not saying, are you, that by then you didn't know where you were heading?"

"It's true—I didn't."

"Oh, come now," he said with a chiding smile. "Within a month you were off to Colfax College. And you took the drama course. No boy makes a move like that without a strongly motivating ambition. And from there on out you went right down that one straight line —radio, motion pictures, television, the Broadway stage——"

"It may look like a straight line to you," Wilder cut him off, "but that isn't the way it was."

"No?"

Wilder shook his head vigorously. "All I ever did was play the ball the way it bounced. And it was no straight line. It was bounce, bounce, bounce"—his hand traced a zig-zag course—"like a pinball game." The thought obviously pleased him. "That's what my whole life has been—a pinball game. Or at least it was until I landed at Crouch Carpet."

"Yes, that's a good description of the way a lot of men do live their lives," he granted, peripherally conscious that the pinball simile might be useful in his book. "But let's go back to that pageant for a minute or two. Are you saying——"

"All right, I'll tell you how it happened," Wilder said wearily, as if finally worn down. "Have you ever been in Iowa? Do you know what it's like—a little county-seat town?"

"No, I'm afraid not," he said, attempting to set a lighter tone. "The closest I ever came to Iowa—I flew over once—on my way out to San Francisco for a medical meeting."

"Haygood's a little county-seat town. Main Street's five blocks long. The depot's at one end, the courthouse at the other. Beyond that—cornfields. Hog farms. On Saturday nights when the farmers come to town, that's all you heard—how's the corn growing, what's the price of hogs going to do. This was back in the Thirties. The corn wasn't growing because of the drought and the Depression had knocked the bottom out of the hog market. Do you remember the WPA?"

"Of course," he quickly agreed, trying to encourage what seemed a breakdown in Wilder's reserve.

"Well, this was a part of it, a handout program to keep these Iowa farmers from worrying so much about corn and hogs that they wouldn't vote for F.D.R. again. Somebody back East thought that the way to do it was to bring a little culture to these poor benighted hog jockeys, so they set up a regional theater program. My grandfather was a political wheel—naturally he got his hand in the pork barrel and came up with a little chunk of fat for Haygood. Two thousand dollars. That wouldn't be anything now, but back then it was a big deal. So they organized the Haygood Regional Theater, and sent out a man from New York to run it, a man named Leslie Dwight. Anybody from back East was bad enough—Wall Street was the abode of the devil—and Leslie Dwight didn't help himself any by turning up with a goatee and a tea-drinker's accent. He was supposed to be a Broadway director—oh, he'd been around the theater for a long time, I learned a lot from him—but the guy had two strikes on him before he ever got started. The only reason he lasted as long as he did was this anniversary business."

Wilder stretched, easing himself into another position. "Most of that country had been settled back in the 1860's, and a lot of the other towns around had been having seventy-fifth anniversary celebrations. Mound City had had a big one and all the Haygood storekeepers were burned up at the business that it had taken away from them. Everybody was trying to find some way to get even. Even before Leslie Dwight turned up, there'd been a lot of talk about doing something, and with that two thousand bucks to start things off—well, that's how the pageant got started."

"How did you become involved?"

"In a little town like that, everybody's involved in everything. You have to be," Wilder said, then conceding, "Oh, I'd been digging into local history, the old Black Hawk story—you know, the eager-beaver kid—and I'd come up with a yarn about a treaty conference with the Indians somewhere near Haygood in the 1830's. You had to stretch the truth a little to tie it in with the start of the town, but still it was enough of a peg to hang a pageant on. And if we did, you see, that gave us a centennial celebration, beating out Mound City by twenty-five years."

"You wrote the script?"

"Oh, there wasn't much writing to it. It wasn't really a play, just a series of tableaux—the Indian camp, the emigrant wagon train, the night battle, the cavalry coming over the hill, the big peacepipe scene, signing the treaty—sure, it was corny, but it was what they wanted. Everybody really got steamed up about it, the whole town. All the women were sewing Indian costumes, the men were working on props—we had eight covered wagons to build for the emigrant train—and then—*bang*—everything blew up. Old man Sheaffer— that's where Leslie Dwight had been rooming—went upstairs one night and caught Leslie with a young boy in his room. I don't know whether there was anything to it or not—I doubt it—but anyway, that was the end of Leslie Dwight. So that's how the ball bounced —right into my lap."

"You stepped in and took over?"

"Somebody had to. It had gone too far to stop."

"But you couldn't have done it if you hadn't had a great deal of natural talent for the theater, not and made it the success that it so obviously was. After all *Life* doesn't——"

"That was the next bounce," Wilder said, a tongue-in-cheek retort. "*Life* had a crew out there working on a story about county fairs. They had an open week, no fairs, so they covered the pageant. They sent a lot of pictures back to New York, they happened to hit the right editor's desk, and there I was in the magazine—a one-week hero. But then I got another lucky bounce. A copy of *Life* happened to hit Colfax just when they're passing out drama scholarships. So that's where I go to college. There was a part-time job open in the radio station—I bounced into that. The war came along, another bounce and I landed in the Signal Corps. Bounce, bounce, bounce, and I'm a motion picture director with my own unit."

"Wasn't that what you wanted?"

"I could have done worse. But it was pure luck. I didn't apply for it. If I hadn't been talking to this particular lieutenant——"

"Oh, there's an element of chance in everyone's life," he granted. "But you stayed on in motion picture work after the war, didn't you?"

"There were a million guys getting out of the service, all looking for jobs. I had a wife and child to support—what else could I do?"

"And I suppose that going into television was no more than another bounce of that lucky ball."

"Lucky or not, that's what it was. I didn't go after it—they came after me."

"You seem to have been a singularly docile young man," he said sardonically. "No ambition, no drive, no sense of direction——"

Wilder laughed, a little burst of sound quickly snuffed out. "Whether you believe it or not, that's the way it was."

"Oh, I can easily enough believe that you didn't always know where you were going next. An opportunity came along—you took it. And at the time, perhaps, it seemed no more than a lucky break. Or as you put it, another bounce of the ball. But there was more than that involved, Mr. Wilder. There had to be. A ball doesn't bounce uphill. It has to be propelled. There has to be energy behind it—drive, ambition, ability—and a sense of purpose." He paused. "You don't land on Broadway by accident."

Unmistakably, Wilder flinched, and he must have been aware of it, because he tried to cover it with motion, lifting his legs, tenting the bedclothes over his knees.

After a fruitless wait for a reply, Aaron Kharr pressed on. "So at the age of thirty-two—" He stopped, his voice suspended, wondering if there was anything to be gained by making the point that the personality pattern that produced a mid-forties coronary was so often evidenced earlier by some kind of revolutionary upheaval in the man's early thirties, deciding against it when he saw Wilder's broadening smirk.

"So at the age of thirty-two," Wilder repeated, a broad mimicry. "I took all my God-given talent and sold it for a mess of potage—right? I could have been a great theatrical director but, no, I threw all that away and wound up as nothing but an advertising man. That's how you've got me pegged, isn't it—the frustrated artist who's eating his heart out because he knows what a mess he's made of his life? That's why you think I've been under all this stress—right?"

For an instant, Aaron Kharr felt his mind bared, the very act of exposure a form of ridicule, yet in the next instant he was aware that Wilder's bitter sarcasm was highly revelatory. Obviously, his attitude was not of recent origin. It could only have been steeped out over a long period of time, an acid reaction to some persistent irritation. Was it something buried in his own mind, a growing cancer of unacknowledged regret? Or was he reacting to someone else's judgment? Could it possibly be his wife?

"All right, maybe I did have a little talent," Wilder went on, his tone easier, but still taut, "—theatrical sense, a knack for direction, whatever you want to call it—but whatever it was, I've made a damn sight better use of it with Crouch Carpet than I could ever have done on Broadway, or in Hollywood, or wherever else I might have landed. I didn't toss anything overboard. I didn't throw anything away. I used everything I had. And I got a lot more satisfaction out of it than I ever had before. I mean that."

"I'm sure you do," he said placatingly, noting with concern that Wilder's self-defense was totally in the past tense.

"Damn it, it's true!"

"There's no need to convince me, Mr. Wilder."

"I suppose you think I'm only trying to convince myself."

He made no reply, waiting out a long silence.

"You asked me this morning why I came with Crouch Carpet," Wilder finally said. "Maybe this isn't the reason I came, but it's the reason I stayed. After that first year—when I saw how much I could accomplish, how much more it meant"—he exhaled wearily—"I guess it's hard to understand if you haven't gone through it yourself."

"I'd like to try," he said, low-voiced.

"Oh, I won't say that I didn't get some kicks out of show business —sure I did," Wilder went on, as abstracted as if he were thinking aloud. "Taking a bunch of actors and a script, bringing a play to life—the way you feel the minute before you go on the air, before the curtain goes up—all right, it's a wallop, sure it is. But it doesn't last. And when it's over, what have you got? There's nothing deader than last night's television show. Unless maybe it's a theater after a play has closed. I remember—" His voice drifted off.

Whatever it was that he remembered never came to light, submerged in a long moment of secret thought. "For some people—a little applause, a few curtain calls, a good line in a review—that's all they want out of life. I know so many of them—actors, actresses, directors, scenic designers—nothing else matters. They'll give up anything, make any sacrifice, scrounge along on nothing, never lose hope—and I'm not saying they're wrong."

"But the theater was never that important to you?" Aaron Kharr asked, by no means convinced.

"No," Wilder said firmly. "I had to have something solid, something that was going to last, something that I knew wasn't going to end when—well, when the projector went off, or the curtain came down."

"And that's what you found at Crouch Carpet?"

Wilder looked away, silent for a long time, finally saying, "All right, suppose I'd stayed with it—the theater, television, wherever I might have wound up—are you saying that if I'd done that, I'd never have had a heart attack?"

"No, not at all. There's a very high incidence among people in show business."

"And what would have happened then? Can you imagine a theatrical producer turning up here the way Mr. Crouch did—telling me to forget it, not to worry, that he was postponing the show until I was ready to take over again? And in the meantime my salary would go on just as if I were working? Doesn't that mean something —to know that the ground isn't going to be cut out from under you the first time you get a little bad break?"

"Yes, of course," Aaron Kharr muttered, reminding himself of how elated he had been by Crouch's action, thinking what a great help it would be to Wilder's rehabilitation, yet now he felt sickeningly disappointed, hardly able to believe that Wilder had fallen back upon such a weak justification for what he had done with his life. He had, until this moment, seen him as a strong character, independent and individualistic, battered but far from beaten, fully capable of bouncing back and taking command again. To see him as he now appeared, abjectly grateful for Crouch's favor, huddling under the corporate umbrella, thinking of the future only in terms of a continuing salary, added up to something far more serious than a simple violation of expectation. Nothing was more destructive of hope than to find a patient sunk so deep that he was clinging to a job as desperately as if it were life itself.

Fighting against despair, he tried to tell himself that he was reading much too much into what Wilder had said, giving more weight to a casual remark than it merited, yet he could not avoid recalling the question that Wilder had been waiting to ask him, hearing it in new context, not as the intelligent and thoughtful inquiry that he had then judged it to be, but as a missed revelation of crippling anxiety . . . Cope was right . . . Wilder was far more frightened than he had suspected.

He had to say something, and he said, "Yes, that means a lot, knowing that you don't have to worry about your job," routine assurance offered without thought, blindly adding, "and knowing that Mr. Crouch won't let you down."

Wilder nodded, his satisfaction so alarmingly smug that it cried out for argument. But what could he say? Nothing. Not now. He had gone as far as he could tonight. He had already talked to Wilder longer than he had planned, pushed him almost as far as he dared . . . maybe one more little point . . . open up the ground for tomorrow . . .

Distantly, he heard a mechanical voice paging Dr. Teeter.

Abruptly, he stood up, his stethoscope out of his pocket before he quite realized what he was doing. Aware of it, he felt himself demeaned by subterfuge, resorting to trickery, hiding behind a ritual of deceptive fakery. There was no need to listen to Wilder's heart, no reason whatsoever. But he was too far committed now to turn back. Bending over, he felt as if he were bowing to failure, weighted down again with an almost terrifying sense of incompetence and inadequacy . . . he had been so sure tonight that he was right . . . but it hadn't worked out . . . again and again and again . . . why, why, why?

« 7 »

Night had come to County Memorial as it always did, less a phenomenon of light than of sound. The hushing mantle had fallen, the last visitor gone from the corridor, the cart clatter stilled, the squawk box cut off. The only sound was the click of Mrs. Cope's knitting needles, and that, endlessly persistent, was noticed only when it stopped.

Judd Wilder lifted his head.

"Want something?" she asked.

"No," he said, dropping his head, slipping back into the mental process that, earlier in the day, he had described to Dr. Kharr as "doing a lot of thinking." He had been in no way dishonest in that statement—he imagined that he had—yet there was little truth in the implication that he had been engaged in any serious self-analysis. His mind, an instrument shaped by long usage to a different end, could not be easily turned in upon itself. What passed for introspection was largely a review of stored memories, necessarily limited to impressions already made and recorded. Even now, preoccupied with some of the *why* questions that Kharr had asked, his search for answers did not go beyond a review of those motivations of which he had been conscious at the time.

All that he had told Kharr about his reasons for going with Crouch Carpet had been essentially true, yet he had been aware then, and was even more so now, that he had not given him the whole story. He had not been deceptive—if Kharr had given him an opening, he might have told him something about Kay, at least enough to let him know what he had been up against—and there was the further justification that Kharr would probably have got the wrong impression. Kay had not really influenced him. He had made his own decision. And no one could say that it hadn't worked out. No matter what Kharr was imagining . . .

His thoughts came full circle again, back to where they had started, that big pitch about wasting his talent in business . . . Kay . . . that night he came home to tell her about taking the Crouch Carpet job . . .

Impulsively, surprising himself, he said, "Do you suppose there's any stationery around? Maybe I ought to write my wife."

"Well, it's about time," Cope exclaimed, stuffing her knitting, stabbing herself with a needle, brushing off a wince of pain. "If there isn't any, I'll get some," she said, on her feet, banging drawers, finding nothing.

"Forget it," he said. "I'll write in the morning."

"You'll do it right now," she said, charging out of the room, back in a moment with a sheaf of County Memorial letterheads, fishing a ballpoint out of her purse, cranking up the bed, a flurry of furious activity that left him with a pen in hand, and a blank sheet in front of him.

He wrote *Dear Kay* and then stopped, beginning a search for words. He thought of an opening sentence and tested it in silent recitation, abruptly diverted by another and stronger voice . . . "*If I were to give you a sheet of paper and a pencil, would you be able to put down—right now, this very minute—a clear statement of what you want to accomplish in the last half of your life?*"

❖ VI ❖

SOMETIME IN THE NIGHT, Kay Wilder had been awakened by the foghorn, a guttural groaning that seemed to come not from overhead but from somewhere deep within the ship, an outcry against some visceral agony, the vessel rolling from side to side as if afflicted by an awful torment, pain expressed in a rising chorus of creaks and screeches. By the time the portholes became visible, cold light filtering into the black void of her cabin, she could hear the shriek of rising wind and feel the shuddering impact of huge waves. She had known then that it was only a storm, not a nightmare, and had gone back to sleep.

When she awoke again it was almost nine o'clock, but the cabin was scarcely lighter than it had been at dawn. The movement of the ship, however, seemed less violent, and she got out of bed, an experimental foray that took her to the porthole. Directly below, she could see the swirling rush of black water, but that was the limit of visibility. Beyond, everything was blotted out by wet-rag clouds. The foghorn was still blasting away.

Surprisingly, she felt not at all queasy, the prospect of breakfast actually inviting. Dressed, she made her way to the dining saloon, the waiter's smile a flattering compliment for fortitude. She was alone at the captain's table, no one nearer than a man, also alone, who sat at one of the small tables directly in front of her. His face seemed familiar, perhaps no more so than dozens of others she had come to recognize as shipmates, yet somehow there was a suggestion of earlier acquaintance in the way he kept looking at her. Every time she glanced in his direction, his eyes were waiting, his questioning expression becoming more and more a demand for recognition.

Dismissing him as a foraging male, remembering what Chris had said last night—"Oh God, these goaty characters that think every divorcee is fair game!"—she ate her grapefruit without sugaring it, accepting acid tartness as penance for the chocolate mousse that she had eaten for dessert last night. Reaching for her coffee cup, unable to refrain from another checking glance, she was startled to see that he had got up from his chair and was coming directly toward her. As a protective reflex she looked away, pretending not to have seen him, a ruse defeated by his firmly insistent "You're Mrs. Judd Wilder, aren't you?"

"Yes."

"Your husband used to be in television?"

Again she said, "Yes," but now as a guarded admission, a reluctant yielding of the anonymity that had been the most appealing aspect of this ocean voyage.

"I'm Dave Keegan," he said, pausing as if expecting recognition, then anxiously adding, "We met only once, I'm sure you've forgotten —I had the rehearsal studio right next to Judd's. When he was doing the Vega Hour, you know?"

"Oh, yes," she said, wondering if shipboard camaraderie demanded that she ask him to sit down.

He seemed embarrassed now. "You're still—I mean, you and Judd—you aren't—?"

"We're still married," she said, trying to control a too-nervous laugh, achieving poise with a firm "Please sit down, Mr. Keegan. You'll have a cup of coffee, won't you?"

He waved off the eavesdropping waiter, but he did sit down. "I've been holed up in my cabin, playing nursemaid to a sick script, so I didn't really look at the passenger list until last night, but when I saw that name—Judd Wilder—you're still living down in—somewhere in Pennsylvania, isn't it? I saw Judd a couple of years ago, one noon at The Lambs. He looked wonderful."

"Yes, he's fine."

"I remember when he took that job. We all thought he was out of his mind." He shrugged it off. "He who laughs last, huh?"

The ship lurched, struck hard, and then hung as if suspended for an awful moment of indecision, setting up an arpeggio of tinkling glass and silver ending with the cymbal crash of a tray of dishes dropped by a staggering busboy. Her coffee cup had spilled and the waiter stepped in to mop it up, spreading a napkin, extending the moment that she needed to comb her memory . . . *Keegan* . . . *Dave Keegan* . . . ?

The name was somehow familiar, yet no more so than a hundred others that Judd had bandied about back in those television days, an explanation no more than accepted when it hit her, a recognition so sudden that she could not choke off a bursting "You're *David* Keegan!"

"Guilty," he grinned.

"Oh, but I—I *am* sorry! Somehow, I never connected—*Dave* Keegan sounds so different—"

"It's one of my better disguises," he said, pseudo-serious. "It's been known to fool even my most persistent creditors."

She laughed, accepting the humor of David Keegan ever having to worry about bill collectors. "Oh, I so wanted to see your play. The notices were so wonderful. And I've always thought John Washburn was so—" Something was wrong. Could she be mistaken? "I am right—you did direct—?"

"I thought for a moment you were talking about my last magnum opus. Or even the one before. The Washburn thing was five years ago."

"Oh, but it can't be," she protested.

"Time flies," he said with a dismissing flip of his hand. "I was thinking about that a minute ago—the old Vega Hour, that must have been 1950. I remember Judd's play, the Ilsa Lang thing—that was 'fifty-one, wasn't it?"

"Yes, 'fifty-one," she said, over-brightly, an almost conscious attempt to slack the tension that she always felt at the mention of that Lang woman's name, quite purposefully changing the subject with, "What's the script you're working on—a new play?"

He put his hands over his face, a mockery of shame, but there was more bitterness than humor in his farcically groaned "Don't ask."

"I understand," she said with a smile, imagining that she did, transported back in memory to those days when the sharing of a director's agonizing over a bad script had been an accepted part of her life.

David Keegan dropped his hands, revealing a face that seemed to have aged ten years in ten seconds. "I'm back to doing television again. Right where I was ten years ago. Except for this one rather horrifying difference—then it was all ahead, now it's all behind."

"You don't really mean that you're giving up the theater, you know you don't," she said chidingly, trying to tell him that she understood these transient moments of depression that all theater people went through.

"It's not a question of my giving up the theater," he said heavily. "It's the other way around. No, it's true. I'm not kidding myself. After my last play—I thought it the best thing I'd ever done—sound, solid, real, true. Ten years ago it would have run for a year. It closed in a week. No, when you get to the point where you can't rely on your own judgment and taste—what's left?"

"You'll be back in the theater," she said confidently.

"I'm not even certain that I can make this television thing go. It's only a pilot, and if they don't pick it up—" He broke off with a humorless laugh. "Now that you've heard my sad tale——"

"It's the weather," she said. "You'll be all right when the sun comes out."

"Maybe so," he said, starting to rise, balancing himself against the roll of the ship. "Look, if you'd be willing to give the sun a hand—will you have a drink with me—before lunch, I mean—the bar at twelve-thirty?"

"Of course," she said, caution dissipated by the promise that escaping a noontime drink with Chris Kemble would stall off, at least for a few more hours, telling her that she would not be going to Spain with her.

« 2 »

On this Tuesday morning, the beginning of Judd Wilder's sixth day at County Memorial Hospital, he received his first substantial packet of mail. There had been a few cards before but they had been largely meaningless, sterile signatures subscribing to mass-produced sentiments as essentially impersonal as the Christmas cards that each year filled Kay's old Waterford punch bowl, registering only as checkmarks on the double-columned list that she kept to avoid the embarrassment of a mismatch between *Received* and *Sent*.

This morning there was a thick stack of envelopes, borne in with a gay mimicry of ceremony, presented by Mary as an offering on a tray, anticipation aroused by her ebulliently awed remark about all the friends he must have.

Riffling through the envelopes, he saw that almost all were from New York, explained when the first note that he read mentioned the *Transom*, Madison Avenue's gossipy equivalent of a little small-town newspaper. Apparently there had been something about his illness in yesterday morning's edition, a hint that had been immediately picked up, it seemed, by every space peddler and time sales-man who had any interest in the Crouch Carpet account. Although most of the notes had to be discounted for a soft-sell sales pitch, they were nevertheless more personal than greeting cards, and there were at least two that evidenced genuine interest and concern, both from men who had had heart attacks themselves.

The last note that Mary handed him—she was standing by, open-ing envelopes—was a flowery epistle from Nick Saltini at Jersey-Hudson Colorplate, an instant reminder that he had forgotten, in the message that he had asked Daphy to relay, to tell Allen Talbott to cancel the order he had given Nick for the cover of the convention program. He was debating what to do, wondering if Mary would let him get away with making a telephone call, when he heard her ask, "Shall I open this for you?"

"Open what?" he asked, the question answered as she lifted what he had before thought a small tray upon which the mail had been delivered, but which he now saw was a thin package, the size of a letter sheet, its brown paper wrapping multi-stamped with FIRST CLASS and INSURED, tape-bound and sealed with red wax.

Perhaps it was the wax seal—there had to be some reason beyond simple premonition for the feeling that his outreaching hand was trembling—but somehow he knew, even before he saw the pen-inscribed return address, who had sent it. That was all there was, only the address, no name, but no name was necessary . . . *Sutton Place* . . .

"I'll just get the tape off," Mary said, perceptive enough to under-stand that he wanted to open it himself.

"All right," he agreed, yet even that small concession seemed a breach of security, threatening a secret area that he had always felt himself called upon to guard with a caution that had never, at least in retrospect, been justified by any real danger. Even during those years when Ilsa Lang had been so much a part of his life, there had always been the impregnable defense of a professionally acceptable relationship between a conscientious director and a star who needed more than simple direction. Whatever that relationship had been, whatever name might once have been given to it, it was something so long lost that it had come to seem hardly more than an illusory dream—until this moment when, seeing that Sutton Place address, twelve years were overleaped in a flash of abrupt materialization.

He had not seen Ilsa Lang—except once across Fifth Avenue, coming out of Bergdorf's—since that afternoon when he had gone to Sutton Place to tell her that he had taken a job in Pennsylvania, that he was leaving New York, hoping that there would be some painless way to make her understand that it was an ending that had to be. But it was she, not he, who had said, "We always knew that it would have to end sometime," her voice low and throaty, projected as if she were reading a third-act curtain line, the business of holding both his hands in hers as she firmly guided him to the door so perfectly performed that it seemed she must have rehearsed it for weeks.

And then he had been outside in the dark vestibule, feeling himself tricked, used and then discarded, pushed off because he was no longer of any use to her, escaping to the street as if he were running away from something that could never have happened. He had walked for blocks before he had even started watching for a taxi, finally flagging one down, and it had been only after that, speeding toward Grand Central and the train to Connecticut, that he had begun to regain his balance, realizing that he had been a fool—yet, in the end, a lucky one.

He had thought of Ilsa Lang in New York the other night only because the blinking VEGA sign had been an inescapable reminder, and he remembered having idly wondered if she had ever again thought of him, stunned now by this evidence that she had somehow remained close enough to him to know that he had had a heart attack, that he was hospitalized here at County Memorial. It was possible, of course, that she had seen it in the *Transom*—as deeply as she was involved with Vega, she undoubtedly followed the advertising press—but that seemed too prosaic an explanation for what, as he watched Mary pry loose the wax seal, seemed a manifestation of that eerily mystic perception which, from the very beginning, had been such an intriguing contradiction of everything that he had expected Ilsa Lang to be.

When Ted Newcomb, the network producer of his television show, first broached the idea of using Ilsa Lang as a guest star on one of their early programs, he had objected as strenuously as he dared, maintaining that no Hollywood actress with only a week of rehearsal could possibly sustain an hour-long live performance, thinking that he was clinching his point when he quoted Huck Joyce as having said that when he had directed *Lady in Waiting*, for which Ilsa Lang had won her Academy Award, he had averaged over ten takes a scene, overrunning his shooting schedule by two months and his budget by almost a half-million dollars. If Hollywood had stopped gambling on Ilsa Lang—she had not made a picture in over three years—why should the network?

There was, it turned out, one very good reason—Ilsa Lang had already been signed to a contract. The sales department, in a desperate pitch to find a sponsor for the program, had already printed an elaborate brochure guaranteeing *"Every Play with a Top Star from Hollywood or Broadway!"* The casting department had found it difficult to fulfill that boastful promise. Genuine stars were hard to come by. Only the has-beens and the impoverished, with everything to gain and nothing to lose, were willing in those early days to subject themselves to the well-publicized terrors of live television. That was what he had expected that first time he had gone to Sutton Place—a once-bright star whose flash fame had burned out —her only asset a tarnished Oscar, yet still able to collect five thousand dollars for the right to advertise her as an *Academy Award Winner*.

He had, by then, been around the make-believe world of theater long enough to see through the scrim-curtain illusion of continuing prosperity that every fading star felt it necessary to maintain, but the solid luxury of the Sutton Place house had gone far beyond expectation. A black-uniformed man had answered his ring, opening the locked grillwork gate on the street and then the shining black-lacquer door behind it, passing him on to another man, similarly black-habited, who had taken him up in an elevator to the second floor. There he had stepped out into a room that exuded an air of solid wealth, not the flamboyance with which set designers always attempted to convey that impression, but rather the special aura of someone to whom money had been no hindrance in the exercise of impeccable taste. Asked to wait, he had stood in the center of the room, slowly surveying it, finding it difficult to reconstruct his image of Ilsa Lang—she had been, her publicity said, the daughter of a village schoolmaster somewhere in Sweden—all but impossible to imagine her as a collector of Persian miniatures, of which a dozen or more were displayed on the walls.

But if fitting the star to the setting was difficult, it had been even harder to accept the reality of Ilsa Lang's appearance as she edged into the room through a half-opened door, wearing a gray skirt and a simple white blouse, her ashen hair drawn back to a knot low on her neck, the overall impression of farm-girl plainness so pronounced that, for an instant, he thought that she must have costumed herself to convince him that she was still young enough to play Hilda. But then he realized that she could not possibly know what the part was—he had, only last night, discovered Kenyon Malling's unproduced play *Dust Bowl* in a pile of unread manuscripts—and as she came up to him, shyly offering her hand, the firm lines of her face and the texture of her skin argued a persisting youthfulness that no makeup could possibly have produced. She had to be deep in her thirties, perhaps as old as forty—he could remember seeing her in *Lady in Waiting*, playing the prime minister's wife, when he had been a sophomore in high school—but at that moment, and afterwards as well, it had been impossible to think of himself as not being older than she was.

In the taxi on his way to Sutton Place, he had resolved to go all out on the difficulties of live television, hoping that he might frighten her off, sparing himself the problem of trying to get a passable performance out of her. With no awareness of having changed his mind, he found himself attempting to convince her that television was not really as difficult as everyone was making it out to be. There was something about Ilsa Lang that cried out for reassurance, a powerful plea for help and support, a need that he could not bring himself to deny. It was that need that had first attracted him, and for all those months afterward it had kept him in a kind of bondage that he had never before, nor since, experienced with any other woman. Of all the later moments of passion and intimacy that might have become high points of memory, nothing had ever been more often recalled than that night of the Broadway opening when, clutching his hands in the wings she had whispered, as if it were the voice of her anguished soul, "Oh, darling, hold on to me—I need you so terribly, terribly much." And no memory was more painful than of that afternoon when she had declared that need at an end.

Mary's scissors cut the tape and the stiff brown paper sprang free. Inside, there was black leather, simply embossed with a thin gold border and an inscription in Arabic letters, seemingly a portfolio that, opened, would reveal a photograph. Cautiously, he raised the leather-bound folder from its wrapping, turning it to shield whatever was inside from Mary's eyes. There was no such need. Opened, he saw only a small Persian miniature painting, hardly larger than the palm of his hand, wide-framed with a figured matting. A slip of paper fluttered out. It was a printed listing cut from the catalogue of some sale or exhibit:

117. BOOK ILLUSTRATION—LATE MONGOL (c. 1500). Although not positively attributable, this remarkable miniature bears some evidence of being from the hand of Behzad of Herat, the greatest master of Persian painting. It depicts an important prince rising from his sick-bed, proclaiming to the awed on-lookers the miracle of his recovery. Particularly notable is the strength of character in the prince's face and the dominance of his powerful presence upon all those about him. The differentiation in countenance and bearing among even the most minor of characters is highly suggestive of the genius of Behzad of Herat.

There was nothing else, no card, no signature, but no further identification was necessary. No one but Ilsa Lang could have sent him such a lavish gift, moved only by an impulsive response to a recognition of appropriateness, as unmindful of implication as she was of cost. He knew that this miniature was worth hundreds of dollars, perhaps thousands, but he knew, too, that unless she had disposed of Arsa Zelenkian's fabulous collection, there were hundreds more like it in that big safe secreted behind the paneled end wall of that room where he had first waited for her. It was in that room, not that first day but later, the safe opened to display its treasures, that she had told him the story of her life: of her child-marriage to the German director who brought her to Berlin, a fiftyish Svengali ravishing a seventeen-year-old Trilby; of the international impresario who had rescued her, promising affectionate protection but treating her as a chattel, selling her in the Hollywood flesh market for half of her earnings; finally, recited as a confession offered in the hope of absolution, an account of how she had found shelter and protection with Arsa Zelenkian, living here in one of the hideaway homes that he maintained in financial centers all around the world. She had not seen him, she said, in almost a year.

That, too, was the night when he had learned that Vega was a secret fiefdom of Zelenkian's, one unit in his worldwide syndicate of cosmetic companies. Confronted later, Ted Newcomb had confessed that the network had known it all along, that signing Ilsa Lang had been an inside pitch to get a sponsor for the show. But by then neither Judd Wilder's prior blindness nor the network's devious tactics could detract from the sense of high accomplishment that he had gotten from Ilsa Lang's first performance on the air, an achievement all the greater because it had seemed, until the last moment, so hopelessly improbable.

In the first act of *Dust Bowl*, Hilda, the heroine, was the cowering daughter of a bullying Midwest farmer, the poor little slavey who was put upon by the whole family, never daring to call her soul her own. In the second act, hit by the Depression, the family fortune blown away in the dust storms, the father gave up, revealing himself as a weak character, threatening to carry down the whole family with him. There had been no real problem up to that second-act curtain, other than to keep Hilda from being totally overshadowed by the show-stealing father. In the third act, however, Hilda had to come out of the shadows, and with a spectacular show of unsuspected strength, take command of the family and her own life. It was upon the playing of that climactic scene that everything depended, not only the justification of Ilsa Lang's starring status, but also the rescue of the play itself from outdated banality.

On paper, that big scene had seemed tailor-made for Ilsa Lang —Kenyon Malling had, in truth, written the original play with her in mind, all but plagiarizing the scene in *Lady in Waiting* where she confronted the King's cabinet—but in no rehearsal had Ilsa Lang risen to anything near what the scene demanded. Blindly certain that she had it in her if he could only bring it out, Judd had gone home with her to Sutton Place, working with her on that big scene.

For four straight nights he was there until after midnight. On the last night before the air show, he had stayed. Kay was out of town, visiting Miss Jessica and taking Rolfe to a Philadelphia doctor, but the sharing of Ilsa Lang's bed had been no fortuitous response to temporary freedom. It was uncontrived, an act of the moment, a seemingly natural extension of the intimacy that had grown out of his drive to penetrate Ilsa Lang's crippling reserve, to find some inner well of power and self-confidence that might be tapped for that last scene.

The next afternoon, the dress rehearsal produced a small miracle. For the first time, Ilsa Lang made the third act believable. But the rehearsal, good though it had been, was no more than a hint of what was to come on the air. Her Hilda was magnificent—even *Variety* had found no other word to describe it—and for the first and last time in television, he had heard spontaneous applause break out from the crew the moment he had signaled from the booth that they were off the air.

There had been an immediate flare-up of talk about producing *Dust Bowl* on Broadway, excitedly fostered by Ken Malling, who was certain that his play would be an even greater success if the brutal cuts necessitated by an hour television show could only be restored. Judd had backed away from the suggestion that he direct. As much as he wanted a Broadway production credit, leaving the relative security of his television job was a gamble that he dared not take for a play in which he had so little faith. He was certain that *Dust Bowl* was too dated to succeed on Broadway, too much a hangover product of the Thirties to find an audience in a theater that was making hits out of *Mr. Roberts, Death of a Salesman,* and *Detective Story.* When Ilsa Lang had called him for advice, telling him that there was a producer who was ready to go ahead, he had told her exactly what he thought, arguing that if she wanted to do a Broadway play, she could surely find a better vehicle than *Dust Bowl.* Later, she had asked him to come up to Sutton Place again —"I need someone I can trust"—but deep in rehearsals for that week's show, trying to make a half-credible romantic lover out of a Hollywood fag, he had begged off, crediting himself with a measure of common sense and virtue that, he was certain, the coming thirteen-week summer hiatus would help him to preserve.

The network assigned him to direct a summer replacement, but it was only a quiz show, requiring little preparation, and he was always free from Thursday night until Monday morning. He had wanted to take some short trips up into New England, but by then Kay was all tied up with the Opera House project and weekends were the only times she could get her committee together. One week, Ben Kassoff had invited him to go deep-sea fishing, and, as always, open to any new experience—a director, Huck had once said, could never have too many of them—Judd had accepted. There had been little fishing but endless talk. They had spent most of their time in harbor, always with a glass in hand, feet up on the cockpit coaming, usually debating Ben's future in terms of some new hare-brained scheme that his mind had hatched. Judd had learned by then that Ben's stories about having once worked as a scenic de-signer were, even if embroidered with some fantasy, substantially true, and he had argued that Ben should forget everything except establishing himself as a Broadway set designer. Early in the eve-ning Ben had edged toward tentative agreement but as the sun went down he retreated into second-bottle cynicism. "What you ought to do, boy, is get the stars out of your eyes and take a look at what the goddam theater really is," he had said. "All this Art-of-the-Theater talk is just plain crap. You want to know what the art of the theater really is? All right, I'll tell you—it's the art of the fast buck. It's the art of all the scrounging bastards who'll suck your blood and turn it into the gold that buys them their Rolls-Royces, and the country estates where they can park Fat Mama so she won't know about the fresh pussy that's always waiting for him in that little Park Avenue hideaway." And then he had said, "Broadway's no different from the rest of the world—look at the bastards," circling the harbor with his stabbing finger, ticking off the names of the big yachts and detailing the rackets of their owners. The biggest ship in harbor that night had been *Omar Khayyam*, the globe-girdling yacht owned by Arsa Zelenkian, in port after an Atlantic crossing.

That next week, unexpectedly, Judd had met the fabulous Arsa Zelenkian in person, a privilege that even some of his upper-level executives were reputed never to have had. Vega had still not signed a new contract to sponsor the show when it went on the air again in September, and when Ted Newcomb had asked Judd to come into town for a showdown session with the Vega people, he had expected that the meeting would be either at the advertising agency or in the Vega offices. Instead, when they got into the cab, Ted had given the driver Ilsa's Sutton Place address.

Somehow he had carried it off, helped by the last minute self-assurance that there was no reason to be disconcerted by facing Ilsa Lang in Zelenkian's presence—after all, he had directed her in the television play that had won first place in the *Video* poll—even managing to surmount his surprise in finding Arsa Zelenkian not at all the man he had imagined. He had visualized a Middle East potentate in ill-fitting Western dress, swarthy and oily-skinned, heavily mustached, hooded eyes guarding Oriental inscrutability. Instead, Zelenkian had turned out to be a polished cosmopolite, clean-shaven and London-tailored, impeccably mannered, lightly displaying all the gentlemanly ease of the confidently rich. Moreover, he was freely voluble, immediately taking charge. But he did wear dark glasses all through the meeting, perhaps because he did not want to risk having his eyes betray his real motive. If true, it was an unnecessary precaution. Transparently, his only interest was in making certain that television would make money for Vega cosmetics. Even before Ted Newcomb had got through his turnover presentation, making his point that the spectacular rise in sets-in-use now justified television as a major advertising medium—the count, by then, had got up to a million sets in New York City alone—Zelenkian had cut him off, showing no interest in the prospective lineup of plays and stars. "It is the commercials that I wish to discuss," he had said. "Last season they were not, in my opinion, of comparable quality to the dramatic content of your shows. If we are to continue, that is something that we would wish to correct. Would it not be possible —this is only a suggestion of course, but it strikes me as having great merit—would it not be possible for Mr. Wilder to stage and direct the commercials as well as the play?"

Ted Newcomb's instant "Of course!" had cut off any chance of protest. Zelenkian had gone on, no less certain of acceptance as he suggested, "Might it not also be wise to allow Miss Lang to act as a consultant in matters of style and fashion? As I am sure you will agree, she has most excellent taste—do you not concur, Mr. Wilder?"

If there had been a barb in that last thrust, it was hidden by Zelenkian's dark glasses, but there was no mistaking the way that Ilsa, after a single pleading glance, looked away and refused to meet Judd's eyes. There was no doubt, it seemed, where the idea had originated.

All through that second season, Judd Wilder made a trip to Sutton Place every week. Despite his earlier suspicions, it was difficult to sustain the belief that Ilsa had contrived these weekly meetings. He could hardly doubt the genuineness of her fear that Zelenkian had thrust upon her a responsibility that she could not discharge—except, of course, with Judd's help—and he had soon found himself in the anomalous position of helping her to support and sustain her relationship with Zelenkian. In his darker moments, away from her, he felt like a pimp, the Sutton Place house a plush brothel. With her, he was less self-critical, but still there was enough of a shadow to keep him out of her bed. He held to his resolve to maintain a business-only relationship, and rather to his surprise, Ilsa gave no overt evidence that she expected anything else. The commercial scripts, which were prepared by the advertising agency but which he almost invariably rewrote, were always approved. Ilsa would sometimes make suggestions, but always tentatively, always bowing to his final judgment. Rather quickly, however, he found himself relying upon her feeling for what would and would not appeal to women viewers. By Thanksgiving, her own hairdresser, under her direction, was doing all the coiffures—a supervisory responsibility that he was more than willing to surrender—and by Christmas she was selecting all the clothes to be worn by the models.

More than once, the network switchboard was jammed with calls from viewers wanting to know where a hat, or a handbag, or even a dress could be bought. The program mail doubled, more of it referring to the commercials than to the play, but whatever reaction that might have aroused under other circumstances was lost under his mounting load of more pressing problems.

The television boom, so long predicted, was finally materializing. A network management that, before, had carried along TV as a hopeful experiment, willing enough to leave it in the hands of low-echelon youngsters, was now moving in to mine the gold. High-level executives were being transferred en masse from radio, a supposedly sinking ship being hurriedly abandoned. At every rehearsal, Judd Wilder glimpsed horn-rimmed eyes watching him out of the shadows, sometimes a lone scout from some newly interested department, more often a committee. His right to select plays, once almost unrestricted, had to be largely abdicated to the new Editorial Department. In casting, where his only previous restriction had been that of providing a bit part now and then for one of Ted Newcomb's revolving harem, now became a running battle with the Talent Department. Censorship by Program Acceptance, exercised to make certain that no viewer, no matter how crackpot, would ever be offended by any word or act, became a growing harassment. Worst of all was the locust horde of cost accountants and efficiency men that now overran the studio, forever calling upon him to explain his every move, making him feel like a thief when he used the last hundred dollars in the prop budget to get the authenticity that a close-up shot demanded, instead of saving the money for a dutiful contribution to the network's profit pot.

Before the season was over, he was spending at least ten hours a week in meetings, losing the equivalent of a full day from the already crushing schedule that was demanded in order to get a new show on the air every week. To save overtime hours on the set or in the rehearsal hall, he started going up to Sutton Place in the late evening, working on the commercials with Ilsa Lang until he had to leave to catch the last Connecticut train that stopped at Sedgefield.

In late February a new pressure was applied. In a meeting with the Marketing Statistical Department, he had taken his first beating with "cost-per-thousand," a new whip that had never before been used on him. With *Studio One* and *Philco TV Playhouse* both below his show's cost, one by 11¢, the other by 7¢, he decided that he had to start staying in town on the night before the show. Kay had accepted it without concern—she was by then working full time on the Opera House project—and Ilsa Lang, evidencing no surprise, had made it seem both right and inevitable. All she had said, responding to his first meaningful kiss in many months, was, "It's been a long time, hasn't it?"

Soon afterwards, the new Program Development Department, exercising its assigned function of "creating new program concepts," had come up with the idea, based on a statistical analysis of last year's audience and critical reaction, that another show starring Ilsa Lang in a Kenyon Malling script would surely be a ten-strike. As he guessed the moment he read the memorandum, a script had been commissioned, Malling's first draft was already in hand, and a tentative approach had been made to Miss Lang's agent. When he got his hands on the script, the first few pages told him that it was nothing but a rewrite of *Dust Bowl,* under a new title, *Head of the House.* The farmer father had been made a factory foreman, the relentless hand of fate evidenced not by dust storms but by a heartless corporation squeezing out its old employees with automation. He had rejected it on the spot, not only because it was only a warmed-over rehash, but also because he could not imagine Program Acceptance approving a script that showed big business in such an unfavorable light. However, since Ilsa had already been told about it by her agent, he took the script along with him that next week when he went up to Sutton Place.

Not too surprisingly, Ilsa already had a copy, but he was unprepared for her enthusiasm. Trying to tell her why it was all wrong, too worn and weary to find the right words, he had made a mess of it, letting her think that he didn't want her on his show again, so anxious to make any sort of recovery that he had raised no objection when she had asked if he would mind if her agent talked to Kenyon Malling about the possibility of expanding the television script into a full-length play for Broadway. He would, he thought, talk her out of it later.

But that next week Arsa Zelenkian arrived back in New York—Ilsa called him to say that he was to go ahead on his own with the commercials—and that was the week, too, when Bill Throck walked out on him. Throck had been his floor manager since the start of the season, serving an apprenticeship that he hoped would put him in the director's chair, an ambition that had plainly gotten out of hand. Every week he had become more cockily argumentative, wasting rehearsal time that could not be spared, infecting the whole staff—and often the cast as well—with a questioning attitude that undermined the absolute control and instant response that a director had to have. That week's show had been a complicated production, calling for some split-second camera maneuvers that were dependent upon a precise set placement that Judd had plotted in the walkthrough rehearsals. When he got into the studio, he found that Throck had ordered a different arrangement. Judd had blown his top—perhaps, as he later agreed, a bit more violently than might have been necessary—but nothing that he had said, nor even the way he had said it, could possibly have justified the way that Throck had ripped off his headphones, thrown them on the floor, and walked out of the studio. He had tried to go ahead without him, only to be confronted with a slowdown by the cameramen who, afraid to actually walk off the job, were nevertheless supporting Throck's traitorous behavior.

Eventually it was settled, but only after the loss of a full half-day of rehearsal, and two horribly demeaning hours with T. Randolph Ames, the new Vice President for Television, whose only knowledge of television production had been gained as the head of a management consultant outfit that the network had retained to find out why its new goldmine was producing so inadequately. Judd had given ground—there had been no other way, the show had to get on the air—knowing well enough what it meant. When the summer season assignments for staff directors came through a few days later, he was not at all surprised to find himself penciled in for a daytime show that, since it was unsponsored, would cut back his salary to the low sustaining level. Although he was too tied down with his remaining four shows of the season to do anything about looking for a new job at once, he knew that his days at the network were numbered.

Vega and the advertising agency threw a season-end party after the last show, but it was more wake than celebration, the word having already gotten around that Vega was going to a Berle-type comedy show in the fall. Unexpectedly, Ilsa Lang appeared, obviously looking for him, and that was when he had learned that Malling had finished a stage version of *Head of the House*. Bernard Solleman was going to produce it, Ilsa said, and she was waiting to sign a starring contract only until she had his agreement to direct—"I can't do it without your help, Judd darling, you know that."

He had been able to resist her appeal, his mind hardened by a chilling awareness that she had turned back to him only after Zelenkian had left town, expecting him to respond like a whistled dog, his tail wagging and his tongue hanging out. He gave her a vague promise that he would come up to Sutton Place sometime to read the script, ignoring her broad hint that he make it that very night. Instead, he caught the train to Connecticut, regarding himself as a strongminded and righteous husband, almost wishing that he could tell Kay about it in order to win her appreciation of his faithfulness.

But when he got home he found that she had put Rolfe to bed with the sniffles and a runny nose, and afraid that it might be summer flu, she had decided to sleep in Rolfe's room in order to keep an eye on him.

By morning, confronted at the breakfast table with Kay's accounting of unpaid bills, he began to have second thoughts about directing *Head of the House*. He drove down to the village, looking for Ben Kassoff, finally locating him out at Harbor Hill, the plush real estate development to which he had climbed from his start in Papertown. Ben, Judd knew, had once worked with Bernard Solleman. "Sure I know Berny," Ben had said. "He's a big Broadway producer, maybe not as big as some, but still he never needs any appointment to see Lee Shubert—Berny walks in, the door's open. He needs a theater, he gets it. His credit's good. He needs cash, he can always dig it up. But you been hearing things about him and you want my honest size-up of the guy, right? So I'll give it to you—straight. Giving him the benefits of all the doubts and looking at him in the best possible light, Berny Solleman is a thieving little bastard who'd pimp for his own mother, and then steal her pocketbook. Sure, he knows Broadway—every dirty little shell-game trick that anyone ever invented—and if you're so stage-hungry that you can't stand it any more, all right, go ahead and sign with him. He'll give you a bellyful of it as fast as anyone you can find."

If he had needed any more strength to resist going back to Ilsa Lang, he had found it. He went home to Kay. Ken Malling was in the living room. Apparently thinking that everything was all set, he had come out to talk about his production ideas. Kay was beside herself with joy. Judd knew this was what she had always wanted, to be the wife of a Broadway director—that was why he had resolved to say nothing about turning down Ilsa's offer—but now with the story out, her excited anticipation had become an unstemmable force. He had tried to preserve a pose of indecision by raising some questions about becoming involved with Bernard Solleman. Ken had argued that he would be fully protected by the terms of his contract, but what had truly blocked escape had been Kay's sudden discovery that it was June 11, the tenth anniversary of their first meeting, the day when she had first watched him from the wings at the Orangerie. After that, everything sentimentally foreordained, there had been no turning back. He had gone down to

Tony's, bought two bottles of champagne, laughing off Tony's scowl when he asked to have them put on his bill. Back, the champagne laced with brandy, they had all gotten a little drunk—even Kay.

In bed, after Ken had finally gone, their lovemaking had seemed more genuine than it had in a very long time, Kay's show of passion almost free of the routine responses that usually made the whole act seem so contrived. And when she had said, "I do so want to help you with your play, dear—please let me!" he had promised that he would. And he had. At least he had given her the chance.

Bernard Solleman provided no staff until rehearsals started, and with all the rewriting that had to be done, all the breakdowns that had to be made, all the schedules that had to be drawn up, Kay's secretarial help was an early godsend. The trouble was that she could not bring herself to stop there. She was forever making suggestions, and with Ken Malling around so much during the day— he had taken a beach cottage at Light Point for the summer so that he would be handy to Sedgefield—Judd had frequently come home from New York to find Ken pounding away on some angle that Kay had given him, forced then to make both of them resentful when he tossed it out. Kay simply couldn't keep her hands off the reins. Worse, she had no real feel for the professional theater. She was still the eager art-for-art's sake amateur, still living back in the Orangerie days.

Ilsa Lang had gone abroad for a month in Switzerland, and when she came back in early August, a word from her was enough to make Solleman hop to and provide an in-town office, a secretary, and the services of his nephew Benny as stage manager. Kay was plainly hurt. He tried to soften the blow by asking her to come in now and then, but that too was a mistake. Driving to get the play in rehearsal—a theater had been booked for a September 28 opening —he was wound to a pitch where he couldn't stand anyone heckling him about why he had done this or that. Kay seemed incapable of understanding that he had to have a free hand. Nor could she understand, after rehearsals started, that he could not take her along every time he went out to lunch with Ilsa Lang. Kay never said anything, of course—she wouldn't—and perhaps he had imagined some of it, but there was no mistaking the fact that every time Kay showed up at a rehearsal, Ilsa, like a musical instrument that had been knocked out of tune, always started hitting false notes.

Perhaps cruelly, but with no choice, he had blocked Kay from going to Boston for the tryout week. He did feel a twinge of conscience at having his hotel room next to Ilsa's, separated from her only by a connecting door that was rarely closed. Kay, had she known about it, could not have understood that nothing mattered but the play. And, in all truth, nothing that happened between himself and Ilsa was anything beyond a sharing of that dedication, their short night hours together a mutual escape from tension grown too strong to endure.

Until Boston, Berny Solleman had not lived up to Ben Kassoff's dire prediction. True, he had been pinchpenny tight on sets and costumes, but Judd's TV experience with cost control had prepared him to live within a budget, and there had been no reason to doubt Berny's statement, supported by a list of all the backers and the money that each had subscribed, that there was not a cent more than $47,000 available to bring the show to Broadway. In Boston, seeing the set onstage for the first time, shocked by its summer-theater quality, he had briefly suspected that Berny was pocketing a kickback from the set-builders, but there had been no real confirmation of what was going on until Ilsa, in an unguarded moment, let it slip out that Arsa Zelenkian had given Berny, not the $5,000 that the backer list showed, but a full $50,000. It then became plain why Berny was so obdurately refusing to consider keeping the play out for another two weeks of badly needed work. No matter what happened on Broadway, even if the play was a total flop, he would come out with a personal take of something over $45,000, and he had no intention of letting loose of another cent of what he had already come to regard as his own money. Judd had wanted to confront him then and there, but Ilsa, bound by a promise to Zelenkian, and unwilling to admit that her Broadway debut had been bought and paid for, would not permit him to use what she had disclosed.

And so Judd Wilder had brought his first play to Broadway, grimly certain that failure had been foreordained by Berny Solleman's greed. Actually, the reviews were better than he expected—one even commented on the appropriately stark simplicity of the set—and having surmounted the danger of a quick closing, he saw the possibility of a reasonable run, not of hit proportions, but still long enough to insure a profit. He needed it badly—he had taken a three per cent share to balance the low salary that Berny had talked him into accepting—but at the end of the fourth week the closing notice went up. There was a rumor, believable enough by then, that Berny had been bought off, making a private deal to vacate the theater for another show that was coming in. If so, it was pocket money compared to what then came out: he had sold the movie rights for $200,000. For a single day, Judd had seen himself freed from his financial worries—his three per cent would be $6000, enough to get him even with the boards—but then, as a climactic disappointment, he learned that an unnoticed phrase in his contract cut him out of any participation in movie rights.

He had considered hiring a lawyer, but Ben Kassoff had talked him out of it. "If Berny can take an international sharpie like Zelenkian for fifty grand, what chance have you got? Charge it off to experience, boy. You were asking for it, and you got it. So how about coming in with me—handling the promotion for Harbor Hill? You could do a hell of a job if you'd put your mind to it."

For several weeks, he had been unable to put his mind to anything. A story appeared that Ilsa Lang had been signed to do *Head of the House* in a movie version to be produced at Inter-Cine in Rome, the studio that had recently been acquired by Zelenkian interests. The film, *Variety* reported, would be directed by Ian Mac-Dougall.

He went into New York every day, trying to contact producers who might have a play for him. He got nothing except the privilege of picking up some luncheon checks that he could ill afford to pay. At home, when some of the overdue bills disappeared, he knew that Kay had paid them out of her own money, but he was unable to further degrade himself by mentioning it. Gritting his teeth, he went back to the network, prepared to grovel before the new Vice President for Television who, by then, had replaced T. Randolph Ames. He was not even given the chance. Nor did he fare any better at the other networks. His credit as an established Broadway director proved more handicap than help in an industry that was trying to discourage employees from defecting excursions into other media. For a day or two he thought he might have a chance with a new package outfit that was starting to do shows on film, a hope blasted when he learned that Bill Throck was one of the partners.

Almost as an act of desperation, he had responded to an out-of-the-blue call from someone at Frederick Coleman & Associates, informing him that the advertising agency was setting up a new department to produce television shows for its clients. Was he free to have lunch with Mr. Coleman? By nightfall he had been hired, so anxious for the job that he had not asked what would be expected of him, committed before he learned that one of his assignments would be the direction of the commercials on Vega's new comedy program. When he tried to get out of it, he was told that that was why he had been called—someone at Vega had suggested him. He had good reason to suspect who that someone was. A few days later a call from Ilsa Lang confirmed his suspicion. She was back in New York. Ian MacDougall, she said, was an impossible director, the film had been indefinitely postponed, and she was looking for another Broadway play. She invited him to stop by for a drink any afternoon he was free. With no compulsion—neither she nor anyone at Vega suggested that she be consulted about the commercials—he resolved not to let it get started again.

And he had held to that resolution until the day that the Vega Hour was unexpectedly canceled, the time preempted for a White House broadcast. Late in the afternoon he had gone to the studio to make certain that the commercial set was being dismantled carefully enough so that it could be used the following week. Walking back along 57th Street, his eye was caught by a showing of Persian miniatures in an art dealer's window. It was no more than a reminder, probably unnecessary—he had only glanced in the window, walking quickly by—but seconds later he was in a telephone booth, not even consulting the directory, Ilsa Lang's number dialed without the conscious exercise of memory.

In the months since he had seen her, something had changed—perhaps Ilsa, perhaps himself, surely the circumstances of their relationship. He said nothing about his job at the agency, nor did she suggest by even the most subtle hint that she was expecting gratitude for having helped him get it, but there was nevertheless a pervading awareness that it was he, not she, who had needed help, and that it was she, not he, who had supplied it. And now it was he who had come to her, wanting something that, no matter how willingly she gave it, was indefinably different from what it had been before. Once, for a shocking moment, something had reminded him of the girl in Miami, and on the train to Connecticut he had felt the black stain of that same self-damning revulsion that he had experienced on the plane coming back to New York from Florida. Then, too, he had been running away from a grosser self, coming back to Kay as if to a soul-cleansing bath, getting off the train at Sedgefield, filling his lungs with the clean air of that spring night, swearing that he would never again see Ilsa Lang—and then he had gone home to find Kay with Ben Kassoff.

Divorce had appeared inevitable, never actually discussed but seemingly delayed only by stalemate, neither of them in a position to take the initiative. Tentatively, never as more than the wary testing of a dangerous prospect, he had tried to talk to Ilsa about the future, feeling somehow betrayed, yet strangely relieved, when she had told him that she was leaving in September to meet Arsa Zelenkian in Beirut. They were, she said, to be married. That was when it had really ended—that was what she had meant that last time he had seen her—and there was no temptation now to imagine this lavish gift as a bid toward renewal. He accepted it as nothing more than the impulsive gesture of a very rich woman, so meaningless that he handed it to Mary with no feeling of restraint, no sense of a privacy that had to be preserved.

Mary examined it, plainly awed, seemingly more impressed by the leather folder than by what was inside, finally saying, "Goodness, this is the most beautiful card I've ever seen. I never even knew they made anything like this. It must have cost a fortune."

"She can afford it," he said, remembering that morning—he was in New Ulster then, a year or so after he had gone to work for Crouch Carpet—when Kay had put the newspaper beside his breakfast plate, folded to expose the story of Arsa Zelenkian's death in a plane crash somewhere in the Arabian desert. "Wasn't he Ilsa Lang's boyfriend?" Kay had asked, so flatly expressionless that he had been able to reply calmly, "I think she finally married him—I heard that somewhere." But there was nothing in the story about a surviving wife, nor was there any mention in the longer story in the *New York Times* that he read after he got to the office. *Time* magazine, that next week, had only a leering line, styling Zelenkian as "a great and good long time friend of Oscared actress Ilsa Lang," going on then to report the spate of international speculation about the future of the Zelenkian empire.

Later, one day in Mr. Crouch's office, he had chanced to see a story in the *Wall Street Journal* about multiple lawsuits in Paris and Athens over Zelenkian's estate, but there was no reference to Ilsa Lang as a claimant. He did not see her name in print until long afterward when it had leaped out at him from the pages of *Business Week*. The story was about Vega Cosmetics, reporting on the company's new venture into door-to-door selling. Mentioned in the course of it was "Mrs. Arsa Zelenkian, the former actress Ilsa Lang, who as principal stockholder and chairman of the board—" Her picture, a single column on a runover page, had been captioned MRS. ZELENKIAN and rightly so, for the businesswoman face that regarded him as coolly as if he were a written-off entry on an old inventory bore little or no resemblance to Ilsa Lang.

Mary asked now, "Shall I leave it here on the dresser?"

"No, put it away," he said, lying back, exhaling when he heard the drawer thump shut. "Is that all?"

"That's all."

"Funny there wasn't anything from New Ulster," he said, recalling Daphy's promise that she would forward the mail from the house.

"That won't come until this afternoon," she said. "I know because that's when I got my letter from Ralph—yesterday."

"How's everything?" he asked, a quick attempt to make up for neglect, aware now that it had been two days since he had shown any interest.

"Wonderful!" she came back, a joyously ebullient exclamation. "We're going to be married just as soon as I can get back there."

"What do you mean—get back there? You don't mean—?"

But it was obvious that she did, clinched when she said, "You don't think I'd run away and desert you, do you? After all you did for me?"

He tried to argue with her, fearful that he might succeed, greatly relieved when she laughed at him and said, "Now you just hush— I'm going to leave this hospital when you do, and not one minute before!"

« 3 »

Kay Wilder's expectation that her before-luncheon drink with David Keegan would give her a way to avoid Chris Kemble had proved a futile hope. She had no more than stopped in the doorway of the bar, trying to spot him, when Chris had waved from the table she was holding. In the same instant, she saw David Keegan rising from the next table. There was no way to avoid an introduction, nor to resist his suggestion that Chris join them, obviously made because Chris instantly recognized who he was, and immediately launched off on a harangue against the New York critics for having so ridiculously misjudged his last play. She had seen it—or so she claimed—and despite the fact that she had never, until this moment, evidenced the slightest interest in the theater, she suddenly became so theatrically knowledgeable that it was almost sickening. Even before the steward brought their first round of drinks, Kay was thinking that if Chris used that word *sensitive* again she would surely scream.

When Kay had had as much of it as she could bear she got up to leave, availing herself of the excuse that she could not be late at the captain's table. Chris and Dave rose as if to follow her, but when she glanced back from the doorway, she saw that they had sat down again. They did not come into the dining room until a half-hour later and when they did David Keegan, instead of returning to his own table, sat down with Chris. It was plain enough then why he had failed in the theater.

"Tomorrow you will be seeing Miss Jessica," Captain Davideau said in French.

"And my son," she added, a response so automatic that she did not, for a moment, realize that she had spoken in English.

« 4 »

A few minutes after Mrs. Cope came on duty at three o'clock, Dr. Kharr appeared. "How would you like to get out of bed for an hour or so?" he asked, acting as if he were expecting him to be surprised, apparently forgetting that it was a promise that he had made last night.

"Sure, why not?" Judd responded, feeling no apprehension until he noted the extreme care with which the maneuver was carried out, the bed cranked down to the same level as the seat of the chair, most of his weight supported by Mrs. Cope as the shift was made, the doctor intently watching his face. For an instant, reaching out to steady himself with a hand on the arm of the chair, he felt a rubbery weakness, relieved by Dr. Kharr's quickly perceptive, "If you're a little wobbly, don't let it worry you. You'd feel that way after five days in bed even if you were in perfect health."

Safely seated, he felt no different, really, than he had in bed, encouraged to confidence by Kharr's surprising explanation that the workload on the heart was at least fifteen per cent less in a sitting position, finally responding to a definite sensing of freedom and release, the feeling of having taken a long step forward on the road to recovery.

Dr. Kharr soon left, leaving him alone with Mrs. Cope, who remained standing beside him. Twice she asked him how he was feeling, her concerned tone suggesting that she did not approve of the idea of his being out of bed.

Attracted by the open window, he strained to look out, a hint to which Mrs. Cope finally responded by giving his chair a shove and a half-turn. Yet the vast expanse of rolling farmland and open sky was somehow disconcerting, a too-precipitate departure from the safely containing four walls of his hospital room. He cut his eyes back to the parking lot in front of the hospital, searching out his car. He located it at once, dust-fogged and rain-smeared, its abandoned appearance a sharp reminder of the circumstances under which he had left it, disorienting because it seemed impossible that what had happened so long ago could still be so vividly recalled.

"There's the afternoon mail," Mrs. Cope said, idly calling his attention to a car coming up the drive from the highway.

He told her that he was expecting a lot of mail, the forwarding of everything that had accumulated since he had left home, hinting that he wanted her to go pick it up. When suggestion failed, he asked her if she would. Hesitant, she finally agreed, but only after exacting a promise that he would not do "anything silly."

Reminded of New Ulster, he remembered that he had not yet called Allen Talbott. By leaning far to the right and extending his arm, he managed to reach the telephone. The operator evidenced no surprise when he asked her to make a long distance call, and the first ringing sound brought an instantly responding "Crouch Carpet." He asked for Allen Talbott. Gloria answered, stunned when he identified himself, sounding as if she thought she was hearing a voice from the grave, so fussed that it took her a long time to get around to telling him that Allen was not in the office. "Mr. Talbott's in a meeting, Mr. Wilder, and I can't—I mean I don't think I ought to—well, he's up with Mr. Stark."

He hesitated, wondering what Allen was doing in Stark's office, but quickly recovered with "All right, you can give him the message. You know the stuff that Mrs. Ingalls called him about yesterday— she did call, didn't she?"

"I guess so," she said, peculiarly evasive. "Anyway—uh-huh, she called."

"There's another order that has to be canceled," he said. "Jersey-Hudson—the colorplates for the program cover. Tell him to call Nick Saltini and ask him to hold up the plates."

"Well, I'll tell him, Mr. Wilder, but—" He heard the gulp of words being swallowed, a blank silence, and then a hurried "Maybe I'd better have him call you back."

Choked by annoyance—as soon as he got back he'd have to really start putting the heat on Personnel to get him a decent secretary —he cleared his throat, wearily agreeing, "All right, have him call me as soon as he gets back," thinking after he heard himself say it that it might not be such a bad idea, after all . . . find out what Allen was doing up in Stark's office . . .

With the receiver held only by his fingertips, he reached out, trying to get it back in its cradle, almost dropping it when Mrs. Cope's voice exploded from the doorway. "Now just what do you think you're doing!"

She came charging in, snatching the instrument from his hand, and plunking it down. "I thought you promised me you wouldn't do anything foolish."

"I'm sorry," he said, with mock contrition and a tongue-in-cheek grin. "I won't do it again."

"Well, you better not," she said humorlessly, holding back the mail as if debating whether he deserved it.

"Doesn't look like there's as much mail as I thought," he said, seeing only a heavy manila envelope and three or four greeting cards.

Reluctantly, she handed him the packet. "Who were you calling?"

"Only the office. There was something I'd forgotten—"

"You'd be a lot better off if you *did* forget it," she cut in testily. "They'll get along all right without you."

"I'll forget it now," he agreed. But the promise was, in itself, a perverse reminder, and he found himself again wondering what Allen could be doing up in Stark's office, diverted when he saw that the manila envelope was addressed in Daphy's handwriting.

Opened, a dozen or more letters spilled out along with a note from Daphy, hurriedly scrawled on a sheet of blue-lined paper snitched from one of the kid's school notebooks.

Dear Judd:

Ray is going to run down with this so it will get off tonight. Got home to find Chuck with a broken (?) nose and two teeth missing. I still don't know what happened. Says they were just having fun. Some fun!

After getting Chuck to the hospital and back, I was so rushed I didn't have time enough to really sort all your mail but I think I got everything that looked important enough to bother you with. I kept out the bad news (bills) and all the junk mail. I'll go over it again tomorrow.

I called Allen Talbott. He wasn't there but I left the message with his girl. Hope that's all right.

Haven't called the newspaper yet but will the first thing in the morning. I'll just tell them to keep sending it until you cancel. All right?

Everybody I've seen here has asked about you and all so glad you're coming along so well.

Ray says he'll hold you to that fishing date. Trout season opens a week from Saturday and he's tying flies like mad. Don't ask me why, he's got a million of them.

I have to quit now or Ray will never get this down to the post office in time.

Get well fast and we'll see you soon.

Affectionately,
DAPHY

P.S. When I was at your place, a man came from Gardner's, something about flower beds. I told him it could wait until you got home. All right? If there's anything else I can do, let me know.

He knew nothing about flower beds. Probably something else that Kay had started and then forgotten all about when that Paris bug bit her. The thought lingered for a moment, fading then, unsupported by any real concern. It all seemed so long ago, so far away, his mind full of fuzzy-edged memories, latent images that did not seem worth the effort of development.

There was nothing really important in the mail, duplicating an experience that he had often had, coming home from a trip, anxious to see the mail, let down when he found so little in it. There were a couple of bills that Daphy had failed to recognize; a letter from the bank, something about the mortgage on the house, but he could let that slide now; a couple of contribution pitches that he would be excused from overlooking; a letter from John Winthrop Oliver, the president of Colfax, asking him to serve on the committee for the Alumni Fund Drive, again something that he now had a perfect excuse to turn down.

At the bottom of the pile he found an envelope with a *Haygood Herald* return address. He opened it with a feeling of guilt, recalling that he had not written his father since that hurried note from San Francisco, telling him that he was not, after all, going to be able to stop over in Haygood on his way back East.

As always, his father had written on yellow copy paper, but he sensed something different, identified as he glanced down the page. Instead of his father's usual meticulous typing, always as clean as a second galley, there were numerous strike-outs and several penciled corrections in a hand so shaky that it was hardly recognizable as his father's.

Dear Son:
 I was disappointed that you did not come as you had promised you would. There were a lot of things that I was waiting to talk over with you.

I have a chance to sell the paper and the way things are going, it may be the thing to do. Last Monday a week ago I was sitting on the toilet when all of a sudden I blacked out. I don't know exactly what happened, but I must have hit my left arm when I fell. It's still a little numb. I'm having some trouble with my eyes, too, and that doesn't make it any easier. It puts a lot of extra load on Oscar, especially with all of the job work that we are getting now. The seed company is giving us all of their label imprinting again and that means a lot of hand composition and stone-work. Oscar is not complaining but I don't like not being able to do my share.

They have been here three times about buying me out. They already have 7 papers in Iowa and are buying more all the time. I don't like the idea of the Herald *being nothing but a chain paper after all I've put into it in the last 42 years but the way things are I don't know what else I can do. I had always hoped that someday you would come back and take over, but I don't suppose there's any hope of that now. There is a lot more job work that we could get, not to mention all the advertising that would come in if someone would just get around and see the stores and give them a little help with their copy. A younger man could make a good thing of the* Herald *if he wanted to. He might not make as much money as he could with a big company, but there are other things in life than that. When you have something of your own no one can ever take it away from you.*

I'm sorry you couldn't come as I would have liked your advice, but I wish you would write me and tell me what you think. They are pushing me to make up my mind and I'll have to decide one way or another before long. Remember me to Kay.

DAD

"Bad news?" Mrs. Cope asked the instant he lifted his eyes.

"Doesn't sound very good," he said, scanning the second paragraph again, telling her what had happened. "Sounds like a stroke, doesn't it?"

Instead of a direct reply, she asked, "Some friend of yours?"

"My father."

"Your father? Why, I didn't even know he was alive. You never mentioned him when I asked you if there was anyone else——"

"I didn't want to worry him," he cut in, a quick cover for the withheld admission that it had never occurred to him to notify his father.

"How old is he?"

"Sixty-nine," he said after a moment's calculation.

"Yes, it could be a stroke," Cope said cautiously. "Hasn't he gone to a doctor?"

"I don't know whether there's a doctor in town any more or not. Oh, I guess there must be someone. I'm pretty much out of touch. It's a long time since I've been out there, and we don't write very often."

"Well, you ought to write him now," she said, righteously critical.

"I will," he said contritely, finding it easier to acknowledge neglect than to explain how he had drifted apart from his father.

"All people get lonely," Mrs. Cope pressed, and then as if everything he had told her before had to be rechecked. "You did say you don't have any brothers or sisters, didn't you?"

"Oh, he's not alone. He married again after my mother died," he said, unavoidably reminiscent, momentarily reliving that day when he came home for his summer vacation, met at the station by his father, who had blurted out with no warning or preparation, not even a prior hint, that he had married Miss Parkhurst. He had not called her that, of course—"Flora Parkhurst" he had said—but she had been Miss Parkhurst to Judd, and Miss Parkhurst she had continued to be, at least in his mind, any other name a too-thin disguise for the old-maid schoolteacher who had been the principal of Haygood High for so long that it was impossible for him to think of her in any other role.

He would not have been surprised if his father had married Mrs. Gorman—indeed, the possibility had occurred to him as a logical solution of his father's problem—but marrying Miss Parkhurst had been not only a surprise unsupported by rationality, but also a move in precisely the wrong direction. Judd's grief over his mother's death, real though it had been, had not obscured an awareness that his father's married life had not been an entirely happy one, due in no small part to Judd's mother's assumption of social and intellectual superiority. By marrying Miss Parkhurst, his father had passed over a chance for a better life, opting for a return to his old henpecked role, a choice that Judd could only interpret as the revelation of a weak man's taste for subservience.

Flora—Judd had eventually come to call her that, the only alternative to an inept "Miss Parkhurst" or a never-considered "Mother" —had swept into the house like a bride twenty years delayed, half a lifetime of frustration vented in an attic-to-cellar renovation. Nothing was left unchanged, every memento of Judd's childhood as completely banished as if his life up to the day when he had left for college had been forever erased.

Strangely, his father had seemed pleased with what his new wife had done to the house, escorting him on a room-by-room tour, only smiling when Flora had corrected his identification of a Currier & Ives print, treating him as if he were an errant pupil who had not yet learned his lesson. His father's old leather chair, as much a part of Judd's picture of him as the wart on his ear, was gone—the new chintz-covered job, he blandly maintained, was really more comfortable—and he no longer smoked his pipe, even at the office.

Committed to spending the summer in Haygood, Judd had somehow managed to get through it, putting in long days at the newspaper office, eating as many of his meals as he could manage at Burlew's Cafe, getting out of town whenever he could invent a reasonable excuse. Being at home was an agony of displacement, made all the more difficult to endure because his father was so obviously embarrassed by his presence. He left a week early to go back to Colfax.

Never again had he spent more than two consecutive nights in the house that had once been his own home. That next summer he stayed East, working at the Orangerie. Then there had been the long lapse of the war years, and by the time he next saw his father he had become a stranger. Flora had induced him to take a trip back East—she was a delegate from Iowa to the national P.T.A. convention in New York—and they had come up to Connecticut for a weekend, arriving warily, his father afraid that he was out of his element in "all this fancy society business," Flora a bit too stridently attempting to prove that she was not. They had left on Monday morning, professing to have had a wonderful time, but they had not come East again and Judd's visits to Haygood had been few and far between, usually a one-night stopover on a business trip, the last time almost four years ago.

"I guess he's retired now," Mrs. Cope suggested.

"No, he's still running the paper," he said, going on to tell her a little about Haygood and the *Herald,* concluding, "He's got a chance to sell out now, and he should, but he hates to let go. It's understandable, of course—forty-two years is a long time, and the paper has been his whole life."

"There isn't anyone else to carry on?"

"That's what he'd like to have me do," he said with a tolerant smile.

"I guess you wouldn't be interested?" Cope asked. "I remember a patient I had once—he was some kind of an advertising man, too —that was his big dream, buying a little country weekly and settling down to run it."

Judd laughed. "I know, there are a lot of fellows who have that dream. I had enough of it when I was a kid, I know what it's like. Oh, it's not a bad life—if it's what you want."

"But you never did?"

He shook his head with a little snort of half-amused dismissal, sobering as he began to anticipate the difficulty of replying to this letter. No matter what he wrote, it would be hard to keep from saying, at least by implication, that preserving what his father had spent a lifetime to build up was hardly worth a second thought.

Dr. Kharr was at the door again, checking on how he felt.

"Fine," he said. "This is a lot better."

Cocking his head, Kharr examined his face. "All right, you can sit up until you've had your dinner."

Mrs. Cope relaxed a little, noticeably less tense now, the smile she gave Kharr an admission that letting a heart patient sit up in a chair was not, perhaps, as foolish as she had thought it.

◆ VII ◆

THROUGH A RAIN-BLEARED WINDOW of the boat train, Kay Wilder saw that they were coming into the suburbs of Paris, the trackside lined now with an almost unbroken wall of colorless buildings, black-splotched by the rain, grayed by the glowering sky. With her face pressed against the glass, she looked ahead for a first glimpse of the Eiffel Tower or the white dome of Sacre Coeur, searching for some Parisian touchstone that would lift her spirits out of the black mood that this horrible day had brought on, anxiously waiting for the rise of anticipatory excitement that she knew she should be feeling.

The same east-racing storm that the ship had outrun during yesterday's daylight hours had caught up again during the night, turning the Channel into a wild maelstrom, her cabin into a pitching and tossing torture chamber. Sometime in the night everything on her dressing table had crashed to the floor, two bottles broken, suffusing the already heavy atmosphere with the cloying choke of perfume. Unable to open a porthole because of the driving rain, she had felt herself confined to a cell so oppressive that sleep was impossible, the rest of the night endurable only because of the promise of the day.

But when the day finally came it was almost indistinguishable from the night, the sunrise hidden by black clouds and a heavy curtain of rain. Weatherbound, the ship had waited outside the harbor entrance for what had seemed hours, dead in the water, animated only by the vibrant death-rattle groan of the foghorn. Gray-faced passengers wandered about as if in a no-man's land, the familiar atmosphere of the ship, so recently gained, lost now in inhospitable strangeness. The dining saloon, last night so bright and gay for the Captain's Dinner, had been a dreary barracks hall this morning, the soiled linen unchanged, the already-tipped waiters sullenly inattentive. With the lounge preempted by immigration officials who had somehow materialized out of the storm, and cabins already stripped to bareness by stewards and stewardesses too anxious to get ashore, the passengers had no place to sit and wait, forced to stand about in huddled clumps, feeling unfairly dispossessed, blank-faced as if preoccupied by the portents of ill-starred adventures ashore.

Kay Wilder had been by no means immune to the infectious gloom, unable to put down a feeling of indefinable apprehension. She had glimpsed Chris Kemble and David Keegan together in the bar, but had not joined them, offering herself the excuse that she wanted to avoid telling Chris that she would not be with her on the trip to Spain, bypassing an acknowledgment that Chris had not mentioned the invitation again since she had first extended it day before yesterday. She had seemed on the point of doing so last night when they met on the way down to dinner, but David Keegan had come up just then, wearing a paisley dinner jacket with maroon lapels, pure honky-tonk Broadway, but Chris, of course, had made a great fuss over how handsome he looked.

Chris and David were somewhere on the boat train, probably still up in the dining car, drinking. They had invited her to join them but not fervently enough to make refusal a problem, freeing her to rehearse her meeting with Rolfe. And that's what she had been trying to do all the way up from Le Havre. But now as Paris crowded in upon her, the train seemingly speeding up as it rushed toward the station, she became frighteningly aware of her inability to anticipate the unknown—and the unknown, rising like a wraith to blur every clear thought, was this faceless girl that kept turning up in Rolfe's letters . . . *"Jo . . . Jo . . . Jo . . . Jo let me use her Renault so I drove out to this weird place . . . Jo knew one of the librarians so I got back into the stacks . . . Jo invited me . . . Jo asked me . . . Jo said . . . Jo took me . . . Jo . . . Jo . . . Jo . . ."*

That was all she knew about her—Rolfe had not even given her a last name—but her mind, demanding a point of focus, kept coming up with a Parisian version of that horrible creature he had brought out to Mount Desert, that little stretch-pants bitch who had so flagrantly flaunted her single attraction . . . nothing had come of that, nothing would come of this, either . . . Rolfe was much too intelligent to let himself be trapped . . . but he was so young, so inexperienced, so trusting . . . *Paris* . . . *Jo* . . . *Jo* . . . *Jo* . . .

Spinning thought dizzied her, so blurring all sense of time and place that she was unaware that the train was pulling into the station until it came to a jarring stop. Through the window she searched the platform for Rolfe, panicked by the thought that he might not be there to meet her, fear persisting as she stepped out, still unable to see him. Far down the platform someone waved, a man in a dark raincoat and a business suit, the collar-and-tie image so mis-fitted to expectation that she did not recognize Rolfe until, as he strode toward her, she saw his face. Even then there was a blank moment, unable to believe that he could have changed so much in such a short time. He seemed not months but years older. When he had left last June, his farewell kiss had been that of a boy submitting to a silly parental demand. Now the gripping of her shoulders and the quick press of his lips on her cheek was the act of a mature man, a practiced rite performed with confidence and poise. She felt suddenly and frighteningly old, the mother of a grown man, forced to submit to the competent control with which he took over, taking her baggage checks and directing a porter with a burst of colloquial French too fast for her to follow. The vague dream of herself as a knowledgeable Parisian showing the city to an awestruck young son vanished then and there.

"How's Dad?" Rolfe asked, his first seriously asked question, earnestly demanding, anything but routine.

"Oh, fine," she said. "All wrapped up in his convention, of course. But how are you? That's the important thing."

"The convention—that's why he didn't come with you," he said, nodding as if he had found the answer to a question that had been bothering him. "How was his promotion trip this year—pretty rough, I guess?" But then, as if knowing the answer, he broke off with "Look, there's something I'd better tell you—you know, about your staying at the hotel."

"But you said you had my reservation. You wrote——"

"It's not that," he protested. "I got your reservation. It's just that Miss Jessica is counting on your coming out there——"

"Oh, Rolfe, she doesn't have room——"

"—and the way things are, I thought you might want to change your mind about not staying with her."

His tone sent a prickle of fear through her. "What do you mean—the way things are? Rolfe, is something wrong?"

He looked at her for a silent moment, a clear prediction of bad news. "There wasn't time to write you. I didn't really know anything for sure until last Thursday, the day you sailed. I went out that afternoon after I got through at the library. I've been doing that a lot lately—you know, stopping by when I can. Sometimes I stay for dinner, maybe sit around and talk with her for a while afterwards. That's what I was planning to do, but when I got there, I saw a doctor's car in the courtyard. And when I got inside, Celia was all upset. She wouldn't tell me what had happened—you know, the way Miss Jessica has her trained never to open her mouth about anything—but I finally got it out of her. She'd fainted—you know, just blacked out. And this wasn't the first time it's happened. Naturally, I waited until the doctor came down. He wasn't going to tell me anything either, but then when I told him who I was he broke down enough to let me know that—she's in pretty bad shape, I guess."

"Oh, Rolfe, what is it? Do you know? Did he tell you?"

He answered with a Gallic shrug, a mannerism as newly acquired as his maturity, showing a compassionate concern that she had never before seen him evidence toward anyone. "All he said really—you know, she's seventy-four and the way she's always lived—I guess it's what you have to expect. But still—" He took a deep breath, averting his eyes. "She's a terrific person. It's meant a lot to me—you know, just having her here to talk to."

"Of course," she said flatly, downing an inadmissible stab of jealousy, recalling how often over the last few years she failed in an effort to get him to really talk to her. "How is she now? Is she in bed?"

"Not her," he said with a rueful chuckle. "Nobody is going to keep her down. If you didn't know, you'd never guess that anything was wrong, that terrific front she keeps up. That's why I thought I better tell you what the score is before you get out there."

"Did you tell her that you'd talked to her doctor?"

"I didn't have to. She knew. You don't hide anything from her. I don't know how she does it, but—I go out there sometimes, all stewed up about something, swearing I'm not going to say anything about it, and the first thing I know she's telling me."

"You're very fond of her, aren't you?"

"I've never known anyone like her. The thing is—" He bit his lip, for an instant a boy again, an illusion quickly lost as he shifted to a firmly adult "I couldn't tell her that you didn't want to stay with her."

"No, of course you couldn't," she agreed, somehow feeling it necessary to excuse herself. "All I was thinking—I thought if I were at a hotel, it would be so much easier to see more of you, that's all."

"Oh, you'll see plenty of me," he said, that shrug again. "About the birthday party idea—I talked to the doctor about it and he said, no, absolutely not. He said it would be a great mistake to get her as steamed up as she'd be if we tried to do something like that."

"Of course," she acknowledged, feeling as if everything was collapsing around her.

"I'm sorry about hitting you with all this. I know it isn't working out the way you wanted, but still—anyway, it's going to mean an awful lot to her, your being here."

Boldly she thrust in, "I hope it means a little something to you, too."

"Oh, sure, it's wonderful," he said. "The only thing is—I wish I had more time to take you around but I'm—how long are you going to stay?"

"I don't really know," she said, desperately trying to put together the broken pieces of her shattered plans. "A lot depends on——"

"Are those your bags?" he interrupted, gesturing toward the waiting porter, and when she nodded, he said, "Come on then," taking her arm, hurrying her on through the thinning crowd. "Now if Jo has only been able to charm those gendarmes into letting her stay parked—oh, good, there she is."

She glanced toward the curb, but before her eyes could focus, Rolfe winged up his coat, sheltering her from the rain, but blinding her to what lay ahead. Then, across the sidewalk, he whipped his coat away as if it were an unveiling, confronting her with a girl whose expectantly smiling face dissipated one fear, but in the next instant substituted another that was even more frightening. This was no little piece of fluff that could be brushed off with a heart-to-heart talk. This girl was smart and alert, undeniably intelligent, exhibiting a clear-eyed boldness that could only be taken as a challenge backed by the confidence of possession.

"Welcome to Paris, Mrs. Wilder," Jo responded to Rolfe's introduction. "We're so happy to have you here," the plural pronoun slipped in like the point of a knife, a cutting proclamation of established intimacy. And then, no less adroitly, the girl was opening the door for her, turning back the front seat, putting her behind, already treating her like a mother-in-law. But there was no possibility of protest, and hunching her shoulders against the rain, her hand up to shield her hair, she squeezed in through the cramped opening, feeling herself badly outmaneuvered when, turning as she sat down, she looked out to see Jo with her head high, boldly facing into the rain, unmindful of the way her long hair was being whipped out by the wind, eyes bright as she called back to Rolfe, who was somewhere behind the car with the porter and the bags, asking him if he wanted to drive, her tone all too boldly proclaiming a man-and-wife relationship.

Rolfe must have said yes because Jo took the other seat, quickly palming the rain from her face, shaking her head to settle her hair, twisting around to offer a smile to which Kay, try as she would, was unable to respond in kind.

"Rolfe tells me that you were raised in Paris," Jo said.

She managed a choked "Yes," burying her face in her purse, blindly searching for she knew not what, settling for a handkerchief.

"You're going to find it a lot different," Jo said, a bright warning. "I know how much it's changed just in the years since we've been here, all the big glassy-glassy buildings that have gone up."

"How long have you been in Paris?" she asked, knowing that she was sounding terribly stuffy, yet unable to prevent it.

"Only these last three years, really," Jo said. "Before that it was only in and out. Oh, we were here almost all one winter—that's when Daddy first came over—but we didn't really move here until he was transferred to the European company."

"Your father is in business here?" she asked, putting the girl in her place as a stranger about whom she knew absolutely nothing.

Jo was unfazed. "Yes, he's with Seaborne Oil, their European subsidiary. But now there's some new trouble in the Middle East so he's gone back there again. It's only temporary. Or at least I hope so, for his sake. He does so like living in Paris. And he had so much of the Middle East before—when he was with the State Department."

"He was in the Foreign Service?" she asked, feeling a weakening premonition.

"Yes, that's how he knew Miss Jessica."

"Then you know her too?"

"Miss Jessica? Oh, of course. For years and years. The first time Daddy brought us—" She broke off, setting a quizzical smile. "Hasn't Rolfe told you? That's how we met. Miss Jessica had been giving me this terrific buildup about this fab boy who was coming over——"

The driver's door burst open and Rolfe shoved in with a husbandly grumble, something about all the trouble that he'd had finding a post box to mail a letter of Jo's, overriding her protest that it wasn't really that important, calling back, "Mother, I just happened to think—were you having your mail sent to the hotel?"

"Of course."

"All right, I'll stop in the morning and have them forward it," he said, starting the motor. "I could go around that way now but with the rain and all this traffic—"

"Tomorrow will be soon enough," she said, thinking that if there was any mail it would be only a letter from Judd, preoccupied with the way Jo was looking at Rolfe, her expression as confidently possessive as a post-honeymoon bride.

Rolfe's window, a crack open, sent back a blast of air, raw and bone-chilling. She shivered, Jo saw it and said, "Rolfe dear—your window."

Instantly responsive, Rolfe closed it, murmuring an apology, not to her but to Jo.

« 2 »

There was more New York mail this morning, a half dozen notes that attested to the all-covering circulation of the *Transom,* and the intensity with which its gossip column was mined by everyone who had anything to sell to advertisers. There was, however, one letter of a different character, and it struck Judd Wilder with stunning impact, all the more so because it was so unexpected. It was from Frederick Coleman, not typed but written in longhand, not on an agency letterhead with an engraved *Office of the Chairman of the Board*, but on his personal stationery, marked only with the address of the cooperative apartment to which, in semi-retirement, Judd knew that he had lately moved.

MY DEAR JUDD:

I have no idea what state of mind this will find you in, nor how receptive you may be to an old man's reminiscence, but I suspect that you are as despairing of the future as I was twenty-two years ago this month. I, too, suffered a heart attack, a rather bad one, and my doctors offered no alternative to a highly restricted life thereafter. The thought that I might never again be able to give full rein to my "creative temperament" was indeed a black prospect, all the more so because I was convinced that the agency could not survive without it.

I was, however, most fortunate in one of my nurses, a Miss O'Connor. She was as Irish as her name suggests, as rebellious against constituted authority as her compatriots so often are, and it was almost entirely because of her influence that I was eventually able to see through the cloud of despair that the doctors had hung over my head. It was through Miss O'Connor's eyes that I eventually came to see myself, not as a man who had been hopelessly crippled but as one who had been warned against what she described as "breaking your heart chasing rainbows that can't be caught, and wouldn't be worth nothing if you could."

I shall not pursue the obvious moral. Suffice it to say that I came out of the hospital with a new scale of values, and a new realization that my precious store of energy was not something to be profligately squandered. From that day forward, I never undertook any task until a tangible goal was clearly visible, and until I had convinced myself that reaching it would be worth the effort. With those conditions satisfied, I have never felt myself restricted in any way, either mentally or physically.

You may think this letter a gratuitous gesture, but having now outwitted the doctors for twenty-two years, and having accomplished during those years almost everything that has made my life worthwhile, I am moved, as my Methodist grand-

*mother used to say, "to testify to the truth, Dear God, as You
have given this humble servant the power to see it."*

> *In all sincerity,*
> FREDERICK COLEMAN

He read it through a second time, seeing Frederick Coleman in a
new light, understanding a great deal more about him than he ever
had before, even some of the tales he had heard about what a bastard the Old Man had been to work for back in the days when, as
one of those meteorically rising stars that periodically cross the
Madison Avenue meridian, he had started his own agency. This
letter made him seem a wiser man than Judd had ever before
judged him—and Dr. Aaron Kharr an even more trustworthy adviser. What Coleman had written was, in essence, exactly what
Kharr had been saying.

Refolding the letter and putting it back in its envelope, he
handed it to Mary. "Keep this out so that I can show it to Dr. Kharr,"
he said, anticipating the pleasure that he knew it would give him.

« *3* »

Much of Kay Wilder's anticipated sense of a return to youth, of a
canceling of all the years that had elapsed since she left Paris, had
been lost at the railroad station. More slipped away as she looked
out at the streets through which Rolfe was driving, a climax of
disillusionment reached at the Champs Élysées, abruptly viewed as
Rolfe maneuvered the little Renault out from behind a delivery
truck and edged it up to the red-lighted crossway. Her memories
were of a beautiful tree-lined avenue, so wide that a trickle of traffic
went all but unnoticed down its broad expanse. Now it was choked
solid with a bumper-to-bumper phalanx of automobiles and trucks.
Where there had once been a beautiful mansion, seen as a fairy-tale
castle from the park bench where Odette in her blue-striped nurse's
uniform had read aloud to her, she now saw the unadorned bleak-
ness of glass and steel, a gross stereotype of the worst of New York.
Nevertheless, glancing right as the light changed and Rolfe drove

across the avenue, she caught a glimpse of the Arc de Triomphe, foggily unsubstantial through the rain-haze and fading light, yet still there. And the bridge across the Seine was reassuringly unchanged, validating memories that began to crowd in upon her. Shifting her position so that she could see past Rolfe's shoulder, she looked ahead through the narrow fan of glass that the windshield wiper was clearing, watching for the corner that had been the key landmark of her youth, the place where she always broke into a run on her way home from school, running to find an end to loneliness, knowing that she would not be softly comforted, yet knowing, too, that the best of all sources of a sustaining self-sufficiency was Miss Jessica's disdain for a young woman who still acted like a child needing a nurse. "Remember that you're a Cannon," Miss Jessica would say, reminding her that there was no place in the Cannon code for tears, nor uncertainty, nor any fear that you might not be able to cope with any situation that presented itself—even something as serious as not being invited to Germaine de Carville's birthday party.

She missed seeing the corner, Rolfe turning before she knew where she was, the aspect of everything changed by two new apartment houses. But then she saw the griffin-topped gateposts that flanked the turn into the courtyard upon which Miss Jessica's house faced. Inside the courtyard, the last of daylight shut away, it was dark enough to make lighted windows reflect themselves in the wet stone pavement, powerfully inciting a score of memories.

Nothing had changed—except in dimension. Startlingly, the stone façade of Miss Jessica's house had shrunk with the years, much narrower than she remembered it, yet the very smallness of the house now gave her what seemed a better justification for having planned to go to a hotel. Miss Jessica had bought this house, she had once said, because there was no guest room—it had been built by a rich international banker as a townhouse in which to entertain his clients, accounting for the devotion of so much space to dining room and kitchen quarters, so little to bedrooms—yet there was, Kay knew, that room under the eaves where she had lived as a child, and now as she got out of the car and glanced up toward its stone-gabled window, her eyes were diverted by the movement of a curtain at the lighted window below it. She caught a fleeting glimpse of a silhouetted head, a sight more disturbing than anything that she had yet seen—an anxious old lady, stealing a peek through surreptitiously parted curtains, would not be a Miss Jessica she had ever known before.

"I'll take your bags up the back way," Rolfe was saying. "I don't know whether I'll get back this evening—I've got this big meeting —but if I don't, I'll see you the first thing in the morning."

She made no protest, and there was no need for more than a murmured response to whatever it was that Jo was saying about the pleasure of meeting her, and then she was climbing the short flight of worn stone steps, feeling as if she were a little out of breath, running all of the way from the corner, slowed now by that edgy anxiety that always persisted until Miss Jessica, with a stiffly formal "Very good," accepted her report of the day's happenings at school.

Memory was so compelling that she almost expected Odette's hand to reach out through the quickly opened door to draw her inside with an encircling arm, oddly surprised by the strange face that she actually saw. This must be Celia, the new maid that Miss Jessica had mentioned in her letters, hired only a few months ago to fill the gap that had been left by old Marie's death, yet Celia had already acquired that peculiarly distinctive manner that marked everyone who served Miss Jessica. Her servants were often remarked upon as being beautifully trained, yet in truth they were hardly trained at all, at least not in the sense of being instructed and drilled. Whatever it was that they displayed was an innate response to Miss Jessica's aura, a reflected dignity that gave them an air of confident assurance, sustained by a fiercely protective loyalty that could never be reasonably explained as a response to either affection or fear, gratitude or anxiety.

"Miss Jessica is waiting for you, Madame," Celia said as she took her coat, her voice warm with an unstated welcome, yet at the same time chilled with a note of warning.

Kay did not need the maid's gestured direction to know that Miss Jessica was waiting in the little upstairs sitting room, the place where she was always to be found at this late hour of the afternoon. And there she was, seen through the open doorway as Kay reached the top of the stairs, standing before her high-backed chair, her erect carriage a brave denial of both age and infirmity. The unnameable garment in which she was dressed raised again, as did everything she ever wore, a question as to where she could possibly have obtained it. It was never imaginable that any of her clothes had been kept in stock by a shop, yet neither was it credible that any acceptable dressmaker had ever turned them out, even for such a strong-willed client. Nevertheless, whatever she wore was always in character, somehow achieving the unlikely combination of patrician formality with undeniable eccentricity.

"Welcome, my dear," Miss Jessica said, the "my dear" as much of an unbending as could be expected.

She had aged markedly since Kay had seen her three years ago on her last trip to the States, and remembering the face at the window, she had to resist an impulse to rush up and throw her arms around her aunt's shoulders. Instead, she gave her gaunt cheek a lightly planted kiss, getting no more than a grimace as a reward, yet knowing that it was exactly what was expected and wanted, that Miss Jessica would have been deeply hurt had it not been given.

"You had a good crossing," Miss Jessica said, a statement that prohibited a negative reply. "And a nice cabin."

"Yes, I'm very grateful to you," Kay said. "And Captain Davideau sends you his fondest regards."

Miss Jessica gave her the curt nod of royalty accepting due tribute, sitting to end the ceremony, her directing hand a scepter indicating a chair beside a small table on which stood the only lighted lamp in the room. "Sit there. I want to be able to see you. How are you?"

"Oh, fine. But how are you? That's much more to the point."

"Nonsense. At my age, the state of one's health is completely without point." She squared her shoulders, lifting her head. "You're not to be concerned about anything those children told you."

"But I am," she insisted. "What do the doctors say?"

"It's hardly news that my various and sundry organs are in no better than secondhand condition."

"But what did they——?"

"After subjecting me to all of the indignities that their nasty little minds were able to contrive, they finally came to the quite astounding conclusion that my heart will eventually stop beating. Extraordinarily brilliant, don't you think?"

"What I think is that——"

"I have, I hope you'll grant, some understanding of the delusions to which we humans are heir," Miss Jessica went on, "but I must admit to being baffled by the pompous arrogance of these young fools who now call themselves doctors of medicine. They're worse than the priests. At least, the priests have the good grace to ascribe their infallibility to a divine source—these doctors take it all unto themselves. Quackery can be rather charming if it's carried off with a sense of humor—I'm sure you remember old Dr. Galliard, that marvelous beard—but these bloodless creatures that the medical schools are mass-producing these days are an awful lot. They seem to have taken on the mission of degrading man—forgivable, perhaps, in a dilettante philosopher or an avant-garde playwright—but when you do it solely to enrich yourself it becomes something rather horrible."

Dissembling loquacity had always been Miss Jessica's defense against talking about something that she wanted to avoid, and Kay made a purposeful attempt to penetrate it, put off as her aunt said, with an imperious flip of her hand, "Bring the tray," an order seemingly addressed to an empty doorway, but no more than given when there was an instantly responding acknowledgment from a miraculously materialized Celia.

"You were impressed with Jo, weren't you?" Miss Jessica made a fresh start, again a question that supplied its own affirmative answer. "And you can see the change in Rolfe."

At a loss for words, "I understand you brought them together" slipped out, all the worse because her tone made it seem an accusation.

"In only one sense," Miss Jessica said with expressionless aplomb. "I introduced them—yes, to that extent, I was slightly involved—but I've no right, really, to take any of the credit." There was a glimmer of a faint smile. "You can believe what I'm sure Rolfe has written you about her—she's a splendid girl, Kay."

She started to speak, stopped by the impossibility of admitting that Rolfe had written almost nothing about the girl, concluding with a taut "Do you think it's serious?"

"They didn't tell you?"

Her heart plummeted. "They're not—oh God, don't tell me they're married?"

"No," Miss Jessica said, a glorious reprieve until she added, "There's been no ceremony. They're waiting for that until the Wallaces go back to the States. Her father is due for leave as soon as he gets back from the Middle East—the Arabs are being a nuisance

again, you know—and Mrs. Wallace is one of those lily-of-the-valley
creatures whose sense of morality needs the support of organ music
and a sextet of matched bridesmaids."

Kay Wilder could not doubt what she had intuitively known from
the first moment that she had seen Rolfe and Jo together, yet she
was stunned by this evidence that Miss Jessica of all people was
condoning it. She felt suddenly and terrifyingly alone, bereft of
any possible support, experiencing something close to vertigo, a desperate need to keep her head from spinning out of control.

"Surely you'd guessed?"

Kay nodded, tight-lipped, looking away, trying to escape those
piercing eyes, yet knowing how futile it had always been to hide
anything from Miss Jessica.

"I suspect I know how you feel," Miss Jessica said in that too-
kindly voice that was always a prelude to punishment. "But I beg of
you not to let them know it. They're in love, Kay. Accept it. I
did—not easily, I'll admit—but I gave them my blessing. And they've
rewarded me by letting me share a little of something that's very
beautiful. It's been a wonderful experience, one that I've never
really known before, and I don't want it to end with—" she broke off
with a hoarse "Come, come," directed at Celia, who had been waiting at the door for permission to enter.

Celia brought in a large silver tray, loaded with decanters, glasses,
and a repoussé urn filled with ice, an elegant display over which
Miss Jessica presided with patrician grace. "What will you have,
Kay?"

"Oh, anything—just some sherry," she said, warning herself that
she needed to stay as clearheaded as possible, unaware until she
saw Miss Jessica's sharp glance that she had unthinkingly invaded
one of her aunt's eccentric deceptions, a secret so badly kept that
no Foreign Service officer had ever been fully accredited at the
American Embassy until he learned that one of Miss Jessica's cut-
glass sherry decanters, the one with the sunburst stopper, contained
the finest sour-mash bourbon to be found anywhere in Europe.

Straight-faced, Miss Jessica asked, "Spanish or Kentucky?"

"Spanish," Kay said, risking a thin smile, accepting the glass that
Miss Jessica poured for her, then watching with alarm as she saw the
liquid level rise and rise in the wineglass that her aunt was filling

for herself from the other sherry decanter, the one with the sunburst top.

Ceremoniously, Miss Jessica raised her glass, a silent toast, drinking then, making it seem no more than a sip, but Kay saw that the liquid level had fallen precipitously. A fabulous tolerance for alcohol had always been a part of the Miss Jessica legend, but neat whiskey by the glassful was surely dangerous now. Kay made no comment, knowing what the response would be.

Miss Jessica sat silent, studying the rim of her glass, abruptly looking up. "How's Judd?"

"Oh, fine."

"I'd hoped that he might change his mind and come with you."

"Oh, he couldn't possibly, not with his precious convention coming up," she said, unguardedly cynical. "After that, he'll be off to the summer markets. Then it will be—I don't know what, but there's bound to be something." She sipped her sherry. "If I'd waited for him to come with me, I'd never have made it—and I did want to be here for your birthday."

Miss Jessica's narrowed eyes were fixed upon her. "That, I take it, is the excuse that you gave him."

"Excuse?"

"I'm not ungrateful, Kay—I'm delighted to have you here—but we've never minced about, you and I, and it's much too late now to start treating each other like strangers. What's wrong?"

"Wrong? Nothing's wrong. What made you think there is?"

Miss Jessica gave her a penetrating look, the same sharp-pointed thrust with which, over the years, she had deflated the pretensions of some of the world's most practiced professional diplomats. She said only, "Your letter."

"My letter?"

"The one in which you told me you were coming."

"I can't remember what I did write. It was only a hurried note——"

"Oh, that was quite evident," Miss Jessica said. "I could almost hear it—closet doors flung open, drawers banging, suitcases thumped down on your bed. All very familiar. You were fourteen then, weren't you—that time you were going to run away with the Marchand girl?"

Kay's laugh came out dangerously brittle. "Have you been thinking that I was running away from Judd?"

"Weren't you?"

"Of course not."

Miss Jessica looked at her fixedly. "I find the alternative even more concerning."

"I really don't know what you're talking about," she said, honestly baffled now, trying to down disquietude by telling herself that Miss Jessica's age and illness had obviously affected her mind.

Miss Jessica lifted her glass. Another sip. The whiskey was more than half gone now. "I've been thinking about something Dr. Galliard once said about women in their middle forties. He was not all humbug, you know. He knew precious little about the science of medicine, I'll grant you that, but he did know a great deal about women. He should. Goodness knows, he was experienced enough. I've no idea how many mistresses he'd had. He once told me how he picked them. Never in their mid-forties, he said. There was too much danger then of their being afflicted with *quarante-manie*—that's what he called it—the madness of the forties. That was when they went through the frantic period, he said—doing all sorts of foolish things, running away from their husbands, chasing after their lost youth, trying to keep their sons from falling in love with someone who might——"

Kay slashed in with a wordless exclamation, no longer able to damp anger with a tolerance of senile aberrations. "I take it that you've been indulging in some long-range psychoanalysis."

Miss Jessica's face went slack, her lower lip trembling, the first time that Kay had ever seen her so hard hit, an awareness that prompted an attempt at apology, dropped as her aunt said hoarsely, "It seems that the mid-seventies are a foolish time, too. Forgive me. I was much too blunt about it. But I have been concerned about you. And these days everything seems so urgent—so little time."

Penitent, yielding to compassion, Kay managed a stiff smile. "Well, you've nothing to worry about. If I'm afflicted with—whatever you called it—it's a very mild case. And well under control. I'm not running away from Judd, or anything else. I'm quite prepared to go on being the same good Crouch Carpet wife that I've always been—or at least tried to be—and no less prepared, I hope, to accept a daughter-in-law."

She was rather pleased with herself for having brought it off so well, confident enough now to go on. "If you've been imagining that I'm in any way unhappy, please don't. I've settled down in my little rut and am quite content with it." So far, so good—Miss Jessica was believing her—but, too confident, something made her foolishly add, "I'll be going in for African violets any day now."

Caught as she was draining her glass, Miss Jessica choked, coming out with a little I-knew-it snort of triumph.

There was no choice now but to go on in the same vein. "I've even been invited to join the Thursday Garden Club. That's quite an honor, you know, after only twelve years in New Ulster. It usually takes at least twenty before they accept you."

Miss Jessica's only reply was a look of weary impatience. With a sigh she switched to "Judd still happy in his work?"

"At least happy enough so that nothing else matters."

Miss Jessica regarded her speculatively, seemingly poised for another thrust, but apparently relenting, said agreeably, "Yes, it's quite extraordinary, isn't it, this fascination that corporate life has for so many men. I've never understood what it is, really—but whatever it is, it's something that has to be accepted."

"I know that—and I have," Kay put in, a bit more than half-consciously defensive.

Miss Jessica seemed not to have heard her, continuing almost without pause. "As much as anything else, I suppose, it's the tribal instinct coming out. Man has always been a pack hunter—it was the only way he could kill a mastodon—and the mastodon had to be killed. He could feed his body on small game, but his soul demanded downing something bigger than himself. And he could only do that by hunting in a pack."

"I suppose so," Kay said absently, thinking that it was a little sad, that worn old mind, once so sharp that her quick-witted epigrams were repeated in embassies from Oslo to Athens, reduced now to pointless dissembling. She leaned back, sipping her sherry, feeling herself given a moment of respite from on-guard concern.

"Men so love to think of themselves as individualists, you know," Miss Jessica continued. "They've fought war after war to preserve that illusion. Yet how do they fight? As individuals? Of course not. They form an army and there they are, thousands of them, all marching to the same tune. And when the war is over, what do they do? Rush home and live exactly as they fought, cheek to jowl with their neighbors, pillorying the fool who dares get out of step. It takes a very strong man to resist it—unless, of course, there are enough of them, and then they all join up, and with placards aloft and their silly little transistors blaring, off they go to start another fight for liberty or freedom or whatever name they choose to give their newest illusion."

"Yes, it's a crazy world," Kay agreed, remembering the news reports on the ship about last week's worldwide plague of riots—governments overthrown, embassies stoned, ambassadors spat upon —easily enough believing that all this disorder had had its effect upon a mind so long preoccupied with world affairs.

"Man can't deny his nature," Miss Jessica went on. "He's a fighter. That's why I've always thought Freud such a fool, this idea of his that sex is the all-important motivation. Nonsense! Let a man hear a bugle and he'll jump right out of his mistress's bed, desert wife and children, and dash off to war. It's always been that way. I've been rereading Martineau lately—the crusade novel, you know—that wonderful scene where Adrienne imagines that Reynald is hiding in the monastery only because he loves her and cannot bear to leave her, when all the rascal is really doing is playing off Godfrey, the Duke of Lorraine, against the count of Vermandois, seeing who would make the best offer for his services." She regarded her empty glass ruefully. "Today, it would be General Motors versus Chrysler—or Crouch Carpet—or Seaborne Oil—or whatever other banner might have caught his fancy."

Kay stiffened, sensing that Miss Jessica's verbal excursion had not been as goalless as she had imagined. Silently, she demanded an explanation.

"But whatever the banner, Kay, you can't stop them from following it. If you try, you'll lose them. All you can do is live with it—and make the best of it. You can't change them."

"I know that," she retorted, words propelled by the force of self-defense too long unexercised. "I know you've always thought that I tried to manage Judd's life. It's not true. It never was. Did I object to his going with Crouch Carpet? Didn't I move to New Ulster? Haven't I stuck it out? Don't I deserve a little credit for that? Don't you think——"

"I'm not talking about Judd."

Small-voiced, Kay managed a thin "What are you trying to tell me?"

"Has Rolfe written you about what he's planning to do?"

She shook her head, an admission too painful to put into words.

"He'll finish out this year."

"But he won't go on——" Her throat went dry.

"Go on and do what?" Miss Jessica asked flatly. "What *you* want him to do?"

She was still speechless.

"Do you want me to tell you what he said?" Miss Jessica asked, her tone a warning that it would hurt.

She nodded, thinking herself too numbed now to feel any more pain.

"You may think me cruel, Kay, but I'm sure it will hurt less hearing it from me than from him." She took a deep breath, expelling it slowly. "He said—these are his own words, Kay—'Mother has never been satisfied with what Dad has done with his life, so I suppose I'll be disappointing her, too.'"

It was no worse than she had expected, and she managed a taut "He has no right to feel that way."

"And then he said, 'Dad will understand, but Mother won't.'"

Kay felt a cry rising in her throat, a scream of a terrible inner wounding, somehow choked back, audible only as a groan of bewilderment. It was a long time before she was capable of asking, "What's he planning to do?"

"He knows now that he doesn't want to spend his life as a scholar. And he's right. That boy doesn't belong in academic life."

"Then he won't go on to Harvard," she said dully, an abandonment of hope, the ending of a dream that had begun when Rolfe had been chosen out of almost a hundred applicants to work in Paris with Dr. McClelland Brook, acting as his research assistant and getting his master's degree at the same time, clearing the way for Harvard and his doctorate. Disappointment triggered anger, but she choked back the words that rose in her throat.

"Say what you want, Kay. Get it out of your system. Better now than later."

"I just don't understand—" she began, instantly aware that she was confirming what Rolfe had said about her.

"If you're inclined to blame Jo—don't," Miss Jessica said. "She's not influenced him in any way. I doubt if she could, even if she tried, and she most assuredly has not. Quite the opposite. Rolfe's a strongheaded boy—there's more Cannon blood there than I've seen in two generations—and Jo is wise enough to know that if she tried to stand in his way she'd lose him."

Only too obviously, Miss Jessica was warning her that she, too, faced that same danger. For a moment it seemed pointless—Rolfe was already lost—yet her store of emotion was too great to be so rapidly dissipated, her love for her son too powerful to be so quickly reduced to impotence.

"He's no longer a boy, Kay." Miss Jessica paused, adding a clinching thrust. "He's as old right now as Judd was when you first met him."

"I suppose so," she murmured, instantly recovering with a firm "I know that."

"More sherry?"

"No, thank you."

"Are you in a mood for suggestions?"

She wished that she dared shake her head. She nodded.

"I've two of them," Miss Jessica said crisply, in firm command now. "The first is this: be extremely careful, Kay, that you say absolutely nothing that Rolfe could conceivably interpret as being even remotely critical of his father."

"But I never have——"

"If you were to say to him, as you said to me, that his father had not been able to come with you because of his *precious* convention—"

Kay gasped, momentarily unable to credit her aunt's madly unfair distortion of that innocent word, then abruptly suffused by embarrassment, less a response to guilt than to her unthinking carelessness for having let that word slip out.

"My second suggestion is this," Miss Jessica continued. "No matter what he tells you that he's going to do—don't question it. Give him your blessing. Tell him that you approve. Or at the very least, that you understand. If you don't, he'll do it, anyway, so you've everything to gain and nothing to lose. It may not be easy, but do it. He's tearing his heart out because he doesn't want to hurt you. That should be some compensation—having someone love you enough to care what you think. Don't lose his love, Kay. There's too little of it in any of our lives to sacrifice it foolishly." She stopped with a pained smile. "I only hope that I've not sacrificed too much of yours, talking to you this frankly."

Suddenly, Kay Wilder found her hands gripping the arms of the chair, physically suppressing the almost overwhelming force that threatened to propel her toward her aunt, to throw her arms around her, to bury her face and hide the relief of tears—but this was something that could never be done, not with Miss Jessica.

« 4 »

In the pattern to which hospital routine had, by now, molded Judd Wilder's life, Dr. Kharr's evening visit had become the regularly recurring climax of the day. Tonight, waiting for him to appear, he felt a certain uneasiness, below the level of conscious anxiety yet positive enough to incite some cautious preparation. Last night's talk had been a good one, the best yet, but toward the end Kharr had started digging into his married life, asking some questions about Kay that had been as awkward for him to answer as they had obviously been difficult for Kharr to ask. It had been an uncomfortable subject for both of them, soon dropped, but something had suggested that Kharr would pick it up again tonight—unless he could somehow be diverted. That was what Judd Wilder was hoping to do with the letter from Frederick Coleman.

Dr. Kharr did not put in an appearance until after eight o'clock, arriving with a rush, purposefully thrusting open the door, plainly anxious to get on with whatever he had in mind. Mrs. Cope, sensing his mood, got out quickly. Cued by the closing door, Judd cut in on the doctor's opening words with "Didn't you say the other night that you knew Frederick Coleman?"

"I met him once, that's all. Why?"

"I thought you might be interested in a letter I got from him."

Kharr reached out for the letter, but his eyes remained fixed on Judd's face, and when he finally looked down and started to read, his expression remained wary. Then, kaleidoscopically, it began to change, distrust flickering out, giving way to puzzled acceptance, blooming into what could only be judged as restrained delight. Surprisingly, he asked, "This appeals to you?"

"Appeals to me?" Judd asked, unable to see what Kharr was getting at. "I thought you'd like to see it. It's so close to what you've been saying."

"And you're accepting it?"

"Do you mean accepting your idea that stress can cause a heart attack? Of course, I accept it. Why not? Have you been thinking—?" He injected an incredulous laugh. "Look, I haven't been arguing about that. The only thing I've ever——"

"Good," Kharr broke in, an effective vocalization of satisfaction, yet coming nowhere near expressing what lay behind the glow on his face, the unmistakable look of a man who had been relieved of some great anxiety.

"Of course I accept it," Judd repeated. "Doesn't everyone?"

Kharr flashed him a bitterly ironic smile, unexplained, going back to the letter again, rereading it. "This is really quite extraordinary, a layman seeing it so clearly, and being able to express it so succinctly—'I came out of the hospital with a new scale of values, and, a new realization that my precious store of energy was not something to be profligately squandered. From that day forward, I never undertook any task until a tangible goal was clearly visible, and until I had convinced myself that reaching it would be worth the effort.' That's the perfect prescription for a man who wants to avoid a coronary."

"It's pretty much what you've been saying, isn't it?"

"But this says it so much better. And coming from a man who has—" He stopped, thoughtstruck. "I wonder if I could use this in my book. I suppose I'd have to get his permission, wouldn't I?"

"Yes, I'd think so, if you were going to use it as a quote," Judd said offhandedly, preoccupied with the confirmation that he had been right the other night in guessing that the notebook from which Kharr had been reading contained a manuscript. "So you're writing a book?"

"Well—trying to—yes," Kharr fumbled, acting now like any starry-eyed amateur forced into the admission that he was dreaming of becoming a famous writer. "I've published a lot of shorter things, of course—medical papers."

"That's what your book is—medical?"

"Well—yes and no. It started out to be a lay book—that's what the publisher had in mind when he first approached me, but there's so much of it that ought to get through to the profession—I really don't know quite how it's going to wind up."

"Then you already have a publisher?" Judd asked, impressed.

"Oh, yes. That's how I got started. This man Le Corte—he's one of their editors—had read a paper of mine in one of the journals. He thought that it might be expanded into a book, so they gave me a contract."

"How long have you been working on it?"

"Quite a while—too long," Kharr said, nervously apologetic. "I should have finished it before now, but it's been difficult to—" He shrugged. "I've never written anything for a lay audience before— the popularized medical thing, you know, isn't very highly regarded by the profession—and all the less so, I'm afraid, when you want to say some things that aren't generally accepted."

"You don't mean your ideas about stress and heart attacks?"

Kharr nodded curtly. "At times the medical profession can be a little—perhaps *restrictive* isn't quite the right word——"

"How about *hidebound?*" he suggested with a smile, afraid that he had gone too far when he saw Kharr's defensive flinch, quickly retreating to a safer "Maybe *conservative?*"

Dr. Kharr hesitated as if debating the propriety of accepting any criticism of the medical profession by a layman, an impression so positive that Judd was surprised when he said, "The real trouble, of course, is that medicine has gone a little science-crazy these days. Everything has to be quantified and numeralized. Truth is only what you can read on the scale of an instrument—and there's no instrument, of course, that will give you a readout on stress. Nor is there any test-tube procedure by which you can differentiate one type of stress from another. There's no mathematical formula in which you can insert a personality pattern for X and a stress value for Y and come out with a positive prediction for an under-fifty coronary."

"But surely there's enough proof——"

"Of course! It's all around us." Kharr snatched off his glasses. "Have you ever been told that if you didn't slow down and take it easier you might have a heart attack?"

"Sure, every doctor that I've ever——"

"Exactly! We acknowledge it in practice every day of our lives. But just try to get a paper published—in one of the big journals, I mean—that singles out stress as a primary cause of coronary occlusion. The best you can get away with is burying it down in a long list of possibly contributory factors."

"But surely you're not alone. There must be other doctors who have——"

"A few," Kharr snapped. "But you don't fight the establishment, not if you want to get along. Take the National Heart Association. They're supposed to be informing the public, teaching people how to avoid heart attacks, but in their newest piece of literature—I've got it on my desk right now—diet, cigarettes, lack of exercise, that's all—not a word about stress, not a word."

"But why would they—?"

"Because the big-name cardiologists are afraid that—" He stopped abruptly, silenced not only by caution but also, it seemed, by the exhaustion of an emotional outburst.

"Do you think your book will change any of that?"

Kharr shook his head, looking away, preoccupied.

"Then what are you trying to accomplish? What will the book gain for you? Do you think that it might be a big best-seller, make a lot of money?"

"No, no," Kharr said, impatiently vehement. "It's just that so many G.P.'s and internists—if they could only understand a little more about what corporate life is really like—the environment in which an executive has to work, the stresses and strains to which he is subjected—" He broke off with a discouraged sigh. "Oh, I don't know, maybe Le Corte is right, maybe you have to go at it the other way around. He thinks there would be a big audience for a book like this among businessmen. But I question whether they'd be interested enough to read it. My experience hasn't been very encouraging. I've talked to so many of them, trying to warn them—oh, after they've had a coronary, yes, then they'll listen, but before that—what do you think?"

"Oh, I wouldn't know what to say," he said, a reflex escape from involvement, yet intrigued by this unexpected reversal of roles, suddenly finding himself called upon for advice and counsel. It was not, however, a strange position; guiding struggling writers had been a part of his whole working life. "The only thought I might throw out—it's obvious, of course—but the first thing any writer has to do, no matter what he's writing, is to decide who he's writing to, what he wants to say, what he's trying to accomplish."

"I know, I know," Kharr murmured.

"Unless he has a clear goal—" he continued, stopped as he saw Kharr's eyes cut to the letter in his hand, aware too late he had unwittingly picked up an echo of Frederick Coleman's words.

Kharr's eyes flicked up, the look of a guilty man embarrassed by detection, a forced smile and a short burst of nervous laughter. "Very good, Dr. Wilder, very good—I concur in your diagnosis."

"I didn't mean——"

"No, no, you're right," Kharr burst out, words flooding as if a dam had been released. "I'm the coronary type. I know it. That's why I left New York. If I hadn't, I could easily have wound up right where you are. But I did break out of it. It may not sound like it, what I've told you about the book—it's not that important to me. I'm not letting it be. If I can bring it off, all right. If I can't, I'm not going to let it tear my heart out—" he caught himself, stemming the flow, a thin smile flickered as he concluded, "either figuratively or literally." He moved as if he were about to leave, a self-conscious escape from embarrassment. Then, startlingly, he said, "Being a Jew doesn't help, you know. We have an abnormally high incidence of under-fifty coronaries."

Thrown off balance by this stunning revelation of the man behind Kharr's professional front, Judd Wilder hesitated, delayed first by the sharp discomfiture that he always experienced when a Jew made any such differentiating remark, then by the flashed memory of Huck Joyce's advice, a long moment passing before he could respond to an urgent need to change the subject.

Kharr beat him to it, evidencing a remarkable recovery of poise, as abruptly achieved as if he had slammed a door. "I wonder if you'd mind doing this, Mr. Wilder—I don't mean immediately, sometime over the next week or ten days—would you be willing to read a couple of chapters and give me your opinion?"

He hesitated, instinctively resistant. "Well, if you want me to—"

"If you're suspecting subterfuge, please don't. This has nothing to do with you. It's not the heart stuff. That comes later. This is at the beginning of the book, the first two chapters, where I'm trying to establish the basic corporate environment—the atmosphere in which the executive operates, the demands that are made upon him, the stresses and strains to which he is subjected. That's the first chapter. Then I go over to his side of it—motivations, goals, his relationship to the corporation. That's an area where I'd particularly like to have your reaction. If you wouldn't mind reading it—I don't mean right now, of course—"

"Sure, I'll read it," he said. "But I'm not at all certain that I'm going to agree with your basic premise."

"You mean—?"

"This idea that the corporation executive is subjected to any special stresses and strains."

"Surely you'll agree that he's under a lot of pressure?"

"No more than anyone else," he said with a smile. "There are a lot of off-base ideas floating around about what it's really like working for a big company—all this guff about life in the corporate jungle, what a terrific battle it is, all the back-stabbing and throat-cutting that a man has to go through to get ahead. Most of it's written by guys who are on the outside looking in. It's a different story when you're on the inside looking out."

"Yes, perhaps I am an outsider," Kharr said, a bit stiffly, clearly sensitive to what he had taken as personal criticism. "But I have seen a great many businessmen, Mr. Wilder, and under circumstances that are conceivably more revealing than their workaday fronts."

"Oh, I know you have," he put in contritely, resolved to be more careful.

"You say that the corporation man is under no more stress than anyone else," Kharr went on. "And that may well be true. We do live in a highly competitive society where everyone has to battle to get ahead, true enough. But as I see it, that's not the point. The differentiation lies not in the amount of stress but in the kind of stress. The man who is in some enterprise where he can direct his own activity—the smaller businessman, or even the head of a larger one that he personally controls—Mr. Coleman, for example, can practice what he preaches. It's quite feasible for him to set these clear goals that he talks about, and never to make an effort to reach one of them until he is convinced that it's worth the effort. Can a man in a big corporation do that?"

"Why not?" he asked, but recognizing that he was on shaky

ground. "What he has to do, of course, is set his goals in terms of what's good for the company."

"Whether he believes in them or not."

"If he can't, he ought to get out."

"Theoretically, yes, that's the answer," Kharr granted. "But for most men it's impossible. Or at least impractical. By the time they wake up to what's happened to them, they're tied down by retirement plans, insurance schemes, stock options, what have you. And, of course, a scale of living that demands a continuing high income. A great many men feel trapped, caught in a situation from which there's no escape, forced to go on living a life from which they're deriving no real sense of fulfillment. There are a lot of men like that in big companies, Mr. Wilder."

"Oh, I won't argue about that. But aren't most of them men who haven't made the grade?"

"Or men who have decided it isn't worth the sacrifices that have to be made to do it," Kharr qualified.

"Isn't that an excuse?"

"Sometimes, yes. But those sacrifices are very real, Mr. Wilder." He leaned forward, a hand reaching out as if attempting to catch something evasive. "This is what really puzzles me—I've done more thinking about this than anything else, and I'm still not certain that I'm on solid ground—what is it, Mr. Wilder, that inspires this obsessive devotion to a corporation, this almost fanatical zeal to sacrifice everything for the good of what, after all, is nothing more than a—well, to put it baldly, a commercial enterprise whose only real purpose is to make money?"

"There's a lot more involved than that."

"What?"

"Don't you think that there's been a lot of satisfaction in what we've done at Crouch Carpet, taking a little bankrupt carpet mill and building it into what the company is today?"

"I'm not talking about you, Mr. Wilder, I'm talking about the general situation. Take the man who comes into a big company, one that's already established and functioning—isn't he immediately subjected to the stresses and strains of trying to remake himself to conform to the demands of the organization? Isn't it true that he has to sacrifice his individuality——"

"You mean the 'organization man' thing?"

"Substantially, yes. Oh, I know that it isn't confined to the business world. It's everywhere. The more highly organized our society becomes, the less any of us are the masters of our own fate. But it seems to me that it's particularly pronounced in corporate life. Surely it's a stressful situation to put a man in a position where all of his natural drives—which are essentially individualistic, of course —are thwarted by organizational procedures that are specifically designed to function successfully no matter who the individual involved may be."

Judd laughed off his confusion.

"Isn't that a primary objective of the modern managerial approach —to minimize the human element?"

"Maybe down at the factory level."

"No, at the executive level, too. Isn't that the essential appeal of the computer—the dehumanizing brain that never takes a day off, never comes in with a hangover, never makes an impulse decision? Surely you'll grant that the dominant tendency today is toward suppressing individual initiative in favor of some sort of mechanized control system."

"Maybe in some companies," Judd said, automatic defense launched before he was struck by a halting awareness of Roger Stark. "Nothing like that has ever affected me."

"No, it wouldn't," Kharr agreed. "Not with the kind of relationship that you have with Mr. Crouch. But suppose you didn't have that advantage. Suppose—well, Mr. Crouch isn't a young man any more—he'll be retiring one of these days——"

"I'll be able to take care of myself," he cut him off, quick laughter outracing a consciousness of concern. "Sorry, Doctor, but you can't talk me out of going back to Crouch Carpet."

Kharr's protest was instantaneous, his distress so great that an all-out effort had to be made to stem it. As forcibly as he could, Judd assured him again that he knew very well that he had nothing like that in mind, trying to make up for his stupid blunder by granting there was, indeed, a lot to what Kharr had said about the stresses and strains of corporate life, assuring him again that he would be more than happy to read as much of his book as he would be willing to let him see.

Eventually, Kharr seemed satisfied, even smiling a little, but he kept glancing at his watch, and when the first break came he got to his feet. "Well, this isn't what I'd planned to talk to you about to-night——"

"But there's a lot to think about in what you've said," Judd con-cluded for him. "It's all solid stuff."

Kharr rose abstractedly, still holding the letter from Frederick Coleman. "I wonder—would you mind if I kept this long enough to make a copy?"

"Of course not. Keep it as long as you want to. I would like it back——"

"Thank you," the doctor said, crisply formal. Then with an auto-matic little smile, saying that he would see him in the morning, he left the room.

Fingering the empty envelope, Judd Wilder lay back, assuring himself that he had not made as much of a mess of things tonight as he had that other time—at least he had got himself out of it—self-criticism quickly giving way to thinking about Kharr, resurrecting some of the surprise that he had felt when, for a moment there, he had let down the bars, revealing the intensity of his own emotional stress, culminating in that oblique but highly significant acknowl-edgment that he was a Jew. It was not difficult to understand the extra stress that a Jew was under, the constant pressure of prejudice . . . Manny Rosen . . . last year at the Merchandise Mart . . .

Mrs. Cope came in, giving him a sharply appraising look. "You all right?"

"Sure. Fine. Why not?"

"Doctor didn't stay very long."

"Oh, he was here quite a while," he said aimlessly. "I guess he had something else to do."

"Uh-huh," Cope said, glancing left as if X-raying the walls, look-ing down the corridor. "I just don't know how he stands it, the hours he puts in. He's still here every night when I leave. I can see him sitting there at his typewriter when I go out. You just wonder what a man like that gets out of life."

"What do most of us get?"

"I guess that's right," Cope said, a sign of weary resignation abruptly caught. "Now what kind of talk is that! You just don't know how lucky you are."

He grinned at her. "You keep telling me that long enough, maybe I'll start believing it."

"Well you better!" She bent to crank down the bed. "Time you got a little rest."

He shrugged, giving himself up to the feeling of a slow falling away, a pleasant submission, his mind blank except for the quick passing thought that at least he had kept Kharr from getting off on that marriage business again.

✦ VIII ✦

KAY WILDER WAS AWAITING her son's promised appearance. Up early, unable to sleep after the rising sun had lighted the east-facing window of her attic bedroom, she had wandered through the death-still house, depressed by its general air of moldering decay, feeling as if she were in a museum devoted to a lost way of life, the trappings preserved but the essence gone.

The dining room, once a wonderland of shimmering glass and silver, seemed misted with a smoky film, everything under an ancient haze that could no longer be wiped away with a dustcloth. There were no dazzling rainbows in the crystal chandelier, no dancing reflections in the mirror-waxed surface of the long table, the silver on the sideboard bronzed with neglect. It was understandable. Celia alone could not match the housekeeping standards that it had once taken three girls to maintain, and as Miss Jessica had revealed last night after dinner, her income from the estate that Jeffry Cannon had left her was far less than Kay had imagined. "But it really doesn't matter now—I've enough, all I'll need," Miss Jessica had said, not morbidly but as a strong-willed acceptance of the inevitable, a lost way of life unregretted, looking to the future only when, as she did time and time again, she turned the conversation back to Rolfe. Despite a distractingly painful awareness that her son had talked to Miss Jessica as he never had to her, Kay had drawn her out, garnering every scrap of information that might help her this morning, thinking when she finally went off to bed that she was as well prepared as she could possibly be, capable of accepting whatever Rolfe told her with no revealing hint of disapproval or disappointment, yet realizing that no matter how well she managed it, it would be only a negative accomplishment, no more than holding the line. What then?

This morning there was an even stronger sensing of futility, a fuller realization that she was not going to find here that lift of spirit that she so desperately needed. Miss Jessica could be right—perhaps she had been running away—but if so, the fault lay not with the running but with the direction she had taken. If there was any hope, it had to come not from a resurrected past but from a new future. She knew that she could not endure very many mornings in this musty old house, waiting for Miss Jessica to appear—a gentlewoman, by the Cannon code, never left her room until eleven —and when she did there would be only a repetition of last night, endlessly going over the same ground, obliquely charging her with being a bad mother and a worse wife. Trying to make Miss Jessica understand would be hopeless. No matter what, she would side with Rolfe, as she had always sided with Judd.

Driven by a kind of despair, Kay yielded now to a thought that had been at the threshold of consciousness ever since sunup. She had never actually declined Chris Kemble's invitation to go to Spain. Chris was, she knew, staying at the Crillon. She could give her a ring, perhaps have lunch with her. She found the telephone and was looking up the number when she heard the sound of an automobile in the courtyard. Dropping the directory, she rushed to the window, unaccountably panic-stricken when she saw Rolfe getting out of the car, feeling herself suddenly incapable of bringing off the deception of approval. She almost hoped that Jo was with him, stalling off that frightening moment when she would have to face him alone. Still, when she saw him start for the door, no one else getting out of the car, she felt a powerful urge to go flying down the stairs to greet him. Suppressing it, she waited in the upper hall, out of sight, ears straining, hearing the knocker, the maid's footsteps, the door opening, and then Rolfe greeting Celia, his voice so reassuringly lighthearted that she moved to the head of the staircase.

Rolfe saw her at once, calling out, "Mail for you," flourishing a letter. He came up the stairs with it, not two steps at a time as he had always done before, a fresh reminder of how much he had changed.

Handing her the letter, he said, "That's all there was. They'll send out anything else that comes."

Recognizing the handwriting, she saw that it was only a letter from Daphy Ingalls, remembering now that Daphy, despite protest, had naïvely insisted that she would send her the name of that wonderful shop where her schoolteacher sister had bought such a beautiful beaded bag last summer. Palming the envelope, she reached out to stop Rolfe, who had already taken a backward step down the stairs. "Oh, come, come, you can't run off again," she said, lightness a triumph over trepidation. "I've hardly had a chance to talk to you. You can't be that busy."

"No, I've got a few minutes," he said, his lack of resistance almost frighteningly abnormal. He had always before been reluctant to talk to her, acting when he was younger as if afraid of what she might ask him, these last few years as if he thought her incapable of understanding anything that he might tell her. There was no holdback now, his boldly confident manner an alarming prediction of what lay ahead.

She led the way into the little upstairs sitting room, regretting the choice of place when she found it so reverberant with echoing memories of what Miss Jessica had told her yesterday, yet now there was sunlight filtering in to dissipate the black shadows, and Rolfe saved her from that awful first moment of silence with an easy "What do you think of—?" the subject silently supplied by a head gesture in the direction of Miss Jessica's room.

"You were so right about my staying here," she said, grateful for the chance to compliment him. "It would have been a great mistake if I hadn't."

Rolfe nodded, no longer a boy flustered by appreciation, now a man who did not doubt the soundness of his judgment. "Sorry about running off last night," he said. "But there wasn't much I could do about it. It was the big meeting—I couldn't pass it up."

"No, of course you couldn't," she said, starting to ask what kind of meeting it had been, quickly deciding that a circuitous approach was safer, "How was it?"

"Terrific," he said, solidly and unequivocally, a startling contrast with her expectation of a noncommunicative mumble. Change was equally evident in the way he seated himself. Instead of sliding down into the loose-jointed slump that had always been as characteristic as the nervous finger-combing of his hair—that, too, was missing—he sat upright, his shoulders squared, his eyes meeting hers. His manner carried no hint of either defiance or challenge, only self-confidence, disconcerting because she could not put down a gnawing awareness that this new maturity was the result of his association with Jo, a physical relationship to which she could not close her mind, momentarily blocking consciousness of what he was saying.

"—so they really have to project their plans for at least ten years," Rolfe's voice drifted in. "It will take three years to get the refinery on stream, and the petrochemical plants can't start up until there's feedstock for them, but you do have to have housing and services for the workers—" He broke off with an apologetic "I don't mean to bore you with all this, but it's such a terrific program. Mr. Purcell had told me a lot about it, of course, but until you actually see it all laid out—it's a fabulous company, it really is."

"Company?"

"Seaborne Oil," he said, showing surprise, acting as if she should have known.

She stared at him, recalling Miss Jessica's claim that the girl had had nothing to do with Rolfe's decision to abandon his academic career. "Isn't that the same company that—?"

Rolfe broke in with a chuckling affirmation. "That was really weird—you know, the way I happened to meet Mr. Purcell. I wrote you about it, didn't I?"

She shook her head, resisting the impulse to say that he knew very well he had not, hardly able to believe that Rolfe had become so much like his father.

"You know my tape recorder—the one Dad got me, the little Norelco? I'd been giving it a pretty hard workout, I guess, and something had gone wrong with the playback. I couldn't bug it out myself so I took it down to a little shop that one of the guys knew about. There wasn't too much wrong, only a short in the switch, so I waited around for him to fix it. He was testing it—you know, playing back the cartridge that I had in the machine—when this man walked in. It's a little shop, not much bigger than this room, so he couldn't help hearing what I had on the tape. It wasn't much, only some notes that I'd dictated while I was reading some Colombier—you know, Edouard Colombier, the guy who's been doing all this work on the projection of socioeconomic trends. I could see he was all ears, and in a minute or two he started asking me questions. Why was I reading Colombier? What was I working on? How did I happen to be in Paris? He introduced himself—Julian Purcell—but that was John Doe to me, nobody I'd ever heard of. Still, he was an interesting man to talk to, so when he invited me out to lunch—a free meal at a good restaurant, why not?"

"He was French?" she asked, offering encouragement that was obviously unneeded. Never had she heard Rolfe talk this easily and freely.

"No, he's American—Boston. But I didn't find that out until afterwards. He didn't tell me a thing about himself at lunch. We got off on socioeconomic prediction—Colombier's trend patterns versus the Bromberg criteria projection—and I guess I did most of the talking. We were there until—oh, I don't know, it must have been three o'clock. And then when we were outside, walking down the street, he asked me to come around to his apartment that next Sunday afternoon for a drink. He said he'd invite Colombier and it would be a chance to meet him. Naturally, I told Jo about it, and when I mentioned who had invited me, this man I'd met—Julian Purcell —she started to laugh. That was the first I knew that he had anything to do with Seaborne Oil."

"Yes, that was quite a coincidence, wasn't it?" she said, an unsuccessful attempt to express full acceptance. As a mother, she had rarely had occasion to doubt her young son's veracity, but as a wife she had learned that grown men often had a childish faith in the plausibility of their tales about chance encounters.

"He's in the Planning Division," Rolfe continued. "They handle the long-range planning for all of Seaborne's expansion programs, everything right up to the point where Operations takes over. That's what's so terrific about it, the way everything is tied together. And then the follow-through—you know, not just the economic side but all the social consequences, the effect that it's going to have on the whole area, the whole country. When you think of what it could mean to Spain—they're so far behind the rest of Europe. When I was down there last week and saw how people were still living——"

"Last week?" slipped out. "You've been—?"

"Oh, didn't Miss Jessica tell you? I was down there for two days. Not two full days, really—we flew down Saturday morning and back

Sunday afternoon. The New York crowd had all come over for the meeting, so Mr. Purcell flew them down in the company plane for a site inspection. There was an extra seat, so he asked me to go along."

"How nice," she said, a badly off-key attempt to sweeten bitterness with a smile. "I knew that you wanted to see Spain—you wrote me."

He nodded vigorously. "You can't visualize what it's really like until you actually see it—you know, not just where the refinery is going to be, but the whole area that will have to be developed. I'd seen the plan, of course—"

He went on talking but she let the words wash over her, thinking what a fool she had been to let herself dream up that fairy-tale trip through Spain with Rolfe, a silly grasping at a last hope, lost now as everything else had been lost, nothing left, not even an illusion of what might once have been possible.

"That's the big advantage of starting from scratch and building a brand-new city," Rolfe was saying. "You can give your people a lot better living conditions than if you tried to shoehorn into some metropolitan area that's already a fouled-up mess—you know, Barcelona or Valencia or even Tarragona."

"You seem to be rather deeply involved in all this," she suggested, certain of the answer, yet somehow, almost masochistically, craving the pain that would come when he admitted how he had betrayed all her hopes for him.

"Oh, not really, not yet," he said casually. "All that I've done up to now is this one little job for Mr. Purcell, coordinating the reports on social demands, some of the things the housing architects will have to take into account, but still it's been a wonderful chance to get the feel of it—you know, to make certain that it's something that I want to go on with."

"Go on with?" she repeated, feeling as if she were fingering a fuse already lighted.

But there was no explosion. "They've offered me a job," he said calmly.

"And you're going to take it?"

He glanced away but his eyes came back to hers before he asked, "If I do, what will you think?"

"Would that matter?" she asked, diverted from her rehearsed response by the memory of Judd asking her what she would think about his taking a job with Crouch Carpet, recalling the falseness of his pretense that his decision had not already been made.

"You wouldn't be very happy about it?"

"Why do you say that?"

"You'll be disappointed, won't you?"

Disappointed echoed like a struck gong, a one word validation of everything that Miss Jessica had told her that Rolfe had said about her. In the night she had thought herself well prepared, but now the rehearsed words came out badly, too stiff, too pat, heard almost as if someone else was saying, "You have a good mind, Rolfe, a wonderful mind—I want you to make the most of it, that's all."

"I don't know about the good mind—maybe yes, maybe no, it's so easy to kid yourself—but whatever I have, I know now that I don't want to bury it back in the seventeenth century."

"That's quite a change from the way you were talking when you left," she said, trying to make it a flatly neutral statement, free of accusation.

"I've done a lot of thinking since I came over here," he said matter-of-factly. "And I never had before, not really. At Colfax, I'd been running so hard, chasing the carrots—you know, dean's list, Phi Beta Kappa, magna cum laude—I'd never really looked ahead to see where I was heading. And then when this came up—a year in Paris, a chance to get my M.A. without rocking Dad's pocketbook too hard—it was another carrot, that's all."

"Oh, Rolfe, it was more than that, you know it was," she protested, remembering the intensity of his drive to get the appointment, the triumphant satisfaction that she had heard in his voice that night he called with the news that he had been selected. Belatedly aware of her vow not to argue with him, she said hurriedly, "I'm sorry, Rolfe. All I meant——"

"Sure, I was steamed up about it," he admitted. "I wanted it, and I went all out to get it. And I don't regret it, not for a minute. It's been a great experience."

"But you don't want to go on with it?"

He looked at her strangely. "If you're thinking that it's only because I was offered this job—" He shook his head. "I'd made up my mind long before I met Mr. Purcell. I don't know when exactly, but it wasn't too long after I got over here. When I found out what it was really going to be like—" He picked at his trouser leg, eyes down, then abruptly raised. "As much as anything else, I guess it was something Dad said. You remember when he was up at school last spring, that talk he made to the business-school guys?"

She felt staggered, unable to offer the response for which he seemed to be waiting.

"Dad and I had been talking—this was at the Inn, before we went over to the auditorium—about what I'd be doing over here if I got the appointment. I didn't really know too much about it then myself, only what Dr. Brook had told me—you know, what an exciting period the seventeenth century had been, the very beginning of the scientific age, the real start of the industrial revolution—Newton, Pascal, Hooke, Guericke, Huygens, Leibniz—I can't remember what all I said, but I do remember saying something about what a wonderful thing it must have been to have lived in an age like that."

She nodded blankly, trying to think where she could have been when all this had been going on, deciding that it must have been when she had been down at that committee meeting, remembering now that Rolfe had been in their room when she got back.

"Dad didn't say much about it then," Rolfe continued, "but in his speech, down near the end where he was talking about modern business and the opportunities that it offered—I don't know exactly how he put it, but the idea was that just as scholars are now looking back to the seventeenth century as the start of the scientific age, three hundred years from now they'll be looking back on the twentieth century as an even more exciting period of revolutionary change. I don't know, maybe you remember—?"

She nodded, remembering only too well, recalling the stab of suspicion that had struck her when Judd had departed from his prepared script, wondering then if it was something he was purposefully directing at Rolfe, aware now how blindly foolish she had been in deciding that there was no danger of Rolfe's ever being seriously influenced by his father.

"I didn't think too much about it at the time," Rolfe was saying, "I figured it was just something he'd slipped in to give a lift to the business-school guys. And it did. Three or four of them talked to me about it afterwards—you know, because he was my father. Anyway, after I got over here it kept coming back to me. I remember one time, we were over in the library—Jo was helping me run down some old character. He'd invented a new kind of weaving shuttle, and we thought it might be a link to the development of the power loom. Anyway, we were working on the journal he'd kept, trying to decipher it—we'd been at it all day—and Jo said something about how surprised the old boy would be if he could come back after three hundred years and find anybody this much interested in something he had done."

"Yes, I imagine he would be," she said blankly, preoccupied with this further revelation of the girl's involvement.

"That's when it really hit me—you know, what Dad had said. I couldn't help thinking what my life would look like to somebody three hundred years from now. Would he give me a second look? Or would he just brush me off—you know, the way we do with all the little seventeenth-century characters who never woke up to what was going on all around them, still living back in the fourteenth century with Wycliffe and Savonarola and Joan of Arc."

"Oh, I can understand that, of course I can. But, Rolfe, the history of science isn't the only academic discipline. There are so many other fields where you could—" His eyes stopped her. They fell to her hands. Looking down she saw that she had crushed Daphy's letter, a betrayal of nervousness that she felt now as a flush of warmth in her cheeks.

Rolfe's poise added to her embarrassment. "Oh, I could teach for a while. Dr. Brook has a fellowship lined up if I want it. But I don't want to make the mistake that so many men do—drifting into something because it's the easy thing to do, and then hanging on too long because they don't want to be a quitter—you know, like Jo's father, all those years he wasted in the State Department." He recrossed his legs, reaching down to tug up a slack sock. "And Dad, too, I guess."

He had tossed it off as a throwaway remark, but she saw his eyes flick up before he raised his head, testing her reaction. She warned herself to ignore it, remembering what Miss Jessica had told her about Rolfe's attitude toward his father. But she had to say something. "What does Dr. Brook think about all this?"

"Dr. Brook? I don't know, I haven't talked to him yet. But I can guess. When we first came over here, that's all he could talk about —how Paris had been ruined by all this horrible Americanization— Coca-Cola, hot dogs, rock and roll, the charm of the lovely chimney pots destroyed by television aerials, the glorious *haute cuisine* debauched by Campbell's soup in the supermarkets—" He broke in with a sharp little laugh, quick-fading. "And, of course, it's all the fault of the big American companies. He's like a lot of people, I guess, thinking that business is something pretty awful, existing only to make money, riding roughshod over anything that gets in the way, not caring what they do to a society——"

"Oh, I know that isn't true," she murmured, unavoidably self-defensive, unable to hear anything that Rolfe was saying without thinking it an extension of the charges that she knew he had made against her.

He was leaning forward now, his eyes brighter than she had ever seen them, his cupped hand extended in a grasping gesture, as if he were trying to contain some enormously important essence. "What he doesn't see—what so many people don't see—the modern corporation is so much more than just commercial enterprise. Actually, it's the primary instrumentality of a whole new civilization. Other societies have been built with other instrumentalities—you know, the city-state, the feudal demesne, the temple, the church— there has to be some way to organize and control man's plural-istic effort. This isn't an original thought—it's the thesis of Colombier's whole argument—and once you see it, you simply can't deny it. The corporation is the most efficient and effective instrumentality that we've ever devised to organize human effort. Take this terrific forward thrust we've had in the physical sciences, this enormous expansion of technology—is it because of a simple accumulation of knowledge? No, it's because the corporation is using scientific research and development to promote the growth of a whole new civilization. There's been scientific discovery for hundreds of years, but so little was ever done about it. Science was no more than an exercise in intellect. It's the corporation that's given it point and purpose. We call this the scientific age, but it's not just science and technology that's changing the world—it's planning, it's organization, it's management, it's direction, it's—" he stopped as if faced with the awesomely inexpressible, concluding lamely, "Maybe that doesn't make much sense to you, but——"

"Of course it does," she said, attempting to convey the impression that he had convinced her, but what he actually had done was to arouse a new concern. What had before seemed a new maturity had now been revealed as a zealot's enthusiasm, a rampant idealism that smacked more of unbridled youthfulness than of balanced judgment, clearly predicting the disillusionment that lay in store for him. Every instinct pushed her toward a protective warning, yet she knew that she dared not say a word.

"Oh, I know it isn't all going to be on that level," Rolfe put in, almost as if reacting to an extrasensory perception of what she was thinking. "As Colombier says, it takes a thousand slaves making mud bricks to build a temple. But if I can—I don't know how much of a contribution I can make, but whatever it turns out to be—anyway, I know now that it's what I want to do. That's where the action is, that's where I want to be."

He had given his last words a slightly questioning intonation, less a challenge than an oblique pleading for approval. Reminded of Miss Jessica's warning that she must support him in anything that he proposed, Kay groped for words. Faster than conscious thought, she weighed and rejected possibilities, suddenly struck by an errant impulse that made her ask, "What does Jo think of all of this?" It was the first time that she had spoken her name aloud.

Rolfe's eyes lighted, his face brightened with a wonderfully rewarding smile, transparently an expression of relief. "I guess you know—"

She nodded. "I'm very happy for you."

"I was hoping that you'd feel that way," he murmured, almost as if unaware of saying it aloud, then hurriedly answering her original question with an enthusiastic "Oh, Jo is all for it. That's the wonderful thing about her, the way she—" He paused, something left unsaid. "I was a little worried for a while—you know, when I first decided that I didn't want to teach. She'd been so wrapped up in what I was doing, helping me on the research—that's the kind of a life she thought we'd have, so I didn't know how she was going to take it. But she was terrific, just terrific. She understood right away. That means an awful lot—you know, having somebody that's really with you all the way."

"Of course it does," she said as fervently as she could manage, handicapped by her inability to down the feeling that all of this was peripheral criticism of her.

"I'm a lucky guy."

"She's lucky, too, Rolfe. It isn't every man, you know, who's willing to let someone share his life."

"Maybe so," he said, missing her point. "But there are so many wives that—you know, like Jo's mother. I go out there and we get talking about Seaborne Oil sometimes, Jo and her father and I, and she just—if she can't change the subject, she walks out. The thing is—you know, he was in the Foreign Service for quite a while and I guess she liked that kind of life. Anyway, it's what she's always talking about. She's kind of a—oh, I don't want to give you the wrong impression about her. It's just that—I feel a little sorry for Mr. Wallace sometimes. It must be kind of rugged—you know, having a wife that isn't the least bit interested in anything you're doing."

She barely nodded, afraid to trust her voice, not really believing that Rolfe could be cruel enough to attack her by innuendo, yet unable to shut out Miss Jessica's voice . . . *"Mother has never been satisfied with what Dad did with his life . . ."*

Distracted, she was unaware that Rolfe was rising from his chair until she heard him say something about leaving. She started to protest—there was so much he did not understand about his father, so many arguments that she could advance to justify herself—but reason quickly sealed her lips, forcing her to endure in silence the injustice of her son's unfair judgment.

Rolfe was on his feet now. "I don't know how you'll feel about this, maybe you wouldn't want to—the company is having this big cocktail party tonight, sort of a reception for the French government people, some of the embassy crowd. Jo will be going and we thought maybe you'd like to—you know, meet some of the people."

Torn by dilemma, she hesitated, trying to weigh the agony of acceptance against the danger of refusal. Almost thinking aloud she said, "I'd like to, Rolfe, I'd like to very much, but I don't think I should—"

"I know—Miss Jessica," he supplied a shade too quickly. "I thought you'd probably feel that way." He looked at his watch again. "I'll be back this afternoon, whenever I get a break. I guess you'll be here."

"I imagine so," she said, forcing a smile. "It's been good to hear about all your plans, Rolfe. I hope everything works out the way you want it to."

His eyes searched her face. "You're not disappointed?"

"Of course not," she said, wanting him to leave now, uncertain how long she could sustain her composure.

She watched him as he went out the door, anticipating that something inside her would burst the moment he was out of sight. But she felt only the dullness of anticlimax, everything that Miss Jessica had told her confirmed, oppressed again by a feeling of frightening aloneness. She remembered now that she had been about to telephone Chris, but what she had planned to say had slipped away, and aimlessly filling an empty moment, she absentmindedly opened Daphy's letter.

Skimming, her interest at such a low ebb that she read without thinking, she was halfway down the page before a glimmer of understanding broke through. Her eyes cut back to the first sentence, struck then by something so powerful that her brain came to a dead stop, all capability of rational thought instantly lost. Responding only to an unreasoned impulse, she found herself out of the room and at the hall window that looked down on the courtyard, struggling with the catch, then pounding on the glass. Rolfe did not hear her. The car was already moving out through the gateposts.

She slumped against the window, pressing her hands to her head, trying to contain the rush of irrational thought that was pouring out from a brain that, suddenly bursting into activity, was now spinning out of control. She thought she heard Miss Jessica's voice, but she had been hearing it all morning, thinking that this was only another echo of yesterday until, too powerfully insistent to be denied, she heard: "What have you done?"

She wheeled to face Miss Jessica's accusing eyes, plainly expressing the belief that she had handled Rolfe badly. Kay started to give her the letter, an unconsidered gesture of self-defense, her hand abruptly stayed by a flash of reason. She took a deep mind-settling breath, slowly expelling it, finally saying, "Judd's had a heart attack."

For a moment it appeared that Miss Jessica had not heard, or if she had, that she had not comprehended. Then, as the slow-dawning resurrection of a long-forgotten truth, she saw the strength in Miss Jessica's face, a rock worn by a thousand batterings yet never changed at its core, immutable, infinitely sustaining.

"How much do you know?" Miss Jessica asked, a demand for facts, a rejection of emotionalism.

"Only what's in this letter from Daphy Ingalls. And she thought, of course, that I knew. Oh, why didn't they let me know! They could have——"

"When did it happen?"

"All I know—" She checked the letter again. "This was written Friday night. Daphy says, 'I'll stop at the hospital to see him on my way up to Cornell in the morning.' That must mean that he's—oh, I don't even know where he is. Friday night and he was in the hospital then. It must have happened on his way back from New York Thursday night. Oh God, why didn't they let me know?"

"You were on the ship."

"But they could have sent a radio message."

"Judd may have told them not to."

"But why would he—?" The question rebounded from hard rock. Struck down, Kay asked, "What am I going to do?"

Miss Jessica's eyes were narrowed now, all-wise, infinitely seeing. Kay waited, prepared by memory for submission to a judgment that could not be questioned, a child again, anxious to be told what to do.

Slowly, Miss Jessica's head turned, a majestic movement. Her eyes stopped at the hall clock, paused for a moment, and then at the same slow pace, returned to Kay's face. "Had you thought of telephoning?"

Kay shook her head, feeling a fool because it had not occurred to her.

"That's what we'll do," Miss Jessica said with a gruff little snort of final decision. "But it's too early yet, only six-thirty over there. We'll have some coffee." She raised her hand, and as if it were the commanding of a miracle, Celia appeared from the dark shadows of the back hall, her face soberly knowing . . . Odette on that morning in 1939 when word had come that the American embassy was telling all United States citizens that all protection was at an end, that if they remained in France it would have to be at their own risk . . .

« 2 »

For many years, long enough so that it had become a deeply ingrained habit, Judd Wilder had awakened to instant consciousness of the day that lay ahead of him. It was then, in the moment before he flung aside the bedclothing, that he had habitually set in motion the mental process that he always thought of as planning his day's activity. More accurately, it was a ceremony of arousal, the ritual of a warrior about to go into battle, the buckling on of his armor and the hefting of his sword, a revival of the martial spirit, a quickening of the blood, all done to induce the rise of courage and a sharpened appetite for combat.

Although he had stopped far short of that endpoint this morning, he had awakened to find his mind occupied with thoughts of the Crouch Carpet Company, a condition so normal that it seemed a phenomenon of recovery. Although he rather quickly assured himself that thinking about the company was temporarily pointless, his mind pursued the prickly consciousness that Allen Talbott had never returned his call. He was sure now that it was no oversight. More and more frequently of late, Talbott had been pulling similar tricks, edging as closely as he dared to open insubordination, blunting criticism by coolly maintaining that he had simply forgotten, but always with a supercilious little smirk that revealed the smallness of the man that, disappointingly, he had turned out to be.

At the time that he had hired him, Talbott had appeared exactly the man he had been looking for, someone who could take over most of the creative work on the field promotions, and eventually shoulder at least some of the burden of putting on conventions. His record had been good—Triangle Club at Princeton, three years with Conventioneers Inc., another three years of Madison Avenue with a heavy emphasis on sales promotion—but like so many of the men who had come and gone before him, failing to fulfill their promise, Allen did not have what it really took. He had ideas, occasionally a good one, but he always faltered on the follow-through. His real trouble was that he was essentially lazy, unwilling to drive himself into that last gut-twisting effort that you had to put out if you were to achieve the sheen and glow that a finished job had to have. Talbott knew he wasn't cutting it—his attitude lately had been that of a man secretly looking for another job—and Judd had hoped, after getting home from the spring promotion tour and finding how Talbott had let things slide, that he would soon find one. Had it not been for the convention coming up, needing someone to keep the rest of the work in the shop moving, he would have eased

Talbott out then and there. Now, with the convention postponed until September, it was a different story. As soon as he got back on the job, he would start looking for a replacement, someone who would at least have the courtesy to return a telephone call.

At that point, Mary had arrived, divertingly bright, closing the door that had stood open during the night, shutting out the rest of the world. But when, a short hour later, the telephone rang, he instantly thought of Allen Talbott. Even before Mary could reach out to pick up the receiver, he was framing his response to Talbott's apology for not having called him back yesterday.

Anticipation collapsed as he heard Mary say, "Dr. Kharr? No, he isn't here. He should be before long—oh, wait, I believe—"

Judd glanced toward the opening door, catching the doctor's quick scowl as Mary said, "It's for you, Dr. Kharr."

"I know," he said impatiently. "Tell them I'll be down very shortly."

Twisting in bed, turning to face him, Judd's greeting was cut off by Mary's anxious, "It's a long distance call, Dr. Kharr—from Paris." And then, as if that were an inadequate expression of its supreme importance, she appended an awed "Paris, France."

Judd's eyes cut to the telephone, then back to the doctor's face, held there for a moment of shared comprehension, broken off when Dr. Kharr, with a curt nod of acceptance, walked around the end of the bed and took the instrument from Mary's outstretched hand.

"Dr. Kharr," he said, waiting then. It was a long wait, interminably extended before his blank expression finally came alive. "Oh yes, Mrs. Wilder . . . No, no, not at all, I'm very happy to . . . Of course . . . Yes, it was a coronary occlusion, but fortunately the infarct is a relatively small one . . . Yes, he's coming along in fine shape, a very satisfactory recovery . . . No, nothing like that . . . I really wouldn't know what to say about that, Mrs. Wilder, but here—I'm taking this call in his room—I'll put him on."

With no more warning than that, Dr. Kharr thrust the telephone toward him, confrontation so sudden that it took a moment to gather enough strength to lift the instrument to his ear. Then, with a surge of willed effort, he caught a strengthening breath and loosed a strong "Hi!"—a pitch-pipe note of confident well-being, a hopeful attempt to block an outpouring of Kay's distraught anxiety.

"Oh, Judd, why didn't you let me know?" burst in his ear, so close at hand that there was a distinct sense of actual physical presence, an intrusion so real that it seemed that Kay was standing at the foot of the bed, accusing him as she had so often done before of having failed to tell her something that she should have known.

"I wrote you," he said, weakly defensive, but her voice overran his, telling him what a horrible morning she had had, knowing nothing but what little there had been in a letter from Daphy Ingalls, not even knowing what hospital he was in, forced to wait until she could call New Ulster to find out where he was. Finally out of breath, she gave him a chance to repeat that he had written her a letter, concluding, "If you don't have it yet, you ought to get it today."

"Oh, I suppose it's because of—" Kay's voice lapsed, a strange hesitation followed by "I'm staying out at Miss Jessica's," her tone suggesting that it was somehow an explanation.

"How is she?" he asked.

"Yes, she's right here," Kay said, a puzzling reply until he realized that she was telling him that she could not talk about her.

"How's Rolfe?"

Again there was a strange hesitation, only partly canceled by a quick "Oh, he's fine," obviously another evasion.

"Is he there, too?" he guessed.

"No, he came out this morning—that's how I got Daphy's letter —I don't know where he is now. We've been calling, trying to get in touch with him. I didn't read Daphy's letter until after he'd gone, so he still doesn't know."

"Know what?" he asked, a perverse response to the realization that she still had not directed a single question to him, not even asking how he was feeling.

"About you," she said, adding then, "Are you really all right?" but now it was a prompted question, discounting the validity of her concern.

"Sure, I'm fine," he said, brassily offhand. "Why not?" glancing toward Dr. Kharr, seeing now that he was standing at the window, looking out, his pretense that he was hearing nothing denied by the rigid immobility of his stance, even more positively by the fleeting side glance that came when he said, "It's nothing serious, Kay. Don't worry about it. By the time you get back, I'll be——"

"That's what I want to talk to you about, Judd," she interrupted.

"I haven't checked the planes yet, but I'm sure I can get one——"

"Don't be ridiculous," he cut her off. "You're not coming back because of this. Why should you?" He had reacted to a faster-than-thought sense of alarm, its meaning inadmissible, escaped now by marshaling the support of reason. "There's absolutely no need for you to come back. You'd have to drive back and forth from New Ulster, forty miles up, forty miles back, and there wouldn't be a thing you could do when you got here. There's nothing to worry about—I'm feeling fine, I've got a nice room, wonderful nurses, if I want anything all I have to do is ask for it. I mean it, Kay, it would be silly for you to come rushing back."

There was dead air, only the sound of the line, until she finally asked, "How long will you be there?"

"Oh, quite a while," he said, gratified that he had convinced her, yet oddly disappointed that it had been so easy. "I don't know yet how long it will be, at least ten days, probably two weeks. I'll write you as soon as I know. Or call you. You can get back in a few hours. You won't have any trouble getting a plane reservation, not west-bound."

"No, I don't suppose so, not this time of year," she said, a faraway tone that, for the first time, suggested the distance that separated them.

"And don't worry. I'm fine. Just having a good rest, that's all. They've postponed the convention until September, so I don't even have that to worry about."

"Well, if you don't need me—" Her voice hung suspended, half a world away.

"I don't need a thing," he said, aware now that Mary had dropped her pretense of tidying up the bathroom, her head turned to watch him through the open doorway. Almost more for her benefit than Kay's he said, "I couldn't be happier."

Again there was dead air, pulsating now with an electronic hum, a wavering sound that so distorted Kay's voice that he could hardly hear what she was saying, something about letting her know when he was coming home.

"As soon as I know," he promised, projecting his voice over the screening noise, pressed now by a sense of elapsed time. "Give my best to Miss Jessica, and tell Rolfe——"

Again her voice was muffled, something missed, but "Take care of yourself, Judd," came through clearly, and then "Goodbye, dear," clipped off by a loud click, the connection broken.

Mary hurried in to lift the receiver from his hand. He released it, closing his eyes, seeing Kay at the rail of the ship . . . *Take care of yourself, Judd . . .*"

« 3 »

Kay Wilder's hand still rested on the telephone, delaying the moment when she would have to look up and face Miss Jessica. Her aunt had turned to the window after the call had gone through, a pantomime of courteous withdrawal, but she had clearly heard every word, and no less certainly drawn her own conclusions.

"Well?"

It was an irresistible command. Kay lifted her eyes. Miss Jessica stood before her, looking down with that truth-demanding expression that had always made deception impossible.

"Apparently it's not too bad," she said, feeling almost as if it were an evasion.

"But it was a heart attack?"

"Yes."

"What did the doctor tell you?"

"He didn't seem to be at all worried," she said. "And neither did Judd."

"So you're not going back?"

"He doesn't want me to," she replied, unaware until she heard herself say it that she had revealed more than weakness. Alarm gave her courage. "He said that it would be ridiculous for me to come flying back when there wasn't a thing in the world that I could do for him."

Miss Jessica's gaunt face was heavily clouded, an expression of frightening disapproval.

Kay rose quickly, turning away. "Oh, I don't know what to do. If I go back—he says he's got everything he wants—it won't mean a thing to him."

"But you know what it will mean if you don't," Miss Jessica said brusquely, emphatically demanding, "Don't you?"

Kay held her tongue, fighting off an impulse to confession, saved from breaking down only by the prohibition of Miss Jessica's too-easily imagined reaction. But she did not anticipate that silence, too, had its dangers, realized when she heard, "I was right yesterday, wasn't I?"

"About what?"

"You and Judd," she said, her voice unaccountably soft, almost sympathetic. "You were running away, weren't you?"

She attempted denial, but her voice broke, a betrayal that left her with nothing to say but "If I was, I didn't realize it."

"Did Judd?"

For a blank moment it was an innocuous question, meaningless until a bomb-burst of realization exploded, leaving her staggered and reeling. "Oh, God, you're not blaming me for—but you are, aren't you?" She had something to fight against now. "It's not true. It couldn't be. Nothing that I've ever done has meant enough to Judd to—"

Unbelievably, Miss Jessica's arm was about her shoulder, and in a voice that Kay had never heard before, she was murmuring a softly comforting denial that she had even thought of blaming her. "These things happen—that's the way life is—and when they do, we have to make the best of them."

Kay clung to her, her face buried in Miss Jessica's shoulder, trying to think of the future. But the past prevailed, invoked by the un-nameable scent that, never more than faintly perceptible in Kay's youth, had always been a part of Miss Jessica's aura, too uniquely distinctive to be anything that could ever have been purchased in a shop, an exotic perfume that, like her clothes, was a completely appropriate contradiction of character, the essence of her being—and never, it seemed, had she been more of a source of strength than at this moment. Clinging to her, thinking without thought, Kay waited for her to speak, hungering for the sympathy and understanding that it seemed she had been waiting for all of her life.

A sigh alerted her, every nerve end tingling with anticipation. Then, shatteringly, she heard: "You'll have to be careful with Rolfe —this is going to hit him hard."

« *4* »

All through the day, Judd Wilder's thoughts had again and again been forced back to Kay's telephone call. When he had hung up, he had thought it a closed incident, something that he would not have to think about again until he was ready to leave the hospital. What he had not anticipated was the celebrity that the call had given him. Heart cases were common at County Memorial, poor grist for the gossip mill, but never before in the hospital's history had a patient received a telephone call from Paris, France.

Mary, after a brief foray down the corridor, had reported that everyone was talking about it. The hunchbacked old janitor, who had never before looked up from his swishing mop, had greeted him this morning with gleeful recognition and a moronic cackle about a man not being able to get away from his wife, no matter how far away he sent her. At lunchtime, the girl on the cart, instead of knocking and waiting for Mary to come out for his tray, edged her way into the room, accosting him with a giggled "You're the one that got a call from his wife in Paris, France, ain't you?" He had no more than finished his lunch when a man with MARTY'S TV on the back of his white coveralls came in to install a television set, insistently offering a detailed explanation of all the electronics that were involved in transatlantic telephone communication.

Not surprisingly, Mrs. Cope knew all about it before she came on duty at three o'clock. Once again, he had to go over the same ground, explaining to her as he had to Mary that there was no reason why his wife should come home before he was ready to leave the hospital. But Mrs. Cope was not Mary, and his explanation left her still looking down at him, hands on hips. Thus challenged, his arguments seemed to lose their force. Perhaps it was no more than the erosion of repetition, a dulling of first effectiveness, yet as the afternoon drifted along there was a growing consciousness that Kay had been disturbingly easy to convince.

He had recognized from the beginning, of course, why she had wanted to go to Paris. Miss Jessica's birthday had been a subterfuge, an excuse no more legitimate than that out-of-the-blue offer of a

Mount Desert cottage had been. It was the same old story, Kay following Rolfe to Paris just as she had followed him to Maine. He had been disappointed, having hoped that Maine had taught her a lesson, yet he had said nothing, accepting the pointlessness of trying to influence her, not only because she was so innately resistant to changing her mind, but also because, as the years had gone by, one subject after another had been eliminated from the area of comfortable discussion. Never since that night when she had unexpectedly come home from Maine, had there been more than surface talk of Rolfe, perhaps because she could not forget her embarrassing loss of self-control, more likely because she did not want to create a situation in which she might be forced to admit that her son was infinitely more important to her than her husband. This truth Judd Wilder had acknowledged—it could hardly be missed—and he could not now escape thinking how different the situation would be if it were Rolfe who was here in this hospital bed. Unquestionably, regardless of any argument that might have been advanced, Kay would already be on a homebound plane.

But this awareness had come and gone, drifting across his mind as another cloud in a broken sky. Like most of his thoughts about Kay, it was no more than a brief perception of something that usually lay well below the level of consciousness. Nevertheless, there was this feeling that he had been thinking of her all day long, positive enough so that he made a conscious effort to put her out of his mind. Television was no help, the only receivable program a soap opera. He tried reading, but found it hard to concentrate. A half-dozen times he started conversations with Mrs. Cope, only to have her dead-end them by coming back to Kay again—or if it wasn't Kay, it was Rolfe.

When the afternoon mail arrived, he greeted it with eager anticipation, only to find there was nothing in it of any interest, not even a get-well card. But there was a New Ulster paper today, and as he scanned the first page CROUCH CARPET leaped out at him, for an instant only the name, the full impact delayed until he read the complete headline:

CROUCH CARPET SALES PARLEY
TO BE HELD ON CRUISE SHIP

Blinking, he stared at the black type, waiting as if expecting a burst of pain, but his mind seemed chilled into insensitivity. Coldly, he read the story under the headline.

Telegrams were dispatched today to Crouch Carpet contractors and representatives all over the country announcing a change in plan for the company's annual sales convention. Instead of being held in New Ulster, as it has been for many years past, the parley will be held this year on a cruise to the Bahamas.

"Not only will the ship-board setting be an aid to more effective deliberation," says Warren P. Locke, Vice President for Sales, "but also the atmosphere will be conducive to a furthering of that intimate personal relationship which has always been such an important factor in the building of our distribution system."

The convention will be held on the M.S. *Holiday*, a luxury cruise ship on the Caribbean run during the winter season. Since it does not begin its summer cruises until June, the company was able to arrange a special sailing. Crouch officials expressed themselves as being particularly gratified at the ship's facilities, thus making it possible to invite more guests than could previously be accommodated in New Ulster.

The ship will sail from New York on Sunday, May 16, and return on the following Saturday. Two nights will be spent at Nassau, and according to Allen Talbott, Assistant Director of Advertising and Sales Promotion, under whose direction all plans are being made, a full program of sight-seeing and shore-side entertainment will be provided in addition to the convention sessions.

The automatic response of disbelief sent his eyes back to the start of the story, but he reread no more than the lead paragraph. What challenged credibility was not the story itself—there was no temptation to question a single detail, let alone its overall authenticity—what defied comprehension was the duplicity of the plot that had been set up to deceive him. He knew now why Allen Talbott had not returned his call, but that was no more than a straw in the powerful wind that swept everything before it, a hurricane blast, ripping and tearing, stripping away the covering of pretense, exposing the fox-sharp face of Dr. Aaron Kharr, cunning eyes glinting behind those masking spectacles, hearing again the voice that had said the convention was postponed . . . *"That's what Mr. Crouch told me to tell you . . ."*

"Who's a bastard?"

Shocked, he looked up into Mrs. Cope's face, realizing that she was questioning a curse so automatic that he had been unconscious of even thinking it, let alone of having uttered it aloud. He cut his eyes away, a movement so powerfully motivated that it twisted his shoulders in a muscle-wrenching spasm, his lips torn apart by a gasping cry, an instantaneous reaction to a stab of pain.

Instantly, he felt the clutch of terror, an iron-banded constriction of his chest against which it seemed he could not breathe, the consequences so terrifying that he dared not attempt it.

« 5 »

This was, as Aaron Kharr had now been reminded by coincidence, the end of his first week on the Wilder case. He had been at his typewriter starting a new chapter—last night's talk with Wilder had been a compelling inspiration—three pages completed and a fourth half done, when the paging call had come.

"Dr. Raggi wants you in Emergency," Mrs. Potts's voice had said over the telephone, precise repetition a reminder of last Thursday night, made even more vivid as, needlessly checking the schedule under the glass top of his desk, he saw that this was again Dr. Harmon Teeter's day of duty. Striding down the corridor toward Emergency, he had wondered what excuse Teeter would concoct to explain his absence today, yet the temptation to rancor was mild, balanced by the realization of how fortunate it had been that Teeter had not been on the job last Thursday. Had he been, Kharr would never have taken over the Wilder case himself, and without the revealing experience of this past week, he could never have summoned the conviction with which he was now driving ahead on his book.

Again as a reminder of last Thursday night, Raggi was waiting for him at the door, admission card in hand. But here coincidence ended. The card, hastily scanned, described one ENRICO VALDES, MALE, WHITE, 56, AGRICULTURAL WORKER, complaining of severe abdominal pain. In the upper left-hand corner there were two flagging checkmarks, a double warning that the subject was both unemployed and uninsured.

"Have you called Dr. Teeter?"

"Yes sir. He will be coming as soon as it is possible, he says."

"Did you describe the patient?" he asked with a gesturing glance at the card.

Raggi hesitated, the question half-answered by the hint of a smirk. "No sir. I am only saying it is a turnpike case."

They were through the door now, in the entrance vestibule of the little suite. Through the open doorway of the examining room he saw the patient sitting up on the table, bent almost double, his arms wrapping his belly as if he were attempting to contain the wild demon that was tearing at his guts.

"You've examined him?"

"Yes, sir," Raggi said, swallowing, clearing his throat. "I would suggest hepatitis, sir, possibly complicated by a gastrointestinal involvement. If you are concurring, sir, would you not think it advisable to begin—"

"Well, let's see whether or not I'm concurring," he cut him off, an attempt at lighthearted mimicry that he would not have made had he been less concerned. He started toward the patient, his eyes already beginning their examination, the man's jaundiced skin color not only confirming Raggi's diagnosis, but also the dimension of the problem that faced him. During his first month at County Memorial he had admitted an indigent patient, unknowingly committing a tactical error of the first magnitude. Despite the hospital's status as a publicly supported community institution, and notwithstanding the straight-faced claim that charity cases justified the size of its annual fund-raising goal, it was rare indeed for any uninsured patient with no visible means of paying his doctor to penetrate the defenses against admission that the staff had erected. In this one regard, at least, County Memorial was a highly efficient institution. The standard maneuver, practiced with a dozen subtle variations, was to claim a lack of facilities, assuring the patient that Marathon General was much better equipped to take care of him, charity confined to a magnanimously free twenty-two-mile ride in County Memorial's ambulance.

For ten minutes, Aaron Kharr examined the patient, aided by the smattering of Spanish that he had picked up in New York. The conclusion was inescapable that this man should be hospitalized at once—in the state he was in, a long ambulance ride would be an unjustifiable gamble—but once he was admitted he would be un-ejectable, there for at least a month, piling up a bill that would never be paid, demanding time and attention that no doctor on the staff would willingly give, least of all Harmon Teeter. Suppressing anger rooted in indignation, Aaron Kharr continued his examination, telling himself that his own responsibility was limited to emergency treatment, the major decision out of his hands, his ear cocked for the sound of the opening door that would announce Teeter's arrival. It came sooner than he really expected it.

Turning back to the open doorway, he saw that Raggi had already given Teeter the card. Watching him as he read, he saw Teeter's moon-face collapse like a punctured balloon, the air hissing out with an asthmatic wheeze. As an act of annoyed rejection, Teeter flipped the card at Raggi's hand, paying no attention as it missed and fluttered to the floor. Almost as an involuntary act, he glanced at the doorway of the examining room, blinking his surprise, a slow inhalation inflating the balloon again, forming a distinctly humorless smile. "Doctor," he said, his little bow an elaborate forgery of respect. "How nice of you to have me called."

"Dr. Raggi called you," Aaron Kharr said, a chill response to crude sarcasm. He stepped aside, clearing the door.

Teeter glanced in, but made no move to enter. "Apparently, Doctor, you've not found this a case of such unusual medical interest that you're justified in taking it on yourself."

Aaron Kharr recoiled, every muscle in his body tensed for counterattack, restrained only by a whiff of Teeter's breath, a cautioning reminder that he must be drunk. In that instant of hesitation, the squawk box over his head burst into life with a raucous "Dr. Kharr, Dr. Kharr—call blue, call blue."

It was the emergency code and he snatched at the telephone, stunned as he heard: "Mrs. Cope wants you right away."

Never had that corridor seemed so long, never that short flight of stairs so endlessly high. It took him no more than two minutes to reach Wilder's room, yet never had so short a time been so terrifyingly extended. In any coronary infarction case, there was always the threat of a sudden and unanticipatible heart failure. No matter how well a patient seemed to be coming along, no matter how good the signs were, there were these freak cases where tragedy struck out of a clear sky. Statistically, the incidence was very low, yet it had always been the shibboleth of his opposition, the prime reason why his ideas on rehabilitation had found so little acceptance. The vast majority of cardiologists still routinely imposed three weeks of immobilization and heavy sedation, unmindful of the damage they were doing, concerned only with that odd case where, if they had made any move toward emotional rehabilitation before the ninth day, particularly if they had let the patient out of bed, blame might fall upon them. The nine-day rule was as endlessly preached to young doctors as if it were some magic incantation against evil. Whatever else it was, it was sure protection against professional censure.

Less than an hour ago, starting a new chapter for his book, Aaron Kharr had launched his newest attack against this "self-serving ultra-conservatism," specifically citing a patently ridiculous application of the ninth-day rule from Sippleton's book, and now, as he hurried down the corridor, he felt as if he were being driven to punishment for having defied the gods, false though they were, who still ruled the medical profession. He was very close to something that he had never experienced before, a sense of impending defeat so total that there was no responding urge to fight back against it, a hopelessness so consuming that he failed to interpret the significance of Mrs. Cope's calming gesture as, waiting for him in the corridor, her other hand on the doorknob, she stopped his rushing progress with a raised hand. Even when she said, "I'm sorry, Doctor, it was just a false alarm," he could not slow the racing of his heart, impelled to push past her through the door, stopped by her quietly insistent "Before you go in, you ought to know what happened."

A new fear stormed up out of the look on her face, given substance as she asked only, "Do you remember that first night, his worrying about this convention he was supposed to be putting on?"

"Yes, of course. But it was postponed——"

"Did you tell him that?"

"Of course, Mr. Crouch asked me to. He said——"

"Whatever he said, they're having it, anyway." She paused, measuring his reaction. "It's in the New Ulster paper that he just got. That's when it hit him—when he saw it. The first thing I knew he was grabbing for his chest, breathing hard. I guess I was a little panicked, but you never know. And it's still only the seventh day——"

"I know," he cut her off, trying to calm himself. "But he's all right now? You're sure?"

"The pain was gone before I got back from calling you," she said. "I went out to use the hall phone because I didn't want to scare him——"

"No, of course not," he said, reaching out for the door.

Mrs. Cope's arm still blocked the way. "What I wanted to tell you —this is what I thought you ought to know before you see him— he's blaming you."

"Blaming me? For what?"

"Telling him that they would wait until he got back to put on this convention."

He felt staggered, as if he had been struck a blow beyond endurance, all the more disabling because it was foul. Recovery was slow, the thought that he could easily enough prove his innocence a weak rebuttal to this evidence that all he had done to gain Wilder's faith and confidence had gone for nothing. At the first challenge, Wilder had refused to accept his integrity.

"Maybe the thing to do is just let him simmer down a little," Mrs. Cope suggested. "Not see him until later."

Psychologically, it was both good advice and a welcome prospect; medically, it was too great a risk. He shook his head. Mrs. Cope opened the door, glanced in, and stepped aside.

Wilder was lying on his side, his back to the door. Aaron Kharr walked up to the bedside, announcing his presence with a firm greeting. For a moment, there was no response. Then, without turning his body, Wilder glanced back over his shoulder.

"I've a suggestion for your book, Doctor."

"Yes?"

"You should include a warning," Wilder said. "When you're practicing all these clever deceptions to assure the patient—be careful —don't get caught."

Tautly, Aaron Kharr said, "I've practiced no deception on you, Mr. Wilder."

"No?" Wilder half turned now, fixing him with a sardonic smile. He reached for the newspaper that lay across his knees, lifted it, stabbed a marking finger at a headline, and flung the paper at him. It missed the edge of the bed and fell to the floor. Aaron Kharr bent to retrieve it. When he stood up, Wilder was on his side again, his face turned away.

Aaron Kharr found the headline and read the story. It occurred to him to argue that this could be only a substitute junket, a holding action to stall for time until Judd Wilder was back on the job again, but he stopped well short of that error, aware that any attempt to explain or justify would surely be taken as admission of his original guilt. Wilder had to be made to realize that if there had been deception it had been practiced not by him but by Mr. Crouch, his own role only that of an innocent message-bearer. "All I did, Mr. Wilder, was to repeat the message that Mr. Crouch asked me to give you."

Wilder shot a glance back over his shoulder, a silent response, but no words could have more eloquently expressed his total rejection of the idea that Mr. Crouch could possibly have deceived him.

Almost instantly, Aaron Kharr saw the measure of his dilemma. Simple justice demanded that the blame be lifted from him and placed on Crouch, yet if he were to make himself the instrument of that disillusioning revelation, he would be responsible for destroying the one thing upon which Judd Wilder's recovery so surely depended: his sustaining confidence in the Crouch Carpet Company, and above all else, his personal faith in Matthew R. Crouch. If there was any explanation—and for Wilder's sake, there had to be—Crouch himself would have to offer it.

He looked up at the clock, checking the hour, wondering if Matthew R. Crouch could still be reached in his office. The thought crossed his mind that the president had not called him since last Saturday, an abrupt abandonment in odd contrast with his intense concern the previous morning, yet until this moment it had not seemed unusual, the more or less expected response of a busy man who, once alarm was banished, felt his obligation fulfilled. Now, there was a chilling suspicion that something more lay behind that silence.

« 6 »

Not a word had been spoken since Dr. Kharr had left the room. As a boy, Judd Wilder had been taught the language of silent disapproval by Mrs. Gorman, and like something learned in youth and never forgotten, the grimly maintained pace of Mrs. Cope's knitting needles was an unrelenting demand for apology. Now, no longer able to resist, responding precisely as he would have done to a spoken accusation, he said, "All right, I was wrong."

Mrs. Cope made no saving pretense of not understanding. "You were very unfair to him."

"I know it."

"He didn't lie to you." Her knitting needles were still flashing. "He would never lie to anyone. If he said that he was only repeating what someone else had told him, it was true."

He started to again say that he knew it, stopped by the difficulty of believing that it was Mr. Crouch who had betrayed him. There were times, of course, when Mr. Crouch impetuously said something that he didn't really mean, something that he didn't expect you to take seriously . . . but it couldn't have been that . . . no, not about anything as important as postponing the convention . . . he must have meant it . . . something had happened afterwards . . .

"Don't you think—" he heard, only that and no more, whatever else Mrs. Cope said blanked out by an ear-blocking burst of awareness. All he could hear was Roger Stark's voice . . . *"I have no doubt that this type of convention was effective enough back in those years when the company's prime necessity was the development of effective contract outlets, but in the light of our current situation and market position, is it not reasonable to at least question . . ."*

That was the point where Mr. Crouch had cut Stark down. But now there was only silence. "That bastard," he said under his breath, low-voiced enough so that this time Mrs. Cope did not hear him.

But the click of her knitting needles had stopped. He stole a glance. She was getting up from her chair. "All right, turn over," she forgave him. "I'll rub your back."

◇ IX ◇

THIS WAS THE DAY of Aaron Kharr's meeting at Baltimore. His original plan had been to spend the first half of the morning at the hospital, leaving about ten o'clock. Up early after a bad night, a change of plan had suddenly thrust itself upon him, incited by the awakening thought that he had still not reached Mr. Crouch. He had called too late yesterday afternoon to catch him at his office, and when he had later telephoned his home, the maid had told him that Mr. and Mrs. Crouch were out for the evening and would not return until late. He had decided then to call him the first thing this morning, but after what he had gone through during the night—attempting to compose what he would say to Crouch had been the prime cause of his sleeplessness—it occurred to him that it would be easily possible, and much more desirable, to talk to him face to face. By starting early, and driving not too far out of his way, he could make a stop in New Ulster. If he left at once, he could be at the Crouch Carpet offices as soon as they were open.

Dressing hurriedly, tiptoeing out of the house so that Mrs. Stine would not hear him leave, he drove to the hospital. Fortunately, Raggi was already there, more than willing to take over and follow through on the few things that he had intended to do himself, hesitant only when he had been asked to make a morning and afternoon check on the Wilder case. This show of resistance, mild though it was, and clearly occasioned by Raggi's unsuccessful attempt to talk to Wilder earlier in the week, nevertheless slowed Aaron Kharr's pell-mell rush. He saw then that Wilder might easily misinterpret his nonappearance. "All right, I'll see him for a minute right now—explain it all," he agreed. "And then you stop by a little later."

With his coat and hat on, briefcase in hand, he started down the corridor. Mary Welch was at the floor desk. Her patient was fine this morning, she said, and when he told her that he had to leave town and that Dr. Raggi would be seeing Wilder this morning, she promised that she would explain everything to him. With a concluding "Tell him that I'll be back by dinnertime and will see him this evening," he dashed for the parking lot.

Reassuring though the nurse's report had been, and as reliable as he knew her to be, he nevertheless felt a twinge of guilt for not having seen Wilder and done something to soften the blow that the newspaper story had dealt him. But what could he have done? What could he have said? Crouch had broken his promise, there was no question about that, but that was water over the dam—the best that could be done now would be to get Crouch to assure Wilder that his position in the company was in no way endangered. That was all he would ask him to do, demanding nothing for himself, neither explanation nor apology, knowing that there could be no redress for the wrong that Crouch had done him personally, putting him in a position where his integrity had been questioned, laying him open to the charge of clever duplicity that was always being made against Jewish doctors. During the night, drawing upon the resources of a thousand insults survived, Aaron Kharr had convinced himself that this, too, was something that had to be endured, swallowed and forgotten.

As he got into his car, he checked his watch. New Ulster was forty-two miles away. On that trip he had made to Marathon, he had averaged thirty-two miles an hour over the road. It was not an easy problem in mental arithmetic, but by the time he reached the highway he had solved it. He would arrive in New Ulster at 9:02 A.M.

« 2 »

Judd Wilder was more relieved than concerned when Mary brought the news that Dr. Kharr would not be seeing him until evening. Apology was an unpleasant prospect, and by tonight the need for it would be washed away. And by then, too, he would be prepared

to make Kharr see that this convention business didn't mean a thing
. . . he had clipped Stark before, he could do it again . . .

"Dr. Raggi will be coming in to see you," he heard Mary say.

"Why?"

"Well, you know, just to check."

"Tell him to forget it."

"Oh, I can't do that."

"Why not? I'm all right."

"It won't hurt you to talk to him for a few minutes," Mary said,
her lips pursed in a petulant pout.

"Why bother?" he said wearily, beginning to be annoyed with her
little-girl behavior. If she was old enough to be a registered nurse
—yes, and pregnant, too—she was old enough to start acting her age.

"He'd appreciate it, I know he would. He's really awfully nice
and—well, I know he felt badly about your not wanting to talk to
him that other time."

"What other time?" he asked, but it was a question without force,
weakened by a vague recollection of having, sometime in the distant past, brushed off Raggi.

"I guess I'm just a sucker for lonely people," Mary said, her little
laugh apologetically contrite. "He's so far away from home, and
with nobody he can really talk to—well, that's the way he always
makes you feel."

"I haven't got anything to talk to him about."

"Oh, but you have. Weren't you in India once?"

"A long time ago."

"It would be like meeting somebody from home. I remember
when I was in training, there was this girl. She wasn't anybody special—I mean, nobody you'd ever pay any attention to, but she was
always so kind of sad and forlorn that I just couldn't help talking
to her. She was from Connellsville—you know, out by Pittsburgh—
and when I told her I'd been there once—well, just being able to
remember this motel where we'd stayed, and talking about this
place where we had dinner—it did her a world of good."

"All right, I'll talk to him," he said, no more than humoring a child
with a promise that was easier to make than resist, hoping that this
would be the end of it.

"I knew you would," she said, beaming, adding as if it were a reward for compliance, "and now I'll get you breakfast."

Buoyantly victorious, she swirled away toward the door, humming as she went out of the room. He sighed his relief, yet there was an instant sensing of emptiness, a vacuum that threatened to again fill his mind with thoughts of Crouch Carpet, forestalled as he forced himself to anticipate Raggi's appearance, trying to think what he could talk to him about . . . *India* . . .

Suddenly, as if it were a memory that had been waiting in the wings, cued to burst upon him at this precise moment, he was in the headquarters hut, searching the stateside mail for a confirmation of his order for two Eyemo cameras to replace the ones that had been lost in the jungle when Mike Findley had crashed, that one paragraph exploding upward from the carbon-smeared page . . .

That was how he had learned that the India-Burma picture had been canceled, leaving him angrily bewildered, hopelessly frustrated, traumatically aware of having paid an awful price for nothing, terrifyingly conscious of personal failure.

Nothing like that had ever happened to him before. Until then his life had been a succession of triumphs, one success building upon another. Ever since his high school days when he had blindly driven through the Centennial pageant and wound up in *Life* magazine, he had lived by a code that guaranteed success to the man who whipped himself hard enough, never let up, and never wasted time worrying about where it was getting him. At twenty-three, he was by all odds the youngest unit director in the entire Signal Corps, sent out to the China-Burma-India theater on an assignment that any of the Hollywood boys would have traded an Oscar for.

Of all the dramatic events that were taking place all around the globe in those early months of 1943, nothing was as certainly filmworthy as the airlift over the Hump that was keeping alive the freedom fight within China. Nothing was more vital to the total war effort, Huck Joyce had said, than getting a picture on theater screens all over the United States that would show the public why the China-Burma-India theater was so important. Congress, with a tunnel-vision eye on Europe, was wavering in its support, and without public pressure there was a serious danger that the whole C.B.I. operation might be allowed to collapse. If Huck had not been tied down by the big brass he would have gone out to make the picture himself—he had said exactly that—and when Judd had been given the assignment, he had felt himself driven not only by a sense of surpassing responsibility to the nation and the whole free world, but also by feeling that he was going out as Huck Joyce's alter ego.

He did not, of course, have the same authority that Huck would have had. He was directing a field unit, not the finished picture —the script was being written and the final editing done back at Astoria—but Huck had told him not to worry about that. "You get the right stuff in the can, Juddy boy, and it will edit itself. Remember that what you're making is a moving *picture* . . . forget the words, it's the picture that will tear their guts out . . . you feel it and they'll feel it too."

Huck's admonition had been more than a figure of speech. Quite literally, he had felt it in his guts, clawed at by dysentery bugs, knotted by unremitting tension, irritated by the never-ending frustration of bad weather, mud, inadequate facilities, lost equipment, choked-off supplies, operational foul-ups, and a lack of communication with Astoria that left him isolated at what was, literally, the most remote point on the globe.

He had lost eighteen pounds in two months, but not a day on the job until, riding a careening jeep, trying to get a close shot of a C-47 spraying mud as it came in for landing, he had been pitched off as if by a bucking horse. For a couple of terrifying hours the medics had thought his back broken, but it had turned out to be only four cracked ribs and some torn muscles. Three days later, his chest cocooned with yards of adhesive tape, he got the shot exactly the way he wanted it, so close to the plane that the curtain of flying mud gave him a beautifully natural fade-out.

After that he had done more and more of his own camera work. Selowski, who had come out with him from the States had turned into a goof-off, and Brinkman, the cameraman he had shanghaied from a news crew, was too emotional to take the pressure of flying the Hump. Anyway, being up there himself was the only way he could be certain of getting exactly what he wanted. After he started flying himself, he stopped losing weight. When he got a note from Sam Springer in Astoria—"That was some terrific footage on the plane going down and the guy parachuting"—his dysentery stopped bothering him.

After the first shock of the cancellation order wore off, he realized that he should long before have guessed that something was wrong. That informal note from Sam had been his last communication from Astoria, not a word about any of the film he was sending back, no comment on his pages and pages of shot-by-shot notes and suggestions for editing. Ultimately, he learned that Congress had come around without pressure from the public, and the propaganda boys, off on some new tangent, had simply forgotten the idea of a theater-release picture on flying the Hump.

As ordered, Judd reported to Calcutta for reassignment. There, wearing what he had been able to salvage out of his mildewed and jungle-rotted kit bag, he had sat across the desk from an immaculately uniformed Major Follett. In peacetime, Follett had been an efficiency analyst for a business management outfit that had made a study for NBC. His specialty, he said, was personnel. His method, demonstrated rather than explained, was transfusing hot-blooded movie-makers with the icewater that so plainly flowed through his own veins. Judd had gone in to see him as a high-flying young warrior, deeply hurt by being temporarily grounded but eager for a new battle. In ten minutes, Follett had degraded him from the youngest unit director in the Signal Corps to a kid who, in those early days of the war when personnel was so desperately inadequate, had unfortunately been given an assignment for which he had neither enough maturity nor experience. Judd had tried to fight back, getting nowhere. "I have only one way to judge any man—on his record," Follett had said, "and to put it frankly, Wilder, your record strikes me as being singularly lacking in tangible accomplishment. No doubt you did your best on the Hump picture, but that doesn't seem to have been enough, does it? But stand by, my boy, and we'll see if we can't turn up a spot that's a bit better suited to your capabilities."

He had stood by for five awful weeks, seemingly forgotten, checking in every morning with bloodshot eyes, reconvinced that there was no escape in synthetic Scotch whiskey or pointless carousing, yet knowing that he would try again that night. His dysentery came back worse than ever, eventually a blessing in disguise because it was through Lyons, the medical officer, that he met Follansbee, who somehow got him transferred to Agra. He was only an assistant director, the unit assignment no more than record coverage of the glider training operation, but at least it got him out from under Follett—and, eventually, out of India.

Although his experience in India was too deeply engraved ever to be truly forgotten, he had shut it out of his mind as effectively as he could, and that original resistance to reminiscence had remained, unreasoned but still persisting, broken down now only by the necessity of preparing himself to talk to Raggi. The memories of place and scene were fuzzily out of focus, sharp only as he found himself confronted again by Follett. But now, as if tricked by a quick lap dissolve, he realized that the face he was seeing was not Follett's but Roger Stark's . . . CROUCH CARPET SALES PARLEY TO BE HELD ON CRUISE SHIP . . .

« 3 »

Glimpsing a signpost—NEW ULSTER 9—Aaron Kharr glanced at his watch. His original calculation of arrival time was not working out at all. Preoccupied with what lay ahead of him, he had driven too fast, losing at least ten minutes that he badly needed to think through his approach to Crouch. He would stop somewhere for a cup of coffee . . . the president wouldn't be in his office this early, anyway . . .

But there were no roadside restaurants and the search served only to speed the remaining miles. Impossibly soon, he saw NEW ULSTER 2. Ahead, there was a traffic light—and seen too late, a diner. He was caught in the left lane, unable to make the turn. Edging to the right, he managed to slip into a break, a place no more than secured when he saw C R O U C H   C A R P E T, free-standing bronze letters on a broad stretch of parklike lawn. Reacting without thought, he turned into a long curving driveway, forced on then by honking horns behind him. An arrowed sign, ADMINISTRATION, identified the two-story building that he was approaching as the company's general offices. Behind it, seen at the outermost point of the drive's sweep, was a single-story building that went on and on, stretching back so far that the trucks at a distant loading platform appeared like toys. Pushed ahead by the traffic stream, he turned into a parking lot, cars cutting back and forth in front of him, a bewildering melee from which he was rescued by the opportune sighting of a vacant space marked VISITOR.

He turned the ignition key, cutting off the motor, but made no move to get out. Familiar though he had felt himself with the Crouch Carpet Company, he had not visualized anything so massive. Now, in hurried reappraisal, it was impossible to equate the president of this enormous company with that vulnerable little man who, only a week ago this morning, had come to him as a humble supplicant, begging him to take the Wilder case. Here on his home ground, Crouch would surely be a very different person, perhaps even refusing to see him, a possibility all the more credible as he saw himself walking in, unannounced and with no appointment, demanding an audience with Matthew R. Crouch.

Propelled by challenge, he got out of the car and strode across the parking lot. Pushing through the revolving door, he found himself suddenly short of breath. Stopped, attempting a deep inhalation, he felt the tight constriction of his chest muscles, an instantly recognized symptom of stress. He took it as a warning to stay calm, not to lose his temper no matter what happened, and walked forward to the reception desk. At the last instant he realized that, in his hurry to get away this morning, he had not picked up the packet of cards that he had had printed when he first came to County Memorial. Boldly, he bluffed it through. "I'm Dr. Aaron Kharr from County Memorial Hospital. I want to see Mr. Crouch."

He expected to be told that the president had not yet arrived, but the receptionist said, "Do you have an appointment?"

"No, but I'm sure he'll see me," he said, confidence overdone almost to the point of belligerence.

But it worked. She reached out for the telephone, dialed a three-digit number. "There's a Dr. Kharr here to see Mr. Crouch." She listened, nodding. "Yes, I think so." She looked up. "You did say County Memorial Hospital, didn't you, Dr. Kharr?"

"Right," he said brusquely, relieved by recognition, yet disconcerted by the rush of events, feeling himself too precipitately propelled toward something for which he was badly unprepared.

"If you'll go up those stairs and turn right, Dr. Kharr. Through the glass doors."

He climbed the staircase, racing his mind in an attempt to outrun an apprehension that he was about to make a fool of himself.

Through the glass doors he saw a reception lobby, luxuriously furnished but strangely sterile, windowless, dark-walled, claustrophobic. No one was in sight, nor did anyone appear as he stepped inside. There were several doors, all closed. He walked to the center table, oppressed by silence, even the sound of his footsteps lost in the deep-piled carpet. None of the chairs looked as if anyone had ever sat in them. He waited. A latch clicked. He wheeled. A man stood in an open doorway. The contrast with expectation could hardly have been more complete or disconcerting. Instead of Crouch, the little supercharged bull terrier that he had prepared himself to face, this man was as hound-thin as a Borzoi, posed in the doorway as if he were about to enter a show ring, transparently conscious of self-exhibition. As if satisfied that his intended impression had been made, the man stepped forward. "Dr. Kharr? I'm Roger Stark."

Aaron Kharr took the proffered hand, but his grip was tentative and uncertain, all strength lost as he heard "Unfortunately you just missed Mr. Crouch—he left for Philadelphia not more than five minutes ago—but do come in, Doctor." Stark smiled then, but as if it were an afterthought, too late to be meaningful.

Although the name *Roger Stark* had a vaguely familiar ring, whatever it was that Aaron Kharr had heard about him had not fixed his position in the Crouch Carpet Company, nor preformed any image of the man himself. This first glimpse, however, was more telling than any prior description. Almost instantly, he saw Stark as another pressing from that newly fashionable mold in which, as he had come to realize during his years at the Allison Clinic, more and more corporation executives were now being cast. John Homer, one of his colleagues at the Clinic, had characterized the type when he had once described an examinee by saying, "Twenty years ago he would have been perched on a bookkeeper's stool wearing a green eyeshade, but now that the number-jugglers have inherited the earth he's a member of the new aristocracy."

Once observed, the behavior pattern of these new patricians was as readily recognizable as their three-hundred-dollar custom-tailored suits, their British boots and their star sapphires. A rather high percentage were Harvard Business—that institution, it seemed, was the Mecca of this new cult of number-jugglers—but whatever the molding influence, the resulting personality was remarkably stereotyped. A man could, if necessary, get by with a degree from a less prestigious institution, but he was lost without a controllably expressionless face. The ultimate betrayal of stature, it seemed, was to lose your cool, the slightest show of emotion impossibly gauche. Under any and all circumstances, it was essential to maintain an appearance of mildly cynical detachment, proclaiming a position apart, a complete lack of personal involvement with either your associates or the company which, as a professional corporate manager, you were currently serving. It was this emphasis on *professionalism*, so frequently vocalized, that had prompted Aaron Kharr to equate these new-model corporation executives with some of the medical men he had known, specialists who had parlayed a frozen face and an aristocratic manner into fame and fortune. With that association established, he felt himself better able to understand them—and equally given to a compulsion toward deflation.

A common vulnerability, he had found, was a pretension of culture, usually evidenced by a collection of modern art—suitably emotion-free and noncommunicative, of course—and it was this thought that struck him as he stepped across the threshold into a room that seemed more museum than office. The atmosphere was in complete contrast to the lobby, ice after fire, chillingly austere, the walls colorless except for the paintings that hung upon them. It was a wildly disparate collection, telling him nothing about the man who had assembled it—except, perhaps, that his purchases had been directed by a computer study of auction prices.

Guided by the touch of Stark's fingertips on his elbow, he found his way to a chair, feeling himself uncomfortably patronized. Reacting as he always did to the threat of being made to feel an inferior, he mentally stripped Stark of his three-hundred-dollar suit, quickly reducing him to no more than another patient in his examining room, nakedly unimpressive, a figure so skeletally thin that it suggested a man self-controlled enough to resist the pleasures of eating, or as a more likely possibility, one who had so distorted all natural desires that he was no longer capable of feeling any hunger except that for money and power.

"Mr. Crouch will be disappointed to have missed you," Stark said, moving around to the chair behind his desk, an exact duplicate of the plywood-and-black-leather creation that Harvey Allison, always sensitive to his clients' newest standards of status, had acquired as his throne.

"I only stopped by for a minute or two," Aaron Kharr said, sidestepping the danger of being put off by initial flattery, remembering that this was a commonly employed professional gambit. "I'm on my way to a meeting in Baltimore."

"Delighted," Stark said obliquely, seating himself with studied grace. "This is something of a coincidence, Doctor, your turning up like this. Only last evening, I was wondering if it might not be possible to have a little chat with you." He lounged back, casually explaining, "Mr. Crouch was good enough to pass along one of your papers. Very interesting."

He murmured an acknowledgment, looking at his watch, setting up an excuse for quick escape.

Stark turned sideways to his desk, lifting a British boot to the leather-upholstered footstool that matched his chair. "You're quite convinced, I take it, that emotional stress is a primary cause of heart attacks?"

"All the evidence points in that direction," he said with crisp finality, hoping to cut it off right there . . . he had missed Crouch, the best thing to do was get out of here as fast as he could . . . but he felt himself forced to add, "at least in these under-fifty cases."

"It must give you a great sense of accomplishment, Doctor, taking a man who's still in the prime of life, and bringing him safely through an experience that often proves so personally destructive."

"Yes, a heart attack can be highly traumatic."

"The essence of your approach, I take it, is to isolate the cause of stress?"

"More or less," he said, uncomfortable. "At least that's the starting point."

Stark lifted his other foot to the stool, crossing his legs at the ankles. "If you've been following the procedure outlined in your paper—I'm assuming that you have—I'd be much interested, Doctor, in your assessment of Judd Wilder."

Aaron Kharr stiffened, pointedly unresponsive.

His silence drew a glance from Stark, and then an oddly flickering smile. "If you're questioning the propriety of talking to me—I'm Vice President for Management, Doctor, with direct responsibility for all phases of our operation. Anything that concerns the company concerns me." The smile flickered again. "You can talk to me quite as freely as I'm sure you would to Mr. Crouch."

"I hadn't realized that Mr. Wilder had been working under your direction. I thought——"

"He's not been," Stark broke in, so quick a disclaimer that it could only be interpreted as a disavowal of responsibility. "No, he's been reporting to Mr. Crouch—nominally, at least. Organizationally illogical, I'll grant you, but up to now—as I'm sure you are aware. there was a long-standing personal relationship between Judd and Mr. Crouch that—well, it wasn't something easily swept under the rug. At least not by a new broom."

Again there had been that strange smile, off and on, and as if glimpsed in a lightning flash, Aaron Kharr saw the suddenly revealed possibility that it might be Stark who was responsible for the breaking of Crouch's promise.

"I'm sure that Judd has told you about his relationship with Mr. Crouch?" Stark ventured, a cautious betrayal of concern that seemed to wipe away all doubt of guilt.

Impulse drove Aaron Kharr toward instant accusation, but he curbed impatience, feeling a rise of confidence strong enough to support a more circuitous approach, half-consciously relishing the prospect of leading Stark on until, at the right moment, he could stick a sharp pin in his self-inflated image of the all-knowing corporate manager. Tentatively he put out, "Yes, relationships of that sort are extremely important—and nothing is more necessary to successful rehabilitation than the assurance that they can be relied upon."

"Quite so," Stark said, almost insolently knowing.

"It's not something to be lightly done, Mr. Stark—to destroy a man's faith in the integrity of a relationship of that sort."

"I'm sorry, Doctor, but your point eludes me."

"I believe you said that you were responsible for all of this company's operations."

"Substantially—yes."

"Then it was *your* decision to go ahead with a convention?" Plainly, Stark had been hit, and before he could recover, he struck him again: "Despite Mr. Crouch's promise that it would be postponed until Mr. Wilder was back on the job and able to take over."

Stark stared at him, silent, but his lips moved, forming the word *postponed*, not as a question but as an abstracted recognition of something overlooked. Slowly, he reached out for the squat little jade Buddha that he was using as a paperweight. "Are you quite certain, Doctor, that such a promise was actually made? I'm not doubting your word, of course, but there's always the possibility of a misunderstanding."

"There was no misunderstanding."

Head cocked, Stark studied the Buddha, the pose of a connoisseur, but his face was that of a man searching for the secret of poise. Apparently successful, he asked coolly, "When was this promise made, Doctor?"

"A week ago today."

"The morning after Judd's heart attack?"

"Yes."

"Am I correct in assuming that he was still under opiates?"

"Naturally."

"Under those circumstances is it not possible that Judd may have misinterpreted whatever Mr. Crouch told him?" Bolder, his voice noticeably strengthened, he went on, "Were you in the room, Doctor? Did you hear what Mr. Crouch actually said?"

He let him hang, making no response until it was clear that Stark was at the end of his rope. "He didn't talk to Mr. Wilder, he talked to me. He told me to tell him that he was not to worry about the convention, that it would be postponed until September."

Stark's hand went slack, the Buddha released. "And you reported that to Judd?"

"There was no reason not to—a promise from the president of his company—I had no cause to suspect that it wouldn't be honored."

Stark offered no response, grimly tight-lipped now.

"When I got that emergency call yesterday afternoon, and found out that you were going ahead regardless—frankly, it was difficult to believe. If I hadn't read it myself—"

"Read it?"

"Apparently you hadn't counted on Mr. Wilder having your local newspaper sent up."

No reaction was visible on Stark's face but his feet came off the footstool, hitting the floor with a carpet-deadened thud.

"At this stage of a coronary patient's recovery, Mr. Stark, when the myocardial infarct is still unhealed, there's nothing that we fear more than an unexpected emotional shock. To hit a patient with something like that—no warning, no preparation——"

"How bad was it?" Stark cut him off, his voice hoarse, a guilty man unable to wait longer to hear his condemnation.

"Luckily, he came through it with no new heart damage," he said, almost regretting so favorable a report when he saw its revivifying effect on Stark's face. "But that's not the whole story, of course. The emotional effect——"

"I know," Stark broke in, getting to his feet, walking to the window. There was a long silence. Finally, over his shoulder, he said, "I'm sorry, Doctor. Very sorry. I regret this more than I can possibly tell you." He turned back, shoulders slumped, hands driven deep in his trouser pockets. "Perhaps I should have guessed. I met Mr. Crouch out front that noon. He was getting back from the hospital just as I was leaving. He did say something about postponing the convention, but I had no idea that—" He broke off and came back to his desk, his manner decisive, his voice full and firm. "There was no alternative. We had to go ahead. As for Mr. Crouch—I'm certain that he was planning to explain it to Judd. He mentioned driving up to see him again. I'm sure that's what he had in mind. Unfortunately, something came up that—this is no excuse, I recognize that, but at least it's an explanation—Mr. Crouch has been very much tied up these past few days. This is the third time this week that he's had to go to Philadelphia. He'll be back this evening, and of course I'll report all this the moment I see him. I know he'll be very much concerned, more than anxious to do anything he possibly can to square Judd away. If you have any suggestions—do you?"

"I don't suppose it would be possible——"

"To postpone the convention? No, that's out of the question. We've gone too far now to—" Stark stared at him. "Does it strike you as being at all significant, Doctor, that Judd should be so disproportionately concerned about something that is, after all, only one of a great many activities for which his department is responsible?"

Puzzled, he countered: "But a very important one. At least that's the impression I got from Mr. Crouch."

"Not as important as Judd makes it," Stark said conclusively. "There was a time, of course—please don't misunderstand me, Doctor, I'm in no way depreciating the contribution that Judd's early conventions made to the company's development—but times change.

Crouch Carpet is past the stage now where major effort has to be concentrated on the contract market."

"Then why did you feel it so necessary to rush ahead and——"

"We're not." Stark caught him up. "What we're doing is in no sense a duplication of anything that's been done in the past. We're not trying to stage a Judd Wilder convention, nor even a reasonable facsimile thereof."

"So he shouldn't be at all concerned—is that what you're saying?"

Stark started to speak but stopped, canceling the possibility of an affirmative reply, silent until his feet were back on the footstool again. "No, he'll be concerned—and all the more so now, of course—unless he can be made to accept the inevitability of what has to be. I've been trying to make him see that ever since I came here, but with very little success, I'm afraid."

"I take it then that your relationship with Mr. Wilder hasn't been too—" he hesitated, searching for the right word, finally compromising with *"productive?"*

Stark's smile was thin and watery, but now for the first time, seemingly genuine. "If you're suggesting, Doctor, that I'm implicating myself as a possible cause of the stress that Judd's been under—yes, perhaps I have been. And if so, I regret it—no man likes to see himself as the cause of another man's serious illness—but if it hadn't been I, it would have been someone else. Companies are living organisms. If they don't grow, they die. And as they grow they change. Change demands adaptation. The man who can't break with the past, who's too inflexible to change, who can't adapt himself to new situations and circumstances—" He spread his hands.

"You're saying that Mr. Wilder has been unwilling to adapt himself to what you want the company to be—is that it?"

"It's not a case of what I want, Doctor. This company's future course is inevitable. When I came here—how much past history do you have?"

"Mr. Crouch gave me a rather full account——"

"Yes, I'm sure he did," Stark put in, his tone a weary acknowledgment of the old man's penchant for loquacious reminiscence.

"—and I've had Mr. Wilder's version as well."

Stark gave him a stabbing glance. "Did either of them tell you that three years ago Crouch Carpet was on the verge of—if not bankruptcy, at least a situation where it was wide open for a take-over by anyone who was willing to step in and pick up the pieces?"

Aaron Kharr attempted to conceal his surprise, apparently without success.

"I thought not," Stark said crisply. "That's why I happen to be here. I was brought in at the insistence of the investment house that financed the rescue operation. No one was supposed to know that except Mr. Crouch, but of course everyone did. Inevitably, perhaps, my presence aroused a certain amount of resentment—the old bugaboo of being taken over by the bankers, you know. It wasn't unexpected, of course, at least in the case of the older men who felt their security challenged by a change in the status quo, but I must say that I was quite unprepared for the reaction that I got from Judd Wilder. In my initial assessment, I'd singled him out as a man—in fact, the only one in the old executive group—upon whom I could count to go along."

"But it didn't work out that way," Aaron Kharr suggested, easily able to see why Stark had failed to get a response from a man like Judd Wilder. But he also saw a new cause of stress, something over and above anything he had considered up to now, and he moved to explore it with a probing "You mentioned going along——"

Stark picked it up instantly. "To put it succinctly, Crouch Carpet had simply outgrown itself. It had outgrown its financial structure, it had outgrown its managerial capacity, it was rapidly outgrowing the market area in which all its merchandising effort was being concentrated. Clearly, the entire operation had to be restructured. As soon as we had the financial situation under control—that, of course, was the number-one priority—I turned to the broader problem of building a sound organization and establishing appropriate controls. It's always difficult, of course, to make the transition from autocratic entrepreneurial management to a closely interrelated and intercommunicating organizational structure, but in this case there were some special problems. Mr. Crouch had not been, in all regards, the classic one-man manager. In certain areas he had delegated very substantial responsibility. This was particularly true in the merchandising area. Mr. Crouch was so impressed with the way that Judd's earlier ideas had worked out that when he came up with a new one, he was almost automatically given a green light—and thereupon went ahead with virtually no managerial control."

"But if his ideas were so good——"

"Please—" Stark cut in. "I'm in no way depreciating Judd's ability nor the great contribution that he had made, not at all. No indeed! The point is this—since Judd's ideas were dominating the company's marketing approach, he was—in effect, at least—setting the pattern for corporate development. The question to be faced was whether or not Crouch Carpet, looking to the future, dared to trust its development to the undirected inspiration of one man. The answer was obvious. Of course not. No man at that level, no matter how able he may be, can possibly be aware of all of the considerations that have to be taken into account. Direction and guidance must come from top management—it can't be the other way around."

"In other words, ideas have to be invented to order," Kharr observed, barely suppressing a more forceful voicing of an attitude that had its roots in a bitter memory of what had happened at the Berringer Institute after the Board had decided that it had to pre-plan all of the Institute's research projects. "Do you really think that inspiration can be——"

"In a well-managed company, Doctor, you don't count on inspiration. Business management is not an artistic enterprise. It's a science, imperfect perhaps, but nevertheless a reasoned response to ascertainable facts. We're not out to win blue ribbons or gold medals. Our goal is not creative innovation, it's return on investment." That cold smile flickered. "The business of business, Dr. Kharr, is making money."

"That's all that matters?"

"Precisely," Stark snapped back, an almost belligerent retort. "If a company doesn't make an adequate profit—" His lips twisted, his expression softening. "You can argue, if you will, the ethical validity of a dominant profit motive—perhaps it's not the noblest of man's goals—but it's either that or corporate death. I'm sure I don't have to tell you, Dr. Kharr, that when the chips are down, the will to live supersedes all other considerations." He shrugged, blinking as if suddenly aware of having lost his composure. "But to get back to Judd——"

"You were saying that he didn't turn out to be the man you'd expected," Aaron Kharr prompted.

Stark hesitated. "I don't know that there's too much point in going into a lot of detail——"

"The more I know, the more I'll be able to help him."

"Yes, as his doctor—yes, perhaps, there is some of this that you ought to know," Stark said. "Well, as I said before, Judd originally struck me as being malleable enough to be molded to a new approach. Since he was reporting to Mr. Crouch I had no direct control over him, but nevertheless I made it my business to have as much contact with him as I possibly could. Unquestionably, he was an extraordinarily talented man—you could hardly argue about his creative capability—but on the other side of the coin, it was equally evident that he did not have an organizationally oriented mind. He was very much the individualistic artist, the virtuoso performer, and in consequence, an ineffective administrator. I don't mean in matters of discipline and control—actually, he ran a rather tight shop—but he was so much the one-man operator that he was building no second-level strength in his department. Even more seriously, perhaps, his interpersonal relationships with other department heads most certainly left something to be desired." He paused, changing tone. "Does this at all fit your assessment?"

"Yes, it's possible to see him in that light," Aaron Kharr granted. "But go ahead."

"As I said, he was reporting to Mr. Crouch so I was in no position to exert very much direct influence, but I nevertheless created as many occasions as I could to talk to him, particularly about the necessity of broadening the company's merchandising approach, and now and then I managed to get in a personal note, as well. At least once, I talked to him quite directly about delegating more responsibility, not only to the men under him but also to men in other departments who, if given the chance, could surely make some contribution. Since Mr. Crouch was present on that occasion, and strongly supported everything I said, I thought that Judd had gotten the message and would respond to it. And for a while it looked as if he had."

"This was when—how long ago?" Aaron Kharr asked, slipping easily into a familiar role.

"Oh, six months after I came, something like that—say two and a half years ago."

"Sorry." He apologized for the interruption. "You were saying that he appeared to have been favorably influenced."

Stark nodded, pausing for a thoughtful moment. "Perhaps I should tell you this—you may find it pertinent. Judd had made a move to leave the company. I wasn't supposed to know about it, but I did. Naturally I was concerned. At that stage—I'll be quite frank about this—my relationship with Mr. Crouch was still somewhat tenuous, and to have had Judd leave would have been most disturbing. Fortunately, he didn't. I don't know why, whether he didn't get the job he was after, or whether the grass on the other side of the fence didn't turn out to be so green after all. In any event, as I say, he decided not to leave. I judged it one of those crisis periods—most men go through them—and I took his decision to stay as an acceptance of the situation, and evidence of his willingness to go along. But that wasn't my only reason for being encouraged. Judd had always been something of a loner, never really mixing with the other company people, so when he decided to build in Vixen Valley—that's our executive housing development—it seemed a good sign."

"Yes, that struck me, too, as being significant," Aaron Kharr said, cautious support, beginning to be impressed with the depth of Stark's understanding.

"And there were other signs as well," Stark went on. "We began to see more of Judd around the country club, and Kay started entertaining now and then for company people, something that they'd rarely done before. But the most gratifying development, at least from my point of view, was a noticeable improvement in his relationships around the company. In interdepartmental meetings, he was much more amenable, much less the rebel—I was really quite encouraged. But then we came up to convention time again—"

Aaron Kharr nodded knowingly, anticipating what he was about to hear, in no way surprised as Stark continued, "—and there he was, the same old Judd again, the unfettered genius riding roughshod over anything that got in his way, paying no attention to anyone else's ideas, all-out to stage another great spectacle, bigger and better than ever, another personal triumph for Judd Wilder, the big theatrical producer."

There was an unmistakable undertone of bitter deprecation, and Aaron Kharr made a conscious attempt to counter it with a smile. "Do you really think that's what motivated him?"

"That had been his background—the theater."

"Yes, I've explored that rather deeply."

"And you don't think that—"

"Oh, I've no doubt that personal recognition is important to him —he'd be less than human if it weren't—but I must say that it's my impression that any urge that he may have toward self-aggrandizement is decidedly inferior to his dominant concern for the Crouch Carpet Company."

"I respect your judgment, Doctor," Stark said coolly, "but I'm afraid my own experience raises some doubts on that point. Let me tell you what happened this year. After almost three years of studying the situation here, I'd come to the conclusion that these big contractor conventions had outlived their usefulness. Granted, they had contributed importantly to building a strong position in the contract market, but that job was substantially done—our penetration could hardly be improved. It was clear to me—and to everyone in the sales department, I might add—that future growth had to come from other areas. What we all thought we should do—well, it's substantially what we *are* doing."

"This cruise you're putting on?"

Stark shook his head. "No, not the cruise—that's only a gimmick that Allen Talbott came up with when we had to move so fast. What's important is the strategy of making a strong first move into some market areas where we've got to improve our penetration. That's what I'd tried so hard to get over to Judd. He couldn't see it. He'd have no part of it. It had always been a contractors' convention, that's what it had to be. To bring in anyone else would violate the whole Crouch Carpet marketing concept. The contractors would resent it. We'd destroy everything he'd built up. And, anyway, it wouldn't work—we'd never get the people we wanted. We'd make fools of ourselves even inviting them. He was really quite emotional about it, terribly worked up. In the end, of course, he got his way—Mr. Crouch is still president of the company—and everything considered, I decided that it was better to go along for another year." There was a momentary break in Stark's poise, substantial enough to let a peculiar expression break through, explained as he said, "That was the first thing I thought about when I heard that he'd had a heart attack—glad that I hadn't forced the issue."

Aaron Kharr nodded, peripherally impressed that Stark was accepting the stress concept, more consciously aware that he was trying to absolve himself from personal guilt, recalling that Crouch had made the same attempt on that morning when he had come up to County Memorial.

Back in the groove again, Stark was saying, "The response we're getting is simply tremendous, far beyond anything we'd anticipated. I was talking to Allen Talbott just before you came in. The morning mail is full of acceptances. On top of all the telegrams and telephone calls that we got yesterday—it looks now as if we're going to have a problem finding enough room to accommodate everyone who wants to go. Of course, that's only the beginning, I know that—we've still got to do a job after we get them on board—but I'm not too worried about that, not with the way we've got this organization pulling together now. I've never seen everyone so steamed up, so all-out to put something over, so united in a common enterprise. No matter what else we accomplish, it's going to be worth doing just for the psychological effect on our own organization. It's a wonderful experience, Doctor, to see an organization catch fire and come to life. It's what you're always hoping and praying will happen, but it's always so hard to find the spark that sets it off."

Aaron Kharr nodded, attempting an understanding smile, ineffectually trying to hide a feeling of total deflation. Choked, he muttered, as an acknowledgment of defeat, "So there won't be any more Judd Wilder conventions."

"I doubt it," Stark replied. "Of course, Judd doesn't have to know that yet—" His voice faded off, revived as he said, "I know this doesn't make your job any easier, but I hope you aren't too discouraged. If you can bring him around, it will be a tremendous service, not only to Judd but to the company, too."

"You mean you want him back?"

"Of course," Stark said, surprised, sounding as if any other reply was unthinkable.

"But on *your* terms."

"A company is a pluralistic enterprise, Dr. Kharr. It can't be anything else. No man can be sufficient unto himself, no department can be a sovereign and independent island." He paused. "If you can make Judd see that——"

"The individual doesn't matter?"

"There are something like eighteen hundred individuals in this company—they all matter. And so do our stockholders, our retailers and contractors, our suppliers, all of the thousands upon thousands of people who are directly or indirectly dependent upon what happens to Crouch Carpet."

Aaron Kharr looked at his watch. "Well, I'm afraid I'll have to be getting along." He rose.

Stark quickly got to his feet. "I'm sorry, Doctor. I'd hoped after reading your paper—" He came around from behind his desk. "To be completely frank, when I heard that Judd had had a heart attack I wrote him off as a lost man. But after I read your paper—the cases you described, the way you'd brought some of those men around, men who would otherwise have——"

"I'm not God," he cut him off, a self-saving retort so often used that it was almost automatic. "The most I can possibly do—the most any doctor can do—is to exert some slight guiding influence, perhaps help nudge a patient back toward the right path again. I've never tried to go beyond that, nor have I ever advocated that it be attempted."

"That's all we're asking," Stark said, extending his hand. "Thank you for listening to me, Doctor. I hope that I've not made myself seem—there are two sides to it, you know."

He took his hand, managing a smile now that he knew he was out of it. "If there were only two sides it would be so much simpler."

"Yes, I'm sure that's true," Stark said, but oddly preoccupied now, walking along with him as he moved toward the door. "There is one last point that should be borne in mind, perhaps. We were talking about it earlier—Judd's relationship to Mr. Crouch, how important that's been to him?"

"Yes?"

Stark seemed strangely embarrassed, oddly out of character, at least the character that he had assumed up to now. "I wish I were free to be completely open and aboveboard about this but—well, it's not something that should be counted upon for the future." His expression was tortured. "Mr. Crouch is not a young man any more —that's not telling you anything that isn't obvious—the age when most men start thinking about retirement."

Aaron Kharr felt a muscle spasm skitter across his shoulders, the sensation of a chill. "Is that—imminent?"

Stark fixed him with a look that made his clipped "It could be" the revelation of a truth that he dared not openly reveal. With that he turned on his heel and strode back to his desk.

Aaron Kharr was out of the building, sitting in his Volkswagen, the motor running, before it suddenly occurred to him that he still had to drive to Baltimore.

« 4 »

Fulfilling his promise to Mary that he would talk to Dr. Raggi was proving a more diverting experience than Judd Wilder had anticipated. She had been right in saying that the Indian was a lonely man, starved for companionship, hungry for conversation. Once they were past that sticky first minute or two when Raggi had stuffily maintained his posture as a substitute attending physician, it had taken no more than a mention of his native land to send him off on a flight of rhapsodical reminiscence.

The India that Dr. Raggi recalled and described was too far removed from Judd Wilder's experience to bring back any unpleasant memories, separated not only by geography—Raggi's home in tropical Kerala was a continent away from the Himalayan foothills—but also by what, at first, seemed a hardly credible difference in age. It was difficult for Judd Wilder to accept the truth that, during the years he had been in India, Raggi had been only a very small boy too young to have been impressed by any but the most fleeting memories of those wartime years.

"Yes, yes, I am remembering these American soldiers coming to Cochin for their holidays," Raggi had recalled. "Our family home, you see, it is very near this waterway—a lagoon I think you would call it—and these Americans, many of them, twenty or thirty I should say, they are renting these little boats from the fishermen, and they are having great sport, racing and swimming and all of that. They are wearing very little clothes, you see, and to me they are looking strange, so I run to my father and say, 'What disease is it that they are all having that their skin should appear as it does?' He tells me that it is not a disease, that it is only because they are white men that they appear so strange to me. So then I say to him, 'But it is not true that they are white, Father, they are all over *pink*, and is not that a sign of fever?' And then he says to me—he is a very humorous man, my father—that I must remember that it is in the nature of the white man to always be in a state of fever about something."

Raggi ended with a burst of self-appreciative laughter, abruptly cut off with a look of concern. "Please, you must not be offended. I am only——"

Judd relieved him by joining in his laughter, agreeing that Raggi's father had been right, asking now, "Is your father a doctor, too?"

"Yes, yes, it is our family duty, my father and his father before him, and for many generations before that. But it is *Ayurvedic* medicine, you see. I am the first——"

"Ayur—what?"

"Ayurvedic," Raggi eagerly supplied. "It is based, you see, on the very ancient writings of the Ayurveda. No, no, you must not smile. You are thinking it is something very primitive, yes? No, it is not that. It is very—I do not know quite how to say it—*sophisticated?*" His black eyes were glowing coals, popping with excitement. "Much of what is very new in Western medicine, has been in Ayurveda for a very long time. These things Dr. Kharr is saying—they are so new, he says, that your medical journals will not yet publish them because they have not been proved. But that is not true. They have been proved in India for many hundreds of years."

"Like what?" he put in encouragingly, warmed by the glow of Raggi's eager proselytizing.

"It is the principle of Ayurveda, you see—it is all very complicated in its application, one must study many years to learn all that—but the principle is simple. Ayurveda says there is no separation between mind and body—it is all one, an inseparable unity of being. An illness of the body is only a manifestation of a disturbance in the perfection of that unity. That is what must be restored."

"You make it sound like psychiatry."

"No, no," Raggi objected. "In Western medicine, you have this separation. It is the psychiatrist who treats the mind and the doctor of medicine who treats the body. How can there be this separation when it is unity that is needed? That is what we say in India."

"So you'll go home and practice Ayurvedic medicine?"

"I am thinking it is possible to combine the two. That is why I am spending this time with Dr. Kharr. He is a very wise man, I think. Most of your Western doctors—they do not have time enough, they say, to be concerned with the mind. Yes, yes, it is true—Ayur-

vedic is very consuming of time. My father—sometimes he is talking
to a patient for many hours. I remember—"

Raggi interrupted himself with the quick laughter of abrupt reminiscence. "I must tell you a very funny story, I think. There is this
minister of state, a very important man, you see, and he is having
this illness. It is the time of the election, and he is feeling so badly
that he is unable to give a nice smile to all of the people—then they
will not vote for him—so he is coming to my father. Always before
he had gone to this European doctor—he was very Western-think-
ing, this minister—but my father is a kind and tolerant man so he is
willing to see him. He comes very early in the morning—I think so
that he will not be seen—and my father takes him into his consulting
room. It is one hour, two hours, three hours, he is still there. My
father rings for the servant to bring the midday meal. All afternoon
he is there. Everyone is waiting. When he comes out the sun is already in the water. My mother is saying—it is very unusual for my
mother to speak in this way because she does not interfere with my
father's practice—but this is a special time, so she asks my father
why it is necessary to spend so much time with this man. So my
father says to my mother—this is what I think is very funny—he says,
'It is not easy to convince a stubborn Congressman that his belly
trouble will not be cured until the taxes on this house have been
reduced.'"

Judd broke into appreciative laughter, apparently a bit too fervently, bringing a worried look to Raggi's face, an anxious, "It is
only a joke, you see. He does not truly mean——"

Squelching the needling comment that Ayurvedic doctors were
apparently no less pocketbook-oriented than their Western counter-
parts, Judd Wilder changed the subject, asking Dr. Raggi how long
he was staying in the United States.

"Only one more month, then I will be going home," Raggi replied
with eager anticipation. "It has been a very long time, you see. Six
years. It is most exciting to think of being with my family again.
Also—" he hesitated, and with a boyish smile of embarrassed revelation concluded, "now I will be having a wife."

"You're being married?" he asked, and with Raggi's eagerly affirmative nod, added, "Congratulations."

"Thank you, sir," Raggi said formally. "Yes, yes, I'm thinking it
will be very fine to be having a wife."

"She must be a good gal to have waited all this time," Judd observed. "Six years, didn't you say?"

"It is not what you are thinking," Raggi said, obviously embarrassed. "My marriage is something that has been only recently arranged—between the families, you see."

"Oh, sure," Judd said hurriedly, embarrassed himself now, trying to pass it off with a tolerant "That's probably as good a way as any."

"Yes, yes," Raggi agreed, a sharply defensive note in his voice as he added, "It is better, I think, than what I am seeing here in the United States. Is it not more desirable to have a rational arrangement than to be pushed into it by the accident of pregnancy?"

Unavoidably, Judd searched the room with his eyes, assuring himself that Mary had not slipped in unnoticed. "I can't argue with you about that," he said, but that moment of prior hesitation had apparently made Dr. Raggi doubt his sincerity.

"You see, sir, we do not accept your Western idea of romantic love," Raggi said stiffly. "It is not that we are denying love—no, no, that is not true. What we are saying is that love is not to be confused with the urge to copulation. Love is not something that comes before, it is something that comes after. You say love is the beginning, we say it is the end. There is something in one of our holy books— 'It is the seed that is planted in shallow soil that dies too soon—it is the seed that is planted deep in the earth that grows ever stronger and bears the best fruit.'" The young doctor's face, dark though it was, showed a warming flush as he stopped, aware that he had been carried away.

"I'm not arguing with you," Judd said, the only thing he could think of to say to put Raggi at his ease.

The door opened. Mary peeped in, quickly withdrawing. But as if it were a reminder of duty, Raggi got quickly to his feet. "Yes, yes, I must go. I had not been meaning to talk so much."

"It wasn't too much for me," Judd said honestly. "I enjoyed it. Come back any time."

"Thank you, sir, thank you," Raggi said, stopping at the door to repeat it.

Mary came in, beaming. "Now that wasn't so bad, was it? Wasn't I right about him?"

"Yes, you were right," he said. "And just to prove it, I'll let you get me the urinal."

She stopped dead, looking at him as if shocked by the suspicion of a bad joke. Then, with a little giggle, she made a quick move toward the cabinet beside the bed.

« 5 »

Somewhere above the cloud-covered Atlantic, seemingly suspended at some undefined point in space, Kay Wilder tried to fix her position upon the map on the center spread of the timetable. It was not really a map, no more than a diagram distorting the hemisphere to support the airline's contention that it flew the straightest line between all points, but it was enough to serve her purpose. She needed something to occupy her mind, a mathematical puzzle to assure herself that she had not completely lost her ability to reason.

But somehow, confused by the time differential between Paris and New York, her little pencil-marked cross was misplaced, no more than made when the pilot's voice came on, announcing that they would be landing in New York in approximately an hour, "I'm sorry that we're going to be a little late," he had said, "but we've been bucking a big headwind ever since we left Paris."

Kay Wilder felt, not that she had been held back, but rather that she had been hurtled through space by some inexorably driving force, as unseeable as the wind, madly spinning the clock. Boarding the plane at Orly, an eight-hour flight had seemed an unendurable prolongation of suspense. Now, with only an hour to go, something within her cried out for a halt, a delay, a chance to think.

She tried to look ahead, wondering how soon she could get a train, recalling that there had been one that Judd used to take, arriving in New Ulster a few minutes before nine—it must have left New York about five—but that had been a couple of years ago. That train might have been taken off, so many of them had been—that was why Judd drove all the time now—and even if it were still running, she'd never be able to make it, that endless drive in from the airport. If she was too late for the last train, what would she do . . . what *could* she do? Go to a hotel . . . more money wasted . . .

Again, as had happened every time she tried to think ahead, the same thoughts came back, inadmissible yet unavoidable, forcing themselves upon her. Her only protection lay in the secrecy of her mind, shielded there from the accusation that she was being a cold-hearted bitch, thinking of nothing but money at a time like this . . . but how could she help it? Someone had to. Judd never had . . . putting all that money in a house . . . *"What are you worrying about, Kay . . . we've got plenty of money . . . and there's more coming in every month . . ."*

That was where Judd had been so wrong, thinking that it would never end . . . but it would end . . . it *had!* They'd pay his salary for a while . . . Sam Harrod . . . everyone saying how generous the company was, still giving him his full salary . . . six months . . .

Again, as unavoidable as it had been a dozen times before, she heard Anne Locke telling her about Marjorie Harrod taking a brushup course, secretly, not letting Sam know yet that she was getting ready to go back to teaching. But what could *she* do? There was nothing in New Ulster. If they had only stayed in New York, all the contacts she had there . . . but that was twelve years ago . . .

Stopping short of panic, she reached out for what had always been a handhold against slipping into terror, the bonds that she had inherited from Uncle Charles. When the estate had been settled, it had seemed a fortune, protecting her against groveling dependence no matter what happened, but now it seemed so little . . . only a year's salary. They'd cut down expenses of course . . . they'd have to . . . $312.80 a month just for the payment on the house . . . oh, God, why had she spent all this money on such a madly futile trip?

Plunging despair reached deeply enough to touch another fantasy, guilt-shrouded now, the old secret hope that she would someday inherit something from Miss Jessica . . . if there was anything left, Miss Jessica would leave it to Rolfe . . . *Rolfe* . . .

She buried her face in her hands, trying to shut out her last glimpse of her son, all that she had seen looking back as she reached the plane, only his back, his face turned away, his arm around Jo, shielding her from the crush of the crowd.

"Ladies and gentlemen, will you please fasten your seat belts. We've begun our descent for Kennedy Airport and there may be some slight turbulence as we go through the clouds."

The clouds closed in, no longer cottony white, a dirty gray now, ripped and torn into wispy shreds. Below, for the first time on the crossing, she saw water, etched glass with no light behind it, a long arrowhead crack that became the wake of a ship when she identified a smoke-pluming spot at its tip . . . Chris Kemble . . .

There was a blur of motion, and then a heavy crunch, a shocking awareness of weightlessness lost, of tons upon tons of metal crashing to earth, the saving silence blasted by a scream of mechanical protest, isolation destroyed by onrushing engulfment of what lay ahead.

"Please remain in your seats until . . ."

The plane came to a stop, a suspended moment, and then all around her people were getting up, hurriedly pulling on coats and clutching for bags and packages, glancing out of the portholes for eagerly sought first glimpses of waiting faces.

Prodded by the hope that she might still be able to catch a train, she got to her feet, suddenly conscious of the couple in the seats behind her. They were sixtyish, small-town, dowdy, and she knew from scraps of conversation picked up during the flight that they had been on one of those horrible city-a-day package tours.

"Well, Mother, I guess this is it," the old man said. "The end of our second honeymoon, huh?"

"It hasn't really been a second one, dear," the woman said, looking up at him, her dumpy little face glowing. "The first one never ended."

Gravely, he bent to kiss her, clinging, oblivious to everything else in the world.

Reacting to an automatic aversion to open sentimentality, Kay averted her eyes, fighting down the silly choke in her throat, deciding again that it would be foolish to call the hospital from the airport —she would never be able to explain over the telephone why she had abandoned everything and come home.

« 6 »

When Emily had suddenly decided this morning that she would accompany him to Philadelphia, Matt Crouch had grudgingly agreed to take a room for the day at the Bellevue-Stratford. Paying for a bed in which he would not sleep offended one of those little hard-core nubbins of moral principle that still persisted from his less affluent days—these damn high-binding hotels wouldn't even give you a day rate any more—but now, returning to the hotel from Elbert Coe's office, he was secretly grateful that Emily had pushed him into doing it. She had been right in saying that he would need a little rest before they started the drive back to New Ulster—and God knows, she had been right, too, in saying that they could afford it, far more right than she could possibly have known this morning.

Fumbling the key in the lock, his hand trembling with the excitement of anticipated revelation, he thrust open the door, hurriedly closing it behind him when he saw Emily, half undressed, her robe disarranged, curled up on the bed, asleep. He saw her stir and thumping down his briefcase, hit her with a jarring "Well, damn it, it's settled!"

Emily sat bolt upright. "Settled? Oh, Matt, you don't mean—?" Out of bed with a jack-in-the-box leap that made her seem twenty years younger, she threw her arms around him. "You do mean it, don't you? Oh, Matt, I couldn't be happier. Even if you didn't get everything you wanted——"

"What do you mean, I didn't get everything I wanted?"

"Matt, you didn't!"

"Wait until you hear what happened. Remember what I said on the way down—about holding out for forty-five dollars a share so I'd have room enough to do a little horse trading? Well, when I got there, who's waiting for me but Harrison Horter——"

"Himself?"

"Yes sir, there he was."

"You'd never met him before, had you?"

"Hell of a nice fellow, too. No damn shilly-shallying around. Right away, he pulls me aside and we go into this little office, just the two of us. So he says he had a hell of a time getting away from New York today, but damn it, he thought maybe if he'd come down himself we could settle this thing. So I says that's fine with me, providing I get what I want. So he asks me what do I want, let's stop this fooling around and make a deal."

"So you said forty-five."

"You think that would have been pretty good, huh?"

"Well, it's more than——"

"So we're standing there, not even sitting down yet. I'm here and he's over there, kind of around the corner of the desk. There's a pad lying here, one of those yellow ones the lawyers always use, so he shoves it over toward me and hands me a pencil, and tells me to write down my rock-bottom figure, and he'll say yes or no, and that'll settle it right then and there. Well, I'm a pretty stupid guy, not knowing anything about all this high finance business——"

"Now, Matt——"

"I'm so stupid, damned if I could remember what it was I was going to hold out for—you really want to know what I wrote down? Guess."

"Oh, Matt," she said, but her impatience was part of the game, playing along the way she always did. "Tell me!"

"Well, first I wrote down forty-eight——"

"Forty-*eight!*"

"—and then, just for the hell of it, I put on an extra seventy-five cents."

"Matt, you don't mean that he——"

"So he says what's the seventy-five cents for. So I says my wife came down shopping today, buying out the whole damn town——"

She burst into laughter. "If you want to know the truth, I didn't even buy——"

"So he says he knows what I mean, and there's not a damn thing a man can do about it, so we might as well shake hands on it, and get the damn thing over with."

Emily shook her head groggily. "Forty-eight seventy-five! Why, Matt, that's almost——"

"Almost, hell! You want to know what it adds up to? I'll tell you. After we pay all the taxes—that's the only way it means a damn thing, after taxes—five million dollars, that's what it adds up to. And *cash*, by God, no damn stock. Five million cash!"

"*Five—*" she began, collapsing then, slumping down on the edge of the bed. "Matt, I can't believe it. You said that if you got——"

"Not bad, huh, for an old fossil that's never been 'profit-oriented.'"

"It's wonderful, Matt, just wonderful," she said. But then her smile clouded. "He called you a little while ago."

"Who called me?"

"Roger Stark."

"Here? How'd he find out—? Oh, I guess I did tell Miss Fox, didn't I? What did he want?"

"I don't know. All he said—"

"Just couldn't wait to find out that he'd made his killing, huh? You know what I was talking about yesterday—wondering why he was staying out of this, letting me come down here alone?"

"Matt, you didn't want him, you know you didn't. You said yourself——"

"This is what he's been angling for all the time, getting me to sell out. I thought so right along, but now I know. Those bastards—Coe and Horter, the whole damn kit and caboodle of them, thick as thieves. Stark was just their damn stalking horse, that's all he was. That's why Coe made me hire him, so they'd have somebody on the inside, knowing everything that was going on. You know what Stark's going to make out of this for himself, all that stock they made me give him? It's no damn wonder he's ashamed——"

"Now, Matt."

"Damn it, it's true. When I think back to some of the things he's done, the way he kept snookering me into——"

"Stop it," she cut him off. "Be fair, Matt. You know that if you'd sold out three years ago——"

"I'm not talking about three years ago. I'm talking about right now."

"Remember that night you came home from New York? After you'd been trying to borrow money enough to——"

"Yeah, and I bet they're damn sorry now that——"

"That's only three years ago, Matt, and now you've sold your stock for five million dollars. I don't think you've got anything to kick about. If Roger Stark made something for himself—all right, he made a lot more for you."

"It's not only Stark. Look at Elbert Coe and that crowd of his. My God, Emily, they're going to make——"

"Oh, hush!" she exclaimed, getting up quickly, reaching up as if to put a hand across his mouth. "You're beginning to sound like an old skinflint millionaire already. Go take a shower."

"Come on, get your dress on. We've got to get going."

She laughed at him. shaking her head. "We're not going anywhere, Matt. We're going to stay right here and celebrate. This is what I've been waiting for all my life, getting to be one of these rich-bitch wives, and now that I've made it, I'm going to start living like one."

As always, she was irresistible. "Well, as long as we've got this room paid for—" He could not help grinning. "I guess if you're going to be one of those, I might as well order up some champagne, huh?"

"Why not?" she said with a grand gesture.

Chuckling, he picked up the phone and asked for room service, interrupted as he was about to give his order.

"Matt, wait. You know what I'd *really* like? A great, big glass of fresh-squeezed orange juice. I suppose they'll charge a fortune for it—"

"Just hold your horses, miss, and I'll tell you what I want," he said to the impatient voice on the other end of the line. "You got any big glasses down there, like iced-tea glasses? All right, you take two of those glasses, and you take the prettiest damn oranges you got in the place, and you squeeze enough of them to fill both of those glasses—that's right, two glasses. And don't you try to fob off any of that damn frozen stuff on me. Yes, that's all—no, wait a minute—send me up a plate of fig newtons. Fig newtons! What do you mean you don't know what they are? Everybody—all right, just send up the orange juice." He banged down the receiver. "Isn't that the damnedest thing you ever heard of—she didn't know what a fig newton was."

"I know, dear," Emily said, a smiling mockery of sincere sympathy. "You work and slave all your life, just so you can have all the luxuries——"

"Damn it, there's nothing wrong with a good fig newton," he shot back, ripping off his necktie and starting for the bathroom. Inside, he called back, "What did Stark say? What did he want?"

"I don't know, dear. He just asked if you were planning to drive home by way of the turnpike."

"Turnpike? What the hell did he mean by that? What did you say?"

"I said that you'd talked about coming down that way because you were thinking about stopping off to see Judd, but it was so much farther—"

"You don't suppose it could be that, do you—something about Judd?"

"I don't know, dear. All he said was that if you did decide to go back that way, to call him before you left Philadelphia."

"I just might at that," he said, reaching in to turn on the shower, grinning, anticipating the pleasure of telling Judd how he'd set things up for him with Horter.

✧ X ✧

SOMETIME AFTER MIDNIGHT, Kay Wilder had come off the Pennsylvania Turnpike and found a room still available at the Interchange Motel, the one bit of luck in a night of successive delays and misfortunes.

Off the plane in New York, there had been a long wait in customs, all of the inspectors huddled in wrangling argument, unconcerned by the delay they were causing the plane's passengers. Finally on her way into the city, the airport limousine had broken down, another half-hour before a replacement bus arrived. During the breakdown wait, she had heard a man talking to the driver about hotels, the driver telling him that he would be lucky to find a room anywhere in New York. At the terminal, the girl at the information desk had confirmed the situation—"Honey, there's about ten big conventions in town and the hotels are just full up. If it was my own mother, I wouldn't know where to get her a room tonight."

Abjectly bidding for help, Kay had told her story, truthful in its essence yet not without an overtone of dramatized desperation, effective enough so that the girl had become interested in helping her. "Honey, what you want is to get out there to your husband as fast as you can—right? Okay, you know what I'd do if it was my husband in that hospital? I wouldn't fool around waiting for nothing. I'd just go right over there to that Hertz desk and rent me a car. I mean it, honey, why don't you? That way you wouldn't have to go to this New Ulster, and then like you said, drive all the way up to this hospital after that. Didn't you say it was near the Pennsylvania Turnpike? So you'd be right there. It's not going to cost you that much more, and wouldn't it be worth something to get to see him that much sooner?"

Fixed in her role of the desperately anxious wife rushing to her stricken husband's bedside, disagreement had been impossible. And somehow, perhaps by suggestion, that role had gained validity as she drove through the night. Before she was off the New Jersey Turnpike, however, she knew that she would be too late to see Judd until morning, and after she crossed the Delaware bridge, stopping to pick up a Pennsylvania toll ticket, she asked the man in the booth about motels. "There's at least one at every interchange," he told her.

She would stop before long, she thought. But she had kept going, telling herself at every exit that she would come off at the next one, then passing it up and driving on, not stopping until she was as close as she could get. "That's right, ma'am, County Memorial's right up the road, maybe three or four miles," the sleepy old man at the motel desk had told her.

Carrying her bag into the room, she felt staggered by weakness, excusing it by reminding herself that it was almost twenty-four hours since she had got out of bed that morning in Paris. But sleep would not come and she picked up the telephone. When the old man answered, she asked if there would be anybody at the hospital who could give her a report on a patient. "Best way to find out's to try," he said, putting through the call for her. The ringing signal had gone on and on, finally stopped by a gruff male "Yeah?"

"I'm Mrs. Judd Wilder," she had said. "I've only now gotten in from overseas and I'm terribly anxious to find out what my husband's condition is. I've had no word since I left Paris."

"I'm just the night man," the voice came back, a disinterested grumble, abruptly interrupted by a sudden comprehension. "D'you say Paris? Paris, France? You the one called him from over there?"

"Yes, I—"

"Yeah, I know who he is, ma'am. Sure I do. Dr. Kharr's taking care of him, ain't he? I guess he's asleep now, but if you want I should wake him up——"

"No, no," she said hurriedly. "I only want to know how he is."

"Oh, he's fine, ma'am. Sure he is. I was seeing him tonight when I was making my rounds, sitting in there watching television with Mabel Cope. That's his nurse, Mabel Cope. No, ma'am, you got nothing to worry about. He's coming along just fine."

She thanked him, quickly vetoing his suggestion that he leave a message that she had called, telling him that she would be there herself the first thing in the morning. Before she hung up, she re-checked the doctor's name—Dr. Aaron Kharr—and learned that he usually arrived early, almost always at the hospital by eight.

With the assurance she had received, sleep should have come. Instead, she lay awake for a long time, physical exhaustion serving only to emphasize how irrationally she had driven herself to get here, a total effort that would probably result only in her being made to look a fool, remembering the time Judd came down with the flu while he had been working on a picture in Albany. She had met his train in Ned's car, borrowed because it had a better heater, blankets in the front seat, a Thermos filled with tea and another with hot bouillon, the doctor alerted to come to the house as soon as she got Judd back to Connecticut. And then he had got off the train, gruffly brushing aside her concern, leaving her to drive home alone . . . "I've got to get up to the studio and see Huck right away."

There had been other memories spun up in the whirlpool of night thoughts, washed away in a torrent that made no distinction be-tween recollection and fantasy, surfacing again in dreams so vivid that there had been no recognizable transition into sleep until, with an explosive sense of alarm, she had been conscious of daylight and the sound of automobiles pulling away from the motel.

Still in the knit suit that she had worn yesterday, the new day only an extension of the night, she sat now in the motel restaurant, sipping her coffee, picking at her toast, looking at her watch every few seconds, driven by the frustration of waiting into an attempt to peel back the top of the little plastic packet of jelly.

"Them things are awful, ain't they?" she heard, only now aware that the waitress was watching her.

"Oh, it's all right," she said, welcoming the chance to smile.

"I know what you mean," the waitress said. "Apple jelly—nobody likes it. I don't even know why they have it. Over to the hospital we used to have orange marmalade. A lot of people like that. But I guess it costs more."

"Hospital?" she asked, inescapably drawn.

"Unhuh, County Memorial. I was there before I came here."

"Do you know Dr. Kharr?"

"I was in the kitchen, see, so I didn't meet nobody. That's why I quit and came over here. Oh, some of the doctors would come down sometimes getting a sandwich or something—who'd you say?"

"Dr. Kharr," she said. "Dr. Aaron Kharr."

"Oh, him. He's that Jewish doctor, ain't he? The one that's living over at Stine's."

"I really don't know anything about him," she said, instantly distracted . . . Connecticut . . . Dr. Rubin . . . that Thursday night when Rolfe had started vomiting, no other doctor available . . . that strange little man that the medical answering service had sent . . .

A reminiscent shudder ran through her, the still raw memory of how stupidly cruel she had been, trying to make conversation by telling Dr. Rubin that she was on the Hospital Auxiliary committee, inexcusably unaware that he was excluded from Sedgefield General's staff by the never-admitted but rigidly enforced rule that withheld full privileges from any Jewish doctor. Nothing that she had been able to do or say, even resigning from the Auxiliary, had erased the awful memory of that icy smile that she had seen on Dr. Rubin's face when he said, "You need have no concern about my qualifications, Mrs. Wilder . . . chicken pox is not, you see, an exclusively Christian disease."

« 2 »

At the moment when the telephone rang, Aaron Kharr was in a most unusual mood, a rare period of mental equilibrium, his spirits neither elevated nor depressed, neither rising nor falling. Remarkably, this strangely neutral state of mind had survived the night, still reflecting the way that his unexpected success yesterday afternoon at Baltimore had neutralized the depressing sense of failure and futility that had weighed him down after his talk with Roger Stark.

The invitation that he had accepted to appear at the Second Annual National Conference on Corporate Health Problems had asked only that he serve as a member of a four-man panel to answer questions from the floor on heart disease. He had not been told until a few minutes before the session started that each member of the panel was to make a five-minute opening statement. The others, all cardiologists, had apparently been warned, each reading a prepared manuscript. All were predictable—the major emphasis on diet—and still uncertain of what he was going to say when he got on his feet, he had looked out over his audience of corporation personnel managers and heard himself ask, "How many of you men have changed your diet enough in the last twenty years to account for the fact that your chance of dying of a heart attack before you reach fifty-five has more than doubled?" He got a three-man look of shocked disapproval from his fellow panel members, but a sudden hush of total attention from his audience. Groping, he had picked up his "hurricane years" concept, and using that as a springboard had gone on to the importance of the stress factor, concluding with the statement that, in his opinion, the increasing tensions of corporate life were a far more significant cause of the rising coronary occlusion rate than any change in diet.

His five minutes more than gone, his point seemingly still unmade, he had sat down with a frustrating sense of awkward inadequacy, and a biting consciousness of the disapproval of his colleagues on the panel. To his surprise, however, so many of the questions from the floor had been directed to him that the moderator, embarrassed, had attempted to divert some of them to the other panelists. It was the "hurricane years" idea that had seemingly struck home, possibly because so many of the men in the audience were themselves in their forties. When the break came at the end of the session, a dozen or more men came forward to ply him with additional questions, not one showing the slightest disposition to question stress as a primary cause of coronary occlusion.

The president of the association had pushed in to ask him to stay over for the dinner meeting, a spirit-lifting contrast with the reaction of his colleagues on the panel, all of whom had left immediately after the session, not one of them bothering to even say goodbye to him. He had, he knew, done himself no good in the profession, but he had proved that when he got his book done, no matter how the cardiologists received it, he would have an audience among corporation personnel directors.

Gratifying though his personal success had been, there was more than that involved. Sitting through the rest of the program had given him a new perspective on the Wilder case. Listening to the speakers, all citing mass studies, he had seen how foolish he had been to let himself be so completely dominated by a single case. For over a week, he realized, he had thought of almost nothing else, a seriously disproportionate allocation of his time. Worse, he had become emotionally involved, something that no wise doctor ever permitted.

Plainly, he should not have allowed himself to be so upset by what he had learned from Roger Stark. The situation might have been different if the point at issue had been Wilder's postcoronary work capacity—more than once at the Allison Clinic, he had talked corporation presidents into giving coronaries a fair chance to prove their recovery—but that was not the problem with Wilder. As Stark had made clear, the die had been cast long before Wilder's heart attack. What had happened—the convention business—would sooner or later have happened anyway. The timing was unfortunate, hitting Wilder at the worst possible period, but that was not unusual—the precoronary behavior pattern often left an aftermath of personal relationships that were a handicap to rehabilitation. There was nothing that any doctor could do about that.

And it had not been all bad. Stark had definitely said that he wanted Wilder back with the company—on his own terms, to be sure—but still Wilder would probably be able to make the adjustment. But that would be up to him. No doctor could be expected to manage the life of a patient.

On the way home, driving through the night, he had reasoned himself into believing that what had happened might even be a good thing for Wilder. It might well be just what was needed to jar him into some real self-appraisal—and what he found when he got back to County Memorial strongly suggested that Judd Wilder had, indeed, landed with his feet on the ground. It was after eleven, Wilder asleep and Mrs. Cope already gone, but her last note on the chart read: "Cheerful and in good spirits all evening."

This morning he had found Wilder in that same mood, trying to shave himself, laughing with the nurse over her attempts to follow his razor with a little hand mirror. He had talked to him for several minutes, giving him every opportunity to bring up anything that concerned him, but there had been no mention of the convention. Conceivably there was still a buried anxiety, but under the circumstances it was pointless to exhume it. And there was even less point in saying anything about having stopped off in New Ulster yesterday. If Crouch came up to see Wilder, as Stark suggested that he would, it would surely be better for Wilder to think the president's visit an act of free volition, untainted by suggestion or compulsion.

And now, as the telephone rang, he reached out for it with alert anticipation, feeling for the first time in more than a week that he was free to give his full attention to whatever turned up, no longer so foolishly obsessed by the Wilder case.

"Mrs. Wilder is here," the girl at the front desk said. "She'd like to talk to you for a minute before she sees her husband."

"Mrs. Wilder?" he repeated, incredulous for a blank moment that ended with an uncontrollable burst of elation, a blast that knocked his mind off dead center, and then like an electric generator sent wildly spinning, loosed a force so powerful that it propelled him to his feet, hurling him toward the door. He felt as if help had arrived at the last instant, a strong ally unexpectedly gained. Here was what he had needed, what he had not had before—the background, the understanding, the support, the end of a single-handed fight against impossible odds.

He broke stride at the turn into the lobby, hesitant for that instant when his flash impression of the woman he saw waiting for him was a too-insistent reminder of those all-of-a-kind women that he had occasionally been called upon to talk to at East Manhattan, the wives of some of Bernathy's prize patients, those twice-married or thrice-married creatures to whom a husband meant no more than another line in the *Social Register*. But would any of those East Manhattan wives have abandoned a European trip and come rushing back to a husband's bedside? Even more tellingly, this woman smiled the instant she saw him, recognition undisturbed by that never-forgotten look—*a Jew in Dr. Bernathy's office?*—that, although he learned to harden himself against it, had always been so deeply wounding.

She was not at all the woman he had been visualizing as Wilder's wife. Her manner radiated unmistakable warmth, her expressed gratitude for all that he had done for her husband too sincere to be doubted. Above all else, he saw a basic intelligence and capacity for understanding that would be of enormous help to him.

"I did feel that I ought to check with you before I talked to Judd," she said now. "I don't want to say or do anything that you might not want."

"That's very thoughtful of you," he said appreciatively. "It's not every wife who understands how important these things can be."

"I'm sure it will be something of a shock to him, my turning up like this," she went on. "I suppose I should have let him know I was coming——"

"Yes, perhaps we should give him a bit of warning before you walk in," he agreed. "But, still, he's coming along so well——"

"He really is?"

"Oh, yes, splendidly," he said, but quickly adding a self-guarding "Of course, there's always the chance of some unfavorable development—that possibility can't be completely dismissed, of course—but as things stand now, there's every reason to expect a rapid and complete physical recovery."

He saw the flick of her eyes, a reaction to the word *physical,* and seeing it as an opening, pressed in with "The real problem in cases like this, Mrs. Wilder—or at least this is my view—is more emotional than physical."

"I'm sure that's true," she said, full acceptance.

Encouraged, he slipped into his standard explanation, starting with "A heart attack can be a highly traumatic experience," going on then to describe the two divergent reactions. Hurried along by her rapid perception, he quickly reached a concluding "So the key problem, Mrs. Wilder, is to help him walk that center line—fearful enough to guard himself against a recurrence, yet not so frightened as to feel that he has been in any way disabled."

"But he can't go back to Crouch Carpet, can he?" she asked, a question, yet her tone presupposed a negative answer.

"Oh, I'd not say that, not at all."

"How can he?" she demanded. "After this?"

"Well, he'll have to make some adjustments, of course," he said, thinking of Roger Stark, edging as close to revelation as he dared.

"But he won't," she said despairingly. "You were in the room when I talked to him on the phone, you heard what he said. Everything was fine—the convention had been postponed until September. If he goes back to that——"

"He won't," he said, cutting her off with a gesture, deciding that he had to tell her at least this much. "There's been a development that you should know about, Mrs. Wilder. I don't want to hold you up, I know how anxious you are to see him, but he may well bring this up——"

"I want to know everything I possibly can," she said, demonstrating her willingness to listen by backing a step, sitting down on the long settee.

He pulled up a chair, twisting it to put his back to the girl at the desk as he sat down to face Mrs. Wilder. "Mr. Crouch came up here on the morning after your husband's attack. He was very much worried about the convention—your husband, I mean—and when I told Mr. Crouch that that seemed to be his primary anxiety, he immediately told me to tell him that the convention would be postponed. Of course I did, and as your husband indicated to you over the telephone, he was greatly relieved. Then this story appeared in your New Ulster paper that they were going ahead and having the convention without him. When your husband read it——"

"How in the world did he get the paper?"

"He'd asked to have it sent up to him. I think it was Mrs.—am I right?—Ingalls? She was here one day and——"

"She would," she said, under her breath, whatever she was thinking overridden by a stronger "That must have hit him awfully hard."

"Yes, for a few minutes we were quite concerned—a severe emotional impact is something that we never like to see—but he seems to have come out of it in good fashion, no ill effects at all. But still it's something I felt you should know. He may well talk to you about it."

"He might," she said, looking away, somehow suggesting that it would be unexpected if he did. "And it was Mr. Crouch who promised that they wouldn't go ahead without him?"

"Yes."

"That must have been terribly disillusioning," she mused, a strain of bitterness edging in as she added, "Judd's always worshipped him so."

Again, he felt pushed toward telling her about Roger Stark, but he sidestepped it, remaining within the boundary of truth by replying, "There's a possibility, I understand, that Mr. Crouch may be coming up to see him. If he does, he may have some explanation."

"No doubt," she said abstractedly picking at the lock of her purse. "Is there anything else I should know, Dr. Kharr?"

He hesitated, suppressing a hundred questions. "I would like a chance to talk to you later, of course—I know you can be of enormous help to me—but for the moment, no, I'm sure your own good judgment will let you handle anything that comes up."

"Do you want to break the news to him that I'm here?" she reminded him, adding with a little conspiratorial smile, "You could tell him that I'm on my way over from the motel."

"Perhaps that would be best," he agreed, rising, acknowledging the soundness of her suggestion, yet somehow chilled by her willingness to wait. He would never be able to understand wives. Perhaps, after twenty-two years of marriage to Judd Wilder, this was the reaction to be expected from an intelligent and understanding woman. Nevertheless, he felt impelled to say, "There is one thing that I might warn you about, Mrs. Wilder. I'm sure it's unnecessary —I know you're prepared for it—but your husband has been through a rather profound experience. Don't be surprised if you find some of his reactions rather different than you might expect."

She looked up at him, searching his face as if trying to find some added explanation or hidden meaning. Then, tautly poised, she asked, "How long will you keep him here, Dr. Kharr? How soon can he come home?"

"I'd rather not commit myself as yet—at least to him," he said. "But for your own information—reserving, of course, the right to change my mind—I'd like to have him here for—oh, perhaps another ten days."

Her only response was a reserved nod of acceptance.

He looked at his watch. "Suppose you give me five minutes, and then come along. Turn left and go down the corridor. It's the last room on the left, number 24." He started away and then stopped. "No, it might be better—yes, wait for me. I'll come back for you."

« 3 »

When Dr. Kharr had told him that Kay would be here in five minutes, it had seemed an impossibly short warning, a sense of urgently necessary preparation heightened by the little squeal of dismay with which Mary had launched into a wild flurry of housekeeping, trying to get the room in order. But now with everything in place, Mary tugging a last wrinkle out of the bedspread, he was still listening for the sound of Kay's footsteps in the corridor . . . waiting . . .

Strangely, a thought of his mother flashed briefly, the association undetected because it came at a level somewhere below conscious perception, not pure memory but the memory of memories, lying awake in a strange room, his first night in a hotel, that night when Herbert Hoover had made a campaign speech in Des Moines. He had been eight that summer, old enough to understand for the first time what *election* meant, how important it was that his grandfather be reelected, why his mother had been away all that fall, reappearing in Haygood only long enough to get Mrs. Gorman's assurance that there was no need for her to worry about anything at home.

There had been a telephone call early that morning, his father coming back to the breakfast table half-smiling, half-frowning, torn as he always was when something threatened to interfere with getting out the paper, finally telling him that someone was sick and his mother had been chosen to introduce Herbert Hoover at the big rally that night in Des Moines. "I guess we ought to go," his father had said. "It will be something for you to remember."

There had, indeed, been something to remember, too much, too many people, too much color, too many bands, too much noise, impression piled upon impression, everything a blur, out of focus until that moment when he had looked up from the front row of the audience to see his mother standing at the lectern. She was wearing something flame-colored, a dress that he had never seen before nor after, her face haloed by the smoke-hazed spotlight, her arm upraised in a command to the multitude. Every eye was upon her and a hush fell as if they, too, had seen for the first time how beautiful she was, as if they, too, were feeling that same choke in their throats, that same burning mist in their eyes. But no one, not even his father, could possibly have felt what he felt when she glanced down at him, a brief instant of recognition that had distilled a hundred unnamable emotions into a joy almost too concentrated to be endured.

He remembered nothing of Herbert Hoover—he had remained a stranger, recalled only as in a picture seen that next morning in the newspaper—nor could he remember returning to the hotel with his father. All that came back was that room where he had waited for his mother. It must have been a room in a suite because there had been an open door, and through it, lying in bed, he had seen his father reading under the bed-light. And it was through that open doorway that he had heard the sounds of his mother's arrival, predicting a joyous release of all the love-laden homage that was bursting within him, waiting to be poured out, sensation building to an almost unendurable climax, raised to a pitch where he had not dared to look when he knew that she was standing in the doorway. And then he had heard, "Oh, Harry, look what he's done to his new suit!" Lying there with his eyes closed, he had heard the slap of her hand as she dusted his trousers, the whip of his coat before she put it on a wire-tinkling hanger. After that there had been only his father's apology—"I'm sorry, dear, I guess it was my fault"—and then the terrible finality of that closing door.

Even if something had suggested an association between that long-ago memory and the way he felt at this moment, he would have failed to credit it, and with all reason. Surely there was no legitimate comparison between his mother, to whom his presence had never been more than incidental, and Kay, who had given up so much to come back to him. If there was any parallel, and even this was unmarked and unnoted, it lay in the difficulty he was having in trying to frame an expression of appreciation and gratitude. There was no precedent, no like experience, no recallable moment when he had ever before felt himself so much the exclusive subject of Kay's sympathetic concern. And because it was something new it suggested change, and change suggested hope, and hope generated something promising enough to produce an effervescent sense of excitement.

"I think she's coming," Mary said from the guard post she had taken up at the door. "Yes, she's—"

He wanted to cry, "Get out, get out, leave us alone!" but he hesitated, and then it was too late. Kay was in the doorway. There was an instant when it seemed that she would come rushing in to throw her arms around him, an anticipation so real that he started to lift himself from the bed, clearing his shoulders for her embrace. But there was an exchange of words between Mary and Kay, no more than a meaningless self-introduction, yet enough to shatter the suspense of expectation.

Kay came up to the bedside, seemingly about to speak, but no words came from her lips. What he had been prepared to say could not be spoken without a voice-warming preliminary. Silence hung over them, not as a communication of something that needed no expression, but as a barrier that somehow had to be breached. But he heard himself say, "I told you that you didn't need to come back," not at all what he had planned, so far from the mark that he had to say something else. "You didn't have to ruin your trip because of me."

"It wasn't ruined," she denied. "I was there long enough to do everything I really wanted to do."

The door closed. Mary was gone. They were alone now. Again, there was silence, pregnant with possibilities. But all that came out of it was Kay's flatly asked "How are you feeling?"

"I'm fine," he said, a vigorous denial of any impediment to affection, lifting his hand. She took it and he started to pull her toward him, a suggestion too quickly taken, her kiss no more than a hurried brush of lips, a public ritual so reminiscent of picking him up at the airport that he almost expected her to ask him what kind of trip he had had. The only strangeness was the reversal of roles, hearing himself speaking Kay's words, the answer no more important to him than it had ever been to her. On his own, he asked, "When did you get in?"

"Last night," she said, sitting now, searching her purse for whatever it was that never seemed to be there.

"You must have gotten an early start," he said. "It's a long ways up here."

"Oh, I haven't been home. Didn't Dr. Kharr tell you? I spent the night at a motel over here. I drove right down from New York. There was no other way. The last train had gone, and there wasn't a hotel room to be had anywhere—all I could do was rent a Hertz. It seemed foolish to drive all the way home and then come back." She was digging in her purse again. "This way I could see you that much sooner." He waited for her to look up. But when she did it was only to say, "It was too late to call you when I got in."

Some uncontrollable impulse made him say, "And I guess you were pretty tired," echoing the excuse that he had so often heard.

"It was after midnight," she said, balling a handkerchief in her hand, snapping the purse shut.

"Rough trip, huh?"

"Horrible. Everything went wrong. We were late getting off from

Paris, and then we had headwinds—the airport limousine broke down, so I missed the last train—it was one of those days." She dismissed it all with a martyr's sigh. "But anyway, I made it."

"How's Miss Jessica?"

"Not too well," she said, catching herself then, transparently conscious of being the good hospital visitor. "It's nothing to worry about."

"What's wrong with her?"

"When you get to be seventy-four, things happen, I guess."

"And sometimes before," he said pointedly.

She did give him a questioning glance, but no more. "There's some news about Rolfe that ought to please you."

"What's that?"

"He's going into business."

"Business?" he puzzled, the incongruity of the news less startling than Kay's unaccountable smile.

"He's taking a job with Seaborne Oil."

"You mean he's giving up on—he's not getting his master's?"

"No, he'll get that. Oh, he still has some work to do, not much—everything's all right, though, there's no question about his getting it—he's just not going on, that's all."

"He's not going to Harvard? He's not going to teach?"

She shook her head, the smile persisting, an unbelievable response in light of all the ambitions that he knew she had for Rolfe.

"What happened?" he asked. "What changed his mind?"

"Oh, I don't know," she said, tossing it off. "As much as anything else—it was you."

"Me?"

"He said he's been thinking a lot about that talk you made up at Colfax," she said. "The one to the business school."

"But I don't see how that could have—" He let his voice fade off, searching his memory, wanting to accept the satisfaction that she was offering him, yet afraid to do so, credibility challenged by the absence of any recalled evidence that Rolfe had been even mildly impressed. "All I was doing was trying to give some of those kids a lift, trying to make them see that working for a big corporation wasn't as bad as a lot of people think it is."

"Apparently you sold Rolfe," she said, the smile still there but taut now, stretched to the point of translucency, thin enough to let him see a dark shadow behind it.

"I wasn't trying to influence him," he denied. "That was the furthest thing from my mind."

"Oh, I know that."

"Then why did you say that I'd be pleased?"

"Aren't you?"

"Well, if it's what he wants—sure."

"He said that if he could get as much satisfaction out of working for Seaborne Oil as you have for Crouch Carpet—he'd be very happy."

"That really throws me," he said, grinning despite a cautioning awareness that it was dangerous to believe that Kay had changed this much in such a short time. She had never before admitted, even this indirectly, that going with Crouch Carpet had not been the life-wasting misstep that she had always tried to make it seem.

Despite a pressing desire to believe, he could not stop himself from saying, "There must be something more than that."

"He's changed a lot in this last year," Kay said. "He seems so much older."

Aimlessly probing, he asked, "What about the girl?"

He caught Kay's stabbing glance, a flash reminder of how upset she had been by that girl in Maine, an impression instantly canceled by the matter-of-fact tone in which she said, "I thought at first that that might have something to do with it, particularly after I found out that her father was with Seaborne, too, but apparently not. Rolfe had met this other man without even knowing that it was the same company. And it's in an entirely different division. Mr. Wallace is in—oh, I don't know exactly, something about their contracts with European firms—and Rolfe will be in the planning division, working on some of their big new projects. They're building an enormous thing in Spain—a refinery, chemical plants, I don't know what all."

"That's where he'll be?"

"He doesn't know yet. It all depends on where they assign him. He'll be in the States for training first, at least a year, maybe longer."

"When will he be coming home?"

"He wanted to come right away, the minute he heard about you, but he had this final at the Sorbonne——"

"That would really have been crazy," he said, trying to make a little burst of laughter sound disdainful, not entirely able to suppress an overtone of satisfaction.

"He'll be coming back the last week in May. At least that's what he's planning now. If everything works out—if the Wallaces can get back in time—they're going to be married in June."

"Married?" he said blankly, unable to believe that Kay could be talking about Rolfe, her voice so flat and dispassionate.

Without even the suggestion of a tremor she said, "You might as well brace yourself—I know you hate big weddings—but you'll only have to go through it this once."

"So she's that kind, is she?"

"Oh, it's not Jo. It's her mother. If it weren't for her, I'm sure they'd be married by now. As it is—" She let a shrug say the rest of it.

"What's she like—the girl, I mean?"

"Jo? Oh, very nice. I'm sure you'll like her. She's very much your kind."

"What do you mean—my kind?"

Kay looked away. "She'll make Rolfe a good wife—at least the kind of wife he wants—that's all that really matters." Her eyes roamed the room. "It's a nice hospital, isn't it?"

"I guess so," he said. "At least this room's all right. That's about all I've seen. I don't remember much about the rest of it." He paused, expectantly, ready to go on.

But she gave him no opening. "I talked to Dr. Kharr for a minute or two. He seemed very nice."

"Oh, sure, he's all right. Kind of an oddball character—I still haven't figured out what he's doing in a place like this—but, no, he's fine. At least he knows what it's all about." He paused again, ready with his story of that first night, prompting her with "If it had to happen, I guess I picked a lucky place for it."

"Your nurse seemed nice."

"Mary? Sure, she's fine. I was lucky there, too—the nurses I got. Oh, in the beginning I had a clinker, a real old zombie, but we got rid of her. I've only got the two now, Mary and Mrs. Cope. She's the real nurse—Mrs. Cope. Wonderful old gal."

"You don't have a night nurse?"

"I don't need anyone at night any more. I don't really need any day ones, either, but——"

"Of course you do," she cut him off. "You've got to have someone with you."

"Well, it would get a little boring, I guess, without somebody around. Dr. Kharr usually comes in at night—I've had some good bull sessions with him—but that's only a half-hour or so."

"Who's been up from New Ulster? I know Daphy was here——"

"Yes, she stopped off on her way to Cornell. But she's the only one—oh, Mr. Crouch was here, but I didn't see him. That was the first day and I was still pretty groggy. Outside of that—oh, I've had some letters, a lot of cards. Daphy has been checking the mail at the house, sending up anything that was important."

Kay appeared shocked. "You don't mean that she's been sending you—?"

"I asked her to. Why not? I'm perfectly all right. There's no reason why I can't——"

"Well, you won't have to be bothered with anything like that from now on," she said with curt finality.

"I haven't been bothered."

"You shouldn't be."

"I'm not, I mean it. I've never been more relaxed in my life. Isn't that what you were always telling me—relax, take it easy? All right, that's what I'm doing."

"I hope so." She shifted her purse. "You're not worrying about the office, are you?"

"I'm not worrying about anything."

She looked at him intently, her doubt a challenge, and he responded with a self-depreciating laugh. "Oh, I was a little steamed up a couple of days ago—I'm going to have to clip Stark when I get back—but I've done that before, I can do it again."

"What do you mean—clip him?"

"Oh, nothing important," he said, conditioned by experience to avoid talking to her about Crouch Carpet. "Nothing that you'd be interested in."

Startlingly, she exclaimed, "I *am* interested," a quality in her voice that he had never heard before, a tone of almost desperate pleading.

Off balance, he fumbled a false start, then asking, "I told you about the convention being postponed?"

"Yes," she said, noticeably tense.

"But then that bastard Stark steps in and sets up a big junket—charters a cruise ship——"

"Roger? But how could he—wouldn't Mr. Crouch have had to approve it?"

"You know how the old man is—Stark gets in there with that snake-eyed pitch—he tried it this year with the budget—I clipped him then, I'll clip him again."

"Judd, please, you mustn't—there'll be plenty of time to worry about that after——"

"I'm not worrying about it." He saw Kay bite her lip. "Look, maybe I have been kind of a steam-up guy, pushing myself too hard on things that don't really matter. Or at least don't matter as much as I thought they did. But I've been doing a lot of thinking. Things are going to be different from now on."

"I hope so."

"When Stark first came, I thought—we've had guys like that around before, these smart operators that come in and snow the old man—give them enough rope and they hang themselves. That's what I thought was going to happen to Stark, so as long as he stayed out of my hair, all right, to hell with him. But it's gone past that now. Somebody is going to have to really knock him off. If we don't, one of these days we're going to wake up and it isn't going to be the Crouch Carpet Company at all. All it will be—well, anyway, it won't be what I want—and I know damn well it won't be what Mr. Crouch wants either."

Kay tried to stop him but he overrode her. "No, let me finish. This isn't hurting me a bit. I know now where I'm going. And I know how to get there. All I've got to do is sit down with Mr. Crouch and make him see what that bastard is doing to the company. That's all it will take."

« *4* »

Helpless, Aaron Kharr watched as he saw Mrs. Wilder come out of the hospital and cross the parking lot toward her car. He had wanted to talk to her after she saw her husband, so anxious not to miss her that he had gone out into the lobby to wait. That was where Teeter had caught him, dragging him into the Chief of Staff's office, pinning him down in a meeting that he could not walk out on.

Jonas Webster was there, Mallaby and Neilson, even old Dr. Leebow, the closest to a full staff meeting that Aaron Kharr had attended in all of his months at County Memorial. Harmon Teeter, his face flushed with the hypertensive excitement of easy money, was reporting on his trip to Harrisburg yesterday. A grant to County Memorial of $75,000 was, it seemed, as good as in the bag. According to Teeter's account he had, with consummate cleverness, turned an initial setback into a successful counterattack on the Washington bureaucrats. True enough, he said, quoting himself, County Memorial did not have an impressive lineup of board-certified specialists to conduct the proposed research, but what did the enabling legislation envisage—another down-the-nose look at rural medicine by a bunch of big-city specialists who had never got far enough beyond the city limits to see a case of undulant fever? What weight would small-town physicians give the findings of men who didn't know what they were looking at?

In the eleven months that Aaron Kharr had been at County Memorial, he had not seen an undulant fever case, and he was certain that no other staff doctor had either, but that detracted in no way from their appreciation of Teeter's winning ploy. He himself had said nothing, sitting silently through all of Teeter's exercise in self-aggrandizement, hoping that by keeping quiet he might get out in time to catch Mrs. Wilder. But it was too late for that now, she was already in her car. Leebow, querulously blank, was asking, "How we going to come out on this, Harmon—that's what I think we ought to know before we get into it. I don't mind saying I always had kind of a hankering to do a little research, but hankering is one thing and affording it is something else. We all got our practices to think about."

"Very good point, Doctor, and very well taken," Teeter said, plucking at his shirt front like a preening pouter pigeon. "This is all very tentative, of course, no more than a round-figure estimate, but I'm sure a couple or three girls could extract all the data we'd need from the case records we already have. Then if we pick up someone with some bookkeeping experience to pull things together and work out the percentages—I don't see how our out-of-pocket expense could possibly be more than twenty-five thousand. That still leaves fifty. My idea would be to divide it—some absolutely fair basis would have to be worked out, of course—but I'd say that no one on our staff would need to be concerned about not being adequately compensated for any time that he might lose from his private practice. After all, it wouldn't be a time-consuming thing. Or at least it shouldn't be, not the way I visualize it. No, Doctor, all you'd be asked to contribute would be your judgment, experience, your long years of training—surely, no one could argue that dedication is not deserving of some material recognition."

Unable to hold back any longer, Aaron Kharr said, "Do I understand, Dr. Teeter, that once the grant is approved, the money is forthcoming—regardless of the character of quality of the research that's actually done?"

Teeter fixed him with a full-moon smile, total except for the steely glitter of his porcine eyes. "I'm sure, Doctor, that with your literary ability you'll be quite able to draft a fully adequate report. Or if you're thinking that you'll not be with us next year, if that's what you had in mind—" He paused, letting the thrust sink in. "I'm sure, one way or another, we'll be able to work it out. Any more questions?"

There were no more questions.

« 5 »

"Come on, come on, it's five after," Judd Wilder called out. "What's all the stalling about?"

Mary turned, caught with a finger-in-the-jam-pot expression. "I think it's awful, having clocks in hospital rooms."

"Can't get away with a thing, can you?"

"Don't you think you ought to rest a little longer this morning, all the excitement you've had?"

"Excitement? What excitement?"

"Well, your wife coming and all."

"Come on, get that chair over here. I'm sick of this bed."

She studied his face. "You are excited, I can see it in your color. I think I'd better take your blood pressure before I let you up."

"It's your fault," he said with a burlesque scowl. "Don't you know there's nothing worse for a heart patient than being frustrated?"

Her smile broke through. "You're getting to be very difficult."

"Just getting back to normal," he laughed. "I'm a very difficult guy."

"I'll bet," she said, an expression of complimentary disbelief. But she slid the chair over, edging it up to the bed so that he could get into it with an almost effortless half-roll, the maneuver that Mrs. Cope had taught him.

"Now, watch out—don't try to lift yourself," Mary said, an unneeded reminder, serving only to sharpen an already present sense of danger. But he made the move, took a deep breath, found it reassuringly painless and gave Mary an I-told-you-so grin.

She pushed him over to the window. "There! Satisfied?"

"Thank you," he said, grinning up at her.

"Can I trust you not to do anything silly if I leave you alone for a minute? I've got to go for clean linen."

"Alone, I'm thoroughly trustworthy," he said, turning to catch the twisted smirk that she gave him when she got it. "Hurry back."

She giggled and went out.

Alone, he looked out, surveying the morning scene, searching for any sign of change since yesterday. The willows along the little creek at the bottom of the hill seemed a shade greener, the field beyond disked now to brown-velvet smoothness, a reminder of the distant tractor sound that he had heard last evening, continuing all the time that Dr. Raggi had been in, not stopping until long after dark.

Closer at hand, coming up the down-slope of the hospital lawn, an old man in a red plaid jacket was pushing a wheelbarrow bristling with garden tools. He stopped at one of the circular flower beds, stooped over and then dropped to his knees, exploring the earth with a flicking forefinger, searching for some sign of sprouting life. He found it, his face blooming with satisfaction. He got to his feet, taking up the wheelbarrow again, pushing on until he was out of sight.

Movement caught Judd Wilder's eye—a car coming down the drive, a Cadillac with the back fins cut off . . . Mr. Crouch? No, it couldn't be. Not Saturday morning . . . he was always in the office until . . . *it was Mr. Crouch!*

There was no mistaking the man who burst out as if released from a cage, identification positively confirmed as he whirled back, calling something to someone in the car. The windshield was light-blurred, but there was a woman behind it, unquestionably Emily Crouch.

Judd Wilder felt sudden panic, unreasoned alarm that quickly related itself to what he had told Kay that he was planning to do. Although he had been sincere enough in saying that he would clip Stark the first time he had a chance to talk to Mr. Crouch, it had not then been an immediate prospect, no more than something to be done at some indefinitely future time. But with Mr. Crouch you had to grab him when you could . . .

A sound at the door jerked his head around. It was Mary, her arm stacked with linen, hiding her face, but the minute she dropped the linen, she asked, "What's the matter?"

"Mr. Crouch is downstairs. I saw him drive up."

"Oh, good grief!" she exclaimed, flying at the bed, tossing pillows, whipping sheets. He tried to stop her, telling her that the bed did not matter, but he might as well have tried to talk down a hurricane, a whirlwind of activity that nothing could stop until, in what seemed only seconds, the bed was remade, the old linen stuffed away. Then, out of breath, she said, "All right, let him come."

But the telephone did not ring. They waited. The grip of excited anticipation slackened, opening his mind to the return of reason . . . he could stall it off easily enough . . . Mr. Crouch probably wouldn't let him talk about it, anyway . . . no, not here, not as long as he was still in the hospital . . .

"He must have stopped to talk to Dr. Kharr."

"He'll be up in a minute or two," he said, assuring himself that Mr. Crouch would not do again what he had done that first day, not even coming up to see him.

"He's the president of your company, isn't he?" Mary asked, a sympathetic attempt to ease the tension of waiting.

"He *is* the company!" he said, a declaration no more than made when he heard footsteps coming down the corridor, a Crouch sound as unmistakable as that explosive "So!" with which he always entered a room.

"Scram!" Judd Wilder said, ordering Mary out with a hurried flip of his hand, countering her flash of resentment with a grin and a wink.

"No more than ten minutes," she said severely, and then as a warning, "I'll be right outside in the sunroom."

But at least she got out, and in the nick of time, slipping through the door only a moment before Mr. Crouch's "So!" exploded, momentarily reverberant, then quickly followed by an equally forceful "Well, I'll be damned! So they've got you out of bed, huh? Say, you are coming along, aren't you, boy!"

He held himself to a reserved "Hello, Mr. Crouch," conditioned by experience to distrust the president's opening gambit as an accurate indicator of his real mood.

"So Kay got back, huh?" Mr. Crouch said as he came around the end of the bed.

Alarm stabbed, forcing out a taut "Did you see her?"

"No, Doc Kharr told me. Saw him for a minute on my way in. Just happened to run into him. Says you're doing wonderful. And you really look it. Hell, boy, if I didn't know different, I'd say there wasn't one damn thing wrong with you."

"There isn't," he said, chancing a smile. "You know me—always goofing off."

"Yeah, sure," Mr. Crouch said, making a great joke of it. He started to sit down on the edge of the bed. "So they're treating you all right, huh?"

"Fine."

"Well, that's good," Mr. Crouch said, reaching out to slap his knee. "Yes, sir, you're sure looking great, boy, damned if you're not."

He only smiled, silenced by the conviction that Mr. Crouch had something on his mind.

"Nice day," the president said, a feeble attempt at small talk, abandoned as he reached out to his knee again, gripping it. "Say, what's this I hear about you being all upset about this cruise business?"

"Who told you that?" he said, a too-quick cover-up for the alarm of sudden confrontation. "Dr. Kharr?"

"Now, don't you worry about who told me. The main thing is—no, it wasn't Kharr. Damn it, boy, you got this thing all wrong. I know, you read what they had in the paper—calling it a convention. Hell, it's no convention. It's just a damn junket, that's all it is. Oh, I guess they'll have some meetings, go through the motions, but what the hell, that's no convention."

"I'm not worrying about it," he said, fencing, waiting for a better opening.

"You aren't, huh?" Mr. Crouch said, surprising him with a look of quickly embraced relief. "Good! Didn't think you were. Just wanted to make sure. Damn it, boy, I've never let you down, you know that. And I'm not starting now. No sir. And I don't want you worrying when—well, you're going to be reading this in the paper, too, I guess. It's bound to get out, you can't keep them from snooping—that's why I drove around this way—I'd rather have you hear it from me than reading it in that damn paper, the way they'll get it all screwed up."

Judd made an attempt to ask what he was talking about, but the question could not be forced out, blocked by the sudden constriction of his throat, tightening as he heard Crouch say, "I hadn't really been thinking about selling—not for a while, yet, anyway—but Emily had been pushing me, telling me I ought to start taking it a little easier. And, damn it, I am coming up to sixty-five. Hard to believe —hell, it don't seem twenty years since I started Crouch Carpet. But it is. Close to it, anyway. So when this offer came along—damn it, boy, there just wasn't anything else I could—"

Judd Wilder's lips moved, but if there was any sound, it was drowned by the battering of Crouch's voice, coming at him now like waves pounding at a ship already sunk. But out of the surf-roar he finally began to hear words again, picking up "—a man can't go on forever—" and then, more clearly, "—the company will go on, that's the important thing."

"You've sold the company," Judd said, too weak-voiced to keep it from sounding like an accusation.

"Hell, no. How could I? You can't sell something you don't own. I didn't own the company. All I did was sell my shares——"

"But that's—"

"All right, damn it, it's twenty-seven per cent. And with the rest of the stock they've got, I guess that'll give 'em control. Somebody's got to have it, and I'd a damn sight rather it was him than some of the vultures that it might have been if I'd just let things ride along. Hell, I could drop over dead any day. And then what would have happened? I've seen it too many times. You get a company tied up in an estate, a flock of lawyers in there picking the bones, all that inheritance tax to pay—you know what happened to Bill Sargent's business. Hell, that was a nice little company, a beautiful operation, and what is it now? Five years and it's nothing. It would have killed me to see something like that happen to Crouch Carpet. This way it'll keep right on growing."

"It won't be the same company without you," he said, his voice leaden.

"Well, that's damn nice of you, Judd," Mr. Crouch said, clearly pleased. "A lot of people aren't going to feel that way, I guess—be glad to see me out of the way—but I'm glad you don't. We had some great times together, huh? You remember that first big government order we got—the whole damn industry sitting back and laughing at us, thinking we'd never be able to pass those tests with a piece of tufted carpet. I was telling Horter about that yesterday——"

"Who?" he asked, the word expelled by the force of surprise.

"Horter," the old man said, blinking. "I told you before—Harrison Horter. You didn't get it, huh? I thought you would." A needle glinted in his narrowed eyes. "You ought to remember him."

"So that's who'll be taking over," he murmured, remembering the luncheon, Horter sitting there like a stone sphinx watching while his hatchet men chopped away . . . "What do your profitability studies show, Mr. Wilder?" . . . "But how do you justify that profitwise?" . . . "Surely you're not saying that profit can ever be a secondary consideration?" . . . *Stark* . . .

"Well, he remembers you, all right," he heard Mr. Crouch say, and now, "You're the only man in the company he mentioned. Yes sir, you're the only one. And the way I got things set up for—you're going to be sitting pretty, boy, you don't have to worry about that, not for a minute."

"I'm not worrying," he said. And, strangely, it was true. There was that same sensation he had experienced in the ambulance, a peculiar detachment of mind from body, feeling as if what was happening was not something experienced but something observed. He was the runner who had escaped his pursuers, giving them the slip, watching now from his hideaway. If he waited, silent and unresponsive, Mr. Crouch would go away. All he wanted to hear now was the sound of retreating footsteps and a closing door.

« 6 »

Stopped by the traffic light at Vixen Valley Road, almost home, Kay Wilder was only now beginning to lift herself out of the depressed state of mind in which she had left the hospital. Then, logically enough, she had charged her mood to a largely sleepless night after an endlessly wearing day, disregarding the incompatibility of physical fatigue with the unthinking need for movement and activity that had propelled her down the road toward New Ulster. There had been no reason to go rushing home, no reason at all, and now as she glanced ahead, catching her first clear view of the Crouch Carpet buildings, there was a seeping acknowledgment that she had been a fool . . . letting her emotions get the better of her, failing to think . . . *think* . . . yes, that was what she had to do . . . think her way through, reason it out . . . there was an answer somewhere . . . *there had to be!*

But her mind was logy and unresponsive, bruised by the beating it had taken, the urge to do *something* endlessly battered against the evidence that there was no longer anything that could be done.

There had been hope until this morning, intangible and undefined, yet supported by the seeming inevitability of change. All the way across the Atlantic, even more insistently last night on the turnpike, she had told herself that Judd would surely be a different man now, expectation raised to certainty this morning when Dr. Kharr had told her not to be surprised when she found out how much her husband had changed. He had meant it as a warning but she had taken it as a hopeful promise, only to be stunned a few minutes later by the crushing discovery that there had been no change at all.

Approaching his room, she had visualized him as a stricken man needing sympathy and support, her role fixed by what Dr. Kharr had said about how much he was counting upon her help, and never in her married life had she felt herself so emotionally prepared for an unrestrained outpouring of assurance and strength and courage. Something, perhaps no more than an intuitive perception, had stopped her at the doorway, a first glance enough to tell her that the chasm between them was as wide and deep as it had ever been. Judd had proved, if anything, even harder to reach than he had been before, separation enforced with that terrifying confirmation of Miss Jessica's charge . . . *"Nothing that you would be interested in."*

After that, everything had been a hopeless struggle against that same feeling of unsalvageable defeat that had struck her down in Paris, all the worse because there was no self-saving explanation. Miss Jessica's accusation could be excused, at least in retrospect, as an eccentric delusion induced by senility and illness, Rolfe's parroting repetition no more than the unwitting cruelty of an unthinking boy, but there was no way to save herself from the full impact of those damning words from Judd's own lips.

As a last hope, built upon what Dr. Kharr had told her about the convention, she had thought that she might find at least a crack in Judd's image of old Matt Crouch as the all-wise, all-knowing, all-trustworthy idol that he had always made of him. But, no, Judd had refused to blame him, transferring all the onus to Roger Stark, still obsessed with that same neurotic antipathy that had been so evident ever since Roger had come with the company.

Driving toward New Ulster, she had been more and more occupied with thoughts of Judd's attitude toward Roger Stark, memory after memory suggesting the answer that she should have given Dr. Kharr when, walking down the corridor after he had come back to take her to Judd's room, he had asked, "Have you noticed anything out of the ordinary about your husband over the past two or three years, Mrs. Wilder, anything that impressed you as being a change in his essential behavior pattern?" She had given him an offhanded negative reply, too preoccupied with anticipation to look back. But that was before she had talked to Judd, before she had caught the significance of Dr. Kharr's question. Once seen, everything had fallen into place, not only the time span that Dr. Kharr had specified—"the last two or three years"—but also the succession of recalled incidents that traced the ever-rising intensity of Judd's antipathy to Roger Stark. She should have recognized it before, seen what it meant . . . but even if she had, what could she have done about it? Judd had never given her a chance . . . no, no, no . . . it was her own fault . . .

The light changed and she made the turn into Vixen Valley Road, visualizing her return to an empty house, feeling herself a runaway caught and hauled back to solitary confinement, punished not for an attempt to escape but for her failure as a wife . . . Miss Jessica was right . . . so was Rolfe . . . and Dr. Kharr, too . . . yes, that was why he had asked her all those questions, proving how blind she had been . . .

A flash of yellow caught her eye, a car wheeling out through the stone gateposts that marked the entrance to Vixen Valley, instantly identified as Eloise Stark's new Thunderbird. Anne Locke was with her, both of them in golf clothes, obviously on their way to the country club, so engrossed in conversation that neither looked in her direction. Having only a moment before reminded herself that it was Saturday—she had to get this car back to the Hertz place before it closed—the thought crossed her mind that it was strange that the Starks were in town this weekend, they so rarely were, but as she made the turn, the clinging image of Eloise and Anne shut out everything except a memory that canceled any hope that she would ever be able to temper Judd's feeling toward Roger Stark . . . that night coming home from the Lockes' cocktail party when she had innocently repeated Anne's remark that Roger had surprised her by knowing so much more about modern art than she had expected . . . Judd flaring back at her in that wildly irrational way, then grimly silent when she tried to defend herself, treating her as he did every time Roger's name came up, refusing to tell her why.

Suddenly she heard the echo of Judd's voice this morning, *"No, let me finish"*—triggering the realization that he *had* tried to talk to her . . . and she, frightened into stupidity, had stopped him!

Perhaps it was a vision less inspired than it seemed, no more than a reaction from the untenability of total despair, yet there suddenly burst upon her an illuminating awareness of the real nature of her error . . . Judd had thought that she was on Roger's side . . . standing against him . . . *of course, of course, of course* . . .

And almost as quickly, seen as an after-image of that same revelation, she saw with equal clarity the mistake that she had so often made when Judd said something about Matt Crouch, automatically discounting whatever it was, trying to make Judd see that he couldn't possibly be the faultless hero that he was trying to make him appear . . . *oh, God, how could she have been such a fool!*

All right, maybe she didn't *understand* her husband—but was that so important? Did it matter why he worshipped old Matt Crouch? Why he hated Roger Stark? She had to accept the way he felt and let it go at that . . . yes, that was what she had to do . . . stand by Judd, no matter what . . . think as he thought, feel as he felt . . . never criticizing him, never arguing with him . . .

Blinking, she saw a car parked in the driveway, an abrupt shattering of the expectation of total aloneness. Pulling up behind it, she saw that it was an old Plymouth, thinking then that she would find Annie inside, giving the house its weekly cleaning on Saturday instead of her regular Thursday.

But there was no sign of Annie in the kitchen, no telltale coffeepot on the stove. She stepped into the center hall, struck then by a screech of surprise that, even before she saw her, identified the intruder as Daphy Ingalls.

Before Kay could speak, Daphy's arms were around her, a smothering big-bosomed embrace that, although automatically resisted, was strangely comforting, a momentary relief from tension. But the greeting over, the spontaneity of surprise exhausted, Daphy backed away, evident embarrassment coloring her explanation that she had only stopped by to check the mail.

"Yes, I know—Judd told me how wonderful you've been," Kay acknowledged, hurriedly burying disapproval under a fulsome "I can't tell you how grateful I am, Daphy. For everything. If it hadn't been for your letter——"

"Oh, goodness, I haven't done anything," Daphy said. "But I am glad you decided to come home, Kay, awful glad. It's a darn shame to have your trip ruined like this, but still——"

"That's not important," she broke in, a more forceful disclaimer than she intended, subconsciously motivated by the feeling that Daphy had always thought Judd a neglected husband, never missing a chance to do something for him that, innocent though it might be, invariably appeared an expression of sympathy. Now, too conscious of harbored resentment, she overdid an attempt to keep it from showing, pouring out a full account of her trip home, reciting all that she had gone through, somehow feeling that she had to prove herself to Daphy, an attempt successful enough to incite a warmly moving "Bless you, honey, I know how worried you must have been," and Daphy's arm, slipping around her waist as she spoke, was an intimacy almost welcomed.

"Well, I guess I better pick up Joanne and get back to my stewing husband," Daphy finally said with a breakaway laugh. "Ray's so worked up about all these rumors—" She caught herself. "I guess you haven't heard."

"Rumors? About what?"

"Well, I don't know if it's true or not—maybe it's only talk—but there's a story all over town that Mr. Crouch has sold his stock and somebody else is going to be taking over the company—you know, one of these merger things."

"Sold his stock? You don't mean—?"

"I don't know, maybe it's just a rumor—you know how these things are, something like that gets started and everybody builds it up until you don't know what to believe. But there must be something to it. Ray got home from the office just before I left. He never goes in on Saturdays any more, but he was so stewed up this morning that he had to find out what he could. They were all there, all the old crowd—Jim and Harold and Ken Davis—oh, I don't know who all. Anyway, Ken told Ray that they've had three strange men going over the books up in Accounting. They aren't from the regular auditors—nobody knows who they are—Roger Stark just brought them up and said they were to be shown anything they wanted to see. And then, too, Mr. Crouch has been shuttling back and forth to Philadelphia all week. He wasn't in this morning, and that's kind of funny, too, because he's always there on Saturday, so it does sort of add up—to something, anyway."

"Yes, it does seem to, doesn't it," Kay said weakly, only now beginning to see what it might mean.

"You're thinking about Judd, aren't you?"

She nodded, beginning to be genuinely frightened. "He's always been so close to Mr. Crouch. If someone else were to come in as president—"

"That's what Ray says—without Mr. Crouch it won't be the same company. Of course, it wouldn't be so bad for Ray—at least that's what I've been trying to tell him—he's got his own work and he can just go ahead and do it, no matter who's president. But with Judd— and some of the others, too, I guess. Ray says that Vance Nichols told somebody that he'll walk out the very minute that Roger Stark comes in."

"Roger Stark? But would he be—I thought you said some other company?"

"Honey, I just don't know, but from what Ray says—I think most of this comes from Frank Whittaker—you know, when Roger first came, all the talk there was about his being brought in by the bankers? Well, it looks now like it was true. They were just setting things up so they could get their hands on the company. And you know the way Roger has wormed his way into everything—"

"Yes, I know," Kay said, struck by this stunning proof that there had been more to Judd's antipathy to Roger Stark than she had imagined possible.

"Well, there must be something to it," Daphy was rattling on. "If there wasn't, they wouldn't have had it in the paper this morning. Of course, they said it was only a rumor, but still they wouldn't have run it if—"

"Paper?"

Daphy gasped out an explanation. "Oh, good grief—Judd'll be seeing it, won't he? Oh, if I'd known anything like this was coming, I'd never have had the paper sent up to him—even if he did ask me to."

Kay bit her lip, trying to fight off the delusion that all of this was somehow Daphy's fault, unable to escape the damning coincidence that it was Daphy who had written to her, Daphy who was telling her this awful news, Daphy who was sending the newspaper up to Judd.

"—you just come over any time at all," Daphy's voice drifted in. "Six, six-thirty, seven—all I'm having is a chicken pie, so it won't make a bit of difference."

"Oh, thank you, Daphy," she said, buying escape with counterfeit appreciation. "But I've so many things to do—" She saw a way out. "And I'll probably be driving up to the hospital again this afternoon. I only drove down to turn in this rented car and get my own."

Self-convinced, she knew it was what she had to do, and the moment she got Daphy out of the house, she snatched up the telephone and placed a call for Dr. Kharr at County Memorial Hospital, curbing impatience by abstractedly sorting through the stacked junk mail while she waited for the call to go through, caught unprepared when she heard a flatly colorless "This is Doctor Kharr."

She identified herself, and then with as much poise as she could manage, said, "I've just heard that there's a story in the morning paper that's going to be an awful shock to Judd. I really think—if it's at all possible to get hold of it before he sees it——"

"If it's about Mr. Crouch selling his stock——"

"He's already seen it," she said, her voice collapsing.

"Mr. Crouch was here right after you left," Dr. Kharr explained. "He told your husband the whole story—or so I'd assume. At least, he knows that Mr. Crouch has sold out and that a new management will be taking over the company. So if that's all there is in the paper——"

"No, there's no point in it then, not if he knows—" she agreed, fighting off a sense of total deflation, finally able to ask, "Have you talked to Judd about it?"

"Yes," he said, his voice suspended, pregnant with a fearsome threat. "He's shaken, of course—he'd have to be, it couldn't possibly be otherwise——"

"Don't you think I should come back, Dr. Kharr? I could easily enough."

"Well, that's up to you, Mrs. Wilder—I can hardly advise you—but for whatever my judgment may be worth, I really don't think it's necessary. Your husband doesn't seem too seriously disturbed, much less so, really, than I would have expected. Apparently, Mr. Crouch did a very good job with him."

"He would," she said, the bitter edge in her voice dulled by the choke in her throat. Somehow, she managed to say that she would see him in the morning, and then with the last of her strength and composure, added a concluding "Thank you, Doctor."

Minutes later, when a buzzing sound finally penetrated the silence, she realized that she had not yet hung up the telephone.

❖ XI ❖

EVERY DAY THIS WEEK—Sunday, Monday, Tuesday, Wednesday, Thursday, Friday—Kay Wilder had driven the forty-two miles to County Memorial Hospital, spent an hour or so with her husband and then driven home again, more convinced each day that her visit had been a tolerated but hardly welcome intrusion upon the snug little world that Judd had built for himself within the hospital walls. For all that she had accomplished, she might as well have stayed in Paris.

With two minor exceptions, Judd had shown no reaction whatsoever to an impending change of management at Crouch Carpet. Last Sunday, the morning after Mr. Crouch had broken the news to him, she had driven up with anxious anticipation, expecting the worst, only to have Judd pass it off with "It's one of those things, I guess." Unable to believe that he could be so genuinely unconcerned, she had attempted a light probing, firmly rebuffed when he cut her off with "There's no use worrying about it—just have to wait and see what happens."

Then on Tuesday there had been a letter from Rolfe, addressed to both of them as his letters always were, but plainly written to his father, a three-page description of what his work with Seaborne Oil would be, a rather boyishly exuberant anticipation of the opportunity that lay ahead of him, all leading up to an expression of appreciation to his father for having opened his eyes to the wonderful life that a big corporation could offer. "I hope he doesn't wake up some day," Judd had said, "and blame me for having given him a bad steer."

"You know you didn't," she had quickly assured him, ready to go on, but Judd had slammed the door with a change of subject, leaving her with only that glimpse of the depth of his disillusionment.

She had tried every day to nudge that door open again but with no success. Judd had not volunteered a word about the company, and feeling herself prohibited from telling him anything that might worry him, she had repeated none of the rumors that she had heard. No one knew anything for sure, it seemed—there had been nothing more in the paper, no official announcement of any kind—and since company-talk was all she heard from everyone she met, there was little else that she could bring to Judd as news from New Ulster. Even when she managed to pick up something that should have interested him, at least enough to fill a few minutes of that long hour, it invariably fell flat. It was not that he was refusing to talk to her; he would talk freely enough about anything that went on within the hospital walls, but that was the limit of his interest. He was living in his own little private world, a tiny domain significantly populated only with Mary, Mrs. Cope, Dr. Kharr—and, these last three or four days, that young Indian doctor who, more successful than she had been, had somehow managed to squeeze his way inside.

Now it was Saturday again, 2:25 on the dashboard clock as she pulled in to park. She was on the schedule that she had adopted early in the week. After hearing Judd's repetitious praise of Mrs. Cope, she had decided that she must meet this paragon. Delaying her arrival until two-thirty made her hour-long visit overlap the change of shifts, giving her a chance to see not only the little Welch girl—a pleasant enough child but hardly anyone who could teach her anything that she needed to know—but also Mrs. Cope, from whom she hoped to learn some nursing secrets that she herself might use after she got Judd home from the hospital.

As a first impression, she had seen Mrs. Cope as one of those manless women to whom the nursing profession offered a license for the temporary possession of other women's husbands. As the week had gone by that estimate had been strengthened rather than diminished. There was, it seemed, no end to which the old biddy would not go to subvert any attempt that Kay made to do something for her husband.

A part of the trouble, of course, lay with Judd. Whatever he wanted, he asked Mrs. Cope first, and with that advantage she could always beat her out. All that had been left for her to do was to bring him books and magazines, seemingly a wasted effort because, as far as she could tell from anything Judd had said, he was not reading. Nor was he watching television—at least the set was never on when she arrived, nor had he once mentioned any program that he had seen, not even the news. When she had asked him yesterday if he had listened to President Johnson's Vietnam speech, he had switched the subject to the old man in the room across the corridor whose prostate trouble, it seemed, was of vastly superior importance.

She had parked today where she always did, beside Judd's dusty Riviera, a reminder that one of these days she would have to find someone to come up with her and drive it home. There were any number of people who would be glad enough to do it, but deciding who to ask suggested itself as something to talk about to Judd, and she got out of her car gratefully adding it to the too-small cache of conversational subjects that she had stored up for today's visit.

As she walked toward the hospital, her eyes caught Dr. Kharr standing in the window of his office, watching her arrival. She raised her hand in greeting and he replied with a gesture that said he wanted to see her. She smiled, nodding to tell him that she understood, but her mood was mixed, a sincere desire to talk to him again countered by a reminiscent consciousness of the discomfiture that she had felt during her last session with him. On Sunday, he had talked to her for more than an hour, telling her how stress could cause a coronary occlusion, explaining his theory of the precoronary behavior syndrome, illustrating it by using Judd as an example, astounding her with how much he knew about him, even some things that she herself had never noticed until he called them to her attention. Despite the embarrassment of acknowledging the doctor's superior observation and understanding, it had been an illuminating experience, enhancing her confidence in him, encouraging her to tell him everything she could about Judd and his work.

She had not seen him on Monday, but there had been a long session on Tuesday, even more revealing than the Sunday one had been, and she willingly enough agreed to talk to him again the next day. Overnight, however, he seemed to have changed his attitude, no longer assuming that the stress that had caused Judd's heart attack had been generated by his job. He had asked her a lot of questions about the past, digging more and more deeply into their married relationship, and in spite of a conscious attempt to be completely honest and forthright, she found herself becoming edgily resistant. She was more than willing to submit to anything that might prove helpful, but the line of some of Dr. Kharr's questioning had begun to make her think that he was more interested in completing a scientific case study than he was in helping her, a suspicion aroused when he dropped a remark about working on a book.

Nevertheless, it was a transient attitude, substantially offset by her appreciation for how much she had learned from him, and she had looked forward to another session. He had not been around on Thursday, however, and yesterday she had seen him for only a moment coming down the corridor as she was leaving. She had a dozen questions waiting to be asked, but now when she found him waiting for her in the lobby, something about the way he invited her to come back to his office made her feel a prickle of apprehension, in no way relieved when, as he held a chair for her, she noticed the top of his desk. Everything had been cleared away except a file folder with Judd's name on it.

Seated he said, "Your husband is coming along very well, Mrs. Wilder, very well indeed. I've put him through a quite complete examination over the past two days—yesterday afternoon, this morning—I couldn't be more pleased with his physical condition."

"That's good to hear," she said, a response less sincere than it would have been had she not noticed that, in contrast to his composed voice, the fingers of his left hand were drumming a rapid tattoo on the file folder.

"So we're at the point now where a decision has to be made," he continued, still in that same controlled tone, but now she saw his right hand go through a quick sequence of nervous movements, finger-combing his hair, pinching his pursed lips, tugging at an earlobe. Then, suddenly taking off his spectacles, he asked, "How does he strike you, Mrs. Wilder—his state of mind, his mental attitude?"

She fumbled for direction, finding it when Dr. Kharr asked specifically, "Has he said anything to you about going back to work?"

"No."

"Nothing?" he asked. "Nothing at all?"

"No, not a word."

Dr. Kharr nodded, his expression suggesting that he was hearing what he had feared might be true. "Has he said anything about Mr. Crouch?"

She shook her head. "Not since the day after he was here."

"Anything about Mr. Stark?"

"Well, the day I got back—I told you about that——"

"Yes, I remember. But he's said nothing about him since?"

"No, he hasn't even mentioned his name."

Again, Dr. Kharr nodded, even more certainly an expression of fear confirmed. "Has he said anything about going home?"

"No."

"Any complaints about the hospital—the food, the service, the way he's being taken care of?"

"No, he seems perfectly content, completely satisfied."

"Too much so, I'm afraid," he muttered under his breath, silent for a preoccupied moment, and then as if thinking aloud, "By now—a man of his temperament—he ought to be tearing down the walls to get out of here." He fixed her with a suddenly focused stare. "What do you make of it?"

"I—well, I really don't know what to say. It has worried me a little, his not being interested in anything except—" She let her voice fade off, thinking that he was not listening.

But he caught her up with "Except what?"

"What's going on here. In the hospital, I mean. It's as if—well, as if he'd put everything else out of his mind. I don't know, maybe it's the best thing for him——"

"No," he cut her off, so sharply that, aware of it, he excused himself with a thin smile. "I've been worrying about it, too."

"He's not been talking to you either?" she asked, surprised when he shook his head, obliquely relieved to learn that Judd's unwillingness to talk about the future was not confined to her.

"It's not an unusual reaction, of course," Dr. Kharr was saying. "In fact, it's a rather common one, the one we see more often than any other—the man who's been so frightened by a coronary that he's more than willing to hole up in a nice comfortable hospital room and let the rest of the world go by. But I must say it's not what I expected of your husband. I thought our problem would be at the opposite pole—trying to hold him down, get all that drive and energy under control."

Tentatively she advanced, "Do you really think it's because he's frightened?"

He looked at her sharply. "You don't?"

"I suppose he could be more frightened than he appears——"

"But you don't think so?"

"Couldn't it be—well, it's not his heart attack that he's refusing to talk about—it's what's happening at the company."

"You think that's what he's trying to avoid—facing up to what's going on at Crouch Carpet?"

"Oh, I don't know—maybe I'm wrong."

"Tell me this—do you think there's any possibility that he might decide not to go back?"

"You think he should?"

"By all means," he said, strongly positive. "At least for long enough to prove to himself that he's not been licked. It's like a man who's been thrown from a horse—unless he gets right back on, he may never ride again." He leaned forward, his hand raised in a gesture of restraint. "I don't want to frighten you unnecessarily, Mrs. Wilder—no, not at all—but I do think you should be aware of how potentially serious this can be. I've seen it so often—the man who uses a heart attack as a convenient excuse to retire into a state of semi-invalidism, consciously or not avoiding something that he doesn't want to face up to. I'm sure it's difficult to see your husband in that light—" His suspended voice made it a question.

"Yes, it is," she agreed, but memory made it a possibility less remote than she was willing to admit, recalling how abruptly Judd had abandoned the theater, all interest as suddenly lost as if a flame had been snuffed out.

Dr. Kharr was saying something about wishing there were more he could do, meaningless words that were no more than half heard until, with consciousness-crashing suddenness, she realized that he had just said, "From here on out, Mrs. Wilder, it's going to be up to you."

Stunned, she groped, "Up to me? What can I—what do you mean?"

"If anyone can bring him around—and I'm sure you can—you're the one to do it. And you can't do it here, I know that. That's why I'm so anxious to get him home."

"Home? You don't mean—not today?"

"There's no reason for keeping him here any longer, no reason at all. All the tests——"

"Oh, I know you wouldn't release him if it weren't the thing to do, but—well, you'd said another ten days."

"Yes, I suppose there are some arrangements you'll have to make, aren't there?" he said, plainly a concession. "All right, suppose we say tomorrow."

"I want him home as soon as possible—of course I do. It's only that—well, I'm not certain that I can give him the kind of care that he ought to have."

"He needs no special care, Mrs. Wilder. He's out of bed now—we've had him walking up and down the hall the last two days. He can go to the bathroom, bathe himself—he's not a bedridden invalid any more. Oh, he should be reasonably careful, of course—avoid any real physical effort for the next couple of weeks. I wouldn't want to see him running up and down stairs, for example —or is your house all on one floor?"

"No, it's two-story," she said, trying to recover her balance, hurriedly resurrecting the plan that she had tentatively made for Judd's care. "We have a first-floor library that's planned so it can be converted into another guest room—"

"Good. That's fine. Let him stay there for—oh, a week or so. It's probably an unnecessary precaution—there are many men doing hard physical labor with hearts no better than his is right now—but still there's no harm in playing it safe. And a first-floor room will be very convenient—a bed where he can lie down whenever he feels tired. He ought to get all the rest he can—a good nap in the afternoon, early to bed—but the real problem, Mrs. Wilder, isn't physical. I'm not worried about his heart, not in the least. And you shouldn't be either. Don't try to turn your house into a hospital, or yourself into a nurse. Don't treat him like an invalid. If you do, that's the way he'll go on thinking of himself." He put on a forced smile. "We've got to drag him out of that cave and get him back in the world again." The smile faded. "I'm sure you understand."

She nodded, understanding well enough, yet torn by the frightening conflict between what he was asking her to do, and the compelling need to establish a new relationship with her husband through the kind of loving care and sympathetic concern that she was prepared to lavish upon him.

"The important thing is to get him talking. Get it all out in the open, all this company business. Talk it out. As soon as he hears himself putting it into words, he'll realize that he's hiding from something that's not half as bad as he's been imagining. Once you get him talking——"

"But what if he won't?" burst out, expelled by the pressure of anxiety. "I've tried to get him to talk all week—he just won't, that's all."

He fixed her with a pinning stare. "How hard have you tried—how seriously?"

"Well, not too, I guess," she retreated. "I was afraid if I asked him too many questions—well, I didn't want it to worry him."

His eyes narrowed to slits. "The only thing to be afraid of, Mrs. Wilder, is that it won't worry him."

Silent, she looked away.

"What *is* happening at the company?" he demanded.

"That's the trouble, it's all so indefinite, just a lot of rumors."

"That you haven't told him about?"

"No, I——"

"Tell him everything you hear, Mrs. Wilder. Good or bad, foolish or not, don't hold back anything. Everything you pick up, no matter how inconsequential it may seem—it's another chance to get him talking. Then he'll start thinking. That's the important thing—make him think his way through. That's what you've got to do—and you can't do it by protecting him, keeping things from him. Don't be afraid of worrying him—it'll do him no harm. Remember what I told you about coronary stress—it's not generated by a tangible anxiety. It's the blind driving that——"

"I remember," she said, trying to cut him off, feeling herself being driven deeper and deeper into a hopeless situation.

Dr. Kharr was not to be stopped. "He may try to do the same thing at home that he's doing here—hole up and shut out the world. Don't let him. Encourage visitors, particularly people from the company, and do everything you can to make certain that they don't treat him like an invalid who has to be protected from the truth. Get them to talk about what's going on, what's happening, what's liable to happen. Ask questions yourself. Bore in. Direct the conversation."

"But I've never——"

"You may think that I'm going too far in telling you all this, but I've seen so many cases——"

"No, I want you to tell me," she said hurriedly. "The only thing is—well, I've never talked to Judd about the company, and I'm sure he'd be terribly suspicious if, all of a sudden, I start—" She stopped, hoping that she had said enough to make him understand.

Seemingly, he understood only too well, his eyes cutting through her like X-ray beams. "Are you saying that up to now you haven't been interested in your husband's business life?"

"It's not that I haven't been interested," she protested. "It's only that—we used to talk things over, years ago—" She was getting in deeper and deeper, trapping herself, so far gone now that admission offered the only escape. "I don't know, maybe it's partly my own fault. Maybe I haven't been as interested as I should have been. But when you aren't told what's happening, when you don't know what's going on—it's terribly difficult to be really interested if you aren't involved."

Quietly, but with telling force, Dr. Kharr said, "You're involved now, Mrs. Wilder. You have to be. There's no one else."

She felt suddenly weak, drained by a debilitating sense of personal inadequacy, a sensation strange enough to be frightening.

"I think you underestimate yourself, Mrs. Wilder," Dr. Kharr said firmly, encouragement that was more meaningful than any expression of sympathy or understanding could possibly have been. "You're so much more objective than most wives are, so much more capable of seeing things as they really are—you'll bring him around, Mrs. Wilder, I know you will."

She avoided his eyes, listening to the echo of his words, trying to hear them as a rebuttal of everything that Miss Jessica and Rolfe had said against her, yet chilled by the implications of *objective*, hearing it as an antonym of everything that she had to be if that wall between herself and Judd was ever to be broken down.

"I wish there were more I could do," Dr. Kharr said. "But there's a limit to how far any doctor can go. I'm sure you understand."

She nodded, and responding to an unmistakable tone of dismissal, got quickly to her feet.

"I'll see you again tomorrow, of course," Dr. Kharr said. "I'll have a diet list for you—a few notes—"

She made a move toward the door. "Have you told Judd that you're releasing him?"

"No, but I told him this morning that if his other tests looked as good as his EKG—I'm sure he's expecting it."

"You don't want me to tell him—or do you?"

"If you'd rather not—?"

"No, I'll tell him," she said firmly, less a show of confidence than a demanded assumption of responsibility, stimulating a kind of false courage that gave a credible semblance of sincerity to the thanks she offered him for being so helpful. But as she walked down the corridor, there was a persisting consciousness that there had been an expression of relief on Dr. Kharr's face as he had turned away at the door, a feeling that translated itself now into a sense of abandonment, of being left totally alone to solve a problem that had already defeated him . . . *"There's a limit to how far a doctor can go"* . . . but there was no limit, apparently, to what was expected of a wife.

The door of Judd's room stood open. Glancing in she saw that the shift change had already taken place. Mrs. Cope was standing on the far side of the bed talking to Judd, interrupting herself with a throat-clearing warning and a silent glance toward the door.

Judd's head came around. "I'd about given up—didn't think you were coming today." His tone was encouraging, tempting her to believe that he might have been disappointed if she had failed to appear.

"I've been talking to Dr. Kharr," she explained.

Judd's expression changed to one of tense inquiry, disconcerting but no more so than Mrs. Cope's flatfooted stance beside the bed.

"He was telling me about the tests he's made, how good they all look," she said, attempting lightness that didn't quite come off. Judd was silent, waiting for her to go on, but she felt no more challenged by him than by Mrs. Cope who, still making no move to leave the room, was regarding her with a grimly tight-lipped expression, almost as if daring her to speak.

Looking fixedly at Judd, but by no means unconscious of Mrs. Cope's ears, she said, "He says he's going to let you go home tomorrow." Quickly she added, "Isn't that wonderful?" but not before she saw that Judd's first reaction was a questioning glance at Mrs. Cope.

« 2 »

All through the afternoon and on into the early evening, Judd Wilder's thoughts had returned again and again to his wife's strange mood today. She had not been continuously in his mind—there had been interruptions and diversions—yet he had, in the past three hours, thought about her more intently than he had for many years. Actually, it was one of the few serious and sustained attempts that he had ever made to understand behavior that he had found unaccountable. In the early years of his marriage he had made similar attempts, but one failure after another had taught him, if only subconsciously, that it was a futile effort. Nevertheless he had acquired —this, too, was largely subconscious—an instinctive anticipation of how Kay would react to any given situation, and it was a violation of this pattern of expectation that had disturbed him this afternoon. Unsure though he was of his ability to interpret her mood, it was difficult to down the impression that she was frightened. But why?

He had not been at all surprised by the news that he was being released from the hospital—only a minute or two before Kay's arrival, he had bet Mrs. Cope that he would be home before tomorrow night—but it seemed that Kay had been caught off guard, disconcerted, as she always was, by anything that made an unanticipated demand upon her. Yet that explanation was challenged by her reaction to his protest that turning the library into a bedroom would put her to more work than it was worth. She had brushed off the work and trouble as being of no consequence, not even obliquely asking for any special gratitude, seemingly thinking only of him, not at all of herself . . . *strange* . . .

Her fear—if fear it was—might mean that Kharr had told her that there was something more seriously wrong with his heart than he had admitted to him. But if that were true, why was he discharging him early? And he was. Mrs. Cope had made that plain enough, saying that she would have brought in something really special for his dinner if she had only known that this was to be his last night. But she, too, was acting strangely. She was annoyed, it seemed, because Kay had been told before she had, a guess strongly supported by the way she had treated Dr. Kharr when he had stopped in for a brief visit on his way home to dinner, giving him only the grimmest of nods when he asked, "I suppose you know that we're sending him home tomorrow?"

In the few minutes that Kharr had stayed—he would be back later, he said—Judd had tried to pin him down to exactly what he had told Kay, but had found nothing to support his suspicion that Kharr was holding something back, nothing to explain why Kay had acted so peculiarly.

Mrs. Cope had not come back into the room immediately after the doctor had left, as she had always done before, and she had been out of the room several times since, no longer apologizing for leaving him alone. Her change of attitude was not, he felt reasonably sure, a continuation of her earlier pique, but was instead the reflection of an accepted ending, a defection reminiscent of Mrs. Gorman on those evenings after his father had said that his mother would be coming home tomorrow.

He had tried to talk to her several times since dinner, but had sparked nothing beyond a little polite chitchat. She was no longer interested. What had before seemed something close to affection was revealed now as a prostitution, something bought and paid for, over and ended when the money stopped. Her only forward-looking remark had been "I hope you're not going to be foolish enough to go back to work too soon," turning his mind back to Kay again, thinking of her in the context of Dr. Kharr's admonition that he spend at least three weeks at home . . . *"and a month would be better."*

If that was what was frightening Kay, the prospect of having him at home day after day for a month, her anxiety was something that he could both understand and share. In ten years, they had never spent two consecutive dawn-to-dark days in each other's company. The last occasion that was at all comparable to what now lay ahead had been that awful month in Connecticut before he had finally grabbed off the agency job. Day after day, he had tried to stick it out at home, always giving up before noon, catching the 11:20 into New York. That was the only way he had managed to get through it, being able to get out of the house, to get away from those accusing glances that Kay would give him every time she didn't think he was looking, always that same "Nothing" when he asked her what she was thinking, always that same rigid resistance to letting him invade her secret mind.

Judd Wilder had never, at least in terms specific enough to be consciously concluding, thought of his marriage as a mistake. He had accepted it as he had accepted most of his other unfulfilled dreams, none of which had ever worked out quite as he had anticipated. He had once thought that having a play on Broadway would somehow cause him to shed his confining chrysalis and permit his rebirth as a new man. That had not happened. Nor, in a different but nevertheless pertinent way, had marrying Kay Cannon turned out to be what he had imagined.

He had vaguely visualized marriage as a duality of being, a doubling of self that would broaden and expand the confining limits of a single life. None of his thinking—if *thinking* it was—had ever been precise enough to demand a subsequent admission of naïveté, yet his disappointment had been tangible enough, and long enough continued, to make him accept the seemingly inevitable conclusion that a true blending of their lives was impossible. The most that he could hope for was a tolerable coexistence.

He sometimes imagined that things might have been different if it had not been for the war, thinking that by the time he got home from the service, his marriage already three years old, Kay's separateness had been too firmly established to be broken down. Yet that had never been a completely tenable explanation. There was something beyond that, something deeply fixed in Kay's character —a penchant for secrecy, her mind an inner sanctum that he was never allowed to enter, filled with private thoughts that she would never permit him to share. Kay's life was her own, lived not with him but with herself, behind those eyes that were always measuring the gap between something that he had done and her own secret expectation.

He had never made any serious attempt to talk things out with Kay, certain that she would have been unable to understand the kind of relationship that he wanted. She would have maintained, as she so frequently had in the old days, that nothing gave her more happiness than a chance to "help" him, yet what she meant by *help* had always been uncomfortably close to *control*. Never had this been more evident than the time he had let her work with him on his Broadway play. He had learned then, belatedly, the true answer to his boyhood question about why his father had so quietly but firmly excluded his mother from the newspaper office. "She's got her own interests," was all that his father had said, not explaining that it was the only way he had found to avoid what would otherwise have been an intolerable situation. Although Judd Wilder had never specifically recognized a parallel between his wife and his mother, he had nevertheless sensed that Kay's consuming preoccupation with Rolfe was somehow akin to his mother's continuing identification with her father, the Senator's political career the dominant interest in her life. As a boy he had easily seen through the transparently false front behind which his mother had tried to conceal the agony she had suffered when his grandfather's Senate seat had been swept away in a landslide defeat, and there was at least something of that recollection behind his feeling that Kay's strange behavior since she had returned from Paris was somehow related to the way that she had been hurt by Rolfe's rebellious abandonment of all of the plans she had made for him. Today, something about her manner had reminded him of that night when she had returned from Maine, coming to his bed with a passion that had been, as he had afterward realized, little more than a rebounding reaction to the demeaning way that she had been spurned. Then, too, there had been an aura of fear . . . but somehow this was different . . . *strange* . . .

He heard footsteps coming down the corridor, instantly recognized as Raggi's, arousing a welcome anticipation of pleasant diversion. Ever since that morning when Mary had pushed him into talking to Raggi, the young Indian had been a regular visitor, poking his head in the door to say hello every time he happened to be down at this end of the hall, at least once a day making a purposeful appearance, settling down for as long a talk as he could manage. Although Raggi was unquestionably motivated by loneliness and a characteristically Indian love of argument, it seemed that a real friendship had developed, all the more certain after Raggi had stopped punctuating every sentence with a too-respectful "sir," all the more genuine because it carried no overtone of professional obligation.

Mrs. Cope plainly disapproved of Raggi's intrusions, frequently discouraging their extension by sitting tight, not leaving when he appeared. Tonight, however, she was on her feet by the time he appeared in the doorway, out of the room as soon as she could slip past him.

"So tomorrow you will be leaving us," Raggi said as he came around the end of the bed. "You are happy, yes?"

Judd shrugged. "I'll still be tied down—a month at home."

"A month?" Raggi repeated, surprised. "This is what Dr. Kharr is telling you? You must be staying home for a month?"

"It's up to me—two or three weeks, a month—depending on how I feel."

"Ah, yes," Raggi said, smiling his relief. "I am thinking it will not be a month."

"I hope not."

"Then you will be returning to your company?"

"I don't know—maybe yes, maybe no. It all depends on how the ball bounces."

"But you are thinking—maybe no?" Raggi pressed, clearly concerned.

"I just haven't been thinking, that's all."

"No, no, that I am not believing," Raggi came back. "You have been thinking very much—yes?"

"A little," he granted. "Two and a half weeks, nothing else to do—you can't help it. Particularly with Kharr needling you into it."

"But that is good, do you not think so?"

He shrugged.

"You do not think it is good—what Dr. Kharr has done for you?"

He started a flippant reply, put off by Raggi's dead-earnest expression, switching to an honest "Oh, I won't say that he hasn't done me some good. Sure he has. He's made me see a lot of things that I'd never seen before."

"You have changed very much since you are here, I think. I remember when I first saw you—" Raggi distorted his face into a caricaturing mask. "No, no, you cannot be ill, you do not have time for such foolishness, you must go to a very important meeting!" He laughed. "Those meetings—now they are not so important—is that not true?"

He shrugged.

"I think you will be going back to your company," Raggi said confidently.

"I've got to make a living."

"It is not that, I think," Raggi said. "It is not necessary that you must be so rich."

"Rich? I wish I were."

"How much is it that you are making each year?"

He recoiled, but quickly forgave Raggi's foreign boldness, replying frankly, "Oh, I don't know—thirty-odd thousand, something like that."

"And you are not thinking that is being rich?"

"After I pay my taxes, all the things I get shaken down for—there's damn little left, I can tell you that."

"But you are having a big house, servants—"

"A cleaning woman two days a week."

"How many cars are you having?"

"Three—but one of them is my son's."

"You are sending him to Paris for his education."

"He's there on a grant that pays most of his expenses."

"So it is not possible for you to live without this thirty-odd thousand—is that what you are saying?"

"I've lived on a lot less."

"But then you are not happy?"

"No, I wouldn't say that. Money isn't everything."

"Ah!" Raggi exclaimed, a bugle call to a new attack. "Yes, yes, that is what you Americans are always saying—it is not the money that is important. That is what you are saying, but I am thinking it is not true."

"All right, what is true?" he asked, encouragement without spirit, finding himself a little too sober-minded tonight to truly relish the verbal jousting that Raggi so loved.

"This company for which you are working, this Crouch Carpet—what is it that they are doing? Yes, yes, you are making these beautiful carpets so that all American people will have wall-to-wall happiness—" He interjected a giggle, appreciating his own little joke. "Is it not true that this company is existing only to make money?"

"You've got it the wrong way around. We make money so that we *can* exist."

"But if it is only to exist, what is the purpose of this existence?"

"What are you trying to do? Talk me out of going back to Crouch Carpet?"

"No, no, please, you must not be thinking that," Raggi said hurriedly. "It is only that I am trying to understand what I will be needing to know when I get back to India. Already in this town that is my home we are having big companies coming to build factories. There is already one where they are making *ganaspati*—it is hydrogenated vegetable oil for cooking, you see. Also there is a plant for making aluminium, and now my father is writing that they are building a very large factory for the making of automobile tires. So very soon, I am thinking I will be having patients like you. If I do not understand this American disease, how is it possible that I will be able to treat it?"

"What do you mean—'American disease'?" he came back, aware that he was laying himself open to a waiting needle, attempting to blunt it with defensive "You're not trying to tell me, are you, that you don't have heart attacks in India?"

"No, no, it is not only heart attacks of which I am speaking," Raggi said. "But since you have mentioned it—only today I am receiving a letter from my father in which he is telling me that he is having such a case, a coronary who is not yet fifty years old. It is not a coincidence, I think, that this man of whom he is writing is the assistant to the managing director at the *ganaspati* factory."

"Is it an American company?"

"No, no."

"Then why call it the American disease?"

A twinkling smile cracked Raggi's mask. "My father is saying—he is a very witty man, I think—he is saying that it is a very communicable disease. Now it is spreading all over the world."

"I thought it was the British who were responsible for all your troubles."

"It is all the same disease," Raggi said blandly. "Only you are having it in a more virulent form. The British—they are still having their tea, but you—no, no, you cannot have such a waste of time. Always you must be driving, driving, driving—push, push, push."

"All right, if we Americans are such a bad lot, why did you come to the United States to get your medical education?"

A twinkle flashed in Raggi's eyes. "When one wishes to study an infectious disease, is it not wise to go to the place where it is endemic?"

He laughed his appreciation of the Indian's debating skill, but countered with "All you're saying is that all the rest of the world wishes that they had it, too."

"Ah, yes—now you will be telling me again that you have the highest standard of living the world has ever known."

"Can you deny it?"

"So all Americans must be very happy—is that what you are saying? No, no, I do not think so. When I first came to New York, that is what I am thinking—everyone will be happy because they are having such a very fine life. But it is not true. In all the world, I think, there are not so many unhappy people as there are in this country."

"If by unhappy you mean dissatisfied—sure, we are. That's why we've gotten somewhere. You don't make progress by squatting down on your hunkers and waiting for the gods to take care of you."

Raggi recoiled as if struck an unfair blow, but quickly bounded back to the attack. "So you say you are getting somewhere. Tell me where it is that you are getting?"

Judd started to speak, but a moment of hesitation gave Raggi a chance to cut him down with "Ah, you cannot tell me. That is the trouble, I think. You do not know. It is like climbing a ladder that has no top. Yes, yes, that is what is wrong in your Western philosophy. For you, life is a ladder. Always you must be climbing, climbing, climbing—up, up, up. There is no ending until you are too old to climb any more."

"Or someone knocks you off the ladder," Judd suggested, an almost involuntary response to apprehensions that, even now, were hardly over the threshold of consciousness.

For a moment it seemed that Raggi would pick it up, but then he continued soberly, "In our Hindu belief, you see, life is not a ladder —it is a wheel. On a ladder, one rung is always higher than another— yes? But who can say that one spoke of a wheel is ahead of another?"

"So you just get aboard and go rolling along for the ride," Judd said with a needling smile. "You don't worry whether or not you're getting anywhere?"

"Where is it that you are getting?" Raggi flashed back. "No, no, I do not mean *you*, Mr. Wilder—I am meaning only this American way of thinking, this illusion that you are making what you call progress."

"But we are. How can you deny it? All you have to do is look around you."

Raggi was shaking his head. "Do you not see—it is only the turning of the wheel? You are believing that you are ahead of anything that has ever been in the history of the world. It is not true. You are not ahead, you are behind. Two thousand years behind. Two thousand years ago—do you know that India was then the richest country in the world? We are having great factories for doing many things —yes, yes, the weaving of beautiful textiles, that you are knowing, I think. But also we are having factories for woodworking, for glassblowing, for metalworking—" He caught a quick breath. "Do you know where the swords and lances of the Roman legions came from? India! Have you read Pliny? Do you not know what he says, what fools the Romans are to be spending all their gold on these fine things that are being made in India. And was he not correct, sir? Do you know why it is that Rome is falling? No, no, it is not for the reasons you are saying in your Western history books—it is because the Romans are sending all of their gold to India. When the gold is gone, there is no more Roman Empire."

"But if India was so far ahead of the rest of the world——"

"Ah, *ahead* you are saying. Do you not remember my question— what spoke of the wheel is ahead of another? Yes, yes, that is what it is—the turning of the wheel. You are now where India was two thousand years ago. Two thousand years from now—where will you be? If you are wishing to see—look at India as it is today. You do not like this—it does not please you to think of not being so rich and powerful?"

"Answer my question," Judd broke in, smiling. "If India was once the richest nation on earth, why did you——"

"Is there more goodness in rice that is eaten from a golden bowl?"

"But if you don't have enough rice to keep from starving——"

"Yes, yes, we are very grateful to you for sending us the grain we must have," Raggi said, a burlesque of fawning gratitude. "Do you not see why it is that we are dependent upon you? Is it not because of these Western ideas that you have inflicted upon us? We are underdeveloped, you say—we must be having all of these things without which it is not possible to be civilized—steel mills, hydroelectric dams——"

"Nobody forced you to——"

"That is what I am saying—it is a very infectious disease," Raggi cut him off, adroitly avoiding being pinned down. "Please, sir, we are not talking of India, we were talking of America—why it is that you must always be climbing this ladder? Is it not wise for a man to have an ending—a place where you can say, I have climbed enough, now I can stop?"

Judd hesitated, blocked by a recognition of personal pertinence, suspecting for a moment that this must be something that Kharr had put him up to doing. Cautiously, he asked, "All right, where do you stop?"

"For an American, I do not know," Raggi said. "In India, it is all arranged, you see. Do you know the *asrama dharma?*"

"No."

"It is our Brahmin way of life," Raggi took off, a zealot's fire in his eyes. "There are four stages in the life of a man—this is what we are believing. In the first stage, you are a *Brahmachari,* a student. This is the time for studying, for learning, for preparation. Then you are educated and it is time for the second stage, the *Grahastha,* the time of the householder. Now you are married and fulfilling your duty to your family. This is the time for very hard working, for great achievement, for the acquiring of material things."

"How long does that last?"

"It is all a matter of your sons. When they have finished their education and are ready to take up their own duties to the family— then it is time for you to become a *Vanaprastha.* This is the third stage, you see. This is the time of letting go, of withdrawal from all of the things with which you were too preoccupied when you were thinking of only what is material."

"How old would you be then?" Judd asked, his earlier suspicion revived. "About my age?"

"No, no, you must not be taking this in a personal way," Raggi said, a hurried disclaimer. "I am speaking only of our ancient wisdom, what it is that we have learned about the nature of man. We are not believing, you see, in your illusion of progress. That is what is so bad, we think, about your Western philosophy. To have it—is this not what you have said?—you must be always dissatisfied. So how can there be happiness? Yes, yes, I know—it is your philosophy that this will come after death—then you will find your way to God. This is what we do not believe. That is why we are having this fourth stage of life. That is when we say a man should find peace—contentment—happiness—before he dies, not afterwards."

Judd remained silent, avoiding the danger of getting into a religious argument, warned by prior experience of Raggi's sensitivity to any criticism of Hindu belief.

"You do not believe that?" Raggi pressed.

Forced, Judd said, "I guess we all have to play the game according to our own rules. In India—if a man can get away with retiring at forty-five—all right, more power to you."

"No, no, it is not retiring," Raggi objected. "It is only the turning of the wheel, the transition from one phase to another. Do you not think there should be a time in a man's life when he can say, 'Now I am through with material things, this moneymaking—that is over, I have done my duty to my family, my community—now I will be doing my duty to myself.'"

"Why can't he do both at the same time? Why do you think—?"

"Yes, yes, in New York, I have seen these men. All of the day they are running their business, pulling strings, making money. In America, this they must be doing always until they are very old. There is no time for anything else. But they are not happy. Something is missing. So what do they do? Rush to the art gallery—buy a painting which they have no time to appreciate—back to business. Rush to the concert hall—sign a pledge to give money for an orchestra they have no time to hear—back to business."

Judd laughed.

"Please, you have said it yourself, night before last, I think. Is it not true—when you are in business, there is no room in your mind for anything else. I am asking you about what books you have been reading, and you are saying you must do so much reading for your business that there is no time for——"

"All right, I'm an unread, uncultured Yankee slob."

"No, no, please—you must not be thinking—" Raggi began, an agonized protest, abruptly cut off.

Dr. Kharr was standing in the doorway, an inquiring smile playing about his face. "Is this a private battle? Or can anyone get in?"

"Come in," Judd called out. "I need help. Dr. Raggi here has me almost convinced that I ought to throw everything overboard, grow a beard and get a begging bowl—" He was stopped by Karr's sharply critical glance at Raggi, torn then by regret as he saw the young

Indian's anguished expression, the look of a man unfairly victimized. Judd attempted quick retraction, but Raggi's face did not relax, even when Kharr said, "If you can turn up another bowl, I might join you."

Raggi, on his feet since the instant of Kharr's appearance, backed away, offering his chair. "No, no, I must be going," he said, rejecting a warm invitation to stay. "I am here too long already, I think."

Judd caught him at the door with a hastily called "I'll see you before I leave," getting a "Yes, yes" that was, he hoped, at least partly forgiving.

Kharr settled down, crossing his legs. "You didn't mean that seriously, did you—that he was trying to talk you out of——"

"No, of course not," Judd broke in apologetically. "It was just a bull-session argument—India versus the United States—what a bunch of materialistic money-grubbers we are. I shouldn't have made a crack like that. He's a little on the sensitive side."

Kharr nodded, silent for a long moment broken only by an abstracted "Yes," finally saying, "I suppose he's told you that he'll be going back to India in a few weeks."

"Yes, he's all set up about it—getting married."

"He's been a lot of help, I'll regret losing him."

"He'll miss you, too. He's quite a fan of yours, you know."

Kharr appeared pleasantly surprised. "Well, I was responsible for his coming down here—I've tried to help as much as I could. I doubt that I've accomplished very much, though—except by way of convincing him that American medicine is at least a thousand years behind the times."

"You mean this stuff that his father practices—what do they call it?"

"Ayurveda," Kharr instantly supplied. "I've been reading some of it—some of the old books that Dr. Raggi had sent over for me. It really is amazing how they anticipated so much of—no, I ought to put it the other way around, I suppose—how much of what we think of as being new is only a rediscovery of what they've known for a long time. Even my own work—the relationship between stress and coronary occlusion—there's a reference in one of those old books that pins it right down, even to citing the nature of the causative stress."

"So it isn't just working for a big corporation?" Judd needled.

"I've never maintained that," Kharr said sharply. "I've never told you—"

"I know that," Judd backtracked. "I was only—"

"Still, it may be more pertinent than you might think," Kharr said. "When you dig back into Indian history, the Chandragupta period, roughly 300 B.C., about the time of Alexander the Great—it's astounding, really, how much of a parallel there is with the United States now. There was great technological development, an industrial revolution, an enormous increase in trade and commerce. And the same kind of a highly centralized government, an enormous bureaucracy that assumed more and more control of the life of the individual—" He broke off with a smile. "There's even a reference, in one of the books I read, to the young students at Taxila—that was their great intellectual center, you know, the Athens of ancient India—they were all rebelling against their fathers because they were interested in nothing but piling up gold and building big palaces for themselves."

"Maybe Raggi's right," Judd smiled. "Maybe that's where we'll wind up two thousand years from now—where India is today."

"Who knows?" Kharr said, spreading his hands. "I hadn't intended to get off on all of this—" He twisted in his chair, recrossing his legs, seemingly at a loss to remember what he had intended. "I thought you might have a last-minute question or two, something that you might like to talk out." There was a questioning pause. "Anything worrying you?"

"No."

"I told your wife that I'd give her a diet list in the morning—not that it's really necessary. I'm sure you understand the guiding principle—just hold down on your total intake of fats, that's all it really amounts to."

Waiting for a pause, Judd asked, "What else did you tell her?"

"Tell her? Your wife? Why?"

"Oh, I don't know—she seemed so jumpy—I thought maybe you told her something that had——"

Kharr was shaking his head. "No, I told her nothing that could have disturbed her. Of course, she was concerned about taking care of you, making certain that——"

"I don't need any taking care of."

"That's exactly what I told her. But it's only natural that she should be concerned. It would be highly unnatural if she weren't. I've seen it so many times—sometimes I think a coronary is harder on a wife than it is on the man who's had it. Don't blame her for being anxious. It's only because—"

"Oh, I didn't mean it that way. I thought there might be something else you'd talked about."

"No, nothing in particular," Kharr said, studying his face, fixing him with an inquiring look that made him uncomfortable. "Your wife is a very intelligent woman, Mr. Wilder."

"I know that."

"She can be a lot of help to you—perhaps more than you realize —if you give her a chance."

"What do you mean—give her a chance? I've always—" He stopped, interrupted by Mrs. Cope's voice . . . *"Why are you always so afraid to let anyone help you?"*

Involuntarily, he glanced toward the doorway, almost surprised to see it empty, Cope nowhere in sight.

« *3* »

Kay had been home for almost an hour, frantically preoccupied with trying to turn the library into an appealing bedroom—despite all she had done, it still seemed hopelessly makeshift—when it suddenly occurred to her that she had done nothing about finding someone to go up with her in the morning and drive Judd's car back.

Judd had vetoed the idea of asking any of their friends—"Sunday morning, weather like this, they'll all want to get out on the golf course"—even more vigorously rejecting the idea of asking any of the boys in his department. "Get one of the kids," he had decreed. "Give him five bucks and a chance to drive a decent car and he'll be in seventh heaven." He had suggested Chuck Ingalls, and as much as Kay wanted to avoid getting involved with Daphy again, she called her now.

"Oh, honey, I'm terribly sorry," Daphy said. "Today's the opening of the trout season, you know, and Ray took Chuck up in the mountains with him. They won't be home until tomorrow night—but, look, why don't I go up with you?"

She talked Daphy out of that, but there was no way to keep her from taking over. "You've got enough to do, getting ready to have Judd home. You just forget it and leave everything to me. I'll find someone."

Daphy called back a few minutes later. "I've got just the boy—Kip Whittaker. You know, Frank and Ella's boy, the one they adopted? Ella says he isn't doing a thing and there's nothing he'd like better. You just stop by their place and pick him up whenever you're ready to go. I told Ella it would be about nine, isn't that what you said?"

She thanked her, concern about what Judd would think quickly overrun by a more pertinent anxiety as Daphy went on, "Honey, don't you think you ought to have someone with you in your car? All that way down here—I know you say Judd's all right, but wouldn't you feel better if you had someone with you, just in case? I'm not doing a thing, and I'd be happy to go along."

"I know you would," she said, thanking her profusely, finally convincing her that it was unnecessary, but hanging up with a new anxiety, a frightening visualization of Judd having another heart attack on the way home, trying to fight it off by telling herself that Dr. Kharr would not be releasing him if there were any such possibility, finally settling for the half-comforting solution of having Kip Whittaker follow right behind her all the way home.

Jumpy and on edge, anxiety translating itself into a sensation of hunger, she went out in the kitchen to find something to eat, struck the instant she opened the refrigerator by the shocking realization that she had overlooked the necessity of stocking up with food for Judd. It was Saturday night, all the supermarkets closing at six . . . only ten minutes . . .

Slamming the refrigerator door, she started for the stairs, thinking that she had to change, at least pull on another dress, stopped as she saw an automobile turn into the drive. She flew to the hall window for a guarded peep . . . *Frank Whittaker* . . . ?

After no more than an instant of debate, she ran up the stairs, the need to change even more positive now. In the bedroom, she whipped off her dress, snatching at the assurance that there was bound to be a little grocery store somewhere that would still be open, giving her full mind to a hurried speculation as to why Frank Whittaker had come to see her. The obvious possibility was that Kip, unknown to his mother, had another engagement . . . but if that's all it was, Ella would have called Daphy back . . . no, it was something else . . . but what? Frank was no close friend of Judd's . . . Ella . . . that time she had come to call . . .

It had been in that first month after she and Judd had moved to New Ulster, the house still a mess, no curtains in the living room because they were still waiting to get the woodwork repainted, the dining room cavernously unfurnished because the Philadelphia storage company had not yet sent up the furniture that Miss Jessica had said they might as well be using. That day, too, she had been caught unaware, up on a step-stool trying to scrub anciently accumulated grease off the hood over the kitchen stove. Then, too, she had glanced out of the window, but there had been no warning recognition of the dumpy little woman she had seen getting out of the car, her meal-sack figure and thick glasses suggesting that she was the adjuster that the dry-cleaning company had promised to send out to examine the bedroom curtains that they had ruined.

But then she had seen the white gloves. And there was something about the way she had said, "I'm Ella Whittaker," that was plainly significant, uninterpretable only because Judd had never bothered to tell her that Frank Whittaker was Secretary of the Crouch Carpet Company. Ella had not come to call, however, as a company wife. She had learned that Kay was both Bryn Mawr and Old Philadelphia, qualifications that merited at least a preliminary investigation of a possible candidate for the grace and favor of membership in the Thursday Garden Club.

Kay had not been invited to join, and three years had gone by before she had even been asked to take a table for Ella's annual Bryn Mawr Benefit Tea, the once-a-year occasion when the creaking doors of the castle-turreted old Coburn mansion were opened to those county women who, in Ella's myopic vision, had so strangely managed to get into Bryn Mawr. "Of course, you were only a graduate student, weren't you?" Ella had once said to Kay, seemingly an explanation for an unpalatable truth.

The Whittakers were always invited if someone was having a big cocktail party, and they usually came for a brief courtesy appearance, but no one ever thought of them as being company people. Daphy was the only Crouch Carpet wife who ever saw Ella at any other time, but that had no particular significance, Daphy being

Daphy. Everyone else was aware of the social line that separated Old New Ulster from Crouch Carpet, and Ella Whittaker gave no one any encouragement to attempt crossing it. Frank, largely unnoticed, lived in a no-man's land between those two worlds. When someone was ticking off the officers of the company for a stranger's benefit, it was the commonest of all errors to forget to name him. He was Secretary of the company, but no one ever seemed to know exactly what he did. He had something to do with stockholders—the only time that Kay could recall Judd ever having mentioned Frank's work had been once when he had laughed about Frank having spent a whole week fussing over a letter to be sent out to the stockholder list—but whatever Frank Whittaker's position in the company, no one ever forgot that he was there because of his wife. As Ella Coburn she had inherited the block of stock that Matt Crouch had given to her father as one of the considerations for a clear title to the property of the old Coburn Carpet Company. She was, next to Matt Crouch, the largest individual stockholder in the company.

The doorbell rang while Kay was pulling a dress over her head, and then again as she reached the first step, still tugging at a zipper. Whipping back her hair, she hurried down the stairs, half-consciously anticipating the face she would see, the blandly forbearing expression that always made her think how different Frank Whittaker might have been if, too early in life, he had not bought security at the price of marrying Ella Coburn.

She opened the door, prepared to feign pleasant surprise, blinking as she found pretense unnecessary. She had never seen Frank Whittaker's face so drawn with concern, his eyes so anxiously anticipatory, so unsure of himself that he fumbled a response to her greeting, starting to call her "Mrs. Wilder," then groping for a uncertain "Kay."

Inside, he said, "I understand that you're bringing Judd home tomorrow," reviving her guess that this was something about Kip being unable to go along—Frank was the kind of man who would be embarrassed by something like that—but when she suggested it, trying to put him at his ease, he said, "No, no, Kip is free to go—he'd be delighted, I'm sure—but if you don't mind—" He paused, swallowing, damping his lips, abruptly blurting out, "I'd like to do it myself, Kay."

"Oh, I wouldn't want you to take your time——"

"I wouldn't be doing anything," he protested. "And I've been thinking of driving up to see Judd, anyway."

"Oh, really," she said blankly, the only response she could manage to such an unlikely possibility.

Sensitive to her tone, he appeared suddenly deflated, collapsing into a chair when she asked him to sit down, dropping the first hint of explanation when he said, "I don't suppose Judd knows what's happening at the company—or does he?"

"If you mean about Mr. Crouch selling his stock—yes, he knows."

"He does?" he said, reviving. "What does he—I don't suppose—how does he feel about it?"

"I really don't know," Kay said, more puzzled than ever now. "I don't think he knows enough yet about what it's going to mean—" She caught a glint in his eye. "Do you?"

He looked at her for a hesitant moment, suggesting that he was about to say, as Judd would surely have done, that it was nothing that would interest her, but Frank Whittaker was a man who had been trained to talk to his wife. "I know what it's going to mean if we let Harrison Horter take over," he said grimly. "I've checked out three of the other companies he's gobbled up. It's the same story everywhere. The minute he moves in, it's a clean sweep—everyone's out—at least everyone who's in a staff job. That's the way he operates—centralized purchasing, centralized accounting, centralized sales—"

He paused for breath, and she slipped in a testing "Your work, too, I suppose?"

He winced a wan smile. "It's not myself I'm thinking of, it's all of us who've spent all these years—Vance Nichols, Ed Lowe, Ray Ingalls—and Judd, too, of course."

She tried to maintain her poise, a screen behind which she could hear Dr. Kharr telling her how important it was that Judd go back to his job at Crouch Carpet . . . but if there was no Crouch Carpet Company . . . no job . . .

"None of his other companies have their advertising departments," Frank said. "Advertising, promotion, merchandising, the whole ball of wax—it's all handled out of New York."

Weakly she asked, "But what can you do?"—more an expression of despair than a question.

He regarded her anxiously. "We mustn't let a word of this get out before we're ready to move."

"Of course not," she assured him. "You think you can stop Mr. Crouch from selling out, is that it?"

"No, we can't do that. But it does look—this is what our lawyer says—there's an excellent chance that we can block a merger with General Carpet. It all depends on our being able to line up enough stockholders who are willing to back us up in a fight. If we had the right kind of campaign, I'm sure we could do it."

"That's what you want to see Judd about?"

"Oh, I know he's not well enough yet to really get into it—" He paused as if hoping for denial. "All I had in mind—if he would only look over this letter I'm planning to send out—" Again, there was a questioning pause. "I've been scratching away at it all day, trying to get it right—but I know it isn't. If Judd could only take a look at it, tell me whether I'm on the right track or not—he has such a wonderful feel for the way the stockholders are going to react. Those letters he helped me with last year—we've never had such a good reaction to anything we've ever sent out, never." He paused. "Do you think it would do him any harm? It wouldn't take him more than ten minutes."

"I suppose it's something that has to be done right away," she mused distractedly, torn by the conflict between an intuitive need to protect her husband, and Dr. Kharr's demand that she keep nothing from him. She could not prevent herself from saying, "It's going to be a strain for him tomorrow—his first day out of the hospital, the long trip home—"

"Oh, I wasn't thinking of tomorrow," he disclaimed. "I know he'll be riding with you—I'd not have a chance to talk to him—but I thought you might feel more comfortable with me along. Kip's a good boy, a fine boy, but still——"

"Yes, I would appreciate that," she said, acceptance triggered by the suddenly realized possibility that, on the way up, she could learn enough about what was happening at the company to really understand what all of this meant. At least, Frank Whittaker would talk to her.

· XII ·

JUDD WILDER'S LAST DAY at County Memorial Hospital had begun
early. Awake at daybreak, he had been kept from going back to
sleep by an apprehension rooted in some deeply implanted memories, all sharing the common denominator of a venture into the unknown—that night before he had slipped out of the house to meet
Floyd Fulton at the fairgrounds when the Farmers Union was
mobilizing its battle force—waiting in the pearly predawn Himalayan light for his first flight over the Hump—Pennsylvania Station
that rainy morning when he had gone down to Philadelphia to
marry Kay Cannon. But there was a difference, too, obliquely recognized as a missing sense of anticipatory excitement. He should,
he knew, be elated by the prospect of going home. He was not. But
neither was he regretting leaving the hospital. There had been a
moment yesterday, first catching Kharr's hint that he might be releasing him, when he had experienced something close to panic, at
least a feeling of a too-abrupt change for which he was unprepared,
but by the time Kay had come in with positive confirmation, he was
ready for it. After that, aware of how completely Mrs. Cope's attitude toward him had changed by the news of his release, he had
accepted an ending. He had said goodbye to Dr. Kharr last night,
trying to thank him adequately for all that he had done for him, but
there had been a naggingly insistent suspicion that Kharr, too, had
lost interest in him, having already relegated him to his file of closed
cases.

Mary, too, must have got word that it was all over. She had never
been late before, ten after seven and still no sign of her, another five
minutes before he heard her coming down the corridor, not walk-

ing but running, breasting the doorway as if it were a runner's tape, a guilty glance at the clock and then an out-of-breath apology.

"Forget it," he assured her, smiling at her too-hurried attempt to get her cap on straight, sensing now that there was something more involved than concern over being fifteen minutes late, certain of it when she turned to him and he saw the excitement in her eyes.

"What goes?" he asked, suddenly sobered when he saw her bite her lip, seemingly a suggestion that the night had brought the discovery that she was not pregnant after all. "You're all right, huh?"

She caught a quick little gasping breath, silent for a split second, then bursting out with "Ralph's coming! He just called, that's why I'm late. He's got the day off and he's borrowed a car—"

She stopped for another breath, giving him a chance to slip in "And you're going back with him?"

"No," she said, instantly vigorous denial. "He wants me to, but I told him I wouldn't—I couldn't. Do you think I'd walk out on you?"

"Suppose I were going home today?"

"But you're not." She blinked as if trying to clear her sight. "You don't really mean it?"

"Sure, I mean it. My wife's coming up for me about ten o'clock."

The last shadow of disbelief faded from her face, loosing a little cry of choked elation, a signaling release of exultant energy that propelled her toward him. For an instant, it seemed that she would throw her arms about him, an anticipation shattered as she swirled away, her open-palmed hands pressing her flushed cheeks. "Oh, I've got to call Ralph right away. I told him there was no use of his coming until—do you mind terribly if I take just another minute? I know I'm late already, but——"

"Sure, go ahead," he said, indicating the telephone.

"Oh, I won't bother you," she said, shutting him out, running out of the room, leaving him alone, apparently forgetting him. When she got back it was almost eight o'clock. But she had his breakfast.

After he had eaten, he decided to get dressed, his tarnished image of Mrs. Cope challenged when he found that, unknown to him, she had sent out the suit that he had worn the night he had been admitted to the hospital. It was waiting for him in the closet, still in the dry cleaner's bag. And when he opened his suitcase, hoping that he still had a clean shirt, he discovered that all of his dirty clothes had been laundered.

He dressed guardedly, going into the bathroom to get out of his pajamas and slip into a pair of shorts, feeling the imposition of a modesty that had not been necessary before. Along with everything else, there had been an ending of his patient-nurse relationship with Mary. All they had in common now was suppressed impatience, two strangers in a waiting room, a young girl waiting for her lover to come and carry her away to legitimate happiness, an old man waiting for his wife to pick him up . . . "What kind of a trip did you have, dear?" . . . "Oh, not too bad" . . .

« 2 »

Even before she reached the traffic light and made the north turn onto the highway, Kay Wilder began her questioning of Frank Whittaker. She found no resistance. Frank was even more willing to talk to her than he had been last evening at the house. Overnight, as he told her quite frankly, he had decided that his best approach to Judd was through her. She could tell Judd what was happening, give him a chance to think about it, and then in a day or two Frank would show him the letter. No prospect could have pleased her more.

Surprisingly, she found it easy to follow what he was telling her about Crouch Carpet's capital structure, even memorizing without difficulty the figures that he gave her for the number of shares of stock and how they were distributed, everything understandable until he got to telling her about the antitrust laws.

"I don't blame you for being confused," he said after she asked him to repeat something. "It doesn't make much sense, I'll grant you that. It's surely not what Congress intended when the act was passed, but nevertheless it's the way it's being interpreted now."

"Two companies that are in the same line of business can't merge —is that what you're saying?"

"Well, they *can*—they do—and if no one complains to the government they may get away with it, particularly if it's an industry where there are a lot of competing companies, and if the two that are merging aren't too well known or too much in the public eye. We think that's what Horter is counting on—he's done it before without getting into trouble—and he'll do anything he can get away with, we know that."

"And once the merger goes through, it's too late," she observed. "That's why you have to move so fast?"

"No, the government can still go back—there are some recent cases where the courts have ordered the dissolution of mergers that took place years ago—the point is that once you let someone in, it's devil-ish hard to ever get them out. They can battle it through the courts, taking one appeal after another—that can go on for four or five years, even longer—and by then, of course, they've gotten all the technical know-how, all the manufacturing secrets, all the market-ing background, access to all the customers. Even if you do get the company back, it's been stripped clean."

"Couldn't they do that without merging?" she asked, testing her understanding. "If they have control of the company—their own man in as president—?"

"But Horter doesn't *have* control," he broke in. "I've gone over and over the register, checking out the ownership of every share of stock. Of course, there's some of it that we can't be certain about—brokerage accounts and all that, you know—but even if he has all of that, and I don't think he does, he still doesn't have a majority hold-ing."

"So if you can line up all of the rest of the stockholders against him——"

"That's it exactly," he said, his tone a congratulatory acknowledg-ment of her quick perception. "That's what I was trying to make Ella see last night. If we can just get this letter—"

His voice was sucked away by the air blast of a passing truck, a buffeting shock that forced her to give full attention to the wheel. Ahead, there was a jalopy, stuttering along at thirty miles an hour. She tramped on the accelerator, whipping around the old car, but slowed down the moment she was safely past—they were already ten miles out of New Ulster, the minutes flying by with the miles, and there was so much that she still had to know.

« *3* »

Dressed and waiting, Judd Wilder sat at the window watching the parking lot. Trying to make the time pass more quickly, he had turned on the television set, forgetting that it was Sunday, snapping it off when he found nothing but a church program and an animated cartoon. He had paged through *Time,* pausing now and then when some story caught his eye, yet reading nothing through to the end, concentration destroyed by a vague unease, no less distracting because it was unfocused.

Mary had been in and out of the room all morning, out more than in, coming back once to tell him that there had been an awful automobile accident on the turnpike, explaining why Dr. Kharr had not yet appeared, destroying the hope that Raggi would stop in to say goodbye before Kay arrived. Except for Mary, not a soul had entered his room this morning, no one to pick up his breakfast tray, no blood-sample girl from the laboratory, not even the old guy with the mop who, yesterday, had still been cackling about that telephone call from Paris, France.

Mary came back, this time pushing a wheelchair into the room. "What's that for?" he demanded.

"You," she said. "To take you to the door."

"But why? I've been walking up and down the corridor for days."

"They said at the desk that you were supposed to use it," she said, uncharacteristically solemn. "It's some kind of regulation. Most hospitals have it. I guess they don't want you to—well, you know—start home all tired out."

He said with a grin, "They want to make certain that I get at least as far as the door, that's all."

She responded with a little smile, brief and uncertain, abstracted by her preoccupation with the open door of the closet. "I guess you won't want to wear your topcoat—it's so warm out—I'll just carry it out for you."

"You seem to be in a big hurry to get rid of me," he said, mock-serious.

This time he got through to her, eliciting an anxious protest, but it was quick-fading, broken off with the self-saving pretense that there was something that she had forgotten out at the desk. He turned back to the window again, his eyes focused on the distant road, a moment passing before he saw, as something of a shock, that Kay's car had slipped into the parking lot without his having seen it arrive. She was getting out now, still talking to someone inside. Her gesture made it plain that she was telling Chuck Ingalls—if that was who she had brought along—to wait for her, but as she walked away toward the hospital, out of his sight now, the car door opened and a man got out, stretching his arms, flexing his legs. It was not Chuck, that was instantly evident, but a moment passed before recognition could surmount incredulity . . . Frank Whittaker . . . of all the people that Kay might have asked . . . *Frank Whittaker?*

Baffled, he found himself lost in another vain attempt to understand his wife, a diversion that drained away most of the anticipation with which he had awaited her arrival. Imperceptibly, his active desire to get out of the hospital gave way to apprehension, its cause unconsidered, full consciousness reserved for this evidence that Kay had disregarded what he had asked her to do . . . taking over on her own . . . *but why Frank Whittaker?*

Hurriedly, he tested possible explanations, finding no tenable suspicion until he recalled that Kay, only a week or so before she had left for Paris, had unexpectedly received an invitation to join the Garden Club. She had brushed it off with a cynical laugh, saying that after being passed over for twelve years she had no intention of giving Ella Whittaker the satisfaction of a humbly submitted application . . . yet she *had* told him about it . . . she wouldn't have bothered to do that if it had not meant something to her . . . and now she had called Frank . . .

Mary came back on the fly, excitedly proclaiming, "Mrs. Wilder's here! I just saw her go in the office—about your bill, I guess."

"I know, I saw her come," he said, abstractedly . . . taking over . . .

Frank Whittaker was standing against the front fender now, a sheet of paper before him on the hood, a poised pencil in his hand, a sight so perfectly fitted to a characterizing image—a proofreader searching for error—that it instantly penetrated the subconscious screen behind which Judd Wilder had shut away all thoughts of the

Crouch Carpet Company. It was, however, a safely peripheral approach, skirting a full-front confrontation, and the memories aroused were all old ones, going back to the days before Roger Stark when Frank Whittaker had handled the annual stockholders report. The week when it went to press had been the high point of Frank's year. Then, like a monk released from his hideaway cloister for Mardi Gras, he had reveled in the excitement of copy being rushed to the printer, proofs being hurried back and forth, all culminating in the climactic ceremony of delivering the first bound copy to Mr. Crouch, an honor that Judd had always reserved for this strange man who, despite what seemed a good mind, was so peculiarly content with his odd-job existence on the fringe of the company world—or so it had always seemed until the day when, out of his placid countenance, a thunderbolt attack upon Roger Stark had so unexpectedly flashed forth.

Frank Whittaker's loss of responsibility for the annual report was not the only deprivation that had been imposed upon him by Roger Stark's appearance on the scene. Although neither a qualified lawyer nor a trained accountant, he was nevertheless a Yale man, the only college graduate in the company before Judd's arrival, and he had benefited from an assumption of erudition that had made Mr. Crouch turn to him in all matters that involved complicated forms or legal language. Thus, tax returns had been under his wing, and legal questions were always raised with him first, his office the liaison point with the company's attorney. It was a problem in that latter category that had sent Judd to his office that day, searching for some action that might be taken against a printer who had defaulted on a contract. He had no more than begun his story when Frank had cut him off with uncharacteristic brusqueness, telling him that he would have to see Roger Stark about it, then loosing that explosion of stored anger and resentment. It had been a momentary outburst, quickly past, but long enough sustained to reveal that he had been stripped not only of all responsibility for legal matters, but also of any involvement in the preparation of the company's tax returns.

Although he was sympathetic, the more so because Frank Whittaker seemed so incapable of fighting back, the incident had made no great impression upon Judd Wilder until now—and now only because, wedgelike, it pried itself into his mind, opening the way for an inrushing flood of questions that he had been refusing to ask himself, all of them centrally concerned with Roger Stark.

"She's coming," Mary announced from the doorway, rushing for the closet, taking out his topcoat with a hanger-rattle of excited preparation.

He started to get up from the chair, his mind abruptly changed by an involuntary glance out of the window, seeing Frank Whittaker still studying whatever was on that sheet of paper. He settled down again, his eyes averted from the doorway, a semiconscious preparation for the feigning of surprise, an anticipation lost when Mary took the play away from him with a brightly exuberant greeting to Kay and a gay announcement that he was all ready to leave.

"Hi," he said, a minimal acknowledgment of Kay's presence. "You took care of the bill, huh?"

"No," Kay said. "Did you want me to?"

"Mary said you stopped in the office."

"I did," Kay said. "To pick up the keys for your car."

Warned by the collapse of one unfounded suspicion, he withheld the question that he was prepared to ask. But now Kay said, "You'll never guess who came up with me to drive your car back," and there was no alternative to a grunting admission that he had seen who it was, no holding back of an accusing "Why didn't you get Chuck?"

"I tried," she said quietly. "But he's still up in the mountains with his father."

Deflated again, he mumbled, "I know, I know," as Kay offered the now unnecessary explanation that yesterday had been the opening of the trout season. "I saw it in the paper," he admitted. "I should have known."

"Daphy insisted on getting one of the other boys for me," Kay was going on. "As busy as I was, I let her—you know how hard it is to stop her, once she gets started on something—and anyway, I didn't think it mattered too much who it was as long as it was someone who could drive. She called back in a little while to say that she'd gotten Kip Whittaker. But then in a few minutes Frank came over, insisting that he wanted to come himself. I really didn't know what to do—I knew you wouldn't want to offend him——"

"No, of course not," he said, and almost as an act of contrition, got to his feet and walked to the wheelchair, seating himself without protest, smiling up at Kay when he saw her look of questioning concern, explaining that it was only because of some silly hospital regulation.

Seemingly satisfied, Kay switched back to Frank again. "I hope you don't mind?"

"No, why should I? Surprised me, but—he's always been a pretty good friend of mine."

Kay was oddly hesitant, silent for a moment. "There's something that he wants you to do."

"Do?"

With a guarding glance at Mary, who was making a hurried last search of the room, Kay bent over him and said in a low voice, "He wants you to look over a letter that he's planning to send out to all the stockholders. He says that if he can line up enough of them to back him up, they can block the merger."

"Merger?" he asked blankly, a question erased by an exclamation of dismay from Mary, who, searching dresser drawers, had discovered his cache of cards and mail. "Oh, I was going to get a big envelope—that's what I'd started out to do when——"

"Here," Kay said, instantly decisive, flopping his suitcase on its side, quickly opening it. "We'll put it all in here."

Digging out the drawer, Mary came up with a double-handed bundle, holding it palm to palm as she passed it to Kay. He watched, surprised when he saw how much mail he had really received, a moment passing before he caught sight of Ilsa Lang's black leather folder, acute awareness striking as Kay picked it up with a puzzled "What in the world is this?"

Dry-mouthed, he said, "Nothing much—a friend of mine in New York, that's all."

"May I see?" she asked, waiting for the nod that he dared not withhold, opening it then, staring intently for a long time, finally lifting it to read the little printed slip that he remembered having tucked under the edge of the mat. Her expression remained unchanged, enigmatic and unreadable, and there was no way to appraise the tone of voice in which she said, "It's a beautiful thing. Lovely. And wonderfully appropriate." But she did not ask who had sent it—she knew—and the sense of guilt that had dried his mouth now became a silencing choke, all the more constricting as he saw the care with which Kay placed the portfolio in the suitcase, protecting it with a padding of cards, closing the lid cautiously, snapping the latch and then giving it a testing tug.

Perfectly composed, she asked Mary, "Is that everything now?"

"I hope so," Mary said, distraught, glancing in the bathroom again, running her hand along the high closet shelf, bending to look under the bed, her face flushed when she stood up with an apologetic "I just don't know what's happened to my mind this morning."

With a forced smile he said, "Yes, you do." But instead of being relieved, Mary seemed all the more at sixes and sevens, making an awkward attempt to carry both his bag and topcoat with her right hand, trying to push the wheelchair with her left. Gratefully, he saw Kay step in and take charge, handing him the topcoat, taking his bag herself, moving a chair to clear the way as Mary maneuvered him out through the door.

No one spoke—it seemed there was nothing more to say, every conversational subject either closed or exhausted—and they moved ahead down the corridor, a silent procession, soundless except for the click of Kay's heels beside him and Mary's barely audible rubber-soled footsteps behind him. This long hall was not strange territory, he had walked its full length three times yesterday and twice the day before, but what came back now was the memory of that first night, lighted milestones in a blue sky. Grasping for reality, he looked up, identifying the round-globed lights, confirming the sky-blueness of the ceiling.

"Goodbye, Mr. Wilder" marked the passing of the floor desk, and he turned his head, trading a smile and a wave with the nurse on duty, getting an added "Good luck" that was plainly sincere, almost too much so, a warning that he might need it. He took a deep breath, slowly expelling it.

"We may have to wait for a minute or two," Kay said as they approached the lobby. "Dr. Kharr was tied up, but he'd left word that he wanted to be called. And I know you'll want to say goodbye to him."

He started to say that he already had, last night, but cut himself off, aware now, as he had not been before, that this was the end, total and final, inciting an apprehension that, had it been acknowledgable, he would have recognized as a feeling of being suddenly cast adrift with neither sustenance nor support.

They were in the lobby now, empty except for the woman at the switchboard who offered a reassuring "He's coming, Mrs. Wilder."

"Thank you," Kay said.

They waited, the silence more and more oppressive until Kay broke it with a nervous "Why don't I go ahead and bring the car up to the door?"

"Might as well."

"I'll be back," Kay said, pushing out through the door.

Still standing behind him, Mary said contritely, "I'm sorry about this morning, Mr. Wilder."

"Sorry? Why?"

"Everything getting so mixed up," she said. "I guess I'm just too excited."

"Why not? This is the big day. You wouldn't be human if you weren't."

"I guess so," she said, as if trying to believe it. "It's just that—there's nothing to be afraid of, I know there isn't—but I am."

Half turning, he saw her hand on the arm of the chair and covered it with his own. "Don't worry, you'll be all right."

She was standing too far back for him to see her face, so there was no warning change of expression to prepare him for the suddenness with which she burst out, "Oh, Mr. Wilder, I don't know what I'm going to do without you. You're the most absolutely wonderful person I've ever known. If it hadn't been for you——"

"Forget it," he said, giving her hand a squeeze, letting his own fall away as he saw that the woman at the desk was watching them with a sidelong stare.

"I just wanted you to know," Mary whispered. "I don't suppose I'll ever see you again——"

Impulse prompted a reassuring denial, but again there was that overwhelming consciousness of an ending without recourse, the irretrievable loss of something that could never be regained. He tried to thank her for all she had done for him, an effort made ineffectual by his inability to strike the right tone, saved from the necessity of a final farewell when Mary whispered a warning "Here's Dr. Kharr."

She started to twist the wheelchair around, but Kharr was already there, rubbing his hands as if drying them after a hurried washing. "Sorry if I've held you up," he said, nervously apologetic.

"I hear you've had a bad morning," Judd said, consciously excusing him, subconsciously stalling off another wrenching farewell.

"Horrible," Kharr said, a brief admission, unpursued. "Your wife—?"

"She's gone for the car."

"I promised her that I'd have a diet list ready," Kharr said. "But there's really no need to spell it out. You know the principle—keep your total fats down, that's all that really matters. Remember those triglycerides."

He smiled, raising his hand, three fingers up, silent proof of a memory too vivid to ever be forgotten.

"Good," Kharr said, crisply professional. "Beyond that—eat what you want, do what you want. The faster you get back to a normal life, the better off you'll be. Oh, for two or three weeks—yes, get all the rest you can—but after that, forget it. There's no need to feel yourself under any limitation, no reason whatsoever. Don't be afraid of that heart. There's nothing wrong with it now. That's over."

"I know that," Judd said, edging out of the chair, feeling that by remaining seated he was convicting himself of a foolish fear. He started to get up, stopped as Kharr said, "Oh, I wanted to mention this—your medical record. I'll make a transcript of it and send it along to your doctor. I have his name somewhere—Hewes—is that right?"

"Don't bother," he said, a flash decision. "He's not my doctor. At least he won't be from here on out."

"That's up to you, of course," Kharr said, obviously discomfited, the way all doctors were when you put them on the spot by criticizing another physician. "But you should have a checkup in a few weeks, if only to——"

"It's only forty miles up here," he cut in with a suddenly inspired thought. "You've spoiled me for any other doctor."

Kharr started to speak, a strangled protest that he had done nothing for him that any doctor could not have done, a long moment passing before he managed a controlled "But I do appreciate your feeling that way."

Kay's car was stopping in front of the door.

Judd stood up, offering his hand. Kharr took it, gripping down, his silence an eloquent farewell. Judd replied in kind, nodding.

He started for the door, Mary hurrying up to push it open.

"Goodbye," she whispered.

He nodded and stepped out into the open air, not looking at her.

Frank Whittaker was pulling up the Riviera behind Kay's car, waving as he braked to a stop. Judd walked toward him, a half-dozen steps before he was stopped by the hurriedly opened door. Frank got out, an awkward unfolding of legs and arms, a delay that added to the strength of a finally released greeting.

"Nice of you to do this, Frank," Judd said, searching his face for some explanation beyond the one that Kay had given him, but the thrust of his eyes, like a punch that had missed its mark, went past Frank's face and in the next instant, as if struck by a counterblow before his own could land, he felt suddenly staggered. It was sensation with no awareness of cause, the transition to illusion so instantly made that he was in no way surprised to see his notebook lying on the floor, clearly remembering that it had fallen from the seat a moment before when he had made the turn at the light . . . *but where was the proof envelope?*

Panicked, he looked down, searching the ground, thinking that it might have fallen out when he opened the door . . . no, it was somewhere in the car. But he dared not bend over to look for it . . . if he did he would faint . . . had to keep his head up . . . walk it off . . . get over to that diner . . .

"By golly, Judd, you're looking fine" crashed in upon him, a voice out of the night, darkness that exploded into sunlight blazing on Frank Whittaker's face.

"Sure, I'm fine," he heard himself say, catching a quick breath to prove that it was true, the return to reality as startlingly instantaneous as the retreat into fantasy had been.

"Would you rather take this car?" Frank was asking. "I can just as easily drive Kay's if you'd——"

"No," he cut him off, a quicker-than-thought reaction to the threat of recurrence, turning away, seeing now that Kay had gone back into the hospital. Through the glass door, he could see her talking to Dr. Kharr, nodding to whatever he was telling her, glancing out every few seconds to check up on him. "No, she'll be more comfortable driving her own car," he said, turning back toward it.

Frank reached out as if to steady him, but his hand dropped away the instant his fingertips touched his arm, excusing himself with a perceptive "I guess you don't need any help."

"No, I'm fine," he said, taking a deep breath, drinking in the warm-cool springtime air, an invigorating draught that propelled him forward. He walked between the two cars and around to the right-hand door of Kay's, feeling a little lightheaded now, and as he reached out for the latch, his hand trembled, his whole body seemingly enveloped in a warm damp mist. Guardedly, trying not to betray himself, he rested his hip against the side of the car. But Kay must have seen it. Pushing out through the hospital door, she dropped his bag, and came running, opening the door for him, disregarding his attempt to make her stop fussing over him, her hand lingering on his arm even after he was in and seated.

Frank had gone back for his bag, putting it in the back seat now. Kay got in the car and started the motor.

"Don't worry, I'll be right behind you," Frank called, his voice fading as he hurried back to the Riviera.

"What was that all about?" he asked, the car moving now.

"Oh, he was supposed to have a diet list ready for me——"

"I didn't mean that—" he began, his voice cut off as, with a last backward glance, he saw that Dr. Kharr had stepped outside the door, watching his departure.

The car turned, cutting off his view until it straightened away for the drive. Kharr had not moved, his face too far away now to be seen, his white coat still a focal point in the widening landscape as Kay made the turn onto the highway.

« 4 »

Squaring away to his desk, Aaron Kharr reached out for the file holder, turned it over, and opened the back cover to expose the last sheet of his notes. With a slowly inhaled breath, steadying his hand, he picked up a pen, tested its point, and precisely inscribed: *4/17— released 10:20 a.m.*

Still exercising taut control, he closed the folder, picked it up, got to his feet and turned to the gray filing case, his own, the one he had shipped down from New York. He opened the center drawer, found the right tab, forced his hand downward to clear enough space for another thick file, and stuffed in the folder. The drawer closed with a dull *thunk*.

Released, he turned back to his desk, snatching the dust cover off of his typewriter as he sat down. Reaching for a clean sheet of paper, he spun it into the machine, backed off to the top of the page, confronted then by a goading blankness . . . if his book was to be finished by September, he had to really drive himself now . . . these last two weeks wasted . . . a whole chapter that had to be thrown away.

A knock on the door snapped the last thin thread of self-control, loosing an explosive release of tension that sparked the quick fire of angry impatience. Clamping his jaws, he choked off an automatic "Come in," hoping that whoever it was would go away and leave him alone.

But the door opened and Jonas Webster looked in, his imperturbable expression a quick-acting sedative that, instantaneously effective, prompted a mumbled apology and the quick clearing of a chair.

"No, I'm not staying," the Chief of Staff said, lounging back against the door frame, hands jammed in his trouser pockets. "Got to get home. Julia's got some people coming in for dinner. Hear you had a bad one this morning?"

He nodded, looking down, trying to fight off the too-vivid memory of the carnage that had confronted him in Emergency, his fingertips still feeling that last chilling quaver of departing life, wondering if this was the moment to tell Webster that he would not be renewing his contract with County Memorial.

The Chief of Staff blocked him with a pleasantly casual "Saw your heart patient leaving. Back to his job, eh?"

"I don't know," he said, on guard, recalling that Webster had talked to Crouch that first day, remembering that he had accused him of having taken the case with a contingent promise. "You remember the president of his company?"

"Oh, yes, very well."

"How anxious he was to get Wilder back on the job?"

"Yes."

"A week later he sold his stock and got out himself."

"I'll be damned," Webster said with a wry chuckle. "Sort of reshuffled the cards on you, huh?"

He shrugged. "At least it didn't turn out to be the kind of a case that I thought it was going to be."

"That's the hell of it—they never do," Webster said philosophically. "But that's medicine. It's like my father used to say—it would be a fine profession, if it weren't for the damn patients. One way or another, somehow they always manage to cross you up."

"Oh, I don't feel that way," he denied. "It's the easy way out, of course—blaming the patient for your own shortcomings. I could have done a better job."

Webster cocked his head. "Have you ever had a case where you didn't feel that way?" He paused. "You set too high a standard for yourself, Aaron. You try to take in too much ground. There's a limit to how much any doctor can do."

"I know that," he said, hearing his own words coming back at him.

"There's only one way to find any happiness in this damned profession," Webster said, diluting cynicism with a twisted smile. "You've got to face up to what you're dealing with—human beings —irrational, self-destructive, greedy, self-centered, and nine times out of ten downright stupid. You can patch them up, salve their wounds, kill some of the bugs that are eating away at them, ease some of the pain of living—yes, that much you can do—but that's all. You don't change them, not one damn bit."

"But men do change——"

"I wonder."

"—and it is possible to nudge them in the right direction."

"Perhaps," Webster said, regarding him silently for a moment. "If you're sure enough of yourself to know what that right direction is."

His eyes strayed to the filing case. "Yes, that's the problem," he admitted heavily, anxiously recalling the advice he had given Mrs. Wilder. "In the end, of course, a patient makes up his own mind."

Webster laughed. "Yes, that's what always gets us off the hook, isn't it?"

« 5 »

Before she had driven a mile away from the hospital, Kay Wilder had decided against talking to Judd on the way home about what was happening at the Crouch Carpet Company. Despite the advice that Dr. Kharr had given her, and notwithstanding the enticing prospect of participation that had been aroused by what she had learned from Frank Whittaker, there was a blocking awareness that Judd was still a long way from being back to his normal self. At least the danger outweighed any possible gain. In an hour, she would have him safely home. Tomorrow, the next day—if he wanted to talk to Frank, all right. But there had been no indication that he wanted to talk to anyone.

True, he had finally relaxed a little, settling back against the seat, no longer edged forward as if he were afraid of her driving, but still he had not said a word about Frank Whittaker. Actually, he had said very little about anything. That was not unusual—she recalled that last drive to New York, mile after mile without exchanging a word—and she felt herself excused from small talk by the need to concentrate on driving. The traffic was heavy, everyone out for a drive on this first really nice Sunday, and there was the added burden of keeping a watch on Frank. Three or four times, other cars had cut in to separate them, and now as she crossed the entrance to the new shopping center on the Marathon bypass, the light changed too quickly, letting her through but stopping Frank. She slowed down, creeping along the berm, waiting for him to catch up.

For the first time, Judd twisted in his seat to look back, surprising her by asking, "What's all this about a letter?"

Prior decision prompted evasion, but there was also an awareness of the demand that Dr. Kharr had made upon her, and when Judd added, "Or don't you know?" an even more insistent need to save herself from the indictment of not having been interested enough to have listened to what Frank had told her.

"Yes, I know," she said. "Or at least I know what it is that he's trying to do." She paused, recalling what she had told Judd earlier, assuring herself there was no harm in repeating it. "He thinks that if he can line up enough stockholders to back him up, they can stop the merger."

"Merger?" Judd asked. "Are you sure that's what he said? There hasn't been anything like that in the paper."

"No, and there probably won't be," she said. "At least until they have to put it up to the stockholders. Until then, they'll keep it as quiet as possible." Afraid that she had sounded too cockily know-it-all she added, "Or at least that's what Frank says."

In the rear-vision mirror she saw the light change, the Riviera starting to move, and she speeded up, conscious that Judd was studying her with a puzzled expression, finally asking, "What else did he tell you?"

"Oh, I don't know—he talked all the way up——"

"But you don't remember," he said, unquestionably an accusation.

"Yes, I remember—most of it at least," she said as lightly as she could manage. "What do you want to know?"

A pickup truck shot in from a side road, demanding full attention for a moment. Safely past, she said, "I'm sorry, dear, I didn't hear——"

"I didn't say anything," he said, still looking at her, plainly testing her now with, "Who's this merger supposed to be with?"

She hesitated, glancing up at the rear-vision mirror for a reassuring glimpse of Frank's face, a subconscious attempt to guarantee the precision of her memory, afraid that the smallest slip-of-the-tongue error would spoil everything. "Well, this man who's bought Mr. Crouch's stock, this Mr. Horter—Harrison Horter—owns General Carpet. Or at least he controls it."

"That's right," Judd said, neither approval nor encouragement, a simple statement that he had not caught her up yet. But he was waiting.

Too far committed to retreat, she went on, "He put General Carpet together by buying three small mills, one at Dalton, Georgia, one somewhere in North Carolina, and one over in New Jersey. The Jersey company had built up a lot of volume, dumping junk carpet into the New York market, but they hadn't made any money. The other two mills were both on the rocks, so he picked them up for next to nothing." She paused, made increasingly nervous by Judd's lack of response. "I suppose you know all of this?"

"Go on," he said flatly.

"What he was planning to do—Frank says this is his standard maneuver—was to float a stock issue and unload General Carpet on the public. All he needed was one big profitable year, but he hasn't been able to pull it off, so now he's stuck with an unsalable property. But if he can merge with Crouch Carpet he'll have a consolidated statement that will look good enough so that he can unload and get out from under."

She had been prevented from looking at Judd by the necessity of maneuvering past a car full of old ladies who had slowed down to gawk at a tumbledown shack rising out of a blaze of blooming tulips. But now, a clear road ahead again, she turned to him, disconcerted when she found his eyes narrowed in surveillance, the hint of a smile twisting his lips as he said, "You really dug in, didn't you?"

"Frank kept talking," she said. "I was interested—naturally, I listened."

Negotiating a corner demanded full attention, but she remained acutely conscious that Judd was still staring at her.

"Has Frank talked to Mr. Crouch?" Judd asked, again a testing question, but nevertheless encouraging proof that he was at least willing to talk to her.

"No one has seen him all week," she replied. "They pulled out Sunday afternoon, he and Emily, and went down to Sea Island. No one knows when they're getting back."

"Then how does Frank know what's going to happen?" Judd asked. "I can't imagine Horter telling anyone what his plans are."

"I asked him about that," she said, grateful that she had, experiencing an encouraging sense of rightness. "He said that he'd been digging into what had happened to some other companies that Horter had bought into—it's always the same story."

"Maybe so," Judd said. "But it doesn't make sense. I know Mr. Crouch too well to believe that he'd sell his stock without making certain that the company wasn't going to be wrecked. It means too much to him. I don't know Horter that well—oh, he's an operator, and all out for the big buck, I know that—but I surely didn't get the impression when I talked to him that he had any idea of dumping General Carpet. They were plowing in a lot of money to modernize those old mills."

Startled, she asked, "You talked to him?"

"I had lunch with him one day in New York. He wanted to talk to me about a job."

She bit her lip, physically restraining herself from asking why he had never told her before, contenting herself with the awareness that he was talking to her now . . . he *had* changed! . . .

But not enough, apparently, to keep him from asking, "I told you about it, didn't I?"

"No."

"It wasn't anything I was really interested in," he said, as if that were an adequate excuse. "I don't know why I even bothered to go over and see him, except that—"

A motorcycle roared past, an interrupting blast of sound, and then another and another, black leather jackets and white helmets, a skinny-bottomed girl desperately clinging to the arched back of a red-bearded giant. "Crazy kids," Judd said, all but ending the hope that he would go on to reveal what he had been about to tell her.

Taking a shaky gamble she ventured, "I didn't know that you had ever thought of leaving the company."

"They came to me, I didn't go to them," he said. "And it caught me at a time when—oh I don't know, I guess I was a little fed up with the way things were going."

"At the company," she said, aimlessly supplying what it seemed that he had left unsaid, startled when he came back, "No, not just the company—everything, I guess. It would have been a chance to go back to New York, and I knew you've never been very happy in New Ulster——"

Protest burst from her lips, but it had a hollow sound, reverberant with the guilt she had felt when Dr. Kharr had questioned her about her marriage, all too plainly implicating her as a cause of the stress that had brought on Judd's heart attack.

"But that's two years ago," Judd was saying. "More than that, I guess, almost three. Maybe the situation's changed, I don't know."

She knew that he was referring not to her but to General Carpet, yet she could not stop her mind from a backward-spinning search . . . two years ago . . . more than that . . . almost three? That summer when she had left him and gone to Maine? No, that was only year before last. It must have been before that . . .

Suddenly it burst upon her . . . *the house!* Of course, of course, of course . . . yes, she had tried to make him realize how foolish it was to tie up everything they had in a house, saddling themselves with an enormous mortgage . . . and Judd had taken it the wrong way, thinking that she was objecting to staying in New Ulster. But she dared not try to explain it now, worrying him about money . . . all those bills piling up . . .

Her ears caught the echo of a questioning "Did he?"

"I'm sorry, I didn't hear," she apologized, trying to excuse her lapse of attention with an anxious look at the rear-vision mirror.

"Say anything about Roger Stark?" he repeated.

She hesitated, warning herself of the danger of telling Judd all that Frank had said about Roger, anticipating the flare-up that it would surely touch off. But she could not remain silent, and the least dangerous revelation seemed to be: "He thinks Roger had something to do with talking Mr. Crouch into selling his stock."

"I thought so," Judd said with what sounded like a chuckle of sardonic amusement. "He's always hated Roger's guts, and now he's worrying about what will happen when he goes in as president."

Thrown off guard by incredulity, she let herself ask, "But you aren't?"

"Aren't what?"

"Worried about—well, Roger taking over?"

"It won't be that much of a change," Judd said easily. "He started taking over the day he came in. This last year or so—you might as well face it—Mr. Crouch hasn't been running the company. Roger has."

"But you've never——"

"Yes, I've been able to keep him out of my bailiwick," he said with a note of grim satisfaction, but it was only the faintest echo of his old belligerent attitude, even that lost as he added a submissive "—until this came along."

She clung to the wheel with a white-knuckled grip, uncertain as to what he meant by *this*. A giant truck pulled alongside, hanging there with a roar that made conversation impossible, giving her a moment to decide whether Judd's reference had been to his heart attack or to the situation created by Mr. Crouch having sold his stock. One alternative seemed as bad as the other. Whatever the reason, Judd's spirit had been broken. She had always wanted him to change, hoping that someday he would be able to see Matt Crouch and the Crouch Carpet Company with dispassionate judgment, to talk about Roger Stark without flying into a neurotic rage, yet fulfillment of that desire was more genuinely frightening than anything that had happened since she had read Daphy's letter in Paris.

The truck finally edged past, the roar fading, and her spirits sank even lower as Judd said, "I know how he feels about Roger—I've never liked the guy either—but you've got to give him credit. He saw what the situation was—Mr. Crouch over sixty and nobody coming along to take over—that's why he took the job. And now it's paying off, that's all. Somebody has to be president. Who else is there? If Frank doesn't want Roger, who *does* he want?"

As disoriented as she was by Judd's all-but-unbelievable attitude, she was nevertheless aware that he was jumping to an unsupported conclusion about Frank Whittaker's motive. "Really, Judd, I don't think Frank's as much worried about Roger as he is about—well, the idea of the company being taken over by General Carpet."

"I don't see how Horter could get away with merging Crouch and General Carpet. The government would be sure to step in. Has Frank thought about that?"

She wanted to say that she didn't know, to get out of it any way that she could, but if she gave up now she would never have another chance. "What Frank's afraid of is that the government might let it slip through unless someone raises an objection."

"All right, suppose Horter does try to pull off a merger—I don't think he will, I don't think he's that stupid—but suppose he does. And for the sake of argument, suppose something blocks it. Where does that leave Crouch Carpet? Mr. Crouch is gone—he's out and he's not going to come back—he's sold his stock. And who owns it? Harrison Horter. So he controls the company."

"But Frank says that he doesn't have control. He says that even with all of Mr. Crouch's stock——"

"Look—" Judd cut her off, half facing her now. "Horter bought his stock and he paid cash for it. I don't know how much because I don't remember exactly how many shares Mr. Crouch had. But it's somewhere around a hundred and fifty thousand. And he paid at least forty dollars. That's what the stock was quoted at the day before—I checked it in the paper. Even if he paid only the market price—he probably paid more—it still adds up to six million dollars. Do you think Horter is fool enough to put that kind of money on the line if he didn't know where he was going? Do you think he'd have stuck his neck out that far if there was any danger of letting himself be clipped by an old futz like Frank Whittaker?"

"But I thought you always liked Frank," she said, groping for direction, staggered by the implausibility of hearing Judd sounding like a financial man.

"Oh, he's all right," Judd said. "I've always gotten along with him —mainly, I guess, because I've always treated him like he really counted. But the truth is—Frank never had a hell of a lot on the ball. If it hadn't been for mama's stock, he'd never have been Secretary of the company. In the old days it was a pretty cushy berth—a nice office, a big title, Mr. Crouch always calling him for advice—he loved it. But then Roger came along and started clipping him back. It's not hard to see why Frank would do anything he could to get even with him."

"You don't think he's really interested in saving the company?"

"What do you mean—saving the company? From what?"

"Well, you know—trying to keep it the kind of company that—well, the kind of a company it's always been?"

Judd leaned forward, his hands on the dash, staring down the road, silent. She waited, feeling as if everything depended on what he said now, but when he spoke it was only a murmured "Maybe it never was."

She said nothing, thinking that silence might prompt him to some explanation. But it never came. Pushing back, Judd dropped his arms, and with a satisfied sigh said, "Anyway, it's not my worry—not for a while, at least."

She looked up at the mirror. Frank was behind her, seemingly pushing her on. "You don't want to see this letter of Frank's?"

"You want me to," he accused her. "Is that it?"

"No, no, no," she cried. "All I want—darling, I don't want you to do anything that—all I want is to have you do exactly what you want to do."

"I didn't know," he said. "You seemed so interested—"

She closed her eyes for an instant, trying to blank her ears . . . *oh, God couldn't she ever be right . . . just once . . .*

"Watch it!"

Her eyes snapped open, an instant of panic, but a twist of the wheel brought her back on the road.

"Anyway, get rid of him today," Judd said.

"Of course," she said, wanting to tell him that she had already prohibited Frank from talking to him today, but knowing that if she told Judd he would surely take it the wrong way.

« 6 »

Kay reached out to open the front door and Judd Wilder stepped forward, a steadying hand on the door frame, a sense of physical weakness mingled with a feeling of strangeness. This house had been his home for more than two years, yet there was an unbanishable impression of seeing it now for the first time.

Getting rid of Frank Whittaker had been easy enough—all it had taken had been a show of weariness, a little nod when Frank had said that he would be seeing him in a day or two—but now there was a vague awareness of error, almost a wish that he had let him stay. He stepped inside and walked to the hall table, steadying himself with an out-reaching hand. Behind him, he heard the front door close, a dull thud cut through with the metallic click of the lock.

"You're tired, aren't you?"

"A little," he said, accepting that easy explanation of a feeling that he had no inclination to define more precisely.

"Well, you can rest now," Kay said, moving past him. "Everything's ready for you."

She had gone to the end of the hall, stopping at the library door, her inward glance a gesture of invitation, a reminder that she had told him that this was to be his bedroom.

He hesitated, forward movement blocked by an anticipatory visualization, seeing the room as he had last seen it, a perpetual accusation of pointless extravagance. When the plans for the house had been drawn, he had insisted on having what he had described only as "a place where I can work," but in the privacy of his own mind, never more precisely seen than as a time-eroded memory of the book-jammed study where he had spent so many nights at Colfax, listening to old Professor Coggle talk about the plays of his beloved Racine. He had visualized a retreat in which he would find something too elusive to be described to an architect, too subtle to be achieved by purposeful design or decoration.

But his failure had not been entirely chargeable to intangibility. There had been, as well, the matter of money, and that had become, in the end, an excusing explanation. Forcing a library into the house plan had added not only an extra 300 square feet to the first floor, and an unneeded equal amount of extra space to the second, but also it had necessitated a larger heating plant, a different roof construction, an extension of the terrace, a seemingly endless listing of extra costs with which the architect had tried to excuse how much the final bids had overrun the top limit that had originally been set. There was no way to get back to that total, he had said, unless Judd was willing to give up the room that, for want of an adequate name, the architect had labeled LIBRARY.

That, of course, was what Kay had expected him to do—she had done her part, she thought, by giving up her service pantry—but at the time, it had seemed that cutting out his room would destroy everything he was trying to achieve by building. An article in *House Beautiful,* picturing a combination library-guest room, had given him a last straw, strengthened when the text had touted the advantages of a first-floor bedroom for a guest too old or too infirm to negotiate stairs. Was it not possible that Miss Jessica might someday come to stay with them? Or his father? Irrational though he knew his argument to be—what he wanted, really, was a room inviolately his own, never to be shared with anyone—he had nevertheless driven through with it, adding the extra cost of a full bathroom, moving the cellar stairs to make room for a clothes closet, hunting out a daybed that, when he finally found one that fitted his image, became the most costly piece of furniture that they had bought for the new house.

The shocking bill—he had ordered it with a special finish and different upholstery, not asking what the extra cost would be—had hit him like a slap across the face, prompting a grudging decision that furnishing the rest of the room would have to wait. Thus it had remained as a largely barren shell, a green hope that had withered rather than ripened, the bookshelves less than half filled, the bathroom rarely used except by Annie on cleaning days, the clothes closet a repository for junk. There were no draperies at the windows, only a scattering of furniture left over from Diversion Street, unusable anywhere else in the house, and that giant daybed, raucously and extravagantly new, so inevitably accusing that he had, consciously or not, avoided bringing any work home with him that demanded the private retreat that he had once so obsessively craved.

"I hope it will be all right," Kay said as they approached the door, seemingly implying that it would be his own fault if it was not.

"Anything—" he began, caught in the middle of the stride that would have carried him through the doorway by a sight that struck as hard as if he had hit an invisible glass door. Staggered, he stared into the room, tempted for a moment to believe that it was only the bed—he had never before seen it opened out and made up, even experimentally—but that easy explanation was denied as the totality of first impression was shattered into a multiplicity of lesser perceptions. He saw the pair of lamps that flanked the bed, a taller lamp standing over a chair from the living room, a fan of magazines, draperies at the windows, pictures on the walls . . . *how could Kay have . . . ?*

Everywhere he looked, he saw something else—the big all-wave radio that he had won as a door prize at an ANA convention, long forgotten but waiting now within the reach of his arm; his old drawing board, still covered with the landscaping plan that he had started but had never had time to finish; his binoculars on the windowsill . . . the bookshelves . . . *what had she done?*

He saw what she had done—spreading the books, filling out the shelves with things that had been so long banished as dust-catchers —the little bronze Buddha that he had found in the bulldozed mud of Chabus airport, the Chinese firedog that he had bought for eleven cigarettes and two sticks of chewing gum. Blinking in disbelief, he saw that Kay had even brought out of hiding the temple fragment that he had lugged home all the way across the Pacific, banished from view because she had thought it too revoltingly erotic, the little stone god figures coupled in endless intercourse—

"I hope it's all right," Kay said. "There wasn't much time——"

"It's wonderful," he said, groping for some way to convert astonishment into appreciation, turning to her then, his mind abruptly blanked by the expression on her face. She seemed someone that he had never known before, staring at him so strangely, her lips parted as if a cry for mercy had already begun. He lifted his hands, an automatic response to bewilderment, but she took it as invitation, and in the next instant she was pressed against him, clutching him before his arms could close around her, clinging to him for what, had it been anyone but Kay, he would have accounted a moment of total panic.

Baffled, he murmured a wordless question, but got only a muffled moan in response. Consciousness broke through, not with an explanation but with a demand for sympathy that, blind as it was, made him reach for her cheek. At the touch of his fingertips her face came up, offering her lips. His kiss began as no more than an automatic response, but in the next instant it was something beyond that, neither describable nor needing description, meeting a tumescence that was at the same time resistant and yielding, fighting back against his own hard thrust, yet at the same time enveloping him with warmth that, catching fire, sent a stiffening tremor through his whole body.

Unknowingly he let his hand slide down from her shoulder to the incurving small of her back, aware of it only when, as if some hidden sensitivity had been touched, Kay broke away with an anguished "I'm sorry, dear, I don't know what's happened to me. I'm just—just tired, that's all. I shouldn't have—I've been trying so hard to do what—"

There was the choking sound of tears in her voice, but she fought off his attempt to see her eyes, twisting her head away, evading his reaching hands with a fiercely determined move toward the door, a muffled "I'll bring your bag in."

He stood looking after her, anticipating her return as he had never anticipated any moment since that honeymoon night at Buck Hill Falls when he had waited for her to come out of the bathroom.

But when she returned with his bag, it was as if nothing had happened, as if twenty years had been overleaped in the length of the hall. "You'd better get some rest now," she said commandingly, completely herself again.

✧ XIII ✧

PUTTING JUDD IN THE LIBRARY had been a mistake. Despite the reward of continuing appreciation—she rarely entered the room without receiving some new expression of gratitude—these days at home had justified Dr. Kharr's concern that Judd might continue the same reclusive bent that had been so evident during his last week in the hospital. Unmistakably, that had happened. She had made the library a new cave, even more comfortable than his hospital room had been, and he had crawled into it with all too obvious contentment. On Monday, seeing what was happening, she had stopped bringing his meals to him, forcing him to come out at least long enough to eat, but there was no way to keep him from returning the minute he finished, retreat excused with the unarguable remark that he should rest immediately after eating.

Her prime difficulty was that he was giving her nothing to fight against. Had there been any discernible anxiety, she could have set out to break it down, but there was not. No matter what she said or did, he accepted it without concern, occasionally offering a mild reservation but never arguing. Tied to the house as she was, leaving only for hurried shopping expeditions, she had little chance to pick up company gossip, and the few tidbits that she managed to find and bring home had not aroused enough interest to encourage further search. No matter what the rumor, it got no more response than what had, by now, become his standard rejoinder—"There's no use worrying about it until we have to"—and the tone in which he said it was, every day, pushing that time of confrontation farther and farther into the future.

She had done her best to implement Dr. Kharr's suggestion that she encourage company visitors, but there were few Crouch Carpet men who were close enough friends to call up with a request that they stop by—she would surely lose more than could possibly be gained if Judd caught her doing anything like that—and the visitors who had come of their own accord offered little hope that having more would do any real good.

Daphy and Ray had stopped in Monday night, and Judd had received them with predictable cordiality, even getting up to welcome them but not advancing a step beyond the door of the library. "How was the fishing?" he had asked Ray, pulling him inside. She might have followed, but it would have been an awkward intrusion, particularly after Daphy had said, "Well, that's good for as long as we can stay," edging back up the hall, virtually forcing a return to the living room. Carrying on a sustained conversation with Daphy was always difficult, made even more so that night by a fruitless attempt to eavesdrop on what was being said in the library.

After they had gone, emboldened by anxiety, she had asked Judd whether he had talked to Ray about what was happening at the company. Surprisingly, he had told her everything that had been said, giving her a verbatim account, challenging her faith in Dr. Kharr's judgment that he was unwilling to face up to what was happening at Crouch Carpet, suggesting the far more frightening possibility that he no longer cared.

That conclusion had been made to seem even more valid the next day when Allen Talbott had dropped by at noon. She had been startled when she saw him at the door, alarmed by the prospect of confronting Judd with a reminder of the convention—it had not been mentioned since that first day in the hospital—and she had taken Allen down the hall with considerable trepidation, slipping ahead to give Judd a minute's warning, only to have him say without an instant of hesitation, "Sure, tell him to come on back." And when Allen appeared in the doorway, Judd had greeted him with a bland "Come in and tell me how your convention is coming along." Allen had appeared far more ill at ease than Judd, seemingly embarrassed by his report that everything was going so well, and he got away as quickly as he could. Obviously, it had been a duty call, made during the lunch hour to give him an excuse for quick escape, and there had been a jittery tremolo in his voice when, at the front door, he had taken his leave with a puzzled "I never thought—I'd never seen him so—he's so relaxed—well, thank you, Mrs. Wilder, thank you."

Twice before he reached his car, he had glanced back as if still unable to believe what he had seen and heard. She could easily enough understand how he felt.

When she went back to the library, Judd was reading one of the Camus novels that Rolfe had brought home from Colfax, the first time in years that she had seen him reading anything other than a magazine.

Frank Whittaker had telephoned on Wednesday afternoon, wanting to bring his letter over that evening, and thinking it might jar Judd out of his disinterested lethargy, she had encouraged him to agree. "Sure, if he wants to come over—why not?" Judd had said, hardly lifting his eyes from the book he was reading. She had resolved to stay in the library after Frank arrived, keying herself up to the brashness that it would demand, let down when Judd casually included her in his invitation to sit down. Since Sunday, Frank had discovered a new vulnerability in the enemy front. He had learned from some source, pointedly unrevealed, that Mr. Crouch had sold his stock at more than eight dollars a share above market price, thus receiving an extra million dollars, a bonanza which the other stockholders had been excluded from sharing. Judd finally took the letter that Frank kept offering him, but gave it only a casual once-over reading, handing it back with an offhanded comment that Frank might be putting himself in a dangerous position by attributing motives to Harrison Horter that were unsupported by any solid evidence. They had talked on then for a few minutes, Judd surprising her by how much he seemed to know about corporation law and SEC regulations, but what might otherwise have been appreciation served only to heighten her concern that he remained so disinterested. Only once had there been a flash of attention, his head snapping up when Frank suggested that the perfect time to strike would be when Roger Stark and all of his fellow conspirators were away on the convention cruise, but the spark in Judd's eyes had quickly dulled, flickering out with a weary sigh that was plainly an announcement that he had had enough.

That was the night she had taken a second sleeping pill, finally dropping off only to awaken sometime before dawn with a stinging garland around her neck, a fiery rash that she had scratched raw in her drugged sleep. The itching subsided before morning, but there was a reminding necklace of red blotches, a warning that she had to do a better job of keeping her nerves under control. She had debated taking a tranquilizer—Lyman Hewes had given her a prescription last winter when she had been having all that stomach trouble—but then as now, she had been unable to bring herself to admit that she could no longer exercise self-control without the frightening help of a mind-dulling drug.

Thursday had been a bad day, the weather gray and depressing, Judd immune to every attempt she had made to lift his spirits. Anne Locke had said that she and Warren were planning to stop on their way home from the club, but they never appeared.

Yesterday had gone a little better, partly because the attrition of continual anxiety had worn her down to an acceptance of the need for patience, but also because it had seemed that Judd was edging out of his cave. He had lingered over breakfast, not hurrying back to the library as he had done every other morning, and before noon he surprised her by suddenly appearing in the kitchen, looking for that old metal box in which he had kept the kit of small tools that he used in India to make his own camera repairs. She had not seen it for years, but almost as a good omen, she found it in one of the basement storage cabinets. When she brought it to the library, Judd already had the back off the big radio, and he had spent most of the afternoon tinkering with it and Rolfe's portable record player, explaining that he was trying to hook them together so that he could get better reproduction, cutting out the little tin-pan speaker in the player and piping the music through the better sound system in the big radio. He was, he said, fed up with radio rock-and-roll and wanted to hear some decent music. They still had all of his good records, didn't they?

Again there was a basement search, more confidently made because she recalled having seen, at the time they moved, the brown fiber suitcase in which she had packed away the classical record collection that, for a few weeks in Connecticut, had been Judd's all-consuming interest. He had known almost nothing about music, a weakness exposed when he had begun directing television, and he had put himself through an all-out cram course, reading one book after another, the record player turned on the minute he entered the house, blaring away until she had been ready to scream at the first note of another replaying of the *Lohengrin* Prelude. The only composer that seemed to interest him was Wagner. She had wanted to tell him that he was never going to develop his musical appreciation by such an obsessive attack, but within a month she had overheard him on the telephone one night, talking to Otto Pilzner, the composer for his show, describing the musical bridge that he wanted by saying, "Do you remember in the Fire Music, the way the strings come in—" And when she had met Otto at the year-end party he had told her with evident sincerity that Judd was the only director he had ever worked with who really understood a composer's problems.

Even before they had left Connecticut, the records had been packed away, and the case had never since been opened. Getting out the records, sorting and dusting them, gave her an excuse to stay in the library, and there had been more than a token of honesty in her statement, made after Judd had everything hooked up and adjusted, that she had never heard the *Lohengrin* Prelude sound so good. She had been in and out of the library all afternoon, music a valid passport, and Judd had not once nudged her out by saying that he was tired and thought he ought to get some rest. After dinner, hearing the Liebesnacht from *Tristan und Isolde,* she had felt herself invited back. And Judd had greeted her with a welcoming smile, even reaching out for her when she sat down in the chair beside the bed. The touch of his hand, electrified by the erotically pulsing swell and fall of the music, had made her think that putting him in the library had been a wise precaution. And yet, later, upstairs and alone, lonelier than she had ever been before, the library had again seemed a mistake. There was no real danger—Judd was as afraid of his heart as she was, protecting himself at every turn—but if there was ever to be anything meaningful between them again, every spark had to be sheltered and tended, preserved as a source of warmth for a new and better future life.

She had decided then that she would get him upstairs tonight—he had come home Sunday, this was Saturday, close enough to Dr. Kharr's casually indefinite "keep him there for a week or so"—and that was still her plan this morning, action delayed only because it was another gray day, Judd's spirits understandably depressed by the weather, and there was no real reason to say anything until late afternoon. But she was getting everything ready for the change, stripping Judd's twin bed, putting on fresh sheets when she heard a car stop out front. Curious as to who it could be—all the regular deliverymen came up the drive—she went to the window, stunned to see Roger Stark getting out of his car.

Jabbed by sudden panic, she went flying down the stairs, the impulse to warn Judd taking precedence over concern for her appearance. She stopped for an instant at the foot of the stairs, telling herself that she must not alarm him. But try as she would, it was still a breathless announcement, and there was no mistaking his reaction. He said the same thing that he had said the day Allen Talbott had appeared—"All right, send him back"—but now his tone was taut, his jaws set, his eyes narrowed in defensive anticipation.

« 2 »

The door chimes sounded, a rising scale of muted notes, struck and then fading away into shimmering silence, yet persisting in the echo chamber of Judd Wilder's mind as the sound of an alarm bell to which he knew that he should be responding. And there was a reaction, but it was hardly more than a reminiscent reflex, a reminding prickle of the on-guard sensation that always flashed in every nerve-end at the prospect of being confronted by Roger Stark.

Weak though that reaction was today, it was strong enough to curl his lips as he visualized the opening of the door, seeing Stark as he had so often seen him come into a meeting room, always that minute or two late that gave him a chance to make an entrance, always that calculated pause in the doorway to make certain that all eyes were upon him, always that cool insouciance that had made him such an unsatisfying opponent. Even in defeat, Roger Stark always managed to make it seem that he had come out no worse than even with the board, treating a sound licking as no more than a minor setback in a campaign that he was certain to win in the end —and now he had.

Despite Frank Whittaker's insistence that the Horter-Stark take-over of the Crouch Carpet Company was still unclinched, Judd Wilder had no inclination to question Roger Stark's victory—if he had not already assumed the presidency, he would as soon as the formalities could be complied with—and he was coming here today as an act of office, the usurper aping the usurped, making one of those sick calls with which Mr. Crouch had earned so much affection from the men in the mill, the form without the substance, Stark's lack of genuine compassion sure to be betrayed by that cold-light smile that would be flickering on and off like a faulty fluorescent tube.

Listening, he heard the front door open, and then the blatantly falsified surprise of Kay's greeting, the demeaning unctuousness with which she invited him inside. Scowling, but uncontrollably curious, Judd moved toward the library door, attempting to catch what Stark was saying, hearing only Kay's too eager assurance that of course he would be delighted to see him. "I think he's up but I'm not certain that he's dressed. Sit down a moment—I'll go back and see."

But she did not come. They had gone into the living room, their voices too muffled to be heard, talking about him but careful to keep him from hearing what they were saying. Frustrated, he went back to his chair, seating himself as a gesture of to-hell-with-it disinterest, a proclamation of the self-sufficiency that had always carried him through, no matter who was ganged up against him. But there was no responding rise of induced courage, a consciousness that slowly made itself felt as a dull-edged recognition that there was no point in generating a lot of adrenaline about something that no longer mattered.

Kay came down the hall at last, a flurry of approaching footsteps and then a quick closing of the door behind her, her face tautly anxious. "It's Roger, all right," she said, acting as if she were expecting him to curse or shout, or crawl away and hide.

"So what?" he said with a shrug. "Send him in."

She stared at him for an anxious moment. "You're sure you won't——"

"Won't what?"

"I'll get your robe," she said with a hurried move to the closet, taking his blue Viyella off its hanger, holding it out, waiting for him to stand. "You won't get yourself all worked up, will you?"

Standing, he said, "Why should I?"

"You shouldn't," Kay said, humorlessly sober. "I just want to be certain that you don't."

"What are you so worried about? Did he say something that—?"

"No, no," she broke in, reaching up to straighten the robe's collar.

"It's only that—well, I know how Roger always makes you——"

He laughed, a quick cover-up. "All right, he's safe. You don't have to worry about him. I won't——"

"Oh, Judd, please!" she protested, no more than a choked whisper but unmistakably anguished, as unaccountable as the way her hands flashed out, gripping him hard, her body pressed tightly against him for a moment, long enough to murmur, "I'm not worried about anyone but you."

Startled by this emotional display, he was still trying to charge it to some reasonable cause when she abruptly asked, "Do you mind if I sit in?" Unthinking he said, "Sure, if you want to—why not?"—retraction made impossible by the instant bloom of her smile, leaving him blinking as she spun around and went out the door. He sank down in his chair again, so preoccupied that he missed the warning approach of their footsteps, suddenly aware that Roger Stark was standing in the doorway, striking an entrance posture that loosed a shrapnel burst of warning memories.

But something was strangely wrong. Like an actor who had lost his sense of timing, Stark stood transfixed, hesitant as if he had missed a cue and was unable to improvise an entrance.

"Come in," Judd said, suddenly feeling a director's sense of commanding control, no more than obliquely recognized yet strong enough to keep him from making any move to rise in greeting.

Cued, Stark entered quickly, a move so hurriedly made that it could only be seen as a violation of character, somehow making "How are you, Judd?" seem almost sincere, validity added by his fixedly anxious expression. There was no hint of that expected pseudo-smile, not even the reflection of an interior flicker.

Kay started to move a chair for him but Stark put her off with a nervous, "No, no, please don't bother. I'm not staying. I only stopped by—" He made a move as if to sit on the edge of the bed, stopped uncertainly, and then with a mumbled word of thanks, accepted the chair after all.

Judd watched him as he sat down, close surveillance made possible by Stark's distractedly unfocused eyes. Seated, he crossed his legs, but there was no follow-up routine, no straightening of a trouser seam, no picking at nonexistent lint, no foot-waggling display of his British boots. Stripped of his cultivated mannerisms, he appeared a man so different as to be almost unrecognizable.

Quite consciously, but for only a brushing instant, Judd Wilder felt himself warned of danger—whatever Stark had come to tell him could only be bad news—yet his own sense of superior self-control was an antidote for fear, potent enough to allow him to sit back in almost dispassionate curiosity, easily maintained as they fenced their way through a Ping-Pong exchange of platitudes about how well he looked and felt, and how fortunate it was that this library had been designed for double duty as a downstairs bedroom.

The small talk exhausted, stranded in pregnant silence, Judd put in, "I suppose I should be congratulating you."

"On what?"

"You'll be taking over now, won't you? Or have you already?"

"There's been no change in company officers," Stark said stiffly, adding a taut "—if that's what you mean."

"But you will go in as president?"

Stark looked down, clamping his nervously writhing fingers into a double-handed fist. "I may, I may not—I don't know." He seemed to mean it.

Until now Judd Wilder had given little credence to Frank Whittaker's idea that Harrison Horter could be thwarted in his attempt to gain control of the Crouch Carpet Company, thinking it a harebrained scheme with no possibility of success, but now it suddenly took on validity. Stark was frightened, and it seemed a logical assumption that he had discovered Frank Whittaker's plot, and that he was here in an attempt to talk him out of helping to further it. Even though he had never had any intention of doing so, it was pleasantly invigorating to have Stark so afraid of what might happen if he did, and he now asked, "You do have control, don't you?" —probing for confirmation.

Stark's eyes came up slowly. "Are you by any chance under the misapprehension that I'm involved in Horter's take-over of the company?"

"I've heard some rumors."

"I'm sure you have," Stark said grimly, silent for a moment. "Would you be interested in hearing the truth?"

Silent, Judd spread his hands, a neutral gesture.

"Until Harrison Horter walked into my office yesterday afternoon, I had never met the man. Nor had I ever had any contact with him, direct or indirect."

Judd stared back at him, distrustful, yet finding it difficult to doubt his sincerity.

Stark broke the grip of his locked hands, flexing his fingers. "I knew, of course, that Mr. Crouch was selling his stock—I had in fact, advised him that it was the thing to do—but I had no idea that it would wind up in Harrison Horter's hands. I had assumed that Tilden, Coe would make a secondary offering, dispersing it widely enough so that no control problem would arise. Actually, that was more than an assumption—I'd talked to Elbert Coe along those lines some weeks before—so I wasn't concerned. Apparently I should have been, but the circumstances being what they were, I felt it best to remain uninvolved. In any event, I know nothing about what was happening until the deal was set. By then it was too late. Horter had the stock."

"But that didn't give him control, did it?"

"No, not in itself," Stark said, more poised now. "But it seems that he had some other holdings as well, not in his own name but stashed away in some hideaways that he controls. He's a very clever operator, very adept at covering his tracks."

"So he *does* have control?"

Stark hesitated. "At the moment—he may, he may not, I'm not sure. I do know that he picked up a rather substantial block here last night—something over ten thousand shares."

Judd barely contained a gasp of shock. There was, he knew, only one block of Crouch Carpet stock like that in New Ulster, the implications so devastating that he could not help asking, "Whittaker's?"

"Yes, I was surprised, too," Stark said. "When he told me last evening that he was going over to see Ella Whittaker—the old Coburn family connection, Frank's long association with the company—I had no idea that he'd be able to jar it loose." A wan smile broke, not that cold flicker but a sincere expression of cynical acceptance. "He walked in with a certified check for a half-million dollars—that was that—she took it."

Too stunned to respond, Judd glanced away, his eyes inadvertently catching Kay's. He had until now almost forgotten her presence in the room. There was a brief exchange of common bewilderment, broken off as Stark continued, "I don't know whether or not that pushed him over the line—it really doesn't matter—if he doesn't have a majority position now, he will before this time tomorrow." He paused. "There'll be an advertisement in the evening paper—a news story, too, no doubt—he's making a tender for one hundred thousand shares. And at the price he's offering, he's sure to get it."

"What's he offering?"

"The same price he paid Mr. Crouch and Ella Whittaker," Stark said. "He picked up a rumor that there were some disgruntled stockholders—I can't see that anyone could have caused him any trouble, his deal with Mr. Crouch was perfectly legal—but in any event, he decided to forestall a possible nuisance suit by giving everyone a chance to sell their stock at the same price."

Without thinking, purely as an attempt to lighten the atmosphere, Judd said with a smile, "Maybe I ought to sell him mine."

A muffled squeak of protest drew his eyes to Kay. She seemed unaccountably concerned, plainly relieved when Stark said, "No, I don't think I'd do that. At least I'm not selling mine for a while. Based on what he's done with most of the other companies that he's taken over I'd guess that he'll drive the market price well above that figure." He paused, his expression tense again. "But there is something else that you may want to think about."

"What's that?"

Stark appeared even more agitated now than when he first entered the room. "I don't suppose you've given any thought to your own future—no reason why you should have—and I know that this isn't the best time to—" He glanced at Kay, almost as if he were asking for approval to continue.

"Go ahead," Judd demanded impatiently. "What's on your mind?"

Stark caught a quick breath, expelling it as if he were coughing a choke out of his throat. "You talked to Mr. Crouch, didn't you? He told you about selling his stock?"

"Yes."

"And the deal he'd made with Horter—the contract that you were to be given?"

He started to ask, "Contract for what?" but choked it back, a glimmer of light breaking, a vague recollection of something having been said about setting things up for him with Horter. *Contract* struck no responsive chord—he could not remember the word having been used—but not knowing what Stark was up to he decided to play it safe with an ambiguous "What about it?"

"It seems there's some misunderstanding about what Horter agreed to do. When his lawyers sent Mr. Crouch a copy of the contract that Horter proposed to offer you, he refused to approve it—and on that basis, he's holding up submitting his resignation from the board and the presidency. Horter is very much upset, of course. He can get around it—a special stockholders meeting, elect a new board and all that—but it will be a long and complicated maneuver, and for quite understandable reasons, he's anxious to move quickly. In any event—I won't say that I exactly volunteered to see you—I tried to tell him that you were in no shape to—"

"I'm all right," he put in. "What's the argument?"

Stark took a scrap of notepaper from his pocket. "I finally managed to reach Mr. Crouch, talked to him long distance just before I left the office." He checked his notes. "It seems there's no disagreement on terms—not less than two years at not less than your present rate of compensation—so it all comes down to a question of who the contracting corporation is to be. It's Mr. Crouch's contention that Horter agreed that your contract was to be with the Crouch Carpet Company. Horter maintains that he couldn't have made such an agreement since he didn't have control of the company, nor was he then, nor is he now, empowered to act in its behalf. He says that his agreement was simply to guarantee your employment for two years—that's why he had the contract drawn with Horter Enterprises. Mr. Crouch comes back and says that it's only a maneuver to get you away from Crouch Carpet and into one of Horter's other companies." He crumbled the notepaper. "So that's where things stand."

Judd looked away, a reaction to bewilderment restrained by a momentarily overwhelming consciousness of how far Mr. Crouch had gone to protect him. Kay was staring at him, blank-faced, offering no suggestion of what his next move ought to be. The only out seemed to be "All right, what do you want me to do?"—asked of Stark with a smile that he hoped would get him by until he could think his way through.

"I know it's unfair to ask you to make a decision now—" Stark's voice drained off.

"What is there for me to decide?" he asked, still a little groggy. "I can't see that it's up to me."

Stark watched him intently as he said, "Mr. Crouch says now that if you're satisfied with Horter's contract it will be all right with him. All he's interested in is seeing that you're taken care of."

"Well, I appreciate his trying to do something for me, of course I do, but I still don't see—" The brain fog was clearing. "Why do I need a contract? Would I be out without one? Is that what you're saying?"

"No, no, not at all. The whole point—Mr. Crouch felt that you might be worried about the future, and that having a contract would give you some extra assurance."

There was a prickle of alarm, inciting the goad of unreasoned anger. "Why? Because he doesn't think I can go on doing my job? All right, if I can't, to hell with it. At least, I don't want to be kept on just because I've got a contract. And particularly one that someone was pressured into signing. If I can't cut it on my own—forget it."

Stark had made several attempts to interrupt, but now that he was given a chance to speak he hesitated for a long moment, finally saying quietly, "You're wrong, Judd. Horter isn't doing this just because he's been pressured into it. He's a great admirer of yours. He was telling me last night about having had lunch with you."

He nodded curtly, wondering if Stark could possibly be as innocent as he was trying to make himself appear, finding it difficult to erase the long-held suspicion that it was Stark who had spied him out that day at the Pinnacle Club and gone tattling back to Mr. Crouch.

"He offered you a job then—he still wants you."

"That's a long time ago," Judd said uncomfortably, skirting the truth that there had been no job offer. And yet it was true that Horter had written afterward, wanting to see him again. "What's he going to do with the company?"

"I don't know," Stark said, and then as if to prove his sincerity, "I wish I did."

"A merger with General Carpet?"

Stark shook his head. "I thought, too, that that's what he was planning. Obviously, he isn't. If he were, he'd wreck his tax position by buying up all this stock—and he's not fool enough to do that. All he'll say is that he never knows how he's going to play a hand until after he's drawn all his cards. I do know that he's bought three small furniture factories and a drapery mill in the last few months. There was a story in the *Wall Street Journal* a few days ago that made it look as if he might be putting together a home furnishings combine. He may be planning to tie in Crouch Carpet, I don't know. With a man like that—if you try to outguess him, you only make a fool of yourself."

"Yes, I know he's an operator," Judd agreed, a cover-up for the bewildering awareness that Mr. Crouch could have knowingly let the company slip into Horter's hands . . . and he *had* known . . . this contract business proved that.

"Of course, his record isn't all bad," Stark went on. "In some cases, he's done a constructive job, picking up weak companies and revitalizing their merchandising. He's a great believer in intensive promotion to a restricted market—more or less the pattern that you worked out for Crouch Carpet—and it may well be that he's thinking of trying something of the same sort in the furniture business. But that's only a guess."

Judd had let him go on and on, certain that Stark was in fishing for a reaction, strongly suspecting that he was trying to maneuver him into leaving Crouch Carpet. "You think I ought to sign up with him, is that it?"

"Well, that's up to you, of course," Stark said warily. "I can see that you might not want to be under as much pressure as you were before, but I'm sure there'll be some spot in the company where—" He broke off with a twisted smile. "I'm really in an awkward position here, Judd. If I were sure that I was staying on as president, it would be different, but as things stand now—" He spread his hands, waiting, finally going on. "I can understand your feeling that you don't want to be paid unless you're able to do a job—I respect you for it—but on the other hand, having your salary guaranteed for two years wouldn't be a bad anchor to windward. And I don't think you'd have to feel that it was something that you hadn't earned. You've done a lot for Crouch Carpet. A bonus for past services wouldn't be out of order, not at all."

"Maybe not," he said aimlessly, avoiding Kay's eyes yet acutely aware that they were fixed on him . . . she'd been so jumpy lately . . . maybe she wouldn't worry so much if she knew that a salary check would keep coming in every month . . .

"But it all depends on what you want," he heard Stark say, startled when he heard a different voice . . . *"If I were to give you a piece of paper and a pencil would you be able to put down right now, this very minute . . ."*

"I don't know yet," he cut in sharply, the illusion that he was talking to Dr. Kharr so strong that he felt something close to shock when he turned back and found himself confronted by Roger Stark. "All I know is that I don't want to be tied down—not yet, anyway."

Stark's face, flushed a moment before, turned gray. "You don't want a contract?"

"No."

Stark regarded him silently. "May I report that to Mr. Crouch?"

Judd shrugged.

Color came back to Stark's face. "If you're satisfied—there's no point in his holding out for something that you don't want."

He started to reply but stopped, thinking of the call that Stark would make to Mr. Crouch. "I wouldn't want him to think that I don't appreciate it."

"Oh, I understand that," Stark said, edging forward on his chair. "And I'm sure Mr. Crouch will, too." He stood. "I'm sorry I've had to inflict this on you, Judd. I tried to duck it but——"

"No reason why you should," he said, his voice strengthened by the feeling that he had gained the upper hand. "I hope everything works out all right for you."

Silent, Stark looked at him for a long time. "For you, too," he finally said, but his voice was so flat that what he really meant was largely obscured.

Kay went out with Stark, escorting him to the door. Alone, Judd Wilder stood for a moment, feeling as if he had been swept up by a storm, fortunate in something beyond simple survival, yet by no means certain that he had not been a fool. He sat down on the bed, and responding to a suddenly discovered feeling of fatigue, kicked off his slippers and lay back. His head fell short of the pillows, an awkward position, and shifting his body to change it, he saw that Kay had already returned.

Watching silently until she caught his eyes, she asked, "Did that tire you?"

"Why should it?" he said, proving his vigor by grabbing at the pillow, thumping it into a wadded support for his raised head.

Kay came up to the bed, tentatively seating herself on its edge. "I hope it didn't bother you—my sitting in? Maybe I shouldn't have?"

"Why not?"

"It might have been easier for you to talk if I hadn't been here."

"It didn't bother me any. I said everything I had to say."

There was a sound in the hall, the clatter of the mail slot in the front door. "There's the mail," he said, but Kay made no move to leave, looking away as she said, "That was a little disillusioning, wasn't it—the Whittakers selling out."

"Don't you remember what I said the last time Frank was here? All that guff about Mr. Crouch selling out the other stockholders—"

"I know," she acknowledged. "But Frank sounded so sincere, so worried about what was going to happen to the company."

"You can buy a lot of sincerity with a half-million dollars."

Kay nodded doubtfully. "Maybe Mr. Horter convinced them that he wasn't going to do anything to hurt the company."

"Then why did they sell?"

"I suppose you're right," she said, silent then, staring out of the window. "Did you know what Mr. Crouch had done—the contract?"

"All I knew—he said that he'd set things up for me with Horter, but he didn't say how."

"Then he knew that Horter would be taking over?"

"Of course. I've said that all along. That's what I tried to tell Frank."

"Still it was a nice thing for him to do," Kay said, a strange quality in her voice, sounding almost as if it were a reluctant admission. "You can't help but be grateful—even if you don't want it."

"Salving his conscience, I guess."

"Do you really believe that?"

"Why did he get out of town the minute he'd signed the deal?"

"Oh, Judd, you know they always go down to Sea Island every spring."

"And he knew that Stark would try to dump me the minute he took over," he said, a solider thrust.

"Do you still feel the same way about Roger, even after——"

"After what?"

"I thought that today—he seemed so concerned——"

"About me?" He laughed sardonically. "Didn't you hear what he said about Horter being so upset because Mr. Crouch was holding him up? All right, here was a chance for Roger to build in with the new boss, pull his chestnuts out of the fire, and maybe save his own skin in the process."

"You don't think—"

"All that guff about not knowing whether he was going to accept the presidency? Don't you know why? Because it hasn't been offered to him, that's why. And he's scared as hell that it won't be. Didn't you see how jumpy he was?"

Kay nodded doubtfully, started to speak, and then cut herself off with a quick-bitten lip.

"Go ahead," he commanded. "Say it."

"I suppose you're right—you know him so much better than I do," she tentatively advanced. "But the things he said about Horter, his whole attitude toward him—he surely didn't make him sound as if he were the kind of man that he wanted to work for."

"Oh, I'm not saying that he likes him. Why should he? This is something that Roger has been working on for three years—building himself in, playing all the angles, clearing the way so that he could move in the minute he got Mr. Crouch out of the way. This was his big payoff maneuver—didn't you hear what he said about advising him to sell his stock? So there he was, only one step from the top— and *bang*—Horter kicks the ladder out from under him. You don't love the guy that does that to you."

"No, I'm sure you don't," Kay agreed. "But why would he—?" She shook her head.

"Why would he what?"

"If he were really trying to build in with Horter, why would he say the things about him that he did? It would be different if you were a close friend, someone that he felt he could confide in—oh, I suppose you're right, you probably are. And I'm sure Roger Stark thought that you'd feel the same way he does about it."

"About what? Horter taking over the company?"

Kay nodded, looking away for an abstracted moment. "I couldn't help feeling—I suppose it's silly—didn't you think Roger acted disappointed about the Whittakers selling out? It sounded almost as if—well, that if Frank had made a fight of it, Roger might have been on his side." She paused. "And then, just now at the door when he was leaving, he said something about how unfair it was that someone could walk in and buy control of a company—all the lives that are affected, so many people who've worked so hard to build up the company, thinking it would be something that was going to last——"

"Fools like me," he put in with a cynical laugh.

"I don't think you've been a fool," Kay said, moving closer to him, reaching out, bridging his body with her arm, her wrist pressing tightly against the turn of his hips. "I'm sorry about all this, Judd, terribly sorry. I know how much the company meant to you, how disappointed you are. I never realized before—" Abruptly, she leaned forward to kiss him, a startlingly impetuous show of affection. But at the last instant her lips changed course, avoiding his mouth and brushing his cheek, a contact that had the effect of discharging a potential spark, neutrality restored as she said, "But it'll all work out. I know it will."

"You want me to go back to Crouch Carpet, don't you?"

"Not unless you really want to," she said firmly. "If you can still feel about the company the way you felt before—all right. But you're not going to take something——"

"We've got to live."

"I'm not worried about that. We'll get along, no matter what you decide to do. We always have, we always will."

"I guess so," he said vaguely, less a reflection of wavering confidence than a groping attempt to understand what had happened to Kay. He had never seen her like this before, hardly able to believe that she could sincerely mean what she seemed to be saying.

"Don't you think you ought to get some rest now?"

His hand lifted, a reflex response to a fear of loss, brushing the soft roundness of her breast as he grasped her forearm, pulling her down to him. This time their lips met, the quick hard thrust and the soft yielding, clinging for an instant that provoked a surge of arousal, a first wave that crested and then broke into nothingness as Kay quickly lifted her head. But she was still leaning over him, her lips fuller than normal and slightly parted, her eyes wide and liquid, her whole expression a tremulous balance of fear against innate desire, sustained for an instant, then broken off with an abrupt "I'll get the mail."

He slumped back, feeling that same emptiness that he so often felt when she had cut the ground out from under him, either insensitive to his arousal or simply not caring. Yet there was something different now, an incongruity that made him wonder if the sex urge that he had felt had been as self-generated as Kay had always before made it seem, always acting as if she were surprised, yielding if he was insistent enough but always putting upon him the burden of arousing her own reluctant desire, occasionally giving him the satisfaction of success, but never before—at least for a very long time—had there been this feeling that arousal had come not from within himself, but as a response to something within Kay, a need that she had rarely revealed, and even less frequently given him a chance to fulfill.

Suddenly, he was aware of his pounding heart, a warning drum-beat in his ear, a frightening reminder of enforced celibacy. Clamping down, he shut off one thought stream and tried to switch to another, attempting to replace Kay's image with Roger Stark's, momentarily thwarted by a question that popped in out of nowhere . . . *what had Kay done with that Persian miniature that Ilsa had sent him?*

He pushed it aside, the answer as unimportant as the question was irrelevant, his only concern a lack of self-control, and even that anxiety persisted for no more than an instant, gone without a trace as he heard Kay coming down the hall, the pace of her footsteps suggesting that she was reading a letter. She was, turning a page as she came up to the doorway.

"Rolfe?" he asked.

She nodded without looking up, still reading as she came up to his bed, abstractedly reaching out to hand him an envelope. "Letter from your father."

Kay was wrong. She had seen only the *Haygood Herald* return address on the envelope, failing to notice that the envelope was addressed not with his father's spatter-dash typing, but in Flora's schoolteacherish hand, the Palmer penmanship that she had tried to inflict upon generation after generation of Haygood youngsters. That was the way he usually thought of her, not as the rarely seen stepmother that she had been for more than twenty years now, never writing to him except for that once-a-year thank-you note after Christmas. He ripped the envelope, a feeling of alarm aroused not only by strangeness, but also by the thick multi-paged packet of letter paper.

DEAR JUDD

I know that your father has written you but I suspect that he had not told you the whole story, and I feel that it's my duty to tell you what the situation really is. I think you ought to know and that is why I am writing.

Four weeks ago last Tuesday morning, your father went into the bathroom while I was dressing. He still had not come out when I was ready to go downstairs, so I called to him. He didn't answer so I went in to investigate and found him lying on the floor. He was perfectly conscious but didn't seem to be able to talk. Needless to say I was terribly frightened and called Dr. Collins right away. By the time he got here, your father was much better, able to talk enough to tell me what had happened (all he remembered was that everything had gone blank) but his speech was slurred and there were some words he didn't seem to be able to pronounce at all. Dr. Collins said right away that it was a stroke, and we got him to bed as soon as we could.

He was a lot better that next day and insisted that he had to go down to the shop to get the paper to press. You know how he is about the paper, so there was nothing I could do to stop him. He came home a little early, all right except for a splitting headache. His speech was better, and Dr. Collins was very much encouraged, and needless to say, so was I.

Everything went along then until that next Friday morning. When I woke up, he was sitting on the edge of the bed rubbing the side of his face and saying that he didn't have any feeling in it. He thought that it had just gone to sleep because he had been lying on it, so he wouldn't let me call Dr. Collins, but I did, anyway. He said right away that it was another little stroke, and that unless your father stopped working and got a lot of real rest, things were going to go from bad to worse.

You know how your father is about the paper, but I did manage to keep him home for three days. Then in spite of everything I did to try to stop him, he started going down to the shop again, and I'm afraid that's what did it. This last one was the worst of all. It's not so much physical as mental, and that's what makes it so hard. Your father has always been so kind and considerate, just a wonderful man in every way, but now he has this idea that everybody is trying to take advantage of him, and when I try to reason with him he turns abusive. That isn't your father, I know that, and with God's help I'm doing the best I can, but there's one thing that's beyond me, and I've got to have your help.

Oscar has been with your father for so many years now that I just don't know what would happen to the Herald *without him, but I'm afraid we're going to lose him unless something can be done. I hate to say this, because I know your father is a sick man and not really responsible, but he's treating Oscar just awful. Oscar has always been the most loyal and faithful man that there ever was, but now your father has got this idea that he's trying to take the paper away from him. Of course, Oscar has always thought that someday he would be given a chance to buy the paper and he had every right to think that after all he's been told, but your father has this idea that you're coming back to take over the paper. I know that's what he used to hope years ago, and with the state his mind is in he has made himself believe it. It's like that with so many things. His mind seems to have gone back to where it was years and years ago.*

What I am hoping, Judd, is that you'll write Oscar and tell him that you have no intention of coming back. I know that will encourage him to stay on, and help to keep him from being too discouraged by the way your father is acting toward him. I know there is nothing more important to your father than the paper (it's been his whole life) and if he were only himself, he would know that it can't go on without Oscar. If he leaves, the only thing we could do would be to sell out to the Bruxton chain, and that would be the last straw as far as your father is concerned.

Please write Oscar just as soon as you can. I know that whatever you say will be a big help. I hate to bother you but I'm so worried that I don't know what else to do.

I hope that you and Kay are both well and that you can come out to see your father before too long. Dr. Collins says that his physical condition isn't too bad at the moment but we never know what God's will will be.

Love to you both,
FLORA

P.S. I'm not telling your father that I'm writing to you and I think it would be better if you didn't mention it either.

When he looked up, Kay was waiting to hand him Rolfe's letter. "He won't be coming home until September," she said dejectedly. "They want him to go to Spain before he—" His face must have betrayed him. "What's wrong, dear?"

He handed her the letter.

« 3 »

Kay Wilder was in the kitchen, speculatively regarding the two trout that lay defrosting on the counter top. Daphy had brought them over this morning, Ray's proof that he had really caught two sixteen-inchers on Kettle Creek. She had planned to do them more or less *bonne femme,* Judd's favorite fish dish, but as keyed-up as he had been all afternoon, broiling seemed a safer bet. She could probably get away with faking the sauce, using very little cream, but even so it might be too rich for the touchy stomach that he always had when his nerves were on edge.

For a moment she considered going back to the library to ask him what he would like, discarding the idea because he would surely think her appearance another subterfuge to get him to talk. She had already made too many such attempts this afternoon; another might be the last straw. Genuine though her sympathy was, she knew now that she could not transform it into a force strong enough to penetrate the shell into which Judd had withdrawn after receiving Flora's letter, a retreat obviously generated by a feeling of guilt. He had not stopped over in Iowa on his way home from California, as he had promised his father that he would do, a lapse made all the more serious because he had done the same thing twice last year. He had not seen his father for over two years, and then only for that evening when, in Des Moines for a promotion meeting, he had persuaded him to drive down for dinner.

Judd had not been in Haygood for at least four years, and in Kay's best recollection, he had gone back only five times since their marriage. He wrote his father only infrequently, never without a night-after-night routine of saying, always as he was getting into bed, that he had to be sure to get off a letter to him tomorrow. This afternoon he had castigated himself unmercifully for not having answered the letter that he had received while he had been in the hospital. She had found the letter for him, digging it out of the stack of cards that she had brought home, and he reread and reread it, muttering to himself about having stupidly failed to appreciate how much emotional stress his father was under, driven as he had been to the extreme of considering the sale of the *Herald* to the newspaper chain that had offered to buy him out. He had given her the letter to read, forcing her to agree that, two weeks ago, his father had been perfectly rational, insisting that his failure to send back a tension-relieving reply had somehow contributed to this last stroke that he had suffered.

There had been, she thought, a more rational cause of concern in the conflict between what Flora was asking Judd to do, and the lack of any evidence in his father's letter that he had ever considered letting Oscar buy the paper. Clearly, the thought had been in Harry Wilder's mind that Judd might come home and take over the *Herald,* a support for Flora's claim of irrationality that Kay would have pointed out had not Judd somehow given her the impression that he might not agree that it was so madly unreasonable. He had said nothing to suggest that he might be considering it, yet he had talked briefly about what a good and satisfactory life his father had had, a revealing minute or two of conversation that she had foolishly cut off with an inadvertent remark that his father faced, on a small scale but with the same essential problem, a dilemma not unlike the one that had confronted Matt Crouch. Once diverted, Judd could not be brought back to the subject, resuming his self-criticism for having failed to write his father, unwilling to accept his own excuse that he had not written because he had wanted to avoid worrying him by letting him know that he was in the hospital after a heart attack.

When she had left him a few minutes ago, Judd had still not made up his mind as to whether or not he would write Oscar as Flora had asked, excusing his indecision by saying that he didn't know enough about what the true situation was. "I ought to go out," he had said. Kay had agreed that he should go as soon as he could, but that was out of the question for at least a month. In the meantime, she knew that something had to be done to relieve the stress that Judd was under. It was difficult to think of anything to suggest, every idea challenged by her limited understanding of how he really felt about his father. She was handicapped, she knew, by her own fatherless childhood, giving her an exaggerated idea of how strong a child-parent bond should be. And she understood, too, how the death of Judd's mother, and his father's subsequent marriage to a woman whom Judd could see only as an old-maid schoolteacher, had created an alienating situation. Nevertheless, she had always suspected—this afternoon had proved how right she had been—that Judd felt a much stronger attachment to his father than he had ever revealed, perhaps even to himself.

The only idea that had aroused even momentary interest from Judd had been her suggestion that he telephone his father this evening. He had objected that he couldn't do it without telling him why he had not answered his letter, but it had not seemed so firm a rejection that she might not be able to overcome it by talking to him during dinner. Visualizing the scene, planning what she would say, she became aware that it would take time . . . Judd always ate so fast when he was keyed up . . .

Decisively, she crossed the kitchen, opening the cabinet where she kept her stock of canned goods, searching for something that she could use for a time-extending first course. She saw a can of Campbell's consommé and reached out for it, stopped as the telephone rang. Turning, she picked up the receiver, the trout on the counter suggesting that it would probably be Daphy, confounded, when a colorless masculine voice said, "Mr. Judd Wilder, please. This is Western Union."

Suddenly dry-mouthed, somehow knowing what the message would be, she said shakily, "Mr. Wilder is ill and can't come to the telephone. I'll take it."

"This Mrs. Wilder?"

"Yes," she said, already confronted by the terrifying prospect of telling Judd.

"Okay, ma'am, I guess that'll be all right," the voice said, turning mechanical now. "It's from Haygood, Iowa—your father passed away suddenly this morning funeral Monday afternoon—signed Oscar."

"Monday," she repeated blankly.

"That's what it says, ma'am—funeral Monday afternoon. Any reply?"

"No," she said. "I'll have to call you back."

Automatically, she replaced the receiver in its cradle. For a mad moment, she considered the possibility of not telling Judd, terrified by what the consequences of such a shock might be. Reason quickly prevailed . . . she had to tell him . . . but how?

She closed her eyes, pressing the heels of her palms against her temples, a physical response to the wild spinning of her mind, a desperate attempt to restore something like orderly thought.

"What was that about?"

Unheard, Judd had come out of the library, standing now in the open doorway of the kitchen. Dumbstruck, she tried to find words that her lips could form. Failing, she stared at him with the unthinking hope that silence might convey what could not be said. It did not.

"It was a telegram."

"Who from?"

"Oscar."

"He's gone?"

She nodded, watching him with horrified expectation.

She had to say something. "Why do you suppose he'd send a telegram instead of calling?"

"It's still Haygood," he said, his poise all but unbelievable. "When's the funeral? Did he say?"

"Monday afternoon."

He looked at his watch. "We might still be able to catch someone at Seven Seas."

It took a moment for Seven Seas to register as the name of a travel agency. "Judd, you're not thinking of going?"

He looked at her, narrow-eyed, his tight lips parted only long enough to say, "Why not?"

"Judd, you can't! It's only been—Judd, it's only been a week since you got out of the hospital."

His jaws were clamped.

"Judd, please! You've got to think of yourself, what might happen——" Horrified, she saw his face, the hard set of a determination that nothing could change.

"Stop worrying," he said commandingly. "It's not going to hurt me any. I can sit in an airplane just as well as I can sit here."

"But the strain——"

"It won't be as bad as the strain of not being there," he said flatly. "I've got to go, Kay. I couldn't live with myself if I didn't."

She knew that he was irrevocably committed, yet she could not stop herself from asking, "Don't you think you ought to ask Dr. Kharr?" His look made her cringe, inciting a desperately defensive "Maybe there's something that he could—some medicine—something—"

"Call him if you want to," he said, a cool indulgence. "I know what he'll say—but whether he does or not, I'm going."

She gave up. "You're not going alone."

He looked at her, the question in his eyes adding still another fear to what already seemed an unbearable burden. "All right," he said finally, the granting of a favor. He reached out for the telephone. "I'll find out when we can get a plane."

She caught his hand. "No, let me do it."

She gripped his hand, resisting the powerful urge to throw her arms around him and loose the flood of sympathy that welled up within her, successfully restrained only because of the intuitive realization that if she were to shatter the thin veneer of Judd's set-jawed poise, her own self-control might be irretrievably lost. "Go get some rest while you can," she said firmly. "You'll need it. I'll see when we can get a plane."

"We'll probably have to drive to Harrisburg."

"I'll find out," she said. "Now go lie down."

He nodded vacantly, turned, and started back to the library, the slump of his shoulders resurrecting her first fears in all of their original potency. The telephone directory was on the little shelf where she kept her cookbooks. Reaching for it, she glanced up at the clock, seeing that it was ten after five—the travel agency would probably be closed. It was. The telephone rang and rang but there was no answer. What now? Judd had said they would have to drive to Harrisburg. Call the airport there. She started to open the directory, looking for dialing directions for long-distance information, stopped as she saw the number she had penciled on the cover. Seemingly without volition—but she did close the kitchen door first—she dialed the number, almost surprised when she heard "County Memorial."

"I wonder—" she groped, then firmly asked, "Is Dr. Kharr in the hospital? This is Mrs. Judd Wilder."

"Oh, yes, Mrs. Wilder," the operator said, an encouraging recognition. "Yes, he's in his office. I'll connect you."

Hurriedly she put together a first sentence, prepared for the expected demand of Dr. Kharr's answering voice. But it did not come. There was only silence, so long extended that she was at the point of hanging up when the operator finally cut in with "I'm sorry, Mrs. Wilder. Dr. Kharr was in his office just a few minutes ago but he doesn't answer now. Do you want to leave a message? Or have him call you back?"

"No thank you," she said, hanging up, resigned to pointlessness . . . there was nothing he could have told her, anyway . . . he'd already told her that he had gone as far as he could . . . *"from here on out, Mrs. Wilder, it's going to be up to you . . ."*

❖ XIV ❖

Assuring herself that Judd had dozed off, Kay Wilder touched the button that let her seat recline, feeling herself momentarily relieved of the fear-free mien that she had vowed to maintain. Last night, accepting the impossibility of changing Judd's mind, she had decided that she must hide every evidence of her concern, doing or saying nothing that would add to the stress he would be under. At best, it would be a horrible trip, brutally wearing on anyone, let alone a man who was only three and a half weeks away from a heart attack.

So far, she had not done too badly, only one serious blackmark against her: that little shriek of horror that had slipped out when, too tense after that long drive to Harrisburg through the early morning fog, she had dropped Judd at the airport terminal building, only to discover when she came back from parking the car that he had carried their two bags inside.

The plane, when it finally arrived twenty minutes late, had been so crowded that they had been forced to take separate seats, and foolishly she had allowed Judd to take the first one they had reached, seating herself two rows ahead of him, putting herself in a position where she could not keep an eye on him without a fear-betraying backward glance.

Departing passengers at Pittsburgh had opened the way to side-by-side seating, but with a forty-minute stop on the ground, Judd had insisted on getting out of the plane and she had not dared to raise a strong enough objection to stop him from what, try as she would, she could not help feeling was an almost suicidal compulsion to drive himself into another heart attack. Behind her mask of unconcerned compliance, she had wrestled with the wide-awake nightmare of his collapse, secretly planning what she would do when it happened.

Safely back on the plane, there had been the small gain of Judd's admission that he felt a little tired, excuse enough to suggest that he try to rest—after all, he had been up since six-fifteen—but not enough to broach the idea of getting a wheelchair at Chicago. That change of planes was what she had tried hardest of all to avoid, but there were no direct flights to Des Moines, no way to avoid a two-hour layover in Chicago. At Des Moines she would have to rent a car unless, as seemed highly improbable, someone took the hint in her telegram and met their plane. Judd had vetoed the idea of asking Oscar to drive down for them, saying that they would need a car while they were in Haygood, anyway, transparently a blind for some unrevealed objection that she was prohibited from exploring.

Closing her eyes against the unearthly glow of cold light that illuminated the interior of the plane, the sun reflected upward from the solid cloud cover over which they were flying—it had been raining in Pittsburgh—she fought off the press of fatigue, fearful of sleep, almost as frightened as she had been last night, afraid that she might awaken to find her nightmare come true. With her eyes closed, the drowsy drone of the plane's motors made sleep too much of a threat, and she prized them open, taking a deep breath that slipped out of control and became an unmistakable yawn.

Instantly responsive, Judd asked, "Tired?"—startling evidence that she had been wrong in thinking him asleep.

"Not really," she said. "It's warm in here, that's all."

He reached up, twisting the little air nozzle, sending a cold blast in her direction. "It's going to be a rugged trip," he said. "That's why I didn't want you to come."

"You know I wouldn't let you come alone," she replied, afraid when she heard herself say it that it might be taken the wrong way, a violation of her vow.

"Maybe you'd like to stay overnight in Des Moines," he suggested solicitously. "We could go to a motel, drive up in the morning."

"Whatever you want, dear," she said, unable to accept the legitimacy of his concern for her, hopeful that he was thinking of a way to save himself. "It might be a good idea. There really isn't any point in getting there tonight."

"I guess not," he said, lost for a long moment in an unshared thought. "Oscar didn't say what time the funeral would be?"

"No, the telegram just said 'afternoon.' If we don't get there until noon it will be time enough—and a lot easier on you."

"I wasn't thinking of that," he said, lost in thought again. "It'll be a big funeral. Everybody in town. All over the county. Dad had a lot of friends."

"I'm sure he did."

"It's different out here, not like it is in the East. Everybody knows you, you know everybody—people are a lot closer. Money isn't so important, that's the big difference. Nobody is out to take you, nobody is waiting to slip a knife into your ribs the minute you turn your back. There's a lot more live-and-let-live, a lot more—it's just a better life, that's all."

"I'm sure it was for your father," she said, alerted to danger, reviving her earlier suspicion that Judd might be thinking of taking over the *Herald*, dismissed then because it appeared so wildly implausible, reconsidered now because what he was saying about Haygood was so reminiscent of how he had tried to sell her on moving to New Ulster in that brief preamble to his abrupt announcement that he had already taken a job with Crouch Carpet. Cautiously, she advanced, "But I remember that time your father and Flora came back to see us, something he said when I was driving him around—" She hesitated, searching for a safe way to recount what Harry Wilder had said about how wise Judd had been to break away from Haygood, more relieved than annoyed when the stewardess suddenly appeared, asking if they wanted coffee.

"Sure, bring it on," Judd said, instantly shifting her longer-ranged fears to the more immediate concern that this would be his third cup. But she dared not object. Bad though all this coffee was, it was less dangerous to let him have it than to remind him of why he should not.

"There's one thing I want—" Judd said after the stewardess had gone. "One thing I *don't* want——"

"What's that?"

"Don't say anything to anyone about—you know, this heart attack business."

"But why—?"

"Just don't, that's all—not a word to anyone."

As the plane roared down the runway, Judd Wilder reached out to
close the porthole curtain, purposefully shadowing his face, another
move to keep Kay from discovering how close to the ragged edge
he had been. He was feeling better now, breathing more easily, but
there was still a hangover tremor in his leg muscles, a frightening
reminder of that rubber-kneed feeling that had hit him when they
were boarding for this last-hop flight to Des Moines.

Guardedly clasping his hands, he hid his thumb's quest for his
pulse, surprised when he felt its measured beat, steady and certain.
Countering the embarrassment of false alarm, he told himself that
he had known all along that it couldn't have been his heart . . . he
was just soft, that's all . . . all that time in bed, no exercise . . . that
godawful wait, the crushing crowd, no decent place to rest . . . that
long walk to the other gate . . .

"Are you all right, dear?"

"Sure. Why not?"

"That must be the most horrible airport in the world," Kay said
with the vibrant tremolo of a shudder. "But at least it's behind us
now."

"How long?" he asked curtly, testing the steadiness of his voice.
Satisfied, he tried a more demanding, "When do we get to Des
Moines, what time?"

"Four forty-two," she said. "There's a stop, you know—Davenport."

"This is really a puddle-jumper, isn't it?" he said, looking around
him now, seeing the interior of the plane for the first time. "I don't
know what it is—an old Viscount, I guess."

"It was either this or wait another two hours," Kay said apologetically. "I didn't think you'd want to do that."

"Oh, it's all right," he said hurriedly, conscious again of how super-
sensitive she was today, taking everything he said as a criticism of
the arrangements she had made. "You couldn't have done any better, I know that. And anyway it'll get us there, that's all that matters."

The lighted signs flashed off and he loosened his seat belt.

Kay asked, "Have you thought any more about staying over in Des Moines?"

"Let's do it," he said abruptly, decision motivated by a sudden urge to delay his arrival in Haygood as long as he could. "There's probably a motel somewhere out near the airport. If there isn't we can go into town and stay at the—" The name of the hotel eluded him and he reached out for a prompting memory, visualizing the lobby, and then as if two contact points had been bridged with the speed of light, he was sitting in that little minimum-rate room with Floyd Fulton, a flashed recollection persisting only long enough to incite the realization that it was the last time he had seen him alive, that drawn face instantly transformed into the lifeless mask he had seen in the Jersey City morgue. And then as if a hidden spring had been tapped, an outlet for the confluence of a dozen underground streams, he found himself swept along in a torrential outpouring of wildly mixed memories . . . that first night at County Memorial inextricably mingled with his descent into that tomb-like gray-walled basement, the harsh burst of green-tinted light and then the old man's talon-clawed hand pulling back the sheet. But the lifeless face was not Floyd Fulton . . . his father . . . the name on the red tag was wrong . . . not JUDD WILDER . . . no, no, no . . . HARRY WILDER . . . *"We commit to this grave thy servant, Floyd Fulton . . . earth to earth, ashes to ashes, dust to dust . . ."*

Dust? There was no dust, only raw earth turned to mud by the rain, a dead-blood brown rivulet running down into the open grave . . . if he only hadn't failed him that day in Des Moines . . .

Des Moines? No, it hadn't been Des Moines . . . Iowa City . . .

"Isn't it the Fort Des Moines?" Kay asked. "Isn't that where you always stay? I remember writing you——"

"Yes, the Fort Des Moines," he said, a quick escape. "I was mixed up for a minute, thinking of something else." He pushed back the curtain, looking out through the porthole, prompted by the gray clouds to say, "I hope it isn't raining in Haygood tomorrow."

"So do I," Kay said feelingly. "That's about all I remember of my father's funeral—the rain—the mud. It was horrible. I used to dream about it."

He stared at her, feeling himself swept along again in that same hallucinatory flood, all the more unbelievable now because Kay was in it with him, sharing that same nightmare. Groping for solid ground he said, "I remember the same thing—Floyd Fulton's funeral."

"He was that foreign correspondent?" Kay asked, her tone voicing her standard complaint that he never talked to her.

He nodded, thinking that he had told her everything there was to know, he must have—as long as they had been married, there could be nothing left that she had not discovered—yet he could specifically recall only one occasion when he had ever really talked to her about Floyd Fulton, that time before they were married when he had told her about Huck having known Floyd in Spain. "I've told you about the first time I saw him—coming into the *Herald* office?"

Not unexpectedly she said, "No."

"I must have," he said, but the force of argument was not strong enough to stem the flood and when he began, "I was only a kid—" there was a quick clearing of his mind, letting him see his father as he had seen him that day, greeting Floyd Fulton who was standing in the doorway with the sun behind him. "It was press day and I was back on the folding machine—" he heard himself say, all consciousness of speaking lost after that, the story coming out as if memory was being directly conveyed without translation into words.

Occasionally, he heard a murmur beside him, an acknowledgment of understanding or an expression of sharp interest, but there were no interruptions until, as he was listening to Floyd Fulton in that hotel room in Iowa City, Kay whispered, "Fasten your seat belt, dear," looking surprised when he asked her why, shocking him back into the here and now by asking if he had not heard the pilot's announcement that they were coming down for Davenport.

On the ground, the spell seemed irretrievably broken, but back in the air again for the short hop to Des Moines, Kay nudged him into telling her the rest of the story. He could not, however, recapture the sense of unimpeded flow that there had been before. He was conscious of words now, picking his way around mental blocks, yet managing to tell her about Jersey City and the morgue, even about the shock of finding his own name on the red tag. Chuckling to a strange sense of relief he went on, "It's a funny thing, but that first night in the hospital—as doped up as I was, that's what kept coming back to me—my name on that red tag."

He heard a little gasp that made him glance at Kay, catching an expression of wide-eyed terror in the instant before it vanished under a watery smile. He laughed at her, surprised that it came so easily, a prelude to the realization that he was feeling better than he had in a long time. "What's the matter? Why are you so—?"

"Oh, darling, I'm terribly sorry, really I am. I've been trying so hard to—" Her hand found his on the armrest, squeezing so hard that he winced, less from pain than from an awareness of how disturbed she was.

"Forget it," he said, an honest attempt to relieve her mind, yet at a level not far below consciousness he was hoping that she never did.

This time he heard the pilot's announcement. They were coming down for Des Moines. This was it. All that remained now was the drive to Haygood. Only an hour . . . as good as he felt now, there was no need to stay over . . .

"Do you see a motel?" Kay asked. "Or do you want to go into town?"

He started to reply, ready to say that it would be foolish not to drive on to Haygood, when he became suddenly conscious that Kay's hand was still on his, gripping down again. He glanced at her, surprised to find her eyes averted, yet even in profile her expression was startlingly strange, readable only as the mirroring of an inner frailty that he had never seen there before, an impression too unaccountable to be consciously accepted, yet something made him twist his hand, freeing it from her grip so that now he was holding hers, and whatever that impulse was, that same unrecognized motivation made him deny that he had changed his mind. "If there's a motel, let's grab it," he said. "It will be easier that way."

He had not said "easier for you," but she must have understood because the glance she gave him was an expression of unalloyed gratitude. In the instant when their eyes met he felt the quickened beating of his heart, not as an alarm signal but as a new force, an invigorating power flowing from a source that had never before been tapped.

But it was more than a momentary sensation, persisting after the plane had touched down and rolled to a stop, inciting the concern with which he watched her as she got to her feet, impelling the hand that reached out to steady her. As they moved out into the aisle, she tried to slip behind him, taking the same protective position that she had assumed all day. Resisting, he attempted to make her move ahead of him, a momentary impasse resolved as the aisle cleared enough to let them move ahead more or less side by side—but it was his hand that was on her arm, not hers on his.

They stepped out into a sodden world, grayed with misting rain driven by a chill wind from which he tried to shelter Kay as they hurried toward the gate to the terminal. Watching her instead of looking ahead, he paid no attention to the little knot of people who were waiting, unwarned when he was suddenly hit with a strange-voiced "Judd!"

Surprised, it took a moment to search out its source, another before he recognized that the man waiting with an open-faced look of anxious expectation was Oscar Nansen.

« 3 »

Shielding her true feelings, Kay Wilder got into the back seat of Oscar Nansen's little Volvo, fitting herself into the space that had been cleared by pushing aside the clutter of cartons that Oscar assured her he would have taken out if only he had known that she was coming. She had not specifically stated in her telegram that she would be with Judd, and everyone had apparently taken it for granted that he would be alone. From a whispered conversation that she had overheard between Judd and Oscar, she gathered that Flora had saved only Judd's old single-bedded room, filling the other two bedrooms with her own relatives. For a moment, the situation seemed to offer another chance to stay overnight in Des Moines, but Judd, with a bold show of that same false-front courage that had frightened her when they were getting off the plane, insisted that they would work it out some way.

As anxious as she was to protect him, she was regretting her promise to say nothing about his heart attack. She could hardly blame Oscar—he didn't know that he was talking to a man who had to be saved from stress and strain—yet it did seem that he had been unnecessarily callous, so lightly dismissing the death of Judd's father, so quickly turning to talk about the *Herald*. They were no more than inside the terminal when he brought up some trouble that he was having with the old Linotype machine, and before their baggage had been brought in, he had detailed a number of other problems in the shop, all of which had apparently been neglected because of Harry Wilder's illness and now required emergency action.

She could understand Oscar—he was one of those self-centered men incapable of thinking of anything beyond his own work, the mechanic concerned only with the tools of his trade—but she could not understand why Judd was not saving himself by refusing to become involved. He had to listen, perhaps, but there was no reason why he should encourage Oscar by asking questions. And he had, digging in as if every problem were his own, his voice crackling, his manner as animated as it had ever been before his heart attack. Because of his demand on the plane that she tell no one what had happened to him, it seemed that he was calculatedly trying to hide it behind a bold front, a masquerade that resurrected Dr. Kharr's warning that it was no more dangerous for a heart patient to refuse to leave his cave than it was for him to come roaring out with his mind closed to what had happened to him before. In the last hour, it seemed, the pendulum had swung from one extreme to the other.

Judd would be under enough strain as it was, coming back to Haygood to bury his father, and now as they started out of the parking lot, she made a determined effort to divert Oscar from any more talk about the *Herald*, asking a hurriedly concocted string of questions about Des Moines and Iowa and the weather, all of which Oscar answered politely, encouraging enough to make her think that she might be successful until Judd knifed in with "What are you going to do about that paper cutter—try to fix it up again?"

"Well, I don't know what to say," Oscar said, abandoning an attempt to pass a truck, edging back into line again. "Maybe we could get a new set of blades somewhere, try to keep it going for a while, but with the price of parts these days—I don't know whether it would pay or not. But a new cutter isn't going to be cheap either. It's up to you, I guess."

"What do you mean—up to me?" Judd asked.

She saw Oscar's head turn to Judd, but handicapped as she was by her inability to see Judd's face, she could only guess his reaction to what Oscar seemed to be expecting. For a long moment, there was only the thumping beat of the windshield wipers. Then Oscar said, "It was sure a relief when your father told me he was leaving the paper to you instead of selling out to the chain. As bad as his mind had gotten, I'd been afraid he might let them have it. They been after it—I guess he wrote you that?"

She saw Judd nod and waited for him to go on, expecting some echo of her own astonishment. They had talked briefly last night about his father's estate, only from the standpoint of whether or not there would be enough money to take care of Flora, but he had made it clear that he surely expected the paper would be left to her. Yet now he gave no evidence of surprise at what Oscar had said, asking for no elaboration, expressing no doubt. But neither was there any word of acceptance, and as the silence continued, she decided that he was refraining from comment in order to avoid offending Oscar by saying anything that would downgrade the *Herald* as a valued legacy.

Encouraged, she relaxed a little, looking out of the window—they were still going through the suburbs, Des Moines a larger city than she had imagined—startled out of semi-complacency when Judd said abruptly, "Can a man make a decent living with a country weekly these days, Oscar?"

"Make a living?" Oscar retorted, sounding as if he had never heard a sillier question. Then, diplomatically backtracking, he went on, "'Course I don't know what you mean by a living. You aren't going to make yourself a millionaire or anything like that——"

"How much money does the *Herald* make? Do you know?"

"Well, it ain't been making what it ought to, I can tell you that," Oscar said emphatically. "The thing is, Judd—I don't want to say anything against your father, a finer man never lived—but these last few months——"

"I know," Judd said. "I get the paper every week. I could see that there's been something missing."

Oscar gave him a sharp glance. "It's the advertising, Judd—that's what's been missing. And that's what you've got to have if you're going to make any money. Real money, I mean."

"But is it there to get?" Judd asked. "Is there really enough business around to support a good newspaper?"

"Sure there is. All you got to do is look through the exchanges and see what some of the other papers are doing. Now you take Mound

City—the *Democrat,* you know? Mound City's no bigger than Haygood. They got no more stores, no more territory to draw from, nothing we don't have, but every week they're carrying seventy, eighty, maybe a hundred more inches of advertising than we are. Two dollars an inch—that's two hundred dollars a week. Fifty-two weeks—that's better than ten thousand a year. Sure, you got some extra expense, but it ain't that much, Judd. Paper and ink is about all it amounts to. As far as composition goes, that's no problem, 'specially with a lot of the stuff coming in already matted. That's the way we get the Super-Sam ad every week. Comes out from Omaha. All we got to do is cast it, mortise in a few price changes and there you are. Nothing to it. If you got it coming in, we can take care of it."

"Which means that you've got to go out and sell it," Judd said, his tone a transparent expression of his aversion to personal selling, a reminder that she had once heard him say that space salesmen had the worst job in the world.

"You don't have to sell them," Oscar argued. "All you got to do is help them a little. You remember Keith Rachow? He took over the drugstore after his father moved to California."

"Sure, he was in my high-school graduating class."

"Well, this big Super-Sam store that we've got now has been giving him fits, running a big ad every week, all full of what are supposed to be specials. Well, you got to fight fire with fire, so Keith comes in one day—mind you now, he's coming in to see us, not the other way around, the way it ought to be. Anyway, he's got a list of what he wants to advertise—can we make up an ad that'll look as good as the Super-Sam? I guess you know what happens. Your father hands me Keith's list, that's all—no layout, no nothing. Judd, there isn't anything around a print shop I can't do, but I'm no advertising man and I don't pretend to be. You understand what I mean?"

"Sure."

"What I'm saying is this, Judd—a newspaper's a two-man job. You got to have somebody back running the shop, and you got to have somebody up front taking care of that end of it. Now you take the *Mound City Democrat.* When old man Casey had it, it used to be just like the *Herald.* You remember him, don't you? Always driving over to borrow a tube of ink or something?"

"Vaguely."

"Well, he died three or four years ago and this young fellow comes down from Minneapolis and buys the *Democrat*. He'd been with an advertising agency up there and he was plenty fed up with it. Said it was nothing but a rat race—I was talking to him at the state meeting—so he bought the *Democrat*. Don't know what he paid for it but whatever it was he says it's the best move he ever made. Yes, sir, right now he's about the happiest fellow you ever saw. Says he wouldn't go back to any big city again for a million dollars. And they got just the kind of setup I'm talking about. He's got a good man back in the shop—Fritz Krueger—and he's got sense enough not to butt in there. So all he's got to worry about is the office—and that's no worry, not the way he's got things going now. We could do the same thing with the *Herald*, Judd."

Judd's noncommittal silence supported the hope that he was at least aware that Oscar's optimism was strongly tainted with self-interest.

Oscar reached out to wipe a misty film from the inside of the windshield. "You were asking if the *Herald* would make a man a living. All I got to say is this—if it won't, why would the Bruxton people be trying so hard to buy it? You know darn well they're not going to buy a paper that can't make money."

"No, of course they aren't," Judd said, his face hidden from her, but she could almost see that narrow-eyed look, that expression of totally occupying interest that had so often signaled the onset of some impetuous but irreversible decision.

"'Course when you're talking about what could be done," Oscar was saying, "it ain't only the paper—you got all the job work, too."

"Dad wrote that you'd been doing pretty well there."

"Not what we ought to be doing," Oscar came back strongly. "Now you take the seed corn company. Sure, we been getting some of their labels to imprint, but that ain't one, two, three with what it could be. I go out there—you know, making deliveries—and this Mr. Coleback says to me, 'Oscar, couldn't you be printing some of these forms instead of our sending down to Des Moines for them?' I say, 'Sure,' so he says, 'How about giving us a bid on ten thousand of these?' So he gives me this form and I give it to your father. I guess you know what happened. He'd just lost interest these last couple of years, not caring any more."

"How much business could you get out there, Oscar—if you really went after it?"

"Oh, I wouldn't know what to guess," Oscar said, wiping the windshield again. "Crack that little window, will you, Judd? We're getting all steamed up."

Judd opened the vent window, starting a windrush sound that made it difficult for her to hear, all the more so as Judd moved closer to Oscar, their heads almost together now. Without too obviously leaning forward she could not completely follow their conversation, but she could hear enough to make it seem that Judd was seriously considering taking over the *Herald*. She had, several times over the years, heard him laugh about some city-born man's dream of getting away from it all with a little country newspaper—"He just doesn't know what it's all about"—but Judd did know, his eyes were open, and the more she thought about it the more it seemed a possible solution of what, yesterday, had been an awesome problem.

Judd had never before shown any desire to go into business for himself, but what had happened at Crouch Carpet had surely weakened his faith in corporate life . . . and he had to do something . . . only forty-four . . . twenty-one years before he was retirement age . . .

They were out in open country now, the rain-misted landscape drearily monotonous if you looked at it with unseeing eyes, yet there was a kind of beauty here too, the quiet charm of a Chinese painting in the way a grove of trees materialized out of the low-hanging clouds, given reality by no more than a delicate tracery of green budding. Beyond, there was a double row of Lombardy poplars that Corot might have painted . . . the beautifully grayed red of that misty-edged barn . . .

A huddle of buildings flashed past, the main street of a bleak little town that offered a gloomy prediction of what Haygood would be like . . . no place looked its best on a rainy day . . . and it was Sunday, too . . .

And there was a further lift of spirit as she heard Oscar's voice saying something about a lot of these little towns drying up. Boldly leaning forward, unashamedly eavesdropping, she heard him go on, "That's the good thing about Haygood, being far enough away from any big city so we ain't getting sucked dry. And then the seed company helps too—forty or fifty people working out there—gives us something besides the farm trade."

"Sure it does," Judd said, echoing her satisfaction, allowing her to sit back again, beginning to see now how well it might work out, how much happier Judd might be. Whether he stayed with Crouch Carpet or went into one of Horter's other companies, he'd still be under someone else's thumb . . . a lot of thumbs . . . all the people you had to please in a big company, the constant pressure . . . twenty-one more years of it . . .

No, this would be better, so much better . . . real friends instead of just people in the company. That was what Judd had been thinking about on the plane . . . "People are a lot friendlier" . . . all the men he'd thought were such good friends of his, but not a one of them willing to drive up forty miles to see him in the hospital. Even this last week at home . . . Frank Whittaker . . .

The miles went by, a new life spun out of the gossamer haze that draped the landscape, fantasy given startling reality when Judd said suddenly, turning and pointing, "That's the fairgrounds, Kay. Remember, I was telling you—?"

"Yes, Floyd Fulton," she said eagerly, let down as she looked out to see a long shed-like building with broken windows and a remnant of black roofing paper flapping in the wind; the barebones skeleton of a grandstand fronting on what, in better days, had been some sort of a race track.

"Doesn't look like it used to," Judd said, apologetically disappointed, but Oscar quickly explained, "We don't use it any more, not since we got the new Legion Park."

They crossed the railroad tracks, Judd pointing out the little depot as if it were a sight not to be missed, asking Oscar if Lars Dyson was still the stationmaster. No, he had died years ago, Oscar said. No, none of the Dyson boys were in Haygood any more. Paul was out on the Coast, managing a Sears store, and Nels was a dentist somewhere in Arizona. No, Haygood didn't have a dentist any more, not since old Doc Fetter had died. But there was a good one in Mound City and that was only eighteen miles.

"Well, this is Main Street," Judd announced, and despite her brave attempt at appreciation, he sensed her true reaction, adding an anxious "It looks a lot better when it isn't raining."

"I know—and it's Sunday afternoon, too," she said, then foolishly adding, "It's a lovely little town," knowing the instant she heard herself say it that she had lost validity by overdoing it. Biting her lip, she saw a brownstone building dead-ending Main Street, a Greek-revival monstrosity that she guessed must be the county courthouse. The memory of Judd having said that his old home was right next door came as a crashing reminder that the immediate present was infinitely more important than the future . . . only a week out of the hospital . . . this was going to be a terrible strain for him . . .

"I guess you don't want to stop now?" Oscar asked, suggestively slowing the car in front of a little one-story building, its narrow front hardly wide enough to accommodate a single door and a show window across which, in now flaking and tarnished gold leaf, HAYGOOD HERALD had long ago been lettered.

"No, we'd better go right up to the house," Judd said. His voice had changed, heavy now, almost to the point of hoarseness.

"Maybe in the morning," Oscar said hopefully, driving ahead.

Judd made no reply, looking ahead, and guided by the direction of his fixed gaze, she saw an old white house in a yard overgrown with the bare brush of untrimmed shrubbery. There were a half-dozen cars out front, one just leaving, another pulling up, someone coming out of the front door of the house, the doorway yellow with a light that cut through the gathering dusk, highlighting a black wreath.

Oscar got out first. "You folks go ahead—I'll bring your bags."

Judd stood staring at the house, seemingly unmindful of the rain. "I guess this is it."

There was nothing she could say, nothing that she could do to ease this awful moment . . . she should never have let him come . . . but how could she have stopped him?

« 4 »

Sitting on the edge of the bed, Judd Wilder looked around him, courting memories that, strangely, refused to be resurrected. This was the room that had been his through all of his childhood, his private domain until that day he had left for college, the wellspring

from which he had anticipated an outpouring of nostalgic remi-
niscences that would be difficult to endure, yet now that he was
here, his searching eyes saw only an odd-shaped little room tucked
into the sharply gabled space over the front porch, much smaller
than he recalled it to be, and almost totally unprovocative.

This was the same old bedstead, the crowning knob on the foot-
board post still flattened from the accidentally scalping blow of his
Boy Scout hatchet, but the scar was covered now with the crackle-
finish paint with which Flora had "antiqued" all of the old furniture,
what lay underneath identifiable but emotionally sterile.

There was the wall upon which he had pinned his pennants and
pictures, but the pink rosebud wallpaper that now covered it was
all but impenetrable to memory. There was the low window through
which, on his knees, he had spied upon the world, but what had so
fascinated him had been lost beyond recall. There was the old book-
case where, behind the stacked *National Geographics*, he had hidden the books that Floyd Fulton had sent him, but he could not
easily recall what those books had been, nor why it had been necessary to hide them, that impelling need lost in a past that was beyond recall. But, somehow, it did not seem to matter. This long
evening had brought a slow awakening, a sensing that his return to
Haygood was an ending of something that had begun on that cloverleaf coming down from the Pennsylvania Turnpike.

He had managed well enough on the drive up from Des Moines,
blanking his mind to what lay ahead by keeping it occupied with
the *Herald*, safely diverted until they crossed the railroad tracks and
started up Main Street, caught up then in a web of apprehension
from which escape seemed impossible. Ahead, there had been that
awful prospect of stepping into a house of death, a confrontation
that he had been madly tempted to delay when Oscar had suggested a stop at the *Herald* office, drawn on by the magnetism of
horror.

The core of his anticipation, all but hidden from perception by
the thick scar tissue of a deep wound—this was his only clear memory of coming home for his mother's funeral—was that awful moment
when he stepped in through the front door, glanced right and saw
that flower-banked casket in the downstairs bedroom, forced then
by the inhumanitarian cruelty of custom to walk in and look down
upon that revolting parody of life, that coldly repellent rouged and

powdered caricature of a face that once had been alive with intelligence and concern and love for him.

This afternoon, coming up the walk, crossing the front porch, he had been as close as he had ever been in all of his life to a scream of protest against the unendurable. Then, suddenly, the door was open and he was inside the living room, surrounded by people speaking his name and shaking his hand, telling him how glad they were to see him again, how happy they were to finally meet Kay, asking him what kind of a trip they had had, making him feel as if he had walked in upon a party, the atmosphere a bit on the formal side, perhaps, but surely nothing like the grief-burdened wake that he had imagined. And there was no casket in the downstairs bedroom.

Unthinking, anticipation based upon memories that had long since lost validity, it did not occur to him that Haygood now had a funeral home until someone asked him if he wanted to go down to this evening's viewing. For an instant, there had been a flashback of that same horror with which he had entered the house, banished when Kay had quietly asked, "Wouldn't you rather remember him the way you knew him?"

Kay's quick perception, and the speed with which she had acted to save him, was close to the forefront of his mind now, gratitude buttressed by his appreciation for the way she had moved in to share burdens that would otherwise have been his alone to bear, particularly that long session with Flora who, when she had come downstairs a few minutes after their arrival, had given him a bad minute or two. Kay had saved him then, too, quickly intervening, edging them out into the kitchen where, sitting at the center table surrounded by all the cakes, pies, salads, meat loaves, casseroles, breads and biscuits—in this regard, at least, Haygood was still Haygood—Flora had poured out the story of his father's illness and death with excruciating precision, sparing him not a single harrowing detail from that morning when she had found him on the bathroom floor until that gasp of life which she insisted upon calling a "death rattle." Had it not been for Kay he would not have been able to endure it. What had to be said, she said; what had to be done, she did. He had never thought of her as being overly compassionate, always a bit too self-contained to give herself wholly to someone else's plight, yet tonight there had been an unmistakably genuine show of sympathy for Flora. And it was equally evident that it had been appreciated. All through the evening, Flora had kept Kay beside her, seemingly feeling closer to her than to her own relatives. When, an hour or so ago, Kay had whispered to him that she was going to spend the night in Flora's room, sleeping in the bed that once had been his father's, he had sensed that it was a truly compassionate act, not merely a solution of the housing problem created by her unexpected arrival. Flora's brother and his wife had suggested giving up their room and going to the motel so that he and Kay could be together, but Kay had quietly insisted that she didn't mind at all staying with Flora, saying that he would be more comfortable in his own room. And until this moment he had thought that he would be.

Now, sitting on the edge of the bed, making no move to start undressing, he felt a kind of loneliness that he had never before experienced, most tangibly evident as a hope that Kay would stop in on her way to bed. Through the open register of the hot-air heating system he could still hear her down in the living room with Flora, her voice too low for words to be understood but the tone unmistakably warm with understanding, inciting a feeling that, had it been acknowledgeable, he would have recognized as being something very close to jealousy.

✧ XV ✧

Awakened by the sun, Judd Wilder experienced a moment of blinking disorientation, unable to fit what he saw to the still persistent scene of a shattered dream. Then, as an abruptly explosive perception, he knew where he was and why he was here. This was the day of the funeral.

Out of bed, he cracked the door for a surreptitiously exploratory glance, assuring himself that the bathroom was unoccupied. Coming out, he saw that the door of the master bedroom stood open, the beds already made. He could smell coffee and bacon and hear the distant chatter of many voices. He took a long shower, the water running cold before he got out, and then dressed slowly, putting on the dark blue suit that Kay had packed for him. As a last-minute decision, he changed neckties, substituting a maroon foulard for the too-somber gray that he had already knotted at his throat.

The house was full of people, an unrecognized couple with two children in the living room as he passed through, someone out on the porch glimpsed through the window, the dining room table filled, most of the faces recognizable from last night, but the names were largely lost except for Flora's brother Fred, to whom he had listened for a long time last night, hearing a full account of his rise from a barefoot boyhood to his recently achieved eminence as president-elect of the Southern Iowa Hatchery Association.

"Morning," he said to Fred, peripherally including the rest of the table, and walked through into the kitchen. Kay, in an apron and with her sleeves rolled up, had obviously taken over, deferring to Flora but plainly directing the two neighbor women who had come in to help. She broke off whatever she was telling them as he entered, quickly coming over to greet him, asking him how he had slept and what he wanted for breakfast, telling him to go in and sit down at the dining room table.

"No, all I want is a cup of coffee," he said, resolutely seating himself at the kitchen table, and then glancing at the array on the counter, "Maybe one of those cinnamon rolls."

Served, he felt the embarrassment of intrusion, relieved when the women finally went back to their interrupted planning of how lunch would be handled. Flora's chief worry, it seemed, was that everyone be properly fed, a problem because the funeral was to be at one o'clock, and although he recognized that her concern was a diversion to fill the void of waiting, he could not down a feeling that it represented a lack of properly displayed mourning, an impression all the stronger because he felt that same deficiency on his own part. His father was dead, he should be consumed with grief, experiencing some peaking of emotion, but he was feeling nothing beyond the detached reaction of an observer watching the events of a ritualistic holiday. But there was still the funeral.

He slipped away unnoticed and walked back through the house. Another carload of Flora's relatives had just arrived, a young girl with a tiny baby packaged in a pink plastic basket, a pasty-faced young husband who looked as if he were still surprised at having found himself capable of siring a child. There were people everywhere he turned, endlessly talking, the mindless chatter without which the human race seemed unable to sustain life, as unthinking as the act of breathing. He heard not a word spoken about his father. All they were talking about, it seemed, was the weather, how lucky it was that they had such a nice day.

Fred was on the front porch, smoking a cigar. "Sure glad to see this weather finally break," he said. "We got seventy-two thousand chicks coming out of the incubators this next week. Don't know how we'd a moved 'em if the weather'd stayed bad. I remember back in 'fifty-seven—maybe I told you last night?"

"Yes, I'm sure you did," he said, avoiding insult by muttering something about having to go downtown. He walked out to the street, turning right toward the business section because Fred was still watching him. As he crossed the first side street, it occurred to him that this was farther than he had walked since his heart attack, but he wandered on, an aimless search for something that had been missing at the house, not knowing exactly what, yet somehow feeling that he would find it on Main Street. Vague though his objective was, it was close enough to awareness to make him realize that he wanted to talk to someone about his father, if only to rid himself of the feeling of aloneness that had come over him at the house. Everything there was centered around Flora; all the relatives who had come were hers. Reason told him that it could hardly be otherwise —his father's only brother had died years ago in Long Beach, a widower with no children, leaving Harry Wilder to die with no blood tie to anyone on earth strong enough to bring any mourner to his grave other than his son. He was that son, and he was alone—except for Kay.

Walking on, he thought of her, thinking how fortunate it was that he had brought her with him, how much easier she had made it for him. And again, quite consciously, he thought of how wonderful she had been with Flora last night, how adeptly she had taken over this morning, how willingly those two other women in the kitchen had accepted her direction and command. What might, under other circumstances, have been taken as a revelation of something missed before, a quality in Kay that he had never adequately appreciated, came through now as a recognition that she had changed a lot in this past month.

And he had changed, too. Or perhaps it was Haygood that had changed. In either event, everything he saw was mismatched with expectation. There was no support anywhere for his prior impression that he would come home to embracing familiarity. He saw, as he had in his room last night, the dim outline of memory's justification, all but lost now under the accretion of the years, the new fake-stone front on the Haygood National Bank as concealing as the age-faking paint on his old bedstead.

Oscar had been right in saying that Haygood had not dried up as had so many of the other little towns that they had gone through on their drive up from Des Moines yesterday afternoon. Insulated by distance from big-city competition, drawing on a wide territory of prosperous farmers and further supported by the payroll of the seed corn company, Haygood had obviously attracted the money-sniffing location scouts of the chain stores. The old Sugar Bowl, once a glittering epicurean shrine and the social center of his high school days, was now a bargain-shouting Coast-to-Coast clothing store, its sign-plastered window display as calculatedly planned to confuse the gullible natives as an Indian bazaar. Sulzberger's Bakery was gone, its wonderful fresh-bread odor lost forever in the leathery smell of a chain shoe store. Only by counting buildings, remembering that it had been three doors down from the corner, was he able to locate Vanderslice's jewelry store. That was where he had picked out the Hamilton watch that his father had given him when he had graduated from High School. Now it was Western Auto.

But the most shocking change was across the street where, like some obscenely enormous growth on the body of the town, the Super-Sam discount store had taken over half of the block, choking the life out of Ellison's Hardware, spreading into the cool cathedral-like interior of what had once been Fielding's Furniture & Undertaking Parlor, going on to devour August Zink's butcher shop and Hattie Rafferty's millinery store. As if dipped in the blood of its victims, everything was now covered with red paint, conquest proclaimed with NOBODY CAN BEAT SUPER-SAM!

Watching from across the street, he saw a fat farmer and his fat wife come out with a loaded wire-mesh cart, dumping its contents into the back seat of a new white Cadillac. He did not know the fat farmer, nor did he recognize the man who stopped to talk to him. Two men came out of Western Auto, neither of their faces even vaguely familiar. A woman got out of a Pontiac station wagon, eyed him suspiciously, and went back to lock up. He walked on, a stranger in a strange land.

The *Haygood Herald* building was a small island of familiarity in an unknown sea, unchanged except that, like a very old man, it seemed to have shrunk in stature with the years. But the door was locked, the curtain drawn. Pressing his face to the show window, cupping his hands to shield his eyes, he looked inside, seeing his father's old rolltop desk, the uncapped paste jar, the festoon of spindled galleys, the old chair with its worn leather back. Almost as a conscious exercise in recollection, he attempted to conjure the memory of that day when Floyd Fulton had appeared, but all that came back was a mind picture of the fairgrounds as he had seen them yesterday afternoon.

Rachow's Drug Store was next door, recognizable despite its new front, and recalling that Oscar had said that Keith was still there, he started to enter, wondering if Keith would recognize him. Guarding against the possibility that he might not, he plotted the purchase of something, anything—a small bottle of aspirin—and pushed in through the door, discouraged by an absence of the redolently druggy odor that he remembered, rescued from disappointment by an explosive greeting from behind the prescription counter.

Keith came out with his hands extended, a hearty greeting that denied all memory of the prissy little four-eyed kid that he had been in high school. His stringy yellow hair was largely gone, his once-thin face filled out with pudgy softness. "By golly, it's good to see you, Judd," Keith exulted, sounding as if he really meant it. "Been a long time." They shook hands. "Sorry about your father, Judd—wonderful man—Haygood won't be the same without him. But it's something we all have to face up to. I lost my father this last year, you know. I guess you saw it in the *Herald*."

"Yes, I remember," he said, bluffing it out, getting away with it.

"That was a wonderful thing your father wrote about him," Keith said. "I guess you remember—about how they used to go out to the lake, that old crowd they used to have, your dad and my dad, Cass Priestly, Otto Backe, old Doc Noble? They're all gone now except Judge Finley."

"He's still around?"

"Oh, sure. Be in here any minute now, getting his day's supply of White Owls. He was asking about you yesterday, wondering when you were coming. You want to be sure and see him while you're here, Judd. Mean a lot to him. He was eighty last month. We had a little birthday affair for him—the Chamber, you know. I'm president this term so I kind of set it up at our February meeting, gave him a silver cigar box and Lou Samuels made a speech. I guess you don't know Lou. He's manager of the Western Auto."

"What happened to the Vanderslices?"

"The Vanderslices? Oh, that's right, they used to have a jewelry store in there, didn't they. The old folks are down in Florida somewhere. Nancy—the wife was saying something about her just the other night—what was it? Oh, I remember now. I guess you know, she married this fellow she met at college? They'd been living out on the Coast. He was with one of these big aircraft companies. Doing real good, too, from what Margie said. She saw them when she was out there a couple of years ago—big house, swimming pool, three cars. Well, they just got a divorce. Sounds kind of crazy, married all those years—you never know, I guess."

"What about Willie Bracken?" he asked, the name suggested by an association with Nancy Vanderslice, remembering that he had cast Willie as her Indian lover in the Centennial pageant.

"Golly, I don't know what's happened to Willie. The last I heard of him, he was in Detroit working for Chrysler. Paul Dyson is out on the Coast, manager of a Sears store."

"Yes, I heard that."

"Nels Olafsen is out in Oregon, working for Georgia-Pacific in one of their plywood plants. Let's see who else was there in our class? Oh, sure—Ken Weidler. That's kind of a funny one. Maybe you heard about it. He'd been with some big chemical company back East, and really getting someplace, too. His father came in one time with this booklet they put out, proud as Punch—had Ken's picture in it. Well sir, here about a year ago, he just walks out and takes this job with the government. Foreign aid or something. I can't remember just where he is now—Thailand, Cambodia, somewhere out there. Crazy, huh?"

"Oh, I don't know—maybe it was the smart thing to do," he said, thinking it a safely ambiguous remark. "The chemical business can get pretty rough."

"I guess so," Keith agreed. "Maybe save him from winding up like Todd Tolken. You heard about him, didn't you?"

"No."

"Dropped dead of a heart attack here about—oh, I don't know, it was last fall sometime. Tough. Wife and four kids, two of them still in college. And he was only—well, our age—forty-four, forty-five—"

"The hurricane years," he murmured to himself, recalling the last chapter of Kharr's book that he had given him to read.

"What was that?" Keith puzzled.

"Oh, nothing important, something I read, that's all," he said quickly, searching for a change of subject. "Nice store, Keith."

"Well, it's not too bad, I guess. Remodeled here a couple of years ago. Put in a hell of a lot of money, I know that, more than I should have. If I had it to do over again—I don't know, I guess maybe I'm crazy hanging on here."

"Competition a little rough?"

"Oh, I've still got the prescription business, that keeps me going. It's just that—this last year or so I've been doing a lot of thinking. With the kids gone—Linda's married, living in New Orleans, and Peter's through pharmacy school and working for Squibb—oh, I don't know, be a hell of a break to pull up stakes and leave Haygood, but if I don't make the break now, I never will. I'll be forty-six my next birthday—"

"I know what you mean."

"You're still with the same company?"

"Yes."

"And doing all right?"

"Oh, sure."

"That's the difference, I guess—a big company keeps growing, you've got some place to go. But when you're on your own—I get a feeling sometimes like a squirrel in a cage, running like hell and getting nowhere fast." He finished with a self-saving smile. "Anything I can get you, Judd?"

"Got some aspirin?"

"Sure, you bet—Anacin, Bufferin, Excedrin, anything you want," Keith said, instantly the wheel-spinning squirrel.

"Anything at all," Judd said. He took a dollar bill out of his wallet, exchanging it for the bagged bottle that Keith handed him, so anxious to get away that he almost said, "Keep the change."

"I'm going to try to make the funeral," Keith said, giving him a clutter of coins. "I was hoping I would get everybody to close for an hour, but you know how it is—these chain-store managers."

"Yes, they've got to go by the book," he said, starting for the door, stopped as he saw a craggy old man about to enter, identification made certain as he heard Keith say, "There he is now."

"Judge, how are you?" He greeted the old man as he opened the door. "I'm Judd Wilder."

Squinting from under his bushy brows, the old man stared at him for the moment that it took comprehension to break. Then, suddenly agitated, he grasped his hands, hanging on as if afraid that he might escape, telling him that he had to see him right away, asking if he would come back to his office with him.

« 2 »

Released at last by the arrival of Flora's sister, Kay Wilder went searching for Judd, hurried by an anxious realization that, in her attempt to protect him from all the pre-funeral turmoil, she had failed to give him the support that he surely needed. Not seeing him on the first floor, she went flying up the stairs. His room was empty, so was the bathroom. But his hat and topcoat were still on the clothes tree. He had to be somewhere around. She went back to the first floor again, seeing now that someone was out on the front porch. But it was only Fred, sitting in the sun with his brother-in-law, talking about the hatchery business. Judd was nowhere in sight.

Fred called out, "You looking for that man of yours?"

"Yes, have you seen him?"

"Yeah, he walked downtown. Said there was something he had to do."

"Walked? But he shouldn't—" She caught herself, stopped short of that prohibited revelation. But her anxiety was apparently too great to conceal.

Fred must have noticed it, getting up now from the porch swing. "You need him, huh? All right, come on, I'll run you down. My car's right out there."

She hesitated, fearful of what Judd might think if she came running after him, momentarily sheltering the delusion that taking his hat and coat might be an excuse, then abruptly aware that that would only make it worse.

Fred had his car keys out, jingling them. "We'll see him around somewhere. The town's not that big."

Abruptly decisive, she said, "I'll get a coat." Finding it in the hall closet, she almost changed her mind. But Fred was already in his car, honking when she stepped out on the porch.

"I imagine he's at the newspaper shop," she said, frantically engaged in the invention of a tenable excuse, hoping that she might somehow be able to make it seem a show of interest in the *Herald*. "It's on this side of the street, down about two or three blocks."

"I know where it is," Fred said, driving directly to it. She got out, finding the door locked.

"Isn't that him?" Fred asked. "Over there in front of the bank?"

Yes, there he was, talking to those two men. He was all right, that's all she needed to know. She started to tell Fred that she wouldn't bother him now, but she was too late; Fred had already launched a booming hail.

Judd turned, seeing her. But instead of withering her with a scowl, he smiled a greeting, said something to the older of the two men, and waved to her to come across the street, an invitation made unmistakable as he advanced to meet her.

He was waiting at the curb, whispering, "It's Judge Finley—something about the paper and Dad's will."

"Oh, Judd, you go ahead. I don't want to——"

"No, come on," he demanded. "It's your life, too."

Her heart leaped with the elation of a freely offered sharing, an emotion too powerful to permit resistance, and then Judd was introducing her to John Bowerman, the president of the bank, and then to Judge Finley, with whom, a moment later, they were walking down the side street toward a door at the back of the building. Although she could not fault the warmth of the old lawyer's greeting, she sensed some concern about her presence, sure of it when she heard Judd say to the old man as he unlocked the door of his office, "There's nothing you can tell me that I don't want Kay to know."

The door opened directly into the office, walled floor to ceiling with lawbooks that looked as if they had been neither disturbed nor dusted for fifty years, the air heavy with the odor of old leather bindings smoke-cured by a half-century of fuming cigars. They sat down around an oak table in the center of the room, Judge Finley with his back to his rolltop desk, his elbows planted to support the weight of his once-powerful shoulders and his still-massive head. Spreading his liver-spotted hands on the tabletop, he said in a shaky voice, "What I'm about to do is no doubt a violation of the law—or at least of legal ethics—but after you've served the law as long as I have, you earn the right to—" His voice drifted off as if the thought in his mind had gone out of focus. Absentmindedly, he reached for a cigar, put it in his mouth, struck a match, and then as if alerted to indiscretion, hesitated, looking at her.

"Please smoke if you wish," she said. "It won't bother me."

He regarded her gratefully, lighting the cigar now, holding it so that he had its smoking tip and Judd in the same frame of vision. "This makes me think of you. How old are you now?"

"Forty-four, sir."

"This is all your fault," the old lawyer said with a rheumy-eyed smile. "That was the first cigar I ever smoked—the one your father gave me when you were born."

Judd murmured a response but Judge Finley seemed not to have heard it.

"We were good friends, your father and I, about as close as two men can ever be."

"I know that, sir."

The old lawyer looked away, his face agonized. "It's not easy, someone who's meant as much to you as he had—" His voice expired in a shuddering sigh. He took a deep breath. "As far as I'm concerned, Judd, your father didn't die Saturday morning. He died two weeks ago. The man who came in here that morning to change his will wasn't the man I'd known all these years. His mind was gone. But I couldn't tell him that. How could I? How can you tell someone that you love that he's—" He closed his eyes, gasping in a deep breath. "I couldn't tell him that he was no longer mentally competent."

"No, of course you couldn't."

"I've been stalling off letting Flora see this new will," Judge Finley said, "and that's something I've no right to do—except, perhaps, the right of justice, and mercy, and not wanting to see an old friend's wife unnecessarily hurt."

She could feel the tension in Judd's clipped, "What's in the new will?"

There was a long wait before Judge Finley said, "The change he made, Judd, was to leave the paper to you—building, equipment, goodwill, everything. I tried to talk to him about Flora—he seemed to have forgotten that she existed. When I said something to him about taking care of his wife, he said that his wife was dead." He put his hands to his face, finally dropping them to say, "He wasn't himself, Judd, not the man I'd known—nor the man that Flora had been married to for twenty-odd years, whatever it's been. And she'd been a good wife to him, as good a wife as any woman could ever have been. I keep seeing her face when—" He closed his eyes as if trying to blank out a horrible vision.

She watched Judd's expression, tautly unrevealing as he asked, "What did he leave her?"

"The house, a little life insurance."

"Nothing to live on?"

"Only the insurance. Five thousand dollars."

"That won't last long."

"Not these days."

Judd asked, "What was the old will, the one that he changed?"

"He left everything to Flora," the old lawyer said, "but with the request—this was not a stipulation, only a suggestion—that Oscar—Oscar Nansen, you know?"

"Yes."

"He wanted Oscar to be given a first chance to buy the paper, paying for it on the installment plan, giving Flora a regular monthly check."

"Why did he change his mind? Did he say?"

"He kept saying—I suppose you know, years ago, he'd always thought that someday you might come back?"

She glanced at Judd, seeing him nod, but his eyes were averted.

Judge Finley went on, "I suppose he thought—if you can call it thinking—that by leaving the paper to you he could force you into coming back."

Judd was leaning over the table, his face shielded from her. "Couldn't this new will be broken?"

"Yes, without question—if Flora wants to contest it."

Judd looked away, "Do you still have the old will?"

With a trembling hand, Judge Finley reached out to tap the ash from his cigar, finally looking at Judd, answering with a nod.

"What would you think about just forgetting that this new will had ever been written?"

A faint smile lighted Finley's craggy face. "As a sworn servant of the court, I would think it a serious subversion of the law. As a man who loved your father—if I had a son, it's what I'd want him to do for me."

Judd took a deep breath, lifting his shoulders, "Thank you, Judge."

When they went out, there were tears in the old lawyer's eyes, but they were tears of joy and relief, emotions that Kay Wilder had no difficulty in understanding.

Outside, walking up the side street, Judd said, "There wasn't anything else I could do."

"Of course not."

"But it surprised you," he said. "Why? You weren't imagining were you, that I'd ever come back here?"

Honesty seemed to demand "I didn't know."

They walked on in silence, frightening until Judd said, "Maybe I was—before I got here." And then, "You know what I was thinking about—sitting there? The hospital—one of Kharr's gimmicks—'Here's a pencil and a piece of paper, write down what you want to do with the rest of your life.' I could never have written, 'Editor of the *Haygood Herald.*'"

Fred had pulled across the street, waiting in his parked car. "I thought maybe you'd want a ride," he said. "It's getting late."

Driving toward the house, Fred said, "How long are you folks staying?"

Without hesitation, Judd said, "We'll have to get away as soon as we can."

"Yes, I was figuring you'd have to get back on the job, too," Fred said. "If it would be any help we could get you as far as Des Moines. Be going that way, anyway. Plenty of room. No trouble to drop you off."

Judd looked at her. "All right?"

"Of course."

« 3 »

She paid the driver and got out of the taxicab, facing the doorway he had indicated, a wide opening into a deeply shadowed vestibule. There were men inside, black-bearded and black-hatted, and she felt herself at the end of courage. But the taxicab had already gone.

Tentatively, she took two forward steps and stopped, feeling herself an unwanted alien in an exotic corner of an unknown world, a mourner excluded by ritual and rite, buoyed only by the memory of having experienced this same apprehension the first time she had ever gone to a Catholic funeral. But this was even more an excursion beyond possible anticipation, a venture into the totally unknown, the end of a mad journey impelled by grief that was so unaccountable that it was almost beyond belief that she was actually here.

She glanced up the street, a subconscious search for an avenue of retreat, suddenly aware that a man had come to the doorway and was now looking directly at her. There was something about his face that seemed vaguely familiar, a family resemblance, and she must have acknowledged recognition because now the man was coming toward her. "You're Mrs. Cope?" he asked, nodding as if he already knew. "I'm Ezekiel, Aaron's brother. Come."

Impelled by the light touch of his guiding arm, she walked through the doorway. The little knot of men parted before her, opening the way. They walked on and on, into a dark room, seemingly illuminated only by the wax-white face of an old man.

"Father, this is Mrs. Cope, the lady from Pennsylvania who has been so kind."

The old man reached out, gathering her hands in his. "You knew him well?"

"I was on his last case," she said, strengthened by the knowledge that this man was a doctor, remembering now that she was a nurse.

"He wrote me that he was working on a book," he said. "I don't suppose that he'd finished it?"

"I don't know," she said. "But I have all of his papers packed up and ready to send. I thought someone would want it."

"I hope so," the old man said. And then his voice choked and the tears came, and she heard a distant sound, a bass voice singing words that she could not understand. But there was no mistaking their import.

"Come," Ezekiel said.

« 4 »

"... *We commit his body to the ground, earth to earth, ashes to ashes, dust to dust, in sure and certain hope of the resurrection to eternal life through our Lord Jesus Christ ...*"

With his head bowed, his eyes closed, Judd Wilder let the words wash over him.

"... *Through Jesus Christ to whom be glory for ever and ever— Amen.*"

There was rustle about him, the sound of movement, but he stood with his head still bowed, a long last moment of waiting for something that he now knew would not come. He had anticipated his father's burial as a totally trying experience, an ultimate testing, and now there was a strong sense of secret guilt in finding himself so self-controlled, so easily capable of mastering what he had imagined as an all but unendurable emotion.

What he felt was more regret than grief, blaming himself for not having been a more understanding and considerate son, yet it was difficult to focus even that feeling upon the casket that had been committed to the earth, much easier to accept Judge Finley's view that the man who had died Saturday morning was not his father but someone he had never known.

There had been little to challenge that self-saving illusion, the funeral service a mercifully impersonal recitation by rote, only one passing mention of his father's name, no grief-provoking eulogy. After all the buildup and preparation—the milling crowd at the house, the pressing convergence upon the funeral home, the long cortege to the cemetery—he felt oddly let down, a sensation not unlike one he had often experienced after the final curtain had fallen on a performance that had proved only a dim shadow of expectation.

Yielding to the pressure of Kay's hand on his arm, he turned away from the grave. The crowd, already signaled by Flora's departure, was melting off, somberly silent until the nearby roadway was reached, then breaking into the babbling chatter that was their proof of life, their denial of death. Everywhere automobile motors were being started, a raucous grinding that assaulted the soft whisper of the warm south wind.

Glancing back, he saw what he had not noticed before, the white marble stone beside his father's grave . . . JULIA JUDD WILDER . . . his father had long ago bought a family plot, three lots, one for him . . . now it would be a place for Flora . . . REST IN PEACE . . .

Kay's hand tightened on his arm, and for the first time he felt the sting of tears in his eyes. Somewhere in the distance, beyond the greening trees, he heard a meadowlark call, a harbinger of spring, a sound from his lost boyhood, a song that he would never hear again.

"Let's get out of here," he whispered hoarsely.

Ahead, Fred was waiting beside his car, looking at his watch. Kay whispered, "Do you still want to get to Des Moines tonight?"

"Why not?"

"I'm all packed."

"Nice service," Fred said. "Real nice."

"Just lovely," his wife agreed absently, watching two women getting into one of the other cars. "I guess I wouldn't a needed this black dress, either, but I just never enjoy a funeral if I ain't dressed right."

« 5 »

Tightly wrapping her robe, cinching the belt, clutching the collar to her throat, anticipating the chill of the bedroom air after the steamy warmth of a hot shower, Kay Wilder cautiously opened the bathroom door, expecting to find Judd lying down as he had promised her that he would do.

Disappointed, she saw him sitting at the window, still in the chair into which he had flopped after he had taken the tub bath that she had hoped would help him to relax. The floor around him was littered with the newspapers that he had picked up in the lobby. He had bought every paper in sight, seemingly no more than a response to habit—he had always been a compulsive paper-buyer, never able to pass a newsstand without reaching out—but now, as something of a surprise, she saw that he had actually been reading. By contrast with this past week at home, when he had no more than glanced at the *New York Times* and never once bothered to open the *Wall Street Journal,* it seemed a welcome return to normality, yet there was an overriding apprehension that it might be a sign of dangerous tension still unrelieved.

"I thought you were going to take a nap," she said.

Instantly responding to the sound of her voice, he said, "Listen to this," reaching out to the windowsill for a raggedly torn sheet. "Speculators who have been crystal-balling the shape of things to come in the Harrison Horter empire," he read, "had one of their hot-tip rumors confirmed over the weekend by an announcement that Horter interests have acquired control of the Casa Corporation. Casa owns a chain of high-quality furniture stores scattered over twenty-one states, and through a wholly-owned subsidiary, operates leased departments in a number of metropolitan department stores. The announcement stated that additional units will be opened as rapidly as possible, a goal of one hundred and twenty fully operative outlets having been set for the end of the current year."

"Isn't that what Roger was telling us?"

"This is the interesting part," he said, flat-voiced, reading on. "The crystal-ball gazers were proved less clairvoyant, however, in their prediction that Horter would make the General Carpet Corporation the key manufacturing unit in a new vertical home-furnishings combine, a rumor to that effect having touched off the recent flurry of activity in General Carpet stock. In a surprise development, a company spokesman revealed that Horter Enterprises has largely divested itself of its holdings in General Carpet, trading its position in that corporation for a controlling interest in the Crouch Carpet Company of New Ulster, Pennsylvania."

"Then he wasn't planning a merger."

"I said that all along."

"I know you did, but——"

"Here's the payoff," Judd said, turning the paper to the window to catch the last of the fast-fading daylight. "The switch from General Carpet, which has concentrated on the low-end market, to Crouch Carpet, reputedly the industry's most successful producer of top-quality carpeting, appears to be consistent with Horter's other recent acquisitions. The three furniture companies that he has taken over in the past three months are all makers of fine furniture, and Annex Mills, acquired last week, makes only top-end drapery fabric. In the light of the Casa take-over, it now becomes clear that Horter is mounting a strong countermove against the industry trend that has, over the past twenty years, shifted much of the high-quality home furnishings business to decorators, while retail furniture stores have generally downgraded their merchandise, catering to the low-end mass market. Although some trade sources are skeptical that this trend can be reversed, others reason that Horter's control of primary sources will put the chain in a much more favorable position. Whatever the outcome, Horter is plainly betting his chips on the newly affluent middle class which, as experience in other merchandising areas is beginning to prove, now offers a market of mass proportions." He tossed the sheet, a casual gesture in the same spirit as his reading voice, giving her no hint of what his reaction might be.

"What do you think?" she asked, a forced show of interest. "Will it work?"

"Oh, the market's there," he said, leaning back, stretching.

"There's a lot of resistance to decorators—too many people are afraid of getting clipped—and there are plenty of cities now, even some pretty big ones, where there isn't a single top-end furniture store any more. But whether or not you can do it with a chain-store operation—" He yawned.

"Why don't you get some rest, dear?"

"I'm not tired."

"You must be," she said, sitting on the arm of his chair.

He looked up, a darting glance, the suggestion of a smile. "When are you going to stop worrying about me?"

"You've had a hard day, you know you have."

"Doesn't that prove it?"

"Prove what?" She reached out to put her arm around his shoulder, but at the last instant, deterred by caution, let it rest against the back of the chair. "Prove what?" she repeated.

Judd had turned away, looking out of the window. The lights of the city were blinking on against the fastcoming night. "Maybe I shouldn't say this—I wouldn't to anyone except you—but today did me a lot of good. On the way out here—maybe you knew, I suppose you did—I didn't know whether I was going to be able to take it or not."

"But you did," she said, emboldened to let her arm fall away from the chair, lightly resting on his shoulder.

"That's what I meant," he said. "If I could take today I can take anything. It's all over, Kay. I'm out of the woods now, back on the main road again. That's what this trip has done for me, that more than anything else—making me see how right Kharr was. It's true, I had been going around in circles these last two or three years, spinning up a hurricane—he's right about that, too—that's what it's really like, getting yourself caught in a hurricane and not knowing how to get out of it."

She waited out a moment of silence, hoping that he would go on. He finally did. "That's something else that today proved—you can't get out of it by running backwards. But still it does you some good, going back to where it all started."

"Of course," she agreed, a barely audible whisper, trying not to divert him.

"I've done a lot of thinking these last two days, trying to figure out what it's all about. I've never done that before. I thought I had, but I hadn't, not really. Things look a lot different when you get far enough away so that you can take a look at yourself—see what you've done, what you haven't done—how much of your life you've spent chasing rainbows. I showed you that letter from Mr. Coleman, didn't I?"

"Yes."

"That's what I've never had—a real sense of values," he said, looking out into the night. "If there was a job to be done—that's all that mattered. I never stopped to think whether it was *worth* doing—it was the *doing* that was important. Take the convention——" A big electric sign came on across the street, a cascading waterfall of light that caught Judd's eyes, seemingly a silencing diversion.

"I know," she murmured, a mindless assurance, but it served its purpose.

"When I first found out that they were going ahead without me—it really shook me. As far as I was concerned, that was it. I'd had it. You remember what I—?"

"But you don't feel that way now," she said, only putting into words what his tone had already made clear.

He nodded. "That's what's so different—getting far enough away from myself to see what a crazy character I've been. It's like taking off the blinders, seeing myself for the first time—the oddball guy you've been putting up with all these years."

"I've never felt that way."

"But you haven't been exactly happy?"

Caught, her instinctive reaction was again denial, but there was a deeper intuitive sensing that this was a moment of demanded truth. "No, not always," she said, fighting the tremor in her voice. "But this last month has done a lot for me, too."

He turned his face to her, an irresistible invitation, and her lips met his, clinging for a moment, then abruptly parted by a sudden awareness of how dangerous this was, the first time in almost a month that they had shared a room. Impelled by fear, she broke away, quickly standing. He looked puzzled, hurt. "Everything is going to be different from now on, darling," she said brightly, an unsuccessful attempt to wipe the frown from his face.

"Maybe too different," he said, almost a question.

"I'm not worried," she said earnestly. "It'll all work out, one way or another. You're well again, that's all that matters."

His eyes were fixed upon her, a searching inquiry, broken off as he got up from the chair. "I'd better find out about planes, see how early we can get out of here in the morning."

"What's the hurry?" she asked, attempting lightness, trying to clear his clouded expression.

He sat on the edge of the bed, his hand on the telephone. "If we can get to Harrisburg early enough, I thought we might drive home by way of the hospital, see Kharr for a minute or two." He saw her anxious look. "I want to thank him, that's all—tell him how grateful I am, how much I owe him. It won't take long, it's not that far out of the way, and I think he'll appreciate it."

"I'm sure he will."

"And I never had a chance to say goodbye to Raggi, either," he said, picking up the telephone, asking for the porter.

Looking for slippers, she opened her train case, forgetting until she lifted the lid that, at the last minute, she had jammed in the collection of old photographs and mementos that Flora had pressed upon her. A picture of Judd fell out, fluttering to the floor. She retrieved it, about to tuck it away when Judd, hanging up with a weary "No, I'll call the airport," asked her what it was.

"Oh, Flora gave me some things last night," she said, sidestepping the threat of sentimentality. "She thought you might want them someday."

"Let me see it," he said, not moving, forcing her to hand it to him.

He looked at the picture, a puzzled smile slowly forming. "Where in the world did this come from?"

"Flora said she'd found it somewhere."

"I'd forgotten this," he said, flattening the time-brittled print over his knee. "It's one of the shots the *Life* photographers took—the night of the pageant—Judd Wilder, the big director, the boy wonder." He put in a little bittersweet "Look at that face."

"Do you know what I see?"

"The Orangerie?"

"No," she said, thinking of Paris, seeing her son's face again. "I never realized before how much Rolfe looks like you."

He seemed pleased, but shook his head. "His feet are a lot more solidly planted than mine ever were. He knows where he's going, he knows what he wants. That letter we got the other day—this kid could never have written that—he never knew."

"I'm not so certain that Rolfe does either," she said. "He'll change, too."

Judd was still staring at the face in the picture. "At least he's not off chasing a rainbow."

"That's not the difference," something made her say. "He fell in love with a smarter girl."

His head came around slowly. "Do you know what I think?"

She shook her head, too dry-lipped to speak.

He looked at her for a long time before he said, "He doesn't know what love is all about. You can't, not at that age. Love isn't something that—do you know what they say in India?"

Whatever it was that had been said in India was never repeated, lost in a flash of fear ignited by the flesh-to-flesh touch of his hand on her breast, consumed in flaring terror as she felt herself in the crush of his arms, borne down by the weight of his body, her mind blanked to everything except the horror of consequence. And yet, as if every nerve-end in her body had been supersensitized by the very fear that impelled resistance, she felt a warming surge go through her, an almost virginal response to the fire-and-ice blending of awful apprehension with irresistible desire. What little rationality remained was given up to a sensing of uniqueness, of youth recaptured, of something happening that had never happened before. And it never had. This was something truly new, not a frantic struggle to achieve the skyrocket burst of passion driven to an exploding climax, but a consuming quest for a oneness that denied self, a unity that became a goal beyond goals. This would be love. And it was.

Slowly, a delayed dawn in the warmth of a tropical night, the light of fear came back. "Are you all right, dear?"

"You should know," he said, his earthy chuckle a restoration of reality, a denial of illusion, a promise of persistence.

"You're wonderful," she whispered, clinging to him, slipping back into the timeless night.

And then she was awake again, abruptly conscious of aloneness. But there was a light somewhere, and her eyes searched it out. Judd was back in the chair by the window, sitting under the floor lamp, a piece of paper on his knee, a pencil in his hand. She watched him for a moment, and then quietly asked, "What are you doing, dear?"

"Nothing much," he said abstractedly, drawing a line, adding a column of figures. "Just figuring out what you could do with a hundred and twenty stores, that's all."